THE

LOVE CHILD.

𝔄 𝔯𝔬𝔪𝔞𝔫𝔠𝔢.

——— " We speak of passions
Of unholy impulse, and the jarring elements
Of human pride."

LONDON:

PUBLISHED BY EDWARD LLOYD, 12, SALISBURY SQUARE,
FLEET STREET.

1847.

PREFACE.

THE great success which has attended the Romance of the "Love Child," and which, from its first appearance, has been most signal, was probably owing to the extremely natural character of the incidents, and to the story generally, being in a great measure so faithful a transcript of human life.

It will not fail to be noted, that the whole story is illustrative of the great lengths to which unbridled passion may lead people, who give way in any one instance to its impulses. The fate of the Countess of Crumbledown is certainly a melancholy one, but we must recollect that, from the first to the last, she has no one to accuse but herself for the direful termination of her guilty career.

We cannot help, likewise, blaming the earl, who was, at all events, weak enough to afford great facilities for the exercise of villany; and in his case we shall likewise perceive how, from the consequences of his first error, consisting of the treacherous part he played regarding poor Emily Whitworth, he became a man, who was, in his most hilarous moments, ever liable to hear

> " That still, small voice,
> Which, 'mid the din of battle and the roar
> Of trumpets, will be heard,"—

the voice of conscience; for he could not, whatever was his after conduct, dream of conceiving that any one, who should view the whole affair with unprejudiced eyes, could acquit him.

For himself and for the publisher, the Author begs to return his best thanks to the public for the great patronage which has been accorded to this work, and sincerely hopes that his future exertions in the field of literature may meet with the like gratifying results.

Wishing to all of them a merry Christmas, and every adjunct that can make that festive season delightful, the Author of the "Love Child," for the present, takes his leave.

London,
  December, 1846.

THE LOVE CHILD;

OR,

THE LITTLE HEROINE.

A Romance.

BY THE AUTHOR OF "VARNEY, THE VAMPYRE," "THE RIVALS," "BLACK MANTLE," ETC. ETC.

[See p.

CHAPTER I.

THE TRAVELLING CHARIOT.—THE BIRTH.—THE DEATH OF THE MOTHER.—THE CHILD OF LOVE AND MYSTERY.

THE soft shades of a summer's evening were just beginning to grow sensibly dark, and the birds were singing their evening carol to the god of day, when there dashed into the high street, or rather what we may truly enough call the only street, of a small village, situated about fifteen miles from the city of York, a travelling chariot.

The horses, from their distressed appearance, had evidently been driven far, and they no doubt gladly paused, when they were permitted, at the door of the only inn the little place afforded.

Of course, such an arrival produced a corresponding degree of bustle and excitement, and the whole powers of the establishment were called into requisition to do honour to the visitors, who came in their own travelling chariot.

The landlord rushed out, and the landlady rushed out. The boots, and the ostler, and the chambermaid, and the cook, all did the same; so that the whole numerical force of the Goat and Topboots, which was the name of the inn, stood outside.

The footman, who occupied a place on the rumble behind, hastily got down, almost before the wheels of the carriage began to cease their revolutions. He opened the door hurriedly, and letting down the steps, he then stood aside, while a young and handsome man, whose complexion gave evidences of recent travel, sprang in an instant from the vehicle.

"What place is this?" he demanded, with the air of a man accustomed to command; "what place is this?"

"Snookins-cum-pipe, if you please, sir, it's called, if you please," said the landlord.

"What an infernal name! Have you accommodation for a lady?"

"For lots o' ladies, sir, though I say it. Here, missus. Green for a lady—green for a lady."

"What do you mean?"

"Green's our best room, sir, if you please; and if a lady who travels in her own chariot don't have green, I don't know who ought."

"Very well, very well. Only, be quick. Have you a medical man in the neighbourhood?"

"A doctor, sir? Lord bless you, yes! Of course, we has. The lady ain't well, I suppose."

"What's that to you?"

"Oh! nothing, sir—nothing; only I —— Green for the lady — green for the lady!"

The landlord rushed into the house, and the young stranger who had leaped from the carriage, now approached it, saying—

"Emily, Emily, be of good cheer. We can remain here until you are better."

"God help me! God help me!" was the reply from a female within the chariot.

"Hush! hush!" said the gentleman, "for God's sake, Emily. With all your feelings, recollect that we are among strangers."

"For your sake—for your sake," she said, in a low, moaning tone; "for your sake I will. Oh, Herbert—Herbert, our sufferings will now commence. Guilt! guilt! guilt!"

"Hush, Emily, hush! Do you want me to place a pistol to my head? If you do, you will go on as you are doing now."

"No, no, no, no."

"Peace, then, for your own sake as well as mine. I am doing the best I can. Do you feel able to walk from the carriage?"

"Yes,—oh, yes!"

"Come, then, I will assist you. Depend upon it, you will soon be better, and will be able to resume your journey."

She wept bitterly, as she, by his assistance, descended from the chariot. Then she glanced around her for a moment before she entered the inn, and with a shudder, said—

"Farewell!"

"Farewell! To whom—to what? Emily, Emily, what do you mean?"

"'Tis nothing! 'Tis nothing.'"

A shudder came over her frame, and, but for him, she would have fallen to the ground. She was a light and fragile form, and with the greatest ease he now raised her in his arms, and so carried her into the inn, calling out as he did,

"Show me the room for this lady. Show it me at once—don't stand staring at me like a parcel of idiots. Which is the room, I say?"

The landlord sprang forward, and rushing upstairs, he shouted,

"This way, sir; this way. Missus, where are you? The green chamber for the lady: No 10. Missus, missus, the lady's a coming."

The stranger followed him, and when he had brought the sick lady into the room, he resigned her to the care of the landlady, who was in such a state of agitation from the shouting of her husband and the suddenness of the arrival, that she did not know what to do.

"Have you sent for the nearest medical man?" said the gentleman.

"Lor, sir, no. You didn't order a medical man."

"Quick, then, now. Quick, send for him. I do order one."

"Yes, sir—certainly—certainly."

Down stairs rushed the landlord, leaving the stranger with the insensible companion of the travelling carriage and the landlady. A close veil, which, until now, enveloped the face of her who was named Emily, was removed, and never had it hidden a more lovely and enchanting countenance. She did not seem to be above seventeen, and she was as beautiful as the warmest imagination can depict.

"Well, I never!" exclaimed the landlady, as she lifted up her hands. "She is pretty! Are you a married man?"

"No—yes—no—that—ah, yes."

"Oh, indeed! Then, perhaps, sir, you'll excuse me if I takes upon myself, sir, to say as this here young lady oughtn't to have been took about in a carriage, in her uncommon delicate situation."

"Well, well," said the gentleman, impatiently, "I know all that. It was inevitable. There is a ten pound note. I shall trust to you to pay every attention."

"No ring!"

"No what?"

"No wedding ring, sir."

"Oh, she—she lost it. Leaning her hand out of the carriage window, it came off—you see. You understand—you—you understand?"

"Oh, hem! I think as how I really does. Howsomdever, females is females, and men is men. I've got a heart a continually a beating in my bosom for all. The poor sweet young thing shall want for nothing here."

"You shall lose nothing by any attention you may pay her, you may depend. Do for her all that kindness can suggest, and trust to me for such remuneration as shall be ample."

"I'm a mother of four myself, sir. My first, you must know, was a seven months', and I often say to my husband ——"

"All of which you shall tell me another time," interrupted the young man. "Now I will leave you with your patient, and I hope we shall be able to proceed to-morrow."

"To-morrow, did you say, sir? Do you think as a young lady is like a wild Injun?—and her first, too, no doubt. If you move from here under a blessed month, I'll eat the bedpost."

"You—you don't think so?"

There came a tap at the door, and simultaneously with that tap it was opened, and the medical man of the village walked in. He bowed to the young stranger, and the landlady took occasion to announce who he was.

"I will leave you with your patient, sir," said the traveller, who seemed to feel very irksome under any scrutinizing glance that might be bent upon him. Having uttered these words, he hastily left the room, and upon reaching the ground-floor, he demanded a private sitting-room, and when the landlord ventured to ask him what he wanted, he said,—

"Send me in some of the best wine you have in the place, and plenty of it."

This was not a kind of order which was likely to be displeasing to an innkeeper; but still it betrayed a reckless state of mind in his customer, which he did not like to see, and which gave him some uneasiness. However, he supplied the wine, and when he did so, he found his guest with his elbows resting upon the table, and his face buried in his hands, as if in profound meditation.

"The wine, sir," he said.

But there was no answer. So, after a pause of about a minute, he again said,—

" The wine, sir."

That having also no effect, he just touched the shoulder of the young man, and again said,—

" Please, sir, the wine."

The young traveller sprang to his feet in a moment, and cried,—

" What now, scoundrel? What now?"

" Sir, I—I—sir, I only brought the wine."

" Leave it then."

He reassumed his former position, and the landlord was glad to get out of the room again with a whole skin.

It was getting very dark now. The sun had completely set, and the evening was becoming cool for the season of the year; but still that young traveller sat with his hands covering his face, while now and then a deep groan would come from the very bottom of his heart, as if to indicate that the subject of his reflection was one of the most painful character. He sat in the dark, for the landlord was afraid, after the reception he had met with, to go into the room again, and so, as he did not ring for candles, he remained in the dark.

Suddenly, however, he heard, or fancied he heard, the sound of hurried footsteps in the inn, and as if some unusual bustle was taking place. Then he sprang to his feet, and uttered the name of Emily in frantic accents.

By the dim light around he just managed to see that wine was upon the table, and at once seizing upon the decanter, he poured out, and drank off rapidly, five or six glasses in succession without any pause. Then he listened again, but all was still.

" This is retribution!" he said. " This is retribution! Oh, God! there are people whom I can never look upon again, without the conscious flush of guilt rising to my face. I may deny the imputation that will be cast upon me,—I may brave out the accusation, if it be made; but yet I know that I am guilty—that I am the seducer of such innocence as surely rarely dwells in a mortal frame. Oh, Emily! Emily! it was on the account of your very trusting purity that you fell."

There was suddenly a flash of light, and the door of the room was opened. It was the medical man, who carried a candle in his hand. He stood upon the threshold of the door, and without saying a word, he beckoned to the young traveller, who sprang towards him in a state of the greatest alarm.

" What—what has happened?" he said.

" If you wish to see her alive, you will go up stairs at once."

The young traveller staggered back a pace or two, as if some one had suddenly planted a dagger in his heart; then a strange bursting sob came from his lips, and he dashed up the staircase like a maniac. To reach the room where he had left the young and beautiful girl, was the work of a moment. There were several women there surrounding the bed. He tottered forward, and, by the light of a candle which one of them held, he saw her who had been his travelling companion lying as if already dead.

A shriek burst from his lips as he pronounced her name.

" Emily! Emily! Emily! Oh, God!"

She heard that sound, although the sounds of this earth and its inhabitants were flitting from her. She saw that face she knew so well, although the film of death was gathering upon her eyes. It was one of those efforts which powerful emotion will wring from almost death itself. She extended her arms, and a smile flitted over her wan features as she said—

" My Herbert!"

He stooped over her, and she clung to his neck. It was but for a moment. The arms relaxed their hold; the small taper fingers slid gently from each others clasp; there was one long-drawn sigh, and all was over. That beautiful girl was dead,—dead in the glorious promise of her youth—dead on the threshold of existence—a rose-bud crushed!

* * * * * * * * *

What pen can hope to picture the agony of him who now looked upon the bed of death! The reality of the dreadful fact seemed indeed too horrible to be believed. He looked from face to face of those who were there assembled, as if imploring some one of them to give him a hope that such was not the case; that she whom he had loved to her destruction, was not dead; that he had not sacrificed her; and that not for him whom she had "loved, not wisely, but too well," had she passed the dread portal that separates life from eternity.

"Emily! Emily! Emily!" he shouted. "Speak, oh, speak to me, Emily, my love, my own only love—my darling Emily!"

"She will never speak again," said a woman who was present. "She will never speak again, poor thing!"

He flung his arms around the corpse.

"Lights, lights!" he cried. "Bring me lights! Nearer and nearer still, that I may assure myself that this is but a swoon; a likeness of death, but not the reality of it. Emily, Emily! you are not dead. Dead! oh! no; that is too dreadful a word to associate with you. Best and dearest, you are not dead!"

They did as he bade them, and brought him lights, which they held so that he had a clear view of the face of her who, but a few short hours since, had breathed the breath of life, and looked into his face for hope and consolation under circumstances which were most awfully depressing.

He could not longer doubt the dreadful truth,—she was dead! The half-closed eyes were fixed and motionless; the lips had lost their ruddy hue—the face was pale, and the nerveless frame had that apathetic look which follows quick on dissolution,

> "Ere decay's offensive fingers
> Have marred the lines where beauty reigns."

A cry of despair burst from his heart, and sinking into a chair, he covered his face with his hands as he said, in a shrieking, wailing tone—

"And I am desolate!"

"Not so, sir," said the woman who had before spoken to him. "No so, sir."

He felt something touch him. He looked up, and saw a new born infant in her arms. For the first time he seemed to think of the possibility of the existence of the child. A low, wailing cry from the infant, however, in a moment convinced him that it, at least, had survived its unhappy mother.

"God of heaven!" he said, "oh, God of heaven! why does this thing live, and she whom I loved ——"

He could say no more, but bursting into a flood of passionate tears, he shook like an aspen leaf.

"Oh! sir," said the woman, "it ought to be a consolation to you that the child lives, although its poor mother is no more."

He wrung his hands as he said—

"Will no one kill me,—will no one kill me?"

That woman who had assumed the care of the child, seemed to take the lead among the others who had been hastily summoned to the chamber of death, and she seemed to be possessed with the opinion that if anything at all would have the effect of calming the tumult of feeling and of remorse which seemed to have found a home in the heart of that bereaved man, that child would. She still pressed it upon his attention, saying,—

"The child, sir; the child."

A sudden revulsion of feeling came over him. He rose, and took the infant in his arms, and showered kisses upon its soft cheeks, while his tears fell like rain upon its face.

"Unhappy one! unhappy one!" he sobbed; "I will live to beg and earn your forgiveness. Let me be alone for—for an hour."

He staggered to the door of the room, and then he paused, and, turning to the woman, he said,—

"The child is a boy?"

"No, sir; a girl."

" God help her! God help her!" he said.

Again he seemed to be on the point of leaving the room, but again he returned, and going up to the bed, he took a long and agonized look at the face of the corpse.

He stooped and kissed those pale lips he so often pressed to his in life. He remembered, at that moment, the time when he had first done so, and being but gently chidden for the act. He remembered how the soft pressure thrilled through him. Oh, that was a remembrance now of agony—that was a re- miniscence now of the past, which added some years to his age, and nearly broke the heart that treasured up such a feeling !

He could not feel but like one who feels himself on the road to some dread- ful doom no earthly power can arrest. He now slowly passed from the room, and went tottering down the staircase. He reached whence he had been sum- moned to the bed of death, and there he sat like one bewildered. They heard him rise, and lock the door. Then all was as still as the tomb.

CHAPTER II.

THE SUDDEN DEPARTURE.—THE AWKWARD PREDICAMENT.

THE presence of the young stranger in the chamber of death appeared to have exerted a calming effect upon all who were there, if we might judge from the increased tumult that took place after his absence.

We do not intend it as any libel upon the ladies, but it is a certain fact, as a general thing, that they have a great propensity for giving their opinions all at once. Probably the excitement, caused by the appearance of him who was supposed to be so largely interested in the direful event that had taken place, superseded all other considerations for a time ; but now that he had given vent to his anguish, and looked his look of despair, the interest in him was of course wonderfully de- creased, and the several dames of the village who had been called in by the land- lady, took it as the advent of a new existence, and became, all of a sudden, active in conjecture.

And yet they spoke in low tones, although earnest ones, for there is something about the presence of the dead which awes commonplace minds into far greater silence and respect than they would award to the sick.

Oh, how all the circumstances were canvassed, and how the dead mother's clothing was criticised, and what a world of elaborate discourse was expended upon the infant, which now lay peacefully slumbering upon the same bed which bore the remains of her whom cruel fortune had doomed never to play towards it a mother's part !

But there was one opinion in which they all agreed, and that was, that it was a dreadful shame, for there was quite sufficient evidence to prove, in their minds, that the young and beautiful girl who had come to an untimely grave, although a mother, was no wife.

The absence of the wedding-ring, which had at first attracted the landlady's attention, was of itself considered most conclusive testimony, although the ease with which the insignia of matrimony can be assumed ought to have deprived it of some of its weight.

"Oh ! it's easy," said one, " to see how the cat jumps. Come what may, or go what would, I would not be without my wedding-ring, for the universe, the Injees, and the Bank of England included. No ; not to please anybody. There has been something very wrong going on here."

"Well, I'd give something," said another, " to know all about it. It must be very interesting. She is what many men would call good-looking, but not to my taste."

"And he is decidedly an elegant man," said the first speaker, " and quite the gentleman."

Then, all at once, they declared together they would give any reasonable sum to know all about it ; after which, the child began to cry, upon which the oldest, and of course the most knowing of the lot, stuffed its mouth with sugar and butter, and put it on its back, to save it from the throes of convulsion whic h it made to swallow it.

" You may depend upon it," said one who had first remarked upon it, " that come where you will, or go where you may, there's loads of what there shouldn't be. Howsomedever, it mayn't turn out a bad affair after all, for somebody seems to have their eyes wide open to the main chance."

This was evidently said in allusion to the woman who had shown the child to the young stranger, and who, by her manner and a certain indescribable appearance about her face, would have been pronounced to be a superior person to her neighbours.

She did not seem to think herself called upon to make any reply to this hint, so that it was entirely thrown away ; the great beauty of such speeches being to get the party to whom they are addressed to reply to them.

And now by this time they knew pretty well how much a yard everything was likely to have cost which the mother had on her, and had settled in their own minds a great many other interesting particulars ; when the landlady, who had left the room for a few moments, returned with such precipitation, that it was evident she had some wonderful news to relate. She sank into a chair, with the very satisfactory exclamation of—

" Oh! my gracious powers !"

Of course she was eagerly questioned by the whole throng ; but, like the oracles of old, she was very obscure ; and it was not until she had recovered and taken a small glass of something neat, that she was enabled to commence her revelations by saying,—

" What do you think ?"

Everybody declared they didn't know what to think ; and then she told them that the gentleman had had fresh horses put into the chariot, and was fairly gone no one knew whither.

Like the chorus in a Greek tragedy, when something has gone very queer, the ladies looked at each other with rueful countenances, and then, with one accord, said,—

" The brute !"

" To desert his own flesh and blood !" screamed one.

" And not," cried another, " to stay and see another poor creature put decently under ground as he has been the ruin of."

" I declare," said another, " as I am a living woman, and a mother of a family, I shouldn't know him again."

" Perhaps," said the woman who had held the child in her arms, " he has left thus hastily on that very account."

" Oh! dear me !" said the landlady ; " my husband's got the letter. It's enough to make any one faint away for a month to think of it. I declare to you all I never was in the state I am in now. He wanted to keep the letter to himself, and take it over to Justice Webb's, but I told him we lived in a public-house, and could have nothing private here."

" But what's to become of the child ?" said every one of them in chorus.

" Look at it," said the woman whom we have before noticed as being superior to the others, as she took the child in her arms. " It may be the child of shame and sorrow ; but saw ye ever one so beautiful ? I am poor, as Heaven knows, and have a profligate for a husband. Will any of you who are in far better circumstances than myself, give this poor little creature a home ?"

" A home, indeed !" cried one. " I think I see the little brat coming within my doors! No, indeed ! Send it to the parish. Mr. Shortshanks, the overseer, is the man for that."

" I should think so," chimed in the most voluble of the party. " Listen to me, female ladies—I declare to you, on the word of a respectable woman, as always has, her ' marriage loins' at hand to show to anybody, let 'em be who they may—Turks or Prussians, or infidels—that I wouldn't have the little wretch in my house for all the universe, the Injees, and the Bank of England."

" Besides, look at the example to husbands," cried a third.

And then they all cried,—

" Oh! good God! Yes."

As if all the husbands in the village were only waiting for this example to become so many Don Giovannis.

At this moment the door opened, and the landlord appeared. He uttered the words,—

" Oh, I've read the letter! What do you think? Mr. Potts, down stairs, has read it too."

Having delivered this piece of oracularism, he shot down stairs like lightning, but it had its effects, for after him flew the gossipping matrons, nor did they stop till they had made their way into the bar parlour, where sat the landlord and the aforesaid Mr. Potts.

This Mr. Potts was rather a great man in his way. He was a bachelor, retired from—nobody knew where, with a small income, to take up his abode in the village ; and a very great pest he became to a variety of most exalted personages in that vicinity.

Mr. Potts opposed the lawyer, and swore he was always wrong ; he opposed the doctor, and declared he could cure the people in half the time, and kill them in a third ; and he was ever ready to split a straw in controversial divinity with the parson.

He knew some manure that none of the farmers knew ; and he abused their rotation of crops in some scientific manner which they did not comprehend, and, therefore, could not answer ; which, consequently, made them angry.

In fact, a more unpopular person than Mr. Potts could not well be, and yet, somehow or another, when anybody had any grievance, he or she ran to Mr. Potts, who was sure to take part against the constituted authorities, let the grounds of the quarrel be what they might.

" Well, well !" said Mr. Potts, as the females rushed into the room ; " what's the row ? what's the row ?"

" The letter !" they all gasped; " he's left a letter."

" He has left a letter," said Mr. Potts, with a shrug, as much as to say, " And a pretty article it is, too."

" Yes, yes; and what's his name ?" cried two or three in a breath.

" John Smith," said Mr. Potts, solemnly. " What he wishes to know, is, which of you ladies will be so kind as to take charge of the infant for one year ?"

The look of virtuous indignation which pervaded the whole phalanx was immense. Mr. Potts even came in for his share of vituperation, for being the mouthpiece to such audacity, and it was with some difficulty he could obtain another hearing sufficient to say,—

" Then, ladies, you one and all reject the offer ?"

Loud cries of " Certainly ;" " Oh, indeed ! Don't you wish you may get it ?" " Send the brat to the parish ;" " Where's Mr. Shortshanks ?" resounded through the body, with the exception of the woman who, up to then, had assumed the care of the infant. When the clamour had somewhat subsided, she spoke, saying,—

" Sir, it is well known to all here that I am poor—very poor ; but I have a feeling of tenderness towards the child that makes me loth it should be committed to the brutality of the parish. I shall not look upon this little creature as a burden, day by day, hour by hour, as they would. God knows I have little ; but that little, if Heaven still spare it me, that child shall share."

" But," said Potts, deprecatingly, " you have, Mrs. Grove, one of the idlest and most drunken husbands in the parish. Besides, you have a little boy of your own."

" My child is five years of age," she said, " and this is an infant. Little Willie will be fond of it. The milk and bread it will eat, we will try to do without."

" Very good," said Mr. Potts; " wilful people must have their own way, of

course.   I suppose, ladies, you are all agreeable that Mrs. Grove shall take the responsibility of this child."

"Oh! yes, indeed," was the cry.   "Birds of a feather flock together."

"And all the disadvantages ?" said Mr. Potts.

"Oh! yes—yes; and lots of 'em."

"And all the advantages ?"

There was a general laugh, but Mr. Potts said gravely—

"Now, ladies! now, ladies!   Who knows but at the end of the year the father
may come back and be tremendously grateful."

This produced another laugh from all the ladies, and poor Mrs. Grove was looked
upon with so much contempt, that, in spite of herself, her eyes filled with tears, and
she held the babe still closer to her breast, repeating her resolve never to part with
it willingly.

"Very good—very good," said Mr. Potts, as he unfolded the letter with great deliberation. "There's nobody says no, Mrs. Grove, and you say yes. I will read to you the very brief note which will be your authority in this case."

Mr. Potts then read as follows :—

"Let the infant be placed in charge with the kindest and most trustworthy of the women whom I left in the chamber of death, provided she will undertake the charge. The enclosed amount, it is hoped, will prove satisfactory for the first year's maintenance.   "JOHN SMITH."

A scream burst from the lips of the ladies, as the contents of this note reached their ears. Several felt faint, and one showed a slight disposition to go into hysterics. It was she who would not have taken the child for "the universe, the Injees, and the Bank of England," who had the courage to ask the question of—

"And—and—good gracious preserve us all! what may this Mr. John Smith think enough for keeping the sweet little dear for twelve months, and in attending to it in such a motherly way as never was ?"

"Fifty-two pounds," said Mrs. Potts. "Here's a fifty pounds note, and two sovereigns, which I hand to you, Mrs. Grove, in the presence of witnesses, as one of the advantages attending the little responsibility."

The ladies who had been very nearly fainting now fainted entirely, and the one who had shown a slight tendency to hysterics went slap into them, as if she had been used to it all her life, and liked it.

The scene of confusion that ensued baffles all description ; there was not one among the lot who would not have gladly jumped at one half the sum. Never had there been such a take in, in that village, in the memory of that all knowing person, the oldest inhabitant.

Mrs. Grove herself was astonished, and some one of the ladies might have snatched the fifty pounds note from her hand and swallowed it, but for the carefulness of Mr. Potts and the landlord, who at once conducted her into another room, the door of which they closed, so as to keep out all disturbance.

Here, Mrs. Grove's first act, instead of any expression of exultation, was to burst into tears, and when she recovered sufficiently to speak, she said—

"Oh! sir, I would rather not take the money. I had no idea of money in the matter. Besides, Heaven only knows what effect such a sum of money might have upon William"—meaning her husband.

"But you are entitled to it, and it shall be yours," said Mr. Potts. "The only way to keep it out of your husband's power, is to place it in the hands of some one you can trust, and draw it, a few shillings at a time, as you may want for you own necessities and those of the child. There's Squire Webb, or the d—d lawyer, or the doctor ——"

"Will you, sir, undertake for me that office? I shall be most grateful to you, and feel assured that all is correct."

"If you wish it, I will. And now don't stand talking here another second, but wrap up the child as carefully as you can, and get home to your own cottage. That you will do your duty by it, Mrs. Grove, I have not the slightest doubt ; nor have I any doubt but the whole affair will turn out very much to your advantage. Take the two odd pounds now, and come to me the moment you require more."

Mrs. Grove borrowed a blanket of the landlady, and in it she so securely wrapped the little stranger, that not the least breath of cold air could get to it. The season of the year, too, was favourable to the infant, for it was warm and genial, so that this child, who might be said to be as much an orphan, to all intents and purposes, as any child could well be, probably had a fair enough chance for existence.

We give Mrs. Grove full credit for not having the least idea of the handsome remuneration which the gentlemanly young stranger had left, and which had been withheld until such a critical moment by Mr. Potts; and such being the case, it is a matter of great congratulation, not only that the poor little infant should have got into such hands, but the money also.

Mrs. Grove had in her own mind but one drawback upon the pleasure which the whole transaction afforded her, and that consisted in a positive dread of what would be the conduct of her drunken and dissolute husband as regarded it, known as he was to the whole village, and to most of the country round about, wherever public-houses flourished, as "drunken Jack Grove"—a most unenviable reputation, and one which caused his innocent and exemplary wife many and many a heartache.

CHAPTER III.

THE PARTY AT THE MARCHIONESS OF FANFARONADE'S IN MAY-FAIR.

LET us leave for a while the little village, with its verdant green, its inn, its little politics and bickerings, its intense gossipping powers, and its goodness as well as its evil, while we turn to a far different scene; and with the less reluctance do we leave the child which fate had been kinder to than its parents, for it had been cast into kind hands, and Mrs. Grove loved it for its own sake, and found in each of its infant cries a loud appeal to its humanity.

We leave it, we say, with less reluctance, because we feel that all a tender mother's care could not exceed that which was being bestowed upon it by her who had not lightly or heedlessly taken upon herself to supply the place of one. And, moreover, Jack Grove, as fortune would have it, had got desperately drunk on that day, and had, in a state of pot valour, assaulted a constable of a neighbouring market-town, who had signified an intention of making him acquainted with the cage.

For this offence he had been adjudged on the following morning to pay a fine of ten shillings, besides five shillings for the offence at law of drunkenness, and the costs, making altogether the amount of seven-and-twenty shillings, current coin of the nation.

Now, as Jack Grove's exchequer amounted to somewhere about half that number of pence, it did not lie within the compass of belief that he could pay it, so for fourteen days was Jack committed to durance vile, as a *quid pro quo*.

Fourteen happy days to his wife—fourteen peaceful days to the whole village, and, fortunately, to the child who had received shelter under that roof which we were about to call his, but which really ought not to be called so, even out of courtesy, seeing that it was only kept over his head by his wife's exertions.

Thus, then, do we feel that, with some degree of peace in our minds, can we leave the "love child," to detail proceedings in London which it is highly necessary to our story that the reader should be made acquainted with.

That we shall be back to the village again, to the cottage of Mrs. Grove, on the day of the liberation of Jack Grove, we promise; when we shall give a faithful record of what he did, and what he didn't—what he said, and what he left alone—of how drunk he got, and what he thought, till he got so very drunk, that he couldn't think at all.

Our metropolitan readers know that at the top of Oxford-street nearly, on the left-hand side going westward, is a narrowish thoroughfare, which leads to a much larger one, called May-fair. This May-fair is considered decidedly aristocratic, for there all sorts of people—of reputation and of no reputation—of wealth and of trickery—of title and of fashion—reside; and many and splendid have been the entertainments which have been from time to time given in that most odd and celebrated locality.

One of the largest, handsomest, and most expensive of the houses was occupied by the Marchioness of Fanfaronade. This female—if we are not speaking in too derogatory a manner of a marchioness, by calling her a female—was tall, wiry-looking, and aristocratic. She had a large face, and an aquiline nose; she was moderately wealthy, and contrived by some mysterious way, although she had five thousand pounds per annum, to live up to the rate of, at the very least, twelve.

How she managed such a seeming impossibility is the lady's affair, not ours; and, as it concerns not our story, we have nothing to say to it. She was, her compeers said, as proud as an empress—her servants said, as proud as Lucifer; but proud she was, and of the most ridiculous thing in all the world to be proud of, namely, of descent, and of her ancestors.

It was to the Marchioness of Fanfaronade that the testy old gentleman, who had been much annoyed by hearing her talk of her ancestors, said,—

"Madam, you are like a carrot. To hear you talk, it is quite evident that the best of you is underground."

The marchioness, we forgot to say, was a widow. The Marquis of Fanfaronade only held out five years after his marriage, and was then quietly consigned to his family vault, leaving behind him three daughters of very tender years.

At the period we write, these daughters were respectively of the ages of eighteen, sixteen, and fifteen. They were handsome young women, particularly the eldest, who inherited all that her mother could pretend to in good looks, with all her pride and heartlessness, and utter selfishness of character. Her name was Annabella, and she was a compound of arrogance such as even in the circles in which she moved is very rarely to be met with.

The second daughter, Julia, was something of the same cast; but owing to not being so tall as Annabella, she did not carry the same weight with her, and could never assume half the arrogant airs of her sister.

The third, Flora, was very much the reverse. She was very beautiful, but timid as a young fawn. She shunned instead of courted admiration, and had certainly amiability enough for the whole family in her disposition. She was the very soul of feeling, sensitiveness, and romance; and how she became so very different a character from her selfish and imperious sisters, must be left to be decided by those learned physiologists and ethical philosophers, who can decide anything, from a pin's head to a mammoth's tooth.

We are simply content to record facts, and a fact it was that Flora was the most loveable and amiable young creature under the sun. She was but fifteen—an early age to be, what is called in fashionable society, " brought out." But her tall, graceful figure, and the beauty and mild seriousness of her countenance, made it look really odd to keep her in the nursery; consequently, at the advice and instance of the Dowager Duchess of Mountmidden, Flora was brought out, in spite of being a good year and a half younger than had been either of her sisters at the period of so interesting a process.

As bringing out a young lady, however, only consists in allowing her to walk from the nursery to the drawing-room, and to leave a card, and receive invites, and as the " mother always knows they're out," it is by no means a serious affair. Indeed, it is but a sort of invite to the men, as if the old hen should say,—

"Now, my men, here's another chick, young and tender. Look at her well. She's a-going—a-going to the highest bidder."

There were ill-natured, as well as ill-disposed people, who did not scruple to say that the advice of the Dowager Duchess of Mountmidden had been of a very insidious character, and that she only advised that she might be brought out, in order that she might, by her superior beauty, interfere with the prospects of Annabella.

Now, Annabella was looking out for a husband, and her mother was aiding her in the search, so that it was just possible that somebody might have sense enough to prefer the real beauty, and the gentleness, and the amiability of Flora, to the showy, aristocratic manners of Annabella, who boasted of that style of beauty which was rather of the masculine order, and which it requires a man of a tolerable coarse intellect to admire.

Thus matters went on for half a season, when an accident happened, or rather two accidents, which caused a great sensation in the fashionable world, and at once provided the Lady Annabella with a husband.

There was an old Earl of Crumbledown and Warelock. His was one of the oldest peerages in the kingdom. He had come over with the Conqueror, and had assisted much in the subjugation of England by the Normans.

We say he had come over with the Conqueror, because the old man himself always used that phrase, so thoroughly did he identify himself with his family and their times, when the Crumbledowns were mailed knights, and really took some hard knocks on their hard heads for what they got.

The old earl was nearly ninety. He had married twice with the hope of a heir to his estates. In the first marriage he was disappointed; but, in the second, he was gratified by the birth of a son, who was now at the age of twenty-one precisely, and who, of course, was heir-presumptive to the ancient peerage of Crumbledown.

Lord Herbert Warelock, or Lord Warelock, as he was commonly called, was eminently handsome, but he certainly had not an abundance of that kind of intellect which gives any firmness and resolution to the character. He was not what one might say, mentally deficient; he could talk well enough; and, considering his station in life, did not make it at all necessary that he should make any great call upon his mental powers, was likely enough, in as respectable a manner as any other lord, to get through his existence, and occupy a place in the archives of his family.

When, too, we come to consider really his high rank, he was not, as all things are comparative, to be called a fool; but then a man who, in the middle class of society, would be unable to get a living, or the slightest attention paid to what he said or did, does very well indeed for a lord or a duke—take the Duke of Cambridge for example, who is only a degree or two, as well as his son, removed from idiotcy; or such a man as Lord Londonderry, of whom Brougham said that he did not believe God Almighty ever made anybody so stupid, but that it must be wilful on his own part. But Lord Warelock was not so bad as these by a vast amount; indeed, he was rather a presentable young man.

The event to which we have alluded as making a great change in the aspect of affairs as regarded the Lady Annabella, was the death of the old Earl of Crumbledown; but as the circumstances deserve a chapter of their own, we will reserve them till our next, and content ourselves by introducing our readers to the evening party which the Marchioness of Fanfaronade gave on the evening succeeding that which heralded into existence the " love child" at the little village inn.

" We are all determined to hang together," said one of a lot of rogues once, and the saying is good as regards the aristocracy of this country. Let the vices, the follies, or the crimes of any one of their number be what they may, they still hang together, and seem to feel the necessity of upholding the dignity of rank as something quite apart from common honesty or common morality.

Thus, such a woman as the Marchioness of Fanfaronade could always fill her rooms with the proudest and noblest of the nobility of England, notwithstanding many of her smiling guests knew her to be a woman of the narrowest principles, and one whom, apart from the rank she held, might well have been despised and detested. Moreover, it was as well known, too, as if she had had the fact placarded in her saloons, that she was giving a series of brilliant entertainments for the one sole object of endeavouring to get off her daughters, always to the highest bidder.

No one had, as yet, had the courage to make an offer to Annabella; but there were about three whom she and her mamma had picked out as men towards whom some little flattering attention should be shown.

One of these, then, was the young Warelock—unexceptionable in point of birth, and the expected possessor, at the death of his father, of one of the most enormous fortunes of any peer of the kingdom. But the young lord had rather a will of his own, and was proof against the whole artillery of charms which were brought to bear against the outworks of his heart by the Lady Annabella.

The party was a most brilliant one. The state apartments of the marchioness's house, as, with an affectation almost of royalty, they were called, were all thrown open, and presented a perfect picture of magnificence. Hundreds of wax lights lent their soft, grateful brilliancy to the scene; and the crash of delightful music filled the air with joyous sounds. And then the ladies, resplendent with jewels; and the gentlemen, many of them in court suits—for there had been a levee on the same day, and the artful and cunning Marchioness of Fanfaronade had calculated upon many of their guests coming in their court costumes—made the rooms look positively regal.

Without, there was an incessant roar, rattle, and dash of carriages. Within, light, beauty, smiles, and music.

The entertainment had not commenced till eleven o'clock, when well-disposed people are in bed; and about one it was at its height, and dancing had been going on for about an hour. Notwithstanding, however, all her manœuvring, the marchioness had not been able to match her daughter with any of the three men she had pitched upon as desirable, and she was in a state of vexation almost bordering upon madness.

Lord Warelock had bestowed some flattering attentions upon Flora, and Annabella had seen him do so. She sought out her mother, and with bitterness said to her—

"I knew it. Men are always attracted by overgrown children. Lord Warelock is talking to Flora, and only look at his eyes, and her pretended timidity!"

"I'll put a stop to that, my dear," said the marchioness. "It shall not be, I can tell you."

"Very good; but as it is not you, you know, to whom he is paying attention, I don't see very well how you can put a stop to it."

One of those noiseless, well-dressed attendants, who glide about drawing-rooms so gently that they are never in anybody's way, approached the marchioness, and stood a few paces off, waiting until she should have leisure to hear him.

"Well, Simpson," she said, "what is it?"

"The prince."

"The who?"

"Beg pardon, my lady, but I can't pronounce his name. The gentleman is coming up, and as he had not been here before, and I thought no one seemed to know him, I thought, my lady, I had better tell you."

"But who is he?"

"There's his card, my lady. I—I don't like pronouncing his name."

"Is it anything improper?" said Annabella, in an eager whisper, as she glanced at the card.

"No, my dear; but it is one of those Russian or Polish names which nobody can pronounce, unless they have been brought up to it from infancy."

On the card was the name of the Prince Adolphe Schreuskiczincki.

Hardly had the marchioness made an attempt to decipher the conundrum of a name, than the groom of the chamber announced the arrival, saying, in a loud tone,

"The Prince Adolphe Skin-sneaky-crunky-iky-sky."

The name appeared to excite considerable sensation among the guests, and many eyes were turned in the direction of the grand entrance to the rooms.

A young man, very plainly attired, and with a sharp physiognomy, entered the saloon. He was met by the marchioness, who bowed to him with some degree of hauteur, as she said, in a tone of voice that showed she must have an answer, while at the same time it was perfectly polite—

"Not having the honour of your previous acquaintance, I am at a loss to know whom I am addressing."

"Lord Warelock knows me, my lady," said the prince.

"Lord Warelock of Crumbledown?"

"Exactly. If you send for him, he will act as my sponsor upon this occasion, I am quite certain."

"I need scarcely say that any friend of Lord Warelock's is most welcome here. He is in the room. Will you permit me to have the honour of accompanying you to seek him?"

"Certainly, madam."

The prince gave his hand to the marchioness, and with far more grace and dignity of manner than his rather brusque mode of talking would have bespoken, he led her towards a window, where Lord Warelock was leaning against the back of a chair, and talking to Flora, with more animation in his countenance than it usually displayed.

"My lord," said the marchioness, "here is a friend of yours who has honoured us by a most unexpected visit."

"A friend of mine!" exclaimed Warelock, as he looked with surprise at the prince with the unpronounceable name.

"Do you not know the gentleman?"

"Not I, Lady Fanfaronade. Not I."

"Your lordship has a short memory," said the prince. "If you will step aside with me for one moment, I will convince you that we have met in Warsaw."

"Warsaw! I never was in Warsaw in my life."

"Nay, nay, my lord, your memory is singularly defective. Pray indulge me with a moment's audience, and I shall be able to convince your lordship you are wrong."

"Gentlemen," said the marchioness, "I think you must be jesting with us."

"Believe me, not I," said Lord Warelock. "This gentleman is mistaken."

"I beg your pardon, my lord, I am not mistaken," said the prince. "I can call to your remembrance some circumstances which will at once convince you that I am right."

He stepped close up to him, and whispered about a dozen words in the ear of Lord Warelock, after which he turned to the marchioness and Flora, saying,—

"May I hope for your kind forgiveness for so much rudeness?"

"Gracious Heaven! Lord Warelock is ill!" exclaimed the marchioness.

"Ill!" echoed Flora; "oh! no, no."

"Hush! You go away directly."

Lord Warelock turned very pale, and sank into the chair which had been vacated by Flora, even while the prince spoke to him; and then he trembled so much, and looked so really ill, that the marchioness would have called for aid, but the prince said,—

"'Tis only the shock, madam, of a sudden joyful surprise, at meeting with an old friend whom he did not at first recognise. His lordship knows me now, and will be better."

"Indeed!"

"Ay; you shall hear."

"My lord, are you better?"

"Yes—yes," gasped Warelock.

"Do you recollect now being in Warsaw?"

"Yes, yes."

"At my father's palace, where we became acquainted, and where the young Duke Constantine was staying."

"Yes—I—I remember now."

"And I am the Prince Schreuskiczincki?"

"You are—you are."

"You hear, now, madam; you hear. I do much regret that I should have caused you any uneasiness. I am but newly arrived in London, and hearing that my friend, Lord Warelock, was here, and that this house was the abode of a lady holding so deservedly and so nobly the position of your ladyship, I made bold to come."

There was something desperately out of the proper order of things in all this, but the marchioness knew not very well what to do or say, except to make the prince, whose name she would not venture upon attempting to utter, welcome, so she said—

"Any friend of Lord Warelock we are most happy to see;" and then placing her daughter's arm beneath her own, she walked slowly away.

Lord Warelock made a passionate gesture as he said to the prince in a low tone,

"Great God, why choose this place?"

"Hush! Are you about to leave or stay?"

"Leave, by all means; and you—you will not remain here?"

"No, I will go with you; but mark me—I am free of this house on the score of your knowledge of me. Betray me, and ——"

"Hush!"

"I was merely going to say that you know the consequences."

"Come away, come away. I will not—I cannot listen to you here. What designs or projects you may have, Heaven only knows."

"And myself. But, as you seem to consider it will be inconvenient here to converse, why, come away, by all means; I have no desire to stay. What amount of curiosity I had has been satisfied. I am quite ready to go."

Lord Warelock left the saloons, closely followed by the prince. He descended the staircase rapidly, and crossed the hall. Then, without calling his carriage, he emerged into the street. When he had got a few paces from the door, he turned abruptly, and said,—

"Now, sir, be you whom you may, you are out of my friend's house, and shall give me an account of what has provoked this insolence."

"Insolence, my lord!"

"Yes; most unheard-of insolence."

"Indeed! You assume a new tone now. I told you I was uncle Joe. Where's my niece? I say, where's my niece, you infernal aristocratic seducer? Where's my niece? You shall assist me, or I will ruin you. The Earl of Crumbledown is in town."

Lord Warelock staggered a little.

"I want to make a good alliance," continued the mock prince. "You descended to affect to love honourably my niece. I ascend, and love Flora Fanfaronade. I want her for a wife; so, you see, I act more honourably than you. I have no present intention of seducing her. Hark you, my lord, I will make a bargain with you. You shall back me up in high life—you shall lend me money—and vouch for my being a prince; and, in return, I will make no effort to discover where you have hidden my niece. Nay, I will so direct the inquiries of others, that you shall not be suspected of having had any hand in the abduction. You will perhaps want to know who I am, and I answer nothing. I have been many things. My wits have always been my trading capital. I have a tolerable education, an amazing stock of assurance, I am civil and friendly to my friends, I am implacable to my enemies. Now you know me, with the exception of my name, which is, Joseph Willoughby. Is it a bargain? You do well to reflect. Such a story as I have to tell your father, would cut you out of all the personal property."

All this was spoken with such rapidity and volubility, that Lord Warelock stood aghast for some time listening to it, and wanted power to interrupt the speaker, who naturally enough thought, from the young nobleman's silence, that he entertained the proposition. Most disagreeably was he surprised when Lord Warelock suddenly turned upon him, and, with one well-directed blow, knocked him down, where he lay so stunned, that the young noble walked away, called loudly for his carriage, and had driven off before he recovered.

CHAPTER IV.

THE EARL'S ANGER.—THE ACCIDENT TO THE CARRIAGE, AND ITS CONSEQUENCES.

THE sham prince, when he did recover himself from the hard knock in the shape of an argument he had received from Lord Warelock, found that some good Samaritan had removed him to the step of a door, and propped him up against the door itself, most probably under the supposition that he was drunk.

There were two or three idle persons looking at him and laughing.

"He's coming round a little now," said one. "A good pumping on him now would be the best thing for him."

"To be sure it would," exclaimed another, "and it would serve him out into the bargain."

"A coach! a coach!" said the prince, alias Joe Willoughby. "Can't I have a coach?"

"Oh! yes, old brick," said a boy; "you shall have two, if you like."

"Whoever fetches me a coach, shall have a shilling," he said. "I am not drunk, as perhaps you may imagine, but I have had a serious fall."

The promised shilling had its effect, and the boy, who was inclined to make merry at the sufferer's expense, became preternaturally grave in a moment, and said,—

"A coach, sir, and a shilling? Oh, yes, sir; certainly. A coach?"

"Yes—yes."

"And you'll give a shilling?"

"Yes, my lad, yes. Get a good-looking one, there's a sharp, fine lad."

Away started the boy, and then Mr. Willoughby rose to his feet. He felt a little dizzy and confused, but that was a feeling which he knew would soon go off, so he walked in the direction which the boy had taken; and as he walked steadily, and exhibited none of the eccentric symptoms of drunkenness, the few people who had paused to look at him went away; so that when the rumble of wheels met his ears, and he saw a coach turn the corner with the boy triumphantly seated on the box, he was alone.

The coach drew up, and the coachman and boy both got down. Mr. Willoughby drew the coachman aside, and said to him in a whisper,—

"Long's Hotel."

"Yes, your honour."

And in got the prince.

"Please, sir, my shilling," said the boy.

"Your shilling?"

"Yes, sir; you know you prom'sed."

"Oh, I might have promised, my young friend. But the longer you live in the world, the more you'll dis-

cover what an immense difference there is between, promising and performing. Drive on, coachman; and if the boy gets up behind I'll stand an extra sixpence to have him lashed well."

The coachman laughed, and put his horses to the trot. The boy, as might fairly be expected, did get up behind, but he got so sweet a cut with the whip that he got down again with a howl, and gave up the affair as a bad job altogether.

The distance was short to the hotel which had been mentioned—an hotel where there is the greatest possible amount of incivility at the highest possible price—and in a few minutes the coach drew up.

It being, however, only a hackney coach, no attention was paid to it by any of the bloated officials of the establishment, so that Willoughby was permitted to alight, and walk into the hall or not, just as he pleased.

"Is the Earl of Crumbledown up or in bed?" he said to a waiter, who was lounging by the fire in the hall.

"The Earl of Crumbledown—and who are you?"

"That is not the question."

"Oh, but it is, though."

"Then there is my card."

The waiter took the card, and when his eye fell upon the word prince, his countenance at once altered, and he said, in such soft bland accents that they seemed to remind one of melted butter going through a fine sieve,—

"Your highness will pardon me, I did not have the honour of knowing your highness. The earl's valet is up, and, if your highness will please to walk into this room, your highness's card shall be delivered to the earl, who I don't think has gone to bed—indeed, he don't seem to be going."

"Indeed!"

"No, your highness; he's been dozing all day on a sofa."

"He is aged."

"Very old, indeed, your highness, very old."

The waiter, now as obsequious as he was before insolent, bowed the sham prince into a handsome sitting-room, and then went up stairs with his card.

The old Lord Crumbledown was an eccentric man. He had outlived a great many natural affections, and his greatest delight was now in annoying everybody, and doing just what nobody else would ever think of doing. He dozed away his time, as the waiter had remarked, almost all day, so he felt no inclination at all to go to bed, and if any one called to see him in the middle of the night, he quite enjoyed it, because it put everybody else out of the way.

His valet was compelled to sleep when he could. He rarely had a regular night's repose, for the old man would insist upon sitting up, and having all the attendance in the night which other people were content with in daytime only.

He had come up to town hastily to make some trifling alterations in his will, for he was always saying that he could not last long; although, if any one else had said so, no doubt it would have been considered a most deadly offence.

Indeed, the only subject upon which the old earl would stand the least contradiction was, upon how long he might or might not last. What he liked was to hold an argument with somebody who would insist upon it that he would last a number of years yet, and see out many of the young fellows who looked upon him as one so very old as to belong to another age.

There were a few persons who always held such an argument with him. They were his valet, his steward, his lawyer, and a very prudent physician who attended him, and who had the tact which some of his predecessors had wanted, to argue with the old earl, in differing with him, and so he got a couple of guineas a-day, and had had them for three years in consequence.

Such was the old Earl of Crumbledown, and when his valet came into his room where he was lying wide awake, he said,—

"My lord, a foreign prince, I think, wishes to see you."

The old man was rather pleased than otherwise, because it just then struck two.

"Prince who? prince who?" he said.

"Prince Srisck—no—Shizrisck—kinki. It's a very hard name, my lord."

"You're a fool!"

"Yes, my lord."

"Show him up. He's a sensible man, or he wouldn't come out at such an hour as this. I hope the house has been disturbed."

"Oh, yes, my lord."

"And everybody wakened up and swearing, and a general tumult and vexation."

"All that, my lord."

"Eugh! then you may show him up. I wonder now if it would be very inconvenient to cook anything? Do you think it would?"

"I should say it would, my lord."

"Then order three or four troublesome made dishes directly"

" Yes, my lord. Oh, how enraged everybody will be. What a tumult there will be below. Such a cursing and swearing ! Oh, dear ! oh, dear !"

This was not addressed to the old earl, but the valet took good care he should hear it, for well he knew how it would please him ; and it did, for the old man laughed in a strange fashion, like some old resuscitated mummy.

" Eugh ! eugh !" he said. " Now I wonder where Herbert is ? Eugh ! eugh ! It's no excuse to say he don't know I am in town, because he ought to find out. He shall make some noble alliance—I will see it done before I go. Oh ! I shall not last long. Eh ? Oh, there's nobody here.   How dare there be nobody here ? If I find that Herbert has made any low connection I'll leave all I have to some infernal humbug of a public charity, and that's not difficult to find, and he shall have my curse along with an encumbered estate."

The old man was silent for a few minutes, and then looking at the fire from beneath his shaggy brows, he said—

" I am only ninety-two. I shall not last long. Eh ? Oh, there's nobody here. What a scoundrel that Truebit, my valet, is."

The door was softly opened, and the valet said,—

" The Prince—a—a-hem !—ceki—&c., my lord."

Mr. Willoughby walked confidently into the room, and the valet lit several wax lights, which had only been a short time before extinguished, because the old earl had been to sleep.

" My lord," said Willoughby, deferentially, " although a stranger to your lordship, permit me to rejoice in this opportunity of paying to you my respects. You are looking wonderfully well."

" Well—well ?"

" Admirably well !"

" Your highness does not know my age—I am ninety-two."

" Indeed !   And yet as hale and well as many a man of thirty."

" No, no, no."

" Your lordship must have an iron constitution."

" No, no, no ; I am going soon."

" Not so ; you will last me, and many more that I could name, out. I am certain, I am of opinion, that when a man reaches your lordship's age he needs a stamina of constitution which cannot be easily shaken. The Lord Meadow-bank was to have introduced me to your lordship ; but I have accidentally heard of a circumstance of such family importance to your lordship, that, without waiting until to-morrow, I ordered my carriage and came here at once, despite the unreasonable hour."

" Unreasonable !   It's the hour I like best."

" Indeed !"

" Yes ; most people make their morning visits at least hours later than this," returned his lordship.

" They do, indeed ; but, my lord, respecting what I came about. Have you seen your son since your arrival in town ?"

" No."

" Then I have. He is very busy, very busy, indeed, my lord. Perhaps you are aware that he has formed a connection, and is now carrying on an intrigue, with a lawyer's daughter, my lord—a man with his couple of hundred a year— a pettifogging attorney—a man not fit to dash the dust from your lordship's shoes ; but his daughter has a pretty doll's face, and so your only son—the heir to your name, your title, your honours, your fortune—has eloped with her, and thus, in the low connection he has made, disgracing you, himself, and a noble name, which until now never knew disgrace."

" God of heaven !" exclaimed the old man as he sprang to his feet, burning from top to toe with anger ; " God of heaven ! curses ——"

" It is true. Whether it will offend you or not, I know not. I respect you, and so I came to tell you."

"My son, Lord Warelock—the future Earl of Crumbledown—the twenty-second

Earl of Crumbledown—form a low connection—a low intrigue—an attorney's daughter! No, no, no! Oh, no!"

"I pledge my honour. I know of my own knowledge, and not from hearsay, that what I have now told you is true."

"No, no, no."

"I am ready to swear it.'"

"Then d———n take all the world!" yelled the old man. "I'll kill him, and the title shall be extinct for ever. Why—why I never heard of but one intrigue in all the family, and, d—n it, that was with Queen Elizabeth."

"Ah, my lord, a queen! There was some excuse for that; but, only for a moment, compare Queen Elizabeth with a pettifogging attorney's daughter."

"I cannot—I cannot."

"It is, indeed, a stretch of the imagination, my lord; but such has been the conduct of your son. He has eloped with her."

"Where is he?" said the old man, with a more than natural calmness—a calmness which looked like one of those suspicious lulls that precede the worst of storms.

"Where is he—where is he now?"

"Your son?"

"Yes, Lord Warelock; my only son—where is he now?"

"I have reason to believe that he is now at an entertainment given at her house in May Fair, by the Marchioness of Fanfaronade."

"Indeed!"

"Yes; I know he was to be there."

"Then there I will seek him. The marchioness is an old friend of mine—a woman of most unblemished family descent. They did not come in with the Conqueror, the Fanfaronades, but they came in very soon after. I will go there and denounce him on the spot. I will leave him my curse to-night, for fear I should not live till to-morrow to bestow it on him."

"You will do well, my lord, to protect the honour of your ancient house, which for ages now has been looked up to with so much reverential homage."

"Yes, yes, yes!"

"What now, if, in some moment of dalliance and foolish fondness, he was to promise to marry the little pettifogging attorney's daughter?"

"A thousand devils!"

"And then carry the promise into effect, and make her Countess of Crumbledown and Warelock, engrafting on the pure stock of your ancient race, which has mingled with the blood of kings, the family of the attorney, whose father before him sold greens and potatoes, and whose grandfather nobody ever heard of at all in this world."

"I shall go mad—I shall go mad!"

"Nay, now, compose yourself, my lord."

"I—I cannot think—I am really mad. D———! what shall I do? My own son—my own son, too. My Herbert—my———"

"But, think of the greens and the potatoes, and the man who never had a grandfather."

With a yell of rage the old man called to the valet, who answered him tremblingly.

"The carriage! the carriage!" cried the old earl; "the carriage!"

"Yes, my lord, yes."

"I will seek him, were he hidden in hell."

"Do, my lord," said the prince; "I would, indeed; and now, I bid you farewell, satisfied, that although the news I have brought to your lordship is not pleasant, yet that, as the representative myself of a noble house, it was my duty to bring it to you."

"It was, it was."

"Good morning, my lord."

"Thank you, thank you; good morning. I shall return your visit to-morrow. Where do you stay?"

"At Lord Meadowbank's."

"Well, well—yes. To-morrow you shall see me; till then, farewell. I am not so old but I can feel a wound against my honour."

The prince, alias Willoughby, left the hotel, and when he reached the street, he shook his fist, as he said, in tones of passion—

"Now, my Lord Warelock, I have brought about your ears a hornets' nest, which may yet induce you to think that you had better have made terms with me. And now, d—n it, what shall I do next?"

He folded his arms, and walked sternly down Bond-street.

The old Earl of Crumbledown, when he was left alone, looked nearly stupified for some moments, and then, as he trembled partly from ague and partly from passion, he said,—

"I have come to town to make some trifling alterations in my will. Before I leave it, I will make a tremendous one. Truebit, Truebit, I say."

"Yes, my lord; the carriage will be round in a few moments. It was a great inconvenience, my lord."

"Hold your d——d tongue. What is it to me; what is an inconvenience to such hounds as you are? Bring me writing materials."

"Yes, my lord."

A writing-desk was opened before the old man, and selecting a scrap of paper, he wrote on it the following words:—

"I, John Humphrey Codman Warelock, Earl of Crumbledown, hereby revoke all former wills and testamentary papers whatever, and leave the whole of my personal property, without exception, to ——; on condition, that within one month after my decease she becomes the wife of my only son, Herbert Warelock, commonly called Lord Warelock."

The blank we have placed in was left by the old man, and after having written this paper, he folded it up very carefully and placed it in his pocket, without attaching to it signature or date.

"Now," he said, "now the carriage—the carriage."

"'Tis here, my lord."

"Truebit, Truebit."

"Yes, my lord."

"Order them to drive to the Marchioness of Fanfaronade's, in May Fair. I intend to die to-night, Truebit."

"To die, my lord?"

"Yes; do not contradict me. I shall die to-night, my heart is broken; and if I miss seeing him, and you should see my son, Herbert, tell him that he broke it; and, but that I would not have extinct in the annals of my country a peerage that has always been assimilated with honour, I would not have made an arrangement which he will find in my will."

"Yes, my lord; but you know you will last out all the young ones yet, my lord."

"That flattery has lost its charm."

"Oh, dear, you are quite mistaken, my lord. You will see me out, and many a faithful servant besides. I often say to myself, when I see some young fellow about thirty, looking as strong as a bullock—'Ah, it's all very fine, but my master, the earl, will see you out!'"

"Peace! peace! peace!"

"Yes, my lord."

"I understand you, and should not be angry that you feed the foible I myself have nourished, but now 'tis past—my race is now run! To the carriage—to the carriage! I want no help!"

The last spark in the candle ever burns brightly. And so it seemed with the old earl, for notwithstanding his very advanced age, he walked more erectly now, and with a firmer step, than he had done for twenty years, ay, than he had done at his last marriage, and he made an effort to look vigorous then, though he was seventy-one when that event arrived.

The servants who had been so hastily summoned from their slumbers, as may be well supposed, were very far, indeed, from being well pleased at the whim of the old earl.   How they cursed and swore as they led the horses to the carriage we do not feel ourselves at liberty to reveal; but certainly if all the oaths had stuck to the stable wall, it would have been difficult, through so thick a coating as they would have made, to have come to any conclusion as to what had been its original colour.   However, they knew that the order once issued must be obeyed, and so they swore as much as they liked and put in the horses.

When all was finished the carriage was brought round to the door of the hall, and then, in a few minutes, the old earl descended to the hall.   His valet was ready with an ample cloak, in which he muffled his master, who then slipped into the carriage.

Now, as we have before had occasion to remark, in the case of Mr. Willoughby, alias the prince with the unpronounceable name, the distance was very short, and the old Earl of Crumbledown would have got safely enough to the Marchioness of Fanfaronade's had not his coachman, when he saw a great number of carriages in May Fair, been seized with a desire to show off a little, and come up to the door with a dash.   And even that might have been accomplished well enough, for coachee was no despicable whip, had it not been that in the hurry of putting in the horses, and being half asleep besides, various errors had been made in the adaptation of the harness, and among others a trace had been left hanging loose, as well as a crupper wanting.   The consequence of this was, that when the horses were put upon their mettle a little, one of them made the, to him, interesting discovery that he was more at liberty than usual, and he thought it would not be amiss for him to walk up the steps of the door.   The effect of this measure was to overturn the carriage, which went on its side with a tremendous crash.

Plenty of assistance was obtained in a moment, and the upper door being opened, the old Earl of Crumbledown was lifted out in an insensible state, and carried into a private room in the Marchioness of Fanfaronade's house.

Then, while a fashionable physician a few doors off was sent for, the news was taken to her ladyship that no less a personage than the old Earl of Crumbledown had broken down at her very door, and was now lying in a helpless state in her house.

To tell Annabella to follow her, and to seek the apartment in which the ancient nobleman lay, was to the marchioness the work of a moment.   She only paused at the door to say to the haughty Annabella,—

"My dear, this is an opportunity of getting the old earl with us, as regards certain affairs we have talked over, which will never occur again.   You must propitiate him—don't spare a few tears, my love.   He is as old as Methusaleh, and I will take care there are no spectators.   Pay him every sort of attention, mind.   All now depends, completely and entirely, my dear, upon your own tact and discretion."

·———·

CHAPTER V.

THE OLD EARL'S DEATH. — THE WILL AND THE TRIUMPH OF THE MARCHIONESS.

THE marchioness knew very well that Lady Annabella might be thoroughly depended upon in any matter which involved any advantages, or any chance of achieving that one grand object of her existence, namely, the getting hold of some man in the noose matrimonial, who could keep up an expensive establishment. The opportune arrival of Lord Warelock's father presented a chance of propitiating him, which, as the marchionesss truly observed, would be not likely to occur again.

Both the Lady Annabella and her imperious mother knew not how the young Lord Warelock was situated. They knew, in common with every one who chose to come at the knowledge of such a fact, that the old earl had, during his long life, been busily engaged by every means in his power in the acquisition of money.

The estates were comparatively valueless when considered in opposition to the immense sums of money which the old man possessed in all descriptions of real securities. Indeed, it seemed to many persons as if he purposely allowed that family property, the descent of which from father to son was provided for by the law of entail, to fall to decay and unprofitableness, in order that he might have the fortune of his successor the more completely at his own entire and absolute control and disposal.

And the very circumstance of his life extending so far beyond the ordinary limits, had enabled him to do this to an almost unprecedented extent.

Allowing to Lord Warelock only as small a sum as was at all consistent with his rank, he may be said to have kept the young man completely in leading strings, and now, in consequence of the revengeful conduct of Mr. Willoughby, alias the prince with the unpronounceable name, he was in extreme hazard of occupying that most unenviable of all positions, of a poor nobleman—a man of exalted rank without the means of supporting it. In such a case what a grievous burthen does dignity become.

The Marchioness of Fanfaronade knew all this, as likewise did the Lady Annabella, and hence if any further designs were to be carried out against the independence of the young Lord Warelock, it became highly necessary that the old lord, who might make the match a desirable one or otherwise, according to his whim and fancy, should be propitiated.

The ladies were not in the habit of attributing much of any good that fortune occurred to Providence; perhaps a suspicion, or a conviction of their own utter worthlessness led them to discard such an idea, but it did seem almost providential to them that the carriage of the old Earl of Crumbledown should upset just at their very door, and that they should have such a glorious opportunity of paying a host of small attentions, which the aged appreciate so much, and which makes them so angry if withheld.

In a word, then, the Marchioness of Fanfaronade, and the Lady Annabella, were fully resolved upon humbugging the old man.

The fall in itself which the old earl had received was nothing. To a young man it would have been productive of no inconvenience whatever, but when we come to consider his extreme age, we cannot wonder that, notwithstanding his well-lined and padded carriage prevented him from receiving any external injury, he was so much shaken as to place even his life in imminent jeopardy.

It is usually a shock of some kind, mental or physical, which suddenly hurries to the tomb those who have outlived the ordinary space of existence. The old earl might have gone through the ordinary routine of life for a long while, had not this unlucky upset of his carriage occurred, and we must bear in mind, too, that this physical derangement of his nerves, caused by the sudden shock and the fright, was now acting along with the mental disturbance he had received from the communication of the prince.

He was in a kind of stupor when the marchioness and her daughter reached the room, from which they were at once careful to exclude every one else. It was the marchioness herself who first tried a little fascination upon the old earl by seizing his hand, and exclaiming,—

"Oh, my dear lord, do tell me that you are unhurt. Oh, could but affection and reverence for you have their will how gladly would I take to myself all the consequences of this dreadful accident, so that such an ornament to nature and to nobility as yourself was spared."

"He does not hear you," remarked Annabella.

"No—so I see," said the marchioness, in so different a tone, that it seemed scarcely possible it could proceed from the same person. "I thought it was as well to try, but the old idiot is insensible evidently."

"Yes. What a fright !"

"He is, indeed. He ought to have been in his grave long ago."

"So I have heard everybody say," added the Lady Annabella. "I have no patience with people who live to such ages."

The mother could not blame the daughter for such a speech. She had brought her up to such feelings, and she had seen, from earliest childhood, such an amount of cold-hearted selfishness in all around her, that it would have required a great power of innate virtue for her to have successfully struggled against such feelings, and been other than what she now was.

"Dr. Weatherby, my lady," announced a servant, and the fashionable physician made his bow and entered the room.

"This old gentleman," said the marchioness, "has had a fall in consequence of his carriage overturning."

"Dear me," said the physician, with a bland smile. "Dear me, he seems very old."

"He is very old."

"Ah—humph—he has fainted. Ah, we will see what we can do."

The physician took from his pocket a small phial which contained some extremely pungent substance, and he applied it to the old man's nose. The effect was powerful and instantaneous, for the features were immediately convulsed, and the old earl opened his eyes.

"That will do," said the physician, "that will do. There is not much the matter, I dare say, my lady. I will write a prescription which, no doubt, will place all to rights."

The old man glanced at him from beneath his low shaggy brows, as he wrote, and when he had concluded, he said,—

"What mummery is this?"

"Mummery, my dear sir !" said the physician. "Really, now, really."

"Who are you, sir, that intrude into my private apartments ? Eh ? Who are you, I say ? There is something fawning and sneaking about you that I hate. Begone—begone."

"Sir, I am a physician."

"I thought so! I thought so! A physician—I have avoided such men as you are for many, many years. Away with you—away !"

"How dare you remain, sir," said the marchioness, "when you are told to go ?"

"Unfeeling man !" cried the Lady Annabella; "why do you not go at once, after what has been so properly remarked by this gentleman?"

The physician, who was one of those who adopted the smiling system, looked rather aghast at all this, and became wonderfully grave all of a sudden.

"Why—why!" he said; "what have I done ?"

"Begone !" cried the old earl. "Begone ! begone !"

"Ah !" added Annabella, "begone ! or must we summon assistance to have you turned with obloquy from the house ?"

"Yes, yes, yes !" said the old earl, catching at the word. "Turn him from the house with obloquy. That will do. The sight of him, like grim death, has added to my fears, and made me full twenty years older than I was; and God knows that were needless—that were needless ! I am old enough—quite old enough !"

"My dear sir, do not say so," exclaimed Annabella, leaning over his shoulder, and making her cheek almost touch the old man's, as she took one of his shrivelled hands in hers. "Do not say so in the presence of those who love, admire, and respect you."

"Eh ?"

"Long may you live, dear sir, and happily."

The old earl turned his glassy-looking eyes upon her as he said, in a clear tone,—

"And who are you, my dear?"

"They call me the Lady Annabella. I am the eldest daughter of the Marchioness of Fanfaronade."

" In deed! indeed! Let me think—let me think! Oh, yes—yes! I remember all now. The prince—ay, and the accident of the carriage."

" Yes, my lord, the sad accident. Some time since it was. Oh! in what an agony of apprehension have I been watching you!"

" Ah, indeed, my dear. And so you watched the old man? Why—why—what noise is that I now hear?"

" There is a dance above."

" And—and—let me look at you; you are young and handsome. Have you left the dance, the music, and the lights, and the flatterers that buzz round the like of you, to tend upon such an old withered leaf as I am?"

" I would not hear another speak so of you, my lord. To me you are the great and noble Earl of Crumbledown and Warelock; the dignified and chivalrous representative of one of the most ancient and noble families of England."

" Am I so?"

" You are, my lord, and one word from you of commendation outweighs a world of flatteries from ordinary lips."

The old man let his head sink upon his breast, as he muttered,—

" A noble girl—a just-thinking girl. Such an one as—as would bear the weight of a coronet as one who felt it not, and yet never forgot 'twas on her brow. Ah, humph! Let me think—let me think."

" Are you better, dear sir?"

" The Farfaronades came in very soon after the Conquest.",

" Let me hope that you are well, dear sir."

" And one Marquis of Fanfaronade fell at Agincourt. Humph!"

" You feel no pain?"

" An old family—an old family and no bar sinister on the escutcheon; a good old family.—Ha!—an ancient race. Is my son here?"

" He is not, my lord."

"I was told that he was here, Lord Warelock—my only son,—you know him?"

"We do, my lord," said the marchioness, who had now managed to get rid of the physician ; "we are always honoured to receive any one who can claim the honour of kindred with yourself."

"Humph—ha !"

"And you are better?" whispered Annabella.

"Humph !"

"You are quite recovered ?"

"Ha !"

The mother and daughter cast at each other a glance as much as to say—was there ever such a tiresome old idiot in this world, and then they were silent for some few moments while the old earl appeared to be in deep thought. After about five minutes, which seemed interminably long, were thus passed, he spoke again to the great relief of the marchioness and the Lady Annabella.

"Bring me pen and ink, " he said.

"Yes, my lord, yes. Oh ! what a pleasure to wait upon you !"

Annabella brought close to him a small table, on which were writing materials, and then the old earl took from his pocket the written paper he had prepared at the hotel. He spread it open before him and took the pen in his hand.

He was about to write, when, with a sudden groan, he fell back, and such a remarkable change came over his countenance, that they thought he was dying at the moment.

"Oh, my lord, my lord," cried Annabella, and almost unconscious of what she did, the marchioness rang the bell so violently, that half a dozen servants rushed into the room directly, as well as several of the guests from the saloons.

"The Earl of Crumbledown is very ill," said the marchioness. "Call assistance."

The old man shook his head, and with the assistance of Annabella, he sat upright again.

"No, no, no !" he said, in hollow tones, "no assistance from any one to me."

The news spread through the saloons with great rapidity, that the old Earl of Crumbledown was below and dying. The consequence was, that a number of the guests came down stairs, some from curiosity and some from sympathy, while messengers were despatched in various directions for Lord Warelock, and some of the most eminent of the fashionable physicians who resided in the immediate vicinity.

The music was stopped, the dancing ceased, and the house began to present a strange scene of confusion of quite a different nature to what had characterised it but a short half hour before.

The marchioness and the Lady Annabella were in despair. Of course, no more fascinations could now be tried upon the old man, for too many were present who would perfectly understand their object ; so that affairs were just permitted to take their own course, with the exception that the Lady Annabella stood close to him, and strove in vain to read the slip of paper which he had taken from his pocket, but which he had now laid his hand over.

The change in the old earl's countenance was now terrible to see. He resembled some revivified corpse more than anything human. His eyes had an awful leaden colour about them, and his cheeks looked cold, wax-like, and so deadly white, that it would appear the blood had completely deserted them. Even the lips were as white as paper, and he looked at the throng that now surrounded him like some old necromancer, who held in his hands the fate of thousands, and had come from the grave to declare it.

Some of those whom curiosity had brought from the room above kept as far back as possible from the old earl as if they feared he might make some sudden dart at some of them, and do them deadly bodily injury. Others, more bold, pressed forward, so that, one with another, there were abundance of witnesses to what the old man might say or do.

He made now several ineffectual attempts to speak, but the words seemed to die away in indistinct murmurs before they reached his lips, and no one at all understood what he meant by them. The Lady Annabella paid the most close attention; but, even with all that, she could not catch the purport of what he said.

"He is dying," whispered several. "Did you ever see such a look?"

"And time he should die," said one; "he has been long enough in the world; not that he has kept Warelock out of the peerage; because, you see, the old man married so late in life, that Warelock is a young man yet."

"True; and he now will be Earl of Crumbledown before he is many weeks older, or I am very much mistaken indeed."

"You are right; and I think every one here is of your way of thinking. Only look at the old man, what efforts he makes to speak."

And so, indeed, the old earl was making efforts to speak—efforts, apparently of a painful character, for his throat seemed convulsed by them. He put up his hand and clutched at his throat, as if by so doing he could assist himself in pronouncing in an articulate manner what he wished to say. This fearful struggle lasted several minutes; and then, suddenly he spoke, so that he could be understood, at all events, by those who happened to be the nearest to him, among whom was the Lady Annabella.

"Where's my son?" he said.

"We have sent for him, dear sir," whispered Annabella.

"He will be too late. Listen all here present to me; for, unless my eyes deceive me, there are many persons here present."

"There are none so pleased as I to see you better."

"Hush—hush! I have no time. The pen—the pen!"

The pen had dropped on the floor, but Annabella quickly raised it and placed it in his hand.

"Who knows," she thought; "old people are eccentric; he may be going to leave me some legacy, or write me a cheque; I would not be surprised at either."

Of a truth she would not have been disagreeably surprised at either, at all events; but she little guessed what was the old earl's real intention. By a glance he gave her he let her know that he did not wish her to look over him while he wrote, and then he filled in the blank he had left in the document he had drawn up with so much precision at the hotel with the name of Annabella Fanfaronade.

When he had done this he signed his own name at the bottom of the document, and holding it up, he said,—

"Who will witness that this is my signature I have this moment in presence of you all written?"

"I, my dear, sir," said Annabella.

"No—you must not."

"Must not!"

"You must not. Do not inquire more, only you must not; but, if you must have it in plainer language, you shall not."

The Lady Annabella drew back with a blank look, as she thought,—

"And this is the old brute, after all, upon whom I have wasted a whole hour's attendance. This is how I am repaid. I have a great mind ——"

What the Lady Annabella had a great mind to do, was what ladies, both high and low, have always a great inclination for, namely, to tell people their minds, which consists usually in an abusive piece of candour. And well for the Lady Annabella Fanfaronade was it that she abstained from such a course. She knew not that she was now at the most critical period of her fortunes, and that a word or a look might at once leave her where she was instead of placing her in a position which her most enthusiastic dreams of ambition had never yet reached.

She was silent. The habitual duplicity of what is called high life had given her habits of self control, and she said nothing, although, as human nature is human nature still, even in a marchioness's daughter, she could have found it in her heart to punch the old earl's head, for putting what she, at that moment, considered such a slight upon her before so many persons.

At the demand of the Earl of Crumbledown for some person to witness his signature, a Lord Whitney, an empty-headed coxcomb, stepped forward, and said,—

" I will do so."

But at that time the old man seemed gifted with a power of seeing into every one's character but that of the Lady Annabella, and he said, abruptly,—

" No, no.   You are a fool.   I want two persons of some sense."

There was a general titter at Lord Whitney's expense on the part of all, except one lady to whom he was paying his addresses, and, of course, she saw nothing to laugh at.   Women never will, of course, acknowledge their own admirer to be a fool.

" You," said the earl, pointing to a gentlemanly-looking man, " and you," indicating another.

These were not titled personages at all.   One was a Colonel Bruce, and the other a Mr. Ducie, and to tell the truth, they were both of them men of some ability. Although amused at the old earl's eccentricity, they were neither of them very well pleased to be selected by him as witnesses to his signature ; but yet it was a matter they did not like to refuse, so, without casting their eyes at all upon the writing that was on the scrap of paper, they attached their signatures to it at once.

The old earl immediately folded it up and placed it in his pocket.   He clasped his hands for a moment together and trembled.

" This is the end," he said, and then falling back upon the couch, he gave one sigh, and expired.

At this moment the first arrival of the physicians who had been sent for came into the room, and no doubt was not a little mortified at finding himself too late.

As it was he tried to bleed the old earl, but that was quite ineffectual.   He was dead, and no human aid could again restore the breath of life to that form which was now but an inanimate lump of clay.

" Yes," said the physician, reluctantly, in answer to numerous eager inquiries, " he is quite dead."

" And nothing can be done ?" said the marchioness.

" Nothing more, madam.   He has died, I presume from the appearances, of old age.   No human skill can avail him now, although I am not prepared to say, but what a great deal could have been done, had time permitted."

All medical men have this piece of jargon at their tongues' end,—that if they had but been a few minutes earlier, of course they could have done something wonderful, which now cannot be attempted.   It's like asking of some dear friend the loan of a twenty-pound note, and being told how very sorry he is you didn't ask him yesterday, when he could have done it with ease, and now very much regrets that he cannot, &c., &c.

" Well," said Lord Whitney, " he was not very civil in his last moments."

" No, indeed.   I call him insane," said the lady to whom Lord Whitney was paying his addresses.

" You are quite right," said Lord Whitney.   " He called me a fool."

" Which brings all to the conclusion of his madness," said the lady.

" You have wonderful penetration."

" Nay, my lord, you flatter."

" I think," said Colonel Bruce to Mr. Ducie, " as we have witnessed to the old earl's signature at the foot of some document, we ought now to see what it is."

" I think so to.   He placed it in his pocket."

" Oh, the old wretch," whispered the Lady Annabella to the Marchioness Fanfaronade ; " what a hideous idea to come and die here."

" And what is worse, my dear, there will be some low man coming, that they call a coroner, and some of the *canaille* from the neighbourhood as a jury."

" Gracious ! I had forgotten that.   We cannot endure it."

" And for nothing, too.   We will not endure it ; I shall have him removed to some hotel or another directly."

" This document," said Colonel Bruce, in a loud tone, so as to command general attention, as he held up the paper he and Mr. Ducie had witnessed —" This document is one of vast importance, and such being the case, I will read it aloud."

This was a proposition that was sure to be acceded to by all, for curiosity had been strongly excited, so there was a general polite murmur of assent, and even Lord Whitney left off whispering tender nothings into the ear of the lady who would not think him a fool, to listen to the contents of the paper the old earl had so unceremoniously rejected his name to as a witness.

In a clear tone, which all could hear with the greatest distinctness, the colonel read the document, which was as follows :—

" I, John Humphrey Codman Warelock, Earl of Crumbledown, hereby revoke all other wills and testamentary papers whatever, and leave the whole of my personal property, without exception, to the Lady Annabella, eldest daughter of the Marquis and Marchioness of Fanfaronade, on condition that, within one month after my decease, she becomes the wife of my only son, Herbert Warelock, commonly called Lord Warelock.   "CRUMBLEDOWN AND WARELOCK."

The reading of this document was listened to with the most profound silence by every one ; but the moment it was concluded, there was such an expression of intense astonishment upon the faces and lips aristocratic, which are taught that the concealment of all natural emotions is the essence of greatness, it was truly astonishing.

But if the general guests were astonished, how much more so must have been the Marchioness of Fanfaronade and her daughter Annabella.   They who had just been abusing the old man, and thinking his coming there to die such an unwarrantable liberty.   They who would have denied house-room even for a day or two to his remains—what must have been their feelings at the reading of that short but most important document?   Here was, at one swoop, all they had been struggling for placed within their grasp.   The lordly husband, and the princely, ay, the regal fortune.   Amazement sat upon their countenances, and it was only the great tact of the marchioness which could have enabled the Lady Annabella to meet such an emergency properly.

Here the generalship of the marchioness at once showed itself, and not greater was Napoleon at Wagram than was she in May Fair.   She saw at once the bewilderment of Annabella, and she feared some sudden ebullition of satisfaction, which would of course have been much repented of afterwards, so she laid her hand upon the arm of the Lady Annabella, and whispered to her,—

" Faint, my dear—faint, faint."

The Lady Annabella took the hint, and seeing at once the great practical utility, and how well it would get her through the business, she fainted away on the instant.

" Very judicious," said an old fat dowager, who was present.   " Very judicious that—Annabella is a talented young person."

This was true, although there can be no doubt of the object of the speech, which was to let everybody know that the fainting was merely a piece of judicious pantomime got up on the spur of the moment, and for which she was willing to give all due credit to the performer who did it so well, and at the exact juncture.

" You see now, my dear," added the dowager, who tapped with her fan the arm of a niece of her's, " how very nicely the Lady Annabella Fanfaronade has got out of an extremely awkward situation.   What could she say?—what could she do?—so she fainted, which was all that was left her ; and now you see she is being carried comfortably to her own room, and has not committed herself in any way by a single word.   I hope, my dear, this practical lesson will not be lost upon you."

" No, aunt."

" Very good, my dear, very good.

The Lady Annabella became everybody's care, and was duly conveyed to her chamber, followed by the marchioness, who, when they were there, said,—

" That's right, my love.   You could not have done it better.   Now, don't stir from here whatever you do, and as soon as I can get a clear house I will return to you, and we will talk the matter over between ourselves calmly and considerately."

" How much do you think it will come to?" eagerly asked Annabella.   " That's what I want to know.   How much?"

"I cannot say; but I have heard it reported that he had more than two hundred thousand pounds currency."

"That will do."

"I should think it would do, my love."

"Oh, how I will mortify everybody! What an agony I will put the acquaintance I have into! How I will make them positively mad! What's the use of two hundred thousand pounds if you don't almost make every one of your acquaintance commit suicide from sheer vexation? I will excite such envy that there shall never have been known the like before. I long to begin—I do long to begin."

With these sweet and amiable feelings we will now leave the Lady Annabella Fanfaronade, of whom, doubtless, the reader has about the same share of admiration as we have ourselves.

CHAPTER VI.

THE HYPOCRISY OF THE MARCHIONESS.—THE DEPARTURE OF THE GUESTS, AND THE ADMIRABLE PLANS TO ENSNARE LORD WARELOCK.

THE marchioness paused a moment or two to think before she proceeded down stairs to the guests.

"Shall I pay them the compliment of asking them to stay or not?" she asked herself; and that question she very quickly answered in the negative. "No, no; they must all go. I must be too much overpowered with grief at the loss of so old, so dear, and so valued a friend as the Earl of Crumbledown, to be able to entertain anybody. Indeed I must not be by any means myself."

Acting upon this determination, the marchioness went into a small room which adjoined one of the principal saloons, and then she rang for a servant, and desired that several ladies whom she named might be requested to come to her. These soon made their appearance, and they found the marchioness with her handkerchief to her eyes, absorbed in grief, which the dowager, who was one of those who came to her, said was exceedingly proper.

"My dear friends," said the marchioness, "I am of course now unequal to anything but tears. Will you say as much to our friends below?"

"Certainly," said one. "Oh, dear, yes. I suppose the little bit of a will will be disputed, my dear?"

"Very likely," said the marchioness.

"But then, you know, my dear friend," said another, "Lord Warelock, now the Earl of Crumbledown, may have his own reasons for objecting to marry the dear, sweet, amiable Annabella."

"Remarkably true," said the marchioness.

"So don't cry, love," said a third; "you think too much of it."

"I won't."

"That's right. There's sad reverses in the world. It is all a delusion, I dare say."

"That's my opinion."

"We don't think the new earl will marry dear Annabella."

"Nor I."

"And we therefore don't think she will have the spending of a shilling of the old earl's hoarded up money."

"That's just my opinion, my dear friends."

"Besides, beauty," said one, "is now likely to attract the new earl."

"True," said the marchioness, "very true; and Annabella is plain, decidedly. So you see, my dear friends, that I am thoroughly grieved at the old lord's death, because, as we can expect nothing from it, our grief must be serious."

"Yes, dear," said one who was ready to burst with vexation.

"Compose yourself, my admirable friend," said another.

"I will endeavour to do so, and, if anything could have the effect of alleviating the sudden pang I feel at the death of so old and valued a friend, it would of course be the tender and the gentle sympathy I meet with from all of you."

"Well, it is delightful to hear your say so."

"I know it," said she. "Oh, how charming is real friendship."

"Very, oh, very. They say the old earl has not so much money as everybody believed, by a large amount."

"My own opinion, ladies and dear friends," said the marchioness, quite confidentially, "is, that he has none at all; that, if he had, the will would be disputed; that Lord Warelock would not marry Annabella; that Annabella would not marry Lord Warelock, and that the whole affair is a delusion from the beginning to the end. We expect nothing, and so you see we cannot be disappointed; and, if it should turn out that the old earl had three hundred thousand pounds, and that the new earl and Annabella—poor young thing—make a match of it, why, I shall not interfere with their natural affections, bless their young tender hearts."

"No, don't," said the ladies, in chorus.

"I don't, indeed. God bless you all."

"And bless you, too, my dear marchioness. By-bye, for the present; we will soon rid you of your guests."

And so with smiles, that, if smiles would kill, would pretty soon have laid the marchioness dead at their feet, the dear friends left her.

"An old designing wretch!" said one.

"A cat!" said another.

"Oh, how intensely I hate her," said a third. "How sure she makes of the money."

"I'd give half a year's income to see her disappointed," cried another. "I have no patience with her—I could have scratched her."

"And so could I."

"Indeed," said the marchioness to herself, when she was alone, "indeed! Bless you all—you are very kind. You think we shall get nothing, do you? I know better—much better. I can see my way very well in this affair; Annabella will be —ah, she shall be, Countess of Crumbledown before this day month."

The ladies performed their promise of clearing the house of the guests. Indeed many had already gone. Some from an instinctive delicacy, which taught them that the presence of the dead should be respected, and that no longer should any attempt be made to keep up the evening. Others went in order to have the satisfaction—and it is to some people an immense satisfaction—of being able to state what had occurred in different gossiping quarters where the news had not yet reached.

The few who remained were those who were rather bewildered, and knew not exactly what to do, but, upon a polite hint from the friends of the marchioness regarding the extremely delicate state of that lady's nerves, they went also, and in another half-hour May Fair was restored to its wonted gravity, and the carriages had conveyed away the guests at one of the most brilliant of the Marchioness of Fanfaronade's soirees.

Death had usurped the place of the living, and a silence, which was remarkably in contrast with the pleasant strains of music and gay bustle that had resounded throughout those saloons so short a time before, now reigned over the whole of that most superb mansion.

The kind and considerate friends of the Marchioness of Fanfaronade never made a greater mistake in their lives than when they considered that after getting rid successfully of that lady's guests, they were themselves in any manner to become sharers in her reflections.

The fact is, she wanted to get rid of them, for she was turning plans and schemes of the most artful and admirable character—schemes which she did not think at all necessary they should be made acquainted with. When, therefore, they made their way back to her, and announced that the guests had taken the hint given to them, and were all gone, they were not over pleased to hear the marchioness remark,—

"Ah, my dear friends, how much I am obliged to you. I will now go to bed at once, and endeavour to compose myself to sleep, and in that sweet forgetfulness to find a balm for my wretched mind."

This was anything but what they wished or anticipated, and one of them ventured to say,—

"My dear marchioness, believe me, that the state of your mind will not allow you to sleep. You had much better think of how what has occurred may, at all events, be turned to some advantage."

"No, my dear friend, no. Why should I look for advantages? In the bosom of my family I live in peace, and, indeed, I much regret that poor dear Earl Crumbledown should have thought it at all necessary to give such a mark of his esteem and appreciation of my poor dear girl Annabella as he has."

"We can, and ought, to excuse anything on the plea of insanity you know, my dear, kind friend. That covers all faults."

"Yes, it does; and, therefore, the bitterness and the envy which this munificence to my poor, dear, amiable Annabella, will produce among some people, I shall ascribe to that cause; for how severely does the scripture forbid us to envy our neighbours."

"Certainly. Oh, certainly."

The marchioness had rung for her own maid while this little dialogue was going on, and when the maid came, she said,—

"Ladies, I am going to bed. My feelings will not permit me to sit up any longer."

With expressions of sympathy on their lips, and thoughts of envy and malice in their hearts, the ladies now left.

Immediately the door had closed upon them, the marchioness hastened to the chamber of Annabella, who she found anxiously awaiting her.

"Oh, you are up, my dear," said the marchioness.

"Yes, I have been waiting for you."

"That is right; I have only just succeeded in getting rid of some of our kind friends, who are ready to cut their own throats from vexation at the impossibility of cutting yours."

"Are they indeed so angry already?"

"Indeed they are; you would have been wonderfully amused had you heard them. It is impossible to conceive anything too spiteful for them to say. They insinuated everything they possibly could that had the remotest chance of making me uneasy, but I flatter myself that I showed myself too old a tactician for them, and that I sent them away devoured with spleen."

"If they are angry now," said Annabella, with animation, "what will they not be when they see some of the results of to-night's proceedings?"

"True, my dear; most true."

"Oh, I will make it my study and my amusement to vex them. They shall never see me, but something rich and rare and new shall awaken all their most envious feelings. In equipages, in diamonds, in everything that money can produce, I will so aggravate them, that, if some take not ill and die of mere chagrin, it shall not be my fault."

"You are quite right, my love; and I rejoice to see that you take these things in such a rational manner. But there is yet much to be done."

"What?"

"It is true that this money is left to you, but it is left on a contingency, namely, that within one month from now you are the wife of Lord Warelock, now the Earl of Crumbledown."

"Well, but if he refuse, the money, surely, cannot be taken from me?"

"I do not know that; I am inclined to think that there would be endless lawsuits about to discover if you, being willing to conform to the wishes of the old man, were entitled to the money, or whether the new earl could take it as heir-at-law, supposing he refused to marry you."

"Do you think so?"

"I do, indeed; and now, Annabella, you see this is a matter well worth our most serious and attentive consideration, and I propose that before we go a step further in the matter, we ought to have the opinion of some eminent lawyer about it."

"With all my heart, mamma."

"Agreed, then ; as soon as the morning is sufficiently advanced, I will order the carriage, and call myself upon Sir Ralph Skeffington, the Attorney-General, who I am sure will give me the best advice."

"But you said you had a scheme, mother."

"So I have, my dear. It is a bold one, but still it is one which I think must succeed, and at all events is worth the trying ; because, if properly tried, it can in no way do us any harm. I say us, my dear Annabella, although of course I mean you."

"Nay, it is us ; for you shall benefit by this wealth. What will three hundred thousand pounds produce annually ?"

"I dare say fourteen or fifteen thousand a year."

The Lady Annabella's eyes brightened as this sum was mentioned, and she said at once,—

"Then I here make you a solemn promise, mamma, to add one thousand a year out of it to your present income."

"My dear, that is more than I ought to expect, and yet not more than your good disposition might have made me believe you would offer. We now quite understand each other upon that point."

"You have my word upon it. If I come into possession of this money, I will secure you a thousand a-year out of it."

"Between us," said the marchioness, "of course there need be no disguises, and therefore I have no hesitation in saying, that such a sum will be very acceptable indeed ; and, besides, in the position you will be placed, you will have it in your power to do so much for Julia and Flora."

"Of course I shall."

"And now, as there cannot be any interference, I am sure they may rely upon you completely."

"You can tell them that I will do all I can to get them comfortably settled in life, and I dare say I shall succeed."

"Good. It is a pleasure, my love, to find that we understand each other so well, and so completely."

"Then, as that is all arranged, ma, what is the plan which you consider so very important, that it ought to be immediately arranged ?"

" Thank you, for reminding me of it. Of course, my dear, the first visitor we shall now have, will be the new Earl of Crumbledown."

" Yes."

" Then what I want is, that you and I should not be taken by surprise, but thoroughly arrange beforehand how he is to be received."

" Very proper, indeed."

" I propose then, my dear, that you see him alone, and that you at once affect so much sympathy with his bereavement, and so much dislike to the way in which the old earl has sought to force him into a marriage with you, that you make him a voluntary offer to give up the whole of the property to him, leaving him free to make his own choice of whoever he pleases to share it with him."

" But won't it be dangerous ?"

" Not at all. Such noble generosity on your part ought to meet with corresponding feelings, and he ought to make you at once an offer of his hand in the handsomest manner possible."

" But if he should not ?"

" Well, then, he ought to say to you, ' My heart is not at my own disposal ; but without any opposition from me, you shall have possession of all that my father has left you."

" Ah ! but in money matters people are not sometimes, you know, neither half so generous nor noble-minded as they ought to be."

" Well."

" Well ! I think it would be anything but well, if he were to take me at my word, and say he was very much obliged to me, and that he should never forget such noble generosity as long as he lived—that he was very sorry it was not convenient to marry me, but would always esteem me as a dear friend, &c., &c."

" My dear, if he could act so shabbily as that, we ought to combat him with his own weapons ; and as you will be careful to make the generous offer merely verbally, and without the presence of witnesses ; and as Colonel Bruce handed me the will of the old earl before he left the house, we can still act as if no offer of the sort had been made, and strenuously deny it."

" That might be done."

" Most easily. Who will believe that it was ever made ?"

" Not one, of course. So I perceive he would but be laughed at for hinting at such a thing."

" And, besides, my love, no man can be evidence in his own cause, so we have him safe, and can try this magnificent experiment without the cost of a sixpence, or in the slightest degree hazarding anything whatever."

" I like the plan amazingly," said Annabella ; " and believe me it shall want none of its chances in my hands."

" That I well know, my dear. You have been well brought up, and I am quite sure you can manage such a little affair with the greatest possible discretion ; so now you have but to remain in until he comes, and then to take care that you are alone with him when you make the offer—that there are no listeners ; and I have, in my own mind, a strong conviction that something very satisfactory indeed will come of it. You may depend, my dear, say what people may, there is nothing like treating a person with affected generosity, especially when, as in the present case, nothing is lost if the experiment should chance to fail."

" You are a first-rate diplomatist, mamma, I will say."

" My dear, a widow with three daughters, and a slender income, must be a first-rate diplomatist, or nothing at all."

" Well, then, if this plan, which I do say is a most admirable one, succeed, I shall consider myself bound to make you a very handsome present."

" Business is business, my dear. How much ?"

" I will double your first year's annuity."

" Making two thousand."

" Yes ; I will give you a thousand pounds down as soon as I am in possession of the money."

" My love, your conduct is admirable—all that I could expect from you ; and it only the more and more convinces me how correct I have been in the manner in which I have brought you up, my dear. You will not spare your tears in your interview with the young lord ; and if anything uncomfortable arises, so that you wish to break up the interview, you can always faint you know."

" Certainly. I think I shall do so at once, if I see he don't come into the offer, and take it in the right spirit."

" Well, perhaps it would be the best thing. Ring the bell first, and then faint just as you see a servant at the door. Besides, that will let me know how the matter stands, you see, and I can talk to him accordingly. So we will consider all that as quite nicely arranged, my love."

" Yes, certainly ; and now as I feel positively wearied, I shall try and get a few hours' rest."

" Do so, my love. You may depend to-morrow will be a very busy day. I call it to-morrow, because it is not yet daylight, but in reality I ought to say to-day, for it's just upon four o'clock."

The marchioness now retired to her own room, and thus this virtuous and exemplary mother and daughter arranged between them how the new Earl of Crumbledown was to be hooked into matrimony.

And let not any of our readers suppose that we have at all overdrawn this picture or too highly coloured it. That would be impossible. The moral abandonment, the want of all common honesty, honour, and decency, which characterises the women of what is called the aristocracy of this country, is beyond all reasonable conception.

The men are certainly deficient in intellect, and many of them of the most brutal temperaments ; but the women, with very few exceptions, know no restraint whatever, and there is nothing to equal the lies they can unblushingly tell, the insolence and dishonesty they can perpetrate, and the vices they can indulge in.

We have said nothing can equal them ; but we must make an exception, and that is, when some female, perhaps the wife of some well-to-do tradesman, becomes inflated with vanity, and apes the vices of the class above her, without having education or tact enough to throw even the flimsy veil over her coarseness which from habit and otherwise the women of the aristocracy know how to assume. When this occurs, it is a lamentable spectacle ; and adieu at once to the peace and the prosperity of the family in which it takes place.

Woman has been very ungallantly defined by a German writer, as an envious animal ; but we cannot go all the way with that gentleman, because we may have found many specimens of such a class, although we must admit that the specimens are many.

We recollect the wife of a tradesman in Bond-street, who being a trifle above the ordinary stature of women, was pronounced by her acquaintances to be a fine woman accordingly, and when any ladies of rank chanced to come into her husband's shop, it generally cost her an attack of hysterics, so great was her envy and anger combined. She would glare at them from her back parlour like an enraged tigress, criticising their dresses, picking to pieces their faces and their characters, 'dare-saying that they were no better than they should be, affecting to despise the barouche at the door, and altogether making such an exhibition of herself, that it was quite a curiosity to see her. But then this woman was ignorant and vain, with a naturally domineering temper, and a fool for a husband, who had given way to her.

It is, however, in the middle classes of society that virtue, innocence, beauty, and real good feeling are to be found. There, free from the arrogance and the vices of the rich, and the vulgarities and fearful intemperances of all kinds and descriptions of the poor, we find that free, unsophisticated, beautiful character, " the true English girl," than whom a more amiable, more gentle, loveable being cannot be found.

These are the creatures that lend the highest charm to poetry, by ennobling the very genius that worships them. These are the beings who make really the high-souled, gentle, affectionate mothers of England—mothers who need no assistance in their duties from a ranting Mrs. Ellis, or from the twaddling pages of a " Chambers's Magazine," both of whom are just about a hundred years behind the age.

CHAPTER VII.

THE PROCEEEDINGS OF THE NEW EARL.—HIS RECEPTION OF THE VERY GENEROUS PROPOSAL OF THE LADY ANNABELLA FANFARONADE.

WHEN Lord Warelock had so far vindicated his dignity as to knock down Mr. Willoughby, the sham prince, and had driven off in his carriage from May-fair, he was for some time in a state of excitement which forbade anything like very steady reflection on what had occurred.

When, however, that state subsided into a calmer one, which it did all the sooner, on account of his feeling that he had done what he ought to do, in at once rejecting the dishonourable proposition of Willoughby, he began to ask himself if there would be an end of the whole affair, or if he who had so successfully personated the prince with the unpronounceable name would feel inclined to push it any further.

The more he considered over the circumstances, the more he became convinced that the latter course was the one most likely to be pursued, and at length he so far settled in his own mind that Willoughby would attempt something, that the question now only became what that something was likely to be.

Then he remembered that the fellow had asserted that the old Earl of Crumbledown was in London; but that Lord Warelock did not for a moment believe, and only set it down as an idle threat, by which Willoughby had sought to intimidate him and drive him to terms.

"It is not at all likely," he said, "that my father would come to London now. He is full enough, I am well aware, of freaks and fancies, but consideration for his health will keep him at his country seat of Crumbledown."

Notwithstanding, however, this consolatory feeling, he felt how much it might be in the power of such a man as Willoughby to annoy him, and bitterly did he regret his own want of presence of mind at the Marchioness of Fanfaronade's party, which had led him to admit the claim of the sham prince to that title.

"Oh, what a piece of folly was that !" he exclaimed. "At all risks, I ought to have at once denounced the impostor, but he took me unawares, and I had no time for thought."

There are some minds which, if taken at unawares, always act truthfully and candidly, without reference to the policy of the matter; and there are others, again, of which order was the Earl of Crumbledown, as we ought now to call him, although he knew not of his own new dignity, which do exactly the reverse, and if suddenly placed in unexpected circumstances, always act disingenuously, and have, perhaps, to regret, upon reflection, that they did not be truthful and candid, from a conviction that, after all, it was the best policy.

Bitterly did the earl feel the scrape he had got himself into by his acknowledgment of the sham prince, and it gave him some uneasiness to consider how he should place himself right with the Fanfaronades, than as regarded what mischief by way of revenge Mr. Willoughby might attempt to do him.

"What can he do?" he asked himself; "but how am I to convince the Marchioness of Fanfaronade that it was a mistake of mine to recognise the Polish prince?"

Lord Warelock was not much smitten with the Lady Flora Fanfaronade, although, probably, if he had been told, " Now, you must positively marry some one, as a matter of compulsion, but you may take your choice," he would, more than probably, have fixed it upon her.

There were, however, circumstances of too recent a nature, weighing like lead upon his spirits, to enable him to enter heart and soul into any new affection. Time might accomplish much, but as yet the wounds of conscience were too green and smarting.

As regarded Annabella, he certainly never had entertained the most distant thought of making her his wife.

It was not that he did not think her quite handsome enough, and accomplished enough, but he was not compelled to marry her because he could not find fault with her; so he had never thought at all about it, although he could not but perceive that the marchioness would not be sorry were he to choose a wife from among her daughters; and he knew enough of the tactics of manœuvring mammas in the fashionable world, to be fully aware that the eldest daughter was always anxiously sought to be got off first.

But then he was in the habit of visiting at many houses in London, where very similar circumstances existed, and where much the same feelings found a home, and much the same system of match-making manœuvring existed as at the Marchioness of Fanfaronade's, and perhaps with the additional disadvantage of not possessing such undoubted illustrious descent as she.

He was in his private room at the hotel where he constantly lived when in London, while these reflections passed through his mind, when Lord Whitney was announced to him.

Much wondering what could induce a visit from him whom he, Warelock, had always kept at a distance on account of his well-known stupidity, he ordered him to be at once admitted.

That was an act of courtesy from one nobleman to another, which could not be avoided.

When Lord Whitney entered the apartment, he said at once,—

"I give you joy. Am I the first? Am I, now, the very first?"

"The first what, my lord?" said Warelock, in surprise. He had it at the tip of his tongue to say, "do you mean the first fool?"

"Ah, yes," said his silly lordship; "I see I am, now. You are the Earl of Crumbledown. I've made what haste I could to tell you."

Lord Warelock turned very pale, for the truth flashed upon him in a moment.

"Yes. Ah, yes," continued Lord Whitney, "you are now the Earl of Crumbledown. The old man is dead."

"Sir," said Lord Warelock, "that old man was my father."

"Ah, ah! I know that, and that's just what makes it so lucky. I came to tell you, to show I had no malice."

"Malice?"

"Yes—some people would have had. What now do you think he said of me just a little before he died? He said I was a fool."

The new earl heard not what Lord Whitney was saying. Notwithstanding for some years past he had been daily, nay, we may say, hourly expecting to hear of the death of his father, the notice of that event came upon him with a suddenness, and a shock which could not have been much greater, had it been totally and completely unexpected. He felt that strange rush of new sensations which any very great and unexpected event always produces, and death most of all, for somehow, let us be how we may prepared for that event, it always comes across the imagination with a painful and a burning shock.

If any one could have been said to be at all prepared for the death of another, that one most certainly was Lord Warelock, as regarded his father, for his very earliest remembrances of him had always pictured him as a very old man, and that the Earl of Crumbledown marrying at seventy-one, should outlive his countess, and see his son and heir of age, were circumstances which nobody for a moment then reflected on as being at all within the compass of belief.

Such, however, had been the case, and the old man for the last ten years had been a wonder to everybody.

Yet the young Lord Warelock felt a great shock at this sudden news of his father's death. Indeed, a far greater shock than he chose to let so unsympathising and stupid an observer as Lord Whitney see.

"Why, you look surprised," said Lord Whitney.

"No, no. Not exactly surprised."

" Then you didn't expect it ?"

" My Lord Whitney, I cannot of course expect you to have any feeling upon this subject, any more than you can expect me to have none."

" Oh ,I—I don't object."

" What may be quite a joke to you, is none to me."

" A joke ! Do you fancy it was to me a joke, to be called a fool before a whole room-full of people? I can tell you, I think it's no joke, but a very gross insult, which, if the Earl of Crumbledown were not dead, I should feel myself most unquestionably called upon to resent, unless the friends on both sides agreed in the admirable suggestion of Lady Mary Flittings, that he was insane when he said I was a fool, and so of course said what was very far from being correct."

To quarrel with such a known idiot as my Lord Whitney, Warelock well knew would be a reflection upon his own sense; therefore he just let him say what he would, without troubling himself about whether it was complimentary or insulting, and when he had an opportunity of getting in a word, he said,—

" My lord, since you have taken the trouble to bring me this news, no doubt you are prepared with every particular connected with it ?"

" Oh, yes—yes."

" Where did it happen ?"

" At the Marchioness Fanfaronade's rout."

" Impossible ! I was there myself."

" It's the fact, for all that."

" Indeed !"

" As I heard it, the old earl's carriage broke down at the door, and did him some damage. He was taken into the house, and there he died, after making one of the most extraordinary wills ever anybody in this world heard of."

" Wills !"

" Yes. What do you think he has done ?"

" I cannot imagine."

" The most ridiculous thing on earth."

" Left you something ?"

" No, he hasn't—I wish he had. He's left every penny he was possessed of to Lady Annabella Fanfaronade, on condition that you and she make a match of it."

" Impossible !"

" Ah, it's all very well for you to say impossible ; but I heard the will read with my own ears. Colonel Bruce and Mr. Ducie witnessed it, and that was how the old earl came to call me a fool. He asked for witnesses to his signature, and I offered myself, and he refused me, because he said I was too great a fool. Now, d—n it, I don't see what amount of wisdom was required in witnessing a signature, if I had been a fool, instead of being, as everybody knows, as Lady Mary says, so very much the contrary."

" Left all to the Lady Annabella Farfaronade !" repeated Lord Warelock, as if doubting the evidence of his own senses in the matter.

" Precisely : on condition that you and she make a match of it. That's how I understood it, and everybody else too who heard it read."

" You must be labouring under some strange mistake. Why, he never saw the daughters of the Marchioness of Fanfaronade. She herself told me she had frequently sent him invitations to her parties, but could never induce him to come, and latterly had not even a civil refusal."

" Ah, well, I don't know anything about all that ; I only thought I'd come and let you know. I knew where you were staying, and nobody else did, apparently, or I should not have been the first."

" My Lord Whitney, I thank you for that courtesy ; but if, sir, this is altogether a jest, I now tell you plainly I shall not consider it as one."

" A jest !"

" Yes, my Lord Whitney, I said a jest."

" You can go and see for yourself. The old earl lies dead now at the Marchioness of Fanfaronade's. If you think I am joking, you will find yourself very much mistaken indeed, Lord Warelock. I beg pardon, I mean my Lord Crumbledown, which, of course, is your title now."

"Excuse me, then," said Lord Warelock. "I must, of course, go immediately to the marchioness's to ascertain the truth of this matter."

"You had better wait awhile. In an hour or two it will be a more seasonable time to make your visit."

"No. This is a circumstance which excuses any ill-timed call. Excuse me, my lord, that I leave you thus abruptly."

Lord Warelock hastily seized his hat, and left the hotel to proceed on foot, a quicker than ordering any carriage, could he reach May Fair. It never occurred to him that the mysterious prince had any hand at all in the affair. The only thing that at all assimilated itself with Willoughby in his mind, was the fact that that personage had said that the old earl was in London, and how he should become aware of that fact before he, Lord Warelock, was a mystery he had no means of solving.

Notwithstanding what he had said to my Lord Whitney concerning the possibility of the news of the death of the old earl being a jest of that individual's, he had no such hopes.

We say hopes; because, although Lord Warelock was very far from being a perfect character, or one towards whom we can feel any amount of admiration, yet he had natural good feeling enough not to rejoice in the death of a father, let the circumstances connected with that death, and the contingent advantages to himself, be what they might.

On his route he bethought him that Lord Whitney had said that Colonel Bruce and a Mr. Ducie had witnessed the extraordinary will his father had made, and, as he knew Colonel Bruce very well, and that he resided in Manchester-square, he thought that, before calling on the Marchioness of Fanfaronade, it would be far better to get a distinct and clear account from the colonel of what had really taken place.

"I shall hear from him what I can rely upon," said Lord Warelock; "and before I go to May Fair, it is far better that I should be prepared by a full acquaintance with all the particulars, than have there to ask questions."

This was so sensible a view to take of the affair, that even to think of it was to carry it into immediate action; so Lord Warelock bent his course to the residence of Colonel Bruce, in Manchester-square.

There he learnt at once from the hall-porter that Colonel Bruce was up, and, having sent his card to him, he was desired to walk up to the colonel's dressing-room. A glance at Colonel Bruce's face convinced him that what he had heard from Lord Whitney, as far as regarded the death of his father, was quite correct.

"My dear Warelock," said the colonel, "spare yourself the pain of making any inquiries. I can guess what you have come about at once; so just sit down, and I will tell you as shortly as can be, consistent with accuracy, all that has occurred this night at the Marchioness of Fanfaronade's, in which you can be at all interested."

Lord Warelock did sit down as the colonel desired, and then he heard a clear and intelligible narrative of all that had happened.

"Now, Warelock," said the colonel, in conclusion, "you must draw your own conclusions, and adopt your own line of conduct. I have told you the circumstances just as they have now happened, and there the matter rests. What could have induced your father to make so extraordinary and so informal a will, I cannot, of course, conjecture."

"Nor I," said Lord Warelock.

"Have you no idea?"

"None whatever. I knew not that he was in town; and as for his leaving the Lady Annabella Fanfaronade sole legatee, I cannot imagine his motive. I don't think that, before this once, he ever saw her in his life."

"You surprise me!"

"Not more than I am myself surprised, I assure you."

"Had you done anything to provoke his anger?"

" Nothing," said Lord Warelock, as a sudden accession of colour came over his face—" nothing that he could be aware of."

" Oh, then, there was something ?"

" I don't mind telling you, of course, that I have been engaged in an intrigue, which has turned out a most unfortunate affair, with an attorney's daughter ; but he knew nothing of it."

" Don't be too sure of that, Warelock. You may depend that that's at the bottom of all the seeming mystery."

" I begin to think it must be so."

" You may depend it is so.   Some one has made him acquainted with the affair, and this has been his eccentric mode of punishing you for it. I wonder you did not think of that at once."

" I now feel that you are right, and I know who has played me this trick. What to say or what to do, I know not.   Can you advise me ?"

" Why, my dear fellow, love and murder are proverbially ticklish matters to advise anybody about ; but you should ask yourself what your feelings are, as regards the lady."

" Entirely of a negative character."

" That is, you do not love her."

" Certainly not."

" Nor hate her."

" Certainly not.   I am profoundly indifferent towards her, and as for making her my wife, such a thought never entered my head."

" Still you know your own affairs; bu , Warelock, you are now the Earl of Crumbledown, and without the personal property of your father, you will be the poorest peer that ever lived."

" I know it.   I know it."

" Then it is seriously worth your while to consider if in an ordinary sort of way you could be happy with the Lady Annabella Fanfaronade for a countess.   She is young—she has good birth, and of course education.   She is not certainly handsome to my mind, but no one can call her plain. Of her temper I know nothing, nor can any man, except by some wonderful accident, know anything now-a-days of the temper of any unmarried woman."

" True, true."

" So, in that respect, you are no worse off than anybody else, who pops his neck into the noose matrimonial."

" But there is something devilish unpleasant in being disposed of in this way among the personalities of an estate in the clause of a will."

" There is, but ——"

" But what ?"

" Current report gives your late father three hundred thousand pounds in English securities alone.   You perhaps are able to judge if that be an exaggeration or not."

" It is much more."

" Indeed."

" Yes, I am certain it approaches nearer to half a million."

" The deuce it does."

" Yes, I am nearly distracted, and know not what to do. I owe about forty thousand pounds among the money lenders."

The colonel whistled as he added,

" My dear Warelock, take advice, then, and marry the half million with the Lady Annabella Fanfaronade attached to it. You cannot help yourself, and after all, you know such a sum will be a great sweetener to the bitters of matrimony."

" I will not decide ; but I will marry her, or blow out my brains. I have no other choice."

[See page 45.

CHAPTER VIII.

THE INTERESTING INTERVIEW.—THE LOVER WON.—THE ARRANGED MARRIAGE.

It was, as Lord Warelock truly said, a most uncomfortable thing to be willed into a marriage, whether one liked it or not. Under such circumstances, even with a thousand predilections in the lady's favour, it is not likely that any swain would grow warmer in his admiration of her charms.

People don't like to be made to do what even is agreeable to them. There is an obstinacy inherent in human nature which forbids them; and when the new Earl of Crumbledown now sought the house of the Marchioness of Fanfaronade, it was with feelings very far from amiably disposed towards the Lady Annabella, who might be said to hold his destiny in her hands.

The extraordinary will which the old earl had left, was just one of those documents which afford the finest possible field for litigation. Some of the most capital and knotty points possible were involved in it.

Firstly, here was immense property left to a certain person on condition that she did something which required the consent and concurrence of another, and she might have said, "Why should I be deprived of a bequest given to me on a condition which I am quite willing to perform, but which I am hindered from doing?"

On the other hand, it might be urged, "Here is certain property left to you on an exact and precise condition; and it matters not whether the non-performance of that condition be your fault or any one elses, so long as it be not performed, for you cannot take the property unless it be."

Then, again, who was to have the property? Was Lord Warelock to take it if he refused to fulfil the precise intentions of his father? while she, the Lady Annabella Fanfaronade, was to lose it, with all the wish and desire in the world to carry out those intentions to the very letter.

And yet if he had it not, who was to have it, for he was the heir-at-law? If the bequest became void, he, as a matter of course, became the only legal claimant.

Under all these circumstances of doubt, trouble, and difficulty, there can be no real doubt in the world as to who would really have it, namely, the lawyers, unless the young earl and the Lady Annabella should come to an agreement between themselves with regard to it.

Perhaps Lord Warelock did not see all these difficulties and troubles which might be contingent upon his father's will as he walked to May Fair, but he saw quite enough of them to give him considerable uneasiness, and to convince him that the affair was a most troublesome one.

My Lord Whitney was right when he said, that by waiting an hour or two, it would be a more reasonable time for a visit to the marchioness, for when the Earl of Crumbledown got there, it was between night and morning, and at an hour when, if any one at all could be justified in refusing to see a visitor, that would be the time.

In these houses, however, if there be not a hall porter, somebody is always up, and the earl was at once admitted without any remark whatever about the hour at which he chose to make his visit.

"I am quite certain, my lord," said the servant who admitted him, "that none of the family are up; but there is a fire in one of the drawing-rooms, and if your lordship chooses to wait there, I will tell my lady's own maid to let her ladyship know as early as possible that your lordship is here."

"Thank you—thank you," said the earl; "do so; I will wait."

He was accordingly shown into the smallest of the drawing-rooms, in which there was a fire, and then he managed to ask the question which had hung on his lips several times, but which he had really not been able to summon courage enough to utter, of—

"In what part of the house lies the body of the Earl of Crumbledown?"

"A parlour below, my lord."

Warelock nodded, as much as to say, "that will do," and then he sat down to wait the appearance of any member of that family towards whom he now stood in so very strange and novel a position.

And he was beneath the same roof, too, now, with the dead body of his father; that father whose last act in life appeared to have been purposely contrived to give him, Warelock, the greatest possible amount of uneasiness.

He could no longer doubt that the man who named himself Willoughby was at the bottom of all this mischief; and this act of vindictive feeling on the part of the old nobleman had taken its rise solely in consequence of what had been communicated to him by that personage.

"Confound him!" muttered Warelock. "Who could suppose, now, that one malicious man could have it in his power to do such a world of mischief; and yet it is so. Probably that fellow has now done an act which is calculated to exercise a fearful effect over the whole of my future life; for whether I wed the Lady Annabella Fanfaronade or not, the consequences of the strange testamentary paper left by my father must be very important."

This was correct enough; and no wonder that he became almost forgetful that death was in that house, as he begun to consider duly the probable and the possible results of what had taken place.

He had not, however, to wait so long for the appearance of any of the family as either he or the servant who admitted him had anticipated. The fact was, that although the marchioness had certainly retired to her chamber, and hoped to get some sleep, she had left strict orders with her own maid that, if Lord Warelock should call, she was to be awakened.

Her own maid had consequently told the porter to knock at her own door in such a contingency, and as all this was done with great exactness by all the parties who were concerned, the reader may imagine the Marchioness of Fanfaronade herself awakening the Lady Annabella, to tell her that the hour for action had now arrived, and she must get up.

" My dear, he has come—he has come !"

" Who, mamma ?"

" Lord Warelock. Get up—get up."

" Well, but surely he will not expect to see me at such an hour ?"

" Nay, nay, my dear, I thought we had settled all that before. You know what we arranged ?"

" Yes, yes."

" Well, then, rise at once, and carry it into effect. Harris tells me he is in the small crimson drawing-room, so you had better go to him, and I will leave all the rest to yourself."

" Well, if I must ——"

" Must ! Why, you seem to object to the unseasonableness of the hour. I can assure you that nothing could be more fortunate. You may depend he is now in that state of mental flurry that he will be far easier acted upon than in the morning. He must be in some state of great excitement, or he would not have come here at such an hour. Remember, dear, all that we agreed upon. If he comes pleasantly into the matter, and makes you a proposal, you manage to touch the bell, and I will be near at hand and come. If he will not act according to our expectations, mind you faint, and that will prevent the necessity of your saying anything else, and at once put an end to the interview, which after that would, of course, become troublesome and embarrassing."

By this time the Lady Annabella had got out of bed, and, being more thoroughly awake, she began to see the affair in the same light as her mother, and duly proceeded to conform to her instructions.

The marchioness herself arrayed her in a simple white morning dress, and leaving her thus quite destitute of ornament, so as to convey the impression to the Earl of Crumbledown that there was no art or design whatever in the getting up of the scene that was about to ensue, she said,—

" Now go, my dear, and good fortune attend you ; for you may depend that the next half hour is the most important in your life."

The Lady Annabella was just the sort of person to go famously through such an interview as that which was now about to take place. She was not of a nervous order of humanity by any means ; she could, like most of her class, lie immensely without blushing, and she had quite sufficient personal vanity to feel the strongest possible reliance upon herself and her own powers.

With a slow step, for she would not flurry herself by any quick movement, she proceeded to the drawing-room, where sat the Earl of Crumbledown in so profound a study that he took no notice whatever of the quiet opening of the door, and was not aware of the presence of any one until the Lady Annabella Fanfaronade placed her hand upon his arm.

He started to his feet, and an exclamation of surprise burst from his lips as he beheld her close to him.

" Lady Annabella !" he said.

" Yes—yes," she replied, as she sunk into a chair close to him, and spread her hands over her face, as if overcome with emotion. " I am the unhappy Lady Annabella."

"Unhappy !"

" Can I be otherwise ?   Oh, cruel ! cruel ! cruel !"

She seemed unable to be more explicit for several minutes, and Lord Warelock was in such a state himself of amazement and confusion, that he knew not what to think or what to say.

However, as she made up her mind that he should now say something by which she should be able to judge what state of mind he was in before she hazarded another remark, he at length spoke,—

" Let me beg of you to be composed," he said, " and tell me the cause of this agitation.   Heaven knows I have reason to be agitated myself; but you, Lady Annabella ——"

Here he paused, and the Lady Annabella looked up into his face with such a well put on aspect of distress, that he could not doubt for a moment but that she was really suffering a large amount of mental anguish.

" My lord," she said, " you are, no doubt, surprised to see me," and she spoke in broken tones, as if struggling to suppress her emotion.   " The hour is unseasonable ; but I must trust to you to place the right construction upon my motives. Your father, the late earl, has breathed his last in this house.   It is that sad circumstance that has brought me here.   Before he died he made a will which—which—excuse me, I shall be more composed soon.   I have risen from my bed upon hearing that you were here, because I felt that not one moment ought to be lost in saying to you what I have to say."

" I shall hear whatever you have to say with the most respectful attention.   I am aware that my father left a will, by which he constituted you his sole heiress on condition ——"

" Oh, spare me—spare me."

" Spare you ?"

" Yes.   Do not repeat that condition.   My lord, I now speak to you as a gentleman, and as a man of unblemished honour.   I never thought a necessity could have arisen for such an interview as this between us.   Whatever my own feelings may be upon this occasion I bury in the depths of my own heart.   Whatever my fondest hopes may have dictated I may not, I dare not say ; but I have one wish in this world which, I trust, Heaven will permit me to see fulfilled."

" And what is that ?"

" Your happiness.   I cannot be the instrument of an injustice.   I cannot, with such feelings, permit myself to take advantage of an occurrence which savours of one."

" What do you mean, Lady Annabella ?"

" I renounce the bequest of your father, and its condition.   You shall have, my lord, to the last shilling, that wealth which you always justly expected, and to which you are most truly and justly entitled."

" You—you renounce it ?"

" I do.   I will take no advantage of that will made at the last moments of your father, from motives of which I know nothing.   I give all up to you, my lord, and I have only to hope that it will conduce to your happiness.   This is what I panted to say to you ; now you know why, at such an hour as this, I have sought you, and when you hereafter think of me, you will place a correct construction on my conduct."

" Good heavens !" exclaimed the thunderstricken nobleman, " do I hear aright ? You renounce a bequest which places you, in point of wealth, above the proudest nobles of the land ?"

" I do, my lord, I renounce it all.   It should be yours, and it shall be yours. I glory in renouncing it, and I would not barter my feelings in doing so for ten times the amount of that fortune which I place entirely at your disposal.   May Heaven bless you, granting you your father's length of days, and such contentment and happiness as this world can afford to you.   Farewell, my lord, farewell. I have done now a duty, to reflect upon which will be a source, to me, of the proudest gratification."

This was, indeed, the finishing stroke to the adventures of the last twelve hours. The earl was so amazed that he winked several times, and looked about him to assure himself that he was really awake, and that, after all, it was not some life-like dream, the various changes and phases of which he was passing through.

Slowly he saw the Lady Annabella moving towards the door, and that sight recovered him. On the impulse of a moment he sprung after her, and, catching her in his arms, he exclaimed,—

"Noble, generous Annabella, can you imagine for one moment that I can be insensible of so much greatness and generosity?"

"My lord!"

"Annabella, share with me that fortune you so generously relinquish—share with me the title which has so recently become mine. As my countess, you shall live to see how much I can and will appreciate the noble mind that could prompt such a generous act as you meditated."

The Lady Annabella burst into tears.

"Nay, dear Annabella, do not weep. You should smile now. We shall be very, very happy. Say that you will be mine, and share with me all that I can call my own, and I shall not regret the strange mode by which I have been enabled to find one who I feel to be so eminently worthy to share my heart, my fortune, and my coronet."

The Lady Annabella played her part well. She first shrunk from the encircling arms of the Earl of Crumbledown, and then, as if the sincerity with which she loved him overcame all other considerations, she sunk sobbing upon his breast.

"You will be mine—you will be mine!" he said, as he kissed her cheek.

"Dare I hope to be so happy?" she said.

And that settled the business completely. The Earl of Crumbledown was done, and had chosen one of the most selfish of women for a wife, because he believed her to be such a miracle of generosity.

The Lady Annabella contrived, unobserved by him, to touch the bell, and then the marchionness came into the room, and pretended to be shocked and amazed to find Annabella in the arms of the earl. Alas! venerable lady, she very nearly fainted; but the earl reassured her, by telling her what had passed, and soliciting her sanction to his choice of Annabella as his countess.

"Bless you both," faltered the marchioness; "my dear children, bless you both. Oh, who would have thought of this? Bless you. My feelings overpower me. Let us see you to-morrow, my dear Crumbledown; and now you go to bed, Annabella; I am sure you will be ill, you are in such a state of agitation."

And thus was crowned with the most complete success the really clever scheme of the Marchioness of Fanfaronade.

CHAPTER IX.

THE VILLAGE AND THE LOVE CHILD.—A SPECIMEN OF ONE OF ENGLAND'S HEROES.—THE DRUNKEN HUSBAND.

HAVING now detailed these incidents in London, with which, sooner or later, it was a matter of importance as regarded our tale that the reader should be fully and entirely acquainted, we once again return to the village where so disastrous an event had occurred as the death of the young and beautiful mother of the infant that first saw the light of day at the little inn.

We took occasion to congratulate the reader and the poor infant whose birth had been marked by such inauspicious events, upon the fact that Mrs. Grove's husband, drunken Jack Grove, as he was familiarly called, was out of the way of mischief for some time, at least, in the county gaol, and there he remained until his time of sentence duly expired, when he was set at liberty, with a strong conviction on the minds of the officials of the establishment in which he had made a compulsory sojourn, that they should soon see him again.

" I needn't say good-bye," remarked the man at the gate, to drunken Jack Grove, as he passed out of the prison ; " for we shall see each other again soon, I dare say."

The polite reply to this was a due consignment of the gaol, its officers, and everybody within to a place too warm to be mentioned by any others than extremely religious people, who may be supposed to be on more intimate terms with its proprietor than anybody else, considering that they have his word so often in their mouths, and that they pay him so much flattering attention, that it is difficult to say which is the strongest motive for attending the parish church —the love of God or the fear of the devil.

But we have not to do with Jack Groves just at present. It behoves us, before we follow that gentleman's devious course, to go to the inn, and see what proceedings were taken consequent upon the affair which had filled the minds of the whole household with wonder, and, in newspaper phraseology, convulsed the village.

The sudden and most unexpected departure of the stranger who had accompanied the young lady to the inn, placed everybody in a dilemma. It was suspected strongly that the landlord, as well as Mr. Pott, knew more about the strange gentleman than they chose to impart to any one else, and that his going was connived at by them both, particularly the former, who, notwithstanding all his pretended surprise, could not be very ignorant of the fact of the departure of the traveller.

Whether or not, though, the host had any very clear notion that he might be involved in very considerable trouble after the only person who could give a concise account of who the lady was, and what she was, had left the place, we cannot say, but certainly there seemed on the following day a very fair prospect of such trouble occurring.

There was the dead body in the house. The dead body of, Heaven knew who, —of one whose name every one there was ignorant of, and, indeed, of whom literally nothing was known, beyond the fact that she had been brought there by some one with the doubtful name of John Smith, and had given birth to a child, and died.

About the manner of her death there could not be much difficulty ; but it was the mystery in which the remainder of the affair was involved, which brought down considerable censure on the head of the landlord.

The news of what had occurred, together with various exaggerations, and a great many actual additions of what had not occurred at all, was soon spread all over the neighbourhood, and in due course reached the ears of the local magistracy, who considered it to be their duty to interfere in the affair.

Accordingly, on the following morning two of the magistrates arrived at the inn, and demanded to know the particulars, which, when they had heard, they both concurred in censuring the landlord for permitting the strange gentleman to go from the inn so very abruptly.

" But, gentlemen," said the landlord, " he paid for all he had, and left money beside, as you hear, for the child and all other expenses, so what could I do or say to him, you know? I couldn't detain him."

" Certainly not," said a respectable-looking man, who had arrived at the inn about half an hour previously, " certainly not ; I think the landlord would not have been legally justified in detaining the gentleman."

" How dare you interfere?" said one of the magistrates, who was rather testy at finding the matter involved in so much mystery.

" How dare I!" said the man, who had thus volunteered his opinion. "This is an inn, and the room we are now in is one of its public ones, or else you would have had no business here, because I had possession of it before you ; therefore, I conceive I have a right to enter into any current subject that may be under discussion here."

" Then you are very much mistaken. We attend here officially."

" And who may you be ?"

" Hush, hush," said the landlord; " these gentlemen are magistrates."

" Well, I cannot help that," said the stranger; " I must say that I have never entertained the most profound respect for country magistrates, and certainly the uncourteous manner with which I have been treated for courteously hazarding an opinion, will not tend to increase my veneration."

" Well, sir, since you have asked who we are," said one of the magistrates, " perhaps you will have no objection to say who you are ?"

" None in the least. I am Thomas Jones."

" And what are you, sir ?"

" The question is rather impertinent; but, if you must know, I am studying the law, and flatter myself that I have made some progress. Now, as regards this affair, you will make yourselves very ridiculous if you interfere too much, and bring upon yourselves some disgrace. The coroner's duty is clearly before him, namely, to hold an inquest upon the body lying dead, with all convenient dispatch, and to return a verdict according to the evidence he shall receive."

" I don't know that," said one of the magistrates. " The child, I think, ought to be taken charge of by the parish, and whatever money is left by the presumed father of it, applied by the proper authorities towards its support."

" Indeed, sir," said the stranger; " I think if you keep a clerk who is more learned in the law than yourself, you had better consult him, and he will tell you that what you now propose is clearly illegal."

" Illegal !"

" Certainly so. Money has been left by a Mr. Smith, as I understand the matter, for the support of his child for twelve months, with a nurse of his own choosing; and let me ask you, then, what right have you to interfere with such an arrangement of that gentleman's ?"

" The child, for all we know, may become chargeable to the parish after a year is gone by."

" But you cannot take me now into the workhouse, and lay hold of my property, for fear I should spend it all and become chargeable to the parish."

" Oh, that's not in point."

" You will find it so. But it is of no use arguing such a point, for the very parish beadle would be able to tell you you were wrong."

" A beadle tell me ?"

" Ah, to be sure; you know better yourself, but your insatiable, prying curiosity is offended at not being able to find out all the particulars of this affair. Now I am really glad I have come by chance, for I shall now stay and look after Mr. John Smith's interests, as I see that some injustice is about to be attempted; I tell you I am studying the law, and it may be as well to add, that I am tolerably well acquainted with parish law."

The magistrate was about to make an angry reply, but the other one, who was a man of much more acuteness of intellect, as well as general information, stopped him, saying—

" Let the affair rest. This Mr. Jones is so far correct, when he says that the magistracy have nothing to do with this affair; I came here to inquire into it, and from what I hear I am quite convinced that no interference of any official person but the coroner is required at all."

" Well, but ——"

" Now, my dear Sir Francis, you may depend it is as I say, and if Mr. Thomas Jones would be sufficiently candid, he would say at once that he is some legal practitioner from London employed to come down here on purpose to see to this affair."

" What ?"

" Now really, sir," said Mr. Jones, with a slight smile, " it's really too bad to attempt to deprive me of the credit due to my goodness of heart in saying I would remain here until all this affair was settled to take the part of the absent Mr. Smith. I don't think it generous of you now."

" Are you here in that capacity ?" asked the irascible magistrate.

" Oh, dear, no. How can you believe what your friend says ? He is only joking. Now confess, sir, and be candid yourself, and say you are only joking."

" Come away, Sir Francis, come away," said he who had made so shrewd a guess as to what Mr. Jones was, and what was the cause of his sudden appearance at the village inn. " Come away, we can do nothing here, and indeed the whole affair at present, until there shall be some new facts come to light, is not one in which, as magistrates, we are called upon to interfere."

By dint of persuasion this rational magistrate got the other away, and when they were gone Mr. Jones got out of the landlord—so imperceptibly that when he had told him everything he scarcely knew he had done so—all the particulars of what had occurred after the departure of the presumed father of the child which was in the care of Mrs. Grove.

" And do you think this woman may be depended upon, landlord?" said Mr. Jones.

" There isn't a better or a more kind-hearted woman, sir, in all the world, I am sure. It's her husband as makes her so poor as she is ; he spends everything in drink, and makes his home, which ought to be a comfortable one, most unhappy. He's in the county gaol now."

" Indeed !"

" Yes ; because he can't pay a fine."

" A good job too. It will give his poor wife some peace. On what day does he come out of prison?"

The landlord told Mr. Jones, who made a memorandum of it in his pocketbook with great care.

" What are you going all for to do, sir ?" said the landlord.

" Oh, nothing, nothing, only I am curious in keeping memoranda of anything that strikes me, and you know it's very interesting to be fully aware of the precise day when drunken Jack Grove comes out of prison."

" Oh, very ; and I don't wonder at it, sir. Shall you stay till the crowner's quest is over ?"

" Yes, I shall. Now, you understand, I'm an idle man, and almost anything does to amuse me, so when I go anywhere and there's anything going on at all out of the common way I am sure to stay till it's all over."

" Exactly, sir. That's just what I should like to do now if I was a gentleman and had shovels-full of money ; I'd go here and there and everywhere, and, as you say, sir, wherever there was anything going on amusing there I'd stay till it was all over."

" The inquest will be to-morrow, I presume ?"

" Why, sir, our beadle told me it would be to-day, if so be as it could be managed at all, and I think the sooner such jobs is over the better."

" So do I. Well, I shall take a walk now in the village and be back in an hour, by which time I hope you will have a lunch ready for me of the best your house affords, and, mark me, I must have choice wine, and if you have it not in your own cellar you must beg it, or steal it, or borrow it."

With these words, away went Mr. Thomas Jones, as he called himself, and when he got out of sight of the inn he inquired his way to Mrs. Grove's cottage of a boy who volunteered for a halfpenny to show him to the exact door, which offer was at once accepted, and when the halfpenny was paid the boy pointed to the door that happened to be within arm's length of Mr. Jones, and said,—

" That's it." After which he ran away as hard as his legs could carry him, for fear the halfpenny should be demanded back again, on account of the small amount of service he had done for it.

" Well done," said Mr. Jones, with a smile, as he tapped at the door of Dame Grove's cottage. " They are not all so green in the country as Londoners imagine."

Mrs. Grove opened the door herself, with her finger on her lips to enjoin silence, for the infant was sleeping, and she thought it was one of her neighbours come to see the child. She had been dreadfully persecuted since daylight by visitors. There was not a woman within five miles round who did not want to see the child, as if it was some natural curiosity, because its mother was dead and its father had gone away in a post-chaise.

Well did Mrs. Grove know that it was useless to set herself up against the tide of popular curiosity; she knew they would all see it, and she was only anxious to get the job over, so she showed it to every one who called while it was awake, but now it was sleeping, and hence was it that she came to her cottage door with her finger on her lips.

When, however, she saw that it was not one of her neighbours, she had an instinctive feeling, in a moment, that the gentleman had come from the father of the infant which had been so strangely committed to her care.

But yet she said nothing, for she preferred permitting him to speak first to committing herself in any way that might be displeasing possibly to him who had committed to her charge the young child, and, according to her estimation of the service, paid her so munificently before hand for her trouble.

"You are nursing a young child," said Mr. Jones, "who was born at the inn in the village here?"

"I am."

"Is it well? and does it seem likely to thrive?"

"It is hard to calculate upon the health or the lives of children," replied Mrs. Grove, "but as far as I can see, the child is a healthy little dear, and as likely to live and do well as any infant I ever saw."

"I am glad to hear it. May I come in and see the infant?"

"It is now sleeping, and it is a thousand pities ever to break the sleep of so

See page 54.

young a child.   As to seeing it, I have welcomed so many persons already to do so, that I am not authorised to refuse you.   I wish, however, if you come on any message from him who is, or who ought to be, the most interested in the child's welfare, you would tell me so."

"What puts that in your head?"

"You do not belong to the village or its neighbourhood."

"Well, but I need not, as a natural consequence, be an acquaintance of the father of the child you have to nurse.   What if no higher feeling at all but the mere curiosity of a stranger who is something of a busybody in other people's affairs should alone have prompted me to come here?"

"You can walk in," said Mrs. Grove; "but I do not think that is your motive."

"Well, well, never mind whether it be or not.   Let me see the child, and bear in mind, at all events, one thing, and that is, that I come to see it with a friendly feeling towards it, which, I dare say, is all you care about."

"It is the child of mystery," said Mrs. Grove, "and I have no right to pry into its history.   I have even in this short time become attached to it, and we naturally feel anxious to know as much as we can of those whom we love."

Mr. Jones looked rather surprised as he said,—

"You were surely not always in your present position in life.   Your language and your manner belong not to this village."

"No," she said, with a sigh; "I was not always what I am now.   Misfortune has reduced me to a class of life which I thought when I commenced it I could embrace with fortitude, but I have long since discovered my mistake. Here is the child, sir.   See how tranquilly it sleeps."

"It does indeed.   It seems a healthy, vigorous child enough.   Alas! alas! poor infant!   It is a pity you were ever born, but being among the living, it is a mercy you are strong and healthful."

"Oh, sir, I am not wrong in supposing that you know something of the history of the poor babe."

"Never mind about that; all I can do is to assure you that you are in good hands as regards remuneration, and that all the care you can possibly bestow upon this child will be well repaid to you with no niggard hand."

"I am abundantly already paid."

"Well, well, never mind that.   But there is one caution I can give you, and which you will do well to recollect.   If any one but myself should ever come to ask you any questions about the infant, you will do well to be cautious how you answer."

"Cautious!   How?"

"Do not enter into the particulars of its birth to any one, and most of all avoid giving any description of its father or its mother."

"I understand, sir."

"With such a caution you cannot do any mischief; but it is just possible that without it some serious mischief might occur."

"To the child, sir?"

"Yes; and to all who are in any way connected with it."

"Shall I see its father?"

"Yes.   He will come—Mr. John Smith; but if ever he does come, it will be at night, so that he will escape the impertinent gaze of the villagers, and be known to you alone; and he will come direct to your cottage."

"I shall expect to see him, and if you, as doubtless you will, happen to see him previously, pray assure him that no care or attention, by night or by day, shall be spared to make the child prosper."

"Of that I think he feels assured himself, and now of course I need scarcely say, that I do not wish you to say to any one what I have now remarked to you, or to take any notice of me at the inquest beyond what you would of a mere stranger, who chooses to interest himself in the matter."

"I will not, sir."

Mr. Jones made a few more casual remarks, and then he left the cottage, and Mrs. Grove felt much more satisfied in her own mind than she had been concerning the child, for, although she had been paid for its keep a whole year in advance, she did not at all like the idea of the infant being on that account wholly deserted by its natural protector, whether in health or in sickness.

"I am glad," she said to herself, as she watched the slumbers of the child, "that this gentleman has called upon me, for it shows that some care is being taken of this little innocent creature, beyond paying merely for its maintenance."

Scarcely, however, had Mr. Jones been gone five minutes when Mrs. Grove had another visitor, who was no other than the beadle of the village, who came to summon her to attend the inquest, which was to take place at four o'clock in the afternoon.

"Mrs. G.," said that important official personage, as he wiped his bald head with an immense silk handkerchief, that was coloured into an imitation of the national flag, " Mrs. G., you will have to attend the inquest, and, on your most solemn and deliberate affidavy, tell all you know about everything and everybody. You will find, Mrs. G., that the laws of your country are no more to be trifled with than I am, and I believe, madam, that, in common with everybody in this parish, you are well aware that I am no joke."

"The inquest at four o'clock; at the inn, I presume?" said Mrs. Grove, calmly.

"Precisely; but let me tell you that it is not a matter to take calm and cool, Mrs. G. It is a serious affair, I can tell you, and one of the onerous and terrible duties of a beadle is to attend at all inquests, and so an inquest is no joke, Mrs. G., cool and comfortable as you seem to take it."

"I never said it was a joke."

"But you looked as if you thought nothing of it, Mrs. G. 'Four o'clock; at the inn, I presume?' says you, as if it was nothink at all."

"The truth is," said Mrs. Grove, "that in this case the inquest does become a mere matter of form, however eminently useful such an institution may frequently be."

"A matter of form?"

"Merely so in this case, because the cause of death is involved in no mystery whatever, you must be aware."

"Come, come, Mrs. Grove; come, come. We don't want no radical opinions here, you know. They won't do."

"Radical opinions! Why, what do you mean?"

"Mean? what do I mean? I'd have you know, Mrs. Grove, that a beadle's not obliged to mean anything. How dare you ask me what I mean? It's like the insolence of the lower classes, when they presume to ask the beadle of a parish what he means."

"It is," said Mrs. Grove; "you have delivered your message, I will trouble you to leave my cottage, for you only disturb the sleeping child."

"Well, I never. That's *quivelant* to turning me out."

"I wish it was actually so."

"I'm a going, and I tell you what it is, Mrs. G., you are not the sort of woman I took you for, I can tell you, a-hem! You don't seem to be at all aware that the friendship of a beadle is better than the countenance of a magistrate. You are a remarkably foolish woman, Mrs. G."

"I am quite content to labour under your bad opinion, if you will please to consider your business here as ended with the delivery of the message which has brought you to my home."

"Oh, very good. Ve—ry good, in a manner of speaking. We shall see what we shall see, and we shall hear what we shall hear. A-hem!"

And with this oracular speech the beadle walked away, trying to look as big as possible, which, after all, was not very big, except laterally, which is a description of greatness that takes away something from dignity, however much it may give to might.

The infant continued sleeping, and as no other visitor came for an hour or two, Mrs. Grove began to congratulate herself upon the fact of having escaped persecution so long, and to think that the curiosity of the village and its neighbourhood was surely at length gratified.

CHAPTER X.

THE VERDICT AT THE INQUEST. — A PERIOD OF PEACE. — THE LIBERATION OF JACK GROVE, AND THE MYSTERIOUS WARNING HE MET WITH.

AT four o'clock, the inquest on the body of that beautiful young creature, who had, at the time of giving birth to the innocent being now in the care of Mrs. Grove, surrendered up her own existence into the hands of her Creator, was held.

Although it was generally well enough known that, as Mrs. Grove truly said in this instance, the inquest was a mere matter of form, since a regular medical man had attended the deceased, and she had died from purely natural and well understood causes, yet the concourse of persons who had assembled to hear those brief particulars placed in an official form was very great indeed.

The beadle, unquestionably, was the most important man there present, and he made such a perpetual bustle in preserving order, that the coroner was compelled at last to tell him, that if he did not be quiet himself, he would have him turned out of the room.

This was a direct hit, in the mind of the beadle, at his dignity, and no wonder that that functionary became, as, indeed, he did, almost officially extinct after it. It was positively cruel.

The first witness examined was the landlord, who deposed to the parties coming to the inn; and then the landlady gave her evidence as to the condition of the young lady, and then sending for the doctor, who attributed the death to natural causes, which he explained in medical terms to the jury, the consequence of which was, that they were just as wise when he had done, as they had been before he commenced his statement.

Then Mrs. Grove deposed to having charge of the child, and the brief note signed " John Smith," in which the money had been enclosed, was produced.

"You are quite certain," the coroner asked at the conclusion, " of all this, that the death of the mother of the child was unavoidable, and in the course of nature?"

" Certainly," said the doctor, to whom the question was put.

" Then, gentlemen," said the coroner, " our duty is very simple indeed."

" I don't see that, Mr. Coroner," said one of the jury.

" You don't see what, sir?"

" That our duty is so simple. Why is not the postillion examined who drove the lady and gentleman here? and why is he not traced at the different places where he changed horses, and all that sort of thing?"

" Because," said Mr. Jones, all at once, " you are met to inquire how a lady unknown came by her death, and not as to where John Smith changed horses."

" That is correct enough," said the coroner; " but, whoever you are, sir, I must beg that you will make no observations, as you are not on the jury."

" I beg your pardon, Mr. Coroner, I know I am wrong. I spoke on the impulse of the moment, in consequence of the horrible stupidity of the remark which was made."

" Stupidity !" said the juryman; " did you say stupidity?"

" Precisely."

" Then I can tell you ——"

" I cannot permit this to go on," said the coroner; " our duty is here quite a plain and distinct one; it is simply to inquire touching the death of a young female whose body we have seen now lying in this house. No one is accused as having been in any way instrumental to her decease, and we cannot enter into the subject of where she came from, or who it was who was with her. We have the most respectable medical testimony that the death was natural."

"If I am an Englishman," said the insulted juryman, "I won't put up with it. My missus wants to know all about it."

There was a roar of laughter at this candid admission of the motive which had actuated the juryman, during which he, in a great passion, moved a vote of censure upon the coroner, and intimated that he dared not go home unless he had some more particulars than he already knew to tell his missus, who was a very fine woman, though rather hasty in her temper."

Upon this, Mr. Jones went up to him, and whispered,—

"My dear sir, don't be offended; I know all about it. You come to me after the inquest is over."

This had the effect of mollifying the irascible juryman, who considered what Mr. Jones had said to be a promise to tell him all about it, when in reality it was no such thing.

A verdict was accordingly returned of "Natural death; but the jury had no knowledge of the name of the deceased."

This was, of course, quite sufficient for all good purposes; as, after the dea hha d been ascertained to have been caused by no violence, the coroner's function se nded at once; but the juryman with the curious wife, who dared not go home unless he had something to tell, hastened to Mr. Jones, and said,—

"Well, sir?—well, sir?"

"And well, sir?" said Mr. Jones.

"You said you knew all about it, you know."

"And so I do."

"What was it then? Tell me."

"Tell you? Did you say tell you?"

"Yes, to be sure; you promised, you know. Don't you recollect you said you would tell me all about it?"

"Nay, my dear sir, you are most decidedly in error. I said I knew all about it, but I was extremely careful not to make any promise of telling you one word upon the subject. Had I so promised, I am such a slave to my word that, you may depend, I should have kept it, let the consequences have been what they might."

The juryman felt that he was completely taken in, and looked rather aghast, but there was no help for it; so he was compelled to go home, with nothing fresh to tell his wife, the consequence of which was, as a neighbour declared, that the bellows was brought against the side of his head several times by the indignant lady with terrific effect, which we consider served him extremely right, if he chose to put up with it.

It was certainly very amazing to all the gossips, far and near, that the most mysterious affair that had taken place in the country for Heaven knows when, should thus pass off so very quietly, and without producing anything like the sensation that was to be expected, or ending in any harrowing or equivocal disclosures.

And yet such seemed to be the fate of the affair. Mr. Jones sent a note to Mrs. Grove, on which were merely written the words,—

"Should anything unpleasant occur, send to X. Y. Z., Lincoln's-inn, London." And from that nothing could be gathered whatever concerning the mother of the child, her name, or under what circumstances she had been so cruelly betrayed.

However, the parson of the parish called upon Mrs. Grove, and would insist upon christening the child, and naming it something; so Mrs. Grove named it Minna, and Minna Smith became, accordingly, the name of the child.

The unfortunate young mother's remains were laid in the village churchyard, and were attended to their last resting-place by almost the whole population of the place, as well as many strangers; Mrs. Grove, too, went to see the mother laid in the grave, and she put on mourning for her, for she loved the little thing which had been committed to her charge, and, from respect to it, she wore the insignia of woe for its poor mother, who thus, in the pride of her beauty, and at the commencement of a life which, under happier circumstances, might have been one of such joy to herself and to others, had gone to that "bourne from whence no traveller returns."

And after this there ensued a period of calmness, during which, notwithstanding the deprivation of its natural nourishment, in the shape of mother's milk, the child throve amazingly, and gave abundant evidences of a strength of constitution which, considering all things, was very remarkable.

But this period of peace was not to last long. Drunken Jack Grove's term of imprisonment had expired, and he was making his way towards the village and his own home.

It was customary, in order to avoid observation, to discharge prisoners, who had served their term of imprisonment in the county gaol, after sunset, so that on the evening—and a lovely one it was—that his sentence ceased to have effect, Jack Grove left the gaol.

When he got some distance, and had done swearing at the gatekeeper, with whom, as we have recorded, he had a little fracas, his impulse was, of course, to endeavour, as soon as possible, to get something to drink. But, alas! no money had he, and as for getting anything on credit, he knew that that was out of the question, for all the publicans in the neighbourhood went upon the unconfiding and selfish principle of pay to-day and trust to-morrow ; and as "to-morrow," in the strict acceptation of the word, never came, they never trusted at all.

"Here's an infernal shame now," soliloquised Jack Grove, as he stood at a corner where several roads met. "Here's an infernal shame—not a drop of drink for a fellow, after he has been in quod for Heaven knows how long, with nothing to drink but water."

This was a most uncomfortable reflection to such a gentleman as Jack Grove, both as regarded the present and the past, and no wonder that it made him swear to a very considerable extent, and make him imagine himself a most ill-used member of society indeed.

What's to be done ? was the question, and it was a serious one ; for the sun had sunk, and each moment the darkness that was spreading around him, was becoming more profound.

And Jack Grove was as ignorant of what had taken place in the village during his absence, and of the altered circumstances of his wife, and the addition to the small family, under what it is a courtesy to call his roof, as any one could possibly be.

Shut up in the county gaol, he had been as it were out of the world completely ; so that all that had gone on, had never penetrated to his understanding, or disturbed his mind in the least.

"Well," he said ; "well, I suppose I must go home, and see what the old woman has got. Confound her, she never once came near me all the while I was in prison, to give a fellow a word of comfort, or a drop of gin or whiskey."

Jack Grove quite forgot to consider how utterly unworthy he was of a word of comfort from a woman to whom he had been a curse and a reproach for years ; but these kind of characters always consider themselves ill-used by everybody.

He leaned back against an old finger-post that stood where three cross-roads all met ; and then he went through what he called a process of thought upon how very unlucky he was.

"Hang me," he said, "if I ain't the most unfortunate fellow in all the world. I am always getting into one trouble and out of another. Here's a nice treat now ! Been ever so long in gaol ; and now, when I have got out, I have not a penny even to get half-a-pint of porter with. It's too bad ; d—n me if I ain't an ill-used man, a very ill-used man, and that's the fact, I feel ill-used."

"Then why don't you resent it ?" said a voice close to his ear.

Jack Groves started and turned round, when he saw leaning against the other side of the direction post, a tall man, whom he was quite sure he had not observed before.

"Who are you ?" said Jack Grove.

"My dear fellow, what need you care who I am, so long as I give you good and disinterested advice."

"Well, but ——"

"Oh nonsense—you are an ill-used man."

"I think so."

"You can't get enough to drink you say; you can't even very conveniently get a living without working for it, and that is a very hard case indeed, as I am well aware of; so I will do you all the good I can. How many years would you like to live, and how much money would you require, to be continually drunk all the time?"

"How long?—how much?"

"Yes, I daresay we can come to some agreement."

Jack Grove began to feel rather alarmed, and he said in a suspicious tone of voice, "I tell you what it is, I did not ask for your company, and I do not want it; pray go your way, and I'll go mine."

"Both our ways are the same," said the mysterious stranger.

"How do you know that? I did not tell you which way I was going."

"Oh nonsense—it's well enough known for all that. You are going to the devil as fast as you can. You ought to be fully aware of that as well as I; but I like you, drunken Jack Grove. You swear such capital oaths; you drink so much; and altogether you are such a vagabond, that you have even my heart."

Jack trembled more than before, as he said to himself, "This must be the devil himself; I have always heard that if he waylays anybody, it's at a cross-road.'

"I say you have even my heart," added the stranger; "and, if you like, you shall be continually drunk."

There was something certainly very captivating in the idea of being continually drunk; but to receive such a boon at the hands of the devil, was, as a matter of course, to consent to becoming his sole undisputed and individual property after a certain period; and that was a proposition that even drunken Jack Grove shrank from."

"No no," he said; "I don't want anything."

"Indeed;" why you said just now you were ill-used, and you looked up as you said it, as if you would accuse your Maker.

"No no, I didn't."

"You did, Jack Grove; beware how you contradict me. Do you accept my offer?"

"No—certainly not. Be off with you. I smell brimstone. I'll have nothing to say to you. I accept nothing from you."

"Beware, then, you have given me the trouble of coming exactly one thousand, and fifty-seven miles, two furlongs, to speak to you; and now I say, beware! Let me catch you drunk, that's all."

So saying, the mysterious stranger darted off, leaving Jack Grove in such a state of agitation, as he had never been in all his life before, and perspiring with fear at every pore, and scarcely able to walk.

"Here's a go," he said, "here's a go; the devil himself come a thousand and fifty-seven miles and two furlongs, on purpose to see me. What will become of me now? He says if I get drunk any more, he'll be down upon me. Oh! I am a most miserable fellow, now I shall be afraid to take half-a-pint of beer. Oh dear! I shall have to reform."

The idea of having to reform, almost brought tears into Jack Grove's eyes, and with many dubious shakes of the head and deep groans, he took his way towards the village in that state of mind which he described afterwards, as one in which a man will give away his life for half-a-farthing, and not care who was the purchaser.

CHAPTER XI.

A DRUNKARD'S REFORMATION.—THE SADDLE AND THE TURNPIKE-GATE.—AND THE REWARD OF CONSTANCY.

UPON such a mind as that of Jack Grove, it was not at all to be wondered at that the effects we have stated were produced; and, probably, a more effective mode of, for a time, weaning him from an indulgence in his favourite potations, could not have been well devised. Not that we say this mode was a devised one, or that the mysterious man who encountered Mr. Grove, was a bit less mysterious than he seemed to be.

We do not at all assert that the strange meeting at the cross-road was contrived by Mr. Jones, for the purpose of throwing the halo of a superstitious protection over the child who was committed to the care of the drunkard's wife.

With not half the spirit that had characterised him, when he left the gaol, did Jack Grove slowly walk towards the village. He shook his head a great many times, as if in a dubious state of thought, and then, with a deep groan, he said,—

" Well, it is hard that a man can't take the least drop in the world, without meeting the devil at a cross-road. I ain't worse than other people. There's loads that wouldn't speak to me, that walk into their wine like winking ; and they never think of the devil, if the devil does of them. And here am I, a poor fellow who has been shut up for a fortnight, and was only thinking of a drop of something in the way of comfort, when the devil himself must come, and want to purchase me out and out. I do call that hard—very hard."

Perhaps Jack Grove considered it harder still, when he came within sight of the swinging sign of an ale-house, which was known by the name of the Saddle and Turnpike-gate, and was situated nearly half a mile outside the village.

" Ah !" soliloquised Jack Grove, as he decreased his slow walk to a positive creep, " ah ! they draw as nice a jug of ale there as any they draw within twenty miles ; but what's the use of that, they go on in the d—d old system—it's all pay to-day, and trust to-morrow ; and what the use of a fellow without a farthing knowing where to get a jug of good ale, if he had the money."

" I'll buy your waistcoat, your coat, or anything," said a voice, some short distance behind him.

And upon Jack Grove turning, he saw an itinerant Jew-dealer in miscellaneous articles, trudging along the high road.

" Hilloa, Moses !" said Jack, " is that you ?"

" Just whatever you like," said the Jew ; " it's all the same in the way of business. You want a jug of ale and have got no money. I'll give you the price of three for your waistcoat."

The offer was irresistible, and the mysterious man at the cross-road was forgotten, and before drunken Jack Grove was a minute older, his waistcoat was transferred to the Jew's pack, and he held in his hand a shilling as its produce.

" If I hadn't known," said the Jew, as he trudged on much quicker than Grove, " that you really wanted the money, I couldn't have given above sixpence, but my feelings always get the better of me, and the money I lose is astonishing."

" Yes," said Jack Grove ; " you may put it all in your eye without seeing any the worse ; but I don't care. Now for the Saddle and Turnpike-gate, and a brimming jug of their finest and best ! I think I see it foaming, and sparkling, and hissing now, as if it were alive. I'll have it. What's life without ale ? I—hilloa ! I'm forgetting my fiend by the cross-roads. What the deuce did he say—if I took another drop he would be with me ? Oh, nonsense, he's got something better to do. There's old Dr. Hartshorn, the vicar, died the other day,—he's got him to attend to ; and yet, I somehow feel devilish uncomfortable. I've got a sort of shivery feel over me. I wonder how affairs are going on at home. It's odd I never heard. What—suppose I was to reform now, and never drink any more. There would be a go. Why, 'twould be the talk of the whole parish ; and instead of being called drunken Jack Grove, who knows but I may be made the beadle of the parish itself at the next vacancy ! D—n it, I will reform. Saddle and Turnpike-gate, I'm going to pass by your door, for the first time in my life. Ale, I despise you, in small quantities. No, I mean I despise you altogether, and don't intend to drink you any more. I have taken a resolution that, instead of one of the crowning pots they sell here—but I mustn't think of it—I won't think of it—I'll keep on the high road to temperance now, and defy the devil."

There came a gleam of light from the parlour of the public-house, it had a rich red glow too, which it borrowed from the crimson curtains that shaded the

windows, and Jack Grove, as he neared the door, heard the delightful sounds, to him, of boisterous merriment within.

He paused a moment, as if he were wavering in his determination; and then he made a sudden rush to get past the door, whistling loudly as he did so, in a vain endeavour to forget the delicious flavour of the ale and the various other compounds for which the house was famous.

"What! Jack Grove, as I'm alive!" said a voice. It was the landlord's, from the door, just as he got past it. "Why, Jack Grove, is that you, passing the Saddle and Turnpike Gate, and here's a new barrel of your favourite ale being tapped, and in such condition to-day as it never will be again? Why, man, are you mad?"

"Hold your row," cried Jack. "I don't want to have anything to say to you; and I don't want any ale."

"Now, my dear fellow."

"You be hanged, and the ale too. In good condition is it?'

"Prime!"

" Then go and smother yourself in it."

The landlord retired into the house, with uplifted hands, and Jack Grove walked on at least twelve steps further ; then he stopped to put his hand in his pocket to feel the shilling, as he said,—

" A man of resolution may venture upon things, another may not. Now it isn't everybody as could have gone past the Saddle and Turnpike Gate as I have done. Now they are all talking about me in the parlour, I know ; and they are just saying I was afraid to stop, because I couldn't trust myself to know when I had had enough. Now, hang them all, if I don't show 'em that I am a different sort of person to what they take me for ; so I'll just go back and let 'em see what a determined, resolute character I have become."

This was an extremely satisfactory mode of getting into the Saddle and Turn-pike Gate, and it was truly astonishing with what rapidity he now made his way into the parlour among some of his own cronies.

There was a great shout, of course, when Jack Grove made his appearance ; for nothing is so amazing to an habitual toper as to find any defalcation on the part of a once boon companion. The landlord had just told them how Jack Grove had passed the door, and his appearance after that was looked upon as a signal triumph of ale over resolution.

" Why, how have you been, old fellow ?" said one, as he handed Jack the brimming pot.

Jack smiled like the infant in " The Angel's Whisper," and placing the pot to his mouth, he took it not away again until he was able to demonstrate, by invert-ing it, and striking the bottom a rap with his knuckles, which made a little bit of froth fall on the floor with a dab, that it was emptied of its precious contents.

" Well, I'm d——d," said the confiding individual, who had handed him the measure ; " how long is it since you've had any ?"

" A fortnight," said Jack, who had exhausted his breath in doing justice to the flagon that was presented to him.

" A fortnight !—why, where the deuce have you been to ?"

" Why, where I was none the better for seeing any of you. It's all very fine to ask me where I've been to ? You all know I've been in the county gaol for a fortnight ; and there I might have rotted for all you cared."

" Oh, dear me ! dear me !" said the landlord ; " and that's human nature, is it ? Dear me—dear me !—it's enough to give one a crick in the neck. I always feel these things round the small of my back ; but never mind, Mr. Grove, never mind, Mr. Grove, we've missed you.—Fourpence."

" Eh ? fourpence—oh !" Jack's eyes fell upon a foaming tankard which the landlord had brought in, in anticipation of the order. He couldn't help laughing, in spite of himself ; the ale looked so cool and inviting, and there was such a mass of hissing bubbles on its surface. How could Jack Grove be angry ! He pro-duced the shilling, and, throwing it down on the table, he cried,—

" Take it, old cut-and-come-again, and bring in the others when this is done with."

" Didn't I say it ?" said the landlord, turning round with an appealing look to the room ; " didn't I always say, the first thing in the morning and the last thing at night, that if you would see a real old English gentleman—one of the olden time—you must look at John Grove."

" Hold your row," said Jack ; " you old toad in a wine-glass ; nobody cares what you said or what you didn't say."

" And he's a funny man, too," said the landlord, as he left the room with a smile ; " remarkably funny, and, oh, such company !"

" Well," said Jack, as he raised his own proper tankard to his lips, " here's the old toast,—' lots o' licker.' "

This toast was duly responded to by the half-drunken conclave ; and Jack was just about to propose another, when the landlord flew into the room like some engineer who had been hoisted by his own petard, and upsetting completely the little man in a high back chair, in the hurry he was in.

" I'm—I'm—I'm swindled. I mean I'm done—I'm swindled. It's all a do, all the world over ; is this the way I'm to pay my brewer ?"

" What now ?" said Jack, as he hit Boniface a whack on the head with the empty flagon.

" Don't do that, sir—don't do that," said the landlord, rubbing the affected part; " it's bad enough to be kicked and thumped by respectable men ; but I won't stand it from a man as brings me a bad shilling."

The melancholy truth in a moment flashed across Jack Grove s mind

" Done again," he said, and then, as if resolved to make something by the disaster, he seized the gin and water of a rather elderly fat individual, who sat next him : he drank it off, holding its owner forcibly by the nose while he did so, so that he was quite incapable of resisting this infraction of the rights of property.

" Two pots and a glass of gin and water, and twopence to the good. What have you got to say now about it ?"

" Catch a funstable—no, I mean fetch a constable ; d—n it, I don't know what I'm saying."

" Catch yourself," said Jack, as he dealt the landlord a blow about the region of the stomach that doubled him up with a great " oh !" and then, thoroughly pot-valiant, out he sallied.

But he went not out alone ; for there ran out after him, a thin, little weazened-faced old man, who called after him as he went,—

" Mr. Grove, Mr. Grove ; a word with you, Mr. Grove, if you please."

" What now ?" said Jack ; " do you want me to put you in one of my boots and stamp upon you? D—me, if your face wouldn't make a good knocker to hell."

" But, Mr. Grove, Mr. Grove ; allow me to say, sir, that you are not at all a destitute man. You know me, Mr. Grove ; my name is Rippon ; you know I've been in the law, and should have been in it still, but for a little difference in opinion the lord chancellor and I had one day. I can tell you, Mr. Grove, you are a man of means—of money, sir."

" That's news," said Jack. " How do you make that out ?"

" Ah ! ah !" said the little man ; " I can make it out fast enough ; and I shall rely upon your generosity, Mr. Grove, completely."

" What's it all about ?" said Jack.

" Why, my good sir, you must know that while you have been so unjustly incarcerated, a singular stroke of good fortune has occurred to your wife ; she has somebody's child to nurse, at a pound a week sterling—current coin of the realm, Mr. Grove."

" The devil she has !"

" Yes, and what's more, sir, she has had fifty-two pounds paid for the first year's bed, board, and washing ; fifty-two pounds—only fancy, fifty-two pounds in a heap—literally in a heap—just fancy you can see them. You needn't be in-debted to nobody for pots of ale, or goes of anything ; you are a made man, Mr. Grove."

" It's gammon," was the very impolite reply to this piece of information.

" Indeed, sir, it is not," said the little man. " I wouldn't deceive a gentle-man with fifty-two pounds on any account. My name is Rippon, you know ; and I assure you what I say is the truth. Your wife, herself, cannot deny it."

" I tell you what it is," said Jack Grove ; " if it's true, I'll stand something handsome ; if it isn't, look out, I'll stultify you, and smash you, and no mistake."

" Ah, ah !" said the little man, " I'll stand the risk. I thought I'd come and tell you, as nobody else seemed inclined. I suppose they thought you knew it ; but I was sure you did not, my dear sir, and therefore I came to tell you, and re-member I was the first and only man that did so, while everybody else was laughing at you, Mr. Grove."

" You're a fool," said Jack Grove ; " and if you come after me another step, I'll fall on you and crush you."

This warning seemed to have some effect upon old Rippon, for he got up an affected laugh, and then walked away, apparently satisfied that he had accomplished something towards putting a few pounds in his pocket.

"D—n it, who knows?" said Jack Grove, who was getting more tipsy, from the potations he had taken, every moment. "It may be true; there are a good many more unlikely things than that have came to pass. Fifty-two pounds! what a calculation to make that into pots of ale. I couldn't do it; howsomedever, here goes, it's no use thinking about it; I'll just see whether it's a fact or not."

"Have you forgotten?" said a deep, solemn voice.

Jack Grove started round, and saw, within half a pace of him, the mysterious-looking man who had accosted him at the cross roads.

"Forgotten! forgotten what?" said Jack, and then a sensation of trembling came over him as he thought how completely he had forgotten the injunctions of his mysterious interrogator.

"Can you ask? Did I not tell you the power I should have over you? I will now tell you more distinctly still if you have forgotten."

"What—what?"

"I can tell you, then, that there is a means of measuring the quantity that every man drinks, and after it has worked a certain amount, I have a certain amount of power over that man, to use him as I please. I was not bound to tell you this before, Jack Grove, but I am now. Will you have twenty thousand for five years, Jack Grove? Money is not much to me. You would be mine in ten years, at any rate, so you may as well accept the offer."

Jack Grove was drunk now, but perfectly sober before, so he felt a little pot-valiant, and he said,—

"I don't want to have anything to say to you one way or another. You go your way, and I'll go mine."

"You have shown," said the mysterious stranger, "that you cannot resist drink. That is just what I expected, and indeed I may add, it is just what I wished. But do as you please; I am bound to tell you that over a reformed drunkard I have no power; but that is a character you will never attain to. You are lost, and you know it."

The mysterious stranger folded his cloak about him—and he wore a very ample one—and he walked away in the contrary direction.

"I don't believe a word of it," said Jack Grove; "I don't believe a word of it. I'll go home, and collar the fifty-two pounds."

CHAPTER XII.

JACK GROVE'S RETURN HOME.—THREATS OF VIOLENCE TO HIS WIFE.—THE MYSTERIOUS STRANGER AGAIN.

WITH this determination Jack Grove hurried onward, until he reached the village, which was situated at some distance; yet he noted little of the distance, for the liquor destroyed all calculation as to distance, and the only thought that crossed his mind was, the probability or the improbability of all that he had heard.

He could not account for what he had heard, nor did he care to do so. Indeed, he was not in a condition to do so.

"Well," muttered Jack Grove, "I don't know, and I don't understand, and I don't want. If she's got the money, good lord! won't they think much of me. I'll go and drink under the governor's nose, and I won't ask him to drink.

"That will aggravate him; but I don't care, I'll teach him to lock me up, and not even allow me a drop of beer; water there was plenty, but no beer. Beer is the best thing in the world. I wish there was no water—not a drop, but all beer, beer. What a glorious idea, if they couldn't serve out water in the county gaol, nor bad tea, nor coffee, nor gruel; all would be beer, glorious happy beer."

And then he began to sing in a vociferous voice, gesticulating all the while vehemently,—" John Barleycorn came from the east," in a voice that would have procured him a round of applause at the Saddle and Turnpike Gate, had the inmates heard it.

All this considerably heated him, and when he arrived within a few yards of the village, he halted, and passed his hand across his feverish face, and endeavoured to collect his ideas, and to clear his lips, by spitting, for they, as well as his tongue, seemed thick and clammy, and he muttered,—

" I am dry, and decidedly thirsty. I wish I had a jug of ale,—cold, mild ale; that would loosen my tongue."

He now endeavoured to steady himself and go forward. It was now getting dark, and as there was no moon up till late, he could not very well see where he was going to.

" What's the odds ?" he suddenly exclaimed, as he made a run, or something between a run and a walk, and in this manner he arrived at his own door. " I thought I should find it," he muttered ; " I thought I could find my way back again. ' Home, home, sweet home.' My voice is always out of tune when I sing that song, 'tis so melancholy and so dismal, and puts me in mind of a blowing up, and all that kind of thing.

" Where's the blessed latch ?" he exclaimed, as he felt all over the door ; " it used to be here, but I suppose it has been put somewhere else ;" at the same time he felt about for it, and after some search he found it. He soon opened the door and walked into the apartment.

Jack Grove gazed at his wife, who sat in some fear expecting him, for she knew his imprisonment was terminated, and his liberation would of course take place, and he would come to her as soon as he found he was at liberty, and without means.

The child was lying beside her, and Jack's eye instantly caught it, and no sooner did he perceive it than he cried out,—

" Ah, 'tis all true, then ; well, who would have thought it ? Come, come, no gammon ; tell us, where are the fifty-two yellow boys ?"

Mrs. Grove lifted up her hands in sorrow at the sight of her husband ; there was no hope that even his imprisonment had done him any good. She said nothing, but waited in silence for the announcement.

" Come, come, mother Grove, don't you know me ? I'm Jack Grove."

" Alas !" said the woman, " for my peace, I know you too well—too well. I would I had never seen you—you are always the same—no better—never any change for the better."

" No," said Grove ; " I was born Jack Grove, christened Jack Grove, and Jack Grove I will die. Come tell me, where is the money ?"

As he spoke he gazed around the cottage as if he expected that fifty sovereigns were a sum that could not easily be hidden from view.

" Money, Grove," said the poor woman, in a tone of reproach ; " when did you last bring me any to keep life and soul together ?"

" What's that to do with what I say ? D—n it, you are deaf !"

" I am not, Grove."

" Then listen to me. Where's the money—I say, where's the money? "

" The money ?"

" Yes, fifty-two pounds."

" What fifty-two pounds ?" repeated the widow, as if she were anxious to escape for a time the result that she fully anticipated.

" What is the use of repeating my words ?" said Grove, with a fierce gesture. " I have heard all about it ; that brat didn't come for nothing—you don't take care of other people's children for nothing ; come, come, out with the money."

" Once for all—I have not the money, John Grove ; and what is more, if I had, the child must live and be cared for ; and a part goes for its maintenance, and the other to maintain that home that you do so little for, save to destroy it and yourself too."

"Do I?—Well, a good job too. But as long as I last, that'll last; and as long as that lasts, why I will last; and when we both go, why one won't grumble at the other. Who's afraid?—I ain't. Come, out with the money."

"I have none."

"Now, if you give me any of your broad-wheeled gammon I shall come the broad wheel over you, and roll you to some tune. I'll not believe that you have aken a child without money, and if you had you should take it elsewhere—I'll have none of it."

"Now, listen to me, Grove. I have this child to nurse, and it will produce me victuals; you spend all your earnings in drinking, and they are few enough, for you are idle as well as a drunkard, I am sorry to say."

"Are you, though? There's plenty as would do anything in the drinking way; now I am moderate, very moderate indeed; I know them as'd drink a cart load."

"The more shame for them; and for you, a poor man, to know such."

"Come, come, no nonsense; and if you don't see quickly about giving me the money, why, curse me if I don't knock you over the head. You had fifty-two pounds for the child, where are they? I'll let 'em see that I have money."

"But it is not your money, Grove."

"What's yours is mine, and what's mine's my own, you know."

"I am to receive what is due weekly, because it shall not be otherwise spent, and squandered away in liquor."

"That's some of your infernal tricks; but I won't stand it, and there's an end on it. Are you going to hand over the browns? Because if you arn't, I'll soon let you see I'm master; I'll give you such a whacking that'll tell you I've come back again."

"Alas! I see it too well; and in what a state you are to come back again—drunk, and just turned out of gaol."

"I couldn't help that; I had not money to pay the damage. Come, come, I'm all right, give us over the dumps, and it's all right."

"I cannot."

"Who's got them?"

"Mr. Potts. I receive them of him when the money is due, and he is satisfied that the child is done right by."

"D—n Mr. Potts, I'll be after him. No, no, he'll be too many for me. D—n me! I'll lick you, you wretch—you toad—you she-toad—you rebellious wife— you—you ——"

"If you attempt to strike me, Grove, I'll seek aid elsewhere, and the whole parish shall hear of it, and point at you for a coward."

"I don't care; and if you do, why, d—d—d—n me, I'll serve you out well before-hand, and to save time I'll begin at once."

As he spoke he made a sudden rush at the poor woman, and would have struck her violently, but he struck his foot against an inequality in the floor and tumbled.

"D——e, I'll give you an extra smack for this; I'll give it yer all out at once. I've saved it up for you, you jade; you may as well stay for it, or you'll get an extra dose of it, that's all. Hurrah!"

At the same time, Mrs. Grove, terrified at the threats of her husband, seized the child, and rushed out of the door, to obtain protection among some of her neighbours.

Jack Grove rushed out after her, intending to beat her most unmercifully; but he had scarce passed the door when he was confronted by the mysterious stranger.

"Oh!" exclaimed Jack Grove; and he staggered back a pace or two, and would have sought the interior of the cottage, but the stranger stretched out his arm, and seized him by the throat, and dragged him forward, saying,—

"Come, come; I am by your side again; you have invoked me more than once. I have power over you."

"What do you want?"

"Merely to give you what you intended to administer to your wife."

'Oh, come. I'll tell you a different tale."

Jack Grove, however, found that the mysterious stranger was not to be foiled, and possessed a strength far beyond his own. In a second he was thrown down with tremendous force, and when he got up he was again struck down with terrific violence; this terrible opponent then dragged him to the rails, and propping him up, administered a severe thrashing by dealing vigorous blows about the head and stomach.

"Mercy! mercy!" cried Jack.

"What mercy would you have shown your wife, drunkard?"

"I'll never do so any more."

"Will you sell your soul? I don't care about money."

"Oh, no, no."

"Well, then, I'll leave you something to remember me by. You forget that I said I'd be with you after such occasions;" and as he spoke, he dealt Jack such a blow on the head, that he fell senseless by the gate.

For a moment the stranger paused, and then, with a shake of his head, he said,

"I have but a poor account to give of affairs down here; yet I see not exactly how to better them. Well, well, I must to London now. I have done the best I can, and all I can. The child is well, and, to all appearance, perfectly healthy, and likely to live, a fact which it is hard to congratulate any one upon, considering all the strange circumstances connected with its birth."

He then walked on hastily towards the London road, and in the course of half an hour he was overtaken by the mail, on the top of which he mounted, and was conveyed towards the metropolis at a good ten miles an hour.

The village and the gossips of the surrounding neighbourhood were now compelled for a time to subsist upon the mysteries that had occurred, for no new ones seemed now likely to take place there, and the events in the life of an infant are of too common-place a character to require a record.

While, therefore, the poor little lone child is passing these, the first portions of its infantine existence, turn we to those parties in London, who have already claimed so considerable a share of our attention, and who are now in the way of claiming so much more.

The fact is, that affairs were making much progress as regarded the immediate matrimonial connexion between the Earl of Crumbledown and the Lady Annabella Fanfaronade.

The strange will which the old earl had made was, in consequence of the peculiar circumstances under which it had been made, of course, almost universally known, and as universally was it commented upon by all those of the fashionable world.

When, therefore, it came to be rumoured, which it was very speedily by the Marchioness of Fanfaronade, that the marriage between her daughter, the Lady Annabella, and the young Earl of Crumbledown, was definitively settled, everybody said how wonderfully prudent the young earl was.

But the real fact was, that wonderful prudence had very little to do with the affair, except so far as the clever manœuvring of the Marchioness of Fanfaronade was concerned.

The young earl went to the marchioness's house in a perfectly undecided frame of mind; and it was only the very admirable manner in which he had been met there that had produced the gratifying result which every one, with a nod and a smile, was pleased to set down to the account of his prudence and his thorough appreciation of the value of money.

And now, we accordingly travel to London to be present with our courteous readers at the marriage of the Earl of Crumbledown.

CHAPTER XIII.

LONDON AGAIN.—THE MARCHIONESS OF FANFARONADE PUSHES ON THE MAR-
RIAGE, AND THE OLD EARL OF CRUMBLEDOWN HAS A SUPERB FUNERAL.

THE new Earl of Crumbledown was most decidedly not what the ladies would call a marrying man; and yet, here he was completely and irrevocably committed to share his coronet with one, of whom as a wife he never once thought, until within the last half hour, in which he made her a proposal.

No wonder that the next morning, when he was awakened by his valet, and informed it was nearly twelve o'clock, he should ask himself if it were a dream or a reality.

So many incidents had crowded themselves into so short a space, that well might they resemble to his mind the rapid phantasmagoria-like changes that had disturbed his slumber.

Within the short period of one sunset and the succeeding sunrise, he had lost his father, become an earl, lost three hundred thousand pounds, regained again that amount, proposed for a wife, and been accepted.

Truly, sufficient for the night were the proceedings thereof, and no wonder that the Earl Crumbledown felt his imagination in a whirl, and his brain somewhat disturbed by the rapidity, by these astounding incidents.

"Is it real or a dream?" he cried half aloud; and his valet, fancying he had addressed him, approached the side of the bed, and respectfully said,—

"My lord."

"Where was I last night, James?" he said.

"At the Marchioness of Fanfaronade's rout, your lordship."

"Humph! and something else astonishing has happened, James?"

"Yes, my lord; your lordship's paternal relative has decided in filling up a niche in your lordship's family. I beg pardon, my lord, but I hope it isn't true about the—the ——"

"About the what James?" said the earl.

"About the old earl giving all his money to somebody else."

"It is perfectly true, James."

James gave a long whistle; for, to tell the truth, James and his lordship had gone through a few escapades together, and hence there had grown up a sort of familiarity which the new earl might find it just a little difficult to suppress.

"Then, my lord," added James, when he had finished his whistle, "we are as poor as ever, and all the difference it makes to us is, that we are the Earls of Crumbledown."

"No, James, we are a little better off than that; we certainly are, as you say, the Earls of Crumbledown; but unless we have been dreaming, we have made up our minds to marry the lady to whom the money was left, and so consolidate the interests."

James had his lordship's dressing-gown in his hand, but he dropped it on the floor with an ominous dab, as he gasped,—

"Did you say marry, my lord?"

"I did indeed. I couldn't very conveniently put a barren coronet on my head, and as half a million of money is a great sweetener of the pangs of matrimony, I thought, you see, James, I would sacrifice myself."

"Very good, my lord," exclaimed James, pulling up the dressing-gown, and looking coldly severe at his master. "You will please quite to understand that I keep a month's warning hanging over your head like the sword of Dan Occulas."

"I presume, James, you mean the sword of Damocles, and that the month's warning is to hang like a single hair."

"Just as you say, my lord. I left one place before, because the lady of the house would interfere with me."

"Oh, well, well," said the earl, as he arose, and commenced the operations of the toilet; "it's all true, and no dream. I have proposed to wed, and have been accepted by the Lady Annabella Fanfaronade. I had fondly hoped that she on whose brow I could have placed my coronet would have been one for whom I could have felt all those tender sensations."

"Which your lordship felt for little Miss Emily Whitford."

"James," said his lordship, sternly, "I have once forbidden you never to mention that name again."

"My lord, I can't forget her; I wore out a pair of buckskin breeches, and made my hands look vulgar for a month, in driving you and her down to that what-d'ye-call 'em place. Have you seen Mr. Vullimay since he came back?"

He d——d James's eyes between his teeth, but made no answer.

James, however, knew too much of his master's secrets, to care whether he offended him or not, and he continued,—

" Upon my soul, my lord, there can't be two opinions about Emily, she was decidedly a nice little piece of goods. I tried after the sister myself."

" You scoundrel."

" Scoundrel! I didn't seduce her—I didn't take her down to a village to be confined—I didn't leave her to be buried by anybody or nobody. What a mercy it would be now, if the small parcel of illegitimacy were to die."

The earl was drawing on a boot, and when he had got it on, he took up its fellow and threw it at James's head, with an aim that brought the heel of it in very disagreeable contact with his cheek.

" You scoundrel," said the earl, " how dare you presume so far upon being a pampered and favoured menial, as thus to utter remarks upon subjects which I have forbidden myself to speak upon. You leave my service to-day."

" Very well, my lord. Then I shall see if the Lady Annabella Fanfaronade will take me as an odd man. I might make myself useful to her, if she should miss your lordship for a day or two. I might be able to tell her where there was the greatest chance of finding you. I have the honour to bid your lordship a very good morning."

" James, you're a fool," said the earl, who dared not part with this man so carelessly. " You don't know when you are well off—remain where you are, but don't anger me by allusions to painful subjects."

" I have no desire to leave your lordship, and was not aware the subject was a painful one."

" Let it drop, let it drop."

" As your lordship pleases."

And thus ended one of the rather numerous fracas between the Earl of Crumbledown and his valet. It is a strange feeling, but it undoubtedly does exist among such persons, that they never can refrain long from exhibiting the power they may by accident have over those whom fortune has seemed to place so far above their reach.

The Earl of Crumbledown's valet gained nothing by quarrelling with his master, except the petty gratification of a small mind, in braving his displeasure, and being able to say afterwards " The earl would have discharged me if he dared.

A more distressing predicament for a man of sense, education, and rank, than to have secrets of an imprudent character at the mercy of the ignorant and unprincipled, cannot be imagined; but if a man stoop to vice, let him be the proudest and highest who ever trod the earth, he will have to sip of that same cup of degradation which the meanest and lowest are partakers of.

Could there be a slavery more galling to a sensitive mind than that to which the Earl of Crumbledown was subjected,—a nobleman forced to put up with the insolence of his valet, whom he dared not discharge?

And has the Earl of Crumbledown so completely chased from his mind those incidents with which the reader has, no doubt, connected him, sufficiently to enjoy his new dignities and his new prospects?—has he forgotten that small sequestered village, with its once poorly appointed inn?—has he forgotten that fragile but beautiful creature whom he handed across that threshold to which she was never to return in life?

Has he forgotten that deathbed, with its appalled attendants standing round? —has he forgotten that sad pale countenance of her whom he professed to love? —and those dimming eyes as they turned their last glance in this world upon him?

No, these are circumstances and recollections that would cling to the mind while memory holds its seat. There is no sepulchre to those until the grave receives along with it all that is mortal.

And yet the world would have praised my Lord Crumbledown—they would have said how kind it was of him to seek to carry away that confiding creature and hide her shame, far from those who looked upon her with contempt. How liberal it was of him to give the sum of twenty shillings weekly for the maintenance of his own child; how kind it was of him to send his own attorney, Mr. Vullimy, under the name of Jones, to see that all was right.

Truly, if two or three whites can obliterate one black, the unexceptionable after proceedings of the noble earl might blot out the great misdeed he had done in the first instance. The intense excitement he had gone through since his return to London probably blunted his feeling and perceptions, but it would be madness to assume he had forgotten.

We need scarcely follow the Lady Fanfaronade in her self-felicitations upon the admirable success that followed her plan, for getting the neck of the new Earl of Crumbledown into the noose-matrimonial. She took good care that the news should travel quickly and in all directions, so that when the Earl of Crumbledown met a friend he looked like the genius of tragedy and comedy rolled into one, for he congratulated him upon his approaching marriage, and condoled with him upon the death of his father all in a breath.

Perhaps, in his heart, the earl echoed the words of James the valet, that it would be a good thing if the little bundle of illegitimacy would die. The sympathies of men with infants are small, and news of the death of his child, now that its poor mother was laid in the quiet grave, scarcely cost him an additional pang.

But it was doomed to cling to life, and to exercise such an effect and such an influence on his future career as he little now dreamed of.

Residing in pure air, and nursed by the tenderest assiduity by Mrs. Grove, it was likely to thrive—as thrive indeed it did, for each hour added to the little thing's health and strength.

And now the earl had two important ceremonies to go through; the one was his father's obsequies, and the other his own nuptials.

Truly, he might have said with Hamlet—" The funeral baked meats did coldly furnish the marriage tables ;" for, in truth, the one followed hard upon the other.

Ceremony forced him to wait a week before the remains of the old Earl of Crumbledown were placed among his already crumble-down ancestors, and then gallantry enforced him to beg the bride to name the earliest day for the marriage, and expediency induced her to name that day week.

" My dear," said the marchioness, " you must name the very earliest day you can ; proverbs are decidedly low, but that which states there is many a slip between the cup and the lip, is decidedly correct. Certainly, the earl cannot, with common decency, go back from his promise ; but then, my dear, the men do so many things with such uncommon indecency, that you are never sure of one till the marriage actually takes place. So, my dear, you had better name this day week, and then, you see, the earl has a whole fortnight to get over his father's death."

This was agreed to by a nod on the part of the lady Annabella, who was nothing loth to drag her fish to land now that she had hooked him ; and so, when the earl next called upon the Fanfaronades, and mumbled some nonsense about naming the happy day, he was met by a most bewitching smile from the Lady Annabella, as she said,—

" Ever impatient—ever impatient."

" As may well be believed," he replied. " Let me beseech you to name an early day, when I can indeed call you mine, &c., &c."

" Ah! my lord, I had indeed hoped that you would yet have lingered, &c."

" But you know, Annabella, that the month expires in three weeks."

" Ah! how times flies! Well, make it this day week."

" Eh! this day week ?" said the earl, as his countenance fell a degree or two.

" I cannot say sooner. Consider, my love, the world's opinion."

" No," said the earl, with a long breath, " you couldn't very well say sooner."

" Ah! what a happy day will that be ?"

" Very."

" We'll go to Rome. Don't you think Rome will be the best place to go to for a little trip ?"

" Oh, yes, anywhere you like," said his lordship.

" Then let it be Rome ; and we'll take dear mamma with us, and Flora can stay at home with the Dowager Duchess of Lincomnoodle—you know her, my lord ?"

" I think I do. She's dreadfully deaf, ain't she, and carries a slate with her that people may make their remarks upon it ; and then she bawls you a reply enough to crack the drum of your ears ?"

" Oh, how facetious you are," exclaimed the Lady Annabella, giving his lordship a number of little taps with her fan on the back of his hand. " Is he not a naughty man, mamma ?"

" My dear, all men are," said the marchioness ; " and we can't expect his lordship to be an exception to the general rule."

It will be seen by this that the Lady Annabella Fanfaronade was playing the amiable in grand style, and not showing her claws in the least. His lordship was so sickened by her tenderness that he was ready to tear out his whiskers by the roots when he got into the streets ; but he was booked, and there was no escape. Marry her he must, and so he resigned himself to his fate with what grace he could.   He felt that human nature would not permit him to go through many more such interviews with his intended.   She was too much bent upon doing the playful kittenish dodge to suit him at all.   Alas ! he had vividly in his recollection the gentle, earnest, soul-subduing tenderness of another.

Every day that passed over his head, instead of obliterating it, only brought up with greater vividness before his mind's eye, the image of Emily Whitford.   There were two pictures constantly present to his mind ; the one as he had first seen her when her beauty had dawned upon his sight with all the magic and charm of its novelty, the other was that small, ill-appointed bed-room of the inn, with the still corpse lying upon the couch where the young mother breathed her last.

And gradually this latter scene found a stronger place in his memory than the former.   Indeed the image of Emily Whitford as first he had seen her and known her, seldom now occurred to him, except momentarily to give him some exquisite pang at a moment when he had been more than usually happy, because more than usually forgetful.

Soon he began to feel, that in this world there is a retribution as well as in the next ; and that if it were true that virtue is indeed its own reward in the delightful sensations to which it will give rise, vice equally brings with it its own punishment in the shape of never-ending remorse.

Once or twice, too, the thought did occur that Emily Whitford would have carried her dignity gently, and imparted a lustre even to the coronet of the Crumbledowns, ancient as it was.

He was not by any means so tainted with that most absurd of all prides— unless it be one of mere emulation—the pride of birth, as had been the old earl his father ; and probably had Emily not loved him merely, she might have occupied the place of the Lady Annabella Fanfaronade ; and in that case, too, the large personal property of the old earl might never have been bequeathed in the way it was.

His marriage, had he contracted one with Emily Whitford, could have been kept far more secret from the old earl than his mere *liason* with her, for all her relations would of course have felt it to be very much to their interest indeed to keep the secret, until the old man's death would have rendered concealment no longer necessary.

And thus, then, was this young man, with an illustrious name, a title which placed him among the highest of the nobles of the land, and personal advantages of no mean order, most unhappy ; for he was about uniting himself for money to a woman whom he felt more and more each moment he never could love, while she whom he did love, had died of a broken heart.

But the marriage between the Earl of Crumbledown and the Lady Annabella Fanfaronade, was a marriage of high life, and in those ceremonies a very small amount indeed of anything in the shape of domestic felicity will always suffice.

It is not as is the case with persons in a humbler, but far more useful class of society, that upon the marriage, and the assimilation of tastes and sentiments between the couple, will depend their happiness or misery through life. The titled couple can easily get rid of the trouble of each other's society ; and it is a well known fact, that many of the nobility and their wives only know occasionally where each other is from the pages of the *Court Circular*, and such was extremely likely to be the mode of life to which our noble couple were likely to come.

But let us get them married, and then we shall soon see how his lordship had bartered his peace of mind, and what a bad bargain he had made of it even for half a million of money in exchange.

The congratulation of his friends sounded to him amazingly like sneers ; and he, for the day or two immediately preceding the nuptials, made a complete hermit of himself, and kept out of everybody's way. But at length he began to see the absolute necessity of rousing himself to go through the affair with at all events that show of satisfaction which should prevent his being actually laughed at.

The idea that any one but his own valet—and from him he could not conceal the damning facts—should know how averse he was to the marriage, was gall and wormwood to him ; and consequently, the evening before, his roused he energies to go through the affair, at all events with apparent satisfaction.

Doubtless the rich and great Earl of Crumbledown was very much envied ; doubtless the people who stood outside his coachmaker's shop, to look at the new suite of carriages, thought, with many a sigh, how much they should like to be Earl of Crumbledown, little suspecting what an aching heart he was about to carry with him to the altar, and what gloomy and bewildering thoughts possessed him on the eve of " the happiest day of his life."

He sat up all the night before. Sleep was out of the question. The very rooms that he was accustomed to had become hateful to him, and therefore he repaired to another hotel, and sent for some old companions to sup with him.

It was true he had an invitation to spend that evening at the Marchioness of Fanfaronade's, but he could not do so. He merely hurriedly glanced over the note of invitation, and than crumpling it up and thrusting it into his pocket, he said,—

" No, no, I cannot—I really cannot. D——n ! I cannot !"

A nice, pleasant state of mind this, for a bridegroom on the evening before his nuptials. But was it to be wondered at, when we come to consider all things, and to scan the motives which really induced the match? Besides, the young Earl of Crumbledown was not a fool, although a man of very weak resolves ; and he rather suspected that he had been cajoled into the offer of his hand by a mock piece of generosity.

Such an idea once engendered, was sure to grow upon him ; and each hour he became more and more convinced that the Fanfaronade family had the laugh against him, and that he was regularly done.

And yet he could not retreat—there was no hope, no chance of that. There he was fixed as fate. It might be the destruction of his happiness to go on, but it was death, or, what was much the same to such a mind as his, eternal ridicule now to pause.

" It must be—it must be," he told himself ; " I am a doomed man. It is my fate. I will henceforward be a believer in destiny, and that no mortal can avoid the inevitable fate that is marked out for him from the commencement of his creation."

It was a wonder that he had prudence enough—which he only just had—to avoid going into some excess in the way of wine-drinking on that evening before his marriage, but he did so ; and when he threw himself upon a sofa exhausted, about an hour and a half only before the ceremony was to take place, he was nearly mad, but perfectly sober. Nevertheless he still told himself,—

" I will go through with it well, and not one person shall be able to guess the real state of my feelings."

CHAPTER XIV.

THE TOILET SCENE.—THE MARRIAGE, AND THE DEPARTURE FOR THE CONTINENT.

THE morning—the eventful morning, as the admiring friends would say—came to pass on which the marriage between the Earl of Crumbledown and Lady Annabella Fanfaronade was to be solemnised.

A marriage in high life is always an event that causes some stir; not that the event itself would cause much emotion, yet it causes a stir from the bustle communicated to it by the many adventitious circumstances by which it is surrounded.

There is such a host of friends and servants who are stimulated to make a stir; the first because of the invitations, and the latter from the favours and presents distributed on the occasion, and the quantity of extra duty and extra drink which always have their effect.

The street was in an uproar, and the carriages lined the way for some distance; horses and men were decorated with large white favours, and everything was new and clean.

The house was at an early hour disturbed by the appearance of friends, and the stir and bustle of visitors.

The Lady Annabella rose early on that morning, and was soon at her toilet, in which she was assisted by her favourite maid; and there, amid all the appliances that art and wealth could bestow, she sat engaged in preparing for that ceremony which was to unite her to an earldom and an immense fortune.

She was certainly good looking, and was by her friends esteemed handsome; but she was haughty and proud, and it was easy to predict that she would carry off her honours with triumph, and that, though led blushing to the altar, she would leave the sacred edifice elated in heart, and with a prouder mien than any less ambitious would assume.

Seated amid costly articles of luxury and jewels of great value, she appeared, like Fortune about to bestow gifts upon the fortunate, not to care for or heed the valuables in which she decorated herself, merely for fashion sake, and because they made a glitter and were attractive, as well as proper to her rank.

"Those jewels," she said to her maid, pointing to a casket which lay near her.

The attendant fetched them, and placed them before her, saying,—

"I am sure, my lady, they are very beautiful, and suit your complexion."

"Do you think so?"

"Yes, my lady. I never saw anything so beautiful; they far outshine those of the Lady Georgiana, who displayed so many at Lady Bellamy's ball. She was all glitter, like my Lady Mayoress."

"What a comparison! But it matters not; the Lady Georgiana and I may not meet very soon again."

"The trip to the continent will then occupy your ladyship some time?"

"Some weeks, or it may be longer; it depends upon circumstances. Travelling may not agree with me."

"Truly, your ladyship; and then the earl's seat, and the parks, and the deer—all that must be very beautiful."

"Yes, they are; that seat is a perfect specimen of our most beautiful country residences."

"Much extent?"

"Yes, yes—vast."

"Such a brilliant fortune! What happiness will be yours, my lady; how many are there that will envy your lot! how they will court the young, beautiful, and wealthy countess!"

"No more in that strain," said the Lady Annabella, but not ill pleased. "No more. I have neither time nor patience. Give me those pearl-drops."

The jewels were handed her; they were real pearls, and worth in themselves a fortune, and were the gift of her intended lord.

"Well, my lady, you may be angry, but I cannot help thinking I never saw you so extremely handsome as you look this morning—positively lovely. I am sure the earl must be a happy man. Not such another marriage as this can take place, for certainly the earl is very handsome himself. Do you not call him very handsome, my lady?"

"Why, I think he is passable, else I would never have consented."

"Passable, my lady—passable! Why, he is positively handsome—not in features only, but he is tall and finely proportioned. I have heard many say so."

"Have you?"

"Yes, my lady; and he is generous—everybody says that; indeed, he is all that could be wished for. To wish your ladyship happiness under such circumstances, would be superfluous."

"I believe there is a prospect of it," said the lady; "but you may now admit my bridesmaids; I hear they are come."

Upon this the officious maid left the apartment to seek the ladies, while Annabella sat examining herself in the glass, and by the smile on her lips, she appeared well satisfied with the inspection.

In a very short time the two ladies who were to take the part of bridesmaids upon themselves, entered the apartment.

There were many greetings, and dears, and kisses—many praises and expressions of admiration uttered upon the occasion; and the two beautiful girls—for such they were—were soon engaged in the task of arranging themselves for the delightful occasion.

"Do you know he is come?" said one.

"The earl?"

"Yes."

"I never heard him; I heard but you."

"Ay; but he came in at the same moment as we did."

"Indeed!"

"Yes, and he is below with a very large party. The street is full of carriages."

"He waits."

"Well," said the Lady Annabella, "he must not quarrel about that. I am scarcely ready. What a state I am in! I have scarce nerve enough to go down to meet them all."

"Oh, but you must exert yourself, my dear Anabella; and remember that such occasions for the display of your courage and nerve do not often happen."

"Nor need they."

"You are quite ready; we will conduct you down. There, lean upon my arm, my dear."

"Thank you—thank you. I shall be better now. We will descend."

It would be needless to describe the guests and dresses and the ceremony—the "Court Newsman" contains all that.

But the meeting was one of rapture; and the Earl of Crumbledown flew to his young bride, and led her into the room, and gazed on her with eyes that expressed the pleasure he felt.

There were many greetings and good wishes exchanged on this occasion, and when some time had been thus spent, and in partaking of a splendid cold collation, the guests arose, and the carriages began to come up to the door.

Then the bridesmaids led the bride into one carriage, while the earl went in another; and then there was a dashing and rumbling of wheels, and such sounds as put the whole place in a stir.

There were many persons who had been attracted to the spot, and who crowded together to catch a glimpse of the bride.

Everybody wants to see the bride; nobody thinks of anybody but the bride; there is a charm in her very dress; and one would imagine, from the eagerness with which they endeavour to catch a glimpse of her, that to do so was to effect a cure for some kind of disorder or that it was some forerunner of good fortune.

"Is she handsome? Is she young? Is she rich? How is she dressed? Is that her? Well, I don't see anything so very extraordinary. She may be handsome to his mind, but she is but so-and-so to mine. To my mind her clothes and jewels are the handsomest. Fine feathers make fine birds, you know."

A variety of these sayings are always on hand for such occasions ; for it is very true that you can't hope to please everybody, and Nature herself will give dissatisfaction to some.

The ceremony was performed in the presence of admiring friends, who always feel elated upon the occasion of somebody's marriage, and yet it concerns them not.

The Lady Annabella Fanfaronade was now become the Countess of Crumbledown. The earl led her to the church door, and they both entered one carriage, and proceeded to the residence where they had started from.

Here was much ceremony, and much wine drunk, and cake eaten, and a variety of parcels made up. The bride shed a few tears at leaving her parents' roof ; and the earl, feeling the full force of the sacrifice, and vowing to be all in all to her, and kissing the tears away, he whispered some tender expression in her ear.

The bride retired for a short time, and then the travelling carriage was ordered up to the door, and a short time was employed in placing some packages, already prepared, on the roof, to be ready for an instant start.

The bride entered the drawing-room, arrayed for travelling ; she bade farewell to her friends, shed a few more tears, and then the earl led her triumphantly to the carriage.

Adieus were uttered—hands and handkerchiefs were waved—but they were soon gone. The horses were put in motion, and the wheels soon rattled over the stones, and then other objects and feelings engrossed them.

The guests now began to leave—carriages were called up, and then rattled off with their owners, who were well pleased with their share of the ceremony—that of a privileged looker-on, and they having been seen at a fashionable marriage in high life.

And well indeed had the Earl of Crumbledown managed to hide those feelings which were, perhaps, from being hidden, only the stronger and the more fearfully harassing. He smiled, as he might, so situated, be expected to smile, and he returned the many compliments that were paid to him as if he really felt them all.

But when the travelling carriage drove off, he felt a dreadful reaction ensue, and he almost fainted, so uncomfortable became his feelings.

It was not so, however, with his countess ; she had achieved all that the highest flights of her ambition had aspired to. She had now effected a marriage with one of very high rank, and she had acquired a very ample fortune. There was no imaginable luxury that might not now be within her grasp ; and she felt elated accordingly.

But the lady had considerable tact, and if the Earl of Crumbledown succeeded in deceiving everybody else, and in making everybody else believe that he wore his chains, willingly he could not deceive her.

She felt quite conscious that he saw through the cheat which had been practised upon him, or if he did not exactly see through it, she felt quite sure that he suspected it sufficiently to give him much uneasiness. But what cared the new Countess of Crumbledown for that? Not a whit. She was quite willing that it should be one of those fashionable marriages which take place so frequently, in which there is not a particle of affection upon either side.

" Let it be so," she thought to herself ; " I have a magnificent jointure settled on me, and I am the Countess of Crumbledown. He cannot deprive me of my money or my title, and, therefore, I am abundantly satisfied."

Youth and beauty who may beguile an hour with these pages, will be inclined to believe that the Lady Annabella Fanfaronade was easily contented when she esteemed money and rank as higher advantages than that pure joy which arises from the union of two fond hearts, who to each other are a world of joy and happiness without compare.

But the faults of her feelings were those of education and of habit. She knew no better. The early career which the pride, the poverty, and the ambition of her mother had induced her to embark in, was quite sufficient to destroy all those finer feelings of the heart which she must to a certain extent, in common with human nature, have had.

She had been taught to consider as one of the first objects of her existence, if not, indeed, the very first, the procuring some one for a husband who had the means of making a handsome settlement upon her. As for affection, that was quite another thing, and in a marriage in high life is very seldom an element in the affair.

Had the Earl of Crumbledown almost at the very altar's foot deserted his wife, it would scarcely have cost her a pang; but that was what for his own honour's sake he was not likely to do, so that the lady was perfectly easy and contented.

"Now, my dear Annabella," said the marchioness, on the evening before the interesting ceremony, "you will not stay more than one month at Rome, you know, and on the route, as you return, you had better visit the principal cities of the continent, and make one week at Paris, so that you will be absent from England altogether about two months, and no longer, you know, and you will get back just at the commencement of the season."

" Yes, that will be a very good plan," said Annabella.

" Well, then, my dear, as the earl has no town house, you had better get him to give me a *carte blanche* to get one for you both by the time you return, and to see that it is fitted, and furnished for your reception, and then you will have no trouble."

" Very good, ma; how much money will it take?"

" I really don't know, my dear; but if the earl asks such a question as that, I shall decidedly decline having anything whatever to do with the affair, you may depend."

" I don't say that he will ask it, but you know, ma, as well as I do, that even what we shall have will not be an inexhaustible source of wealth."

" Why, good gracious, my dear, what are you thinking of?"

" The main chance."

" What! with half a million of money! Now really—but putting money out of the question, of course you must have a handsome house to live in. What are people in trade made for, but to see that their superiors have about them every comfort and convenience?"

" That's very true, ma, certainly, and of course I quite agree with you in it. I will speak to the earl about it, and I dare say he will be very glad to get you to take it off his hands."

" Do so, my love; and," added the marchioness to herself, " if I don't make a couple of thousand pounds for my trouble, it will be something very singular indeed."

She might just as well have made this remark aloud, and so avowed what were her intentions as far as the Lady Annabella was concerned, for the other guessed well enough her mother's real motives, knowing as she did from experience the scheming and crafty nature of her relative.

And indeed Annabella had no particular objection to her mother making a something in a quiet way, in addition to what she had promised to give her as a reward for her extremely successful diplomacy in the matter of the marriage.

After a time, however, the Lady Annabella meant to keep a good eye upon money affairs, for she knew well, as she had already taken occasion to remark, that even the amount of money at her disposal was not quite an inexhaustible mine of wealth.

But we will now leave these titled personages with all their faults, their follies, and their petty meannesses, to shift for themselves for a time. Other, and better specimens of humanity imperatively demand our attention as well as our respect.

CHAPTER XV.

THE WHITFORD FAMILY.—A MOTHER'S LOVE, AND A FATHER'S GRIEF.—A NEW ASPECT OF AFFAIRS.

THERE are some persons connected with the progress of our narrative with whom our readers have not yet been made acquainted, but who are of essential importance in the course of those events which render the existence of the Earl of Crumbledown one of so much calamity, and so full of mischievous results.

Allusion has been several times made, in the course of the few last chapters, to the fact that she whose peace and happiness had been for ever ruined by the young Earl of Crumbledown, until she had at last found rest in the grave, was the daughter of an attorney.

It is, then, to the family of Emily Whitford that we intend now to introduce our readers, that family which has been bereaved of its dearest, brightest treasure.

Already is the reader aware of the singular interview between the Earl of Crumbledown before he arrived at that dignity, and Willoughby, the Polish prince, who, with such wonderful audacity, intruded into the house of the Marchioness of Fanfaronade.

This man, it will be recollected, terrified the then Lord Warelock by representing himself as the uncle of her whose melancholy death we took occasion to record in the early part of this work.

In so representing himself he uttered no more than the truth, according to what custom warranted him in doing ; he certainly was the uncle of Emily Whitford, but it was by marriage ; that is, he was the husband of her aunt, and, according to the mischievous and absurd practice of calling people relations who obtrude themselves into families by marriage, he acquired his title of uncle.

But a more different man than the father of Emily there could not be than this same Willoughby.

He was a bad man, in every sense of the word ; tricky and desperate ; not without talent, which might have made him respectable and respected, had he chosen to exert it in any honourable career of industry : but, being totally destitute of principle, he became one of those men who might have been honourable and respected at one half the pains he took to be neither the one nor the other ; but as we proceed we shall see quite enough of Jonathan Willoughby, and at present we will turn to the contemplation of more agreeable characters, although their hearts' best affections are under a cloud.

No doubt it was an intrepid writer or orator, be it which it may, who first asserted the fact, that there could be such a thing as a decidedly honest and conscientious lawyer ; of course, the general principle, that all lawyers are rogues, stands untouched by a few examples of the contrary, and as it has been our fate, in the course of our career of authorship, not unfrequently to present to the reader specimens directly the contrary to the one we are about to mention, we are all the better pleased to be able to do justice to an individual like Mr. Whitford.

Erasmus Whitford was a decidedly honest man, and about as unfit to be a lawyer, or what is termed a man of business, as any human being could possibly be.

He had a sad habit of giving advantages instead of taking them, and there was a prodigality of feeling about him, and a liberality in all his dealings, which were very sad foes to his well doing. Need we add after this, that he was a poor man, and had the worst sort of business ; namely, clients who never paid him.

He always had some business or another on hand, for which he never got anything, which he undertook because somebody or another had got ill used ; in truth, poor Mr. Whitford was the knight errant of solicitors, however rare such a character might be.

Of course, he married somebody as poor as himself, for such a man never makes anything by such a speculation. He was fortunate that he had two children, for such men generally have stupendous families ; these were both girls, and the eldest, alas ! was poor Emily, the mother of the love child, and who now, with all her pains, all her anxieties, her remorse, and her sorrows, was in her grave.

But this was a fact unknown to her family. It is worth while now to contrast two pictures. The reader can fancy the bustle and the excitement contingent upon the Earl of Crumbledown's marriage ; fancy that at its height, with all its glittering paraphernalia, with every face wreathed in smiles, and all realizing such an aspect as if there were no such things as want, or grief, or misery in the wide world.

Then turn abruptly from this scene to another, which we shall lay before the reader.

At the back of Camden-town, to the east, are numerous streets of small third or fourth rate houses, little brick and mortar attempts at the genteel, which, when first built, no doubt, looked neat, if not handsome ; but which, in a few years, in consequence of the poverty of the tenants, became sadly deteriorated.

The landlords of these houses soon discovered that they had the worst and the most unprofitable property in the world. The houses are not good enough for people with ample means, they are not cheap enough for those who depend upon their daily labour for their daily bread, and who never dream of attempting to make any show beyond their means.

The consequence of this is, they fall into the hands of an intermediate class, who cannot labour, and who live a life of continued anxiety in an endeavour to hold a position which they have not the means of accomplishing.

These are people who would be glad to pay, and who are all sanguine that they can pay, that something or other will turn up in the chapter of accidents that will enable them to do so; but, alas! the good fortune never arrives, and from house to house they go, anxious and troubled people ever. Such, unhappily, was the Whitford family.

And the troubles of the Whitford family brought with them no recompenses; they would far rather have paid every one than not, and were not the class to congratulate themselves upon getting rid of any claim illegitimately.

Their style of living, however, afforded a remarkable proof of the saying, that under all circumstances and conditions some comforts are to be found, and some feelings of happiness. The Whitfords found this in themselves, for a more united and affectionate family than they were could not have been found. We do not name this fact as a particular virtue in them, because, where the elements of union and affection are not, it is quite impossible the results can appear. We merely state it as one of the circumstances in which this family was placed—that there was not one bad member in it.

Of course, we do not count Mr. John Willoughby, the uncle, by courtesy, or the folly of custom.

In the growing beauty and accomplishments of their children Mr. and Mrs. Whitford had always found a consolation for every evil in life; but they had yet to learn how a dangerous a gift was beauty to children circumstanced as theirs were. It did not enter into their imaginations to consider how that very beauty would attract the eye of a libertine, and, possibly, become the bane of the future existences of those whose developing charms they watched with so much interest and satisfaction.

It might almost be said that Emily Whitford could have traced her fall to the height of morality that prevailed in her father's house. An untruth, even by implication, was there unknown. Secrets were as rare as sovereigns, and, Heaven knows, they were rare enough, and hence she became terrified at herself upon the first trifling dereliction of that duty, which she owed to the simplicity and sublimity of truth.

The acquaintances of the Whitfords were but few, but it was on a visit to one of those few that the unhappy Emily, whose evil star must have been in the ascendant, made an acquaintance with the then Lord Warelock, which ended in her own destruction, that is to say, her destruction in this world, for she was far from morally guilty, and that Heaven, which sees into the hearts of its creatures, would need an exercise of its justice and mercy.

A trifling accident in the street rendered the assistance of a stranger's arm a very great assistance indeed; that stranger was Lord Warelock, and he became at once fascinated by that truly transcendant beauty of the attorney's daughter. They say affection begets affection; but, if it do not go so far as that, it, at all events, begets favourable consideration, and is an extremely good letter of introduction. The impressement of manner which characterised Lord Warelock in addressing Emily Whitford, was so very different from the even gentle tenor of the affection with which she was treated at home, that it irresistibly attracted her imagination.

She certainly did not keep secret that she had nearly fallen in the street, and slightly sprained her ancle, and that she was indebted to the assistance of a stranger to reach her place of destination; but she quite omitted to mention that she had made an appointment with that stranger for the succeeding evening, and that she had been seduced to do so at his earnest solicitation, which chimed in too well with her own inclination.

From this trifling circumstance may be dated the whole career of misery she went through. Her having not at once mentioned this circumstance, rendered it difficult for her to mention it, and that difficulty increased so much on her mind, hour by hour, that she felt at last that it was impossible to do so, and that, for the first time in her life, she had an important secret to keep from those who loved her best. She met Lord Warelock, little suspecting his rank in life, for he disguised his lordly patrimony with the humble appellation of John Smith. As John Smith he wooed her, and as John Smith he won her. The acquaintance-ship had lasted one year and a half only up to the period of the connecting incidents where our tale commenced with that most distressing scene at the little country inn where Emily Whitford breathed her last.

She had been absent from home some months, however, before this occurrence. In vain had the most active and persevering search been used for her. In vain had such rewards been offered as were in the humble means of the Whitfords. She was not to be found.

Then, despairingly, they offered a larger sum than they ever in their lives saw, caring for nothing, thinking of nothing but the recovery of their child. All, however, was non-effectual; nothing could be done, and nothing was heard of her.

Lord Warelock, during the lifetime of his father, had always considered himself dreadfully poor, because, in the course of eight years, he had to raise forty thousand pounds among the money lenders; but it may easily be conjectured what abundant means he had for foiling all attempts of the Whitfords to discover the hiding-place of Emily.

Alas, it was a simple one; now, had they known where to pitch upon it, a fresh mound of earth in the village churchyard marked the spot where she tarried, and there at least she was at peace with herself, with her seducer, and with the world.

This unexpected blow of fate would have been enough to destroy the Whitford family, had they been at the very pinnacle of worldly prosperity; but struggling as they were, it reduced them to hopeless poverty and degradation.

By some means best known to himself, Jonathan Willoughby had discovered who was the seducer of her whom he called his niece, and that discovery he had endeavoured to turn to his own benefit, as we have seen, instead of communicating it to the bereaved family.

We now delay presenting the picture we promised to the reader no longer. It is simply this. At the moment that the Earl of Crumbledown was pledging his vows at the altar to the Lady Annabella Fanfaronade, the Whitford family were sitting in one room, looking disconsolately at each other, in a state of starvation.

Jonathan Willoughby had made himself singularly active in affecting to endeavour to discover the retreat of Emily, and he made a point of calling upon the Whitfords every day, to tell them how very unsuccessful he had been, and what exertion he had made to be otherwise.

He now came in, and seating himself with an air of mock condolence upon almost the only whole chair which the place afforded, he said,—

" No news, and I am fatigued to death; but where's the odds? I told you I would do the best I could, and I am doing it."

" We know that, Willoughby, and of course we are much indebted to you, and shall never be able to reward you."

" Oh, bother, never nind that; virtue, you know, is its own reward, and vice may be truly said to be *vice versa*."

" Exactly," said Mr. Whitford; " where have you been trying now, Willoughby? And yet I needn't ask you, and yet I am broken-hearted now; and as you have not succeeded, it is of little consequence where you have failed."

" Ah," said Willoughby, not heeding the latter part of this speech. " I have been here, and there, and everywhere. I have been east, west, north, and south, but not yet the least clue."

" It is wonderful and strange, and frightfully afflicting," said Mr. Whitford, as he wrung his hands despairingly. " If somebody could assure me she was dead, I think I could make up my mind to that."

" Well, I can't hear anything one way or the other, but that's the most improbable of all. I think she's alive, you may depend, and all safe enough somewhere; besides, how can you doubt it, after you have heard she was seen with a stranger?"

" Yes, yes, it may be so—it may be so," said Whitford; " but I know not what to think.   We took down in writing what our neighbour Mrs. Anderson said, about seeing Emily during the thunder-storm eight weeks ago.   It is here; I will read it to you."

" Well, well, do so," said Willoughby.

" It is this,—

" Mrs. Anderson says she was coming across Hyde-park, when a terrific thunderstorm came on—it was very sudden, and the rain fell very heavily, and she made the best of her way towards some trees that grew near the carriage drive, and before she could reach it, a carriage drove up, as if to obtain a momentary shelter from the storm.

" It was so violent, that she stopped for a moment or two under a solitary tree, instead of going to reach the clump of trees; but finding this insufficient to afford her any shelter from the drifting rain, at that moment she left it, and proceeded towards the trees under which the carriage had taken shelter.

" She reached there, and looked at the carriage, and at that moment the lady inside turned to speak to the gentleman who sat with her, and she instantly recognised Emily Wharton.

" She paused for a moment, but being certain of her identity, she hastened forward with the intention of speaking to her, but some words were spoken to the coachman, who whipped his horses, and with some difficulty they were induced to start, as the rain came very heavily in their faces, and the lightning was very vivid; and thus Mrs. Anderson could not gain an opportunity to speak to her."

" Ah," said Willoughby, " you have read that to me twice or thrice before, but I don't see that anything can be made of it; and, after all, that good lady may have made a mistake, you know; and if she has, why, there's an end of that."

" True, too true," said Mr. Whitford; " it is extremely possible what you say."

" And the matter is, then, as mysterious as ever; but never mind, Whitford, you know if anybody finds anything out about it, it will be me, so don't go bothering anybody else about it, for that will be the worst thing you can do.   Leave it all to me, Whitford, and if she can be found, she shall be found; but above all things keep strangers out of family affairs."

" Mr. Willoughby, Mr. Willoughby," said Mrs. Whitford, " what can it matter to us, so long as our dear child is discovered, who discovers her?"

" Oh, I beg your pardon there," said Willoughby, " it's quite another affair. Look how you would be harassed about the rewards you offered, if anybody but myself were to succeed; you may depend you would find it a very serious thing."

" And what is to become of us all?" ejaculated Mrs. Whitford.   " Poor Whitford has not been in a state of mind to attend upon anybody, or to do anything, and the consequence of course is, all business has been neglected."

" *Nil desperandum*," said Willoughby, laying down eighteen pence on the table. " There are three of you, and that makes sixpence a-piece, you know; so don't talk of being destitute, for that is all stuff."

" With this exception," said Mr. Whitford, " we are absolutely pennyless. Eighteenpence, therefore, compared with nothing, is quite a sum of money.   We thank you, Willoughby; we are quite sure it is all you have to offer."

" It is," said Willoughby.   " May I be smashed if I have more than another fourpenny piece; but I shall earn a trifle to-morrow, so it don't matter, you see, and now I must be off; but before I go, let me caution you again, not to set any one hunting after Emily but myself, or you will get into hot water, you may depend."

" Alas," said Whitford, " we have no one who would do so much for us if we wished."

"So much the better," muttered Willoughby, as he left the Whitfords.   " I am in hopes of driving a good trade yet in the matter, for I believe the young Earl of Crumbledown has got Emily somewhere in secret keeping, and he surely will be willing to keep such a secret from the ears of his new wife."

It will be recollected that Willoughby, under his assumed title of a Polish prince, had been the means of inducing the old Earl of Crumbledown to disinherit his son, and in reality he, Willoughby, might take to himself the credit of bringing about the marriage between the new earl and the Lady Annabella Fanfaronade.

We do not mean to say that Jonathan Willoughby anticipated any such result, or really felt disposed to take any credit to himself, for being an agent in its production. We only state the fact.

Of course he could not possibly foretell what the old Earl of Crumbledown would do, consequent upon receiving information of the intrigue into which his son had entered. He could not foresee that the Lady Annabella Fanfaronade would be so great a gainer on the transaction, or that, after having made his very eccentric will, the old nobleman was going to be so obliging to the lady as to die suddenly, before sober judgment and calmer reflection should come to his aid, and probably induce him to rescind that remarkable document.

We say all these things were far beyond Jonathan Willoughby's control, and he could have no notion that his late visit to the hotel where Lord Crumbledown was doing his best to make everybody so uncomfortable, would be productive of such results. But like a man who from the top of a steep hill loosens a large stone, and sends it headlong into the valley below, he could have no notion where it would stop.

The communication which Jonathan Willoughby had made to the earl, had about it no ulterior design that was all in accordance with that gentleman's genius, or his usual mode of conducting his affairs.

It was a pure piece of spite contingent upon the row he had had with the then Lord Warelock in the streets, and, like most pieces of spite, was very much repented of after it had been executed.

Willoughby, upon calm and sober reflection, was indeed truly sorry for what he had done. Not sorry on account of any mischief or evil consequences he had brought upon any one. Not sorry because he had so far agitated the mind of the old Earl of Crumbledown, as to break down the flimsy tottering barrier which separated him from eternity; but he was sorry, and bitterly sorry, too, that he of all men should, upon the impulse of a moment, have done anything whatever which was not to him productive of some immediate advantage, or promising of a remote one.

Jonathan Willoughby always was in the habit of telling himself that revenge would keep, and was a commodity which by no means became the worse for time in such a mind as his, and therefore he was in the habit of treasuring up what he was pleased to call his wrongs, although they mostly consisted but of the proper and legitimate opposition which more honest people than himself gave to his designs.

In the course of four-and-twenty hours he felt his mistake. The circumstances attendant upon the death of the old Earl of Crumbledown, and the general tenor of the extraordinary will he had made, were quite sufficiently notorious soon to reach Jonathan Willoughby's ears, and then he held solemn council with himself as to what he should do.

His first notion was to go to the new earl and stop the marriage, or threaten to stop the marriage, by hinting at a disclosure to the bride of the intrigue he had had with the attorney's daughter.

"But then," reasoned Willoughby again, "brides are not so particular; and, after all, she may graciously say she don't care a straw who he intrigued with before his marriage."

This was a potent argument; and, we must confess, we think it a very reasonable one. Brides are not so particular; and we should not like to lay a heavy wager that any marriage could be broken off by any statement whatever of the moral delinquencies of the bridegroom.

Most certainly the Lady Anabella Fanfaronade would have had no such scruples as these.

"But,"—and there is a but to everything—"but after marriage," thought Jonathan Willoughby, "it's a different affair altogether; and however liberal and forgiving a young lady may have been of her lover's irregularities before matrimony, she seldom extends so much charitable consideration to his gallantries afterwards."

And so Willoughby resolved upon waiting until the marriage was concluded, and the happy pair had returned from the continental excursion contingent thereon.

"Then," he said, "I will see what can be made of the earl's fears. Common feeling will not then allow him to wish that such an affair should reach the ears of his wife; and, moreover, it is more than likely that he will have Emily Whitford in keeping somewhere, and if so, he shall pay me well for keeping the secret."

It must be borne in mind that Jonathan Willoughby had no information of the death of Emily. He had acquired a knowledge of her acquaintance with the Earl of Crumbledown, and when she disappeared from home, he put this and that together, and jumped at once to a correct enough conclusion then—namely, that his lordship had persuaded her to elope with him.

Beyond this he knew nothing; he lived in hopes of finding Emily, but he never once thought of looking for her where alone she was to be found, namely, in the grave.

Such, then, was the state of affairs at this period. The earl and his countess are proceeding to the continent, a presumed extremely happy and well satisfied pair, although we and the reader happen to know to the contrary, and that these turtle doves are extremely ill matched, although, to tell the honest truth, we have no great sympathy for either of them.

Emily sleeps calmly in the village churchyard. She at least is happy in being freed from the scene of mortal strife, which, after what had occurred, must have ever been to her one of sadness and self-reproach.

The child—that little innocent which destiny has preserved, despite all the untoward circumstances attendant upon its birth—remains with Mrs. Grove, and is hourly thriving.

And Jonathan Willoughby, like some great general who don't know exactly at the moment what to be at, is waiting his time and the development of mere circumstances.

This scoundrel had so large a connection among gentlemen of his own stamp, that he generally succeeded, with the assistance of one and another, in procuring almost any information he wished, and no wonder, then, that he was very much astonished that he could get no tidings at all of Emily Whitford.

He began very much to admire the way in which she must have been hidden by Lord Crumbledown; and in proportion as his, Willoughby's, difficulty in discovering her place of retreat appeared insurmountable, did his admiration for the talent which had so well hidden her increase.

Like a man who attempts, with a high appreciation of his own powers of fascination, the decoying from the paths of virtue of some one who rejects with scorn his attempts, and then fancies, because he has not succeeded, that the fortress of chastity he has in vain attacked, must be impregnable, Willoughby considered Lord Crumbledown one of the cleverest fellows in the world at conducting an intrigue, because he foiled him.

"I'd have laid a hundred pounds to a sixpence," he exclaimed, "that in seven days I would have found out where Emily Whitford was concealed; but I can't, and therefore she must be uncommonly well taken care of, that's all I can say about it."

But the sojourn of the newly married pair on the continent is now drawing rapidly to a close; and Lord Crumbledown, being heartily sick of his wife, and of everything else abroad, becomes anxious to return to England.

From a letter which he sent to his friend, Colonel Bruce, we may judge of the state of his mind; but before we communicate that letter to our readers, and record his arrival in England, we have a few words to say of the Whitford family, and their wretched situation and prospects.

CHAPTER XVI.

THE DISTRESS OF THE WHITFORD FAMILY.

NOTWITHSTANDING the promises of Willoughby, Mr. Whitford felt but little confidence in his fulfilling them—not that it ever entered into his mind that he would not endeavour to keep his word by discovering the place of concealment of Emily Whitford, but he began to despair of such being within the compass of probability, or even possibility, under the then existing circumstances.

Willoughby, they thought, was their friend, and had their welfare at heart, and yet he could not do what was impossible. He had himself to look to ; and they conceived that, according to his supposed means, he had acted with generosity, and had troubled himself greatly about Emily. It was, as he said, a family affair, and he felt for the honour of them all, and he had done all that he could, and would do more, at least he would try.

"And yet," said Mr. Whitford, "I doubt whether he will be able to bring me any tidings about Emily. He can't be everywhere, and she may not be in London; I would I could hear of her."

"Ay, and so do I. Alas! poor, dear Emily, what could be the reason she has left her home thus? The poor child could never forget her mother so entirely, and be so regardless of her agony as all this. Surely, Whitford, some harm must have come to our Emily. I am very unhappy."

"Unhappy! why, yes," said Mr. Whitford, "it is a most unhappy affair altogether, and one that has cost me more misery than anything I ever yet met with; and this is not all it has done, and where it will end I cannot tell. Alas! we are poor in the midst of our trouble. Poverty is an evil we could endure among ourselves better than we can parted in such a manner. I fear we cannot avert approaching ruin."

"Ruin, indeed!" said Mrs. Whitford. "I see nothing else. I can't tell what this is but ruin, Whitford. I could endure it, but for you and Emily. To see you pushed about after all, indeed, grieves me. I can't bear to see it."

"I will go out and see what can be done—that is, if I can do anything at all; and then I will return in a short time. I have not many places to go to, and am not even fit to go to them. However, there is no choice. Something must be done now, else we shall sink altogether."

So saying, Mr. Whitford brushed his hat, and, with a melancholy countenance, he left the house.

That morning Mr. Whitford walked from house to house—places where he had been in the habit of calling upon business—but he found that there was nothing at all left him to do; there was, in fact, nothing but cold looks, and in some reproaches because of neglect; and when he attempted to justify himself, he was met with an indifferent remark, and an intimation that it was business they were speaking of, and concerned about, and not of private affairs.

Tired and wearied, Mr. Whitford turned his steps homeward, with a yet sadder heart. He knew not what he could do—nothing seemed to prosper. Sorrow and misfortune were in the ascendant, and he must succumb.

These were not evils enough for one day, and poor Whitford, when he came home, was doomed to meet with more disagreeables.

"Well," said Mrs. Whitford, "what fortune have you met with?—though I need not ask you; your face tells me you have met with nothing but evil."

"Indeed, my dear, I have met with no good fortune, I may say; nor, indeed, any that could do us any good now or hereafter. I have met with the usual rebuffs, and have no more to hope."

"Good God! you don't say so, Whitford?"

"I do, my dear. I have not sat down since I left here this morning; and, I assure you, that I have not met with one kind word; all seem alike to set their faces against the father who is bereft of his child."

"Alas!" said Mrs. Whitford, "it is really a lamentable thing. It is hard enough to suffer, but worse to be slighted b███████ou suffer. However, we can but suffer; but sit down and have something to ██ █ t is not much, nor what we have been used to, for the money that Willough██ █t would not do much. Mary and I have had our dinners, and have saved yours, as we were not sure at what hour you would return."

"That was right," said Whitford; "and I am but too thankful to think there is anything at all to be had, for, I must confess, that had it depended on me, I should have disappointed you."

Mr. Whitford sat down and ate his dinner, and Mrs. Whitford sat looking at the miserable fire that slumbered in the grate, and then at their daughter Mary, who sat down and was watching her father as he ate his dinner.

"That, at least, is a blessing I hardly anticipated this morning when I got up," said Whitford, as he finished his dinner, and turned towards the fire. "I would I were sure of getting one like it on this day week. We must not despair, though I cannot tell on what food hope can live upon."

"True enough, Whitford, for us, who are now divided and poverty-stricken. It has been said that union is strength, but all the union in the world won't make the pangs of hunger any easier to be borne, or less painful."

"No, I believe not, my dear. But we have not come to such an extremity."

"Very near it."

"Very true," said Whitford, with a sigh.

"What I regret is, that our poor little Mary should be compelled to be a sharer in our misfortunes, and linger her life thus."

"'Tis past help, my dear; we must do what we can; but that will be more in the way of endurance than aught else: she cannot do more than share our home."

"And that, alas! will soon be taken away from us, I fear."

"What induces you to think so, my dear? But why do I ask such a question? We have no means, and even to keep a house is out of the question; and yet I know not how it is, even in the utmost depth of wretchedness there is a house, or something that passes for one, and surely they will not allow us to sink below the worst."

"I know not, but the man has been for the rent since you were out."

"Ah! the rent; well it ought to be paid, but we haven't got it yet," said Mr. Whitford. "I am sorry for it—we owe it, and ought to pay it. But he will perhaps wait until we can do something and get the money. I wish and will pay every one, my dear."

"I know that, Whitford; but that is the thing I find most difficult to impress upon their minds, and yet harder to believe."

"It is very odd," said Mr. Whitford, who really did not see why people should misdoubt him; "but people are very suspicious in cases where none is justified; they would ask the same favour themselves."

"They would, but somehow there are many people who don't mind taking, and yet they never will give."

"Some how or other I think we always meet with those kind of people. However, when evil fortune has done its worst, we may hope for some respite in this world."

"We may; but when will that happen?"

"If we could but recover our lost child, I could look upon all other evils with equanimity," said the unfortunate father.

"The landlord, or rather Mr. Cross, the agent, has been here."

"Indeed!"

"Yes."

"And what does he say?"

"He will call again."

"If he wait it will be a mrrcy, for I have been too unsuccessful to-day to be able to give any promise as to any specific time of payment. I will the moment I have the money."

"That is what I told him."

"And what did he say?"

"That he could not take that for an answer at all, and would come and see you."

"See me!"

"Yes; he would not say any more to me; he said it was quite useless."

"Well, what I shall say to him will be very little more explicit; I suppose, though I must submit patiently, for the man has waited several weeks, and I owe him the rent. He has a right to demand it of me."

"Ay, there he is," said Mrs. Whitford, "there he is. I wish he had not come just yet. I wouldn't tell you before you had your dinner, lest it should disturb your appetite."

"To be sure these misfortunes are not likely to remove one's natural appetite, though I must confess they do not diminish one's wants."

At this moment there was a rough knock at the door, and Mrs. Whitford arose, and opened it, saying,—

" Come in, Mr. Cross, Mr. Whitford is at home, though I am sorry to say he is not better able than I was this morning to give you an answer."

" Sorry for it, ma'am, but can't help it myself ; I ain't no business to help it."

Mrs. Whitford shut the door, and then resumed her seat by the fire.

" Well, sir, what are you going to pay ?"

" Really, Mr. Cross, you shall have the money as soon as I can get it."

" Very well ; can you get it by nine o'clock to-morrow morning ?"

" I cannot indeed."

" I must get it for you, then."

" Really, that will be more than I can expect from a stranger," said Mr. Whitford, looking very hard at Cross, and not at all understanding what was meant.

" Oh, it's the usual end of all these affairs. My notion is, if you can't pay one week, you can't pay two, and three's out of the question. So if it isn't quite ready by to-morrow at nine o'clock, I will help you to get it, and put a broker in and sell the sticks."

" Good heavens ! Mr. Cross, you will not be so hard upon one as that ? Give me a little time."

" So I will till to-morrow morning."

" Yes, but that is too short a time. We wish to pay everybody ; we are honest, though poor. Nobody shall suffer by me."

" May be, or may be not," said Mr. Cross. " I come here for money—rent, and not to inquire after your character. I don't care for any man's character, so I get the rent. He may be good, bad, or indifferent to other people, but if he pays me, I'll speak of him as I find—he's a respectable man, and I'd swear to it at the Old Bailey."

" Well, but Mr. Cross, I do not want you to do anything of the sort for me."

" I couldn't do it if you did. I should be compelled to say I didn't know no good on you."

" That may be ; you may suppose so if you like—there's no objection to that that I know of ; but though the song says ' Poverty's no sin.'"

" I tell you 'tis a very great crime !"

" Indeed ! then I'm truly guilty."

" The more's the pity. But you'll find if poverty's no crime, all its consequences are punished as misdemeanours ; for if you get into debt you'll be quadded, and I must sell the sticks ; and it's no use of your begging unless you can beg the money from some one."

" But we have had a serious misfortune, and what between one evil and another, I have really got no money."

" So much the worse—I want money."

" And so do I, Mr. Cross," said Whitford.

" Exactly, we all want it ; but I want what is due."

" I cannot give it you if I haven't got it."

" That's true ; but what business had you to get into debt ? People are always running into debt because they haven't got it to pay ; that's what I call being dishonest. You never hear of a man who has got money getting into debt."

" He has no need."

" Well, then, it's only your scabby sheep as ain't got it that gets in debt, and so says my principal—you must have it."

" Mr. Cross," said Mrs. Whitford, " will you not afford us some little more grace ? We shall be turned into the streets if you don't show us some mercy. For my sake, and this poor little child here, have a little patience, and all shall be paid."

" My good woman," said Mr. Cross, with a waive of the hand, " if I were to have pity, as you call it, I should be a very bad collector, and not worth my salt to my principal. I'm a collector, and not a dispenser of charity."

" We don't expect ——"

" There, that'll do," said Mr. Cross ; " I shall see you to-morrow morning at nine o'clock ; if you are any later with the tin, why it won't do, unless you pay expenses."

"But Mr. Cross ——"

"But Mr. Fiddlestick."

"There, don't say any more," said Whitford to his wife, "it's no use."

"Mr. Cross, are you a husband?"

"Yes, ma'am, unfortunately I am."

"Are you a father?"

"So my wife tells me; and I know I've to support a blessed lot of kids, and that'll spoil any man's temper, much more a collector's, who's crossed at every other house he goes to."

"Well, but you must have some ties—something to love and ——"

"Oh, yes, I have all that."

"Well, then, as you would wish for ——"

"Oh, you needn't mention it, I can drink at any time; but it's no use your asking when you can't pay the rent. You can't stand ——"

"Stand—I don't mean stand," said Mrs. Whitford; "I was about to beg of you, by all the ties you hold most dear ——"

"Ah, that's all very well; the ties I hold most dear is, my glass; and I own, though brandy's dear, yet I don't grudge the money. But it's no use stopping here—it's great cry and little wool, as the devil said when he shaved the pig."

And with this speech, Mr. Cross, the collector, walked out of the room without uttering another word, but merely looking round the room, taking a bird's eye view of the furniture, and giving an ominous shrug of the shoulder, as much as to say,—

"There ain't enough here to fetch the money, much less to allow it to run any longer."

When they were left alone, Whitford and his wife gazed at each other sadly. It was some minutes before either spoke; and then Mrs. Whitford said, with a deep sigh,—

"I had scarce expected this. Do you think he will keep his word?"

"I hope not, but I fear it," said Mr. Whitford. "He seems to be a hard-hearted man, and yet he may think the threat will produce the money, which we wouldn't pay with a less urgent threat."

There was but a dismal prospect before these unfortunate Whitfords, who might be looked upon as a wholly destitute family, and utterly ruined beyond any hope of recovery. And moreover, they not only suffered in circumstances, but they had a greater misfortune in the loss of their daughter, which they felt so acutely that it in some measure blunted all the poignancy of their other feelings and misfortunes.

CHAPTER XVII.

THE COLLECTOR OF RENTS.—THE BROKER AND HIS MAN.—THE SEIZURE FOR RENT.

THE evening was a cheerless one to the Whitfords, and night was broken and filled with unpleasant dreams. The threat of the collector had almost deprived them of the power of sleep, and when they did it was to fall into an uneasy slumber from exhaustion, and they rose somewhat later in the morning.

"Dear me," said Whitford, "'tis very near eight o'clock, I declare; I have slept late this morning."

"And yet," said his wife, "I don't see what we could do by early rising; you have nothing to do, and therefore neglect nothing."

"That's very true," said Whitford—"very true; the more one can sleep the more one escapes of wretchedness. What shall we do for breakfast this morning? It is a curious inquiry, for I believe we have none of Willoughby's eighteenpence left?"

"None; yet I think, though, there are three farthings on the mantelpiece."

"And that is wholly inadequate to the procuring of us a breakfast. I am afraid little Mary will for once go without one; poor thing, she can't understand it, I dare say."

" I tell you what, Whitford, we must get one."

" Must."

" Yes."

" I should be glad to know how. Point out the means, and I will do it."

" We must part with some of the few things we have about us to raise a few shillings, and enable us to obtain food."

" But the landlord will take them all in a few hours, and nobody will buy under such circumstances, you know."

" I'll put together some articles of linen—alas ! there are none too many—and we must pledge them."

" I never thought of that," said Mr. Whitford; " I will do it. For since the things must go, we may as well part with some, so as we can get them back again when we are more fortunate."

Mrs. Whitford sighed as though she feared that that would be a long time before it arrived, if ever it did.

Whitford arose and dressed himself, and Mrs. Whitford, before she did so, collected together a number of articles, which she folded up in two moderate sized bundles, and giving them to her husband, said,—

" There are the remains of all that is good or valuable we have left ; obtain all you can on them, for my mind seems to have forebodings of the worst ; we must make it last as long as we can, lest we have no more."

" I will," said Whitford ; " and when I return I will bring in the necessaries with me."

" Do so ; I will be dressed, and have the breakfast laid and water boiling."

" Poor Whitford," muttered Mrs. W., as she looked after her husband as he descended the stairs with a good-sized bundle under each arm; " he has not been used to such scenes. I would have gone for him, had it not been that I should have caused him some uneasiness, and I can get all ready by the time he comes back."

It was near three-quarters of an hour, or nearly half-past eight, before he came back, and Mrs. W. became uneasy at his absence, but about that time she heard him coming up the stairs, and he entered the room and brought in his hand several articles that were necessary.

" I feared," she said, " that something had happened to you, you were so long."

" Yes, my dear, I had to wait the shopkeeper's convenience, and was then treated with insolence by his shopman. I suppose these people, who live upon the wants of those who are distressed, imagine that they are fully entitle to treat their customers with incivility and brutality."

It is a well known fact that by far the greater portion of these individuals in the metropolis are the only tradesmen who think of treating their customers with a degree of insolence that would ruin any other tradesmen, and cause his shop to be deserted ; but not so with the pawnbroker, who, notwithstanding the legitimacy of his profits, does draw them from the hard earnings of the very poorest, who have nothing to show for the money they pay him ; indeed, they purchase from him merely the use of money, and therefore get nothing substantial, and therefore, of all tradesmen, he is the most ruinous to his customers ; and yet this man, so subsisting, will treat those who support him with a degree of harshness and incivility one might expect from an Algerine to a slave.

This is well known to all who have suffered misfortunes, and none feel them so acutely as those who have been used to a better mode of life, and who cannot see any vast amount of respectability either in pawnbroking as a trade or means of living, or pawnbrokers as men. The necessities of the time alone justify the existence of such locusts.

" Ah !" said Mrs. Whitford, when she saw how much poor Whitford felt the treatment he had received. " Ah, thank God we have at least obtained the money ; we have a breakfast ; sit down, and it will be ready for you ; there, Mary place your father a chair."

Whitford disburdened himself of his purchases, and they sat down with some appetite, for they had no supper on the previous night.

" Where to go to I know not to-day," said Whitford ; " but it is no use stopping at home. By the way, there is nine o'clock striking ; that man said he would be here, did he not ?"

" Yes."

At that moment they heard a knock at the street door, and the heavy footsteps of more than one man upon the stairs.

" He is as good as his word, at all events ; and we may expect the worst."

Mr. Whitford looked very blank at this intimation, and Mrs. Whitford herself seemed much moved, as she said,—

" I suppose we shall now be turned out of our home. Emily, you know not what you have done, or the misery you have inflicted ; but, alas! I will not blame her, she knew not the consequences she entailed upon her home, and she may herself be suffering worse."

The door was now opened by Mr. Cross, who gave a premonitory knock, and then, without waiting for the customary invitation to come in, walked in, followed by the broker and his men—two rough-looking individuals, who were by no means troubled with bashfulness or civility.

" Well," said Mr. Cross, " I have come—you know I agreed to give you till nine o'clock—for the sum of two pounds five shillings. Is the money ready ?"

" Indeed I have not got it."

" Well, if I had been you, I could not go on eating and drinking in that way. A man who can't pay his debts, especially his rent, ought to be too much ashamed of himself to eat and drink ; it looks like living in the face of his landlord. You astonish me."

" I am at a loss to understand what you would have me do."

" Go without—starve ; or, at the most, eat but bread and drink but water."

" We have, unfortunately, but little more ; however, if your duty is so imperative, do it, and do not attempt to insult our poverty with ill-timed and unfeeling remarks."

" Ill-timed ! well now, I like that," said Mr. Cross, very sharply. " I'm to be told I am ill-timed, am I? but you shall see I am in very good time, in a brace of shakes. I tell you what, when could I be better timed? not at all, not at any time ; haven't I caught you in the fact? and what better time is there ? but a man who comes for money is always ill-timed, when the creditor don't want to pay."

" But I do want to pay."

" Then why don't you ?"

" Because I have not the means, just at this moment, though I should be able to pay all in a short time."

" It's all very well," said Mr. Cross, very slowly ; " but it's all mere moonshine ; it's the old story. Where there's a will there's a way—that's an old saying and a true one—and if it were to go over another week it would still come to the same end, and another week's money owing ; in the meantime, the sticks may walk, and if they didn't, and I rather think from experience they would, they wouldn't then pay the rent, much less the expenses ; what's your opinion, Mr. Cohen ?"

" Why, s'help my goodness," said the Jew, " I shouldn't like to buy all in the room for four-and-twenty shillings, including the peacock's feather on the mantel-piece."

" Then," said Mr. Cross, " I'm let in for it again, and my principal will blame me, and tell me I'm ruining him, because I don't or won't get in the money ; but, lord, he don't know what a difficult thing it is to get money from lodgers—in some cases 'tis like getting blood from a stone."

" You haven't the money?" said the broker, turning to Whitford ; " if you have, you had better pay it to Mr. Cross ; it'll shave you the expenses."

" If I can't pay one, I can't pay the other."

" Then, my dear sir, I must make a beginning,—my time's valuable ; go-a-head, Mr. Cross."

" Make the seizure, Cohen.   I've done all that I can do for them."

" You are as good a man as any in the business.   I've known you these twenty years, and have done business for you during that time, and I can't tell how many distresses there has been put in—but about three hundred and forty a-year —and it always makes you dry."

" So it does, so it does," said Cross, wiping the back of his hand across his mouth.

" Let me shee," said Cohen; " one table and four chairs—the chairs all defective, won't fetch sixpence a-piece ; crockery—odds and ends ; two candle-sticks—odd and old ; bedstead—old, and no doubt buggy.   Ah, the worst of these things is, they won't fetch no money ; people expect to buy them for nothing."

" What do you think of it ?" said Cross.

" Oh, the only thing will be the bed ; and I don't think there is more than enough to clear the expenses, s'help my good gracious me."

" When you have done making the inventory, you had better leave the man in possession and come next door."

" Oh, no ; leave that job next door."

" I can't, time's expired," said Cross, opening his eyes very wide at Cohen's request.   " But why do you ask such an out of the way thing ?"

" 'Cause they've got the malignant typhus there, I'm told, and the boy is as black as my old coat," said Cohen, with a shrug.

" That's catching."

" It just is, I believe you."

" We'll go another day," said Cross, " else our business may stand still for want of ourselves, and then they would come and go in a pretty style, I'm thinking."

" S'help my good gracious me, what a lark it would be ; they'd be delighted ; and what a job for the next collector to get the arrears.   I'm thinking he might as well go to Aldgate pump, and seize the ladle for it."

" Have you finished ?"

" Yes.   Here, Smith, I leave you in possession of this place, and you must not leave it till you have leave ; there must be nothing taken out of the room upon any pretence whatever."

" Very good," said Smith ; " I'm yer man.   I knows all about it."

" Is this man to remain here ?" inquired Mr. Whitford, of Cross.

" Of course he is," replied Cross.   " What do you think he is brought here for, merely as a scarecrow ?   No, no, I means what I mean.   Don't I, Cohen ?"

" Indeed you does, Mr. Cross, s'help my goodness ; but there's no mistake about you, Mr. Cross.   Nobody ever had to complain of saying one thing, and doing another, in business, I'll take my davy of."

" Then I and my family must leave."

" We can't study your convenience, and considering how you pay your rent, I rather think that will be best thing you can do.   Smith will be all alone, to be sure, but he ain't afraid of going to sleep in the dark—are you, Smith ?"

" I should think not.   I've been in a cellar afore now, half full of sweeps and sut, but I wasn't afeard of the black gentlemen.   And I can say the more room I has, the more I shall like it.   I haven't had any backey yet, and I'll blow a cloud."

Then as coolly as possible he lit his pipe, and taking one of the chairs, sat near the door smoking, and Cross and Cohen left the room.

For some moments afterwards Mrs. and Mr. Whitford seemed stupified with amazement and sorrow.   All that passed seemed like a hideous dream, and ever and anon they lifted their eyes to each other, and then to the man who sat coolly smoking.

At length Whitford arose, saying,—

" As we must quit this, my dear, we may as well do so at once."

"It makes no difference to me," said the man. "I'm comfortable enough; don't put yourself out of the way on my account."

Mr. Whitford deigned no reply to this piece of insolence, but looking at his wife, he said,—

"You had better dress yourself and Mary, and take such a change with you as you may be allowed, and we will leave at once."

"I don't mind," said Smith, taking the pipe from his mouth, and spitting between the bars with much precision. "I don't mind your taking some linen, but I must see it all, because, you see, some very pretty things may be carried away in that manner—jewels, and such things."

"Had I any jewels," said Mrs. Whitford, "the rent had not remained unpaid."

"Very likely, ma'am," said Smith; "can't help it, but must do my duty."

Mrs. Whitford said no more, but taking the only few things she had now remaining, and placing them all on the table, unfolded and folded them up again before the man, and tied them up in a small bundle, which she left on the table, saying,—

" That I wish to take away with me.   Are you satisfied with it ?"

" Oh, wery perfectly," said Smith, " quite right.   I knows it, cause I see it."

Then placing her bonnet and shawl on, and dressing Mary, she turned to Whitford, who was then standing ready to go, but almost stupified, and said,—

" Are you ready ?"

" Ready," he exclaimed, starting, and looking at her; but he soon recovered himself, and said, " ah, yes, I am quite ready.   I will take the bundle, and then we can go—be careful of the stairs."

" You are off, then—ain't you coming back again ?" said Mr. Smith, " cause I shall lock the door, and nobody ain't at home to anybody."

" I shall not return," said Whitford, who walked down stairs, followed by his wife.   " Whatever the things may fetch over the rent, will be swallowed up in the expences, and they will be sold for so little among these men, that nothing will there remain for me to receive."

So saying, he left the house, and in company with his wife and daughter, Mr. Whitford quitted the neighbourhood.

———

CHAPTER XVIII.

THE SEARCH OF THE WHITFORDS AFTER A LODGING.—DISAPPOINTMENTS AND REFLECTIONS.

Mr. Whitford walked for some distance in silence.   His heart was too full, his feelings were more employed than his mind ; indeed, he could not think, at least with precision, and images of the past filled his mind, while he walked along by the side of his wife and child.

They, too, were melancholy and sad, and too much occupied with the sadness that sat upon their souls, to engage in conversation, and thus they all three walked about for miles.

The day was up, and the streets were filled with the neighbouring population, all busy, and hurrying to and fro, as if life and death depended upon their speed ; the streets seemed all alike, filled with human beings, of whom there were countless thousands—go where they would, they met them—turn into this street, or go into that, it was all alive with human beings.

If the bye streets were not all equally filled with grown people, they made up, ay, more than up their number in juvenile population, the most noisy and troublesome of the two, by very far.

They had walked about for nearly two hours in this manner, when Mrs. Whitford first recovered her speech, and said to her husband, when they had reached a more quiet spot than usual,

" Whitford, where are we, and where are you going to ?"

" I really don't know where I am going to, but we are now in the city, or very nearly out of it.   I suppose we must see about getting some kind of lodging, be it ever so humble."

" Yes, we must have something we can call home; if it be ever so lowly and abject, still it will be all in all to us, and I think poor Mary will be glad when she sits down."

" Ah, poor child, she is no doubt tired.   Well, Mary, can you walk a little longer, and then we'll stop somewhere and have some dinner—it will not be long ; 'tis half-past twelve, now, and we shall get into a more humble neighbourhood soon."

" I can walk father," said Mary.   " I am not tired yet, but can walk well enough."

" Well, my dear child, you shall not have to walk farther than I can help. Come, my dear," he said to his wife, " we will make for the east end of the town ; I think there there may be some chance of getting things cheaper."

" Very well, Whitford, wherever you go there I am content to follow. I would we were there now, for I feel that I could sit down in any place which we may call our own, and free from intrusion. Misfortunes, indeed, limit one's wants and wishes in many respects."

" Yes, but it limits the means of supplying them, and that is what I most fear, as it may not only limit, but destroy the very means of supplying these."

" Well, we must do our best, and hope for the best; we shall not, I hope, be entirely deserted. What a fortunate thing that we were able to raise a few shillings before those men came this morning to seize upon our few things."

" Ay, it was fortunate, indeed; this will last us some time, and, perhaps, before it is exhausted, I may be fortunate enough to procure a supply from some more legitimate source."

" I hope you may, I am sure; but we must not despair, for some turn of fortune may overtake us yet."

" It may, and I hope it will not be a worse turn; however, here is a lodging to let. Let me see, what does it say? A furnished lodging. Inquire within. Very well, we will."

The street was a long, narrow, dingy-looking street, full of small houses, which were nearly all alike. Whitford knocked at the door, and as no one answered it, he knocked again louder than on the first occasion. At length a dirty slip-shod girl came to the door.

" Who do you want ?" exclaimed this specimen of the east, after she had surveyed them all with extreme care.

" You have a furnished lodging, haven't you ?"

" Yes, oh, yes; 'tis the lodgings you want, is it ?"

" Yes," said Whitford, " it is."

" Oh, then, I'll send up Mrs. Rogers," and she immediately ran down stairs, calling out to Mrs. Rogers, saying,—

" Here's somebody after the lodging."

Upon this intimation Mrs. Rogers came up; a stout woman, with a white face, and very red hair; a dirty white cap, and an indescribable apron, with the corner of which she kept continually wiping her mouth.

As she walked leisurely up stairs, she surveyed the applicants for her apartment as though all the world were in league to obtain them from her by some means that were only to be discovered by her vigilance.

" Oh, you want to see the lodging ?"

" If you please."

" Walk this way and you can see them. Let me go first, and then I can show you the way."

" These stairs are none of the largest, and are very awkward," thought Whitford; but he said nothing about that.

" This is the room," said the woman, looking down upon them as they came up.

Mr. and Mrs. Whitford looked round the room. There was a turn-up bedstead that looked somewhat like a moveable cupboard, four chairs, that had seen service, and two of them creaky, a few cheap chimney ornaments, two small tables, and a coal scuttle, and an indescribable coloured and pattern carpet.

" You see," said the woman, " it is a very snug room, and very comfortable; the grate draws beautiful, and it doesn't smoke at all, leastways, only when the wind is in the east."

" And what may you ask by way of rent ?" inquired Mr. Whitford.

" That will depend whether you find your own linen and crockery."

" No, we could not well find anything."

" Then it would be eight shillings a-week," said the female, " and dirt cheap it is, too, at that price; my husband says that it ought to be another shilling, at all events."

" Ah !" said Mr. Whitford, " I dare say they are well worth it, but the place wouldn't suit us."

" Indeed !"

" Yes ; I do not intend to go to such a rent as that," said Mr. Whitford ; " it is beyond my means altogether," he added, turning to his wife.

" Yes, yes ; this will not do."

" I could not think of taking less," said the woman ; " there's none in the neighbourhood at that price, with such accommodations."

" Indeed !"

" No, I am sure of it."

" I am sorry to have given you so much trouble, but I couldn't tell that until I saw it."

" Very good," said the woman, as she followed them down stairs, and slammed the door after them.

" I wouldn't have considered the place so much," said Mr. Whitford, " as I did the rent. It is enormously heavy, and beyond my means so much that it wouldn't be prudent to have taken it."

" I think not, indeed."

" We must go on farther ; this, you see, is the Commercial-road, but we may as well stop somewhere and obtain some rest and food, poor little Mary seems tired."

" And so am I. I do not wonder at her being tired, poor thing, she hasn't been so far before, I believe."

" No, I think not ; but here is a kind of coffee-house where we may get something, and yet it will be crowded with people. I will get some boiled beef and bread, we can then enter some quiet public-house, where we can sit ourselves down, and rest for an hour, without being thrown into a profuse perspiration by the steam and smells of a score of different dishes."

" As you please, my dear, we have no right now to be particular ; choose, therefore, some quiet place, where we can converse together."

They walked on for some distance, until they came to such a place as they thought would suit them. Entering into a small neat parlour, they all three sat down, and Mr. Whitford having ordered some ale, which was brought to them, he set about apportioning out the viands the best way he could do so.

" I don't know," he said, " but I feel tired, and am very hungry, though what I have seen and gone through this day is enough to destroy all desire of food."

" Exertion, both of mind and body, must require some support," said Mrs. Whitford ; " but where do you intend to go now ?"

" Somewhere down Wapping," said Whitford ; " there are places there at all prices, but here I haven't seen anything that is likely to suit."

" Where did you learn anything about Wapping ?" inquired Mrs. Whitford.

" Why, you see, I have had several, I may say, a good many, poor clients."

" You have had too many, the more the misfortune," said his wife, sorrowfully.

" Ay, that is true enough ; but then you see they were not to blame for that ; if any blame were to be given to any one, it must be to those who made them so, and to me, who took them as such."

" Yes, that is the fact, I believe ; and you often found out that you had been deceived by them."

" I must admit I formed a wrong estimate of character in some cases ; but we are not always infallible, and misfortune is no crime, you know ; however, as I was saying, in answer to your question, how I came to know Wapping was this,—I had a poor client, he was a sea-faring man, and had been the master of several vessels. Well he was thrown into prison, and certain papers of his seized, and the creditors endeavoured to compel his wife to give up certain property that was to be her's and her husband's ; and then, after her death to go to the children. They had no business with the papers, nor with the property, and they had some fraudulent purpose in view. They were Jews, and he was a seaman, and, no doubt, they believed he could be frightened into anything. He was induced to sign a paper, by which he believed they were entitled to all ; but he discovered that the money had come to him, and there were arrears that would pay all his debts more than twice over, and he began to consider he had acted unwisely, and think they had defrauded him, which they had; however, he believed there was no remedy, and he gave it up as a bad job; but his wife came to me and explained the whole circumstances. Of course, I at once agreed to undertake to get the matter settled, and informed him that the document was illegal, and of no use, and they must give place to him. Great was their joy when the discovery was made, and he afterwards received his money, save a small portion that had been spent; and, moreover, I got my costs, for the man was willing to have done anything to have obliged me. It was during my walks backwards and forwards to him that I found out that part of the town."

"And what sort of place is it?"

"It is near the river, mean, and crowded with innumerable streets, cross and direct, alleys and courts, that it is but reasonable to expect that something should be found to suit us."

"It is a strange place, then. Is there any business in that quarter?"

"Yes, as much in it as any other. There is a very large business carried on there, and great numbers of sailors live there while their vessels lie in the river."

Thus they talked away the time, and stayed more than an hour and a half to rest and refresh themselves.

"I wonder," said Whitford, "if there will be any good fortune for me; whether the same evil stream of ill luck will follow me now. It is time a change was made."

"Yes," said Mrs. Whitford, "it is time; but I expect that we shall have to wait patiently. Had we better not see about renewing our search of an abode in this new land?"

"I think we had, my dear, if you and Mary have rested enough."

"Yes, I think she is ready, and the sooner the better, for if it gets night I should begin to despair of obtaining one to-night, and what should we do in such an emergency?"

"We can obtain a bed somewhere, I dare say," said Whitford.

"Yes; but at what a price. I would sooner walk through the streets all night; we should reduce ourselves to starvation in so short a time, that it is fearful to contemplate."

"Do not talk of it," said Whitford; "but, come, we will see what can be done. I am wearied of the search; but we surely cannot walk about for the whole day without coming to something that will do."

They left the house somewhat refreshed by the rest and food they had, and proceeded in their search of a lodging.

How many streets they went up and down it is impossible to say; but they continued to do so without intermission the whole of the afternoon, and how many they went to it is impossible to say, but to many did they go, but not one could they find that would suit them.

The great inconvenience was the amount of rent they required for such miserably furnished rooms, that they could not conceive anything worse; and, therefore, determined that they would get the cheapest that could be got, since that was enough for them, and it must contain all that they deemed such as were really and absolutely necessary.

Some places the rent was lower than others; but there was the same amount of inconvenience for the same amount of money. Everything was of the worst and most poverty-stricken character, and of the same scanty and half-worn-out appearance.

The people, too, who owned these places, were all of them very suspicious, and seemed to think they came on purpose, either to steal the worthless things they possessed, or else to take some inexplicable advantage of them.

However, despite all these disagreeables, they still persevered in their intention, and contrived to knock and ring until they were almost ashamed to touch a knocker, or handle a bell, and began to think there was something in their very appearance that betokened the number of places they had entered.

At length they came to one; it was a low dingy-looking house, not low on

account of its height, for it was taller than many others at the other end of the
street. It had several stories, and had an air of comfort, notwithstanding its
miserable dirty, dingy, and wretched appearance.

The street was filled by a moving population of nondescript appearance, and
whose respectability was as invisible as their means of living.

"Well," said Whitford, "I do begin to despair now. A furnished room to
let, eh; well, we must do something, and if this won't do, we must take it if it be
ever so poorly furnished and inconvenient; we can look out afterwards, and suit
ourselves, when more at leisure, and our time less occupied, and our necessity
not so great.

———

CHAPTER XIX.

THE NEW LODGINGS IN WAPPING. — THE PRETERNATURALLY FAT LANDLADY.
—THE ATTEMPTED MURDER ON THE THAMES.

Mr. and Mrs. Whitford waited at the door for some minutes before any one
came to answer the summons, and when they did hear some one coming, it was
at such a slow rate, that they were at a loss to imagine what could be the reason
of so slow an approach.

At length the door was opened, and a female of considerable dimensions
opened the door. She appeared to be preternaturally corpulent, and would easily
have been imagined to be about to add one, at least, to the number of the population of the neighbourhood.

"You have a lodging to let?" said Whitford.

"Yes," said the fat woman, "we has. A comfortable two-pair back as
ever was. Come in—come in. I'll show you up."

Mr. and Mrs. Whitford walked into the passage, and followed the fat woman,
who waddled about with more activity than could have been imagined, and they
began ascending the stairs, which creaked and swagged very much.

"The lodging is a very comfortable one," said the woman, "but small, to be
sure; that is, it is large for the money, though I am almost afeard you may think
it not genteel enough; but there's been very genteel people in before. The aunt
of the last lodger had a sister who married the mate of a Sunderland vessel;
quite respectable people, I assure you."

"Indeed!"

"Yes, but they met with their reverses; they were unfortunate as well as
other people."

"There are none without their misfortunes," said Whitford, "nor are we;
however, we must put up with them, and endeavour to get the better of them."

"Ay, just as the sailors do against a bad wind, tack and tack about until they
get the better of it, or the wind changes."

"That's right enough, and if there is any prospect of the wind's changing,
why it is cheering," said Mr. Whitford.

"Now that's what I call a sensible remark," said the woman; "but here we
are; this is the door, yon half the landing belongs to this room, and half to the
next."

This was very evident, for the place was ornamented by a cracked earthernware
pan of good dimensions, and a broom, a pair of pattens, and a cradle, which
hung up over head.

"That, you see, belongs to the next room; you can do the same, for there is
room you see, and I never allow one lodger to encroach upon another—it ain't
pleasant."

While she was speaking, she took from a pocket-full of miscellaneous articles
the key of the door, and after turning it about six times the lock performed its
functions, and the door opened.

"There's a little catch in the lock," said the woman; "but then, you know, by perseverance you can easily open the door. Walk in, if you please; it is small, but very comfortable."

"We do not want a large place," said Mrs. Whitford; "we need only comfort and cleanliness."

"Then you'll be sure to find that here, ma'am; we are all clean here, and very comfortable; there's me and my husband, we is comfortable when he isn't drunk and quarrelsome."

"Indeed!"

"Yes, ma'am."

They looked round the room;—there was what is called a turn-up bedstead, with a tattered quilt hanging before four chairs, no carpet, a fireplace, in which were a poker, shovel, and small fender,—one small table, and a little crockery ware in the cupboard.

"How much do you ask for this apartment?" inquired Mr. Whitford.

"How little, I should say; but first, let me see, there's the washing day for this room is on a Friday, the next room on a Thursday, and the first floor on Tuesday and Wednesday, but we accommodate one another."

"A very good plan. But about the rent."

"Oh, yes, the rent; why, then, three shillings can't be any way dear for the accommodation you have here."

"Well," said Mrs. Whitford, looking at her husband, "we may go further and fare worse."

"Indeed that's very true, ma'am; very true indeed, a very sensible remark."

"When can we enter, then?" inquired Mrs. Whitford; "that is the most important of all."

"Whenever you please," said the fat woman; "they are empty, you see, and when they are let why I have no further trouble about them, except to receive the rent, which is quite a pleasure from regular lodgers."

"We shall be regular enough," said Mrs. Whitford; "but, first, do you find everything—linen and everything?"

"Yes, everything; you can have a change once a fortnight."

"Very well; then I suppose I must give you a deposit?" said Mr. Whitford.

"We always look for it," said the landlady.

"If I give you two shillings that will be enough, I presume?"

"Yes, that will do, sir; thank you," she added, as she took the money and placed it in her pocket, and drew therefrom a small glass, the bottom of which had been knocked off and it couldn't stand.

"This is a very dry bargain," said the landlady, "a very dry bargain."

"Eh!" said Mr. Whitford.

"It's a dry bargain, but we must alter it, and wet it."

"Do what?"

"Wet it."

Mr. Whitford paused; he didn't precisely understand what was meant, and he gazed upon the movements of the landlady with a kind of awe difficult to be defined.

She stooped down and made some suspicious arrangement of her lower garments, and tucking her hand up above the elbow, she appeared to be busily employed about something or other, and in about two minutes she slowly pulled from the same place a long bladder about as thick as a sausage.

At first, neither Mrs. nor Mr. Whitford could at all understand what it was, and were much alarmed; however, their unpleasant feelings were soon dissipated, for she seized a string in her teeth, and untying it, she said,—

"This is some of the best Hollands you ever tasted in all your life; it comes from the Saucy Ann, a rakish-looking vessel, but the hands are all tight and right as trivets; there's never an exciseman as knowed anything about this. There, sir, taste that."

At the same time she presented a glassful to Whitford, who knew not what to do; but conceiving it was done out of civility, he at once accepted of the proffered glass. He took it, and smiling a good understanding between them, at which the landlady nodded and laughed in a mysterious manner. He then said,—

"I must applaud your taste. I have very seldom tasted the equal of that, and never the superior, it is really good."

"Superb, I should say."

"It is, but you carry your cellar about you," said Whitford.

"Ha! ha! ha! what a funny man your good gentleman is, ma'am," said the fat woman, as she presented the glass to Mrs. Whitford in turn. "It will do you good, it's good against lowness of spirits, cramp, colic, and misfortune; now, do try it, my dear ma'am. Don't let me stand alone, it will be unsociable. Sorrow is dry, dear; come, come, a little will do you a great deal of good; it's a remedy against all evils, however bad."

"Yes, my dear, a little will, I think, do you good, after the worry and fatigue of to-day."

"I am sure it will," said the landlady, and thereupon Mrs. Whitford did take the glass, and sip some of it, though she declared she feared it would do her more harm than good.

"I'll warrant it shall do nothing of the kind," said the landlady, "it's too good to do ill. Have one more glass, sir," said the landlady, as she emptied the glass down her own throat, and then filled it before there could be any answer made to the offer.

"Why, you won't say, no; I have filled it on purpose for you; drink it up and make haste, for there's the knocker a-going, and I'm wanted below about something or other. I must go and empty my cellar, and blow my bags out with wind, else they'll say I'm up at one time and down another."

Mrs. Whitford looked at the landlady, but couldn't understand a word she said, which she perceiving, said,—

"You see I ain't always so stout as this; that is, underneath. I am wrapped up in bladders, and when them is empty—and they are full of hollands just now—I am obliged to fill 'em full of wind, and to make sure of being always alike, leastways, I am so to all appearance."

So saying, she replaced the bladder and glass, and at once waddled down stairs to answer the door, which had been in a state of agitation for some minutes.

"Well," said Mr. Whitford, "of all the strange females I ever saw she is the strangest. I couldn't imagine what she is about."

"Nor I; however, she does not seem a bad hearted woman; and we have got a lodging, and that is everything at this moment. It is small enough, and there is but little comfort in knowing we are not even owners of this little; but it can't be helped."

"What shall we do about fire?"

"Make one, to be sure. We must have a few coals and things in. A good cup of tea and a fire will do all you can desire towards making you comfortable and easy. I will go out and get these things in, and then we can sit down for the remainder of the day, and talk over our plans for the future."

So saying, Mrs. Whitford left the room, and, proceeding to a neighbouring shed, procured the necessary fuel to obtain a fire, and having seen that taken home, she purchased some necessary articles of food, and this done she herself returned.

As she had expected, there was a fire, and the kettle on, and Mary said to her mother,—

"I had such a job to light the fire, and it smoked horribly; but it is better now—the water is down very low in the back kitchen—I thought you would like a fire."

"Yes, my dear, I am glad of it, tea will be a refreshing thing to me. I am so glad that we have at last found a place to sleep in and live in without going any further."

"I began to entertain serious fears," said Mr. Whitford, at last, "that we should not find any place before night."

"And so did I," added Mrs. Whitford; "but, thank God, that trouble is over, and here we are in a new home, at all events."

See page 66.

"Yes, a new home," said Mr. Whitford, looking around him, "I see; but I must not complain; we may find it a happy one, if not a more fortunate one than that which we have been turned out of."

"It may," said Mrs. Whitford, "all I hope is, there's not more than the usual quantity of bugs and fleas in this neighbourhood."

No. 13.

"It is quite impossible to say anything as regards that," said her husband; "we must take all the chances of Providence about that."

Thus the evening passed among them, and thankful did the unfortunate and sorrowful family seem for so much shelter and comfort as that which they had.

*   *   *   *   *   *   *

The night after that on which they had entered the new lodgings at Wapping, Mr. Whitford came home late. He had not gone out till late in the afternoon, and did not expect to return till late; he was, however, later than even he expected.

Mr. Whitford had been to many places, and had been detained, for his walk was much longer than he had anticipated, and his walk back again took him much longer than he expected, for he had miscalculated his distance.

The streets were much deserted, and here and there only a shop was open; and, at length, nothing but public-houses were open. He walked along, and every now and then, as he passed the end of a short lane that led to the river, he could feel the fresh breeze, and hear distinctly the different sounds that proceeded from the river.

It seemed lonely and dull, and, once or twice, he thought it would be a place where any crime could be committed, and the criminals escape from the consequences and baffle pursuit.

Just as these thoughts passed through his brain, he thought he heard a cry for help, not a sound was heard far or near, all was quiet. The sound was not a very loud one; it might be that it was a stifled sound, and the unfortunate creature might be perishing for want of aid.

He paused, but he heard no more; all was quiet and still. He stopped and listened, but the sound was not repeated, and he had almost determined to go on and take no notice of it, especially as Mrs. Whitford and little Mary would be most anxious for his return.

"There can be no harm in just going down here," he muttered; "it will not take a minute, and I can hear the water; it is close at hand."

He turned down the lane, which led to some of the wharfings, where there were some coal barges moored off.

The night was very dark, and he could scarce see but a few yards, and, after much peering and peeping about, he saw two men standing on the edge of a barge, the one attempting to throw the other overboard.

It was some moments before he could succeed; but he did at length, and Mr. Whitford heard the splash of the body in the water. The man then listened attentively, and then stole away before Mr. Whitford could recover from his horror and surprise; he, however, dashed forward over the barges, and was fortunate enough to seize the unfortunate man as he was trying to spring up to the edge of the barge; he was just sinking when he pulled him up, and, after a moment or two, the man said, in a gruff and quick voice,—

"Thank you, sir—thank you."

"I will raise an alarm."

"No, no; on no account do so."

"But the man attempted to murder you?"

"He did; I know him—I know him."

"Then give him up to justice—denounce him to the police."

"Oh, dear, no," said the man; "lend me your arm till I get into the street. I know the man, and he intended to murder me; but I shall live to punish him more effectually than justice could ever succeed in doing. Thank you, sir—farewell, and do not mention this occurrence."

So saying, the man turned away, leaving Mr. Whitford in a state of amazement. The man had a singular look—dark and fordidding. He had a strange cast in his eyes; or, rather, they both seemed turned towards his nose, and, take him for all in all, he was not by any means one of the most prepossessing of individuals. He did not carry what Lord Chesterfield calls a letter of introduction in his face.

As he went home—alas! what a home—Mr. Whitford, notwithstanding all his benevolence of heart, and kindness of disposition, felt extremely doubtful whether, in following the natural dictates of humanity, and in rescuing the man from a watery grave, he had done or not done any good to society.

But this, to such a man as Whitford, was but a passing thought, and almost as quickly banished as an unworthy one, as it was conceived.

"It matters not," he said, "what he is, or what he was. My duty to him was plain before me. I had to rescue him from the peril in which I found him, and not to reason upon his usefulness or otherwise to society. I have saved him, and that is sufficient."

As for anything in the shape of reward for saving the life of a fellow-creature when it was in his power so to do, Mr. Whitford never looked for it. The act itself brought with it its own gratification, and, in the pleasant feeling that he had done so, he quite forgot that there was a Humane Society in existence, who would have, no doubt, bestowed upon him, after a great deal of trouble and solicitation, a copper medal, of the value of three farthings.

When he got home he mentioned how he had saved a not over good-looking man from being drowned, and the incident formed a matter for conversation during the scanty meal which, by some extraordinary means or another, had been placed before them.

It is an extraordinary thing in London, and one of the most extraordinary which the immense city can present to the curious observer, how some people, and whole families, contrive to live at all.

We find people, without any visible means of subsistence, yet existing somehow or another from year to year, in a manner as inexplicable often to themselves as to anybody else.

They rise in the morning not knowing where to breakfast; as for dinner, it is too remote to be thought of, and yet, somehow, and somewhere, they do succeed in breaking their fast. Something in the shape of breakfast turns up by some extraordinary accident, and then something else in the shape of dinner.

Each day appears to be the last on which any imaginable resources can arise, and yet each day produces something in the chapter of accidents, and so on these homeless, pennyless, friendless people go from day to day, from month to month, and from year to year, existing in an extraordinary manner, which no wonder at last gives them a sort of blind and superstitious reliance upon what fortune will do for them when there seems nothing in the shape of any known tangible or human resource to turn to.

This would now seem to be the sort of life which the Whitford family were condemned to lead. Heaven help them in their miseries, for they really possess social virtues of a high order—virtues which, had fortune in some happy mood smiled upon them, would have placed them high in the estimation of the good and the generous.

CHAPTER XX.

THE EARL'S LETTER TO COLONEL BRUCE.—THE ARRIVAL OF THE EARL AND COUNTESS IN ENGLAND.

LEAVING now the Whitfords and their fortunes for a time, not from any inclination we have to do so, but because other personages of our story demand our attention, we proceed to lay before our readers a letter, which we mentioned some chapters back, and which was addressed by the Earl of Crumbledown to his friend Colonel Bruce, from Rome.

It will be recollected that it was this Colonel Bruce to whom the earl, when Lord Warelock, went for advice under the extraordinary circumstances of his father's will.

The letter was as follows, and it quite sufficiently betrays the state of feeling which existed between the newly married pair :—

" Rome.

" My dear Bruce,—You wrote to me, I find twice, and, I have just got posses-sion of both your letters at once.

" The postal arrangements in the Papal States are, like every other arrangement in them, of the most infamous character ; and, therefore, you must not be sur-prised at my not receiving your letters in proper course, and I was going to commit the Hibernianism of saying, you must not be surprised if you never receive this letter at all.

" I find your first letter commencing with a few ironical congratulations. I must confess I did not expect such from you, however my enemies might con-spire to offer me such an insult.

" You congratulate me, do you? You call me a fortunate dog? Well, if I really thought that such was your opinion, I would cut your acquaintance as a man who had lost all that discernment for which, in ignorance, I had given him credit.

" But such is not your opinion. You know that I am not a subject for any congratulations. You know that I am by no means a fortunate dog.

" Pray, for argument's sake, in what am I fortunate?

" Am I fortunate in getting possession, under the most uncomfortable circum-stances, of some only of that money the whole of which ought to have been mine with no disagreeable conditions at all attached to it?

" Am I fortunate in wedding one of the most thoroughly heartless and selfish women of the world that you can paint to yourself?

" And yet you think, or pretend to think, me a subject for congratulation!

" Bruce, you ought to have more charity. I am shocked and astonished that you, of all men, should congratulate me.

" But, true, we are in Rome. In what they call the eternal city. I think a more appropriate name would be the infernal city. I don't mind to you confess-ing the fact ; but the real truth is, that I cannot get up any raptures about his-torical reminiscences, or classical ground, and all that sort of thing. What is more, too, I don't believe in one half of the pretended raptures of other people—one half, did I say, I don't believe in five per cent. of them.

" I am in Rome, but of the two I would most decidedly prefer being in Pall Mall.

" What is Rome to me, or I to Rome? Just nothing. I was so bored with the history of Rome in my school days, that I have ever since had a cordial hatred to it. The very name to me is suggestive of wearisomeness, and tasks, and *ennui.*

" And after all what is there to see and to admire here?

" First of all Rome is dirty, ill-paved, badly ventilated, and ill-supplied with all those comforts of existence to which Englishmen are accustomed.

" Then the population is composed of three classes. These are the nobles, as poor as rats, and as proud as Lucifer ; there is the priesthood, as assuming and impertinent as anybody can be, and there is the peasantry.

" All are dirty, absolutely and filthily dirty ; men, women, nobles, shopkeepers, priests, and peasantry, all are dirty to an extent which, to the imagination of an Englishman, is perfectly horrifying.

" The houses are ingeniously contrived always to be too hot or too cold, and if you are for a few hours in any one of them, you have the enjoyment of the alternations from one to the other of these states a great number of times.

" Then there are the antiquities which I do not admire, and cannot get into any raptures about.

" You know I don't care one straw about Caligula and the Cæsars, &c., &c., and, therefore, it is dreadful to me to meet some idiot who has come first from the perusal of 'Gibbon's Decline and Fall of the Roman Empire,' falling into pretended raptures and exclaiming,—

" ' Here stood the mighty Augustus ; here Cæsar, with his eagle eye, looked across the plain. Alas ! mighty Rome, what art thou now ?' &c., &c.

" So much for Rome, and now for the domestic sources of happiness which I have.

"The countess and I quarrelled *en route*. Our first serious disturbance was at Paris.

" We found what we ought to have before suspected, that we had no tastes at all in common ; that we differed upon almost every subject, domestic, literary, political, and general, and of course we disputed about some nonsense that in itself was not worth the words wasted upon it, but which served amazingly well as a peg on which to hang a wrangle. After a time she said to me,—

" ' My lord, I very much am induced to think that you married me from widely different motives than affection ;' to which I replied,—

" ' Madam, you yourself must be well aware of the circumstances under which you have become my countess, and I hope you will not deprive yourself of any merit that is due to you for your really clever management of that affair.'

" ' Well, my lord,' she said, ' since we have commenced this topic, and as it is none of the most agreeable, I think we might come to a thorough and a complete understanding upon it.'

" I wondered what she was going to say, but I must give her the credit of saying that she did not keep me long in suspense, nor was she otherwise than perfectly explicit when she did speak.

" ' I dare say,' she added, in a voice of perfect composure, and she was putting on her glasses as she spoke, ' I dare say, my lord, you thoroughly understand the whole transaction.'

" ' Perhaps,' I remarked, ' your ladyship will favour me with your version of it, and then I can compare it with mine, and be able to come to a more accurate judgment.'

" ' Oh, certainly, certainly. The old earl's money, you see, was left to me, on condition that we married. Now, as matrimony requires the consent of two persons, it was a condition which I alone had it not in my power to fulfil, and it become necessary, to avoid endless litigation, for you to marry me somehow or another.'

" ' Litigation, madame,' said I. ' You offered to put an end to that by resigning your claim to the earl's money in my favour.'

" ' Yes, my lord ; but you will recollect that there were no witnesses, and if there had been, a mere verbal piece of generosity is non-effective in the eyes of the law, and considered a mere flourish of speech.'

" ' Then, madam, you had no intention, in case I had not offered you my hand, really to resign the property in my favour ?'

" ' Not the remotest.'

" ' Indeed !'

" ' Not the remotest. I hope you have detected no incipient insanity in my disposition, which can induce you to believe I contemplated for a moment any such nonsense ?'

" ' You would have litigated the will, then ?'

" ' Most certainly ; but it was much better to marry you. I wanted a coronet, of course, and here was one within my grasp.'

" ' Then you tricked me into this marriage solely on those selfish and personal considerations ?'

" ' Solely, sir. And at least you will give me credit for one great virtue—if for only one.'

" ' And pray what may that be ?'

" ' Candour.'

" ' Yes, madam,' said I, ' the candour of deceit, when it is too late for me to profit by it. For duplicity, if you please, I can give you ample credit.'

" ' Well,' she said, ' I had certainly hoped that the candid and open manner in which I have spoken would have induced a similar feeling in yourself, and that, perfectly understanding each other, we might have been far above any common-place domestic quarrels ; but I see you will not.'

"'Madam,' I said, 'I married you from an appreciation of your generosity.'

"'Well, but you altered your mind, my lord, and I really think you have no reason whatever to complain. You wanted money, and so did I. I wanted a titled husband, likewise, and I got him. You got all you wanted, and I got all I wanted; therefore really I do not see why we should not always meet each other with the utmost possible civility.'

"And thus, Bruce, did our conversation end. To contend with such a woman, or to argue with her, was useless. I have been compelled, in order to avoid making myself a laughing-stock to all the world, to be civil to her, and were you to see us, you would be amazed at the extreme politeness which characterises our conduct towards each other.

"You have heard me very frequently launch out into all sorts of invectives against those marriages of convenience, so common in England, where the heart has no concern in the matter, and now you perceive that no one could by any possibility have made a match more perfectly coming up to such a description than I did myself.

"And yet you congratulate me!

"Now, mind, Bruce, I enter into all these particulars to you, and tell you how I am situated just now, that when I return to England, which will be very shortly indeed after you receive this letter—if you receive it at all—that you should say not one word upon the subject.

"The countess and I when in London, will, I dare say, keep separate establishments, so that we shall not be at all in each other's way; but when we meet accidentally, you will perceive what an uncommon amount of mutual politeness will be called into action.

"Do not write to me in answer to this, for we are *en route* homewards, and a letter would be certain to miss me.

"I shall give you a call immediately upon my return, and am

"My dear Bruce, yours faithfully,

"To Colonel Bruce, London.   "CRUMBLEDOWN."

This letter, we trust, fully explains to the reader the relative position of the Earl and Countess of Crumbledown, and with the exception that they did not keep separate establishments in London when they returned, the earl had pretty well painted the mode of life which they were likely to lead.

Now the Earl of Crumbledown suspected all that his lady had told to him; but there is something revolting to human nature in the unblushing avowal of such an amount of selfishness and chicanery as that possessed by the countess.

No wonder that a feeling, almost of hatred towards her, took effect in the earl's mind in lieu of that of indifference merely.

She was now an avowed liar and *intriguante*; she made no scruple about it, and he, for some days afterwards, almost shuddered when he saw her.

The return to England was as rapid as plenty of money freely expended in travelling arrangements could possibly make it, and the white cliffs of Albion therefore soon came upon their sight.

They landed at the Custom-house, where a carriage was in waiting to carry them to the house which the Marchioness of Fanfaronade had, during their absence abroad, amused herself by preparing for their immediate reception.

Of course, in the pursuit of this matter, her ladyship did not forget to make duly the handsome profit she had earned to herself when first she started the magnificent idea of getting the house ready.

The earl, under the circumstances, could not refuse to allow the marchioness to assume the task she had set herself. He knew that she could do it well, and, therefore, as the money with which it was to be done might truly be said to be much more his wife's than his, he let it be so.

The Lady Annabella was as well aware as her mother of the object the latter had in taking so much trouble; but the reader will not have failed to perceive that in the general conduct of the Lady Annabella there had been anything but a wish to behave in a niggardly manner towards her illustrious parent.

We can accept of it, if we like, as rather a good trait in the Countess of Crumbledown's character that she felt so much gratitude towards her mother for managing matters so well for her.

And as the lady has no great assortment of good traits of character to choose from, we may as well set this down as one, for fear it should be a long time before we have the pleasure of finding another.

And, truly, well had the Marchioness of Fanfaronade executed her commission as regarded getting a house ready for the newly-wedded couple.

She rented a mansion in Hanover-square, which, as George Robins would say, presented to the discursive imagination many opportunities for improvement.

Having, then, a carte blanche as to expense, her ladyship took care to fit it up tolerably handsomely.

She netted herself by the transaction about eighteen hundred pounds, and the house was a perfect scene of luxury and magnificence. The furniture was superb, and the decorations in the very best taste. Everything was finished, and the whole place ready for immediate occupation some few days before the arrival of the earl and countess from the continent.

The Marchioness of Fanfaronade had her suspicions before they started that some little interruptions to harmony might occur before they got back, but she was not quite prepared to find that such a thorough understanding of indifference had been come to. With, however, the tact of an old stager in such matters, she saw it in a moment when the travelling carriage halted at the door of the new house and the earl handed out the countess.

There was that frigid look about his face which could not be mistaken, and the marchioness said to herself,—

" Oh, it's all understood and arranged now, is it? Well, well, perhaps it's all for the best; I am glad to see he takes it in its proper light."

Taking it in its proper light meant, to the Marchioness of Fanfaronade's ideas, being as cold and as distant as he liked, but, at the same time, perfectly polite; that was all she required.

And such moderate wishes were evidently doomed to be gratified, for the earl bowed to her with great courtesy and hoped, in a very bland tone of voice, that she was perfectly well, to which she replied she was, and paid him a compliment upon his amended looks, to which change of air had certainly added something.

CHAPTER XXI.

THE CONFIDENTIAL COMMUNICATION BETWEEN THE MOTHER AND DAUGHTER.
—THE VERY MYSTERIOUS NOTE FROM MR. VULLIMAY.

The Earl of Crumbledown merely made some alterations in his dress and he left the house, promising to return to dinner.

The countess was accompanied by the marchioness, her mother, to the superb dressing-room which had been prepared for her, and when there the latter said,—

" Now, my dear, you have not, of course, seen much of the house yet; but, from what you have seen, tell me how you think you will like it."

" Very much indeed," replied the countess. " I was quite sure it would be perfect before I came to it."

" My dear, you are very good to say so. Of course it was a matter in which I could not very well make an error; but now, to quit that subject and come to one of much more importance, upon what sort of terms are you and Lord Crumbledown, my love?"

" The very best."

" Indeed !"

" Yes; the very best."

" Well, of course you know best."

" Precisely."

" I suppose his lordship quite understands, now, his precise position ?"

" Oh, yes ; we had a dispute in Paris, and as I foresaw that unless some immediate and satisfactory explanation was come to we should be continually indulging in the same low amusement, I thought it best to be explicit."

" And what did you say ?"

" I told him, without the shadow of a reservation, the real state of the case,—that I married him for the title, and to prevent litigation concerning the property."

" Really !"

" Yes, and since then we have been perfectly polite to each other."

" Well, then, my dear, as it has turned out, you have adopted a very good plan. It was a little hazardous to go so far at once ; but the result, of course, justifies you, and, I suppose, now you will lead a very comfortable life indeed. How does he seem about money matters ?"

" On that head I have nothing to complain. If anything he is what we may call foolishly easy on that point."

" It's a good fault."

" An admirable one. I do not think I shall have to spend any of my own allowance ; he seems always willing to disburse any amount for which he is asked, and, as he makes no question about its uses, he may as well pay for all my private expenses, and so save my own money."

" Precisely, my love ; you take a very proper view of this subject indeed, and I quite feel a pleasure in seeing how correctly you seem to understand these little matters of domestic management."

" I have had so able an instructress in yourself."

" Come, now, no flattery, my dear. You know I have always had your interest at heart, and have always, through good report and evil report, ridicule or praise, endeavoured to do the best I could for you."

" I know it."

" And now, all I require at your hands, since you have settled so comfortably and have so brilliant an establishment at your command, is to do what you can for your sisters."

" Certainly."

" If you see a chance with any really eligible man, you will, of course, do your best to fix him."

" Yes, of course ; you may depend upon that. The best way will be for one of them to stay with me one week and another the next, so that we shall soon find if any real chances occur. Should anything offer which looks advantageous, and is, upon inquiry, satisfactory, I will at once communicate with you, and some means can be adopted to prevent the animal from escaping the bait which we can prepare for him."

How great was the mother's pride to find her daughter had profited so much by the admirable bringing up she had had.

The Countess of Crumbledown was to the full as unscrupulous, and as tricky, and as heartless as the Marchioness of Fanfaronade ; indeed, she bade fair to exceed her mother in those amiable qualities. She had, if there was any difference sufficiently tangible to be spoken of, a quicker wit and greater downright assurance, so that, when the mother might have but partial success, the daughter was likely wholly to carry her point.

The marchioness could have shed tears of gratitude, so pleased did she feel at the prospect which presented itself now of getting off her other two daughters eligibly. She was fully aware of the immense advantages to a younger sister of having an elder one well married, and, like some old hen who has brought her brood of chicks in safety over the trials of earliest childhood, she looked forward to exciting the rancour of many a manœuvering mother whose arts and schemes had not been so fortunate.

As the Earl of Crumbledown had passed through the hall of his new house on his arrival, a note had been handed to him, which he opened and read as he walked upstairs to change his clothing.

See p. 71.

The contents were simply these few words,—
" Mr. Vullimay's respects to Lord Crumble-down, and he begs to state that all is well as regards he knows who, who is decidedly thriving, and concerning whose continued existence there can now be no doubt whatever. Nothing particularly amazing has occurred. Mr. Vullimay will wait upon his lordship at any time to render a closer account."

The reader understands well to what this note refers, and so, of course, did his lordship, who, when he had read it, at once thrust it into his pocket.

Now it so happened, that in changing that coat, he forgot to remove this note from its pocket, and that it remained subject to the prying curiosity of any one who might chance to find it.

Now certainly no one but his lordship's own valet had any right to interfere with his lordship's apparel, but as the marchioness had been in the new house in order to see that all was correct for some days, she had brought her new maid with her, and that unscrupulous personage took an opportunity of examining the earl's pockets when he had gone out, and in one of them, as a matter of course, she found the note from Mr. Vullimay.

It was immediately read by her with avidity, but melancholy to relate, she could make nothing of it.

" Well!" she exclaimed, " how very provoking, to be sure. I wonder who ' who' is, now? I'd give something to know."

Then, after some moments' consideration as to what was to be done with the note, she said,—

" I'll take it to the marchioness; she may be able to tell me what it means. I'll tell her I found it on the floor of the earl's dressing-room. I really now should like to know who ' who' is."

The new maid at once sought her mistress, who was with the Countess of Crumbledown; but that circumstance infused no delicacy into her mind, and she at once said,—

"Here is a note, my lady, I found on the floor."

"A note?"

"Yes, my lady, it's addressed to his lordship, the earl."

"Then what have we to do with it?" said the countess.

"Oh, my dear," remarked her mother, "we may as well see it. As a general rule, my dear, always get as much general information as you can about your husband. There is no knowing when it may turn out amazingly useful, you know, and a stray note or letter, should never be despised."

"I really care so little," said the countess, "about him, that I cannot bring myself to be interested."

The marchioness read the note twice, and then she said,—

"Well, I certainly cannot comprehend this. Read it, my dear, and see what you can make of it."

The countess read it listlessly, and then, as she returned it to her mother, she said in a voice of perfect indifference,—

"No, no—I don't understand it."

"What can it mean? All is right as regards he knows who."

"Yes, my lady," said the maid, "it's very clear to me."

"Is it?"

"Oh, dear, yes, my lady. Of course he knows who is some—a-hem! a female, my lady—a-hem!"

"Likely enough," said the countess, "but it's really of no consequence."

"Certainly, my love," said the marchioness; "it is not of any consequence what intrigues a man has, so long as he keeps them quiet and respectable; but still, as a matter of necessity, it's always as well for his wife to know something about them."

"Ah! to be sure—to be sure. There may be something in that."

"There is more in that, my dear, than you imagine, I can assure you. The more you know of these sort of matters, which your husband, of course, would fain keep from your knowledge, the more power you have over him, in case of any little disputation going on. You understand me?"

"I think I do."

"Very good. Then, for your sake, my dear, I must say I should very much like to know who is the 'who' in this note."

"But what possible means is there of discovering?"

"Why, dear, it certainly is not very probable the earl would tell you if you were to ask him, nor, under all existing circumstances, would you like to ask him; but still something may be done. I should advise that you return him the note, and watch his countenance to see how he looks when you do so. He may, if it is of no consequence, volunteer an explanation; but if it is an intrigue, you will be able to gather as much by the confusion of his looks."

"It shall be done."

"You found the letter on the floor, Maria?"

"Oh, dear, yes, my lady, close to the pocket of the coat which the earl had just taken off, my lady."

"Oh, indeed! You mean, Maria, that you found it in the pocket?"

"In the pocket? lor, my lady, how could you think that I could feel in the pockets of the earl, my lady?"

"It is of no consequence, as it happens, Maria, but this is a kind of thing which might have been dangerous to you."

While this colloquy was going on at the earl's new house, he had made his way to his friend Colonel Bruce's, and finding that gentleman at home, they, over a bottle of wine, entered into that sort of confidential chit-chat which ensues between persons who are quite sure they can thoroughly trust each other—a very rare state of things, by-the-bye, although frequently believed to exist when such is not the case.

"Of course I received your most lugubrious letter," said Bruce, "and had a good laugh over it."

" A laugh ?"

" Yes, my boy; you did not surely expect me to weep over your matrimonial miseries ?"

" No ; but still I cannot see what there was to laugh at."

" Oh ! everything ; and shortly you will laugh likewise, to think how you could have been so foolish as to make miseries of such matters. Why, my dear fellow, I would marry to-morrow, if I could manage as well as you have."

" Indeed !"

" Ay, indeed !"

" Bruce, I have heard you hold a different line of argument."

" Yes, years ago, when I was a young, green stripling, but I have met with a few misadventures in life that have taught me better things now. I am sure that the philosophy of indifference is the only true and practical one."

" And you think that a road to happiness ?"

" A road to what ?"

" Happiness."

" My dear Crumbledown, expunge the word from your vocabulary, if you please. Like Macbeth's airy dagger, you will find that there's no such thing as happiness. I perceive you have not got far enough in the philosophy of human life, to know what to base your best interests upon."

" Pray explain."

" Yes, short and simple. You go about in the vain hunt for happiness, and there's your grand mistake."

" Mistake ?"

" Yes, mistake. Listen—there's no such thing as durable happiness. There may be for a moment a gushing feeling of joy in the heart at some circumstance that affords us more than common satisfaction, and which for a few seconds of time overpowers reflection ; but how soon, how very soon it fades away."

" That's true enough."

" And then you soon discover that it is not without its alloy. You may depend that happiness or pleasure, call it what you will, so that you express the feeling, is a negative state of things, which pain and misery are positive."

" You think so ?"

" I know so. When we feel highly gratified at anything, it is only because it happens to be peculiarly divested of disagreeables. It is nothing in itself which we call happiness, my dear fellow. The grand thing is, to be in such a state of mind, if possible, about anything and everybody, that let what will happen, one don't care a straw. That is philosophy."

" And would you break up all those tender ties that bind society together ? Would you deprive life of all its sympathies and best feelings ?"

" Tender fiddlesticks! . What nonsense you do talk, Crumbledown. The more interest you have in anything, or in anybody, of course the more you multiply your chances of discomfort. Say that there is one person in the world to whom you are warmly attached ; the consequence is, that your happiness and heart's ease are not only at the mercy of what may happen to yourself, but likewise at the mercy of what may happen to that person."

" Yes, but ——'

" No, no. The subject admits, I assure you, of no contradiction, and so, to come round to where we started, I say you have made a fortunate marriage, because you really don't care one straw about your wife."

" Well, that's an odd conclusion."

" It may sound like one, but you will find it amazingly true. When you are from home now, what anxieties have you ? None whatever. So long as you can say to yourself, the Earl of Crumbledown feels tolerably comfortable, you are all right ; and what a blessed state of mind, now, is that to be in. Here you have all the advantages of matrimony in the stakes it gives to a man in society, with the same feeling of freedom as if you had never slipped your neck into the noose."

" When you say that I can tell myself as long as the Earl of Crumbledown is well, I need care for nothing, you forget that I have a pledge of affection from one concerning whom, certainly, all anxiety is now at rest, but who has left in my heart a remembrance which will never be effaced."

" You allude to your intrigue with the attorney's daughter?"

" I do."

" Does the child live?"

" It does. I have a note here from Vullimay, my solicitor, to the effect that it not only lives, but is likely to live, and to do well. I had the note here somewhere, but I cannot find it; I hope I have not dropped it at home."

"You should be careful of those matters."

" Oh, there were no names in it. It was a most careful and diplomatic note as ever was penned; and now, I recollect, it is in the pocket of my other coat, which I came to town in, and changed previously to coming here; so it is all right."

" It is better to destroy at once all such little memoranda, Crumbledown; you don't know what the curiosity of women might prompt them to undertake, if such a document was found."

" I will be careful for the future; but the note is quite harmless; and now, Bruce, what would you seriously advise me to do as regards this love child?'

" Let it be where it is."

" It is a gossiping country village; and I cannot make my appearance there, I suspect, without being known immediately, and made a complete show of as the wonderful and celebrated father of the child who was born at the inn, and who is to be seen, all alive, for the small charge of nothing at all."

" Upon my word," laughed Bruce, " you seem to have a full appreciation of some of the pleasantries of your situation. How long were you there?"

"Some hours."

" And with persons all the time who were likely to recognise you?"

" Certainly not. I was in a style of dress purposely adapted for concealment, and I did not then, as I have, and do now, wear moustaches. I have several times had doubts with regard to whether I should be recognised again or not; but yet I fear to make the trial."

" That should not I."

" You would not?"

" Certainly not. There is every probability of your not being recognised, you may depend. You go at night to a country inn, as plain Mr. John Smith, and considerably disguised, both purposely; and, no doubt, by the state of agitation you were in, and you are seen by a few people, who, as the Earl of Crumbledown, never could have the least suspicion that you were one and the same person."

" If I were sure ——"

" Sure you cannot be till you try."

" Yes; but the danger!"

" You can try without proclaiming who you are, and if you find yourself at once recognised as John Smith, you need not say who you are, but you can leave at once."

" True; I might do that, certainly."

" Of course you might; and I will go with you, if you like. You know that my cousin, Lord Blenketh, has a country seat close to that very village you named to me as the one where, in consequence of the increasing illness of Emily Whitford, on that eventful evening of her death, you were compelled to stop."

" Yes, I am aware of that fact."

At this moment there was a tap at the library door, in which this conference was going on.

" Come in," said Colonel Bruce; and a servant appeared with a letter upon an elegant silver salver, which he respectfully handed to the colonel, who laid the letter on the table before him.

" Use no ceremony with me, Bruce," said the Earl of Crumbledown. " That letter, may be, contains something that demands your immediate attention."

" No, no; I see by the seal it is from my cousin, Lord Blenketh, and, no doubt, would keep. However, if you will excuse me for being so rude, I will just glance at its contents."

"Oh, certainly."

Colonel Bruce opened the letter, and after a minute's perusal of it, he said, aloud,—

"Well, this is singular enough. Read it, Crumbledown—read it."

He threw the letter across the table to the earl, who read as follows:—

"My dear Bruce,—I wish you to do me the favour of ascertaining for me where letters can be addressed to the Earl of Crumbledown, in London.

"I understand, from the public papers, that he is expected in town immediately from the continent; and I wish to tender him an invite to come with you and his lady to spend some time at Elm Wood. Pray find this out for me, and I will send him an invitation in due form. I remember him very well at college as a very decent man.   "Yours, faithfully,

"To Colonel Bruce.   "BLENKETH."

"What say you to that?" inquired Colonel Bruce, when Lord Crumbledown had finished reading this letter.

"Why, that it comes oddly and opportunely."

"Certainly it does. Will you empower me to write to Blenketh, saying that I have seen you, and that you accept his invitation."

"By all means, as far as I am concerned. But, you see, he mentions the countess there, and, of course, I cannot answer for her ladyship."

"Humph! I suppose her dignity will stand upon a formal invitation from Lady Blenketh. Well, well, I will manage that by writing to my cousin. It is, you see, quite impossible for you to go without her, and so recently married as you are, too."

"I suppose it would create gossip?"

"Of course it would, and that to a very tolerable extent too. 'What would the world say?' as the man in the play remarks."

"Very good; I shall leave it all in your hands; and I do hope that I shall be able to visit the child of Emily Whitford without the disagreeable adjunct of being by any one recognised as its father."

The earl had promised to be home in time for dinner, and as it now wanted but an hour to that period of the day, and as he had to dress, he rose to go, saying, as he did so,—

"Then we quite understand all about Lord Blenketh's invitation. I, of course, accept it, and you will write to Lady Blenketh, saying where Lady Crumbledown can be written to."

"Precisely—precisely. Adieu."

"Adieu—adieu."

CHAPTER XXII.

JONATHAN WILLOUGHBY VISITS THE EARL OF CRUMBLEDOWN, AND MAKES TERMS WITH HIM.

THE distance was so short from Colonel Bruce's house to the new and splendid mansion which the Marchioness of Fanfaronade had had fitted up so tastefully for the Earl and Countess of Crumbledown, that the earl had walked in preference to ordering the carriage.

It took him not above ten minutes to return, and when he reached the doorstep of his own house, it wanted more than half an hour yet to dinner time, so that he was just congratulating himself that he had ample time to dress, when the hall porter said, respectfully,—

"My lord, the gentleman your lordship was to see is in the waiting-room to the left."

"The gentleman I wanted to see?"

" Yes, my lord."

" What gentleman ?"

" Mr. Jonathan Willoughby, my lord."

The earl was so taken by surprise at the impudence of Willoughby in calling upon him, that for a moment or two he was silent. When he did speak, he smothered his anger as well as he could, and said,—

" Upon what pretence did he affect that I wanted to see him ?"

" He produced your lordship's card with an appointment written upon it. I hope, my lord, we have not done wrong ?"

" Never mind—never mind. What room do you say ?"

" This way, your lordship," said a footman, who opened a door to the right of the hall, and ushered his master into a handsome apartment, which was substantially furnished as a best waiting-room.

And there, sure enough, was Jonathan Willoughby with his back against a table and a chair before him, on the back of which he rested his hands. Probably he thought he might as well be prepared in case the Earl of Crumbledown should meditate a renewal of the attack he had made upon him in May Fair, and in such a case to be behind a tolerably heavy chair was an uncommonly safe and eligible position.

There was on Willoughby's countenance that expression of insolent assurance which is commonly assumed by such men when they know they are engaged in a transaction which can only be carried through by an amount of impudence such as few possess. He looked as if he would have said,—

" Say what you will, do what you will, I am not to be got rid of but on my own terms."

The Earl of Crumbledown was not a man of the most decided character in the world, and he wanted that precision of intellect which enables some men to make on the spur of the moment, the very best resolve that the circumstances in which they are suddenly thrown admit of.

When he came into the room where was Jonathan Willoughby, he had no fixed resolve or notion of what he intended to do. He was only angry, and felt that the presence of Willoughby was a most audacious intrusion.

Before, however, he could utter one world, Willoughby spoke, and he spoke so firmly and so clearly, that the earl almost unconsciously paused to hear what it was he had to utter with so much confidence.

" My lord," said Willoughby, " when last we met, I committed a very great error, for which, in the first place, I beg your lordship's pardon. I got angry, and in my anger I took a step which my calmer judgment by no means justified. The quietness of my conduct for the last two months ought to convince your lordship that there is no vindictive feeling on my part. I have not only myself been quiet and passive, and allowed your lordship to spend your honeymoon in peace, but by my personal influence I have kept others quiet, when I could have raised a storm about you with which the press, and society at large, would have rung again ; and which would have reached you, let you be as far off as you possibly could. Your lordship feels that you have been let alone. You have heard nothing to discompose you. Not a breath of scandal has assailed your name. I repeat, you have been let alone, and it is through me and my exertions, that such has been the case."

There was ample truth enough to make some impression upon the Earl of Crumbledown. Moreover, it was spoken extremely well. He felt more vexed, but not quite so angry as he had been ; and now that Willoughby paused after this speech, which of course was a mere exordium to something else, the earl said, rather in an impatient than an angry tone,—

" Well—well—well, what is to be the end of all this ?"

" The end, my lord," said Willoughby, " may be gathered from the commencement. Your lordship may well believe, from the two months of peace which you have had, that I have the power to stop even the tongue of rumour, and absolve you from the disagreeable consequences which publicity, as regards your intrigue with Emily Whitford, would be sure to entail upon you."

" Go on, go on."

" That point, then, being settled, the future is entirely and completely in your own hands, to order as you please."

" How do you mean ?—What do you mean ?"

" I mean, that for a consideration, I am your lordship's very humble servant, to command, and will, as I have hitherto done, persevere in shielding your lordship from the unpleasant exposure which otherwise must ensue, and which I, and I only, have the power to avert."

" In plain words, then," said the earl, " you want to be paid for keeping secret the little affair concerning Emily Whitford."

" Your lordship is as good as a conjurer," said Willoughby.

" And don't it strike you that this is a very rascally proceeding, Mr. Jonathan Willoughby ?"

" It does ; but if your lordship had not given it that name, I should not have liked to take so great a liberty. It is a rascally affair."

" And yet you have the impertinence to carry it on."

" Nay, it is your lordship's impertinence as well as rascality. It is a rascally affair to seduce a young and innocent girl, as you say ; and my impertinence, measured by your lordship's, sinks into utter insignificance."

Lord Crumbledown bit his lips, for he found himself very far indeed from being a match to Jonathan Willoughby in an encounter of wits. He was fairly caught in his own snare, and he could not help feeling a sort of consciousness that any speeches concerning honour or morality must come with an extremely ill grace from such lips as his.

He paced the room twice in silence, and then, suddenly turning upon Willoughby, he said,—

" This is all folly ; you want to be paid for keeping the affair quiet, now it don't matter much to me whether it is known or not. These things are a few days' talk, a little lampooning in the Sunday papers, and then they die a natural death ; so, as I say, I don't care much about it ; but still I have a choice, and of the two, I should prefer that it was not known."

" Precisely, my lord."

" But mark me, I will not be teased by you continually. This must be our first and our last transaction."

" As your lordship pleases."

" What do you demand ?"

" My lord, I had a situation in the law, which, since this affair, I have been compelled to give up."

" Why so ?"

" Because my feelings had received so severe a shock, in consequence of the seduction of my niece, that I found myself unequal to the duties of my profession, and therefore was in honour bound to resign."

" You will oblige me by avoiding the hypocrisy of using the words honour and feelings, if you please," said the earl ; " I presume that a natural love of idleness induced you to give up your situation if you ever had one, when you fancied anything was to be wrung from me."

" No, no ; that is taking a very artificial view of my heart ; but we will let that pass ; I cannot expect fine feeling from your lordship. For now three months I have earned nothing, and that has been all on your lordship's account. Let me see, four times four are sixteen, and three times sixteen are forty-eight ; we will say fifty, for the sake of simplicity in numbers ; that makes the back debt fifty pounds."

" What do you mean ?"

" I had hoped it was plain to the meanest capacity, my lord ; I have lost fifty pounds by being out of employment for three months, and that is what I call the back debt, and which I have no doubt your lordship will discharge at once, before we proceed to business."

This was an amount of impudence that was enough to stagger anybody. It would almost seem, but that he looked so grave and serious, that Willoughby must have uttered such a speech as a kind of experiment, to see how far his lordship's fears of exposure would carry him.

Lord Crumbledown looked at Willoughby for some moments in silence, and then in a voice which he strove to make calm, he said,—

"If you do not leave this house immediately, I will order my servants to turn you out, without much regard to your personal convenience in the process."

"You may certainly legally turn any one out of your house you please," said Willoughby, "always provided no more violence is used than is necessary; but if you do turn me out, I will at once communicate the name of the seducer of his daughter to Mr. Whitford, and you will to-morrow be called upon to defend yourself, in an action at law, for damages. The mere costs of both sides, all of which you will have to pay, will come to much more than any demands of mine; I, therefore, as a man capable of knowing that two and two make four, put it to your sober judgment, whether it is not far better to purchase immunity than to pay a much higher price for exposure?"

The earl's exasperation softened down again. There was no gainsaying the words of Jonathan Willoughby. He had all the argument completely on his side, if his lordship of Crumbledown had all the passion.

"How much do you want," said the earl, "to free me for ever from your presence, and the consequences of the—the ———"

"Seduction ———"

"Well, well, the seduction."

"Two hundred pounds."

"Monstrous!"

"Very good; I have the honour to bid your lordship good day."

"Stay a moment. What security have I that, if I pay you so much money, I shall be secure?"

"The security of the experience of the past. What has saved you hitherto but my will that you should be unmolested?"

"Hark you. You shall have the money, but if you play me false, I shall, perhaps, be able, by a liberal expenditure in some other quarter, to make you repent deceiving me. Wait here, and I will bring you a check for the two hundred."

"Am I to have the fifty, then, in cash?"

"The what?"

"The fifty, back debt."

"Why, you include that."

"I beg your lordship's pardon, I did no such thing. The two hundred is quite a different transaction, I assure you. You can draw a check for two hundred and fifty while you are about it."

The earl cast a withering glance at him, and then hurriedly left the room, feeling that he had no resource but to comply with the fellow's conditions; unless, indeed, he chose to risk all the uncomfortable consequences of a disclosure of his intrigue.

When he was alone, Willoughby folded his arms, and looked composedly around the splendid apartment in which he was. To him it was splendid, although it was, in comparison to many of the rooms of that mansion, but a very plain and poor affair indeed.

"Humph!" he said; "I rather think I have managed this little affair amazingly well. Not a bad morning's work this, I take it. I feel decidedly on most uncommonly good terms with myself."

Jonathan Willoughby walked up to a large looking-glass, and looked at himself, then he nodded his head, as if he would have said,—

"Jonathan Willoughby, you are an uncommonly clever fellow, that's what you are, and no mistake in the world."

He was not, however, left long to congratulate himself thus upon the way in which he was turning to account the distresses of his family connexions, for the earl was to the full as anxious to get rid of him as he could be to finger the cash which was to be the reward of his silence.

Crumbledown walked hastily into the room with the check in his hand, and laying it before Willoughby, he said,—

" Now, sir, I believe our transactions together are at an end completely, and we are clear from the necessity of any further communication of any kind or description whatever."

" Most certainly, my lord."

See page 87.

" There is the door, then, sir."

" I can see it plainly.   It is a large handsome door, which is not at all likely to escape observation."

" Good day, sir."

" I have the honour to bid your lordship good day."

With a swaggering air Jonathan Willoughby left the room, and going through the hall with an air as if the whole place belonged to him, he left the earl's house.

"The scoundrel!" muttered the earl; "to think now that I should be open to the demands of such a man!—An infernal villain!—Hang him!—And yet the affair is well over."

He hastily glanced at his watch. It was only one minute to the hour of dinner.

"No time to dress," he said. "I must dine as I am, and let the countess and, I presume, the marchioness, who, doubtless, dines with us to-day, and every other day, for all I know, stomach how they may the breach of etiquette of dining in boots and a frock-coat."

He then made his way to the dining-room, and it did not require the skill of a conjurer to see that his lordship was considerably chafed and out of humour.

There was nobody there, however, who cared whether he was out of humour or not, so nobody thought it worth while to ask him what it was about.

The only remark that was made concerning his appearance, came from the lips of the marchioness, who said to the Countess of Crumbledown across the table,—

"My dear, do not men dress for dinner now?"

"I really cannot say," replied the countess. "I never trouble myself to look."

The dinner passed off uncomfortably to the earl. To be sure he was studiously polite to the ladies, but he was none the more pleasant-minded really on that account.

When the ladies retired, and he was left alone, for being the first day of the arrival from the continent, there were no gentleman visitors, the earl uttered between his clenched teeth a fervent,—

"Thank God!"

The fact was, that whatever amount of ill-will—and it was tolerably considerable—he was likely to have against his wife, he cordially and distinctly hated his mother-in-law, the marchioness.

To her he attributed (and the reader happens to know how right he was) all the chicanery by which he had been induced to marry one whom he never had esteemed when he knew her least, and who, now that he knew her intimately, he had neither respect nor affection for; consequently he hated the marchioness, and if there was any one thing concerning which he, the earl, was likely to make a vigorous stand, it was as regarded the perpetual presence of his mother-in-law in the house.

After what the mansion in Hanover-square had cost, he did not like the idea of being turned out of it, which must have been the case had he still persevered in his intention of having separate establishments, and if he continued to inhabit that house, he felt that the continual presence of the marchioness would to him be a bore of the first magnitude.

But as yet he could not very well say anything about it, because he had only the experience of one day, and he could not from that possibly take upon himself to say that the intended being there always.

As, however, he sipped his claret, he made a mental determination, that if she remained over a week, there should be what is vulgarly called a row.

And yet what matter could it make to him? None in the least. If half-a-dozen disagreeable, prying, intriguing, odious old women were in the house, he had plenty of means of getting out of their way. But then he was querulous, and had been much annoyed just then, so he did not take a very correct view of anything at all.

Little did he suspect that his house, and his name, and his standing in society, were all to be used as a means of pushing off the remaining daughters of the Marchioness of Fanfaronade. Alas! when he thought of Julia, who for a moment had fixed his attention on that eventful night of the rout in May Fair, what a pang would cross his heart, and how fervently, more than once, he exclaimed,—

"Ah! I should have been happy with her!"

And this is ever the way,—

"Man never is, but always to be blessed."

We, under all circumstances, can always fancy something which would have completed our happiness. To be sure Julia Fanfaronade was a very different sort of person from her sister, Annabella, and with her the dream of romance with which, like most other young men, Lord Crumbledown started life, might have been to a certain extent realized. But it so happened that at the very moment she, Julia, was beginning to awaken in his heart a tender interest, those circumstances were occurring, which with such fearful rapidity changed the whole current of his existence.

He had seen her at the marriage, and he had fancied she was paler than of yore; but since then he had not looked upon her face. He knew not if the lily had usurped the rose on her cheeks. He knew not if she had felt in the slightest the pang of blighted hope.

He was married to her sister, and never more dared he insult her by look or word savouring of affection of a warmer character than that which a brother might feel for a sister. Henceforward she was to him nothing, and if he had, by the few words he had spoken to her on the evening of the rout, awakened any feeling akin to love for him within her breast, she was now compelled by virtue, pride, and honour, to stifle them for ever.

But what must she think of him now? What opinion would she have of the man who had evidently admired her more than he had admired her elder sister, and then married her elder sister because she was left a large legacy?

" Does she despise me ?" asked Lord Crumbledown. " Does she despise me ? She cannot do so more than I despise myself for stooping to this golden divinity. Oh! that I had had courage to let Annabella take the money, and to go myself, as I might have done, with all the eclat of such an act around my name, into public diplomatic life; but I was foolish, and I am now reaping the fruits of my folly."

The reader must not omit to remember that Lord Crumbledown was dipping deep into a bottle of claret while he thus spoke, and by the time he had seen to the bottom of the second bottle, he became rather sentimental about his situation and prospects, and could almost have shed tears over what he considered his melancholy condition.

Hear this, ye sons of labour and misfortune ! Here was a man with an income of five-and-twenty thousand a year, almost ready to cry, he was so miserable.

Who shall say that happiness in this world is not pretty equally meted out to the poor as to the rich ? All stations in life have their own peculiar anxieties, and the only circumstance that induces one class to envy another is, that they cannot know the peculiar miseries of those whose mode of life they are not accustomed to.

The Earl of Crumbledown went into his library at last, and then seating himself in a capacious easy chair, he soon fell fast asleep, and forgot all his miseries.

CHAPTER XXIII.

JACK GROVE'S DETERMINATION, AND JOURNEY TO LONDON.—THE SUBSCRIPTION
IN THE VILLAGE, AND ITS RESULTS.—THE PORKMAN.

BUT what is our drunken friend, Jack Grove, doing all this time? Has he turned a teetotaller, or has the seeming and supernatural being who attacked him afforded him the means of becoming more drunken, or frightened him into the fact of being more temperate?

We shall see. After the drubbing he got, and which certainly seemed to him to come from fists that had sufficient material about them to do away completely with all impression that they were in any way of a ghostly character, he felt for a time uncommonly uncomfortable and serious.

He requested, with all possible humility, of his wife, that she should allow him to come into the cottage, and sleep in peace. He made, too, a great number of promises of amendment for the future, and if he could have been trusted to perform one half of what he promised, we might safely say that Father Mathew would have travelled at any time a long day's journey only to look upon his face, and to hang, with his own hands, a medal round the neck of such a disciple.

A promise from Jack Grove of sobriety was something, so Mrs. Grove at once extended the hand of forgiveness to him, and permitted him to come into the cottage.

"Lor!" said Jack, "what a fool I am, to be sure! There isn't, though I say it, a nicer cottage in the whole village, or a more comfortable fire-side than this, and yet what a wretch I am! What a dreadful wretch I am to be sure!"

Mrs. Grove had by far too much regard for the truth to contradict him, and as he would have it that he was a wretch, she let him be without saying one word to the contrary.

"Ah!" he added, "it's astonishing the effects of drink! The more you drink the more thirsty you get."

"Ah!" said his wife, "I am sure of that."

"Yes—yes, and now—come, now, a draught of ale."

"What? Ale after all your promises of amendment!"

"Well, but who now do you suppose is the soberest man in the village, wife?"

"Anthony Grove."

"Very good, very good. Do you mean now to tell me that Anthony Grove don't take his glass of ale?"

"Yes, he takes his glass of ale; but nobody never thought of objecting to a glass of ale in moderation."

"Very good, very good. That's just what I want now; a glass of ale in moderation. D—n me if I care what I have it in as long as I do have it."

"Ah!" said his wife, with a sigh, "I thought how long your temperance would last, John."

"Did you?"

"I did indeed. Now, I tell you what, I shall have some hopes of you if now instead of ale you will have a nice cool glass of pump-water."

"Pump what?"

"Pump-water."

"Oh! you mean with a quartern of brandy in it?"

"No, indeed I don't. I mean the water, and the water only. Now, Jack, take your choice; you shall have the water, and something tasty for supper, or you may leave the place."

"Well, I'm sure; when a woman is wilful I suppose she must have her way. Now, wife, to convince you that I do intend to reform, I will have the pump-water."

Tears of joy started to the eyes of Mrs. Grove as she said,—

"Will you indeed, Jack!"

"Yes, I will."

"Then I really shall have some faith in you."

"And will you tell me then all about the child you have got to nurse?"

"I will, John, I will, since you promise me that you will be sober and happy, as I am sure you may be, if you like."

It was a piece of desperate duplicity on the part of Jack Grove about taking the pump-water. The fact was he felt extremely anxious to know all about the child from his wife, upon whose account he knew he could rely, and he was well aware that unless he exhibited some symptoms of amendment from his drunken habits, he was not very likely to procure from her such information at all.

It was certainly a serious sacrifice for a man like unto Jack Grove, to drink pump-water, but there was a great object in view, and for that he was for once in a way willing to make so stupendous a sacrifice.

And Mrs. Grove was as good as her word. She did get a jug of pure, cold, beautiful pump-water for Jack, who took the same with about as much relish as he would have done upon taking as much salts and senna, or castor oil.

" Well, Jack, you have indeed taken some," said his wife, " and by the time I see you are determined thoroughly to persevere, I shall keep no secrets from you."

" But I have persevered."

" Oh, no."

" But I say, oh yes. D—n it, I have drank a good half pint of it, and if that is not persevering I'll be hanged if I know what is."

" When I see, John, by a month's experience, that you really mean to be temperate, I shall have great hopes of you, and not only shall you know exactly the amount of what I get for nursing the child, but you shall never be without a shilling for any reasonable purpose."

" D—n it!" said Jack, rising in a great passion, " and have I actually drank half a pint of pump water for nothing? You said you would tell me all."

" And so I will, if you persevere."

" Persevere, and be d—d. It would put me in my grave in a week, and perhaps that's what you would like."

" John, I would rather see you in your coffin than as I once saw you."

" How the devil was that?"

" In the kennel, drunk, and all the ragged boys of the village laughing at you, while you were too insensible even to know what a sad subject of ridicule you were."

" How devilish kind."

" It is kind; although I do not, and cannot expect that you should as such now recognise it. Do you imagine that in the long and sad experience I have had of your intemperance, I do not know well how far to trust you? Alas! too well, too well, John Grove. We were once comfortable in our home, and very happy—by far too happy to last. I feared always that some misfortune was impending over me."

" The deuce you did."

" Yes; and it came. For the first time one day I saw you in a state of intoxication, and then I foresaw all that was about to happen, then I foresaw the misery we should have to wade through, and I understood then the whole warning which the depression of my heart had given me."

" Psha! stuff!"

" John, you cannot now deny that such was the fact. It is out of your power to deny it. I made inquiry, and I ascertained that that was not the first time by many that you had reduced yourself to such a brutalised condition."

" I tell you what it is, wife," cried Jack Grove, " if I want any preaching I can go to church, but d—n me if I have it at home."

" I am not preaching, John. Oh! would that I had the power of preaching you to temperance, I would not then cease until I had accomplished that great object. My words, now, are merely those of lamentation."

" Lament for yourself; I don't want anybody to lament for me."

" Indeed, and in truth, I do lament for myself, John. Can you look me in the face now, and deny that duplicity was in your heart when you drank the water?"

" Duplicity?"

" Yes, John. You wished to deceive me by a show of amendment, in order that you might get from me the full particulars concerning this sweet babe, and then upon these particulars you hoped to have founded some course of conduct that would have tended towards supplying you with the further means of intoxication."

" That's your opinion, is it?"

" Yes, and your's too, John. Can you say it was not so?"

" Yes, I can."

" Oh, no; oh, no. Your eyes are on the ground as you speak; you have not yet sufficient confidence in evil to look me in the face, John, while you utter that which is untrue."

" Yes I have, though."

"No, no. God help me, and you too. I never thought that it would come to this, John."

"Come to what, and be hanged? Here's a nice reception to meet with when one comes home. A jug of pump water, a sermon, and some snivelling at the end of it. Upon my soul, this is a very inviting sort of cottage; I wonder I don't come to it oftener, really."

"Better for those who inhabit it, John, that you never came to it at all, unless you came an altered man."

"Oh, I have no doubt of that," said Jack. "You would like to wear a widow's cap, I have no doubt, but I am tough enough yet to last a considerable time longer, I can tell you; you won't get rid of me half so easy as you think."

Mrs. Grove sat down, and covering her face with her hands she wept bitterly in the affliction of her heart.

"Where's the boy?" suddenly exclaimed Jack Grove. "Where's the boy? D—e, what have you done with our own boy? Have you smothered him, to make room for this new brat of somebody else's?"

"He is at a neighbour's cottage for a night or two."

"Oh! you are afraid he should disturb this one, and so you have turned him out, have you?"

"No, no. I am forced to pay so much attention during the night to this motherless infant that I feared to disturb little Harry, and that is the reason why he sleeps at a kind neighbour's."

"Gammon!"

"As you please; as you please."

"Oh, it's as I please now, is it? Well, then, fetch a pot of ale."

"No, no, not here; not here."

"Then I'm off; and mind you, I know pretty well all about this affair of the brat you have to nurse, and that you have money, if you don't give me some of it I'll do something, perhaps, to make you."

"You are mistaken, John; you are mistaken. I will tell you this much, in order that you may see how futile it will be of you to make any endeavours of that sort: Mr. Pott supplies me with just enough money at a time to provide me with necessaries for myself and the child. If from him you can get more, you are welcome."

"Mr. Pott, eh? D—n Mr. Pott; what has he to do with it? What need he meddle with my affairs?"

"Your affairs, John?"

"Yes, to be sure. Who told him to put his finger in the pie? Some money, I know, has been left for the keep of that child, and what business has he with it? it ought to be in your possession."

"But not in yours; and so, fearing that by force or fraud you would possess yourself of it, I requested Mr. Pott to take charge of it, and dole it out to me in such small sums as I required."

"How much was it?"

"Fifty pounds."

"Fifty pounds! why, dame, it's a fortune! Fifty! Lord bless me! fifty pounds, and I ought to have had it. What's a man's wife's is a man's. I'll see if there ain't some law in the land, to get the money out of his clutches. A likely thing, indeed, that I am to be deprived of what's my own."

"How can you call it yours? You left me and our child here to starve for all you knew, or all you cared. I was getting even victuals from the charity of the neighbours, whose sympathies were awakened by a knowledge of the fact of how I had been treated by you; then a stranger offers me a child to nurse, and I gladly accept the trust, for the sake of a subsistence. What, then, can you have to do with the matter?"

"Oh, argufy away, it won't answer; argue me out of my seven senses if you can. When once a woman begins argufying there's no such thing as stopping her, I know that. Give me what money you have."

" Give you ——"

" Yes. Come, out with it."

" I will not."

" You will not ?"

" It belongs to this sleeping babe, and again I say, I will not. Go to Mr. Pott, and see what answer you will get from him."

" D—n Mr. Pott ! If you don't give me freely what you have, I'll take it by force, I tell you ; I am the stronger of the two, so look out."

" Beware !" said his wife, solemnly. " Beware ! already have you been interrupted in violent intentions by one who may or may not be mortal ; for all I know, without the cottage door even now there may be some one ready, as before, to interrupt you."

Jack Grove shrank back, for he had, in the anger of the moment, forgotten the mysterious stranger who had made so strange a proposal to him, and then given him such a drubbing, apparently because he would not consent to it. He spoke in a lower tone, and one which betrayed that his fears were excited.

" What do you mean ? You didn't suppose I was going to strike you."

" What has happened may again happen," said his wife.

" Stuff ! I'm off. I sha'n't stay here ; what you won't tell me I must learn from others, that's all. You'd better have told me all about it, and then you'd have been sure I knew the truth ; but you can't tell what others have told me, or may tell me. I'm off. You'll see me to-morrow, I dare say, and so shall that Mr. Pott, who makes himself so infernally busy about other people's affairs. He shall find Jack Grove an ugly customer, and perhaps he'll be glad to get rid of the responsibility of having other people's money in his hands. We shall see ; we shall see."

His wife made no reply. She was intently occupied in hushing off the infant to sleep, for it had been disturbed by the last words of Jack Grove, which were uttered in a loud tone. When he found that she was not disposed to answer him, and continue the disputatious conference, he opened the door of the cottage, and, with a bitter oath upon his lips, dashed out.

Jack Grove had not the clearest idea in the world as to what he meant to do. All he had made up his mind to, was that indefinite resolution which is comprehended in a determination to do something, and that that something should be of a violent character.

He bethought him, after a time, of a man who lived on the outskirts of the village, and who was always ready to give any information to anybody which would suffice to set people by the ears, and towards his cottage, or rather hut, for it was little better, Jack bent his steps.

This man's name was Cliff, and he got a living ostensibly by catching moles ; but there never was any doubt in anybody's mind but that he combined with that genteel, but not over remunerative employment a little practcie in snaring hares, &c. In fact, Cliff might have been, with great justice, called Ned Cliff, the poacher, instead of Ned Cliff, the mole-catcher.

To this worthy, who was as cunning as any three cunning fellows rolled into one, Jack Grove went, and after calling lustily for some time outside his house, for other means of making himself heard there were not, a small window was opened, and Ned Cliff popped out his head, with the interrogatory of,—

" What now ?"

" I want to speak to you."

" What about ?"

" About the money that was given to my wife."

" Oh—oh ! and the child. Yes, to be sure. Oh, come in."

" What, in at the window ?"

" No, stupid. Wait a moment, will you ?"

Ned Cliff soon opened the door of his hut, and invited Jack to enter, who did so with great willingness, for he had a tolerable notion that there might result something to drink from the visit.

Very briefly Ned Cliff informed Jack of all that occurred at the inn on the occasion of the birth of the child, and although Jack found that it tallied tolerably well with what he already knew, Ned Cliff told him more particulars than he had as yet heard, and assured him of the fact of the fifty pounds having been left.

" And how am I to get the money ?" was Jack's response.

" No how," was the brief reply.

" Humph ! that's a comfort."

" Glad you think so."

" Come, Ned, no nonsense. What would you do, now, if you was me ?"

" Get as much money as I could."

" But how can I get it from Mr. Pott ?   You know him as well as I do; if he he says he won't part with it, why, you know, he won't, and there's an end of it."

" I didn't say get it of Pott."

" Who from, then ?"

" The father of the love child."

Jack looked in his face for some moments in silence, and then he said,—

" D—n me, if I know who is its father, or if it ever had one."

" No.   At present I dare say you don't, but your place will be to try and find out.   Now, my suspicion of this affair is just this—the father of that child is some worthy man, perhaps a man of high rank, and he thinks he has managed the whole affair as snug as possible ; but, if I were in your place, I would go to London, and I'd find him out, if I turned over every paving-stone in the city to do so."

" You would ?"

" I would, most certainly.   He is a tall young man, with a brilliant set of teeth. I saw him, and looked keenly at him.   You will find him, it's my impression, among some of the highest."

" But it's rather a queer thing to go to London in search of a man you know no more of, than that he is tall, and has a good set of teeth."

" It would ; but I can give you a letter of introduction to a friend of mine, who may be able to assist you."

" Ah ! then, indeed, I may have a chance ; only there's another little difficulty in the way."

" What may that be ?"

" I have no money."

" Well, that is awkward ; but I tell you what you must do.   The whole population of the village, you know, would be uncommonly glad to get rid of you."

" Well."

" Then raise a subscription among them, on the promise that you will be off for London, and never come down here any more.   I will subscribe a shilling to begin with.   Here goes."

Ned Cliff wrote on the top of a slip of paper :—

	£.	s.	d.
Edward Cliff, with a firm conviction that when Jack Grove gets to London, he will either be hanged or transported, and never trouble the village again	0	1	0

Then he said,—

" Take that paper round, and my opinion is, you will gather enough to start you on your journey."

" It's uncommonly flattering," said Jack.

" Never mind that.   It will answer your purpose."

" Well, well.   Have you got anything to drink ?"

" No.   Be off with you, I'm tired of you ; and, besides, I've got some business to transact."

Ned rose, and opening the door of his hut, he pointed out, and Jack Groves, who knew well that, unless he went out at once, he should be turned out with greater speed than gentleness, left the place saying,—

" Thank you, Ned.   You are a rum fellow, but hang me if I don't think you have put me in the right track.   Thank you."

See page 77.

CHAPTER XXIV.

THE COUNTESS OF CRUMBLEDOWN SHOWS THE EARL THE MYSTERIOUS LETTER.—THE [VISIT TO LORD BLENKETH'S COUNTRY SEAT.

THE Countess of Crumbledown was not at all unmindful of the advice which her diplomatic and exceedingly clever mother had given her to take an opportunity of mentioning to the earl that such a letter had been found as that which had been extracted from his pocket by the unscrupulous waiting-maid, and which he began to feel some uneasiness on account of the loss of.

Just before, in consequence of the lateness of the hour, he had been compelled to make his appearance at dinner in undress, he had gone to his dressing-room to procure that letter, and had been vexed and surprised to find it was not in his pocket.

Still he could not pretend to say that any one had abstracted it therefrom, but he thought that he must have dropped it.

The same valet who had lived with him before the death of his father, the old earl, was now in his service, and he well knew that on his discretion he could depend, so that when that individual denied all knowledge of the note, the earl could come to no other conclusion than that he must have dropped it either at home or in the street.

If he had dropped it at home, the question arose of, into whose hands had it fallen, and there, of course, even conjecture was at fault.

It was nearly ten o'clock in the morning, after having been twice asked if he would partake of tea or coffee, that he left the balcony, and strolled listlessly up stairs to the dressing-room.

As he went, he heard the sound of a pianoforte playing, but he felt not at all interested, because he imagined it was his accomplished wife.

Upon entering the magnificent apartment, however, he saw his countess sitting on a couch, conversing with her mother. A glance towards the piano, told him that it was Julia Fanfaronade who was playing.

A couple of wrong notes, suddenly struck, perhaps tended to convince him that she was was aware of his presence, and the sudden " why, Julia," of the marchioness, let her know that the discord she had produced was at once detected.

The earl paused a moment, and a painful bewildering feeling came over him. He then advanced towards the instrument, where Julia, who had risen, still remained, and with what self-possession he could muster, he said,—

" I was not aware you had honoured me with a visit, or—or I should have been here sooner."

The Lady Julia did not look in his face. She affected to be busy in looking for some piece of music, and she managed to say with tolerable composure,—

" I came at my mother's request to see my sister."

" And I hope I may claim the honour of—of ——"

" Of what?" said Julia.

" I—I was going to say some portion of your regard."

" Oh ! certainly, as you say, some portion."

Then having found, or pretending to have found, the piece of music she had been in search of, she commenced playing a loud and brilliant air, which completely put all idea of conversation to the rout.

The earl felt mortified.

" She despises me," he said to himself. " I can see that she despises me;" and then, but for self-love, he was very near adding, " and well she may ;" but he stopped the thought, and walked over the room to the sofa, on which were seated the countess and his mother-in-law.

" I ought to apologise," he said, " for not joining you sooner, but—but having some letters to answer, I was compelled to sit in the library until later than I really intended."

There was a thickness about his voice; and an amount of colour upon his face, which sufficiently indicated that if he had been writing letters, he had taken care to moisten his labours with tolerably copious libations of wine.

" Talking of letters," said the countess, fixing her eyes upon the earl's face with all that self-possession which an insolent woman can so well assume. " Talking of letters, one has been found by one of the servants addressed to you."

" Indeed !"

" Yes. A very mysterious letter."

" Mysterious ?"

" My dear, you had better show it to the earl," said the marchioness, coaxingly, " and then he will, no doubt, in pity to female curiosity, explain to us what it is all about, and so rescue us from the endless maze of conjecture."

" It is here," said the countess, as from a table she took the letter, and handed it to the earl.

" Ah ! ah ! ah ! to be sure," said Crumbledown, " I know. Yes, I dropped it, but being, you understand, of no consequence, that was why I dropped it."

" Indeed ! how odd."

" I mean, being of no consequence, I did not take so much care of it as I otherwise might. That's all."

" But what does it refer to ?"

" Oh ! what does it refer to ? You want to know what it refers to ?"

" Yes."

" Then it refers to my private affairs, concerning which, I don't intend to be explicit to any one."

As the earl uttered this speech of defiance, he turned upon his heel, and nearly upset the footman, who had stolen behind him with the coffee-tray.

" D—n you," said the earl.

The footman hastily retreated, and then Crumbledown walked towards the piano again, at which the Lady Julia was playing, as if her life depended upon the expedition with which she could get through a very intricate composition.

When the earl was out of ear-shot, the countess turned to her mother, and said in a low tone,—

" This won't do."

" Certainly not, my dear."

" I cannot, and will not be snubbed in this manner."

" Of course not, my love."

" But, I am."

" Why, yes—certainly. Leave it to me. You see the earl has evidently been drinking took much wine, and it is quite useless to say anything to him now. You would only get replies from him which would make matters worse."

" But something must be done, mother. I cannot submit to such conduct. If anything is to be said between us in that style, it shall be said by me."

" Of course."

" It's all very well to say of course, but that don't mend the matter. See how attentive he is to Julia."

" Never mind that, my love, you are the countess."

And the earl of Crumbledown was indeed attentive to Julia. He posted himself behind her chair, and while her eyes were dimmed with tears of vexation, that she could hardly see the notes in the page of music from which she was playing, he would talk to her in a tone and manner that was wonderfully sinking him each moment in her esteem.

The fact was, that in her agitation, she had no idea that too much wine was the provocative to his loquacity and odd demeanour. And as far as he was concerned, he had got evidently worse, since coming from the dim and quiet library into the brilliantly illuminated drawing-room.

The chandeliers and the music seemed to have made him many degrees worse, and at times he now scarcely knew really what he said.

" And so," he remarked, " you did not come to see me ?"

The only reply to this, was the conversion of a piano passage in the music to a forte one.

" You come at your mother's request to see your sister. Ah ! Julia, I would I were a glove upon that hand."

" Is he mad ?" thought Julia.

Julia said nothing, but she thought it wonderfully cruel of her mother and sister that they did not one or both of them come to her rescue from the really serious persecution she was enduring.

" And you will not answer me ?" added the earl, with maudlin sensibility, as if he were about to cry ; " you will let my heart break while you play the pianoforte. It puts me in mind of Nero playing the violin, while Rome was in flames."

" He must be mad," thought Julia.

" Do you remember," he added, "the route in May-fair? Ah ! Julia, you were not so cruel then. Then I could speak to you, and you would bend upon me those eloquent eyes, which have ever since been present to my imagination, as the stars of my brighter, happier destiny."

This was too much for mortal sufferance. Compliments were all very well in this way, and might have been put up with, but downright love-making from the man who was but two months married to his sister, and who, to a certain extent, might be said to have played the coquette as far as she, Julia, was concerned, was rather too bad.

With a loud crash of octaves she concluded the tune she had been playing, and then rising, she said, with dignity,—

"My Lord Crumbledown, I have the gratification of saying that I have not heard all you have uttered, and that what I have heard I do not understand."

This speech, although it was uttered quietly, was still sufficiently loud, now that so sudden a cessation of the music had taken place, to be heard by both the countess and the marchioness, although they were some distance off.

A deathlike silence succeeded it. The earl was confounded and half-sobered by the shock of the very ungentlemanly position in which he found himself. The lady Julia had scorn and contempt upon her countenance, as she now no longer hesitated to look at the man who had, in a few brief moments, thoroughly succeeded in eradicating from her bosom the last remnant of a tender feeling towards him.

The Marchioness of Fanfaronade looked astonished, and the Countess of Crumbledown, notwithstanding all her affected indifference towards the earl, felt, at that moment, such a wild rush of angry and jealous feelings, that she had the greatest difficulty in keeping down a sudden exhibition of her wrath, which would not, perhaps, have been of the most ladylike character.

The marchioness, as being the most indifferent person present, was the first to speak, and she made an effort to get over the disagreeable affair by saying,—

"Julia, my dear, I think, as you say, it is getting late, and we had better order the carriage at once."

"Order the carriage at once, mamma, by all means," said Julia.

"What the deuce is the matter?" said the earl.

"Perhaps you will be so good as to inform us," remarked the countess. "Julia, what was it? The earl appears to have lost his faculties. What have you to complain of, Julia?"

"Nothing," said Julia. "Have you ordered the carriage, mamma?"

"Yes, my dear."

"I am a fool," said the earl. "Julia, forgive me; and, on my soul, I declare to you I knew not what I was saying."

Julia made no answer; and the countess observed,—

"But the question is, what did you say, my lord?"

"Never mind what it was; I could not tell you for I don't know. If Julia will be offended, I cannot help it."

"I have but one feeling upon this subject," said Julia, "and that prompts me to decline, for the future, the honour of the acquaintance of the Earl of Crumbledown, and to declare this to be my last visit to his house."

This was a declaration which was so decidedly at variance with the plans and projects of the marchioness, that it was not to be supposed for a moment that she could hear it unmoved. She altered her tactics; and now, instead of trying to smother up the affair, she resolved, if possible, to have an explanation and a reconciliation as quickly as possible, before after-reflection should, perhaps, render the feelings of Julia more embittered than they were even now.

The countess knew enough of human nature to be perfectly aware that after-reflection upon any subject matter of insult was more than likely to dress it up in some of the vivid colours of the imagination, and to render a reconciliation almost impossible.

Therefore, as no strangers were present, which she considered a most blessed occurrence, and as the servants, with ready tact, had left the apartment, the marchioness thought to herself now or never this quarrel must be arranged at once, or, probably, it will never be arranged at all.

She darted across the room in a moment, and seizing both of the hands of Julia in her own, she said,—

"My dear, you must perceive in a moment the cause of all this."

" The cause, mother ?"

" Yes, the condition of the earl."

" What condition ?"

" Why, my love, he has taken too much wine, and is not master of himself. What he has said to you, I don't know ; you can tell me another time ; but, depend upon it, he had no sort of intention of insulting you ; he knew not what he said, evidently ; so think no more about it."

" If," said Julia, " the Earl of Crumbledown is first to deprive himself of the power of knowing what he says, and then, under cover of that obliviousness of intellect, to say those things which I cannot hear, I had better avoid his company. You could not, mother, have possibly supplied me with a stronger reason for never entering the house again."

" But consider, my love."

" I do consider."

" Nay, nay. You know all men will, at times, make themselves so ridiculous ; and, I assure you, you ought not to view the matter in so serious a light. He could speak, but he had no reflection left."

" Speech to such a man, then, is like a drawn sword in the hands of an idiot," remarked Julia, with a shudder. " I have no desire to feel the keenness of its edge."

" Well, well ; look over this little matter."

" But why should I be compelled to make an acquaintance with any one contrary to my inclinations ?"

" To please me, my love—to please me."

" This is ungenerous, mother."

" Nonsense—nonsense, my dear. You will think differently to-morrow. My lord, how could you be so foolish ——"

" Or so criminal ?" added the countess ; " I am inclined to think that wine and folly have an equal share in this transaction."

" Are you, indeed, madam ?" said the now sobered, and half-maddened earl. " You, no doubt, draw that moral from attentive consideration of your own habits of thought and conduct."

" No, my lord ; a perception of the character which combines vice with folly never occurred to me until my acquaintance with you."

" Indeed ! Then you have made a remarkable exhibition of which way your tastes turn, by bestowing on me the honour of your hand. A bitter tongue in a woman is generally considered as quite conclusive evidence of a bad heart."

The marchioness sank on the couch which was nearest to her, and pretended to be deeply affected, while poor Julia looked from one to the other of the matrimonial disputants with terror and amazement.

" Don't be alarmed, Julia," said the countess. " The Earl of Crumbledown is only endeavouring to excuse himself for insulting his wife's sister, by showing how much more he can insult his wife."

" In which," said the earl, " his wife is so great an adept that he despairs of entering into anything like hopeful competition with her."

" Do you want to kill me, all of you ?" said the marchioness ; " oh, do you want to kill me ?"

Nobody made any reply to this. The probability was, that, except Julia, nobody cared whether the dispute had that effect upon the marchioness or not.

And now, for the time, the earl and his amiable countess appeared to have exhausted the " keen encounter of their wits ;" for they were both silent, although they both, by their looks and attitudes, appeared as if, upon very slight provocation indeed, the contest of bitterness and invective would again be commenced.

" Oh, dear—oh, dear !" added the marchioness, " that I should live to see this day. My children, I cannot leave this house until I see peace among you again. This is too dreadful for me."

" I know of no war," said the countess, coldly. " The earl is the best judge, I dare say, of the line of conduct which will most conduce to his domestic happiness here."

"And the countess," replied the earl, "is no doubt well aware of the best mode of attaching to her a husband, after she has caught him."

"It is not every one who marries a beggar," said the countess, "who is taunted afterwards with her catch."

"A beggar, madam?"

"Precisely.   A beggar—a man who was living upon the sufferance of the Jews—really ——"

"Now—now—now!" almost shrieked the marchioness.

"The carriage, my lady," announced a servant.

"Do as you will among each other," said Julia.   "I go home, and thank God I do, to leave this house, which I hope never to be necessitated to enter again. Mother, I am going home."

The Lady Julia left the drawing-room, and hastened to the carriage. For a moment the marchioness hesitated as to whether she should stay and endeavour to reconcile the earl and the countess, or leave ; but sound policy, now that Julia was gone, dictated the latter course, and, without another word, she left the drawing-room to the exclusive possession of its owners, who then had an opportunity of carrying on their quarrel in any way they might choose to fancy.

CHAPTER XXV.

THE MOCK RECONCILIATION, AND THE DEPARTURE TO THE COUNTRY.—THE FEELINGS OF THE LADY JULIA FANFARONADE AND HER DETERMINATION.

THE marchioness had done decidedly right in leaving the earl and countess to settle their affairs alone.

If any matrimonial dispute take place in the presence of a third party, ten to one but it becomes really serious, when, alone, the fitful flame of contention might, in a few moments, have burnt itself out.

There are many ladies who, knowing their husbands to be proud, haughty, intellectual men, succumb to them completely in private life, and so lead an existence of peace and pleasure, for there are hundreds of men who will easily be led by an appearance of being given way to.

But we have often noticed imprudent wives who will take an opportunity, when strangers are present, of saying flouting and ungracious things to the man towards whom, when they are alone, they dare not so behave.

They seem to rely upon the pride of their husbands to put up, before strangers, with indignities which it would be bad taste to repel at such times. This is a course of conduct as common for women to pursue as it is awfully dangerous, where the husband happens to be a man of ingenious understanding and of stern resolves.

Such a man will not always accept the humiliation and the tears of his wife, when the company is gone, as an atonement for an insult while it is present.

It may do once—twice—thrice—ay, twenty times ; but some time, when the wife who so plays with her husband's affections least suspects it, she will find that she has lost them for ever.

We caution the ladies against this sad mistake of giving way to their husbands in private, and defying them, and saying anything which they know will be hurtful to their feelings in public. Precisely the reverse should be the line of conduct pursued.

We are far from wishing that any wife should be a slave to her husband's caprice, —we are far from insinuating that a wife is but the domestic of the husband ; such a state of things is equally degrading to both ; but if a man be a man of intellect sufficient to assume the control of his family and affairs, a piece of worse taste than his wife attempting to contend it with him cannot be imagined, except it be her doing so in public, where pride and good breeding disarms him.

To those men who suffer themselves to be henpecked, we say nothing at all, and offer neither consolation nor advice.

We are glad to see them on all occasions, and on all subjects, snubbed and mortified. They deserve all they get, and they merit the contempt of every one who becomes aware of their condition.

But, ladies—you who wish to be happy wives, and to pass your days serenely with your husbands—always defer to them before strangers. There is no man so brutally insensible but he will appreciate such a piece of delicate consideration.

And then, dear ladies, you know you have abundant opportunity of giving him a curtain lecture afterwards ; and is not that a sweet and an enduring, and a delightful consolation ?

When the Earl and the Countess of Crumbledown were alone they no longer thought of being witty and severe at each other's expense—all that had been intended for the Marchioness and for the Lady Julia Fanfaronade ; but now, as they had no listeners, it was really, they considered, not worth their whiles to be abusive.

There was an ominous silence of a few minutes' duration, during which, no doubt, they were both busy in considering how the affair was likely to end.

The fact was, that the earl felt how much he was in the wrong—indeed he was doubly wrong.

First of all was he wrong in making such remarks to his wife's sister, and, secondly, the bad taste of making them in his wife's presence, was perfectly inexcusable.

Now that he was sufficiently sobered to view his conduct rationally at all, he could view it in no light which did not show it very much indeed to his disadvantage. And as for the countess, she had sense enough, although, as is too often the case, just a little too late, to see her error.

She had no wish to separate from the earl, but she just wished to live with him on civil terms, and now she much regretted that she had been betrayed into uttering such cutting invective as had come from her lips. In fine, they each were now waiting with some anxiety to know what the other would say.

As for anything in the shape of affection between them, that was long ago exploded ; but interest governed the countess, and a sensation of being most decidedly and unequivocally in the wrong, was having its effect upon the earl.

It was he who at length spoke, and he said,—

"It is not for me to dictate what course your ladyship may now think it proper to pursue."

"Course, my lord ?"

"Yes ; after what has passed, I presume your indignation will dictate some violent proceeding."

"My lord, can you say that I had no cause ?"

"Since, my lady, you have asked that question temperately, you shall he i t answered candidly. You had cause."

"My lord, since you are so candid, it would ill become me to be otherwise. I deeply regret that the cause induced me to be so intemperate as I was in addressing you."

"Then the best way is to let the matter rest ! D—n the claret, I had drunk too much of it, and really knew not what I was saying or what I was doing. I have offended Julia, but if I were put upon my word of honour to repeat what I said to her I could not do so."

"Of that I entertain no doubt whatever."

"You need entertain none. The confusion incidental to the piece of folly—for such it was—has sobered me. I regret, very much, that I should, in a matter for which I am so much to blame, be the means of producing any family disensions, and probably you will feel inclined to say so much to your sister."

"I shall take the earliest opportunity of so doing, and whatever may be our own subjects of disagreement, it will, I think, be both pleasant and dessirable to keep them to ourselves."

"Most certainly."

"The agreement which we came to at Paris, I think, may be well thought of and carried out."

"An agreement of perfect indifference, in which I entirely agree with you. I hope this will be the last time we either of us commit ourselves by using any recriminatory speeches."

How very polite now the earl and the countess were. The earl took his coffee with all the grace imaginable, and no one, to have looked for a moment at that pair, could have supposed that, only a very short time before, they were abusing each other, grammatically certainly, but with that one exception, quite as grossly as any of the vulgar commonplace could, with whom they would have been by far too dignified to associate.

But so it is ; human nature will be human nature, let us disguise it how we may, and under what lordly titles we may. And while this happy pair are sipping coffee from cups of silver, let us glance at the two apartments thrown into one, in which they sat.

The rooms in this house were of a most handsome and spacious dimension. The lofty ceiling was decorated round the sides by handsome designs and broad gilding that were at once attractive and rich, while the chandeliers which hung from them were encircled by wreaths of flowers and figures that appeared as though the one was made for the other.

The walls were covered with rich and splendid pier glasses, the frames were of the choicest and most magnificent patterns, while the girandoles were placed in various parts that appeared to require their aid, or where they at all added to the general effect.

The patterns, designs, and execution of all the various works that filled the apartment, were of the finest and most elaborate character that can be conceived or executed. The artisan had not been stinted for time or money when he was told to execute such works.

Everything was of a piece. The curtains and hangings corresponded ; each of its kind appeared the best and the choicest ; but elegance and refinement seemed to chasten the richness of the furniture, and tastefully to harmonize and blend it together.

The hangings were magnificent, while the couches, ottomans, chairs, and settles, all were of the most gorgeous and costly materials and pattern.

Soft carpets covered the floors, upon which the foot might fall without any fear of awakening the faintest echo ; the ear received no sound from the tread.

The fire-irons and fenders, the bell-ropes, the curtain-ropes, all displayed a taste and magnificence that are seldom, if ever, surpassed ; while here and there were pillars of various kinds, on which were placed plans and designs of the chastest and most faultless patterns.

It was indeed a receptacle of everything that was great, beautiful, and magnificent. The cornices of the windows were as grand and rich as could be ; gilt mouldings of carved wood, from beneath which hung the most beautiful embroidered and damasked drapery, that could be produced ; the blinds to keep out the rays of the sun, and to subdue the light, were of the most curious and beautiful construction.

The furniture, too, was composed of such things as only could be procured by wealth ; all that was beautiful, costly, and rare, were there, while flowers and vases were placed in profusion.

Such was the style of decoration of that house which contained a couple so incongruous in their tastes, and yet so alike in some things, as the Earl and Countess of Crumbledown.

There wanted the heart and soul to enjoy the glitter and the beauty of all that was around them, and many a happier heart than either of theirs, beat beneath the humble thatch of some lowly cottage, which the Earl of Crumbledown would have scarcely thought a shelter good enough for one of his hunters ; and his lady, decidedly not good enough for the favourite Italian hound she had brought with her from the continent.

So much for taste !

The earl was glad to bid his lady good night. Of course they had their separate bed-chambers. That is a refinement which surely some day will become almost universal among decent people.

The earl then repaired to his library, and, after walking to and fro some time

See page 124.

thinking if he should go out or not, as he did not feel inclined for bed, he looked from one of the windows and made the agreeable discovery that it was a miserable wet night.   This decided him, and, drawing his chair closer to the fire—for there was one in the stove—he snatched up the first book that came to hand, and commenced attempting to withdraw his mind from the several harassing subjects that distressed and perplexed it by a perusal of the following narrative :—

A loud and shrill whistle rang clearly through the forest, and startled the deer from their lair, and the timid hare from her form, awoke the dull echoes in the forest, when again all was quiet.

A tall form, clad in forest green, stood beneath an aged oak ; by his side hung a strong sword, a horn, a quiver of arrows, and across his shoulders was hung a long bow ; in his hand was a small silver call, or whistle, while two good hounds stood beside him.

The last echoes died away before he moved, and then he glanced an eagle's glance among the trees, by which he was environed.

The morning's sun had just tipped the hills, and spread a golden hue over the sky, and the forest leaves were tinted by the same.

He gazed around, and seemed to pause a few moments as if in expectation of seeing some one or something. Presently the echoes were again waked up by the same shrill sound, and when all was again still, a third time were the same sounds made to startle the timid hind, and then the forms of men were seen issuing from the forest glades, making their way towards the old oak tree, where stood the strange forester.

When they had gathered round him to some number, he said, in a loud tone,—

"Foresters, you know the Baron of Breerwood?"

"We do."

"And you have heard of the beautiful daughter of the baron, the once betrothed of Sir Giles de Norville?"

"We have, we have."

"But," said one of them, "she cannot abide the knight; he is a fierce man, one who fears no laws, human or divine."

"That is true," replied the other. "Now you know the young Lord of Bernar's Hall?"

"We do."

"Then the young lord, Sir Henry Bernar, is in love with the Lady Alice of Breerwood, and his love is returned—why should two such lovers be parted?"

As no one spoke, he continued,—

"And yet, by decrees of parental authority, she will be compelled to marry this man—this Sir Giles, who is our bitterest enemy, and a preserver of the forest laws, and who is rigorous in his punishment for any offence."

"He is, the tyrant."

"What, think you, will be our fate when he shall become master of Breerwood and its dependencies? We shall be hunted like the game itself, and no season of rest allowed us."

"But he cannot stir us from the depths of the forest," said one.

"He knows not the intricacies of the forest," said another.

"But he has hounds that will track our footsteps, to the uttermost den we can creep into—it will be a war of extermination."

"How can we help it?"

"Listen to me. If any other lord become master of Breerwood, our situation would not be so bad; if, for instance, Sir Henry of Bernar's Hall were master of Breerwood."

"Ay, ay."

"Then this very day, towards evening, the marriage will take place between Sir Giles and the Lady Alice, and could we prevent it, we should save ourselves from ex ermination."

"But how?"

"Thus. The young knight, Sir Henry, wishes to prevent it, and carry off the lady, and with our assistance he will do so."

"Has he not followers enough?"

"He has; but does not wish them to know anything about it save a few, because he wishes it not to be known."

"And we are to bear the brunt of the affray?"

"Yes."

"And have to encounter the hatred and revenge of such a man?"

"We have to do so already, and therefore that is nothing new; but it will not be so then, as Sir Henry will challenge the knight to mortal combat, and he has cause enough to do so. We all know Sir Henry Bernar's generosity and valour, and I have no doubt of the result."

"Nor have we; and since he will venture himself in the fray, I will venture too."

"All, all."

" 'Tis well, then. We may as well take the precaution of being disguised."

" Ay, ay."

" Then we will make the attack on the party as they ride out in the chase. Sir Henry desires that Sir Giles may not be wounded, for he has a deadly feud with him, and intends him for his own arm," said the stranger.

" Wherefore should he care about how he fell?"

" Because he has found out that Sir Giles murdered his father."

" And he murdered my father and my brother," said one of the foresters, stepping forward ; " and you all know I have sworn to be revenged, and when opportunity serves, I will lay that man dead."

" Well, then, you must place yourself alongside of Sir Henry, or else you will not have the opportunity left you."

" That I will. When do we meet?"

" In two hours time we shall see them crossing the Birchwood hill, and we will encounter them in the hollow."

" On this side ?"

" Yes, this side. In two hours time be beneath the large beech tree in the hollow."

" We will—we will."

The men departed as they came, in different directions, and the forester was soon left alone.

" 'Tis well," he said ; " and when Sir Giles dies, then I may once again appear in the world. My enemy will be gone, and right may once more take the place of might."

He paused again, and looking at the bow, he muttered in a low tone,—

" I will to Sir Henry, and then he may be prepared to meet his enemy, as I am mine. He will use his sword right willingly to-day."

He left the spot, and was soon lost among the thick trees.

*   *   *   *   *   *

Beneath a large birch-tree, whose beautifully nodding and waving plume-like foliage was a picture—a feature in the landscape—a principal one, in fact—beneath this tree were ranged about fifteen men, the foresters, but disguised as peasants, and with them were the forester and Sir Henry Bernar.

" Now, my friends," said the latter, who had been speaking to them. " And now let me advise you to stand clear of the sword of Sir Giles. He is a brave man, though a base assassin, and being thoroughly protected against attack, he has all his time to attack you, and you have no armour."

" I have. Leave him to me. He murdered my father, and I will have my vengeance for his infamy—for the injury he has done me."

" He shall not escape," said a forester, in a deep tone. " He shall not escape. I, too, have a score to exact from him."

" Indeed !"

" Yes—he slew my father."

" Did he ?"

" Ay, and my brother."

" And he dishonoured my sister, and robbed me of an inheritance," muttered the tall forester. But he was not heard, and he moved away from the spot, and casting his eyes to the hill, he saw that the party were approaching.

" Under cover, lads, under cover—they come. I will give the signals. Sir Henry, come with me."

In a very few moments the whole party were concealed close to the brushwood that lined the road, at the same time that Sir Henry and the forester crept close to the roadside, sheltered in part by a spreading doddered oak.

This party consisted of but the knight, Sir Giles, his squire, and a party of six horsemen, well armed, and accoutred.

They rode along in security, and were all conversing together.

" The Lady Alice," said the squire, " will come in a litter ; she is too unwell to walk."

" Indeed," said Sir Giles, " she will in time get over that humour, when she leaves her father's halls, and comes to mine."

At this speech a loud whistle was given by the forester, and the knight instinctively flew to his sword ; the whole party moved on at a rapid rate, but the arrows flew fast, and three of the party were dismounted, and their horses slain.

With a loud shout the party rushed from their hiding-place, and commenced a furious attack upon the party.

The contest was hand to hand, and the party being well armed, defended themselves for some time, but those who were not engaged, took deliberate aim with their bows, and soon diminished their numbers, and the others cried out for aid.

" Do you intend murder, villains !" exclaimed Sir Giles, " or do you want money ?"

" I mean death," said Sir Henry ; " you slew my father, recollect that, and now is the hour of retribution."

" Sir Giles, you slew my father, because he refused to become an assassin, and my brother also," said the peasant, " and now is the moment of revenge—revenge !"

" And look upon me, Sir Giles. Do you know me ?" said the forester, baring his head.

Sir Giles uttered a cry of terror and surprise, and stepped back a pace or two.

As he did this, the peasant with one sweep of his sword severed the head from the body of Sir Giles, who fell instantly a corpse, and at the same moment the remainder of the escort were either killed, or had taken to flight, and they were masters of the field.

" And who are you, brave forester ?" exclaimed Sir Henry, turning to him, " and what is there in your countenance that should strike terror to the heart of that assassin ?"

" I am the owner of his estates ; he was my guardian, and believed he had murdered me, and seized upon my lands as his own.

" I am Sir Tracy de Norville, the owner of this property, and the estates around. I had a sister whom he married, and then he divorced and dishonoured her, and then he murdered her, and held the estates as his of right, through her."

The estates were restored, and much of Sir Giles's property was awarded as a compensation to Sir Tracy. The Lady Alice was united to her lover, Sir Henry, and all were happy, who but a few weeks before bore a very different aspect.

The foresters one and all became the retainers of Sir Tracy, but at the same time preferred living in their sylvan retreat, under his protection ; and whenever Sir Tracy wanted their aid, they were willing and stout allies, who never shrank before an enemy.

The hour of twelve striking, warned the earl that his usual period of retiring to rest had occurred.

It was not his usual period in London, but somehow, what with the fatigue of almost daily travelling, and the difference in that particular of the manners and customs abroad, he had seldom been out of bed after midnight for some time.

Now, therefore, he rose with a feeling that it was late, and betook himself to his own chamber, as displeased, uneasy, and generally miserable a man as probably could have been found within some distance of his house.

*   *   *   *   *   *   *

The earl and his countess met at breakfast. They hoped each other were well, and they made some indifferent and casual remarks about the London weather. How very pleasant and polite they both were!

Then the earl commenced opening a packet of letters that had been brought to him, and the countess looked languidly over the *Morning Post.*

Thus an hour passed away, and then the countess rang her bell for an attendant to go and tell Davies, who was her maid, that she was coming to her dressing-room.

The earl rose, and opened the drawing-room door for his lady's exit. He would with far more pleasure have held open the door of the family vault of the Crumbledowns to admit her.

She bowed slightly and so did he, after which, he walked to his own dressing-room, in order to prepare himself for the street. He had as yet called on no one but Bruce, and now he ordered his horse, that he might make a number of morning calls in answer to the host of cards that he had found at his new house, awaiting his coming from the continent.

The morning was delicious, for with the sunrise had cleared off all the clouds of the preceding night, and no trace was left behind in the heavens, at least, of the many troubles and disagreeables of the over night.

However, there was a coolness and freshness which was much more genial now, and warmer than it was at a much earlier hour, yet there was a remarkable clearness and freshness in the air that was pleasing, and extremely healthful to those who came under its influence.

The park was a scene of gaiety and splendour; there were many individuals in the ride, who were galloping their horses, whose coats exhibited the warmth they had caused by the severity of the exercise.

People seemed gayer and happier. A fine fresh morning seems to have an effect more or less upon everybody—it seems to influence the spirits, and there can be no good reason why it should not be so.

Warmth and sunshine influence animal and vegetable life, and why not human, since it differs not from the former, save it has something more—and that something more, the mind, is mainly influenced by the state of the body.

There were traces of the storm on the earth, for though the streets, in many places, were washed thoroughly clean, yet there could not but be in many much dirt, which, as the number of passengers increased, the pavements became dirty and muddy, while the roads were filled with mud, and an accumulation of other kinds of filth.

The park, too, was wet and soft, and the rain and wind had brought down a larger quantity of leaves than usually fall at this time of the year.

The clouds were few; and what there were, merely added life and beauty to the scene. The heavens were nearly cloudless; and the sun's rays, as that luminary rose higher, became more and more powerful, and threw great heat upon the earth, tending to make the place drier and more beautiful.

The people, for a time, assumed a serene gait, and all seemed lively and gay; it was a day stolen from the autumn, and added to the summer.

"How much should I," thought the earl, as he cantered from one end of the drive in Hyde-park to the other, "have enjoyed such a morning as this in a barouche, with the Lady Julia Fanfaronade, who, I suppose, I have now offended past all redemption, and shall never see again."

These were extremely vain regrets indeed, and such as the Earl of Crumbledown showed no great amount of wisdom in encouraging; but there are numbers of men, and we are inclined to think that he belonged to the category, who, let their situation in life be what it may, must have some pet misery of their own.

Here was a man of twenty-five thousand a year, and one of the oldest peerages in the kingdom, groaning for what was unattainable, according to the old established usages of human nature.

And so he made himself quite melancholy, until two or three morning calls had, to some extent, dissipated the crowd of blue devils that had congregated around him.

Some people's grief, though, bears a strong resemblance to their money, and with both it is lightly come and lightly go. So was it with Lord Crumbledown; as the morning advanced, and he had indulged in several calls at houses where he was familiar enough to be told that the family were at home, instead of, according to etiquette, being provided with an excuse for merely leaving his card, he got quite into good spirits, and as he cantered along past the gate of Kensington-gardens, he caught himself saying, in a careless voice,—

"What do I care? I shall take things easy, and not trouble myself about my countess, so long as she don't trouble herself about me; and when she shall be so ill-advised as she was last night, when she asked me about Vullimay's letter, as to interfere too urgently, I can treat her with some such answer as she then had, only couched in perhaps more courtly terms than that was, which I blame the claret for."

Lord Crumbledown was by no means a man given to intemperance. It was sheer vexation which had induced him, on that evening of his first arrival in town, to indulge to the extent he did in claret, and such a circumstance was not at all likely to occur again.

He hoped, too, and fully expected, that his peace would be made with the Lady Julia Fanfaronade. He tried to believe that some lingering feeling of affection for him would plead in his favour, and he told himself that a woman sooner forgives an insult that involves any admiration of her, than any other species of indignity whatever.

This was a sentiment he had heard pass the mouths of libertines; and even as he quoted it, he had sense enough to feel how decidedly inapplicable it was to females of a higher order than the most vulgar.

Upon such a person as the Lady Julia Fanfaronade, it could not be supposed to have any effect.

But, upon the whole, the earl succeeded in recovering his good humour, and in getting, in a manner of speaking, reconciled to himself.

"To-morrow," he said, "I hope we shall be able to start for Lord Blenketh's country seat, and then I can steal an opportunity of looking at poor Emily's child."

This was a thought which brought a transient feeling of melancholy across his mind; but if, as we have seen, he so soon got over the first shock of the death of that young and beautiful girl, who had gone to the grave in the very spring of her youth, because she had loved and trusted him too well, we cannot be surprised at his very soon mentally escaping from the pains of any sudden recollection of how or where she had died.

There is, however, a natural instinct which binds a parent to a child, which inclined the heart of even the selfish Lord Crumbledown towards the little child, which had no friend in the wide world but himself.

He made a mental resolve that at all events he would do his duty by that infant, and the more so that it was a girl, and with a strange inconsistency, his cheek glowed with indignation at the thought, that if he did not take great care, when it grew up it might, in consequence of the isolated and invidious position it would hold in society, fall possibly a victim to some seducer.

"I will take good care of her morals," said Lord Crumbledown.

That was certainly an admirable sentiment from the father of an illegitimate child; however, nature is a capital hand at seeing the mote in others eyes, and overlooking the beam in its own.

CHAPTER XXVI.

THE STORM.—THE MEETING UNDER THE TREES.—THE FAMILIAR RECOGNITION.—THE HASTY DEPARTURE FROM LONDON.

THUS amusing himself, as if he could have stood up before any one and said,—

> " Let the galled jade wince,
> Our withers are unwrung,"

when, in reality, he could have found few men, even among his own class, who could have matched, in any episode of their lives, so detestable and heartless a seduction of female innocence as he had been guilty of, Lord Crumbledown reached half the distance between the gate of Kensington-gardens, and the Oxford-street entrance to Hyde-park, when he was suddenly, in common with many other equestrians, as well as pedestrians, startled by such a clap of thunder, that he nearly fell from his steed, and the frightened animal reared, and showed by its agitation of manner, and the quick, strange movement of its ears, how much terrified it was.

"Hilloa!" cried a gentleman on horseback; "is that you?"

The earl turned, and saw a young nobleman with whom he was on habits of tolerable intimacy, and he said,—

"I did not see you, Leslie."

"No, I have been cantering after you; but you are better mounted."

"Indeed! I thought in that you yielded to no man."

"Nor do I usually; but the fact is, I make a favourite of a horse, and keep him too long, they tell me."

"Very likely—very likely, indeed."

"Are we going to have a storm?"

"I think we are."

There was no doubt about it now, for another peal of thunder, of far more intensity than the first, struck upon their ears; and then there came down suddenly some heavy drops of rain.

"We had better ride on," said the Honourable Adolphus Leslie, who was the young man who had spoken to the earl.

"We shall not reach a better shelter than these trees will afford us," said Crumbledown; "very few people are killed by lightning, so I shall risk it, I think, by riding under, till the shower is over."

"Agreed; and if, as the Turks say, it is our *kismet*, as they name fate, to be killed by lightning, of course we cannot help it, let us be where we may; and, therefore, with that comfortable assurance, here goes."

The reader is, no doubt, well acquainted with a row of trees forming a long belt of wood to the right of the walk from the Oxford-street, or Tyburn gate entrance, as it is sometimes called, of Hyde-park, to the beautiful gardens of Kensington-palace."

It was under the boughs of these trees, that the Earl of Crumbledown and his young friend, the Honourable Adolphus Leslie, sought for shelter; and as many of the branches met overhead, they were likely enough to find it, from a mere summer shower especially.

And now the storm came on with a vengeance, and both the young men congratulated themselves even upon the temporary shelter they had procured.

The storm came on with great violence, and the rustling wind swept through the trees, and large and heavy drops of rain came pattering down among the leaves of the young trees, and a heavy clap of thunder suddenly startled them, and a flash of lightning came across them, and startled their horses so much that it was with difficulty they kept their seats among the young trees, which were rather in the way when the horses were capering and jumping about.

"I think we had better dismount," said Leslie; "we shall certainly be thrown among these trees; if down, we can quiet the animals."

"Very well. I begin to be of your opinion."

Before, however, they could execute their resolve, another livid flash of electricity, followed by such an awful, ear-splitting, crashing report, that seemed to rock the very foundation of the earth, and boomed, and rolled away in the distance. The echoes were long in dying away.

The horses began to rear and snort; they trembled, too, and shook with fear, and profiting by a moment like this, the two young men dismounted from their steeds, and stood soothing and patting their necks.

"It is certainly very dreadful; but who on earth would have anticipated such a termination to so fine and so beautiful a morning?"

"It is merely an autumnal storm that rides upon the clouds, and shows itself as it passes along. It cannot last long."

"It had not need, for my horse will never remain here if it do."

They could say no more—the rain fell heavily, but not thickly, and the park seemed to smoke for a time while it lasted, and the air seemed to be filled with the most terrific sounds, and the most vivid lightning which played about in all parts of the heavens; but by means of covering the eyes of their horses they held them tolerably easy and gently, until the storm was leaving them.

The din had been too great to admit of much conversation, but now that the storm clouds were evidently passing rapidly away, and the sky was getting each moment perceptibly lighter, they looked at each other with feelings of satisfaction, and Crumbledown said,—

"Well, Leslie, I never was caught out in a worse land storm than this—at least in England."

"Nor I.   Look how terrified the horses are!"

"They are indeed ; and mine worse than yours.   But who have we here?"

Two men in a tilbury approached the trees ; they had evidently with their ill-depended vehicle gone through the whole of the storm.   They were saturated with the rain, and it would seem as if the horse had had a fall, for one side of him was covered with mud, and some portion of one of the wheels was evidently in a dilapidated state.

The whole affair looked just about as wretched as it could look, and as they came quite near, one of the men said to his companion,—

"You call this a nice, easy going, comfortable horse, do you?   D—n me if I buy him."

"But you know you threw him down yourself, sir," said the other man, in a tone of insolence, just a little tempered, so as not to make it a thoroughly quarrelsome one.

"I threw him down?   How the devil could I throw him down, when I was seated here?"

"Yes ; but ——"

"Oh, you be hanged, and your horse too.   You may mind him while I go under these trees, and try to shake some of the mud out of my hat and clothes. Who would have thought now of such a treacherous morning?"   -

"I think we can ride on now," said the Earl of Crumbledown, in a restless fidgety tone of voice, for in the man who now got out of the chaise, and rapidly approached where he and Leslie were, he could not fail to recognise his tormentor of the preceding day, Jonathan Willoughby.

"As you please," said Leslie.

"Very good.   Will you re-mount?"

"Yes, yes."

Lord Crumbledown himself re-mounted, and was in the very act of turning his horse's head towards the road-way, when he was espied by Jonathan Willoughby, who, with a tone of malicious satisfaction, cried,—

"Hilloa! my Lord Crumbledown, is that you?   Well, it is some consolation to be caught in a storm in such good company, at any rate.   How is the countess and my lady, the mother marchioness?"

Jonathan Willoughby, no doubt, had by that time in the day fortified his stomach with a sufficient quantity of strong drinks to enable him to have impudence enough for anything, or probably, as an acute man of the world, he might have seen how little he had to gain, and how much he had to lose, by thus publicly accosting, and indeed insulting Lord Crumbledown.

"Do you know him?" said Leslie.

"No—yes.   That is, he is a scoundrel!   That's all I know of him."

"Why, you ain't going to cut an old friend?" cried Willoughby.   "Oh! how like the world!   *Oh! tempore! oh! mores!*"

"What can the fellow mean?" said Leslie, with perhaps a little spirit of mischief in his disposition.   "Look at him again, Crumbledown ; perhaps after all you may have known him, and now forget him."

"I have said I know him," remarked the earl, with some slight asperity of manner, "and as I know him for a rogue so I know some other people for fools, and cut them accordingly."

"Oh, indeed!"

"Certainly."

The Honourable Leslie could not but see that these last words were intended in a great measure for himself.   Had he been an elder, and a more experienced man than he was, no doubt he would have merely smiled at the result of the momentary state of irritation into which the Earl of Crumbledown was thrown at being accosted by one whom he did not choose to know.

As it was, however, he was infected with that young man's foible, the desire to retort upon any one an ungracious speech, or a malicious and savage observation.

See p. 142.

"Oh! indeed, my Lord Crumbledown," he said. "You go upon, I think, a very foolish system. If I meet a fool in the park I think nothing of joining company with him."

"Birds of a feather," muttered the earl.

"My lord?"

"Sir?"

"I thought your lordship made an observation."

"I did make an observation, sir, which I hereby presume I am entitled to do, without being catechised."

No. 18,

" Come, I say, my Lord Crumbledown," shouted Jonathan Willoughby, "you are, I dare say, a judge of horse-flesh ; give us your opinion about this nag in the d—d chaise. He's been down, and that fellow of a stable-keeper says I threw him down, and be d—d to him."

The Earl of Crumbledown was by far too intent now upon his dispute with the Honourable Adolphus Leslie to take any notice of Jonathan Willoughby. He was rambling with the idea that Leslie, seeing how much annoyed he was at being spoken to familiarly by such a man as Willoughby, had sought to make him look more ridiculous still, in order that he might have a good story to tell at the clubs.

If there be anything which human nature finds it more difficult to forgive than another, it is the being exposed to ridicule. When even the sensation that such is taking place finds a home in the breast, it remains, and increases each moment until the imagination dresses it up into an offence of the most monstrous magnitude, and having no similitude whatever to its original shape and proportions.

There might still have been a reconciliation between the young men, but as Lord Crumbledown turned his head to make some conciliatory observation, he saw, or he fancied he saw, which was the same thing, a covert smile upon the face of Leslie, and his first idea was, " D—n the fellow ! does he think he has got so much the better of me that he is enjoying his laugh ? I must alter this state of things." Then aloud, he said,—

" May I ask you a plain question ?"

" Yes, my lord."

" Are you disposed to insult me ? and were you laughing at me ?" demanded the earl.

" As for a disposition to insult any man," was the reply, " I repudiate it, utterly ; but you are aware there was a codicil to Magna Charta which enabled people to laugh whenever they pleased."

" To which," said the earl, " was added a clause enabling people to choose their own acquaintances. It may sound a little harsh from me to you, boy as you are, but for the future do not presume to address me."

" Presume ? Truly it requires a rash amount of presumption to address a man as little encumbered with brains as the Earl of Crumbledown. As to the reproach of being a boy, if it means that you are, in contradistinction, a girl, you are a desperately ugly one, which, perhaps, accounts for the success with which you have assumed the outward semblance of a man."

" I can always applaud wit," said the earl, " but nonsense pals dreadfully upon the ear."

" Indeed ! and so accustomed to it as you must be."

" Perhaps you may hear from me, sir."

" At which I shall neither be pleased nor angry."

" Good morning, Mr. Leslie."

" Good morning, my Lord Crumbledown."

They mutually touched their hats, and then separated.

" That fellow has called me a fool," thought the earl ; " what am I to do ? Confound his impertinence. Am I to put up with it, and cut him, or call him out ?"

" I cannot be insulted in this way," were the meditations of the Honourable Adolphus Leslie. " If any man, who happens to be a few years one's senior, is to be in the habit of calling one a boy, and crowing over one, on account of that very doubtful advantage, life would be a succession of insults, and to have an independent opinion would be a matter of impossibility. I will call on my friend, Major Longshanks, and take his opinion upon the matter."

And thus did Jonathan Willoughby become a bone of contention between two persons, who, no doubt, equally despised him, and who now would have been extremely loath to admit that such a personage could have been in any way a ground of quarrel beween them.

But that great effects from trifling causes spring, is well known, and we should not at all be surprised if the Earl of Crumbledown found himself involved in a duel all about nothing.

If such should be the case, and it seems all to depend upon the tastes and habits of Major Longshanks, we suspect the readers will be inclined to think that the cutting speeches which were uttered to each other by the young men were but too true, and that when in courteous language they each intimated an opinion that the other was a fool, they were each in that instance at least wonderfully correct.

But we shall see. Major Longshanks may not be a man who is fond of duels; but, as the lady says in the farce, " Then, again, you know, he may."

And now the earl, as he got cooler upon the matter, almost succeeded in dismissing it entirely from his mind; and when he reached his own house, he found that letters of invitation had come from the Blenkeths, pressing the immediate departure of himself and the countess to Elm Lodge, where a distinguished selection of guests were already assembled.

Town was dull; and, therefore, the Countess of Crumbledown had, before the earl returned from his ride, made up her mind to accept the invitation, and when she mentioned it to him, she was very well pleased to find him in the same mind, so that the oddly-matched couple looked really quite amicably at each other.

" As we have not been," said the countess, " long enough in town to unpack even our luggage, or in any way to settle ourselves, it appears to me that the best thing we can do is to go off at once to Lord Blenketh's."

This, too, chimed in well with the earl's own feeling on the subject. He wished to be out of London, and he wished to look upon the face of that babe, which he could scarcely be said to have yet seen, so transient was the glance he had of it at the inn, where the tragic occurrences connected with its advent into this world took place.

He, however, made a merit of consulting the countess's wishes; and he said,—

" If it is more agreeable to you to start to-day for Lord Blenketh's, I shall have very great pleasure in accompanying you. We can easily get post-horses put to the travelling carriage, and a very few hours will take us there."

" Do not let me disturb any of your arrangements," said the countess; " but, if equally agreeable to you, we will dine early, and go."

" Certainly."

The requisite orders were at once given; and as there was no want, in the Earl of Crumbledown's establishment, of that most accelerating of all arguments—money—everything was ready for a rapid flight to Elm Lodge within an hour of the time when they were ordered.

An early dinner—or rather what might, considering its situation as regarded that meal, be called a lunch—was partaken of, and then the earl, gladly enough, turned his back upon London, and Mr. Willoughby, and the honourable Adolphus Leslie, and every other trouble which beset him in the great city.

" At least," he said, " I shall be free from absolute annoyance for some time; and, besides, it will be giving the Lady Julia Fanfaronade time to recover her indignation at the scene in the drawing-room."

It was still daylight when the travelling carriage of the Earl and Countess of Crumbledown reached the country seat of Lord Blenketh, which, although known by the unpretending title of Elm Lodge, was, in reality, a place of very considerable pretensions, and with ample capabilities, if need should arise, for the entertainment, within its lordly precincts, of a monarch and his court. But we must defer its description to another chapter.

CHAPTER XXVII.

THE OLD COUNTRY SEAT.—THE ARRIVAL.—THE COUNTRY LANE, AND THE LOVE CHILD.

ELM LODGE was a perfect specimen of a gentleman's country residence, which, while it possessed all that is prized in its ancient structure, was well fitted for the residence of a nobleman, from the art and elegance with which it had been adapted to the age and character of the time of its present owner.

Everything that, in modern refinement and luxury, was deemed necessary and proper, here found its appropriate place.

The house was ancient and even beautiful in its structure, while its interior had all the advantage that great wealth and taste could offer such a place ; for while we have gone back in the art of building houses for the wealthy, we have increased the amount and beauty of many of the articles that are in use by modern refinement.

It was an ancient looking place, and the old timber trees that grew all around it, bespoke it of many ages standing.

The worst of modern houses is the difficulty of obtaining good trees ; they take time in growing, though the houses take but a short period in building ; but it is the old timber trees that bespeak the age of the place, and give it an air of grandeur and respectability which modern built places cannot allow.

Indeed, the difference of the two may consist in this—the one tells of a long time of prosperity and respectability, while the other can only boast of a new made respectability.

Elm Lodge had many fine trees, whose lofty tops had often bent beneath the winter's storm, and often might the winter's wind be heard rustling through their leafless branches with a mighty sound as of a rushing torrent.

The old lodge, as it was called, bore all the appearance of grandeur and wealth, and was, moreover, picturesque and beautiful, from its style, its situation, and prospects.

There was plenty of room in the lodge, and it would accommodate any number of visitors who might be called together by any sudden and great emergency that might arise among people who are well off, and of the oldest and most highly connected families of distinction.

It is singular ; but all those old halls—baronial residences—have vast capabilities, which, when seconded by great wealth, come out in strong relief against the known and limited extent of the modern buildings.

But, then, they were built in times when hospitality was a more universal virtue than it is at present—when men of distinction travelled with more extensive retinues than they do now—and at a time when there was less commercial wealth than there is now ; and when, indeed, the owners of such places had not their wealth locked up in such mysterious things as the funds, three-per-cents, and so forth ; but they held land and oxen, and the produce of the land also.

Hence, there was always plenty, come who may ; and there was always plenty of room for the unexpected guest.

Elm Lodge was, in the hands of its modern owners, always the pleasant place that the gentry went to, and were always pleased when the season came when a visit could be made.

Lord Blenketh was a liberal man in the article of hospitality to his visitors ; and the grounds were so extensive, the trees so old, so large, and the shrubberies so beautiful, the gardens and walks so tastefully laid out, that the greatest number of guests could always find plenty of room to wander about in solitude and silence, if they were so minded.

There was abundance of amusement and room for them all, so they were not compelled to be continually in each other's presence, but they had time to recover the fatigues of a long conversation, in which their spirits might have become exhausted.

There were, too, many beautiful walks in the neighbourhood, where the guests might wander undisturbed.

Here it was that the Earl and Countess of Crumbledown arrived to spend a short time on a visit with many other visitors, for the lodge was to be full, and it was known that it would take many, indeed, to fill the old building, so capacious as it was.

The village was in an unusual state of excitement. The number of guests that arrived was very great, and as soon as the sound of wheels and the tramp of horses were heard, every head in the village was popped out from its respective door, and the usual sagacious remarks of the owners were heard and given with gravity and deliberation, that amazed the younger portion of the community, who were all excitement at this unusual bustle and stir.

"Look at the handsome greys," said one; "how they slip along with that chariot; there's nothing better than a team of greys."

"Oh, nonsense!" said a groom; "I know better than that. There, look at them four—dark bay, black manes and tails and feet—ain't they beautiful?—well-matched, every vein to be seen standing out of their silky coats; there's no colour equal to a dark bay—these are the horses to go—sound wind and limb; and they'll last longer and thrive better than any other colour, and are altogether a better and a hardier animal."

"Ah, that's all very well; nobody knows anything about that; but if I were a lady, I would have greys."

"And I wouldn't."

"You have no taste."

"Hold your tongue, you jade, or I'll give you something to talk about."

"Oh, you are a nice man—ain't you? You ——"

"There," said a bystander, "I wouldn't quarrel about what you will never have, under any circumstances, and fight over a bone in another dog's mouth—eh?"

This effectually silenced all squabbles of the loving or unloving pair.

In the mean time, carriage after carriage arrived—not that the guests were to arrive, or were expected to arrive, on one day; some had been there days, and others would not come for several days. Just the tenth of them came on this day, and hence the unusual bustle and excitement that prevailed.

Among the guests who came were the Countess and Earl of Crumbledown, and they were preceded by outriders, who came rushing through the village at a rapid rate, and exciting a vast deal of attention from the villagers.

Then came the carriage, drawn by four fine greys, and this dashed along at full speed; the dust was thrown up in clouds, and the curs in the village set up an universal shout, and ran barking and yelling, while the vehicle remained in sight.

The earl and countess were welcomed to Elm Lodge by its noble owner; and the avenue of elm trees, whose great age was fully borne out by their size and height, seemed alive with human faces, for many stood between them to see the visitors arrive.

The earl and countess were soon received in the ancient building, and conducted to the apartments that were destined for their use during their stay at Elm Lodge.

The morning was spent in following the noble owner about, and in awaiting and exchanging congratulations with other guests, and being introduced to strangers, and strangers introduced to them, until the dinner bell rang loud and sonorous over the whole building, and could be heard all over the grounds.

This signal was attended to, and the large saloon, or dining-room, which was capable of containing at least a couple of hundred guests, was laid out in mos magnificent style.

Everything that convenience or luxury could suggest, was there to be found. It was, indeed, the home of all that was *recherche*—all that could be conceived as useful or ornamental to the occasion.

And then, as to the viands—there can be little said of them; they were such, as such guests had a right to expect from such an entertainer as the wealthy Lord Blenketh.

The viands were delicious—nothing was thought of or imagined, but what was there at hand, and none could complain of the attention, or of the abundance and luxury that prevailed.

When this scene was over, and the wine had passed a few rounds, the Earl of Crumbledown and Colonel Bruce arose, to walk about the grounds awhile.

Several other guests did the same, therefore there was nothing singular or premeditated in this; but these two gentlemen were sitting together, and expressed a mutual desire to walk in the open air, the day being so fine and so tempting.

"I will walk with you," said the Earl of Crumbledown, "for I feel warmed."

The two gentlemen left the dining saloon, and were soon out in the garden, and then they walked into the more secluded spots.

"The ancient appearance of those trees are to me extremely grateful. All seems quiet and shady, and though the air is warm, yet it is very refreshing to me."

"It is so; by the way, you know this neighbourhood very well, I believe?"

"I was here some time ago, as you know," said the earl.

"Exactly—I know the occasion. Have you any objection to stroll over the lane, it leads to the village?"

"None. I am not likely to be recognised. I think I should like to go and see the child, and the woman who has it in charge."

"Very well. I think that can easily be done. You are very differently dressed, and got up now, to what you were then."

"I wore no mustaches then."

"You'll not be known."

"I think not. How will you get out of the ground?" inquired the earl.

"We can make a gap, or get over the hedge easy enough. I remarked a place somewhere here, that would do well."

"Exactly. Then here it is, I suppose," said the earl, pointing to a place.

"Yes, I dare say it is."

They both jumped into the lane, and walked towards the village for some moments in silence. A few thoughts seemed to be passing through the earl's mind, that were of a sombre character. No doubt he remembered well the occasion of his former visit, and the melancholy events that then took place, and they could not but have a saddening influence upon his mind even at such a moment.

The lane they were walking in was exceedingly picturesque and beautiful. Large trees, and wild flowers were creeping about in profusion.

The sweet scents from the gardens and the fields now filled the air, and the cornfields were filled with labourers, that were busily employed in the harvest just then commenced.

"I think," said the earl, "this place seems remarkably beautiful, and would deserve to be protected from intrusion."

"That would be impossible, because the place is public, and the common people have a right to come here."

"That is true enough."

"Here you see is a woman," said Colonel Bruce, "sauntering along with her child, no doubt to give it the benefit of the air."

"It may be so," said the earl. "By heavens, 'tis the very woman who had my child to nurse."

"Indeed!"

"Yes," said the earl. "I wonder if she will recognise me. If she do not, no one else will."

"She will not, I think, when you consider the difference of your appearance at that time and the present; there can be no fear."

"No, none. Let us go forward and address her," said the earl, as he walked slowly towards Mrs. Grove, who was unconsciously walking along.

"You have a fine child there, my good woman," said the earl, as he reached her.

"Yes, she's a sweet girl, sir," said Mrs. Grove, dropping the earl a curtsey, at the same time she looked very hard at him.

"It seems very healthy," remarked the colonel. "It's a healthy spot about this neighbourhood, I dare say—is it not so reckoned?"

"Yes, sir."

"Is that your own?" inquired the earl, looking at the child attentively.

"No, sir."

"Indeed!" said the colonel; "who's is it, if there is no secret about it?"

"It belongs to some gentle people, who placed it in my hands to nurse, and take care of."

" Which you do, no doubt; and a better proof of that cannot be, than the healthiness and heartiness of the child, for it seems both."

" Yes, sir, I do my best by it."

" No doubt. Pray, who is it that has the pleasure of calling that infant theirs ?"

" Some people who are well off in London, and I know nothing more."

" Their name. Don't you know that ?"

" I have heard, but know nothing about them; they pay me handsomely, and I endeavour to do my duty by it, which I would do, for the child's own sake; for I love it—it is so sweet tempered."

" Accept that," said the earl, taking some money from his purse, and placing it in the woman's hand, " and use it as you will, freely. I am fond of infants, and I delight in seeing them well taken care of."

Before Mrs. Grove could reply, the earl and Colonel Bruce had turned from the spot, and were retracing their steps back again.

" You are evidently not known," said the colonel.

" I am not, as she has failed to recognise me."

CHAPTER XXVIII.

WILLOUGHBY'S MANŒUVRES.—THE HORSE AND TILBURY BUSINESS.—THE APPOINTMENT.

Two hundred pounds in the hands of a clever, designing, and unscrupulous individual, is a large sum, and much can be done with it, and so Willoughby found; and, indeed, he knew that well enough already, or else he had not long retained that sum in putting himself in such a style as he believed would aid him in deceiving the world as to who or what he was, and in making such a figure as might throw him on some track of maintaining it, and making a fortune.

He determined upon keeping his vehicle, and for that purpose set about the cleverest way he could imagine for that purpose. Having arranged all with respect to himself, his personal appearance was graced by a fashionable suit, and really improved under his tailor's hands, and it may be reasonably concluded that the tradesman himself was not bettered by the bargain, eventually; indeed, it was part of his plan to make his two hundred pounds last as long as they would, by any and every device that he could think of, and he was by no means deficient in invention for that purpose.

He also resolved to reside at an hotel, where he could have all the ease and delights of a highly fashionable home, with a tenth of the cost, and with none of the many disagreeables that attend the actual possessor of a large establishment.

" Yes," muttered Willoughby, as he gazed at himself before a glass, and picking a small speck off his coat, " I may do now; I am unexceptionable, from beaver to boots. I must push my fortune now. I must make a hit somewhere. I must—let me see—yes, I must get a tilbury. Ay, let me see, a tilbury or a cab—ay, one or the other. Let me see; a cab's out of date, and it wants too much attention. I don't want to have the trouble of servants; I can get them when I want them, whenever occasion may serve. And now, about the tilbury; ay, if I could get one of a private party, why I would, of course, do him; or if I go to the coachmaker's, I might get one remarkably cheap, and give them a bill, payable at three months, or thereabouts; but—but one I must have, and will put it up at livery; I shall know then the expense I am at; my income will run all the further."

Accordingly, he perused all the advertisements for a day or two; but being dissatisfied, he went to a coachmaker's at once, and having procured what he wanted, he desired it might be sent at once to his hotel; but seeing an insurmountable difficulty in the way of payment, he gave some general directions, and left the place.

However, one disappointment was nothing at which Mr. Willoughby was likely to feel at all poignantly, but rather settled in his own mind a resolution to obtain the thing elsewhere, and even upon more reasonable terms.

Chance favoured him, and he had an interview with a gentleman who was about to pass over to the continent, and who was desirous of getting rid of a new turn out. He had not many weeks purchased it, both horse, harness, and tilbury,—all once new.

"This," thought Willoughby, "will do well; and now for the arrangement of affairs. I must not be too knowing, but appear on the wrong side of intelligence in this affair."

Accordingly, he introduced himself as one who was coming into large property; that, indeed, it was already his, but he could not withdraw it from the hands of executors until a few weeks passed over; as persons trusted with the administration of another person's affairs, would not be hurried beyond what legal forms required them.

"And now, sir," he said, after some conversation with the individual whom he intended to dupe; "what is the price you ask for it?"

"Seventy guineas for the whole affair; and I assure you, on the honour of a gentleman, it cost me nearly three times the amount."

"Well, sir, I do not doubt your word. I should like to see and try the vehicle, and the horse; and if you have no objection, I should like a veterinary surgeon to see the horse, an individual, upon whose opinion I have much reliance; my own judgment I have much doubt of."

"Very well, as I mean nothing but what is fair, I have no objection to such a proposal. When will you try him?"

"To-day, or any day you please."

"Then let it be to-day. I am leaving England the day after to-morrow, therefore the sooner it is parted with the better."

Accordingly, they both sallied out, and driving through the town, they ran down the Edgeware-road, until they came very nearly to the town of Edgeware, where they stopped, and then rattled back to London.

Willoughby expressed himself satisfied; and promised to call the next day to see the horse, and bring the veterinary surgeon with him.

He immediately pounced upon a man whom he knew, and on whom he could rely in the case of a do; and the next day he again called upon the same individual.

The horse was brought out, and admired, and pronounced to be good; but there was something about it that made him inclined to think it a bad-tempered animal.

"I cannot help thinking," said the farrier, "that there is something about the animal—that he is bad-tempered, and the near leg seems as though it were tender."

"He went well enough yesterday."

"He did," said Willoughby, "and exhibited no signs of bad temper or otherwise, then."

"Well, I should like to see him in harness, and then I can form an opinion in less than half an hour's gentle ride."

"I suppose there can be no objection to that," said Willoughby, turning to the owner.

"Oh! none; but I suppose this will decide you, and you will be ready to settle with me at once, as I have no more time to spare, but shall send him away."

"Oh! if there's no grave defect, I shall look upon the horse as my own, and the bargain is struck between us, and that, upon payment of the money demanded, I shall have the thing as it now stands."

"Yes, conditionally to your being satisfied, the thing is yours."

"That is what I mean. In half an hour or less," said Willoughby, "I will return, and settle this affair with you, or I will return the concern."

So saying, he stepped into the vehicle, and both he and the farrier drove off to become thoroughly satisfied of his temper, and also to prepare a bill of exchange for fifty pounds, and an offer of cash for the remainder.

"I am only doubtful," thought Willoughby, "how far I ought to pay money at all, but give the bill. Let me see—a wrong stamp will by no means render the affair less complete."

Having settled all this in his own mind, he drove back to the house, and, with a wave of the hand, motioned his companion to drive on, which, by previous concert, he did.

See p. 160.

"Well," said the gentleman; "how have you settled—are you satisfied?"

"Quite—quite; he warmed the horse, and I sent it on to prevent keeping it waiting, while we were settling, fearing it might catch cold."

"Very good; and now about the seventy pounds," said the gentleman.

"Yes, certainly," said Willoughby, screwing his features up, and pulling out his purse; "I have it here. By-the-bye, I told you my ready money was locked up, and I should not get it till the law's delays shall permit me."

"Well, sir ?" said the gentleman, in a very freezing tone, as if he feared there was something wrong.

"Why, I have not got all the cash ready at my hand at this moment, but only part; but I dare say, sir, that it can make no difference to you if you have part now, and a part a few weeks hence."

"It is a ready money transaction."

"So it is."

"But that is not ready money."

"It is almost the same thing."

"But I am going to leave England to-morrow, and may not be back for many weeks, perhaps months – it is monstrous."

"My dear sir, be patient—be patient; these expressions are not at all applicable to the case. I cannot understand them in a personal light, else I must send another individual to arrange the business with you, for I cannot permit such language or inuendos to pass."

"You may do what you like, but it is a very shabby occurrence."

"Will you accept of the bill—a bill for fifty, and the remainder cash?"

"No, I must have all cash."

"I fear I cannot oblige you. I have laid out so much already; but here is the bill for fifty, and the cash with me; a receipt, and the whole affair is settled."

"But I won't have the bill. I'll have the whole concern back again."

"Indeed!"

"Where have you sent it to?"

"It is now on its way to Windsor, I dare say; but I can send for it and have it sent back, since you desire it. I am not so very anxious about the property."

"Very well, send for it. When will you send it back?"

"The day after to-morrow."

"Good God! and I am to leave London to-morrow morning. This will never do, I must have the money. This will never do."

"You cannot have everything, my good sir; and had I thought ready money had been of so much importance to you, I would have borrowed it, or got this bill discounted, which I could easily have done in the city."

"I wish to Heaven you had!"

"I will do so now, and see you again before you go out of town to-morrow."

"Oh! no, no," said the gentleman; "upon second thoughts, I will take the bill and the cash, twenty-three pounds ten."

"The receipt."

"But I cannot give a receipt, as it will make the bill appear void."

"Oh, no; but say the transaction was settled by bill and by cash; that is the truth, you know, and there can be no difficulty."

The injured owner did write out the receipt, and took the cash and the bill. Willoughby pocketed the receipt with inward satisfaction, and left the house, congratulating himself upon the *do* that he had so successfully perpetrated, and rejoined his friend, the horse-doctor, in the next street, where he jumped into his newly-acquired tilbury, and dashed away, leaving his friend with a handsome fee for his trouble in the transaction.

He immediately drove to his hotel, and, after showing it about, drove it to a livery-stables, where he had it put up.

This was a successful beginning; and Mr. Willoughby, with these accessions, seemed the very model of an intriguing man of the world. His personal appearance and address were in his favour, and he had a good knowledge of society; and, now he had begun, he thought he would lose no opportunity; and he, moreover, expected a pretty long run thus, by what he would wring from the hands of the earl, for he fully looked upon that young nobleman as a mine, from which, by duly working it, would be obtained a stream of gold, by which he could live, and enjoy life.

The next day he sported his new vehicle about; and, as he was a good driver, he felt much pleasure in driving about the busiest scenes in London.

He had been in the city, and was driving down the Strand, when some one called out to him to stop; but he took no notice of the hilloa, for he thought it was not intended for him, and, if it were, it could only come from some person whom he did not wish to know; he, therefore, increased his speed, and dashed along at full speed.

"Hilloa! hilloa! stop that tilbury—stop that tilbury—stop that tilbury!"

Notwithstanding what was said, or being alarmed from some unknown cause, or whether it was panic or what, but Willoughby, instead of stopping to ascertain what was the matter, struck the horse, and proceeded onward at a very rapid rate; but with all this speed he could not escape, there were too many things in the way—vehicles of all sorts blocked the way.

"Stop that tilbury—stop that tilbury—stop him—stop him!" were cries that followed him very close, when he found, suddenly, that there was a momentary stoppage that stayed his progress, but it soon cleared, and he was about to start on afresh, when several people rushed out, and seized his horse's head.

"What's that for? Leave go my horse's head; take your hands off the bridle, or I'll give you the whip."

"Stop him! wait awhile, my swell—you've run over somebody."

"Who? I have run over nobody. Get away, you scoundrel."

"Wait till the gentleman in the miscellaneous togs comes up; him as is dressed in the mop cuttings, I mean; here he is. What's the matter, sir—anybody killed?"

"No—no; I only want to speak to this gentleman. Drive on, Willoughby," and the individual, who was not inaptly said to be dressed in mop-cuttings, got into the tilbury amid the laughter of the mob, and to the chagrin of Willoughby, who at once recognized the individual whom Mr. Whitford had rescued from the river.

"In the name of God!" said Willoughby, "what made you get such a mob round me?"

"You wouldn't stop."

"I didn't know it was you; and I didn't know that it was I who was wanted."

"What made you run away, then?"

"I'm hanged if I can tell you; but some sudden impulse—if I had thought, I would have acted differently; but you are in bad trim, and will do me no credit."

"No, I know that; but you and I are old acquaintances, and I am sure you are glad to see me."

"Oh, very."

"Well, then, in that case, there's no harm done; but I have a very great deal to tell you, and it will take some time to do so."

"Indeed! Can't we meet somewhere else, and speak over these matters?"

"We can, if you choose to do so."

"I would do so, then. Where shall it be? but let it be in the evening."

"That will suit me. By the way, you are in excellent case; you have been successful, while I have been, as you can easily guess, the reverse, and am badly off, because I am hiding for a little time, and am not anxious to be seen. You remember the old deserted inn some distance to the left of the Borough, near the plot of ground called the Island, in Bermondsey?"

"I do."

"Well, come to me there, about nine. I am secreted alone in that place; do not be observed if you can avoid."

"I will not."

"And how, just lend me a few shillings, for I am quite out; but you will not fail to come according to your appointment?"

"I will not; you may depend upon that. Here is the silver—it is all I have—good day."

The man descended, and Willoughby soon shot past his questionable friend.

CHAPTER XXIX.

THE DESERTED INN IN BERMONDSEY.—THE MEETING.—THE AGREEMENT.

WILLOUGHBY was pleased enough to get rid of the man who had so suddenly thrust himself upon him in so unceremonious a manner; and whose habiliments were wretched, tattered, and miserable in the extreme. His features were dark and forbidding, with a decided and ungraceful turn of the eyes inwards towards the nose; and his head was surmounted by a hat that served most appropriately as the capital of the column.

It was some time before he thought himself free from the eyes of people; who could tell that such a person had been with him.

This individual had known Willoughby some time before; and they had both been engaged in the same schemes, and were free from the consequences, no doubt, because they were successful; and, if not, it was known who were the perpetrators of such deeds.

There could be no doubt but that this man had some influence over Willoughby, derived from his knowledge of some secret, which, if told, would probably consign him to a prison, or else bring disgrace upon his head; this much is certain—he was not a man likely to be influenced by anything that arose either from sympathy or feeling. No—no; he was the last that was likely to be moved by such things.

Willoughby drove to his stables, and then walked to his hotel, where he remained for the remainder of the day, and then towards night he began to consider about keeping his appointment with the questionable individual beforementioned.

It was near eight o'clock when Willoughby quitted his hotel, and, throwing a cloak over him, he made towards the Borough, a strange place, which few who live on the other side of the river know anything about; indeed, few ever go there. There may be some kind of communication and traffic carried over, but I think it is known almost exclusively to its inhabitants.

There are many places that are in ruins, and many that are wastes; sometimes turned into gardens during the summer, and over which pigs and dogs luxuriate in winter—dust heaps and receptacles for rubbish of all kinds, however unsightly or disagreeable it might be.

The neighbourhood is called Bermondsey, and is composed of long, rambling, indescribable streets, intermixed here and there with these things, or these places of disagreeable and unsightly appearance.

Near one of these stood a large, rambling house. It had been formerly an inn, and that, too, within the memory of man. It was a strange old building, very large, and very rambling; and had long since been condemned as dangerous; and, as if in verification of this opinion, a portion of it had given way.

Whereupon, the authorities, to show their vigilance and care of the public, had boards erected before it, to prevent the mischief that might arise, if any unfortunate vagrant were to sleep beneath its gateway, by the falling of the material.

At the back there were means of entrance; but it was somewhat difficult and disagreeable, being an open space, very deep to get down into, and very uneven, full of holes, and covered with all sorts of mess and mud.

Such was the place that Willoughby found, after he had carefully examined it, and turned from side to side, that the ill-looking individual had appointed as their meeting-place.

"Well," he muttered, "this is as strange and miserable a place as ever I saw. I wonder what induced him to come here?—not to hide himself, because that would be done better in my opinion elsewhere; however, every one to his fancy. I believe that this place is much worse than it used to be; it was very bad years ago; but now it is much worse."

He walked to the other side of the way, muttering as he did so,—

"I sha'n't go in, unless he comes and shows me the way. I am not going to break my neck, or drop into some muddy hole up to my neck and no one near to help me out. It must be poverty alone that induces him to choose such a place as that for his retreat."

The evening had set in squally, and it rained occasionally, sometimes lightly, and sometimes it came down at a very rapid rate; the streets were dull and empty; but few passengers were about at that hour.

Willoughby, at all events, found there was but very little to disturb his meditations, and he wrapped the cloak around him, determined that he would remain an hour at least; and, in case he should not see him, he would leave the place, and not see him again, but forget the whole affair; he had been willing to meet him, and had come there to do so, but he was absent.

"This is infernally tiresome though," muttered Willoughby; "I must try some scheme or other for attracting his attention, for, after all, he may be in the house, but not be seen."

He walked into the road, and, picking up a stone, he threw it into one of the windows, of which there were many broken.

This produced the desired effect, and it was soon after thrown into the street again, and Willoughby could see a face which, after a time, said,—

"Is that you, Willoughby ?"

"Yes."

"Come round the back way."

"I can't, unless you come to help me."

"Very well," muttered the same voice; and Willoughby thought he heard something like a curse or two, as he turned away.

"Ah, you may swear; it's no use grumbling, I can't and won't go over that ground by myself, because the falling into any well is unpleasant, more especially so chilly and cold as I am, waiting in this miserable weather."

He came to the end of the boarding, and there he waited for some moments, till a cautious footstep approached.

"Here I am," he muttered—"all right—there's nobody nigh."

"It is all right. Jump down."

"Jump down, eh ?"

"Yes."

"Jump where, though? that's what I want particularly to know, and can no more tell than if it were into the bottomless pit."

"It is not more than four feet."

"Can't you give me your hand ?"

"No, no; d—n it, no; jump—it is soft."

"I dare say it is," said Willoughby; "all I fear is, it may be too soft."

However, urged thus, he did jump; it was not worse than he had anticipated, for he did not sink above five or six inches in the muck and rubbish that filled the place.

"Come this way," said the man; "come this way, and we shall be unobserved; people pass and repass this place often enough; had it been fine, I dared not have come out to you."

"Then I had dared not to come," said Willoughby, "and we should have missed each other, which would have looked shabby on your part, for I came to oblige you."

"Then oblige yourself, and take care where you are going to," said the individual, who squinted most terrifically.

"With pleasure most unfeigned," said Willoughby; "but how the devil could you bring me to such a place as this ?"

"It is secure."

"But you might have told me what kind of place it was, and I would have made some provision against the filth that I have to encounter, as you know you will spoil my clothes, and my wardrobe is as precious to me as ever Walter Raleigh's cloak was to him; and I am in no such way of getting my fortune as he had, and, therefore, I am not seized with such a sudden fit of generosity."

"Well, well, come along," said the man ; "and don't stand there making as much noise as a boy at a bonfire."

"An uncommon simile, it must be admitted ; but who on earth told you that ?"

"Your infernal clatter will bring down the whole neighbourhood on us presently ; here, get up here, and go in."

"Go in ?"

"Yes."

"No, thank you ; as it is all in the dark, I would sooner see you go first, and then, you know, I may be able to form some practical notion of its possibility."

"You fool !"

"Come, come ; you are scarcely civil to your visitors, and I shall go back again."

"Are you such a fool that you don't know me before to-day ; do you expect to find me here, in distress and danger, standing bowing and uttering civil speeches, when your infernal folly may betray me? Come in, or go away, which you like. I brave you."

"Well, well, then, come ; you needn't be in such an infernal ill-humour, but just step in first, and I'll follow you."

"Then just step up to that place there, and then I can fasten the place after you ; else anybody can come in."

"Very well," said Willoughby ; "is this it ?"

"No, a step higher."

"Will this do ?"

"Yes," said the stranger, springing up, and forcing him in.

Willoughby tumbled forward, and fell a short distance, and then jumped up, terrified at the mode of ingress that he had been forced to adopt, and fearing worse consequences.

"Now," said the man, coming in, "you might have done this without half the fuss ; but, now you are in, come, follow me."

"And where to ?"

"You shall see."

"But what do you mean ?"

"That I ain't a going to be trifled with ; you wanted to play with me outside, now I'll show you I won't play."

"I didn't mean anything of the sort," said Willoughby.

"Very well, then ; come after me now ; I have got a light below stairs in one of the cellars, where we can see and speak in comfort."

"Very well," said Willoughby.

They both now descended the stairs, and, after many turnings and twistings, they came to a passage, which carried them some yards, when the stranger stopped, and opened a door, saying,—

"Here we can talk, and say what we will, without being in any fear that we shall be overheard by any one."

"That's a comfort," said Willoughby, looking round at the miserable, damp walls, which were shining and wet from moisture and age, and it appeared to be very rotten.

The stranger closed the door and secured it, and then said,—

"Here we are then, Willoughby ; met after so long a time, and a longer separation."

"Why, I thought you had been dead, and I believe you must at least have been cooped up somewhere or other, for some little friendly deed or other ; but you are nearly as bad."

"Why, yes, I am not in exactly the best trim I would be in," said the man, looking down at his dress, which certainly was something of the very worst that could be.

"And how came you to get into this trim ?" inquired Willoughby ; "there is a cause for everything, and there must have been one in this case."

"Undoubtedly. I was attacked, and I fled. I have been hiding here for a night or two. I have most essential reasons for not being seen."

"I can easily understand that."

"You have known that, before to-day, you have had more than friends who have been after your tail?"

"Yes, yes, but I was always careful as to what I did, or who I trusted."

"Yes, you were."

"And I always kept on the windward side of the law. I was always safe."

"Yes, you were; but I suspect that in more than one instance you might even now be nailed if they were certain to pounce upon the right man," said the stranger.

"But there is no one bad enough to betray me; but I don't think there is anything that can hurt me, if the worst come to the worst; in fact, I am sure that they cannot."

"I am mistaken," said the man; "but it matters not; but what are you doing now?"

"Nothing," said Willoughby; "nothing at all; merely upon the look out, you know."

"Indeed! I am upon the look out, too; but it is a poor look out for me; and, moreover, I am doing nothing. Look at my clothes and tell me how they thrive upon nothing. How does it happen that you thrive so well upon it? the stock cannot cost you much."

"Well, well; but you see I am doing nothing; literally nothing. I have done this much: done a gentleman out of a tilbury and horse, and I have done a tailor."

"Couldn't you do one for me?" asked the stranger.

"Why, now, how the devil could I carry you about and recommend you; it would not do; you would be given into custody for attempting to obtain goods under false pretences; it would never do under any circumstances."

"Well, well; but what are you doing?"

"I have told you."

"That will not do for me."

"There is nothing more to tell you."

"I say there is."

"There is not."

"Now, Willoughby, I can tell as well as possible, that you have a good thing in view. You would not be so lavish of yourself if there was not something going forward that is worth while."

"Indeed you are mistaken."

"I am, am I?"

"You are, on my honour."

The man said nothing more, but he walked up to Willoughby, and suddenly darted his hand, and caught him by the throat, exclaiming, as he did so,—

"You know, Willoughby, that I am by far the strongest, and can as easily throttle you as tell you so; and I will do so if you will not act fairly by me, and tell me all."

"I will—I will. Upon my soul I will."

"Well, recollect I am the judge of whether you are doing so or not."

Willoughby, who knew the character of the man he was dealing with, and he believed him both able and willing to do all he threatened, at once candidly admitted all from first to the last; even the money he received.

"Well," said the man, "you must give me some money, and we must go shares in the produce of this mine."

"But it's not fair."

"I think it is fair."

"I would have no objection to aid you, but you know what a set you are in league with. They would ruin and spoil everything, and everybody. It would be madness."

"You need fear nothing further on that head," said the stranger. "I have wholly left them. Indeed they do not know that I live."

"Indeed!"

"Yes; they threw me into the river, when we quarrelled, and they attempted my murder, but they failed, and I have escaped from them unknown, and I shall let them think I am dead."

"Well, then, here is twenty pounds. You must get your clothing changed, and to-morrow I must see what I can do for you, and how I can make you useful in this affair."

They had some more conversation of a similar import to the former, and they both parted for the night.

CHAPTER XXX.

JACK GROVE'S SUBSCRIPTION LIST, AND HIS SUBSCRIBERS.—ROOM PREFERABLE
TO COMPANY IN CERTAIN CASES.

In his first fury Jack Grove cursed the donor of the first shilling, and the kick, exclaiming against him, the poacher, the villagers, and the whole world, and then he quitted the spot in a transport of rage.

However, he kept possession of the shilling, and the paper, and then, after having walked some distance, he sat himself down by the road side, and fell into a reflective mood, and began to chew the cud of sweet and bitter thoughts, the latter, however, manifestly prevailing, and giving an unamiable character to his imaginings and his wishes.

"Now," he muttered, "this is all a man's to be born for, is it? Why was I born at all? I don't know, I am sure, and I can't see what I have got by it; and I suppose other people want to get rid of me. D—n them! D—n him! and d—n them! and d—n all the world!" said Jack Grove, slapping his thigh with energy.

"Now, here's a feller would give a neighbour a shilling, and a kick. Yes, a kick and a shilling, and what for—would any one believe it? Why, to get rid of me; to help to send me away from my native place, and to get rid of me for ever.

"Was there ever such heartlessness in the conduct of one neighbour to another? It is worse than ever I believed in; and why? I am sure I can't tell. I never did him any harm, nor anybody else, that I know of; and yet everybody seems to want to get rid of me. Well, well, I don't care if they do, and as they don't care about me, where's the reason why I should about them?

"There's none—none at all. I will go, but no thanks to them, and if I don't succeed why I will come back again, whether they like it or not.

"Then as for this here paper," said Jack Grove, turning it over and over with a great deal of gravity, "it's no compliment to be sure, but then I may be able to get some shillings, and shillings are agreeable and useful. They ain't no offence. There's no insult in a shilling," said Jack Grove.

This was an undeniable proposition, and Jack Grove turned the shilling over, and then struck it mechanically with his thumb-nail, and sent it turning over and over in the air, and before it could fall again, he exclaimed in his usual tone,—

"Heads."

Down came the shilling in the palm of his hand, and he slapped it on the back of his left hand, exclaiming, earnestly,—

"Heads it is. Well done. Now I have a great mind to go round and collect some of 'em. Who knows but I may collect a hat full, and then I shall have a glorious time of it. Lord, Lord, what a many pints of ale I shall have when I am on the road. There's many a public-house between this and London. I wonder when I shall get there?

"But first about the shilling business," said Grove, looking at the coin; "that's the thing. Yes, I'll go round, and show 'em this paper, and gammon 'em over a bit. It will be a very good plan. I don't care what they say, or

what they think ; there'll be no working a dead horse for the money, and if I get
it I'll go and start this blessed day for London, and leave this blessed place.

"If I should meet with the father of this child, why, I will make him tip up
handsomely ; if, as he says, he has any mystery about him, why he'll be afraid of
me, and that's why he must help me, and keep me on.

"Well, a fortune's to be made in London ; it's a great place, and if a man is
fond of ale there, why, he isn't looked upon as the only man who likes good
things. However, I'll go back with the paper, and see what I can do. It ain't
pleasant, but what matters ? it will soon be over, and then I shall be the gainer,
and a good jug of ale will wash away all unpleasantness that may arise. However,
bar kicks,—yes, bar kicking," said Jack Grove, rubbing himself.

He got up, and began his walk towards the village, filled with a good many
reflections in his own mind upon the prospect of success that lay before him,
and the probable chances there were of very unpleasant refusals.

While thinking upon the various chances and doubts which beset his under-taking, he came to a farm-house, not far from the village.

It was an old-fashioned, tumble-down, built-up-anyhow kind of place. There were all kinds of out buildings huddled up, and built close to the house; cow-houses, and piggeries, from which came reeking smells, and cries of trouble of the various inhabitants.

"I may as well begin here," exclaimed Jack; "the old farmer is a gruff customer enough, and very unlikely to give me a shilling; and yet there's no knowing. I'll try, and if he should kick, why, I'll leave too quick for him."

Having thus made up his mind to one course of action, he set about putting it into practice, and crossed over the wooden conduit for the waste water that ran by the road-side, and walked up the little path until he came to the door, which was open; but there was a kind of wicket below, made for the purpose, one to keep children in or out, as was deemed most advisable for the time being, and the other one was to keep the fowls out, as they had a great propensity to come in.

The farmer and his wife were seated on either side of the table, and were both enjoying what was called a little private chat, and were arranging various plans they had formed, when Jack Grove leaned across the wicket, and said,—

"Good morning, farmer Hodges."

Farmer Hodges looked up to see who it was that had accosted him, and when he saw him, he felt annoyed,

"Good morning, mistress," said Jack, to the farmer's wife; "a fine season this."

"A fine season for a working man to be lounging about in, truly," said Mrs. Hodges, tartly.

"Mustn't be hard, missus," said Jack. "I haven't got work, or else I should work."

"And who do you think will employ you, you good for nothing fellow?"

"What, drunken Jack Grove," exclaimed the farmer, "what do you want—work?"

"No, master."

"I believe you. You are the vilest vagabond in the whole parish. Ay, in the whole country, and that is saying much, you know, Jack."

"So it is, master; and too much, I think."

"And the most drunken into the bargain," said the farmer's wife. "He has a good-hearted, industrious woman for a wife. He's quite a disgrace to her. See how he has neglected her, and how he starves her. I am sure I wouldn't be a trifle towards putting him in prison."

"Thank ye, ma'am," said Jack; "but prison don't improve poor people; that I know from experience; a prison ain't a good school."

"It is a bad place, but it is good enough for bad people," said the farmer's wife.

"All I say is, bad people only get worse there," said Jack, doggedly.

"They never get any better, and they ain't sent to be better," persisted the far-mer's wife, growing angry; "the fact is, they're sent there to be punished. A pretty thing, indeed, if people had to pay towards keeping a county goal, and then be told they must pay for making them better as well. A fine thing, indeed."

"You are such a disgrace to the place, Jack," said the farmer, "that I wouldn't mind paying another penny in the pound increase of county-rate, to send you out of the country, or even hanged."

"Thank ye, farmer. I think I had better leave this part of the country."

"I wish you would. You should have my good wishes for your reformation and prosperity elsewhere, but here your example is contagious."

"Well, but I should want help; if I were able, I'd go to London."

"And why?"

"Because I think I could do better there, and once in London, I would never return."

"How happy would Mrs. Grove be."

"Oh, hang her—she may do as she can. She'll do well enough—she's all for herself."

"And you for the publican."

"No; I'm fond of ale, that is, good ale, I'll admit. I'll own that much, but nothing else; but look here, farmer, read that paper, and that will tell you all about it."

The farmer took the paper, and turned it over two or three times, and then read in a rumbling tone the words,—

"Subscription—hum—for Jack Grove—hum—to enable him—hum—to leave—hum—his native place. A very good thing," muttered the farmer. "To leave his native place, and do something for himself in London. One shilling, eh? you've collected that already?"

"Yes; you see I have made a beginning."

"And do you really mean to go, Jack?" inquired the farmer.

"Mean, farmer—ay, I just do. Let me get enough, and I'll engage that I never come here again. The place don't suit me, and neighbours have taken a dislike to me. I shall leave, and never return any more—I don't think I'm safe among enemies—let me get away, and I'll do better elsewhere."

"Well," said the farmer, "there's some truth in that, for whatever may be your intentions, you have been so long idle and drunken here, that nobody will believe in your reformation."

"May be not, farmer."

"I think it the best thing you can do; and where you are not known, you may succeed in getting work, and in abstaining from your most constant sin. You may be better, Jack Grove."

"I hope so, sir."

"And I think, better or worse, that it will be the best that can happen to his wife."

"Well, farmer, have you a mind to help a poor fellow at a pinch; for, fail or succeed, I never come here again."

"Never!"

"No, never."

"If you fail, you'll come back again."

"No, farmer, my mind's made up. If I fail, nobody here shall know it. They will say they know why, and that I shall not like. No, no—I shall keep my misfortune to myself, and not let people laugh at me, and enjoy it."

"If you succeed?"

"I sha'n't come then."

"And why not?"

"Because I shall leave behind nobody who cares for me, and I won't trouble them who do not, to share in my prosperity."

"Very wisely resolved; but I fear you will not keep your word."

"Indeed I will. Will you help me, farmer?"

"Well, I'll put down a shilling, too—'twill be well laid out."

"And I will give one, too," said the farmer's wife, "for his wife's sake; but mind you," she continued, "you are not to get drunk with the money, and say you won't go."

"Oh, no," said Jack Grove. "Oh! dear, no, I wouldn't do such a thing; besides, I mean going, and no mistake—there's no use in stopping."

"Very well; but mind, if you don't, you'll be put in gaol for getting money under false pretences, mind that."

"Oh! yes, ma'am, I'll take care of all that."

"Three!" said the farmer, handing him the two shillings and the paper, "that makes there. I hope you won't be seen in this neighbourhood after sunset."

"You may depend upon it," said Grove, "that I'll leave this place as quickly as I can; there's nothing to induce me to stop. I shall be off as quickly as I can; you may depend upon me."

"Well, go on and prosper, and you will never do that if you don't become sober."

"Well, now," muttered Jack, as he turned into the high-road, "there's a pretty set of unneighbourly creatures. If a man only takes a little drop of anything, see how he's talked to. I don't care a d—n for any of them, and if they don't do what I want, I will return here in spite of them all. I'm not to be done or frightened so easily as they may think. Oh! no, Jack Grove ain't such a fool. And there's that farmer's wife—why, who knows what she may take on the sly? and I've seen him drunk before now, so there ain't much to boast of as he seems inclined to do. It's all moonshine about sobriety—they all get drunk when they like, but they've got more to do it with, and that's how it is that they are never complained of while I am always in for something or other. Well, well, I've got three shillings—that will do. Every fresh name that goes down is a help, and more will follow suit."

He tossed up the money in the air, high over his head, and watched them as they came down, crying out heads.

"Two heads and one woman," he said, as he stooped to picked them up. "Go on and prosper. Women again—I shall do. This is devilish lucky, and much easier than loading a dung-cart, at one shilling and sixpence a-day."

Elated with this idea—this comparison of the industrious hard-working labourer with his own situation, he again walked forward, determined not to allow any chance to escape him, and every place where there was any prospect of a shilling being in the house, and the inhabitants able to give it, in he went and presented the petition.

It was astonishing how willingly people subscribed to the list, and added their shillings to each other, for the purpose of getting rid of him, Jack Grove, for ever.

Jack on several occasions couldn't credit it; he couldn't believe it possible, and yet he placed his hands in his pocket, chinked the money up and down, and found the proceeds of his labour—it sounded musically enough, and made the whole affair appear very real and positive.

There could be no mistake about it—there he was, and there was the money; and how else could it have happened, that he had so much money in his pocket?

"I couldn't have earned it. No, no, I have borrowed it—eh! borrowed it—no, that's not the word—nor have I begged it; but I tell you what I have done, I have raised it for a certain purpose—yes, yes, I have raised it—that's it."

Well satisfied with his own ingenuity in thus accounting to himself for the possession of such a sum, he looked about with the view of ascertaining what places yet remained.

"Ah! there's the parson; d—d if I don't go in and have a turn with him—he may be gammoned by a little of the dismals; I'll go in and try—it will be good fun."

The parsonage stood by the road-side, and was a nice little road-side place, with a garden, orchard, and paddock.

The parson himself was seated at his door, reading a book, and Jack Grove opened the little gate, and walked up towards him. The parson looked up at him, and said,—

"Well, Grove, what do you want here?"

"Will you look at that paper, sir?" said Jack, as he handed it to him.

The parson looked at it very hard for a time, and then he returned it, saying,—

"You have collected a goodly sum, Grove—how do you propose to use it?"

"I intend using it for the purpose mentioned in the paper, sir."

"I am glad of it."

"Will you give me a trifle to help me on the road, sir? I hope to be able to reach London, and there do some good for myself."

"And what hindered you from doing something for yourself here?"

"Drink, sir," said Jack, after a pause; "it was drink, sir. I have had so many companions who do the same thing, they will not let me do otherwise if I remain here."

"Well, then, Grove, I would advise you to go," said the parson, coolly.

"Won't you give me a trifle?"

" Assuredly not. You have been a drunkard all your life, and such you will be, go where you may. Never believe in reformation; it must be disinterested to be pure and sincere; but this is not—you only make it a pretence to obtain money. You need say no more, it will save some trouble. You can go."

CHAPTER XXXI.

THE DEPARTURE FROM THE VILLAGE.—AN INCIDENT OR TWO ON THE ROAD.—THE RICK-BURNERS.

JACK GROVE saw it was useless to say anything to the parson, who knew his character too well; but he was very angry, and couldn't help saying,—

" If I had been as drunk as King David's sow, you ought to have been the last to have said anything about it, since there's Scripture for it."

" Scripture doesn't say that David's sow was always drunk," said the parson, quietly.

" You be d—d!" said Grove, turning round, and slamming the gate after him.

He did not stop to listen if the parson made any answer to this; he walked on rapidly, and now he found he had gone through all that he thought at all able or likely to give a shilling for his journey.

" Oh," said Jack, " it hasn't been such a bad thing after all; some of 'em gave me more than a shilling; they took like smoke. Oh, I put on a good face, and had no more kicks."

" What's that?" muttered Jack, looking up at the sign of a public-house. " Oh, I know, the Whisp and Whistle. Well, I've been pretty hard at it all day, and I may as well go in and have a crust, and a drop of ale; it's good drink they sell here. Well, to be sure, to think I didn't know I was so near it."

" Let me see—yes, this is the road off, and the house is a good one, out of the village and all. Yes, I will drink a pot, and give them curses enough for a legacy."

He walked up to the door, which was up a couple of steps, and walking into the parlour, he saw several that he knew.

" Ah! Jack Grove! how are you, Jack Grove?—hav'n't seen you since you were in gaol."

" Indeed!" said Jack, " then you needn't advertise it, you know, or somebody's mug and your face, will become friends. I don't stand about trifles, you know, when I begin."

" It's all very well, by way of a joke, Jack; but if you do mean anything by that, you know I can fight as well as you."

" Who talked of fighting?" said Jack Grove. " I came here to have a jug of ale, and some cold meat and bread."

" Very well, have it in at once, then."

Jack Grove, however, turned out again; he knew the man he met there; he was as drunken as himself, and had a propensity to quarrel, and that, to one of Jack Grove's disposition, was a fearful thing; not that he minded fighting, but he well knew that there was every probability of his being well thrashed by this man.

He travelled on about two miles, and then he came to another public-house; it was near sunset, and he determined to enter, and have something to eat and drink.

" I never walked so far before," he muttered, " with so much money in my pocket, and so little to drink. I think, now, I deserve a little by way of encouragement. I ought to treat resolution; I can't go on this way; man must fall, unless he takes something to keep up, there's no mistake about that.

" Let me see—yes, two-and-forty shillings, that's it. I have counted them over and over again; they are all good. Well, I can get to London well with this."

He turned into the house, and having sat himself down, he ordered some ale and cold meat; these were brought him, and drinking a hearty draught of the ale, he set about the masticating process, and while he was thus employed, the landlord came.

"What! Master Grove," said the landlord; "I thought I should never see you again."

Grove looked up, and exclaimed,—

"What's that you, Tipple? How came you here? Why, I can't go anywhere, but what somebody's sure to know me. I'm known everywhere."

"Oh!" said a man, who was sitting opposite; "you are such a well-known character, that you will be known everywhere."

"That may be; I am pretty well known, I believe."

"Well," said the landlord, "how have you been all this while?"

"Oh, very well; but how came you to be here in this place?"

"Why, you see, I had a quarrel with my old landlord; he and I couldn't agree at all; he wanted me to pay a heavy sum for renewing my lease, and I wouldn't; the house was not worth it, you see, and so I came here at the end of the time."

"Is this a new house?"

"Yes, quite."

"I never saw it before."

"Very likely; but you never came out so far as this. What's the reason, eh?"

"Oh, I'm tired of the old quarters; and I am going to make a fortune in London."

"The devil you are!"

"Yes, I am."

"Are you sure you can do it?"

"Well," said Grove, "I can't say I'm sure of it; but, if I can find some friends that I think I can, I shall do well enough. You see, everything depends upon introduction, now. I know that when I'm once there, and have got their good word, why, you know, I'm done and settled—my fortune's made, in a manner of speaking."

"No doubt; you know very well what's what, by this time."

"I do, I believe yer. Another pint, and then I'm off."

"Some of the old sort, eh?"

"Yes."

The ale was brought, and the landlord said, "I've brought a double measure; if you please, we'll sit down together."

"With all my heart; but ——"

"What?"

"I don't know what I was going to say; but, let me see—what were we talking about just now, before you brought the ale?"

"Your journey."

"Oh, well, if I get on as I expect, I may come down and take a house somewhere hereabouts, near the old spot, you know."

"I see."

"Or, perhaps, in London."

"You'll let me know—won't you, where you're at? I'll come and see you, wherever you might be."

"Would you, though?"

"Yes, I would."

"I'll let you know where, depend upon it, if I should succeed, as I believe I shall."

"Very good. How do you travel—tramp it?"

"Yes."

"Very good exercise."

"Yes, it will be a good training against I have any work to do."

"Have you any money?"

"Yes, plenty," said Jack, striking his hand against his pocket, and making the money rattle.

"You'll stay, won't you," said the landlord, " all night?—there's no moon."

" No, I must be off; and that, too, at once."

" No; surely you'll stop and have another jug,—old acquaintances, you know."

"Yes, but I must be walking, you know. I have a long journey before me; and I must be off. Well, good-bye; I shall see you some of these days again, I hope."

" Yes, you will," said the landlord; "but you'll pay before you go—won't you?"

" Eh?"

" Pay."

" I have paid."

" No, you haven't."

" I have paid you. I paid you one-and-threepence—that's enough—ain't it?"

" You haven't paid at all. Come—come—hand over the browns."

" I have."

" Now, I tell you what it is; you had better pay at once, or I'll send for the constable. Isn't this too bad, gentlemen?" said the landlord; " here's this man come in to have refreshments and rest, and now he wants to go out again without paying for them. Ain't that too bad?"

Of course everybody said it was too bad; and three or four of them said they wouldn't mind kicking him well enough; and if he didn't pay the landlord, they would do so.

" Well, I'll pay," said Grove; " but I know I did pay him; but it is no use, I suppose; it's a dead robbery, that's all about it."

Grove paid the money a second time; the landlord, seeing that he would not be there again, thinking he would make the most of him.

Leaving the house, he sallied out, and cursed and swore as he walked along the road for some distance. The sun's rays were glancing across the country, and even full upon his face; he felt hot and drowsy, and could scarcely speak plain, and the further he walked, the worse he found himself.

Seeing a waggon on ahead, he made after it, determined to get a lift if he could, and have a sleep on the top.

By the time he got up to it he was nearly out of breath; he hailed the waggoner, who was deaf, and inquired if he would give him a lift onwards.

" How far?" inquired the waggoner.

" How far are you going?" inquired Grove.

" That's what I axed thee," said the waggoner, getting in a rage at not understanding, or not being understood, it was all one to him.

" I ax you how far you are going?" bawled Jack Grove; " are you deaf?"

" Deaf, and be hanged to thee," said the waggoner, who didn't like any allusion to his deafness, and who always denied it.

" Yes, deaf."

" I'll show thee if I be;" and he began to lay his whip across the legs of Jack Grove, who danced with rage and pain, and, seeing a gate close by, he scrambled over it to save himself from any further discipline.

The place Grove had jumped into was a rick-yard, where there were several stacks of hay; some of it new and some of it old, and one stack was about half cut.

Upon one part, that had been newly cut, he threw himself, and thought he would rest awhile, and recover from his smarting.

" I wish I could have got close to him," muttered Jack Grove, " I'd have given him something that would have made him convinced that he was deaf. Curse him, there was no doing anything with that whip, it cut one to the bone, and the very flesh is up in lumps—curse him!

" This is a very comfortable birth, I think I will wait here till to-morrow, till daybreak, and then I will walk on; yes, it will be a nice place to sleep in; there's no wind to get at one here, all is as comfortable as a fox in a hen-house.

" D—n that landlord," said Jack Grove, who had nearly dropped asleep, and suddenly recollected the first disaster, " he's a robber, he robbed me, plain enough;

he knew I paid him—he must have been sure of it. Half-a-crown there; that's too much, I sha'n't reach London if I go on in this manner; but I'll never enter his house again, he's lost his customer."

He now fell almost into a doze, when a loud barking awoke him, and a man entered the rick-yard with a dog, and having put some things to rights, he then went away; but he did not see Grove, who thought it was unnecessary to show himself, or make his presence known.

"Hah!" said Grove, "a pretty day this has been to me—plenty of things have happened to me. Let me see, first, there was a shilling and a kick—well d——n the kick—the shilling was a shilling, and was followed by a good many others, all of them given, however, with the hope that I should never come back again. I see, a pretty set they all are, not one of 'em worth a bunch of radishes.

"Then left, with two pounds two in my pocket—got robbed of fifteen pence—got thrashed by a deaf waggoner. Well—well, that will do for a beginning.

"I'm getting sleepy. This will be a very nice place to pass the night in—the harvest moon and all, providing there's no disturbance; and I can't see why there should be.

"Two pound two—yes, two pound—two pound two."

Thus Jack Grove fell fast asleep on the hay-stack, muttering over to himself the amount of money he had contrived to collect; and this being, with regard to money matters, a grand day to him, he could not very well forget the money he had obtained.

The sun sank, and the earth was, for a short space, in a very uncertain light; the moon rose as the sun receded; but, as it was a new moon, there was but little light derivable from such a source as that; but yet it did throw enough to light the traveller on his way.

That night Jack Grove had slept some hours; the fumes of the ale he had drank, were sufficient to make him cling to a harder bed than the one on which he lay.

However, deep as was his sleep, and long as it had lasted, it was not to remain entirely undisturbed.

That night, or rather towards the morning, there came into the rick-yard three men, all of whom were disguised.

They had owed the farmer who belonged to the ricks a grudge, and they came now to pay him off. Their motions were slow and stealthy, and they held a short whispered consultation together, and they were thus employed some minutes.

Then collecting some rubbish, and piling it lightly up against the stack upon which Jack Grove lay, they prepared to set fire to it.

"Get some more sticks," said one; "the hay will lay too close."

Some sticks were brought, and were mixed up with dry hay, and then they paused, and taking a box of matches from the pocket of one of them, it was ignited, and the men instantly decamped from the spot.

Jack Grove lay all this while unconscious and asleep; however, his sleep was very light, and the noise the men made when they quitted the yard awoke him, and he lay quietly enough, expecting to hear more, and so he did.

About a minute afterwards he thought he heard a strange noise.—he couldn't tell what was the cause of it, and it felt warm.

He lifted up his head, and giving a great cry, he sprang back, and rolled on to the ground.

The cause of this was, no sooner had he lifted his head up, than a tall roaring and rushing flame of fire met his gaze; he could not tell what it was, it was so unexpected, so unlikely, and so far from his thoughts.

Besides, it was hot and terrific; not a sound could be heard at that moment but the roaring of the flames, which seemed to nim awfully loud, and nothing met his sight but the red devouring flame.

The effect was instantaneous, and Jack Grove had nearly fainted with excessive fright. As it was, he could scarcely rise off the ground in time enough to prevent being scorched by the devouring flames as they rushed onward and forward, catching on every straw, and there was fuel enough for it there, Heaven knows.

He rushed from the spot, and with the utmost precipitation quitted the rick-yard, for it would be dangerous to be found there.

See page 172.

CHAPTER XXXII.

MORNING ON A COUNTRY ROAD.—MEETING WITH AN OLD ACQUAINTANCE.—AN UNPLEASANT DILEMMA.

So great was the precipitation with which Jack Grove quitted the burning haystacks, that he scarce saw where he was going, but he rushed along at a desperate pace in the same direction that the men had taken, and then were pursuing, with great care and caution.

They observed Jack coming, and, believing he was in pursuit of them, they increased their speed to get out of his way to the utmost, but yet Jack gained upon them, and, before they could make up their minds as to what they would do, Jack gained so much upon them that he was amongst them in less than a minute.

However, there was no time to consult with each other, and the one nearest to Jack knocked him down and then left him.

How long Jack Grove remained in this state, it is difficult to say ; but, when he did open his eyes, he seemed very confused, and daylight met his gaze—at least, it was daybreak : the sun's rays were chasing the night clouds from the skies, and making them beautiful from the many gorgeous colours in which they appeared to be dressed

Jack began to think—at least, he tried, but found the process very difficult, and he tried several times, but could not do so ; he tried again, and endeavoured to re-collect the occurrences of the previous day, and that which occurred last.

The events all came back to his mind, one after the other, but he thought over the same ground again and again before he could at all explain the cause of his present situation.

He knew he had fallen out, somehow or other, with somebody, who well whipped him, and then he recollected going to sleep, and how he awoke with the fire. Yes, Jack remembered all that, and that he ran away, which was most reasonable in him to do.

He recollected all this, but how he became insensible he could not understand ; he received a blow on the head, but how or wherefore he had no means of knowing. It was true it might have been accidental, and he might have run against something or other and produced a state of insensibility, such as he suffered under ; but then, what could he have run against ?—there was the question.

The ale he had drunk was strong enough to produce such stunning effects ; the moon was up, and yet that was too far off to be any probable cause of his discom-fiture ; he had observed nobody, and therefore felt persuaded that there was some unexplainable mystery about the affair.

Jack sat upon the grass and looked around him with a rueful visage.

"Well, I don't know," he muttered, "how it is, but it seems as if all the world took a pleasure in combining against me ; and what for, I am sure I can't say ; I never did any harm to anybody, and why should anybody do harm to me ? I suppose I may as well ask who it was that knocked me down, if it were any-body, and shall just as well get an answer."

He got up and began to look around him, and, seeing the high road at some distance, he made directly towards it.

"How I came here, I don't know. Oh, I ran away from the fire !—ay, ay. Well, if I go on this way, my journey to London will teach me a few things ; I shall know a great deal, if I don't die in learning them. I should think I must live to a good old age then, when I have once got over the hardship of learning."

Jack now reached the high road, and once more plodded his way towards London. It was early, yet the morning could hardly be said to have broken ; the mists still hung over the low places, and it was easy to see the tops of the trees as they rose out of the white vapour that floated beneath them, looking like islands and mountains in the midst of the ocean.

The hedgerows held their glittering pearls ; the gossamer webs hung like a mantle upon the bushes, retaining the moisture that floated over them, and ap-pearing in the sun's rays like beautiful silver-frosted net-work.

The dusty roads had a slightly deepened tint, for the dew had touched them too ; indeed, all nature wore a garb in accordance with the hour—all was quiet and still.

It was a beautiful moment, such as the lover of nature would delight in, but one which had few charms for such a spirit as that of Jack Grove.

He came to a public-house—it was the Rising Sun ; but no one was astir, and he said, as he shook his head,—

"Ah, the Rising Sun, indeed ! there's nobody rising there ; 'tis the early bird that catches the worm—they'll catch no worms there. But that's the way with them landlords : all they think of is, to eat, drink, and sleep—receive your money, and give no change.

" There now, they are not up to aid the traveller ! here am I, not been in bed since yesterday, and now I want breakfast, and there's nobody there to give a bit or a sup to me, now I am dying for it. It is a scandalous shame. I won't wait here ; I'll go on, and obtain it elsewhere. There's one customer they have lost."

Satisfied with this, Grove walked on at a brisk pace, for the morning air was fresh, and he was chilly. It was some distance, nearly five miles, to the next market town, where he intended to breakfast.

"As soon as I get my breakfast," said Grove, " I'll get half-an-hour's nap, or I'll walk on till dinner time, and then I will have a nap ; but I must not promise too much ; I'll do what I can, and stick to that—it is by far the best."

Thus satisfied, he walked on at a brisk rate, and felt himself warm and much better for the exercise. He walked on with an increase of speed, and in a little more than an hour and a half, he came within sight of a pretty, neat, country roadside town.

' Here," muttered Jack, " people are astir. It is market morning, and it is all astir with people who come to sell and buy."

Though Jack had no pretence to belong either to one of these classes or the other, yet he entered into the spirit of the place ; he appeared to be interested in both the buying and selling department, and wandered about with the air of a man who had some heavy purchase to make, or some great sale to effect.

" D'ye want a hoss, master ?" said one, seeing him look at one.

" Why, that depends upon the price," said Jack, standing and surveying the animal. " What do you want for that animal ?"

" What will you give ?"

" I can't be a buyer and seller too."

" What do you say to forty for 'un ?"

" Forty !" said Jack. " Round 'uns or kidneys ?"

" Thee be'st a fool !"

" I should be if I was to be done at that rate. Why, forty for a horse that's good for nothing at that price !" said Jack. " You are doing business, this morning ; and, if horses fetch such a price as that, I shall do no business here to-day.''

" I should say not. You haven't the means."

" Come—come, none of your jokes," said Jack, slapping his pocket and causing the money to sound.

" Well, you won't get a better hoss than this—he goes with his head and tail up."

" I dare say."

" Sound, wind and limb."

" I dare say."

" Only five year old."

" Ah, he's too good for me. I want something not quite so good."

" You had better go buy a hass, or put the saddle on your own back," cried the man, enraged at being got out.

" I must call again at your shop, when you are better stocked and I have more time," said Jack, as he turned away.

" Vot will you puy, ladish and shentlemens—good peoplish, vot will you puy ? Here's all shorts of tings—every descriptshun you can imagine. Razhors, shizsors, and knives—peautiful knives that will cut—ay, good peoplish, they will cut like nuffin whatever, upon the vord of an honesht trader."

The voice that ran on thus struck familiarly on Jack's ear. He listened awhile ; for he could not then recollect where he had heard him before, and he could not get near enough to see him.

" Now 's yer time, good peoplish, to make all pargains—now 's yer time. I must have de moneysh—my familish ish starving, and I want de moneysh.

Who'll puy—who'll puy! All shorts of tings—real pargains. Cottons, tapes, and ladish gold wedding rings. Here are handsome rings with real studs. Come puy, come puy, pretty maidensh—come puy for your shweethearts. All shorts of tings—all shorts of tings."

Then came a long list of miscellaneous articles, that he uttered with amazing rapidity, and which he continued to do, taking breath at such long intervals that made people laugh.

By this time, Jack Grove recollected the Jew very well, and, coming before him, he was confirmed in his suspicion it was the same man who had given him a bad shilling, in exchange for his waistcoat, outside of the Saddle and Turnpike Gate.

"Hilloa—hilloa!" said Jack.

"Vell, my tear, vhat can I do for you—anyshing in my vay?"

"Yes, something in your way."

"Vat ish it, my tear?"

"I want a shilling of you."

"A shilling! I vant a shilling myself. Come—come, don't dishturb me. You mind your bushiness, and I'll mind mine."

"Don't you know me?"

"Sho help me, father Abraham, I never shaw you pefore now in all my life."

"Why, you old rascal, how dare you tell me such a lie?"

"Now, my good mans, don't dishturb me. I don't want to have your company."

"But I want your's, and will have it though, if I fetch an officer."

"I hope a conshtable will come, and shee how you dishturb the market."

"What do you mean by giving me a bad shilling? Answer me that, you old billygoat, will you—tell me what you mean by that."

"I give you a bad shilling?"

"Yes, you."

"Oh, the reprobate!" said the Jew, clasping his hands and looking up to Heaven. "If any of our peoplish had said anything of dish short, they would have been shtoned, sho help me, Abraham!"

"What's the man done?" inquired a countryman, standing by. "I'm danged if I stand by and see a Jew or a Christian hurt, unless he's deserving of it."

"Ay, what's he done—what's he done?" said a dozen voices.

"I sold him my waistcoat for a shilling the other day, and he gave me a bad shilling."

"Sho help me, Abraham, I never shaw the man pefore!" exclaimed the Jew.

"You old thief! do you mean to say I did not sell you my waistcoat?"

"Yesh, I do—I do. I never shaw you afore. I never had any waistcoat, and never gave you a shilling, good, bad, or indifferent."

"Oh, you rascal."

"Ah, it ish all very well to call namesh, you know; but I never shaw you pefore, and that ish all I know about it."

"You bought my waistcoat, and you gave me a bad shilling in return, and I'll have it out of you somehow, either in money or licking."

"I won't fight."

"You shall."

"I won't. Go for de offisher, and take dish man to prishon, he want to make de noise."

"Come, come, leave the man alone; he isn't interfering with you."

"Where's the waistcoat?"

"I never had one," said the Jew.

"And the shilling?" asked one of the bystanders.

"Haven't got it now," said Grove. "I gave it away."

"For nothing?"

"No; I had ordered some ale and things first, of the landlord of the Saddle and Turnpike Gate, then I paid him the shilling."

" And he took it ?"

" Why, he told me it was bad."

" But still he took it ?" persisted the man who started the question.

" Yes, he had it, I tell you, and I didn't ask it back again—it warn't of no use to me ; a bad shilling ain't of no use to any one, as I knows on," said Grove.

" Did you give him another ?"

" No ; I hadn't got another, else I wouldn't have sold my waistcoat."

" Indeed ! you were very hard up ?"

" Yes ; I wanted some beer."

" And sold your waistcoat, that you might get some beer, eh ?"

" I did."

" You had it, eh ?"

" Yes."

" There," said the Jew, " he says he sold his clothes to get drink, and I dare shay, ladies and shentlemans, he got drunk, and, after all, the shilling vot he got was good enough to pay for it, and he had his shilling's worth—vich vay it vorsh I can't tell, no nobody elsh. Good peoplish, am I to be dishturbed in dish way? I am an honesht man, and may I eat grash like Nebucadnesshar, if ever I shor de man before."

" Why, d—n my ——"

Jack Grove could get nothing more out of his adjuration, for at that moment he felt his hat suddenly come down upon his head, and envelop it to the chin, scraping his nose fearfully, and utterly spoiling his speech.

" Pump upon the impostor," said one.

" Strip him, and tie him to a post with a halter," said another, " and then give him a taste of the cart-whip—he deserves it."

" Good peoplish," said the Jew, " I wouldn't do any man harm, not even de wicked man who would steal my good name, by vich I live, and get my pread ; let him go his ways, and let him remember that he has failed to injure an honesht man."

" Hurrah, Jew ! well done, Jew," said the mob ; " I'm danged if he ain't the best Christian, after all. An honest Jew, by George !"

" Honeshty ish always de pest policy," said the Jew, triumphantly. " I alwaysh act sho—dat ish vhen I can, depend upon it, good peoplish—dat is de way to live, and let live."

" The Jew's the best man, after all. Why, what a sneak he is."

" Give him a kick for luck."

" Give him a chivy."

This was no sooner said than done, and first one hustled him, and then another, until he could scarce stand ; he received a blow from every one he came near, and, but for the appearance of the constable, who rescued him from the crowd, they would have shown him no mercy.

They considered he had attempted to impose upon the Jew, and to accuse him falsely, and that he must be drunk, and they would have probably knocked him about, until he could no longer stand. As it was, he had received more than one bruise.

" It seems to me," said the constable, " you have been playing the fool."

" They've all set upon me at once, the cowards ; take them all into custody ; they are all robbers, and all of 'em have been striking me."

" That's a decent request," said the constable, " to tell one man to take a whole mob into custody—it's a likely thing, indeed ; besides, they say you are an impostor, and if I take anybody's word, it would be their's ; however, here we are, at the boundary of the town ; start on, and don't be found here one while, or they'll serve you out in the same style, and perhaps worse."

CHAPTER XXXIII.

JACK GROVE IN A REFLECTIVE MOOD, AND HIS ANTIPATHY TO ALL HUMAN NATURE
BUT HIS OWN.—THE JOLLY LANDLORD.

THE constable gave Jack Grove a hearty push when he ceased speaking, and
sent him along for several yards before he could stop himself, and when he did, he
looked round, and seeing the constable standing with his staff in a threatening
attitude, Jack Grove, with all the stinging consciousness of being an innocent and
injured man, in this instance, and with all his belligerent propensities strong upon
him, thought it wise, on this occasion, to pocket both insult and injury, and, with an
inward consciousness that it was no use to complain, he walked on.

Jack Grove walked some two or three hundred yards before he even drew a long
breath, to ease his pent-up anger, and he walked nearly half a mile before he spoke,
and then uttering a tremendous oath, he slapped his thigh, and said in a voice of
suppressed anger,—

" Well, then, d—n all the world, both Jew and Gentile. I never was so regularly done as this—this is a regular do. Well, everybody seems to take a pleasure
in doing mischief upon me, d—n them all. No, I shouldn't wonder at all if I were
taken up and hanged for burning the hay-ricks—it's just as likely as not, now
things have taken such an outrageous turn. Anything, no matter what, may be
done to an injured man; get him down, and anybody may knock him about. Ay,
I have been striving all my life against fortune, and she has always been against
me, and I know she has had no cause to do so. I have done the best a man can
do, and I can't do more, and it's no use of women talking about a man's having a
jug of beer now and then. A man can't always be working, and no rest or play,
and I won't. I don't want nothing but what's right. There's few men now that
would have gone ever since last night, and walked the miles I have walked, without
anything either to eat or to drink,—there's no mistake about it. Here's a d—d
pretty state of things. I wonder what will come of the country, when a man not
only gets robbed, but gets knocked about if he complain of the robbery—this is a
very pretty thing, I am sure. I wonder what they will say and do next?"

Jack walked on in silence for some distance, and looked about him with a
savage air, as if he could have done any deed at that moment, by way of
revenge, that would have swamped the whole world.

" Ah!" said he, " I should like to make 'em all feel—all of 'em, d—n 'em!
But I'm both hungry and dry. I wonder when I shall meet with the next house
—I mean public-house. I am dying with hunger and thirst!"

It was, indeed, an occasion of a most extraordinary nature that had kept him
from food or drink. Indeed it had been a series of strange accidents that had
occurred to keep him so many hours out of a public-house, and which had
hurried him from place to place in such a manner.

He walked along the road with these unpleasant monitors constantly calling
to his mind the fact of his wants, and they induced him to keep a sharp eye on
the road in advance, with the hope of being able to detect something in the shape
of a roadside house.

It was near ten o'clock in the day before he saw anything of the kind, and
about that time he got to the top of a hill, the road at the bottom taking a
turn to the left; but this part was hidden by a small wood, or rather a plantation
of trees, that had been allowed to stand for some ages. The trees were all tall
and fine, and ran along for some distance on either side of the road.

However, above the tall trees, among which was a rookery, and the sable
inhabitants of which could be seen sailing in circles over the tree tops, descending and ascending, he could perceive the eddying smoke of a number of houses,
as if it were something in the shape of a village.

" Ah!" thought Jack Grove, " it's quite time to meet with something. I had
no idea that going to London was so dangerous and difficult. However, they

want to prevent my getting there, but they sha'n't. I'll go, and stay, and come back if it suits me.

"There's plenty of life on the road, after a fashion; at least, I hope there's no more of the same in London."

He slowly descended the hill side, and when he came to the corner of the road, at the bottom, he found a small, but neat village before him, containing a score or two of houses. Indeed it almost amounted to a town.

At this Jack Grove was well pleased, and mending his pace, he said,—

"This is promising, and I'll have a good breakfast here, at all events. There must be some places where the inhabitants ain't all fools, or rogues; at least, they'll let one have one's money's worth for the money."

On he pushed, and soon came within ear-shot of the rookery, when the cawing noise of the rooks gave perceptible notion of his approach, and beyond them again was the Rook's Nest public-house.

"Ay, and I'll make it my nest for a short time to come," muttered Jack; "and I hope the Rook's Nest will afford good accommodation."

He came to the door; there was the sign swinging to and fro from a tall post. It was a puzzle to the inhabitants to tell what the picture really meant, and it was an inquiry that had never yet been satisfactorily answered, save by the landlord, who assured his hearers that the strange, black, hulking animal, covered with feathers, and ornamented with a corpulent beak, was meant for a rook, and that he was holding his head on one side to look into his nest, as he was pleased to call a dark-looking hole that seemed very like a well.

There was a long trough for horses, filled with water, and several empty crates, ready for the reception of corn or hay.

Jack Grove walked up a couple of steps, and then into a passage, when he saw the landlord, who was coming out of the parlour.

"Good morning, sir," said the landlord, a jolly, red-faced Boniface,—"good morning. A fine morning—beautiful weather to walk in. Tired, sir? Will you sit down, sir?"

"Yes," said Grove, "I will sit down; for, to say the truth, I am tired."

"Yes, sir," said the landlord, throwing open the parlour-door. "Good accommodation for man and beast here, sir. Walk in."

"I only want accommodation for man."

"And that you can have at the Rook's Nest, I assure you, sir, though I say it."

"Ah!" said Jack, as he threw himself into a seat, and drew a long breath; "well, I am tired, and hungry, and thirsty too."

"I can cure all those complaints, sir. I am a good doctor, though I shouldn't praise myself; but I wouldn't mind making a bet that I could cure those disorders in half-an-hour."

"I dare say."

"That is if the patient would help the doctor. We musn't work at both ends of a team, you know, or we shall both be in the same position."

"Well, what's the prescription?" said Jack.

"Is the fee limited?" inquired the landlord, with a knowing look.

"Anything within reason."

"Well, I should prescribe cold boiled pork, with plenty of mustard, and good white bread."

"Very good."

"That's the solids, you know."

"And the——"

"Draughts, eh?"

"Yes."

"Why, they must be composed of some strong double-malted October."

"Excellent."

"That is," said the landlord, "providing the patient is not too weak. You are not much reduced, are you?"

"No; I've got more room than I want; so please to fill it up."

"A pint, to begin."

"Exactly; that's the sort. Go along, crutches, and bring the victuals."

The landlord turned away, and left the room, and during his absence Jack was engaged in looking round the room. There were several pictures, painted in very strong colours, and those being employed that contrasted most vividly, and altogether produced a remarkable effect, and in some cases rather alarming; for certain gentlemen and females had such flame-coloured garments and features, that the beholder would at first imagine they were being devoured by that element, and were suffering all the pangs and torments said to be felt in a world of which nothing is known.

"They are fine pictures here, at all events," said Jack. "That fellow with a red nose, there," he said, apostrophizing a half figure, with a jug of ale, with an improbable, not to say an impossible foam at the top, running over, "that fellow seems happy enough. I wonder if they'll ever draw my portrait in that style. I don't expect such things can last long, though; there's always something to disturb such scenes of comfort. My eyes, though, it would be a kind of paradise like."

He turned from the contemplation of the happy man on the wall, and watched the door, for he heard the landlord approaching with the promised prescription for his ills.

The door opened, and in walked the landlord with a tray, on which were some fine white bread, a glass, and a jug of ale; and on a good sized dish stood a leg of boiled pork, or rather, what remained of one.

"There," said the landlord, "there's a meal that'll last you till night. I always like to eat a good meal. I'm none of your stingy sort that eat only now and then, and when I do, come to a little bit of meat that wouldn't fill the maw of one of them rooks yonder."

"That's right," said Jack, helping himself plentifully to the meat and bread, and cutting what was called in those parts, a thumb-piece, of something over what the landlord's notions of heartiness reached.

"You can't do better, lad, than eat it all if you can, there's more to be had where that came from; a whole joint or a bit of one makes all the same to the jolly old cock at the Rook's Nest—all's one to him; as long as it's paid for, what's the odds?"

"None at all," said Jack; "eat, drink, and be merry, as I've heard the parson say; be honest and frugal, said his wife; and so they went on, this way and that all day; she scolding and growling, and he jolly and happy; she couldn't kill him, and she died out of spite."

"Lord, lord, what a good wife she must be," said the landlord, "to be so obliging. Well, I declare, if all the scolds in the world would do that, it would clear off nine-tenths of the women, and they'd become quite a scarcity. Why, what a price they would fetch in the market; it would only be a rich man who could afford to have a wife then."

"I'd sell my wife at a moderate price," said Jack, "and lay out the proceeds in jugs of ale."

"And make the fortune of the landlord of the Rook's Nest?" said that individual.

"With all my heart, if good ale would do it," said Jack.

"And what do you think of that, eh?" cried the landlord, as he saw Jack finish the ale and look into the jug for more.

"Uncommon good and strong—let's have another jug; I shall have done with meat by that time."

The landlord seemed to think he might very well spare the remainder, but went for the ale, and when he returned, he put down the ale, and Jack leaned back in his chair and pushed the table from him, saying,—

"There, I've had enough, landlord; the ale I shall drink at my leisure, for I have had a long walk, and intend to rest awhile."

"That's right, lad," said the landlord; "ease and comfort, ease and comfort, that's my motto, and it's the best I know on."

"So it is. I'll have two chairs against this window, and I can look out on the road as long as I like; and then, when I am tired, I can have a nap—that's the way to be easy and comfortable, I believe, ain't it?"

"Yes, I think so," said the landlord. "I respect you, I do; you are a trump of the first water—the fore horse of the team—a regular leader, and no mistake."

The landlord now left the room, and carried away the tray, and left Jack Grove to himself; he leaned back in his chair, and supported his head upon his hand, and began to feel the effects of repletion, and would no doubt have fallen asleep, but he was well aware of the ale that he had yet by him, and which would spoil if he fell asleep; he therefore remained gazing upon the few chance passengers who came by, and watching the gambles of the fowls that basked in the sunshine before the door, and sipped his ale with the air of a lord.

"This is all very well," said Jack to himself; "all very comfortable indeed, only it won't last. I could sit here all day long, and eat and drink in comfort;

but it can't be done, that's the worst—it can't be done. Well, I deserve some kind of enjoyment after my terrible night's adventures, which were brought to a conclusion by that infernal Jew this morning, d—n him!"

He muttered several curses, and seemed to drop into a deep reverie, and from that he dropped into a deep sleep.

How long he remained thus he could not tell; but when he awoke he felt somewhat alarmed, because he remembered the length of the journey that he had before him, and he called for the landlord, who soon came in.

"Hope you've enjoyed your nap," said he of the Rook's Nest.

"Have I slept long?"

"About two hours."

"Two hours?"

"Yes; I thought it would help to add to the efficacy of my prescription. Besides, as you were tired, this sleep would do you good, so I wouldn't wake you up."

"It is all right," said Jack; "bring me another jug. We will square accounts, and then I will jog on the road."

"Very well, sir; you shall have it with pleasure, immediately."

The ale was drawn and brought, and the reckoning paid, the jug emptied, and then Jack, a little after one o'clock, took leave of the host of the Rook's Nest, and his comfortable parlour, and turned into the road, with the determination to proceed to London as quickly as he could, and that he would make a long stage of it before he would again halt, and that, perhaps, for the night; but everything would depend, Jack thought, upon his own feelings after he had travelled another ten or fifteen miles further.

CHAPTER XXXIV.

THE MYSTERIOUS MAN IN THE LONE VILLA.

PAUSING now for one moment in what might seem the ordinary course of our narrative, we must beg the permission of our readers, and presume it to be granted, while we proceed to introduce to them a new character, or at all events a character under a new aspect, who is to exercise some influence over the fortunes of those in whom we feel interested.

A short distance from London was (we regret we cannot say is, for recent building speculations have levelled it with the dust) a villa residence, which had acquired an evil repute, in consequence of its principal inhabitant having committed, under mistaken views, a murder within its walls, to which offence he had added suicide upon discovering his mistake.

For such an event to have taken place in connection with any building is quite sufficient to give house-hunters a decided preference for some other locality.

The consequence was that, although the owner of the villa would have let it to any one a most decided bargain, he could not rob it of its reputation, which was considered an addendum of no trifling importance, in the shape of a drawback upon its charms.

The fact is, that the villa was a most charming place; and yet, there it remained, a melancholy example of the evil effects of giving a house a bad name,— and, had the late tenant been living, most certainly we consider the landlord would have had good grounds for an action against him for special damages.

This state of things had gone on for nearly fifteen years, during the whole of which time the villa, which was called Rotswood Villa, was to let.

To be sure it could not be said to have been untenanted all that time, for various persons had been placed in it by the landlord to shew the premises; but these one by one had given up the dubious trust, on the ground that at night there were strange noises, and that, more than once, when they had dropped into unusually profound slumbers, they were awakened by the most hideous yells that it is possible to conceive; and when they started up in an agony of fright, and gathered courage to look through the house, which they declared they did, but which, by the way, we consider to be a very doubtful proposition, they found no one whatever, or the slightest trace of any human being.

This then was not a state of things that made Rotswood Villa even a desirable property or residence at nothing a-year and one's taxes paid.

The indefatigable George Robins would have found it a difficult task to get a purchaser for such a property, unless, indeed, with that versatility of genius which he possesses, he were to hold it out as " a most delightful and recherche retreat for a nervous gentleman, or a timid lady, and a residence replete with food for the imagination."

However, at length, nobody even would take charge of the villa, and thus, for about the last six years of its forlorn state, it had been forlorn indeed.

What a strange and wonderful effect non-habitation produces even in a short time upon a house. A year or two will almost suffice to make it look as if it required pulling down and building up again before it could be fit for human occupancy ; but when that year or two swells into fifteen, we may well conjecture what a serious state of dilapidation the villa had fallen into.

There it stood, a monument of crime, and a dreadful bad speculation to its owner, who, to be sure, had made several insidious attempts to get rid of it to confiding purchasers at a distance, and always failed, for, somehow or another, before the purchase was concluded, they heard a something of the character of the place, and declared off accordingly.

At length, in despair, the owner had ceased to consider it as a calculable portion of his property, but had been known to go occasionally on a Sunday and look at it from the road way ; on which occasions, people averred that he muttered something usually, which could not, except by the rule of contrary, be construed into a blessing upon Rotswood Villa, or a pious wish for the repose of the soul of its late occupant.

Stagnant was its fish pond ; drear and covered up with tangled weeds was its once beautiful garden ; and the plants—some of them originally wild denizens of the forest, which, by cultivation, had become civilized—now that they found themselves neglected, grew wild and reckless again, and resorted to their old bad habits of straggling here and there and everywhere, and looking by no means trim and neat in their personal appearance,

Birds built their nests boldly on the very window-sills, and not a boy of the vicinity would—although the temptation must have been prodigious—venture to rob the robin of its young within the precincts of the haunted villa.

To be sure, in all communities of people there are restless individuals who must be peculiar in some way, and who will not think like other people, or act like other people, and so it was as regarded occasionally one out of the small rural population which was in the vicinity of the ill-omened villa.

It so happened once, that a hardy fellow, who swore he believed in nothing, and, to use his own language, " wasn't afraid of nobody," made a wager that he would take a mattrass with him and sleep all night in the villa : but somehow or another he saw something, or he heard something, which gave him, as the gossips in the neighbourhood said, a turn, and he came away quicker than he went ; and afterwards he used to shake his head when Rotswood House was mentioned, as if he had something mysterious to say if he liked, but, from some sufficient cause, preferred keeping it a profound secret.

After this the villa, or rather the ghost which was supposed to inhabit it, was allowed to have all its own way, until one night, when there had been an alarming quantity of rain for some hours previously, and then the wind blew a fearful hurricane, there came to the only public-house which the place afforded a melancholy-looking strange man, who, in appearance, did not prepossess anybody in his favour.

This man wanted a bed for the night ; but so sinister was his aspect that the publican would not own to having one disengaged at any price, and told him he was very sorry, but that, as he closed at ten o'clock, he must really trouble him to leave.

" And," said the stranger, with a slightly foreign accent, " can I not, in the village, procure a night's lodging ?"

He made such a hideous grimace as he spoke, with a set of features that were far from pleasant when in a state of serenity, that the landlord replied,

" I should say you would find it difficult."

" Yes," said a man present, who considered himself as the wag of the place. " Yes, you would find it difficult, for there are children in almost every house."

" And what of that ?"

" Why, people don't like the children frightened out of their wits. There's Rotswood Villa, now, if you want a quiet night's lodging ; and they do say that there's still in it Tom Murchison's mattress, that he took in one night to sleep on, but left behind him because he came away in a hurry."

" How kind of you," said the stranger, " to suggest it to me ; but I rather think I shall prefer walking on to London."

He abruptly left the public-house, and certainly no one had the least idea that he would go to the haunted villa ; but, as we intend to follow him, our readers will perceive that such indeed was the route he took.

The positive hurricane of wind that had succeeded the rain which had fallen so plentifully, roared and blustered through the branches of the old trees, which made a kind of woody belt next the roadway, and immediately in front of the villa. The uproar was tremendous, as bough dashed against bough of those huge chesnuts that had been planted at the time the house was first built, and never shorn of their wile-spreading branches.

It was but a park paling of rent oak which separated this belt of old trees from the roadway, and over that any one could get with the greatest ease.

The stranger paused for some moments, and gazed at the mansion, huge and dark as it appeared against the night sky, for several minutes, and then he said to himself, in a low tone, or what, at all events, amid the tremendous uproar made by the wind, sounded like a low tone,—

" It might do—why not ? I may go further and fare worse. A deserted house ! The very place to suit me ; and whatever terrors superstition may have invested it with, I will take good care sufficiently to improve upon to make it not likely to be an abode in which I shall have many visitors, except by my own special appointment."

He then, without further hesitation, surmounted the park palings, and found himself beneath the trees, the leaves from which for many an autumn had now been allowed to rot where they fell.

There might or there might not be difficulty, for all he knew, in finding an entrance to the actual house ; but, from the manner in which he walked on it was quite evident that he feared nothing whatever, and had none of the superstitious fears about him which, to so many minds, peoples any solitude with an undefined terror.

The principal apartment of the villa had three windows, which opened upon a terrace, that ran along on one side of the building, and was just raised above the garden about six feet, so that as many stone steps reached it easily.

Up these steps, then, which likewise ran the whole length of the terrace, the stranger strode, and then he proceeded to try the various windows, until he found one of them which yielded to some slight violence, and came open.

There was at once a tremendous rush of wind into the house, and the violent slamming of several doors succeeded, awakening echoes throughout the deserted rooms, and making an uproar that, if not at the moment attributed to its right cause, would have been sufficient to make any one pause before advancing further into that deserted place.

" Now," said the stranger with the sinister aspect, as he walked into the large apartment, and proceeded to close the window after him, " now, such a simple circumstance as that of all those doors banging about in consequence of the inlet I allowed the wind to get, I dare say would have been enough to have caused a capital story to get current all over the neighbourhood of supernatural noises in this place."

His next step was to produce from his pocket the means of getting a light, and he ignited a wax taper, by the aid of the light from which he looked cautiously around him at the room in which he was.

It had evidently at one time been a handsome apartment, but now the once gorgeous papering was, from damp, half streaming from the walls, and the roof had, in several places, so far as regarded its plaister, given way, making a heap of rubbish on the floor beneath, the dust from which had crept upon every available resting-place.

There was no grate in the fireplace of that apartment, and, take it altogether, it was as cheerless and wretched as any place enclosed by four walls could possibly be.

A very cursory inspection of this place sufficed to show the stranger what it was, and seeing a door at its further end, just swinging upon its hinges, it being no doubt one that had assisted in making the uproar when the gust of wind was admitted, he walked over the heaps of rubbish that lay in his way, and reached it.

This door opened upon a small sort of corridor, from which several rooms evidently branched, and as the stranger had no knowledge of the building, he could have no choice but such as caprice might dictate to him, and he accordingly took the first one he came to.

This led him into an octagonal-shaped parlour, which was in much better order than the larger apartment he had just left, and here there was a firegrate, which, by the eagerness with which he advanced towards it, seemed a welcome sight to the stranger.

He placed his taper upon the marble chimney-piece, and then looked around him for some moments, until in a corner he espied a cupboard. To proceed to it, and wrench out a couple of deal shelves with which it was fitted, was the work of a moment, and these, by the aid of a huge clasped knife, which he took from his pocket, he cut into slips. By tearing paper from the walls he now regularly laid a fire, and the crackling of the wood, and a bright flame up the chimney, soon lent to that apartment a more cheerful aspect.

He put out his wax taper as the flame from the burning wood lent light to the room, and then he seemed to be for some moments completely immersed in thought. He paced the room with agitated strides, and then he muttered,—

"Yes, yes; I will make some compromise of the matter with her, if I find her deserving of it, but if she is as cold, as bitter, and as selfish as report speaks her, I will leave her no more than she is justly entitled to, and that will be nothing. I will, if I can, be generous; and, if I cannot, I will be just. What a shock my presence would be to her. Well, well, I have not travelled so far by land and by sea for nothing. I have not cherished in my heart a purpose which, when far away, formed the constant subject of my meditation, to waver in it now that I am in England."

The light flame from the wood fire began to subside, then advancing towards the door of the cupboard, he dashed his foot through the panelling, and soon succeeded in laying more fuel upon the rapidly consuming pieces of which he had first availed himself.

CHAPTER XXXV.

THE ALARM.— THE CRY IN THE DESERTED VILLA.—THE MORNING.

WHEN the strange man with the sinister aspect found that the fresh wood which he had heaped on the fire was rapidly kindling, he looked around him for something that might serve the purpose of a seat; but the place was denuded of furniture, with the exception of something which looked like a huge bundle of old rags in a corner.

Upon approaching this, he found, from its shape, that by courtesy it might be called a mattrass, and then he recollected what he had been told at the public-house.

"So," he said, "then this is the mattrass of the person they mentioned.

Well, it's a good thing he has left it behind him, for otherwise I should have had to make rather too intimate an acquaintance with the floor boards."

He dragged the apology for a mattrass towards the fire, and, doubling it up, he made for himself a very comfortable seat at all events, upon which he sat, drying his saturated garments, and gazing at the fire, for nearly an hour.

The constant looking at a fire always induces a sleepy sensation, and it did so with this man, who began to close his eyes, and to nod occasionally, as he now and then pushed further into the blaze a protruding piece of the wood with which he had made so free.

Finally, although he did not lie down, he dropped off into a deep sleep, with his head resting upon his breast, and the bright glow of the wood fire, from which now scarcely any flame issued, casting a ruddy radiance upon him, and upon the walls of that apartment, which for many a long day had not brightened with anything half so cheering.

He long he slept he could not tell—it might have been an hour, or it might have been two, for all he knew, when he was suddenly aroused by such a yell, that he sprang to his feet as if he had been electrified, and, on the sudden and surprised impulse of the moment, he gave an answering cry.

Then all was as still as the grave.

He stood for nearly five minutes in the same attitude which he had assumed when first he rose, listening with an intensity that at last became absolutely painful, and then he drew a long breath, as he said, in a hurried tone of alarm,—

"What—what was that?"

The sound of his own voice, faint and low as it was, seemed to give him courage, and he rose to his full height, abandoning the crouching position which had characterised him while he listened so intently, in case there should come any repetition of the sound.

"What was that?" he repeated; "was it real, or only a dream? Yet I was not dreaming—no, no; and when I sprang up, the loud tone was still in my ears. It was no dream. No, no; and yet, what could it have been? By Heaven, I never in all my life heard such a cry as that."

His sleep had brought a chilling sensation over him, and he shuddered as he approached nearer to the fire, upon which he cast some fresh pieces of wood that he had laid ready by the side of the grate.

"No wonder," he added, "that this is a deserted house, if people who attempt to sleep in it are to be awakened by such terrible cries as that which even now seems to be actually thrilling through my brain. It requires some amount of nerve to stand that. How very strange, too! Now, if I were given to superstition, which Heaven knows I am not, I should believe that something supernatural could only have produced such a terrific sound as that which scared me from my sleep."

He was silent for some few moments, and then he asked himself the question,—

"And yet by what ordinary mortal means could that cry have been produced?"

This was a query he found it difficult to answer, and he caught himself glancing round him with that shuddering sort of suspicion of not being quite alone, which will sometimes, in even the apparent solitude of a chamber, come across the best and the boldest, and the most rational and argumentative of us.

"Pho! pho!" he cried, as if ashamed to detect himself in such fears. "What have I to fear? It must be a silly and badly-employed spirit from another world, that could find no better amusement than in aimlessly awakening any one by such a terrific sound as that. But, after all, perhaps, when in the broad light of day, which has so strong an effect in dissipating such fancies, I come to examine this house thouroughly, I may find some rational means of accounting for even such a sound as that which has disturbed me."

What those rational means of accounting for the dreadful yell that had awakened every echo in the house were to be, entirely baffled all conjecture; and, after some time spent in fruitlessly endeavouring to get up some hypothesis upon the subject, he gave it up in despair.

He sat down by the fire again, which he fed sufficiently to enable it to light up the apartment with its bright flickering flame for a considerable time, and a strong disposition to sleep again came over him.

The remembrance, however, of the yell that had before awakened him, clung to his imagination, and was a great foe to repose. Whenever he found himself just dropping off into a slight slumber, he would start awake fully, and rouse himself to listen.

Those who have passed a night listening in momentary dread of some sound of fear or summons of an uncomfortable character, can well imagine what must have been the feelings with which he sat by that fire now, for the remainder of the night, wishing so greatly to sleep, and yet dreading to do so to an extent that induced him to become alarmed the moment the drowsy influence fairly crept over him.

He endured this state of anxiety for some hours, and then, as he thought that he heard from some distant part of the building a slight noise, he sprung up to his feet again, saying,—

"I dare not sleep—I dare not sleep, for my dread of that dream or that reality—by Heavens! I know not which to call it—coming over me again. It seems to me as if such another sound as that would go nigh to driving me distracted."

He opened a small bundle which he had with him, and took from it a flask, containing some foreign spirit, a draught from which he took, and then, rummaging among the contents of the bundle, he at length produced a book, and sitting down by the fire, he said,—

"I will at least make endeavour to shake off the thick-coming fancies that beset my brain, by withdrawing my attention from them."

The book he had, though, was far from being of an order to clear away any of those cobwebs of the brain woven by superstition. It contained legends and poems upon the very subject which had been made prominent in his mind by the yell that had come, as his fancy told him, from no mortal lips, to disturb his repose.

The first page his eye lighted upon, contained a legend in verse, entitled,—

THE VISION OF THE LOST LOVE.

I saw it at the midnight hour,
When all around was still,
Save the gentle sighing of the wind
Which swept adown the hill.

My straining eyes no form could trace,
And yet I knew 'twas there,
The melody of happier worlds
Was floating in the air.

I heard the voice, I saw no form,
It was the loved one's tone;
A shadow passed across my soul,
And then I was alone.

I leant against an aged tree—
Once—twice I gasped her name;
Loud blew the winds—the murky night
In double darkness came.

"This," said the stranger, "but feeds the imagination; and yet it is at such a time, and in such a place as this, that such things should be read. I will not be so much the slave of my own fears, as to shrink even from the page of fiction."

The next article in the work was a legend, that soon enchained his imagination. It was as follows :—

The morning was hazy and foggy, and as yet the sun had not risen, and a dense blackness seemed to hang over the river. No sound met the ears of the men, as they lay secured from the weather among some bales of merchandize, save the rippling of the water, and the creaking now and then of the cordage.

"I say, Jem," said one of the men, "there will be no moving about ye awhile."—"None. It won't be light these two hours; and then it will be bu very dim, while this fog continues."

"And that it will do so for some hours, I am sure of," said the third speaker "this reminds me of some of the fogs that I have seen in my own country."— "Holland?"

"Oh, no; I do not come from Holland; I come from Germany, where th Hartz Mountains rise high in the skies, and where there's as many wonders a you will find in the deep."—"Say you so; then Germany must beat the Southern Ocean all to smash."

"And so it does. Why should it not? I am sure it has more of the in. habitants of the other world, and many I know who have seen them, too. Ah there's been wild work in the woods of Germany before now."—"So there ha been in many other parts of the world before to-day; and so there will be, so long as there is any place where spirits can live."

"You may say that there's no part of the wide world but what has got its tale to tell."—"I believe you. I have seen some things that you would hardly believe; and I have heard some things that would astonish you—that have, in. deed, happened to my own family."

"How! your family? I didn't know you had any."—"Yes; I have had a family—that is, not of my own; but I belonged to a family that have had some things happen, that I would have disbelieved myself, but for the fact of seeing the effects myself; and seeing's believing, you know."

"So they say; and yet I have heard even that denied. You know, now-a-days, they won't allow anything if they can help it. Why, they won't believe in the Holy Ghost, soon."—"I dare say not."

"But what about your family? You have something strange, then, have you not, to tell me?"—"Well, I may as well tell you; we've nothing else to do now, for an hour or two. Is there any more grog afloat? This fog creeps down one's throat like smoke."

"So it does. Here, messmate, drink, and expell it; you will clear your throat as well as if you had used a bottle brush."

The man, who was a light-headed German, who had been so long in the service of the English that he spoke the language correctly enough for one in his station drank his grog, and then said,—

"My father lived near the borders of the Hartz. There's few of them who live there that haven't stout hearts; because it's no use, if they haven't, in living there at all; men won't do any good in a place where much evil and some good fortune is to be found; but only to be found by the daring and the brave of heart.

"My father died when I was young. He had some strange doings in the Hartz Mountains—everybody knew Herman Leitzer, the hunter. Yes, he was known about there, and a pretty good thing he made of it; but he was a wild, careless fellow, who never heeded the morrow, but let it take care of itself.

"He was very much respected as a good hunter, and a bold man, and few would have risked an angry word with Herman Leitzer, who was not a quarrel-some man; but he could take his own part at any time. He had, it was said, some compact with other powers; but of that I know nothing, save that he died when I was young. Since that period I have had the particulars of his death. He had been from the forest some days, and carried on a bit of game, and had earned no money at all; and he found that there was but little chance of his getting any more, unless he went out and earned it. He swore he would go to the Hartz Mountains, and if he didn't get the money out of spirits of the Hartz, why, he would maintain they never existed, or hadn't the power. He was gone three days, and every one gave him up for lost, believing he was lost, or having met with some accident that thoroughly disabled him, he was left to die where he fell.

"This was a melancholy reflection to his friends, and his brother and some others went out into the forest to endeavour to discover his body, if possible, and to save him should he be alive; of this, however, there was but little chance. However, strange to say, they had the luck to meet, but sorely wounded and knocked about; he had dragged himself along, and then stopped where he was until he was found quite exhausted.

How he came by his wounds he would not tell—he would answer no one; but all who saw him said they could not imagine any way by which they could have been given; no mortal instrument, said they, ever inflicted such wounds.

See p. 181.

My father refused the aid of the clergyman who came to see him, and used to lie looking at me; and once or twice I thought there was a dreadful shudder ran through his frame, and he seemed in a dreadful state of bodily and mental suffering —I can recollect that much, at all events.

I was young then—scarce five or six years old—but I can't forget those dreadful looks; and that is really all I recollect of my father.

" You didn't know much of him, then," said one of the men who were sitting round him.—" Very little, indeed."

" And you didn't lose anything by that, I dare say ; but here's peace to his memory."—" Peace to his memory," said the German ; " and peace I fear he wants, but that's neither here nor there, messmate."

" No ; go on."

Well, then ; the night before my father died, my uncle went in with him and had a long talk. I couldn't see or hear them, but it was a deep, earnest conversation, which lasted more than two hours. I was then admitted ; my father was very weak and exhausted—he seemed in great pain.

" Guthrie," said he to me, " your uncle will take care of you ; you must see that you are a good boy ; you will have no father soon."

" No, father !" I said. " Why?"—" Because I am dying, boy ; a few hours more will be the last I shall breath—your uncle will be a father to you, Guthrie."

" Yes," said my uncle ; " I will see he wants for nothing ; and put him out in the world as if he was my own son."—" I know you will," he said to my uncle ; and then, turning to me, he continued,—" You must be as dutiful to him as a son ; do that, and you will deserve the blessing of your father."

Some more was said by way of advice ; and my uncle made the same promise in other words, and then I took a farewell of my father. My uncle remained with him till the morrow, and then the sun rose upon the corpse of my father.

" He was dead, then ?"—" Yes, he was."

" Was your uncle with him when he died ?"—" Yes, so I am told ; but it didn't much signify to me ; I didn't understand that matter at that time ; but I left the house and entered that of my uncle.

My uncle followed the same kind of life my father did, but he was a steadier and more fortunate man ; but he was, if anything, more bold and resolute. I have known him do things but few men would have ventured to have done, and which none would have performed successfully, and escaped death. On one occasion, I recollect, he was out in the forest ; I was with him, but he was out of ammunition —the last charge was expended in firing at a buck. A fine creature he was, too ; got a head of antlers as large as a branch of an oak tree.

Well, he had wounded the animal in the haunch, and it limped along, bleeding very fast.

" Keep up, lad," said my uncle to me ; " the blood will show you the way we go. I shall follow ; he must drop from weakness."

On we went ; my uncle kept ahead of me for some time, and I kept up better than I had any hope of doing, for I kept him tolerably well in sight.

The stag was evidently tiring, for I could see now and then its horns above the underwood.

He now stopped and turned to bay, and my uncle hesitated ; he did not like to leave the animal, and yet he knew that to approach it was not only dangerous, but certain death. A wound from a buck's horn, too, is very dangerous : men often die from it.

Well, he stood looking at the animal, and dodging away as it ran at him, for it was very fierce and savage.

" Ah, boy," he said to me, " I would hamstring him if I had my hanger with me."—" He must fall soon," said I.

" He may live in pain and misery a day or two," said my uncle ; " and then we lose him after all."—" What can be done ?" said I.

My uncle paused, and I said not a word for more than a minute or two, during which time he looked at me several times very hard.

" I tell you what can be done, Guthrie," said he ; " but have you any nerve ?"

" Any what ?"—" Any nerve ; can you do a dangerous thing and not be afraid of a few kicks ?"

" Yes," said I ; " I will do it, or try to do so."—" You mustn't try, lad ; if you do it at all, it must be done ; my life will be lost if you fail, and your own too, most likely."

"What is it, then?" said I; "tell me first, and I will tell you whether I am sure I can or cannot do it."—"Why, I can seize the buck by the horns for a moment or two, and then you must take my knife, which is sharp and pointed, and run it between the ribs, just behind, and a little below, the shoulder-joint."

"Yes," said I, "I could do that, I know."—"He will kick and plunge."

"I'll do it, I'll do it, uncle; give me the knife in readiness first," said I; "so I shall have to run in and do it at once, the moment you hold the horns."—"That's right, boy, I think you will do it; and when you have done that, you may draw the blade across his hind leg, so that you cut the sinews in two."

I took the knife, and stood behind my uncle, who watched his opportunity, and when the stag had turned his head to smell the wound in his hind quarters, my uncle rushed out suddenly and seized the animal's horns.

"Now, Guthrie, quick—quick!"—"Here I am," said I, plunging the knife close up to the hilt, and then the stag gave a plunge round, carrying my uncle.

"It's done, uncle," said I; and I drew the knife across the leg, above the hock.—"I know it's done," said my uncle, reeling back, having let go his hold, and sheltering himself behind a tree; "the plunge he made told me how he felt it."

"It's gone home, too," said I; "for I couldn't push it in any further; and then I hamstrung him."—"Right, lad; you have done more than some men would have ventured."

"What, when you held his horns?"—"They wouldn't have trusted to me; they wouldn't believe I could do it, and they would have run some danger."

Well, there lay the buck. He was some time in dying, for he was big and strong—but he bled to death; and when he was gone, my uncle took off his antlers and gave them to me, saying,—

"There, lad, take that, it is your trophy—you deserve them; we will now go back to the cottage."

And he took the buck on his back, and slowly walked home, having first disembowelled him to lighten the burden; but as it was he went very slowly.

Well, my uncle, as I have said, was an extraordinary man; and, after a time, a gloomy spirit seemed to come over him, and he became reserved and morose.

Day after day came and went without any change whatever; and I found out that my uncle had some misfortunes hanging over him, and he wanted money.

He always lived freely, and above what he could afford. There were none who came to his table but what were welcome, and came again, and he never stinted at any time, and he could not bear to act differently now.

I stood by one day, and heard him speak to himself. I listened, and heard distinctly the following words:—

"I don't see why I should not succeed, if he failed; he didn't act as I should have done; he was not so steady; he had too much spirit, and too little judgment; and, I think, I can succeed. At all events, I'll try; anything is better than disgrace. Well, well, I'll try—I can but die as my brother did before me. I'll invoke the spirits of the Hartz, and obtain their aid; and then the terms—I'll not stick at them—they shall be accepted."

Then my uncle said to me,—

"Guthrie," said he, "I am going into the forest this afternoon, but I shall not take you with me."—"Indeed, uncle. I should like to go with you."

"But you would not like sleeping in the Hartz Forest all night," said my uncle; "you would be fearful."—"Have I not slept out in the forest before now?" I inquired; "I have done so very often with you, uncle."

"Ay, with me, lad, you have; but you have not alone, and I should be obliged to leave you alone."

"And why not take me with you, uncle?"—"Because you cannot go with me. It is not fit you should; you cannot face those that I have to face; you cannot understand; however, say no more about it."

"But, uncle, I dare sleep in the Hartz Forest alone. Give me a gun, and I'll sleep in any part of it."

"You will, lad?"—"Yes, I will, and think nothing of it either."

" You shall go, my lad ; you shall sleep in the Buck's Oak, and if I come not back by the sun's rise, then you must come after me, and seek me out, for I shall want your aid, as your father needed mine."

I thought nothing of it then, but agreed to do as he bade me, and in the evening of the same day we both took our walk into the Hartz Forest. It was fine, and the sun was setting ; the moon, too, was rising, so that as one light failed, another supplied its place, and all was well. We walked towards the forest, but not a word did my uncle utter as we went along. He rambled about as if he wished to pass away the time. We came near the Buck's Oak, a famous place for shooting bucks—beneath that oak tree my uncle often shot his game. There were some famous grazing grounds, and the animals would come there to feed.

" Here, Guthrie," he said, " you must sleep above in the branches. Do you think you can sleep safe ?"—" Yes ; quite."

" Well, then, you may as well get above, and let me see if you can rest there ; but, first, you see yonder path ?"—" Yes ; the one that leads to the haunted cavern ?" said I.

" Yes ; did you know it ?"—" I have been there before now."

My uncle was silent for some moments, during which he looked at me, and seemed to muse, but at length said,—

" Yes ; that is where I am going. If I be not come here by sunrise, take that path and come to me. I shall want your aid, and perhaps more."

" Shall I shoot a buck against you come ?"—" No, lad ; never mind. Now, as you understand what I have told you, get up, and I will then leave you."

With my uncle's aid I did get up into the tree, and then upon a large branch I laid down ; there was room enough for two. I took the gun my uncle handed me up, and he bade me good bye, and left me, taking the path he had spoken of, and was soon out of sight.

I waited the whole of that night without sleeping a moment, and saw the sun rise above the tops of the trees, bright and red, and shedding its beauty around. It is strange, but looking at the sun rise above a forest, is somewhat similar to the sunrise at sea—all is quiet and still—no moving forms ; but at sea all is nearly one colour. Now, in the forest, it is different to my mind,—much finer than sunrise at sea.

All that night in the moonlight, I saw many a fine buck browsing about ; and one animal I shall never forget. He was larger than even I thought they ever grew, and came and poked his nose among the branches in search of acorns, he was so tall. I could not resist the inclination to hit him with the but of the gun, and speak to him. I did so, and it produced an electric shock amongst the whole herd ; they startled, gazed upward, and were almost petrified to see me. Had I been on the ground, they would have smelt me, and I should not have seen them. Off they went like a whirlwind.

When I saw the sun rise, I remembered my uncle's words, and went in search of him. I came to the haunted cavern, but, before I reached it, I saw a man lying on the ground. I went up to him—it was my uncle. I looked at him—he was in a worse condition than my father. I felt him, and he was alive. I poured some wine down his throat, and he revived.

" Thank you, boy," he said ; " I shall get home now ; but it is all over with me ; I am a dead man."

" Who has done this ?"—" The spirits of the Hartz," he said ; " but no matter ; help me up, and I will go home. Say nothing of this to any one, Guthrie ; it's a bad job for me, as well as for you."

I helped him home, and he was placed in bed ; but he refused all religious consolation, saying,—

" It is of no use your attempting to preach to me. I won't believe we can find anything so bad as you would say we can, nor can I understand your promises of the future—you can't tell, only what you conjecture—I'll have none of it."

" Boy,' said he to me, " you have done well. I would I could leave more than a beggar's portion for you ; but I can't. Take, however, this ring—it was your father's, and was mine ; and, remember, it is made of fairy gold of the Hartz mountain."

* * * * * *

My uncle died, and was buried, and they found that he had left more debts than his goods would pay. I was sent away, and then ran away to sea, where I have been ever since.

"Your uncle went where your father did, I suppose?"—"Why, yes, I should think so ; but I can't well tell where that is."

"Well, now the fog clears off, and I expect we shall have our work to do now." —"Yes; the time of our watch is nearly out; and, if so, we shall soon be relieved. Well, here's rest to the soul of your uncle—he wasn't a bad sort of man, after all," said another.

"No ; he was a good man to me," said the German, who rose up, and walked away.

* * * * *

The stranger looked up from the book he had been reading. The first faint colours of the dawn were perceptible through even the dirt begrimed window of the room in which he was. His spirits revived at the sight, and he exclaimed,—

"I will make this my home, despite even that yell, which has so scared me, and, if it come once a night, I will endure it. I have that to do that requires some such an abode as this."

CHAPTER XXXVI.

STARTLING EVENTS.—THE PROGRESS OF THE PLOT.

Now that we have made the reader aware that there is such a person as this lonely man, with the not by any means prepossessing physiognomy, residing at the deserted villa, and likewise given, as we hope, a tolerable insight into his character, we may leave him, with an assurance that this digression, as it seems, was absolutely necessary, inasmuch as he was to play a part in the drama of real life we are presenting to the readers.

And that part happens to be one which would make it extremely inconvenient to introduce him during its progress, so that now, when such a man appears upon the scene, our readers will know something of his character.

That a day of retribution was coming, or, indeed, to a certain extent, had come, for that young, proud, weak, and, in many respects, prejudiced young scion of nobility, who had blighted one of nature's fairest flowers, our readers have perceived; but not yet has he suffered what he shall surely suffer for his deep iniquity.

We call it deep iniquity, for can there be a deeper iniquity than that of alluring from honour, and happiness, and respect, a young and trusting girl, whose very virtues, inasmuch as, by banishing art from her own mind, they banish a suspicion of it in others, become arrayed against her.

Let the seducer, if he can, lay his hand upon his heart, and truly say that he is satisfied with his poor and his unmanly triumph. Let him, if he can, say that he has felt none of the adder-like stings of that conscience which doth make cowards of all such. But he cannot. No, he dare not. With a hollow smile, and a mirthful affectation of glee, he may speak of the treachery which he has been guilty of; but there is that secret monitor within him, which too plainly speaks of a well-deserved retribution.

Such men as Lord Crumbledown fancy too often that, by surrounding themselves with all the insignia and all the allurements of rank and wealth, they, in a manner of speaking, confer upon themselves some sort of patent privilege to behave with whatever amount of heartlessness they may think proper.

In no country on the face of the beautiful earth is money more idolised than it is here in England ; but still there is a national spirit, which is growing each day stronger and stronger, and revolting at the crimes of an aristocracy, which, for the last hundred years, has been growing more and more vitiated.

And such is now the constitution of society, that, as surely as wrong is done, some kind of retribution or another will overtake the wrong-doer. As in commercial transactions, it has been said that, " in England, pay-day always comes," so is it in those matters which more concern the feelings and the morals. The day of retribution always comes. It may be long before that day arrives ; years may elapse, and may have seemed to blot out all the consequences, and almost the memory of a wrong done ; but still let the evil-doer congratulate not himself upon such a seeming disposition of events.

Let him not tell himself that he has escaped—let him not hilloa before he is out of the wood, or congratulate himself that he has been a villain without the consequences of villany, even because his victims sleep the long sleep of death in the silent grave. The day of retribution will still come.

And so Lord Crumbledown felt that it was coming ; and many and many a time he thought over that sad scene, when she whom he had taken from her home in all the fresh springtide of her beauty, and made so wretched, took her last despairing glance at him ere the film of death gathered over her eyes for ever !

How frequently did he recall to himself that glance, and endeavour to find some consolation for it, if he could, rather than condemnation.

" She forgave me !" he would tell himself sometimes. " I am sure, very sure, that she forgave me, or I could not feel so easy as I now do upon the subject of that most sad episode of my existence."

But did he believe himself when he thus talked of being forgiven ?—or was he but, as is too common with human nature, laying some flattering unction to his soul, of the fallaciousness of which he was but too well assured?

Such, we are inclined to think, was the case ; for, as a man may, by blinking and winking, destroy his accurate visual perception of some object, or confound its subtleness and render it extremely indistinct, so can he, eventually, if he have a mind to do so, to a great extent, accomplish a similar result, as regards some circumstance, to look at which calmly and with discrimination would hurl him to the verge of despair.

And this was just Lord Crumbledown's position, as regarded that event of his life with which our readers are so well acquainted. He dared not look at it exactly as it was ; but he was compelled, when a consideration of it did cross his brain, to surround it with as much sophistication as possible.

We do not mean exactly to say that he was one of those most despicable of all characters, who plunge into intrigue for the mere purpose of achieving that most doubtful reputation among the worst class of society, who hail with delight any one guilty of such an amount of iniquity. No ; he was bad enough, but not so bad as that.

He had loved the poor victim who had loved him, not wisely, but, alas ! too well. She had been the victim of his passion, not of his mere pride of conquest ; and, no doubt, had she been in a rank of life which his prejudices would have enabled him to consider equal to his own, he would gladly have made her his wife.

But it will be noticed, in a highly civilised community like our's, that many a man is too proud to do an act of common justice to himself and to another, but not at all too proud to commit the greatest amount of moral devastation.

A scion of the ancient race of the Crumbledowns could not stoop to marry an attorney's daughter, for fear of sullying the brightness of a name which had descended, with a title attached to it, through so many generations ; and yet, by some strange hallucination of intellect, it was not considered a tarnish upon that honour, of which they affected to be so chary, to seduce trusting and affectionate innocence.

Surely this is the very cant of disgusting hypocrisy ! and yet there is not, we will be bound to say, one of our readers who will not feel the truth of what we have asserted in this brief digression, into which we have been naturally led.

*   *   *   *   *

Our readers will recollect that we left Colonel Bruce and the Earl of Crumbledown on their way home from that sweet green lane, in which they had met, accidentally, Mrs. Grove, with that child of love and misfortune in her arm. The colonel had congratulated his lordship on not being recognised by the nurse, but the earl had his own suspicions for all that; and, knowing, as he did well, that Mrs. Grove was not a woman of every-day stamp, he thought possibly that her prudence might have had a larger share in producing her conduct in the lane than her forgetfulness.

"And is it your genuine opinion, Bruce, that she knew me not?"—"Why, my dear Crumbledown, you saw that she did not know you—can there be two opinions upon the subject?"

"Yes, Bruce, there can. That woman is a woman of intellect, and of education likewise, far beyond her station. By her marriage with drunken Jack Grove, I understand that she has been dragged down from her proper sphere to one far beneath her."—"There was certainly something in her style and manner which bespoke cultivation."

"Yes. And did you not note how she fixed her eyes upon me?—and the infant, too, that seemed to look upon me with an old familiar gaze! Oh, how I longed to press it to my heart—to weep over it—to call it mine, and to address it by the old and dear familiar name of its poor, poor sacrificed mother! Bruce, you cannot tell what were my feelings at that moment, and I cannot describe them to you."

"They were natural," said the colonel, after a short pause, "and as creditable to you as natural; but you must never forget, my dear Crumbledown, that you have done the best you can in the matter. The mother of this little thing is dead; and you know you had half a million of good reasons for marrying the Lady Arabella Fanfaronade."

"Yes; a heartless, selfish, cold, designing woman, whom, to say that I do not love her, is to say the least, for ——"—"Hush! that's quite sufficient; you needn't add anything else. But, my dear Crumbledown, you always forget those half million claims that she possessed."

"That money should have been my own, as well you know."

"Of course I do. It should, might, could, and would, have been your own—only it wasn't. Come, come, Crumbledown, you know I'm your friend; take some of the sours of life along with its sweets—mingle them judiciously together, so that they may go down comfortably, like an effervescing draught. You have done your duty by the child; the mother is beyond your care. You were with her, you say, when she died, and, as you told me, she died with ——"

"A blessing upon her lips for her seducer! Yes, I was with her. Oh! Emily, Emily, can that scene ever be blotted from my memory? I think I see her now lying, in all the palor of death, with her eyes bent upon me, striving to speak; while—while ——. But I cannot pursue the picture. Oh, Bruce, if I could but for one moment have asserted the simple honest dignity of manhood, and trample upon this pride of birth, that made me think it a piece of guilt to love one of the best, the gentlest, and most devoted of human beings, I might have been very happy.

"Yes, and enormously sentimental for six weeks—love in a cottage, and the baker cutting off the supplies for the want of his bill being paid. Crumbledown, Crumbledown, I consider it one of the greatest of social iniquities to pun upon anybody's name; but, believe me, your sentiment would have crumbled down to the smallest possible atom in the smallest possible space of time."

"No, no, no."

"Ah, but I say yes, yes, yes. It's only the sight of this child, you know, that has excited all these slumbering feelings in your breast; rouse yourself, man—rouse yourself; only consider in what a princely manner you can provide for this little offspring of an early attachment. And if its mother could look from her grave ——"

"Hush, hush! speak to me not in such a strain. I must visit this woman at her cottage—so transient a glimpse as this of my child is not what will satisfy me. I must and will see her, and question her more closely as to its well-being. I do not think I run any risks, for, by the Heaven above, I believe she knew me."

" As you please; a wilful man must have his way. I don't think you ought to presume too hastily upon being recognised. Recollect that years have passed away, and you are considerably altered in personal appearance, in addition to wearing a moustache, which you did not then; however, if you think that this woman is one who can be thoroughly relied upon, trust her, and then you can go as often as you like."

" I've half determined upon such a course; and, notwithstanding all your raillery, Colonel Bruce, I can assure you that I have never ceased to regret sacrificing myself at the altar of mammon in the way that I have done."

" Really, you don't say so," said the colonel, as they ascended the steps of Lord Blenketh's mansion, and strolled into the billiard-room.

The Earl of Crumbledown was correct in his conjectures. Mrs. Grove did recollect him, and it was prudence and not forgetfulness that made her play the part she did in the country lane where she had met him.

She had become tenderly attached to the infant which had been so strangely committed to her charge, and much she, in her kind and womanly nature, wondered how its only living parent could have so long remained away, and not looked upon the sweet face of the little angel God had given to him

It wa only a strong feeling for the welfare of the little innocent itself, that had enabled her to act as she had done, and then, although the father of that child of chance had not shown to it all the personal affection which she would have expected, he had been far from failing, in any of those more substantial attentions, which consisted in paying liberally for its maintenance, and carefully providing that it should want for nothing.

But do not let the reader suppose, for one moment, that Mrs. Grove was actuated by the least selfish feeling in this business; there is something in the physiology of women which begets a tenderness for the babe they nurse, almost equal to that which they would feel for one of their own; and such was the deep and overweening affection which Mrs. Grove had for the love child, that most probably had no funds at all been forthcoming for its support, she would have willingly worked for her young charge, and maintained it at her own proper cost.

And therefore was it that she showed some consideration towards the father, who, perhaps, she thought, had he been alone, might have shown more for his child; but certain it is, she tidied up her cottage with unwonted care, as if she fully expected some visitor, for a strong impression came across her, that not a long time would elapse ere the father of the babe she loved so well would cross the threshhold of her humble dwelling.

In a country place, such as that was where Lord Blenketh's lordly mansion was situated, it is not to be supposed but that not only he and all the members of his family were well known, but even such visitors as had been in the habit, season after season, of spending their dignified leisure at the magnificent domain, were quite well recognised, gossipped about, and made the common subjects of conversation at many a cottage fireside.

In fact, in the country, what occurs at the " great house," occupies to the full as great a share of the attention of the villagers, as in town do the movements of the court.

The merest particle of gossip finds a ready circulation, and trifles light as air are canvassed and dismissed as if they were subjects of the greatest possible moment and importance.

Even Mrs. Grove, albeit she was not one of those who most delighted in gossipping, or in prying into the affairs of her neighbours, could not be ignorant of the personal appearance of many of Lord Blenketh's visitors. For example, she knew Colonel Bruce well by sight, but as regarded Lord Crumbledown, that was only his first visit there, as we are aware, and therefore she had no means of identifying him, except just as the person who had given into her charge the love child.

The more she thought over the matter and compared his general appearance with that of the gentleman whom she had seen at the bedside of the dying girl at the inn, some time before, the more she felt convinced that she was right; and so, with a

See p. 186.

great amount of nervousness, he waited for some more positive attention on his part to the infant than he had yet bestowed upon it.

And that she had not long to wait for. The evening crept on apace, and about half an hour after dusk, there came a tap at her cottage door.

" 'Tis he—I am certain it is he," she exclaimed; and her heart beat tumultuously with fear and hope—fear, that he might make some arrangement that would deprive her of the care of the child, to whom she had become so tenderly attached; and hope, that he would approve of all that she had done, and give her some positive assurance of being its nurse for a long time to come.

She opened the door noiselessly, for the babe was sleeping; and then she saw, in a moment, that her anticipations were correct, for the Earl of Crumbledown entered the cottage. He was closely muffled up in a travelling cloak, the coolness of the evening giving him a good excuse for wearing such a garment; but Mrs. Grove could see that he trembled as he entered her humble dwelling.

Yes, he, the proud earl, and the descendant of so ancient a race, and rolling in wealth—he who had stood, unabashed, in the saloons of palaces, and in the presence of royalty, shrunk like a guilty man, as he was, before the quiet gaze of that humble but noble-hearted woman.

"You—you—this morning," he said, stammering in his speech—"you succeeded in interesting me about the child which you carried in your arms."

She made him no reply, but conducted him to a little cot, tastefully hung round with flounces of coloured chintz, and presenting the very picture of cleanliness in all its appointments, and, holding a light above it, she merely pointed to the slumbering innocent, who there lay.

The babe was sleeping. One fair, rounded arm lay over the coverlet of the bed; the radiant hues of health sat upon the cheek, and the quiet, regular breathing gave ample indication of the calm and gentle nature of the repose which had wrapped its senses in oblivion.

The earl was human; and surely that alone, without our attempting to invest him with any attributes of an extraordinary nature, will be sufficient fully to account for the effect which such a picture had upon him. He forgot all caution; he forgot all intention of concealing who and what he was; but, obeying the mute invitation of Mrs. Gore, he walked to the side of that little cot, and gazed upon the slumbering treasure that lay within it, as if his whole soul was entranced at the sight. A visible and strong emotion came across him; and, dropping upon one knee, he stooped quietly over the sleeping innocent, and gently kissed the velvet cheek.

"God! it is like her," he said, in broken accents; "my poor, lost—lost Emily!

He rose and staggered to a seat, and then, clasping his hands over his face for a few moments, he seemed lost in painful retrospection.

Mrs. Grove did not speak. She considered it no business of hers to make any remark whatever upon the scene which was taking place; although it not only confirmed her in her suspicions as to who the visitor was, but likewise gave her much pleasure to see such an exhibition of feeling from him.

After a time, however, the emotion which had so suddenly taken possession of him, passed away; at least, it passed away sufficiently to enable him to speak rationally to Mrs. Grove, and he said,—

"I have no doubt you think my conduct strange and inexplicable, or perhaps you guess the true explanation of it. I feel that not only is it useless for me to keep any longer a secret from you what my own emotion has betrayed, but that I may safely trust you with it."—"You may, sir, safely trust me," replied Mrs. Grove. "My affection for this dear child will be a sufficient guarantee that you may."

"I believe you most implicitly. I am that sweet babe's father. I am he who, on that awful night when its unhappy mother breathed her last, entrusted this only remembrance of her, except that which is enshrined in my own heart, to your charge."—"I will not say, sir, that I did not guess as much."

"Did you recollect me when we met in the lane, then?"—"I did, sir, although, of course, that remembrance only amounted to a strong suspicion that you were what I am more pleased than I can tell you to hear that you avow yourself to be."

"This declaration of mine to you, remember, will be the only one I make upon the subject to any one. Therefore, you will feel that it devolves entirely upon you to keep a secret which, if once you divulge, will have the effect of depriving you of the care of this babe, to whom, I believe, you are firmly attached."

"I am, sir, indeed—I am, indeed. Your confidence would have been respected by me, under any circumstances; but if you had sought for any argument more terrifying than another to me, you could not more effectually have found it than you have, sir. The child is dear to me—very dear to me."

Mrs. Grove wept as she spoke, for the very notion of the possibility of the little creature being wrested from her charge was terrible to her.

"Be tranquil upon that head," said the earl. "I have ample cause to be abundantly satisfied with all that has occurred, so far as you are concerned. Now and then I will come down here quietly, and at night, to see the babe."

"You will be always welcome, sir. But now, as you have so far placed confidence in me, may I ask, not from idle curiosity, but from the strong interest I feel in the future welfare of this dear little one, who you really are."

He hesitated for a few moments, during which he thought that, if he refused such an amount of information to her, she could, if she chose, most easily obtain it of any of Lord Blenketh's servants for herself, so he said,—

"I am the Earl of Crumbledown."

"Then, sir—my lord, I ought to say—you have both the power and the will to place this dear one in a position of life her beauty will warrant her in hoping for and gracing. Oh, she will—she must be happy."—"Nothing shall be wanting on my part," said the earl, "to promote the happiness of one who is already so dear to me. I must now leave you, and with many, many thanks, too." He once more approached the cot, as he added,—"I do not like to awaken it." But he said these words in a tone of voice which showed Mrs. Grove that he was very anxious to see the little one awake, so she gently took it from the cot and aroused it. The child opened its beautiful eyes, and fixing them upon the face of the earl, it gently smiled. A smile it was that reminded him of the child-like beauty of its poor, deluded mother, ere he had achieved her ruin. Oh, how like a dagger it went to his heart!

"Nature teaches it to love you," said Mrs. Grove.—"No, no," he cried; "nature will teach it to hate me; and yet kindness may do much; and even you, dear little one, may forget your mother's worst enemy. Farewell."

He clasped the child to his heart, and then turned towards the door of the cottage, when he paused for a moment to place a purse, heavily laden with money, upon a table that stood close at hand, and he said,—"You will call the child Emily; it was her poor mother's name." Then, without waiting for a reply, he rushed from the cottage.

Mrs. Grove, however, laid the child in the cot again hastily, and called out to him,—

"My lord, do not leave me money; take this purse away with you; it may be to me a fatal gift. Already, by your liberality, am I more than well paid. My lord, I pray you to pause a moment. I do not want money. He is gone—gone! Oh, why did he suppose this was necessary?"—"Eh?" said a voice near at hand, "God bless me, Mrs. Grove, what is all this about? It's really enough to make one's hair stand on end. Who is that that you call my lord? and what money is it?"—"Mrs. Green," said Mr. Grove, "that is my business, you will perceive; and as it happens to be of a private nature completely, I must decline troubling you with it."

"Oh, it's no trouble, Mrs. Grove, I assure you; I'll just slip a turf on my fire, and then come in."—"I thank you, but I have nothing to tell, and something to think of alone."

So saying, Mrs. Grove shut and fastened her cottage door on the inside, to the great chagrin of her next door neighbour, who had just heard enough to stimulate her curiosity to the utmost, but not enough really to found any opinion upon, except it might be one detrimental to Mrs. Grove's morals.

When the kind nurse of the love child once more had the cottage to herself, she sat down, and, what was very rare, indeed, for her, she wept for some time. The fact is, the interview with the earl had altogether agitated her very much, and her tears were a great relief.

"My poor, dear little one," she sobbed; "and so your father occupies so proud a position, does he? And there will come a time, surely, when you, too, will occupy a high station. He loves you now, and well he may, for what beauty is to be at all compared to yours?"

She kissed again and again the unconscious infant, which smiled in her face, and then composed itself to rest. The anxious question now arose in the mind of Mrs. Grove what to do with the money which the earl had left.

"I am well paid," she said, "for the maintenance of the child. Indeed it may be called my own living as well, for I have never since my marriage known one half the comforts that have been mine since the liberal allowance which has been so regularly paid to me for the infant. What can I want, then, with this money? and what can I do with it? We have both of us all that we require."

Upon examining the contents of the purse, Mrs. Grove found that it contained a sum exceeding twenty pounds, and the thought came painfully across her mind of what a dreadful temptation such a sum being known, or suspected to be in her possession, would be to some of those bad characters of the neighbourhood, who had once been the associates of her husband, to robbery, or even to murder.

"I must hide it," she said, "until I see him again, and then implore him to take it back again, and free me from the danger of possessing unhallowed gold like this. Where can I place it?"

She considered for a time, and then she decided upon placing the purse and all its contents, in a little earthen jar, and burying it in her garden in some spot where she should be able to pitch upon it in a moment.

The spot she selected was immediately beneath a plum tree, and taking no light with her, for fear of betraying what she was about to any inquisitive neighbour, she soon dug a small hole, sufficient to hold the money, and covering it up with earth, she then left it.

It was quite a consolation to her to feel that she had gotten rid of so tempting an object of cupidity, and she could not help thinking to herself with what avidity her drunken husband would return home if he could but suspect for a moment what a mine could be worked in the little garden at the back of his humble cottage.

Meantime the Earl of Crumbledown made the best of his way now back to Lord Blenketh's mansion, where he hoped that his absence would not have been noticed, although he felt that it was rather a breach of etiquette, considering that he was making his first visit, to be absent for so long at such a time of the evening.

To Colonel Bruce, however, he had communicated his intended visit to the cottage of Mrs. Grove, and he relied upon him to make what excuses for him he could, should Lord Blenketh make an inquiry.

It wanted but a few minutes to the dinner-hour, as he ascended the steps of the mansion; but as he had thought it possible that he might be kept later than he intended at the cottage where his beautiful child resided, he had taken the precaution to dress himself for dinner completely before he started; so that all he had to do was, to go for a moment to his dressing-room, get rid of his cloak, and then to walk down stairs to the dining-room.

The family of Lord Blenketh, as well as most of his interesting visitors, were already assembled there, and a glance from Colonel Bruce let Lord Crumbledown know that all was right. He walked across the room to pay his respects to Lady Blenketh, when, as he passed a young lady of the name of Russel, who always prided herself upon being a perfectly natural character, and upon saying and doing just what come uppermost in her thoughts, she alarmed the whole company, by uttering a loud shriek.

"Good God, what's the matter?" said Lord Crumbledown.—"Oh! where have you been, my lord? It's I who ought to say 'Good God!'"

"Where have I been?" ejaculated Crumbledown, in some confusion. "I—I really Miss Russel, don't understand."—"No, of course not. What can this be? Oh, dear! oh, dear!"

There was something hanging half way out of Lord Crumbledown's pocket, which the natural Miss Russel pulled entirely out, and, lo and behold! it was a baby's cap, which she held up to the observation of everybody.

"Why, my lord, where did you get it?" said Miss Russel.

The ladies looked blank, and the gentlemen laughed in spite of themselves. Too well now did Lord Crumbledown remember having had a great deal of trouble to get his handkerchief into his pocket, as he sat down in Mrs. Grove's cottage on a chair, where were some of the child's things. The awful truth dashed across him in a moment. He must have put it in likewise, in his agitation, and hence had the natural Miss Russel a charming opportunity of making no little confusion, and no little laughter.

CHAPTER XXXVII.

THE DINNER AT LORD BLENKETH'S.—THE SUSPICIONS OF THE COUNTESS.

"DEAR me," said Lord Blenketh, as he advanced, and looked at the cap through his eye-glass, "it's a very remarkable thing."—"But what is it?" said Miss Russel. "My lord, can you guess what it really is?"

"Why—why—ah! to tell the truth, Miss Russel, it looks like—like ——."—"No it don't."

There was a general laugh, and while Lord Crumbledown was covered with confusion, and knew not what to say, Colonel Bruce, with an air of easy assurance, came to the rescue, and addressing Miss Russel, he said,—

"Now, what a cruel trick of yours this is! Really you have no compassion in your wit."—"A trick of mine, colonel? Oh, you brute!"

"Nay, now you know it was. Come, come, Crumbledown, you must forgive your fair but facetious young friend; you must indeed. She has certainly had a laugh against you. You own the delinquency, Miss Russel?"—"Indeed I do no such thing," exclaimed the natural Miss Russel, who was by no means pleased to have the tables thus turned upon her by the diplomatic colonel.

"It is no trick of mine, I can assure you."—"Well, Miss Russel, after that of course I dare not say it was. Will you allow me, however, to beg your acceptance of this singular article, which nobody can give a name to, as a sort of memorial of this event, which has caused so great a sensation?"

Miss Russel, with all her talent which she thought she possessed, had not tact sufficient now to hide her chagrin. She felt that she had got the worst of the war, and with a forced laugh, she said,—

"Oh! very good. I'll stick it on to the fly-leaf of an album."

The dinner put an end to anything further being said upon the subject, but there can be no doubt that the confusion of Lord Crumbledown's manner awakened a number of curious surmises. The fact was that there were no young children in the mansion at all, so that there he could not have obtained the cap; and, notwithstanding her polite pretended indifference to all that had passed, Lady Crumbledown puzzled herself during the whole of dinner time to think if it were really some practical jest played off by some one upon Lord Crumbledown, or anything else which, in its full explanation, would be to her interesting, and curious to know of.

She scarcely knew enough of Miss Russel to come to any decided opinion as to whether or not she was likely to have perpetrated such a not over-refined joke; and yet the improbability of her doing so in such society was almost too glaring to admit of the supposition for a moment. But Miss Russel was dreadfully galled at the colonel's insinuation, that she had placed the cap in Lord Crumbledown's pocket, and when the ladies retired to the drawing-room, she took the opportunity of approaching the countess, and saying,—

"My dear Lady Crumbledown, I do hope you acquit me of placing that child's cap, which indeed it was, in the earl's pocket?"—"Really," said the countess, with admirably acted nonchalance, "it's of so very little consequence one way or the other, that I beg you will not mention it."

"I only wished to tell you, madame, that Colonel Bruce was quite wrong in his insinuation."—"Very good."

The countess had got all the information she could from Miss Russel, and, therefore, she treated her with an insolent hauteur, which was part of her nature, and which she always put on to persons of whose rank in life she was dubious; but, for all that, she made up her mind that there was something connected with the history of the child's cap of a suspicious character.

The Marchioness of Fanfaronade, who was at the party, for she had, with all the insolence in the world, come, as if it were a matter of course, notwithstanding she was certainly not invited, took occasion to speak of the matter to her daughter, saying,—

"My dear, of course you do not intend, for one moment, taking the least notice of, or making the least inquiry concerning that affair of the cap."—"I must own that I should like to know where he got it."

"Yes, of course; but let me recommend you to pass it off in silence. It's some low affair, you may depend. I have once or twice remarked that he was a man somehow of low tastes."—"And I too. He is almost radical in some of his opinions; and can anything be worse than that?"

"Nothing, my dear, nothing. Alas! I have had a note from Julia, and, I grieve to say, that I cannot get her to forgive and forget the conduct of the earl on that unhappy night when he took too much wine."

"I did not expect that she would look over it," remarked the countess. "The fact is, you know as well as I, that Julia is an exceedingly wilful person, and I strongly suspect that she will, some of these days, make some low alliance."

"It's dreadful to think of, but such a thought has come over me with perfect horror more than once, and such opportunities as she might have, too! Why, there's the old Duke of Dunderhead admired her, I am sure, and she almost ridiculed him. The imprudence of some young people is desperate. And now, my dear, let your suspicions of the earl be what they may, say nothing to him. I have remarked that he is a man who will not bear speaking to; but, as I have always said all along, find out as much as you can, because you never know a moment when a knowledge of your husband's infidelities may be of great importance to you."

The countess gave in her adherence to this advice, and so, for the present, the affair rested; although Lord Crumbledown fully expected that something would be said to him by his lady, in her usual cutting, ironical style. When, however, he had seen her twice alone, and she had not alluded to the circumstance, he took heart in the matter, and considered that either from carelessness concerning it, or principle, she had no intention of making it a subject of discussion, and so long as she arrived somehow at that conclusion he cared not how she reached it.

"I consider now," said Lord Crumbledown, to Colonel Bruce, on the following morning, after they had talked over the affair of the cap, and the former had related the particulars of his visit to Mrs. Grove, "I consider now that fortune smiles upon me, colonel, for I have got rid of my torment who I was telling you of, named Willoughby. The child is perfectly well, and I am in a position now to visit it without fear, whenever I like, while Lady Crumbledown and myself are on the most delightful terms of cold, frigid, ice-like civility any one could desire."— "Terrible!" said the colonel.

"Terrible! why?"—"Because every wise man should tremble whenever he feels in such a pleasant state as you have depicted yourself to be in, for when fortune is smiling, you know that every change then must be for the worst."

"Well, of all the Job's comforters that ever I came near, you are the ——" —"Come, come, don't say that; I only wished to moderate your transports a little. I saw the looks of the Countess of Crumbledown while that little episode of the cap was going on, and be assured that she will try her woman's wit to find out what it means, before she is many days older."

"You think so?"—"I do, indeed. And now I am well aware of what an argument you rely upon, for the purpose of coming to a different conclusion. You fancy that she is too indifferent to care one straw about whether you are engaged in an intrigue or not, but do not lay that flattering unction to your soul. All the effect that such a feeling produces, is to enable her to save up what knowledge she may acquire concerning you, to some fitting opportunity for making it tell well."

"I believe you are right there."—"I know I am, Crumbledown; you and I are sufficiently old friends to enable us to talk freely upon such matters. So be cautious, for no stone will be left unturned by your wife and her mother, to find out what you are about."

"Then I had better not visit Mrs. Grove again, while I remain here?"—"Decidedly not."

"I will take your advice, colonel. I know you have made mankind your study, and that you have come to some correct conclusions upon the subject."—"Yes, I have made mankind my study; likewise, I can tell you I should not be at all surprised at some one being put upon your track to-day, if you go much from the house."

"Woe be to whoever I find filling the office of a spy upon my actions."—"No, no, do nothing rash. The best thing you can ever do under such circumstances, is to let them have their labour for their pains. And now, I presume, you will not feel inclined to protract your visit longer than absolutely necessary?"

"Certainly not, although there are enough people here to enable me to get out of the countess's way, yet I have no wish to remain. In London, I can more probably get rid of the pleasure of her society than I can here. There are one or two resources in the metropolis, which we cannot possibly find out of it."

"I suppose you are of the same opinion as the witty Rochester, who, when a dog once nearly bit a piece out of the calf of his leg, and then ran off, could not for some moments find any malediction upon the animal sufficiently strong, to be fully expressive of his indignation, until at last he exclaimed,—'D—n you, I wish only that you were married, and lived in the country.'"

"Good, good. There is no place like London, or some such great capital, when the 'souls' happen to be not quite congenial; so, my dear colonel, you can give a hint to your cousin, that many urgent affairs in London call me soon there."—"I will, I will."

"Many thanks. By-the-bye, is it not extraordinary that the family of Emily should suffer themselves to be so completely hoodwinked by that fellow Willoughby, whom I have paid so well to leave me alone?"—"It is rather so; but do not congratulate yourself too soon, and above all things, Crumbledown, do not be so foolish as to think you have got rid of Jonathan Willoughby."

"Why, hang the fellow, I gave him his own price."—"Yes, for the time, no doubt; but when he has squandered, as doubtless he will squander, all the sum you gave him, what do you suppose he will do, but come to you again?"

"Then I will let the matter take its course."—"That must be considered; but if I might advise you, you should turn him over to me, and I think I shall be able to make a better and a more permanent bargain than you would."

"My dear Bruce, if I might so far trespass upon you, of course I should be most obliged. My feelings are, I know, too much interested in the affair, to allow me to do myself common justice. I am much beholden to you; but whom have we here with such a belligerent aspect?

CHAPTER XXXVIII.

THE INVITATION.—THE INTERESTING COMMUNICATION FROM THE MARCHIONESS OF FANFARONADE TO THE EARL OF CRUMBLEDOWN.

THIS exclamation of surprise arose from the fact of one of Lord Blenketh's servants approaching to where Lord Crumbledown and Colonel Bruce were enjoying this *tete-a-tete*, accompanied by a singular looking being, who now paused, and assuming a theatrical kind of attitude, waited the result of some message, which was to be delivered by the servant, before he himself made his appearance any nearer.

"What is it?" said the colonel.—"It's a gentleman, sir, who has come all the way from town, to speak to the Earl of Crumbledown."

"To me?" said the earl. "From what I can see of the gentleman, I am pretty sure I have not the honour of his acquaintance."—"This is his card, my lord," added the servant, as he handed a card to the earl, on which he read,—"Major Longshanks, Dragoon Guards."

"You can give my compliments to Major Longshanks, and say that, although

I have not the honour of his acquaintance, I shall be very happy to see him, if he has any communication to make to me."—"Yes, my lord."

The servant went to the visitor, and repeated what Lord Crumbledown had said, upon which he immediately stepped up to that nobleman, and, making a very elaborate bow, he tendered to his acceptance a note, which he held in a very mincing sort of manner between his finger and thumb.

Lord Crumbledown took it with some degree of surprise, and opened it. While he was reading the contents, Major Longshanks threw himself into another strong attitude—he seemed affected with a complete mania for them—and looked up at the sky, as if he had nothing whatever to do with the contents of the epistle he had brought.

"May I remain, or shall I leave you?" said Colonel Bruce, in a low tone to the Earl of Crumbledown.—"Certainly remain, Bruce. What, now, do you really suppose that gent. has taken the trouble to come all the way from London about?"

"Not being a conjuror, I really cannot say."—"Why, to bring me a challenge!"

"A challenge!"—"Yes, to be sure; and all about a matter which I had completely forgotten. I had a few words in the park with a young puppy, and it appears he has thought over them until he has worked himself up to the necessary pitch requisite to induce him to send me challenge."

"And what do you mean to do?"—"Oh, I really don't know. It would be too ridiculous to fight upon such a cause of quarrel."

"Say, then, that you will attend to it when you come to town."—"Very good."

Lord Crumbledown advanced to Major Longshanks, and said,—

"You, sir, will probably oblige me by saying to your friend that I will attend to the little affair he calls to my remembrance here when I come to town."— "When you come to town!" echoed Major Longshanks. "I am sorry to say, sir, that that won't do exactly. You must permit me to remark that an affair of honour admits of no delay."

"Except the parties insist upon delaying it, and then, I believe, it becomes a matter of necessity that it is delayed."—"But, my lord, I fully expect your lordship will put me in communication with some gentleman on your behalf."

"When I come to town. Good morning, sir."—"Well, but ——"

"Good morning," said Bruce. And the discomfitted Major Longshanks was left to make good his retreat how he best could.

"I'm glad of this," he said; "upon my word, it's capital. I don't see why I should not make a personal affair of it, really. It's an insult to me now, and I must ask about for some friend to take him a challenge. I wonder now if anywhere near here there is a military depot of any sort. I must inquire. Hilloa, you there! is any regiment quartered in the vicinity?"

"Regiment, sir," said the servant whom he addressed; "do you mean soldiers?"—"Yes, yes, to be sure."

"Oh, yes, in the village; there's the Dashandatem Militia, sir."—"D—n the militia!" cried Major Longshanks; and he walked away deeply insulted that any one should have mentioned the militia to him.

This affair, now that it was for the present over, almost slipped the memory of the Earl of Crumbledown, so immersed was he in matters of real importance, in which his feelings were greatly interested; but it will be found that, trivial as it did appear, it was calculated to be still more troublesome than it at first promised it possibly could be.

The earl now was anxious to get to London. Like all men who are not quite happy in the domestic relations from any cause, he was enormously fidgetty, and never liked remaining long in one place; so now he wished, if possible, to induce the countess to leave, without seeming to make too much of a point of her so doing, in consequence of his desire upon the subject.

He anticipated some difficulty on this head, and he was at all events too well aware of the usages of society, and too awake to what might be said of him, to leave without her; so he took an opportunity that very day of speaking to her upon the subject.

The opportunity of so doing arose in the drawing-room, where he saw her seated alone in the deep recess of a bay window.

See p. 198.

He approached her to her very great surprise, for, if the Earl of Crumbledown showed tact, perseverance, and constancy in anything, that thing certainly was, in always getting as far from his wife as possible.

"What now?" she thought to herself, as she saw him lounge towards her. "What can have happened?"

When he had entered the recess of the bay window, he said, with an air of the most courtly civility,—

"My lady I fear that business, however ungracious the word may sound, will compel me to curtail my visit here."—"Indeed!" she replied.   "Well, the country, to my taste, is always vapid; and, even when London is deserted, I prefer it."

"Then you have no disinclination to name an early day for leaving here, and proceeding to town?"—"None in the least, my lord; and I do not think I shall leave the metropolis again, until after my accouchement."

"After what?" said the earl, as he almost fell down with the suddeness of the shock of this announcement.—"After my accouchement," coolly repeated the countess. "Really, my lord, you seem quite overcome with joy."

"No—yes. I—that is, not knowing—oh, of course, very much overcome, my lady—certainly—of course—exactly."—"How very clear and lucid an explanation."

"D——n!" muttered the Earl of Crumbledown, between his clenched teeth; and then, without anything further than a sort of half bow to his countess, he walked away from the bay window.

Poor, afflicted Lord Crumbledown! he really hated his wife so heartily, that the idea of her bearing to him a child was most distasteful to him, and overthrew all his philosophy in a moment. Somehow or another, he seemed never till now to have taken into account not only the possibility, but the extreme probability, that an heir to the ancient name of Crumbledown might be presented to him by his countess; and now that she spoke so confidently upon such a subject, the shock to him was as great as if such an occurrence scarcely lay within the compass of ordinary belief.

"Good God!" he said to himself. "I am now to be hampered with a child, who may have, for all I know, all its mother's detestable selfishness and cold-hearted, calculating villany. Oh, why did I ever stoop to marry this woman? Oh, why did I sell myself——"

"For half a millon," said Colonel Bruce, who stepped up to him and touched his arm. "My dear fellow, you are not usually in the habit of thinking aloud. What has induced you now to commence such a proceeding?"—"Oh, I admit the folly; but I have had ample provocation."

"Of what nature?"—"I—I don't know how to tell you the extent of my mortification. Would you really have imagined—yes, of course, you may imagine it very well, and wonder what I could have been thinking about, not to look forward to such events; and yet I am dreadfully annoyed."

"Well, I am waiting with a patience which ought to recommend me to a crown of martyrdom."—"Then, in brief, my dear Bruce, Lady Crumbledown has been talking about—about—d—n it! her accouchement."

"Oh! is that all?"—"All—all! and is not that enough, disliking the woman as I do, to drive me mad? and yet you coolly ask me if that is all."

"And well I may. Come, now, Crumbledown; you view this affair in a wrong light. You, nor any one else, cannot accuse me of being in any way a partisan of Lady Crumbledown; but you should remember that she is your wife, made so, too, by your own voluntary act and deed. The child she brings to you will be entitled to your affections."—"I dread an affinity in disposition between the mother and the offspring."

"Stuff—stuff! Education in the cold-hearted school of the Marchioness of Fanfaronade's philosophy has made the Countess of Crumbledown what she is; and there can be no occasion, even if she should present you with a girl, why it should partake of its mother's acquired indifference of habit."—"If it be a boy, she shall see little of him."

"Time enough—time enough to talk of all that, Crumbledown; and, detestable as proverbs are, allow me at least to call your attention to one which inculcates the propriety of not reckoning one's chickens before they are hatched."—"True enough—true enough. Be it so. I will, with what patience I may, endure, such evil fortune as the arbiters of destiny have in store for me."

CHAPTER XXXIX.

JACK GROVE REACHES LONDON, AND TAKES UP HIS RESIDENCE AT THE SAME
HOUSE WITH THE WHITFORDS.—HE CONSULTS JONATHAN WILLOUGHBY.

WITHOUT pursuing Jack Grove's various adventures by flood and field particularly, let us suppose him, one pleasant evening, on the outskirts of London,
towards the north; but the pleasures of the moment much drawn upon by the
knowledge that the last few coins were speedily like to disappear from his pocket
almost as soon and as certain as that the sun would shortly set, and leave him,
Jack Grove, like other sublunary mortals, to the guidance of the lights that
were left them.

And these, Jack Grove found out afterwards, were very different from what he
had before seen in his village, as he was used to call the place he came from;
but presented a very different spectacle to anything that could be seen anywhere
about England.

However, there was Jack Grove, standing on Hampstead-heath, aud gazing
around him on everything he saw. He looked at the Castle, and thought it a
mighty fine place; and he had no manner of doubt they drew fine ale. But
then Jack hadn't much money to spare, and though he was not a man to
stand upon trifles—that is, when they interposed between his thirst, and the
means of quenching it—yet, he had been liberal, and he, for once, determined
to be prudent.

This was an honest resolve, and one which he was sure to keep, so long as the
motive presented itself in stronger and more vivid colours to his imagination
than the foaming tankard of cool ale. But when this latter did usurp the place
of the former, which our readers know well that it did, then Jack Grove drowned
remorse for broken resolution, and regaled his inward man with the best brew
time and circumstances would permit him to procure.

Thus he went on for the last few miles; and now he stood on Hampstead-
heath, and paused a few moments beneath a great tree, where there was a seat,
sat down, and looked about him for some time in silence.

There were long shadows cast before him, and the pond looked bright and
cool. A gentle breeze swept across the heath, and subdued the intense heat
that would have been otherwise experienced from irradiation. There were an
enormous number of donkeys on the heath, and these attracted Jack Grove's attention; he could not have believed anything of the kind if he had been told of
it; but now that he saw it, it was quite another thing. Seeing, with Jack
Grove, was believing.

"Well, well; bless my heart, who would have thought of anything of this
sort? Would they believe me if I were to tell them this at the Saddle and
Turnpike-gate? In course they would; but I wouldn't—not I. Why, how
precious fond of asses they must be up in London here. Surely, they must
fetch a good price.

"Let me see—if I were to set up a breeder of asses, I might make a fortune
—buy them up in the country, and bring them to London, where we are sure to
get a good sale; but then I want capital. Ah, well, I must get that somewhere—I came here on purpose—that's the Castle, eh? Well, it's just such a
castle as I should like, and not that sort of thing they tell us of, with high walls
and deep cellars, though there can be no doubt there would be good storeage for
all casks.

This was a subject upon which Jack Grove's thoughts ran for some minutes,
without any interruption. At the end of that time, he came to the conclusion that
two-and-fourpence was not a sum to speculate with upon such projects.

Rising, therefore, from the seat he had occupied, he walked towards the town
of Hampstead, giving a longing look behind at the Castle, where he had more
than an inclination to return to taste the ales that were spoken of in large characters upon the wall.

"Never mind," thought Jack Grove; "I don't care a straw about it; though, to be sure, good ale is not to be sneezed at, any time, especially when a man's thirsty. Now, I was, and I am; but I have much to do. I don't know where I shall sleep. What a steep place this is. I wonder they didn't build the town at the top, where there is plenty of room, and all level, too. They don't know how to build here; but there, it was all done in the dark ages, I dare say, and that accounts for it. We don't do things in this way in the place where I come from."

This was satisfactory and gratulatory; and the feeling of superiority that came over Jack Grove was so great, that he saw "The Brewery" written on a house-front in large characters on a whitewashed wall, with seats in front; and he at once went in for a pint of ale, determined to sit down and enjoy himself in the front of the house.

"The best ale?" said the fat hostess, as she leaned her hand upon the tap. "The best ale did you say, young man?"

"Yes; give us a pint of your best; you brew it yourself, and you ought to have it good."

"We do have it good, young man, and no mistake about it, either; we only brew the best."

"Ah! I know all about that," said Jack Grove, "all about it, and no mistake. Here, take the damage out of that shilling; I dare say I shall want change soon."

The money was examined, and the change given, when Jack looked at it very gravely, muttering to himself, "Eightpence a pot!—well, I never paid such a price before; but I shall find it all in the strength."

Having assured himself of that, he went outside and sat down on a form, where there were some other men, who had sat down for a similar purpose. He tasted the ale; that is, after his own style, by swallowing one-half, before he paused to find the effect it had upon his palate; and then he seemed lost in doubt and perplexity.

"Well," he muttered; "I don't know what to make of it, I am sure; it seems, somehow or other different, and not exactly the same. I dare say it is strong. Ah! there's the sun, yonder, he's going down; that reminds me I have to go to London, and get a lodging. I wonder how far it is—not far, I believe. Lord, what a place it seems, yonder, all smoke and chimneys; that will not be far off; and yet—and yet ——"

Jack Grove's soliloquy was broken in upon by some man at his side saying,—

"Ah! there's a few on 'em there."

"A few what?" said Grove.—"A few houses; see what miles of chimney-pots there are, and the smoke that fills the air; it is astonishing," said the man, "that so many square miles should be covered, closely packed, with human habitations."

"You don't mean to say that?" said Jack. "Why, how far is London from this place?"—"It begins just over the bridge, in Camden-town, though that is not old London, though it is part of modern; and then it runs on in streets of houses, without any stop or stay, for Heaven knows how long."

"Well," said Jack Grove, "I must be going. I suppose the road lies straight afore me."—"You can't miss it; if you do but keep straight on before you, you will see plenty of houses, and lights, too. You'll be astonished, especially as you have never seen London before."

"Never seen London afore? What do you mean? How do you know that?" inquired Jack Grove, in amazement.—"You are a countryman—a yokel—every-body can see that in your face, if they but take the trouble to look at you. You'll find everybody will read you."

Jack Grove made no reply; he didn't like this, and he began to see that, however great a man he was in his own village, still he was a much less man in London, or even in the outskirts.

Now this was an unpleasant discovery, to say the least of it; and Jack drank up his ale, and rose from his seat where he had been sitting, and deliberately walked down the hill towards the George. Here was another tempting place to rest; but Jack Grove felt that he could not rest at every two hundred yards.

A little below the George, he caught a glimpse of the red clouds that surrounded the setting sun, in all their beauty and variety. The evening was serene; he felt none of that gentle breeze he had felt upon Hampstead Heath; it was sheltered and warm; the gardens were full of beauties of one kind or another, and some of the tall trees threw immense shadows across the road, until they were lost in the distance beyond.

The ale and the atmosphere had made Jack uncommonly warm, and had it not been that he recollected that it was fourpence a pint, he would have gone into the Load of Hay, which he passed in dudgeon.

"The Load of Hay," he muttered; "what loads of money they charge here; why, in a very short time, I should have nothing left, though I couldn't buy anything better than ale. Ah, well, there'll be plenty of places in London for ale, I'll warrant, more than I can drink.

"Good Lord!" he suddenly broke out, as he walked down the road towards the turnpike; "good Lord! if I should find him out, I will have a barrel of ale upon the strength of it, put close to my bed, and then I will have my fill of the best ale that can be had for money."

Thus ran Jack Grove's mind upon ale, nothing but ale; indeed, in mind he was aleing it all the way down the hill until he came to the turnpike, and then he passed over the bridge into Camden-town, and thence through the High-street, into the Hampstead-road, and at length he found himself in Tottenham-court-road.

Here Jack paused, and looked around him; this was a scene he had not seen before; he was taken aback—completely astounded.

"Shops on this side, shops on that; why, where do all their customers come from? They can't be all shops in London; there must be a few private houses, else where can the king and his ministers reside? This will never do. Let me see; doctor's shop, public-house—doctor's shop, public-house—doctor's shop and public-house. Well, I'm hanged," he muttered, "but people hereabouts must be as fond of physic as they are of ale. What a pretty turn out, surely; I never saw such a sight; well, I never saw so many things for sale in all my life before."

Jack Grove wandered on and on, without either knowing, or being much concerned, as to where he was wandering to. It mattered little to Jack Grove; he was Jack Grove go where he would, and he was as well in one place as another. Moreover, he believed that he should have an equal chance of making a discovery by wandering on without any plan as he should have by going on with a plan.

As he had neither rudder nor compass, he let himself drift about at the caprice of the moment; there could be no means of guidance; he troubled himself nothing about it—he was equally at home in one place as another.

"It's no use of my worrying myself," he argued; "I am as well off here as anywhere else; and, moreover, I am as likely to come to mischief anywhere else as here; so what's the odds as long as I'm happy? I'll take it comfortable and easy, come what may. Ease and comfort, a place to sleep in, something to eat, and plenty to drink, is all I care for."

However, this was what he had to win; and how to do that, Jack Grove trusted to his own cunning to procure. He had a notion that he had only to come to London to secure a handsome independence from the pocket of another—not requiring any exertion on his part, save a kind of negative exertion, if such a thing can be—the abstaining from doing anything; and to win an independence of such a character, was, in John Grove's opinion, a matter worth seeing after; more especially since he had been so ignominiously kicked out of the village, and people had there shown a decided inclination to give something to get rid of him.

"They don't know me, else they wouldn't have used me so," he muttered; "they don't appreciate my talents, that's clear; however, before I die, if I be lucky, I shall be able to show them what I am; they'll be rather astonished when they hear that John Grove can take his pint and pipe, and never soil his hands with work. I know they'll repent, I'm sure of it. But then I'll not have anything to do with them, far from it—I won't see or speak to them. Yes, yes, I will; I'll see them, and they shall see me. I'll tell 'em, too, what I think of them, and how I live and enjoy myself. It shall be a perpetual Sunday with me; I'll wear good clothes, and drink nothing less than the best ale that can be had.

"I'll go to the magistrate, and snap my fingers in his face," said John Grove, with a jerk of his body that brought him into violent contact with a carter.

"Dang thee, thou fool!" said the man, hitting John Grove a violent blow on the head with the brass handle of his whip that made him stagger. "Dang thee, can't thee see where thee art going to—Gee, whoa!"—

The man went on with his team, leaving John Grove in a state of mental confusion and bodily affliction.

"If he had stopped a minute longer," said Grove, as he rubbed the afflicted part, "I would have given him something to have carried away with him. What did he mean by assaulting me? Well, if this is London manners, I say they want people to come from the country to teach them a bit."

Thus John Grove soliloquised, and stared at everything he saw, and still kept moving forward, he knew not whither, nor did it seem to concern him much.

By this time he had proceeded along Holborn for some distance, and now the lights began to move about the streets—the shops were beginning to light up, and the lamp-lighter might be seen running along with his ladder, running up, and then down again, with inconceivable speed.

"Ah!" quoth Jack, "I expect it would puzzle the people about our place to find work for a lamp-lighter; a candle-snuffer lives in each house, it is true, upon the same plan that every Welchman is his own cook, because they toast their cheese."

The place was getting every minute more and more crowded, and people were hurrying to and fro, as if all the world depended upon their individual speed.

"What a hurry everybody is in, surely," said Grove to himself, as he walked down Holborn-hill; "and what a lot of horses there are, to be sure. I wonder where they find stables for them; I haven't seen any yet."

Thus Jack Grove wondered and wondered, until having nothing but ale in his stomach, and no food, he began to think that something solid would be as well, and rest for a short time quite as desirable.

Acting upon this idea, he turned into a bye street, and there saw in a shop window a variety of cooked meats, and an inviting display of other edibles, and beyond, a number of long tables, on which were spread many plates, and offered a tempting appearance to the eye.

"Ah!" said Grove, "I own that is all very well, but what a price they put upon them kind of accommodations. Oh dear, they would ruin me, at least as I am. A steak cooked at the tap-room fire! there, indeed, I may do; besides, there is a drop of beer to wash all down with."

So saying, he turned from the tempting display, and walked into a butcher's shop and procured some steak, which he carried to the Goose and Gridiron tap close at hand, where he had it cooked, and with it he ordered some of the compound called London porter, which he did not quite relish, seeing it was a new drink to him.

Here he stayed nearly half an hour, and then he again arose and pursued his journey, whither he knew not, but he went onward. As chance would have it, he still pursued the same line of streets; he made towards the same point of the compass, and proceeded on an easterly course, which he steered as near as the streets would permit him, which, however, was not very much out of the proper direction.

He moved on through Newgate-street, having given a passing look at Newgate, which he considered was a very different affair to the place in which he had been confined for assaulting the constables.

"That is something like a prison," muttered Jack Grove; "one, too, which looks as if you once got in, you would never get out any more. That is a place I would rather not enter, for fear they should not be able to open the gates again; and who knows but a man might die of starvation, and nobody know anything of it?"

This was a moral reflection to Jack Grove, who thought that had he done the same thing in London, how very uncomfortable he would have found it.

"Well," thought Jack, "I am going Heaven knows where; there is no end to this long place. Lord, how many miles have I walked through all these streets? I am sure I can't tell. Who would have thought London had been such a plaguy way through? I must see where I can lodge, for to go on in this manner I can't. Let me see, two-and-fourpence I had at Hampstead—one pint of ale there, another in London, a steak and a pot of porter, leaves me about the odd fourpence; a very excellent way of laying out money, because it's to advantage. Then I have a few shillings sewed up in my waistband,—about six more. Well, I suppose I must pull them out. O'd rat it, but it's bringing the bank low—all cash payments, and no receipts, make a queer account. Well, well," he said, "here goes; I'll walk yet awhile; I can't get a lodging in these large streets; they are all too fine and too big to suit my pockets. By Jove, if I don't find this child's father, I shall be in a pretty state; but never mind, luck's all—here goes again."

So saying, he walked on at an accelerated pace, until he got into the east end of the town. When at London-bridge, he listened to the mournful yet rushing sound of the water against the piles of the bridge for some time, but he turned from that and walked through Thames-street, which he found to be quite a change from what he had already seen, and which quite amazed him.

"They make the streets very narrow," he thought, "and the houses very high. What a miserable place to live in! Who could sleep with such a noise?"

Thus looking about him, he passed through the Tower Hamlets, and then into the streets leading to Wapping, and when he came there, he was amazed at the appearance of the shipping that every now and then appeared to his sight, over the top of some house, or at the corner of some street.

This seemed to puzzle Jack Grove, and he looked about first on one side, and then on the other, but he could not see exactly what he wanted.

"I don't want to lodge at a public-house," said Jack, "because I shall soon be quite destitute of all money, and I ain't got too much now; beside, there are so many, I should like to give them all a turn, one after the other, and then I shall know if one is better than the other."

There was some philosophy in this; and, besides, Jack knew very well there would be much danger in having the tap so near, that he would seldom be in a state approaching to sobriety, much less to one that was entirely so.

At length Jack espied the words, "A lodging to let for a single man," in a window. It attracted his attention in a minute, and he took a survey of the house. It was of a nondescript appearance, a tolerable height, and several windows on a floor; but Jack's eyes couldn't tell him which windows belonged to the house, for they were made all so near one another.

"It's no use looking now; I may as well go over and inquire at once, since I must do it. I may as well begin at once as by-and-by, for I am very tired."

Jack crossed over the way, and again read the bill.

"For a single man, eh? Well, I am a single man—I ain't got no wife with me—she ain't worthy to be the wife of a man like me. I'm a single man now; who knows to the contrary? I'm sure I sha'n't say anything to the contrary, and who else can?"

This was satisfactory; so he walked up to the door, and gave a terrible dab with the knocker, which amazed even himself, and he felt inclined to walk on again, but somebody being behind the door, it was opened at once, and the inquiry of, "What do you want?" pronounced before he was prepared for it.

"Eh," said Jack,—"eh?"

"What do you want, young man?" said a slip-shod girl, who might have been deemed a servant in a very reduced situation in that scale of society, and now become porteress to a paupers' asylum.

"What do I want?" said Jack Grove, recovering himself a little, while he asked an unnecessary and superfluous question. "Why, I wants a lodging for a single young man, to be sure. Don't your bill say so? or is this next door?"

"Oh, I'll call missus," said the girl; and she turned away to the stairs-head, and down which she shouted, "Missus—missus!"

"Well, Mary?"

"You're wanted, mum; there's a man as wants to talk about the lodging. Will'ee come up to him?"

"Yes," said the woman below; for it was a woman, as Jack could now well tell by the voice; and, in another moment, he heard the woman coming up stairs at a very moderate, and with a somewhat heavy but soft foot.

Now Jack Grove could hear this, and, being a judge of cattle, as he expressed himself, he could tell that she was a "big 'un," as he expressed it.

"She's of a good stock, and will fat well," thought Jack. "What a pity no use can be made of fat people as I know on."

"If you please, mum," said Jack, "I see you have a lodging to let for a single man. I have knocked to ask the terms, and to be allowed to see if the place fits me."

"Yes, young man, you may. You see, the room 's small, but uncommonly comfortable—clean."

"Any fleas, mum?" inquired Jack, as he followed the bulky female up more than one pair of stairs.

"Fleas, young man!" said the female,—"fleas! I tell you, young man, that nobody has any fleas in my house, save what they bring in with them; the very cat is free from 'em, except when he sleeps out a' night."

"Any bugs, mum?"

"Bugs, young man!" said the landlady, with huge disdain, "bugs, indeed! Have I lived in this parish these five-and-twenty years, and paid scot-and-lot for fifteen, to be asked such questions as that? Do you think I would have a bug in my place?" And then she added, in an under tone, "Not if I can help it."

"I didn't mean to say you had, mum; only, as I'm a stranger, and didn't know the places about, I asked the question. I don't know the place as well as you do, mum," said Jack, in a deprecatory tone.

"We need all live and learn," said the landlady, who was not very hard to please. "There, this is the room. You see it is very snug and comfortable—very snug."

"Yes, mum, so it is snug. I couldn't well swing a cat round here, but that ain't of no consequence, and houses here are built in as small a space as possible."

"Yes, that is it, exactly. You see—God bless me! I didn't know that I left the Hollands here, dear me."

"Hollands, did you say, mum? What is that, a spirit, eh—something to drink, good stuff, eh?"

"Yes, very beautiful and choice, I assure you; there ain't any of it to be had, out of this neighbourhood, genuine. There, taste that," she said, as she poured out a glass full, which she handed to him, "there, taste that, and tell me what you think of it. Is n't it beautiful?"

"Ah!" said Grove, after he had swallowed a glassful of it with the greatest conceivable gusto, "I never tasted anything like it; it is prime."

Jack Grove smacked his lips—looked kindly on the landlady, and then on the bottle; the hint was at once taken, and the landlady said, in a gentle tone,—

"Ah, dear me! Well, so you like it, do you? Come, have another glass, and then the bottle 's out. I dare say you never did taste the equal to that in all your life; i'ts over-proof—the strongest you can get."

"I can very well believe that," said Jack Grove; "this is the best I ever tasted. Really, this is a good neighbourhood now, where things are to be had so good, and the females so handsome; they are not so everywhere."

"Dear me, what will not the men say?" said the fat landlady, with a sigh and a simper. "Ah! my handsome days are all gone by; some ten years ago, when I was a girl, and could dance on the green—then I was considered passable. I should do, I have heard say, in a crowd with a little pushing."

"Ah, now," said Jack Grove, soliloquising and looking at the mantel-piece,

"that's where it is: we never are believed—as if we wanted to make out that women are what they are not! Why, bless my soul! I should no more have thought of saying such a thing as you have said, than I should have thought o flying; but I tell you, once for all, you are the best looking woman I have seen for some time. But there, it's no use telling you what I mean. What's the rent of this room?"

"Five shillings a-week," said the landlady.

"Ah," said Jack, "and not dear, either, in a respectable house. Any more lodgers?"

"Yes; but there's only one family next you. There," she said, pointing to the door, "there lives as decent and respectable a family as ever you saw—quite respectable, I assure, and well brought up, sir."

"As you say so, I am sure I cannot do wrong in believing it. I am glad to have such neighbours. One feels more at home, and secure, with such people; for f one brings home anything of value, why, it is safe."

"Oh, yes, perfectly safe—quite safe," said the landlady. "Do you think the room will suit you?"

"Yes, suit me very well—very well, indeed. You see, I shall want to come in to-night, because I am just come to town. I have some business to attend to in the morning, and I shall like to be up in time, and to get to bed early, as I am tired. Can I come in at once?"

"Yes, you can come in at once. It's usual to have a reference as to character at first; but, I dare say you are a honourable gentleman, and will pay your shot like a gentleman, without any trouble to us."

"Ay, that I will; there can be little doubt but what I shall be right glad to do so, to keep my berth in such a place. But if you were to write to my uncle, who is a town-councillor where I come from, he would give you a character, I am sure."

"Oh! never mind," said the landlady; "you are a stranger in London, are you not?"

"I am," said Jack; "but I am by no means a stranger to the world. I have been in many places, a great many places; and where they know me they take their hats off, and say 'good morning, Mr. Grove.' I'm respected, ma'am. I say it that should not say it; but if I don't who is?"

"That's very true; but then you see we have our customs here. I wouldn't ask a gentleman of your appearance for such a thing, but we do as a regular custom. I mean the deposit, when you agree to take a lodging."

"Oh! yes, ma'am,—I'll deposit myself—can't do better—with all my heart; and that's the thing I most value on earth, I assure you."

"Oh! I dare say you have a good heart, I'll be bound. You are a funny man, I declare. Well, as you take possession of the room at once, there can be no doubt about your intentions, so we'll drop the deposit; but I tell you I have not let a lodging before for ten years, come the twenty-fourth of next September, without having a deposit."

"Well," said Jack, "I said before you were a handsome woman, and you wouldn't believe it. But I tell you you are; and, more than that, you are not only good-looking, but you are handsome at heart;" and here Jack Grove struck his breast. "You know the old saying, 'of handsome is as handsome does.' Now, if I was to say all I thought, I dare say you would say I was romancing. I am sure you would."

"Oh! dear, what a man, to be sure! But don't talk so loud; the Whitfords will hear you."

"The who?"

"The Whitfords—the lodgers in the next room; they are very respectable people, and I am sure they would never believe that anybody could say so much without meaning nonsense."

"Oh! what people do live in the world! However, I will at once take the room; and now, my name is Mr. John Grove; so if anything arrives, you will know who it is at once."

"Certainly. Shall I leave you a candle?"

"If you please," said John Grove; "if you please. Though while you stop here I have no need of candles, or anything of the sort; your eyes are light enough for me."

"Lor, bless the man!" said the landlady, putting down the candle; "talk about coming out of the country, why, if you had been bred and born in London you could say no more. Why, I've known real Londoners who would not have said half as much."

So saying she opened the door, and, with a gratified countenance, she left the room, saying,—

"Your bed is well aired, young man; it was slept in last night, and if you want anything, you can come down stairs, and call for me."

"Thank you, ma'am," said Grove, and the landlady disappeared. "Now," he continued, as he gazed round the room, "if it was quite empty I couldn't swing a cat; no, that I couldn't; but, never mind, here's as much room as I want, at all events, and I shall be in good hands. The landlady seems a respectable woman, and will listen to reason."

Jack Grove sat himself down on the edge of the bed, and began to count his money, when he heard voices in the next room. Jack paused, and going to the wainscoat, he found he could hear what was said, and by the ingenious contrivance of putting out a knot in the wood, he found he could almost see into the next room. At all events he could hear one voice, and that voice a man's.

After a few moments Jack Grove sat down in a chair, and placing his ear against the hole, he, in the words of the novelists, disposed himself to listen, and heard the following conversation :—

"I tell you what, Whitford, leave it all to me ; she's my niece, and if there's justice to be had—if she's to be found at all, depend upon me for finding her. I know every nook and corner in the kingdom. There ain't a place that you can think of that I don't know."

"Yes, Willoughby, I know your good intentions ; but, God knows my patience and my wants don't keep pace with your success ; or, rather I ought to say the reverse ; your success don't keep pace with my wants and hopes."

"That can never be expected, Whitford ; you cannot do so yourself. I am anxious to save you much trouble and harassing fatigues, for I well know that your means are not such as would keep life and soul together, when great fatigue of body and mind have to be encountered."

"They are not, indeed. We are now at starvation point, Willoughby, and what are we to do?"

"I am at a loss to tell ; but you had better keep quiet, and I will do my best for you, you may depend upon it. What little I can afford, you shall have, but that you know, as well as I can tell you ; there is all I have, save one shilling, which must serve me for supper and breakfast, and then I must chance dinner."

"I don't know what we shall do for rent," said Whitford ; "and I wish you had been successful enough to secure even a trace ; but you have not even done that."

"I don't know how you can imagine that these things can be done so easily. You might as well have commanded a first-rate success in your business as an attorney ; and yet you did not."

"I know ; but, then, what can a man do whose mind and happiness are destroyed?"

"Exactly. You would have done no more than I have, and you would not have gone the systematic way to work I have gone. I have done some extraordinary things, I have, in my time, certainly."

"I dare say you have ; but that is no consolation to a man who has been bereft of his child, and is in an agony of doubt and dread respecting the fate she has met with."

"It is this much consolation to you, Whitford, that if I am baffled, it arises from no want of skill or energy. I could tell you a thing or two that would amaze you. I have been engaged in a different branch of the profession at times to what you have.

"I have been compelled to adopt a little sharp practice, I can assure you. People require a little cleverness now and then, else there would be no understanding the world, and the profession would be no better thought of than so many old women.

"I once undertook an affair purely for the honour of the profession, because it was an exciting piece of business.

"One day a man came to me to know if I would undertake a case he had in hand. It was a delicate affair, and one in which he had no proofs; all must rest upon cunning and stratagem. I at once agreed to it, provided it placed me in no uncomfortable position.

"It was this :—Two men had been for some years in partnership, and had become insolvent—were bankrupts, and had got their certificates. However, their insolvency was a fraud, and they had both agreed to withdraw, for several years, a large sum of money, and one of them was to invest it in another name, until they had cleared off all.

Then, when they obtained their certificates, they were to commence business again, and begin the world anew, or retire upon an annuity for the remainder of their lives, which they thought would be better than remaining in a business that might leave them, after years more of hard labour, in no better situation.

One of the parties, I have told you, had possession of the money, and he confided it to his wife's brother, who had secured it so that no one could touch it, or even discover it. This was just what they wanted, and they declared that nothing could be better than the arrangements made.

But, you see, some men are sharper than others, and they are more easily duped, and it requires a thorough man of business to place the whole lot in a right light. However, I was the man applied to, and I promised to do my best.

"Now," said I, "I know but of one plan that will enable me to get this money from this third person," for I must tell you that the fellow had refused to give up the money, and defied them to their teeth, saying,—

"You have done wrong; you have defrauded your creditors; this money is not yours, 'tis mine; you gave it to me, and I shall keep it; now do your best and worst."

It was in vain to argue with such a man; he was invulnerable, and would, upon no account, turn a favourable ear to them, or to his sister's entreaties; they were a bad set, he said, altogether, and he would defy them all, and he did.

They came to me, and asked my advice as to what should be done. I told them they must be candid, and tell me the worst of the affair, that by doing so, I might be able to assist them, but from the laws they could expect nothing.

" What are we to do?" they exclaimed.

" You must either follow my advice, or give the whole affair up as a bad job, and never expect to see another farthing; it would be a complete and entire loss."

" Well," said the man, " what would you advise me to do in the affair? I can't do anything without money; and my late partner thinks it's a done job between me and my brother-in-law, when I have acted as fair as can be."

" Do you know where he is?" I inquired.

" No, I do not; for since I have obtained my certificate, I wanted to see him and ask for the money. I have met him, it is true, but then I cannot tell where he lives."

" Give me some clue," said I, " as to where he goes, what are his habits, and everything about his friends, and I'll soon find him out. What is the amount of money he has of yours?"

" Three thousand pounds, and seven hundred of my own," he replied; " and then we shall have the three thousand pounds to divide between us."

" Very good," said I; " but as this affair is not a legal one, I must have all the personal assistance from both you and your partner. I cannot make the thing a subject of action at law, that would involve both you and him in pains and penalties."

" It would," he said, " and that is what makes him so sure of this money; he knows I cannot stir without injury to myself. Men like him are not easily moved."

" I'll move him, if you'll follow my advice. You and your partner must give me written confessions as to the nature of the transaction, and then you shall see how I will punish him. I'll have the money."

" But, how? A confession is a dangerous weapon; it may do me more injury than you can ever do me good. I would rather not do that."

" I cannot conceive that your objection can be of any value. You have acknowledged to me all that you would have to put on paper, which would do you no more harm than the oral confession, if I were inclined to use it."

" But of what use," said he, " can that be to you?"

" I will show you," said I; " I can represent myself as a solicitor belonging to the bankruptcy court, and this confession I will declare I have had given me, as you are both promised pardon upon condition that the money is given up, and having found him out, I will give him the option of at once refusing the money, or suffering transportation, or years' imprisonment at the least, for the fraud upon the creditors. I will also say you have made the confession wholly and solely to punish him."

" And what if he would not do it then?"

" I don't know what course to proceed, except to call your creditors together, and tell them the truth, or to allow this man to enjoy the money quietly."

" Well," said he, " I must see my partner about it, and ask his consent, and if he will, I will sign the confession; but just give me a rough draft of the kind of instrument you want; I can take it to him, and get it settled at once."

I did as he requested me. I gave him the draft of the confession, and he carried it away with him, but I did not see him for two days, and then he and his partner both came down to me, and we had a long conversation together; they were both desperately afraid of the confession—anything but that.

However, I told them that nothing else would do. A confession, written and signed by them in the most official form, would do; for a man of his character—that is, the one I had to deal with—would not easily be frightened; he would stick to the money as long as he could.

" One single suspicious circumstance spoils the whole affair; he's sure not to give it up, if he suspects, and then your trouble goes for nothing, and I know the secret."

They looked very blank at each other, and then, after a time, one of them placed his hand in his pocket, and pulling out a paper which he unfolded, said,—

" Well, as there is no other method, we must consent to this. Of course we have nothing to fear from you?"

" Oh, nothing at all," said I; " your success is mine. I fear as you do; if you do not get your money, I get none too. So we fairly understand each other; we have no hope or expectation but what is in common to us all."

" Exactly; we all row in the same boat," they said.

" We do," I replied; " and for [that reason I am unwilling to attempt anything without a prospect of success. If you'll pay me for my time and attendance in other attempts, I'll do it; but I am sure it would be useless."

" Well, here is the confession," he said, giving me a paper, which shook in his hands as though he were giving a warrant for his own execution; " here it is; you must make what use you can of it, to the end we have in view."

" Of course; for any other I should not get paid. Well, now, have you any information as to where I can find out this man, for I must do that?"

" Yes," he answered; " here are a few written remarks, as well as a description of him. I think you'll find him out by that. He is a cunning man—a crafty man."

I took the paper, and read the memoranda made thereon; and thought, however cunning and crafty, he must be uncommonly so if I were not able to overcome him. I set about the work, as a trial of skill. Something for profit and fame, and I determined to be a winner.

Well, sir, I looked after the gentleman, and it took me just three weeks to find him. I could not tell where he lived for a long time. At length I discovered him, by a curious means, not often thought of—but more of that another time.

I had some interviews with him before I could at all bring him to consider the matter. He laughed at me when I told him I had a confession; that both partners had given me their words that such was the case.

" Well," he said, " as for the fabled confession, and pardon for the past, I do not believe the former has been made. Now, if you had the confession with you, I might have deemed that something was really meant by all these people."

" Oh, well," said I, " do not think I come here to you, with a tale I am unable to verify. Now I had the confession regularly made before I stirred in the affair; besides, the court would not sanction my troubling myself without them."

" You mean to say, you have the confession with you," he said, growing a little pale as he spoke.

" Certainly I do," said I, as I took it out of my pocket-book, and laid it before him. " There it is," said I, " and you can read it at leisure, and make out what you can of it. You see the sum is a large one, and will produce a very decent dividend among the creditors, who will, of course, not care much about prosecution, for you are no friend of theirs. They have given a promise of indemnity, provided that they enter heart and soul into the recovery of the money, or the production of the offender—that is, yourself; for all, acquainted with the affair, agree that you must be by far the greatest scoundrel of the lot, and one who has not even that honour supposed to subsist among thieves."

At this he looked very blank, and didn't seem to know well what to do. He shifted, and was uneasy in his seat, and talked about his innocence, and all that; but I laughed in his face, and he was much irritated at this, I could see, but that was of no consequence to me. He suppressed it before me—he dared not show it; but he was evidently fearful he had got into a very serious scrape, which might end in imprisonment.

"Well, what do you intend to do?" I inquired, coolly, as I refolded the confession up and placed it my pocket-book; "what do you intend to do about the money?"

"I haven't got such a sum as this—I never had it," he replied. "I have not the means of doing what you demand, were you requiring what is right; but I have no intention of paying at the desire of others."

"Then you mean to deny you ever had the money?"—"Yes, I do. I never had this money, and they know it, and they cannot prove I had."

"They can. Their united testimony would be sufficient to convict you; but we can trace the money in your hands, and what you did with it for some time. You placed it in another name, not your own, in the Three per cents., and now you have placed it in the Four, in a third name, at least two thousand pounds of the money; and the other in the Three-and-a-half Consols, and the Bank Stock. Now, will you tell me we have no proof as to what has become of the money? Moreover, I am well acquainted with the name of the broker you employed."

"You are," he said, somewhat taken off his guard.

"Yes, Mr. Jones. Now, tell me—are you willing that I should give you into custody; and also, do you feel disposed to chance the results of a criminal trial?"

"I cannot answer this now," he said. "I have business to attend to, and I must leave the consideration of this affair to another day. I cannot waste more time in it now."

"Nor I," said I. "I perfectly understand you; you mean to get out of the way; but this cannot be permitted; you must not stir out of this house. I have an officer on the outside, into whose care I shall confide you, on a charge of aiding in secreting a bankrupt's effects, which you know will come very severe; and all your effects will be seized to pay expenses, and to make the original sum good."

He staggered to a seat, and seemed to tremble violently; and, after a moment or two, he again arose, and came to the window, and looked into the street. I understood what he meant in a moment, and so I went up, too. I had taken the precaution to station an ill-looking fellow close against the window; he was leaning his back against the support, and was watching the door.

I tapped at the window, and the man looked up at me. I pointed to the man beside me—he winked, and nodded his head, as much as to say he should know him.

"Well," said I; "you have seen the confession, and you have seen the officer. We know where the treasure is, so can find it. So, you couldn't gain anything if you thought of going through the imprisonment; and then, after your release, regaining the money. You can only suffer; we shall gain the same either way; only we want to obtain the money without trouble, and to save ourselves that trouble, we are willing to grant you pardon, and not visit your treachery with the punishment it deserves."

Again he sank down upon the chair irresolute, and unable to decide. He looked first one way, then the other; but no inspiration came any way; he was just in the same position as he was before ; and then, seeing him irresolute, I determined to end the matter at once, by saying,—

"Well, sir ; you have had time enough, ample time. Will you or not, consent to an act of justice voluntarily, or will you compel me to call in the officer, for I will waste no more time ? I think sufficient grace has been afforded you already and now or not, it is your time to accept the mercy offered you."

I arose, and walked to the window ; and was about to beckon to the man, when he said,—

"Stop—stop ! Do you promise me you will take no further proceedings against me—that I shall be released from all trouble or consequence in "this affair ?"

"I do so promise you," I said. "If I had not such an intention, I should never have had so much conversation with you ; but you would have been in gaol upon a criminal charge."

"I will give it up immediately," he said, pulling out a drawer. "I have the money all here. I was about to quit the country, and had secured the money, so that I could carry it away at a minute's notice, when the time arrived."

"And when did you intend to go ?" said I.

"As soon as the next packet sailed, which I expected would be in a day or two, and then I should have been on my road to America, for I had been badly treated by my brother-in-law, and was resolved, in return, to punish him."

I counted over the money, and got it quite clear ; it was nearly all in notes, save about three hundred pounds in sovereigns ; then I took and placed them in my pocket, and when all had been satisfactrily arranged, I said to him,—

"Well, sir, this matter is at an end now. I have made you a promise, and I will keep it ; you may now consider yourself released from this unpleasant affair, and I wish you a very good morning."

I don't know whether he really thought that it was only a bit of pleasant cleverness that had been played off upon him or not—I cannot tell—but he appeared, for all the world, like a man who had received a hard knock on the head, just enough to stun without throwing him down ; he stared and stood still, and his mouth stopped open as if he had forgotten to shut it, with one arm extended, and the hand clenched.

He appeared as though he had assumed an attitude for a sculptor or a painter ; he moved not, and while he stood thus, I walked out of the house, gave the man a sovereign for the part he had acted, and then proceeded at once to my banker's, and there I deposited the whole of the money I had thus received from my stupified friend.

That evening the two partners came. I saw they were in high glee ; they had evidently seen the man—the brother-in-law to one of them—and had heard the news. They expected to obtain the cash, but they did not expect to find the kind of man they had to deal with. I was not so easily to be sold as that ; I knew I had got a good thing, and I would retain it.

I considered myself in the position of a man who, having found a treasure, is beset by others, who want to snatch it from him, each having no more right to it than himself, and this was my situation exactly.

"Well, gentlemen," I said, "to what may I owe the pleasure of this visit ?"

"Why, Mr. Willoughby," said one of them, "we have seen my brother-in-law."

"Have you ?" said I ; "and what did he tell you ?"

"He told us you had got the money—that he had given up every farthing ; and how confoundedly stupid he did look, to be sure ; I never saw a man change so."

"Change !" said the other ; "change, indeed ! He was not the same man ; the fright he has been in has had such an effect upon him, that he seems quite beside himself, and swears all kinds of vengeance against us all."

"But you have nothing to do with it, you know ; he ought not to blame you ; you could not help my calling and frightening him out of his wits and his money."

"Our money," said one.

"It's our money, Mr. Willoughby, because he never had any of his own, at least, to that amount, or anything like it. No, no; he thought to have the fortune; but you do deserve your share of the money, for I never saw or heard of anything so well done before—he was completely out-generalled."

"You see," said I, "that all this is because I have been bred to the law; but I thought you said he was a very cunning and crafty man—did you not?"

"Yes, we did say so, and certainly he was; but you have altogether beaten him. Mr. Willoughby, you have done wonders; I am sure we shall never be able to thank you enough for what you have done, which has been done so cleverly too."

"Ay, very cleverly—very cleverly, indeed. I never expected to see any of that money back again. However, there is now a chance for us; we may face the world again."

"You may face the world again, gentlemen," said I, "as soon as you please. It's very pretty, and very pleasant; but I think you may go the same way you came."

"Eh? eh?" they both ejaculated at once, opening their eyes a little way at a time.

"What is your pleasure with me?" I inquired.

"Our pleasure with you, Mr. Willoughby! Why, you know very well what we come about. The affair about which we have already seen and spoken to you ——"

"That affair," said I, "gentlemen, is at an end, quite at an end, and entirely done with. I have no further occasion to consult you about that any more; it is done."

"Yes, we know that full well."

"Then why do you not leave the place, and cease to trouble me any more about a matter that is quite settled and done with? I am busy."

"Come, Mr. Willoughby; I do not wish to be intrusive, but, though this matter is quite settled, and done with, as far as regards my brother-in-law, yet, as far as regards ourselves, it is quite a different matter; we have yet to settle."

"Have you indeed?" said I.

"Yes; we have not yet received our money, and it is for that purpose we have come here this evening; if you will have the kindness to do that we will take our leave."

"You must do that without the money," said I; "for, to tell you the truth, I have no money of yours at all. I never received any of you."

"But you have for us," said the other; "and that makes a great difference. Come, Mr. Willoughby, do not play with us. You will get a good round sum by the affair."

"Yes, rather," said I. "But a clever man cannot work for nothing. What I have got I intend to retain, as a memorial of the transaction, and also as a nest egg for the future."

"You do not mean to say," he said, in an excited tone, "that you will not pay over to us the money you have this day received, eh? You cannot mean that. Why, you would not be so base as to rob us?"

"Oh! dear, no," said I; "certainly not. I would not rob you. I will pay the money to the rightful claimant. I rob, indeed! I spurn the very idea of such a thing. It's abominable!"

It would be a difficult matter to describe the intense disappointment expressed in the countenances of the two worthies. They were in a bath of perspiration—unable to speak, gazing into each others faces as though they were able to gain comfort in that way.

"Not pay us any money?" said they, at length, as if by one impulse; "not pay us any money, eh?"

"No," said I; "I have none of your money, and I owe you none. Don't talk to me; and, as for robbery, I never yet robbed a creditor, and, I am sure, I would not use another man so. Now, gentlemen, my conscience is clear, quite

See page 206.

clear—I have to reproach myself with. I have a sum of money, and I will pay it when the owners can come to me, and say, that is my money, and honestly come; then I will tell them, bring your action, and prove what you say; then I will refund, but not till then."

"This is too bad; why, sir, you have robbed us."

"I rob you? get out of my office; I'll not hear a word about that. Now go, sir, and make a complaint before a magistrate, and obtain redress."

"Well, I never heard the equal of this. Well, but Mr. Willoughby, you undertook the job knowing all about it, from beginning to end. You should not have undertaken it, if you were so shocked; you did all that was asked you until you got the money, and then you suddenly stop."

"And time enough, too. You have no right to the money, nor he either ; I shall retain it until a bill is filed in chancery ; and then I have doubts if they can compel me to pay what I don't owe ; I gave no receipt."

"Well," said they, "we'll try some plan."

"Perhaps you had better go to some other clever person, who will be able to help you ; but, in the meantime, you must be aware I have a document in my pocket that would place you in Newgate for a short time."

There was another pause of some moments, and blank dismay was depicted so forcibly, that I could scarcely help laughing.

"Good God !" said one, "what shall we do ? we intended to leave the country, and now we are reduced to beggary and ruin ; we shall not even be able to earn a miserable existence."

"Very sorry for it, gentlemen," said I, "but you should have thought of that before you became bankrupts. Always look before you leap, and you will seldom fall into the same misfortunes you would otherwise do ; therefore, be cautious for the future."

"Once for all, will you not help us even in a trifling degree ? Do not let us go complete beggars from your door. We are ruined and undone men ; spare us something to get out of the country, and we will never trouble you any more ; you shall never hear our names again."

"Well, Whitford, to make a long story short," said Willoughby, "I gave them five hundred pounds between them, and compelled them to give me a receipt for the whole amount.

"That is what I call doing the thing cleverly ; there are few men who would have done all that as well and cleverly as I did ; and as to finding out the man after he had hidden himself from everybody so cleverly, it was a work of time and great labour."

"I hope you may be as fortunate with our daughter ; poor, poor girl, I am in an agony about her. I would to Heaven I knew where she was," said Whitford.

"I wish I did, too ; you should not desire to know a second time, for you should know it at once. I would, too, I had some of the money I once had, I would make you all happy, somehow or other ; but the will and the means seldom travel hand in hand ; that is the worst of it."

"Oh, dear, dear," said Whitford, "I would I knew what to do. I am, at times, almost beside myself, and can't help thinking that the more inquiries that are made the greater the chance of a discovery. It must be so."

"My dear Whitford, you are wholly in error—wholly in error ; let me assure you of the fact. Now, though I say it, and I don't mind saying it among friends, that there is not a better man in all London than myself to discover matters of this kind ; and I know that you cannot do worse than make too many inquiries when there are reasons for secresy ; then, you may depend upon it, they very easily take alarm, and you lose your object. No, a few well-laid plans and inquiries are by far more likely to succeed than many random attempts to gain information."

"Well, well, we must trust to you, Willoughby, for everything ; and, for Heaven's sake, do your utmost—do your best."

"My dear Whitford," said Willoughby, shaking him by the hand, "rely on me ; I am incapable of deceiving you ; indeed, no man would do so, in the absence of all motive ; and, Heaven knows, my motives all bear the other way. Farewell ! and take care of yourself ; I will see you again soon, news or no news."

Jack Grove listened to all this in intense astonishment, with his eyes and mouth wide open, and he thought that Willoughby must be the very incarnation of all that is clever and cunning ; he never heard or dreamed of such another man ; indeed, he did not believe such another could by any possibility exist.

"He's the man for my money," said Jack Grove, as he slapped his thigh ; "he's the man for me ; he'll do it, I'll warrant, and do it well, too ; but he won't get over Jack Grove as well as he got over the other two chaps. Ah, no, I should think not."

He rose up from the sitting posture in which he had been listening, and determined he would essay to introduce himself, which, considering the ease and freedom of Mr. Grove's manners, was no difficult task, and one which would be easily, and, to himself, pleasantly accomplished; so, snatching up his hat, he ran down stairs after Willoughby, who had just shut the door, and had scarce got three yards from the place, ere Jack Grove touched him on the arm, saying,—

"Beg pardon, sir, but ain't your name Willoughby?"

"Eh, young man, what do you want with me?" exclaimed Willoughby, surprised at being recognised in this quarter by any one; "oh, yes, what do you want with me?"

"You're a very clever man, ain't you?—a cunning man."

"Come, come, my good man, don't stop me with your nonsense; go about your business, and let me go about mine, else I shall do something that will make you more foolish than cunning," said Willoughby.

"But I want to consult you," said Jack Grove.

"I dare say, but I must consult my own ease; my good fellow, if you want money, you won't get it; therefore, go away, before I give you in custody for a vagrant."

"Confound the man," said Jack Groves, suddenly breaking out; "I haven't asked you for anything, but I overheard all you said at Master Whitford's."

"What do you mean?"

"I live in the next room to Mr. Whitford. I overheard all you said about your being such a very clever man. I want to know if you will help me to find out the father of a child."

"I believe, my good man, you had better consult the mother of the child."

"Ah, but she's dead," said Grove, "and that's why I have come to London, on purpose to find out who the father of the child can be, because I know he's somewhere up here."

"And what is your object in discovering the secret of the parent of this child?"

"Why, you see, I know this much, he wants to keep it a secret; because he's left no name down there, and if I can find him out, why, I expect it will be as good as a fortune to me."

"I see, my man—I see what you mean. You are an acute man. Confide in me, and if I can assist you I will. But, unless you tell me all you know, I shall not be in a situation to advise you. I have often heard of such cases."

"Have you?" said Jack Grove. "Well, I expect they do occur now and then; but I came up on purpose to find him out. He gives a pound a week to take care of the child."

"Ay, a pound a week to wet-nurse the child?"

"No; dry-nurse it. But I'll tell you all about it. There was a lady and gentleman came to the inn there, and then the lady was taken ill, and the babby was the consequence, and the consequence of that again was the mother died."

"I see. What was the mother's name?"

"I don't know—I never heard," said Jack Grove; "and yet, I think, I have heard her called Emily. Yes, that was the name, I think. She was buried down there, and then the child was placed in my wife's hands to nurse."

"Your wife's?"

"Yes. She was to have fifty-two pounds a year, which is in the hands of Mr. Potts, who gives it to my wife once a week, and they make matters up some how or other between them; and I have come away."

"To make your fortune by yourself?" said Willoughby.

"Yes," said Jack Grove, in a confidential tone.

Willoughby thought there was more in this than was at first sight apparent, and he determined to amuse Grove, and enjoin secrecy, at the same time he drew from him all he knew.

The name of Emily was a proof in his mind that they were the parties he was in search of. The father of the infant was the Earl of Crumbledown, and the mother Emily Whitford. He made his mind up upon this point. This, in his mind, fully explained the reason why he could not ascertain the place where the earl had placed

Emily. Now she was in her grave, he could well see it would have been difficult to find her place of concealment.

Having made an appointment with Grove, and cautioned him against saying a word to any human being, he gave him a small sum of money, and quitted him, leaving Jack to return to his lodging, to treat himself to some beef, and all upon the strength of his apparent success.

CHAPTER XL.

THE RETURN TO LONDON OF THE CRUMBLEDOWN FAMILY.—AN UNWELCOME PRESENT.

THE advice of Colonel Bruce, and the countenance of one who, like him, was so conversant with the world, and yet not vitiated entirely by it, was certainly of the first importance to such a man as the Earl of Crumbledown.

The fact is, that the latter was just one of those persons who may be led for good or for evil by the individual who will take the trouble to exert a great sway over them, and had Colonel Bruce been as evil a counsellor as he was a good one, no doubt the most disastrous consequences would have resulted to the Earl and Countess of Crumbledown.

It needed but a very slight thing indeed to completely mature the feelings of the earl into such a thorough and implacable hatred of his wife, that he would have thrown off that mask of civility which he had worn towards her now for so long, and which the colonel told him was the least that it behoved him to pay to her in the way of attention.

So it was, that he was reasoned by Bruce into a better way of thinking as regarded the matter of which Lady Crumbledown had given him notice, and he began to look forward to the consequences of his marriage, in the shape of offspring, with better feelings.

" Well, well," he said to himself, " the child may not be like the mother. It does not by any means follow that it should or ought, and, at all events, I can love it even as well, perchance, as I love poor Emily's child, which has so large a share of my very best and dearest affections."

Upon the whole, he thought it would be better not to visit the love child again before he left the country, and in this opinion his friend Bruce agreed, saying,—

" You know with what great facility you can at any time come down on horseback here. It is but, after all, a sharp ride of a few hours ; so, as you say, it will be quite as well to run no risks."

" Exactly. I will not visit it again until I have got the countess to town ; for although I really care very little indeed whether she knows or not of the affair—for I am convinced she has no feelings whatever to outrage or affect—still I do not want the thing made a town's talk."

" Certainly not ; for one of the contingencies of its becoming so would, of course, be to bring down upon you Emily's family, with no end of invectives and threats ; and Heaven knows what it might cost to choke them off, if money would do it at all."

" And money would not."

" Oh, then, there is an additional reason for caution ; so when do you leave ?"

" As quickly as the necessary preparations can be made. Her ladyship, evidently, has no affection for a country life. No doubt she sighs for the fashionable sort of half dissipation of a life in London, so that from her I shall receive, of course, every facility in winding up the visit here."

The Earl of Crumbledown was right enough in his estimate of his lady's predilections for a town life in preference to a country one.

What could such a woman as she seek or desire in green fields and stately trees? What to her were the rich hues of the sunrise, or the glorious tints that pervaded the western sky when it sank to rest? Absolutely nothing. She admired a chandelier in a London drawing-room much more ; and as to being up so barbarously early as to see the sun rise, it was a thing she could not think of for a moment, and would not.

No; the pleasant hedgerows, the scents of flowers, the songs of birds, had no charms for her vitiated taste. She preferred the railings of a fashionable square to the green bank "whereon the wild thyme blooms." The bouquet scented by some court perfumer was more grateful to her feelings than the scent of the sweetest flowers that ever nature made fragrant with glorious essences; and as for the songs of birds, what were they compared to an Italian aria at the opera?

No, no; the Lady Crumbledown had no taste whatever for the unsophisticated pleasures of the country. Not for her were those delightful sights created, or those sounds made to fill the sunny air with joy.

If she had been told that God made the country, and man made the town, she would, probably, have shrugged her shoulders, and said, with all due respect and reverence for the former work, she certainly rather preferred the latter.

Such was this fashionable woman, full of false tastes and vitiated ideas. A being made for the artificial state of society in which she lived; knowing of no other, and not wishing to know of any other. So that any proposition that carried her back again to where she was sure she should feel no ennui, from places where she was so sure that baneful feeling would possess her, was certain to be abundantly welcome.

We need not take up the time of the reader by describing with how many civil regrets, as hollow and worthless as they were civil, the departure of Lord and Lady Crumbledown from Lord Blenketh's gave rise to, but at once suppose the ill-assorted pair seated in the travelling carriage, and being taken to town again as fast as four good horses could accomplish that purpose.

They were not likely to be extremely agreeable companions to each other on the journey to town, but they were for the first stage or so, at least civil. After a silence of a considerable time in duration, the earl said,—

"I presume you will not now leave London again until—until—" he found that confounded word accouchement, ever since she had uttered it, to be the most abominable one that he could utter. But her ladyship, when he paused, released him from the difficulty, by adding,—

"Until after my accouchement? certainly not."—"Oh, ah! I have some thoughts of a short continental tour."

"With all my heart. Have you, really?"—"Yes—I—I think I shall get tired of London, somehow, soon."

"No doubt of it. I think of passing a few months in Paris next season. Perhaps I shall have the pleasure of seeing you there. Mamma will be with me."—"Will she, really. What a pleasure that will be to me, to be sure!"

The countess fully understood the sarcasm with which these words were uttered. She could not be off from doing so, but she would not affect to see it, so she merely replied,—

"Yes, I have no doubt whatever on that head. By-the-bye, in her last note to me, she states that Julia is about to be married."

"Julia—married!"—"Yes, I suppose she may marry if she thinks fit. Her suitor is a younger son, to be sure, but he has great expectations for all that, and they say will be one of the leading men in the Commons on the assembling of the new house."

"Oh! indeed. I am very glad to hear it, very glad. I—I am sure, as a relative, I am very glad to hear of Julia's happiness."—"Mamma was quite sure you would be, and the more especially as Julia and you did not very well agree once."

"Not agree!"—"No; you remember the night when you had taken a little too much wine. Since that occasion, mamma tells me Julia has never spoken of you, unless compelled, and then it has always been with a tone of contempt, from which mamma supposes that she got over all feeling of resentment, having exchanged it for the other state of mind."

"Your mamma is extremely kind to give you such information, and you are equally so for retailing it to me."

"Oh, you are extremely welcome. I am sure no one could be more so than you are to anything that I can tell you of a gratifying character."

"I can only repeat my thanks, saying, at the same time, that although I do not repay the Lady Julia Fanfaronade with the contempt you tell me she chooses to feel for me, yet I cannot help entertaining some of that feeling as regards others, who care not how they, for mere sport, trample on the best feelings of other persons."

" An amazingly proper sentiment," said the countess, as she leaned back in the carriage, " and not at all badly expressed, my lord."

After this they were silent nearly the whole of the way, for the fact is, the lady had nothing else of half so disagreeable a character to say to the earl ; so she left the wound to rankle which she had inflicted, and would not divert his attention from it, by any other more trifling infliction.

It was night when they reached London—these most strangely wretched persons—and the lamps were lit, as they drove up to the door of their town-house.

As for the earl, he merely stayed at home long enough to exchange his travelling dress for an evening costume, and then, without a word to the countess of where he was going, or when he would return, he left the house.

His intention was to have made his way to one of the club-houses of which he was a member, but he found himself in such a fretted state of mind, in consequence of being shut up so long with the countess, that he felt how very unequal he was to behave himself in company with anything like hilarity, or common civility, so he altered his plan.

He turned into a gaming-house. There he thought he should be able to substitute one excitement for another; and at that table of green cloth, where fortunes were lost and won, he thought that at least, at the expense of a few hundreds of pounds, he might succeed for a time in forgetting even the very existence of his countess.

There were a number of players present, and some high stakes were played for before the earl adventured. At length he laid a twenty pound note on red, and by a nod to the man who superintended the table, intimated that that was his bet.

" I'll go you halves, my lord," said a voice at his elbow, and he had the mortification of beholding Willoughby.

" Scoundrel," said the earl, " how dare you accost me ?"—" Stop, my lord, stop. That's an awkward expression to use to a friend, rather. I beg you won't do it."

" How dare you address me ?"—" Because I have some more information about Emily Whitford. Now I do know what has become of her—now I do know how it was that she eluded my search. Well she might, my lord—well she might, when she was hidden in the grave."

The earl looked flushed and angry, but Willoughby kept his eyes upon him, and added, hurriedly,—

" My lord, the case against you is ten times worse than as if she merely lived with you as your mistress. The world will now—if the world through your own imprudence should come to know of the affair—think, and declare that the victim of seduction came to death, in consequence of the grief and shame of finding how much she had been deceived. You will be branded as a murderer as well as a seducer, and an evil reputation will stick to you while you live."—" Peace, peace."

" As you please, my lord. Name your own hour and place of meeting with me to-morrow, and I will convince you of what I know."

" What is it to me what you know? You know that telling me of it does not drive it from your memory. What do you want with me ?"—" I could not think of wronging your lordship's sagacity so much, as to suppose for a moment you could not guess what I wanted."

" You have been already paid for silence."—" Yes, on one point ; but the philosopher as he pursues a course of experiment, and discovers fact after fact, expects to be paid for the last one, without reference to those that have gone before. Now, fact one, was to find out what I did, that your lordship was the seducer of Emily Whitford. To have had that intelligence promulgated far and near would have been inconvenient, and your lordship paid me for keeping it to myself—and I have kept it. You cannot say that I have broken faith with you ?"

" Cease this jargon, and say at once what it is that you require."

" Nay, but your lordship wanted an explanation, and naturally asked me for one."

"No! no! no!"

"Well, but for my own honour's sake, allow me to say, that fact two, in the course of my investigation, is, that Emily Whitford is dead."

"Hush! hush! why do you take a pleasure in repeating that name which is associated in my mind with the most painful, the most agonising recollections?"

"As your lordship pleases. She is dead, then, and that is fact two, for which, as a reasonable man, I require, at all events, some sort of compensation for the trouble and expense of coming at, and all on your account too. Your lordship has not the least idea of the trouble you have given me; because, you will perceive, that I had no idea she was dead, but only admirably well hidden."

"Enough, enough; come to the Travellers' Club to-morrow at twelve."

Willoughby, now that he had succeeded in making this appointment with the earl, did not say another word, but merely bowing his head, he at once left the place.

"The villain haunts me," said Crumbledown, "and, I suppose, will continue to do so; and I have no resource but to kill him or to pay him, so I must do the latter, and even submit to his confounded extortions."

With a desperation, now, which he seldom evinced at an amusement to which he was not much addicted, the earl began to play, and, strange to say, he left off a winner, although not to a large amount.

Probably he was permitted by the proprietors of the table to take away something as a bait for him to come again; for although he certainly had been there before, and had played, yet he was what they called a shy bird, and one whom they considered wanted a little coaxing on, before much could be done with him.

At an hour in the morning when many of the more respectable inhabitants of London were thinking of getting up, the Earl of Cumbledown went home, and so he passed his first evening in town, after his arrival from the country seat of Lord Blenkett.

This was indeed a very bad beginning, but the peer, it will be seen, as well as the peasant, if he have not in his own house the comforts of that domestic society which a man naturally looks for, will seek for excitements in lieu of them, abroad. The one at the expense of health and fortune in a gaming house, and the other with the same sacrifices to the extent of his resources, in the tap-room of a public-house.

CHAPTER XLI.

MR. WILLOUGHBY KEEPS HIS APPOINTMENT.—A STORMY INTERVIEW.

THE Earl of Crumbledown would gladly have given Jonathan Willoughby at once a considerable sum, if, by so doing, he could have induced him to relinquish all further claims upon him, and take himself off completely.

But that was not likely.

It was unlikely, because Jonathan Willoughby would not be so easily induced to relinquish the charming resource he found himself possessed of by means, so easy and pleasant to himself. He, the earl, was as good as an annuity to him, and he would have been much less of a calculating man than he was, if he even dreamed of selling out his interest in the earl, because he could not exactly tell what the earl was worth to him.

Moreover, had the earl been willing to try, there was no reason on earth to suppose that Jonathan would not accept of any decent sum which the earl might offer; but there was no bond by which he could be compelled to keep his bargain; he would take the price, but to observe the conditions was quite another thing, and formed no part of his nature or inclination to attend to.

This being the case, the earl determined that the smaller the sum he was to give him the better, since it would have to be renewed as often as possible, as he could find leisure or occasion to come and extort money from him.

"How he can obtain his information I cannot imagine; it is a mystery I should be glad to solve; if I do not find it out I shall be exposed to a continued run of this fellow's insolence and extortion. If I could obtain the information I might stop his impositions, or at least, limit them, and that would be something; though I cannot obtain an indemnity, I might obtain something towards it, and if I cannot escape him, yet, I may render him less noxious than he is."

Filled with these thoughts, he sat in the club-room, in the Travellers' Club, somewhat fidgetty, and watching the hand of the clock with something approaching to an air of desperation, as if he had made up his mind to something disagreeable, and was anxious for the time to arrive, that would place him beyond any further annoyance upon that subject.

"My lord," said one of the members present, "you look as seriously at the clock as though you expected an unpleasant interview."

"An unpleasant interview! What do you mean?"—"Why, suppose you had an assignation with a young lady's mother instead of the young lady herself; that would not be so pleasant an affair, I think."

"It would not; but I have not any such felicitous expectations. So you are in error."—"It must be business then," said the lounger.

"It may be; but being business it is my own, and in that case I shall not make it a matter of amusement to converse about it; but I have nothing of the description you speak."

"Well, my lord, I wish you a very good morning."—"Good morning," said the earl.

The lounger seeing he could make nothing of his lordship, quitted the club, being conscious he had not been able to shine or say anything that was good.

At that moment a waiter entered the room, and seeing his lordship apparently engaged, he waited a few moments in silence before him, until the earl looked up.

"Well?" said the earl.—"If you please, my lord, a person of the name of Willoughby waits to see your lordship. He says he has an appointment with your lordship. He is below."

"Show him up," said the earl.—"Yes, my lord," said the well-trained waiter, and in another moment he had left the room, and proceeded with his message to Jonathan Willoughby, who was himself waiting below.

"The earl desires you will walk up, sir," he said. "He will see you if you please to come this way."

"Yes, of course he will," said Willoughby; "of course he will. I come on purpose to see him; he could do no less."

The waiter made no reply to this speech of Mr. Willoughby, but he led him to the room in which the earl sat, and then opening the door, admitted him.

"Ah!" said Willoughby, as he advanced towards the earl, "you expected me, no doubt. I am a man of my word, my lord, and you, I see, are here to your time."

"Well, what do you want with me?" inquired the earl, very tartly, for he could not but feel annoyed and vexed at being, in a measure, compelled to admit this man to his presence, and as much on acount of his assumption and insolence as the object with which he came.

"What I want with your lordship is very easily guessed, and I could easily explain to you at length the great benefit that is to be derived by secrecy; but I dare say you are pretty well convinced of that before now."

"Granting that to be the case, I do not expect continually to be paying you for the same thing over and over again; but once paid, the matter I must consider done with."

"Well, my lord, for the present we must consider such to be the case. Your lordship was pleased to pay me for one secret, not for keeping two."

"Two!"—"No; you remember very well I first told you that you had seduced Emily Whitford."

"Well," said the earl, "I gave you a hundred pounds, or something very much like it."—"Yes, yes, we won't quarrel about what has been; but if we must quarrel, it shall be about what is to come; but I think we shall please each other better than quarrelling, by being good and quiet friends, mutually obliging to each other."

"Friends, sir?"—"Yes, friends, my lord. I'm your friend."

"You are an infernal extortionate scoundrel!"—"Never mind me, my lord," said Willoughby, coolly. "I am in no way offended. I can listen, and when you have done, why, I can go on, that's all. We shall be very well pleased with each other before we have done, and have mutually a good opinion."

See p. 211.

"My opinion is, you are a great vagabond," said the earl, very angrily; "that is my opinion."

"I would not dispute your lordship's opinion. Birds of a feather, you know, is an old saying, my lord, and may in some measure account for our friendship."

"What do you mean?"—"That your lordship's soul—that is, if you have one—is not of the purest material, for it is sadly daubed over on the score of morality, and would fetch but a poor price if bought for its value, especially when we view it in relation to the Whitford affair, which doesn't make you appear very much like a saint; but that is all the better for me."

"If you have anything to say to me you had better say it at once. What have you to tell me?"—"Simply that Emily Whitford is dead, and I want some money; the last I had of you is gone."

"Gone?" said the earl.—"Yes, to be sure. How long do you imagine it would last? I find it goes; besides, much of what I had was spent in your service."

"You scoundrel! how dare you utter such an enormous lie!"—"Enormous truth, you mean. Now, listen: I have spent much of this money to discover this second piece of information, and I want to be paid for this also."

"How did you obtain this information?"—"One thing at a time, my lord. Hand over the cash. Say two hundred pounds; that will do to keep up appearances."

"Two hundred you won't have; I haven't got it at hand," said the earl. "Half that sum I can give you; but, understand, the pitcher that oft goes to the well may come back broken at last."

"So it may, my lord. Your lodrship must be something of the dilapidated utensil spoken of, else you would not be so good a friend to me. Well, a hundred pounds be it. You can make it more another time, you know; and next time you'll contrive to have the cash at hand, and then we'll have things more agreeable."

The earl took out of his pocket-book the sum named, and, crumpling them up, threw them across the table to Willoughby, who took them up, and, after examining them, counted them over.

"Well," said the earl, "how did you obtain the information of Emily Whitford's death?"

"How, my lord? Did your lordship say how?—because, if you did, I cannot bring myself to satisfy your curiosity—the same 'how' being my own particular business; and, there being more than a probability that it may be similarly useful to me, I do not feel inclined to rip the goose up for the sake of having the eggs at once."

So saying, he made a familiar nod to the earl, and, turning on his heel, left the earl more chafed than he had been for some time; nor was Willoughby less so, for he had received some hard words from the earl.

CHAPTER XLII.

THE DUEL BETWEEN THE EARL AND THE HONOURABLE ADOLPHUS LESLIE.—THE CONGRATULATIONS OF LADY CRUMBLEDOWN, AND A PAINFUL INTERVIEW WITH JULIA FANFARONADE.

As may be imagined, the interview that he had with Jonathan Willoughby by no means tended to give him that happy equanimity of mind so necessary to personal comfort and happiness. The Earl of Crumbledown was very much ruffled in his interview with his tormentor, Willoughby, whom he considered in the light of his evil genius; though not one of such a magnitude as to cause him to tremble, yet it is one that caused him to feel uneasy, and to leave something upon his mind that was not at all times calculated to restore ease and serenity.

To be bearded to one's face, and have one's pocket picked in the way of extortion, was too bad. It is enough to ruffle the temper of the most patient man in existence, and the Earl of Crumbledown had no such pretensions; moreover, to feel that one is in the power of an unscrupulous vagabond, who is ever on the watch to pounce upon some one circumstance of one's life to enable him, under the threat of exposure, to rob us, is far from pleasant.

The insolent familiarity, too, of Willoughby hurt the pride, as did his freedom of speech hurt the self-love of the young nobleman; and, perhaps, irritated him more than the other parts of the adventure.

"The scoundrel!" he muttered, "to talk in that way to me; but, then, what can I expect from a man who can condescend to gain a living by common robbery and extortion?

"Where can he obtain his information?" inquired the earl of himself, as he sauntered up and down the club-room. "Heaven above knows, for I cannot form even the slightest guess. It is mysterious, inexplicable to me, certainly, for I know of none, save Bruce, who is perfectly aware of all that has passed. However, it is useless to make any further attempt to divine this mystery; it must pass, until, in some lucky moment, it is revealed."

In a kind of gloomy and irritable disposition, he left the Travellers' Club House, and proceeded homewards; and then he entered the house in a some-what subdued manner.

"There is a gentleman who wants to see you," said the servant, as his lord-ship entered the library.

"Who is it?"—The servant, by way of reply, handed him the card, which he read and commented on as follows,—

"Major Longshanks—who the devil's Major Longshanks? Stop! let me see —oh, I recollect, now; it is Leslie's friend, by Jove. I had forgotten all about that cursed foolish affair."

He paused a moment in thought, and then, turning round to the servant, he said,—

"Show Major Longshanks in."

The man disappeared, and, in a few moments more, he heard the footsteps of Major Longshanks as he walked towards the library, where the earl was wait-ing to receive him. When the major entered, he touched his hat with a grace that did honour to the profession, and he said, with a great show of courtesy,—

"My lord, I have the honour to wait upon you from my friend, the Honour-able Adolphus Leslie. I heard you were in town, and thought it would be better to remind your lordship that the affair stands over for your convenience."

"I am certainly beholden to you, Major Longshanks, for the care you have taken; in the multiplicity of other affairs it had been momentarily forgotten; but it would scarce have been so long."—"I thought some such accident likely to occur, and, therefore, came to remind you of it."

"I am your debtor for your courtesy, certainly," said the earl. "Has any-thing new turned up with regard to this affair?"

"Nothing that I know of; the matter stands just where it did, with the ad-dition of the delay on your lordship's account, which, however, has not injured the affair at all, and we shall all be able to proceed with it, just the same as if it had just happened."

"Well, Major Longshanks, what shall we do next? What is it you now ex-pect of me?" said the earl, not in the best of humours, but with all due respect and courtesy for the redoubtable major, who was truly a man of war.

"Are you prepared to apologise?"—"No, sir."

"Well, then, if you will give me the name of your friend, I shall be obliged, my lord; that is the usual course of things, and a very proper one, too."

"I hardly know where to find my friend—the one I desire more particularly to meet you in this affair—save at the Travellers' Club; if you will allow me to send him to you, it will save you some disappointment and trouble."

"I care not for trouble, my lord, when I have business of this nature in hand; though I certainly have no stomach for disappointment. I will accede to your lordship's suggestion."

"I will go myself in search of him, so that no unnecessary delay shall take place."

"I expect as much from your lordship. Will you be pleased to furnish me with the name of the gentleman you intend sending to me, and then I will wait at home until he comes."

"Colonel Bruce."

"I shall have great pleasure in seeing Colonel Bruce. Good morning, my lord," said Major Longshanks, who bowed most formally as he left the room.

"Good morning, major," said the earl, in the same style, but not so low as the major in his obeisance.

"Was there anything so absurd," muttered the earl, "as this silly affair? I must see Bruce, and get him to take that affair in hand, and see if it can be settled, which is very doubtful, for Major Longshanks seems a thorough war-horse, and unwilling to permit the chance of a fight to pass by, without making it a positive affair."

"Colonel Bruce is below, my lord," said a servant, who, at that moment, entered the apartment.

"Ask him to walk up."—"Yes, my lord," said the menial, and he left the room to obey the commands of the earl; and, in a minute more, Colonel Bruce entered the room.

"Ah! Bruce," said his lordship; "you are the very man I want to see. I was about starting out to find you."

"I am glad I have saved your lordship the trouble," replied the colonel; "but what has happened?"—"Why, that infernal Leslie's friend, Major Longshanks, has been here, and, it seems, he means fighting."

"Ah! Major Longshanks is an old war-horse; and it will be difficult to shake him off; if there be any prospect of a fight, he is sure to press it forward with all his power, though he may seem to act with the greatest courtesy; it is so cold, his civility is quite freezing upon these occasions."

"Well, you had better see him for me; you remember the circumstances?" said the earl,—"Yes—yes; you had some words of no moment with him in Hyde-park"

"I did. I was annoyed by some circumstance at the time, and he chose to be more prying and malicious than pleased me; and I said I knew some people to be fools, and a few words of cold courtesy passed, and that is the whole affair."

"It is absurd enough; but, I suppose the truth is, he felt himself a little vexed, and has applied to Major Longshanks for advice; and he, instead of cooling the young gentleman's ire, has tended to increase it, until blood letting becomes necessary; but, after all, it may turn out nothing; these affairs are not very serious."

"As for that," said the earl, "I care not much about it; but the sooner now the matter is settled, the better."

"Exactly; it will grow in strength with its age. I will at once seek out Major Longshanks, and see what can be done in this very absurd affair."

Some little more conversation ensued upon the same subject, and then Colonel Bruce left the house to seek out the redoubtable major, the guardian, for the time being, of the Honourable Adolphus Leslie's honour.

This gentleman he found at home, and introduced himself by saying, when alone with the major,—

"I have the honour to call upon you, at the instance of my friend, the Earl of Crumbledown."

"His lordship has been expeditious; I was sure he would; it is quite a pleasure to have to deal with such a gentleman as his lordship."

"No doubt. I came in very soon after you had left his lordship's house, and that is how I am here so quickly after you, as his lordship is of opinion, that, where no impediments exist, the affair had better be brought to as speedy a conclusion as possible."

"The very best opinion that could be hazarded," said the major; "and now, Colonel Bruce, permit me to ask if you have any apology to offer on the part of your principal, for the insult which my principal has received?"

"You cannot intend to say the words spoken in haste, formed an insult of any colour."

"I know no greater insult, Colonel Bruce," said the major, coolly, "than can be given in one hasty word; and, therefore, that is enough upon the fewness of the words."

"Certainly, if an accommodation could be entered into, which is alike honourable to both parties, it would be far better than placing two valuable lives in jeopardy, for a word so spoken."

"Herein lies the difficulty," replied the major; "what will satisfy the one, will be considered to infringe upon the honour and courage of the other; and I can see no medium course; but if you are prepared with one, we can discuss it. As to jeopardising men's lives, why, you see, affairs of honour cannot be conducted on the harmless principle."

"Certainly not; but some consideration might be had to the cause and trifling nature of the quarrel."

"From trifling causes great events may arise," said the major, and then he took a pinch of snuff.

"Well, sir, we may as well arrange the meeting," said Colonel Bruce, who saw that the major was inclined to become obstinate, and thinking he had done enough already to bring about an accommodation.

"It is your privilege," said the major, "and we will assent to anything you may propose."

"Then to-morrow morning, an hour after sunrise, in the fields adjoining Maiden-lane, leading to Highgate."—"That will do very well. If you had said sunrise, I should have deemed it better," said the major, "there is less chance of an interruption."

"Be it sunrise. Pistols I presume?"—"Certainly; I agree to that."

"Good morning, Major Longshanks. The fields to the right of Maiden-lane, if you please."—"Good morning, Colonel Bruce. I know the spot perfectly well and will conduct my friend there in good time."

Bruce left the abode of Major Longshanks, well convinced that the major would be as good as his word. He then immediately returned to the earl, and informed him exactly what was to take place, and promised to call for him an hour before the hour named for the appointment, after which the colonel left the earl, to make what preparations he chose.

*　　　　*　　　　*　　　　*　　　　*

The colonel called for his principal. The parties met in a hollow, dell-like spot, situated about half way up the lane; and having acted with all due courtesy to each other, the seconds placed their men at proper distances, and then placed the murderous weapons in their hands.

There was a pause, and neither spoke. The word was given, and both fired, but no result followed. A second discharge was necessary to satisfy the belligerent appetite of Major Longshanks, and then the parties left the ground; Colonel Bruce accompanying the earl, and the other two gentlemen likewise left in company.

*　　　　*　　　　*　　　　*　　　　*　　　　*

"My lord," said the countess, who met the earl as she was going up stairs, "I sincerely congratulate you on your safety. How dreadful it would have been had anything happened to you."

The countess smiled, and continued her walk up stairs, while a word too impolite to repeat was upon the earl's lips; but he immediately walked down stairs with the intention of quitting the house, but he met in the passage with the Lady Julia Fanfaronade, who had just come in, and appeared in some distress.

"My lord, are you here?" she exclaimed, as soon as she had entered a side room on the ground floor. "I—I—that is, I was told you were mortally wounded!"

"And you came to see me, Lady Julia. This is kind, and more than I deserve."

"My lord, I am mistaken; but I heard of your duel with the Honourable Mr. Leslie, and it was reported you had just been carried home in a dying state."

"Lady Julia," said the earl, and he was about to proceed, but he saw she was much distressed and annoyed.

"My lord, I must beg you will say nothing of my visit here. I have not even seen my sister—the countess—permit me to pass, my lord. Your lordship is well and I must leave."

The Lady Julia was hardly conscious of what she did; but her object was now to get out of the house, since she had been led to the commission of an act she would not have done had she been aware how false the rumour was of his wound.

CHAPTER XLIII.

A FEW MONTHS OF PEACE.—THE LITTLE STRANGER AND THE CONGRATULATIONS.—
THE MEDICAL OPINION.—A SUDDEN THOUGHT ACTED UPON.—THE NURSE.

AFTER the disclosure to the earl of the interesting situation of the countess, and the prospects thereunto attached, the earl began to imagine that he should have some few months' peace, during which time he could, unmolested, dispose of himself as he pleased.

This most auspicious event was like to be a comforter to him in some respects; but he had none in particular respecting the thing itself. He considered it rather a bore than anything else; he could not but be pleased, however, with the prospect it afforded him of his own personal ease and comfort, for, of course, it would not be prudent and decent for the countess to be seen out.

This was what he anticipated; but he found his account not in this quite so soon as he had anticipated, for the countess continued to see much company in her own apartments, besides the carriage drives, which were considered necessary for her health; so that there was no want of gaiety, news, and scandal, at the Countess of Crumbledown's.

The earl, in the meanwhile, amused himself about town, when one day he was met in the street by a club acquaintance, who had met the countess at a mutual friend's—the Honourable Augustus Spoon, who thought he could be witty, and said to him—

"Oh, my lord, I saw your amiable countess last evening."

"Did you?" said the earl.—"Yes, I did. How charming she appears! But, I say, my lord,—why—you—you really oughtn't—but I suppose you want a heir to your title and estates; well, well, it's very natural."

"You are running on in a string of riddles," said the earl; "half of what you have said, if said plainly, might be understandable, with some care."—"My lord!"

"If you had spoken plainly, I might have known what to say in return, but I can't."

The Honourable Augustus looked puzzled, and rather red in the face, when at that moment Colonel Bruce came up and released him.

"Are you engaged, my lord?" said the colonel.—"No, Bruce, no."

"Then I have something to say to you of importance," said the colonel.—"Good morning, sir," said the earl to the Honourable Augustus Spoon, as he took Colonel Bruce's arm.

"Good morning," said the individual addressed, with a blank air, and then they separated.

This was what he had hoped to be the happiest moments of his married life, and he felt himself annoyed by the congratulations of his friends upon a subject in which he felt no cause for delight; indeed, it was like to be a very great source of annoyance to him.

The weeks passed away, the Earl of Crumbledown scarcely knew how; his rounds of pleasure, as he called them, which might by some be called dissipation, drowned all knowledge of the event and its results.

However the earl might spend his time, that of the countess was rapidly coming round, and the event was each day coming nearer and nearer, till the hours only were counted.

The earl was not considered a very good husband upon the occasion, for his only anxiety seemed to be to get out of the way from the scene of his troubles, and devoutly did he hope to be absent when the event took place.

*   *   *   *   *   *   *

The earl had been to the opera. That was very wrong, but the truth must be told, he had been to the opera, and we cannot say where afterwards; however, he had supped out, and that, no doubt, was the sole cause of his being out at that hour of the night, or rather darkness, for it was past midnight, and another day had begun.

He came home, and with the assistance of his valet, he got into bed, and fell to sleep, not dreaming of the events that were happening around him; he was innocent of the presence of " doctor, and nurse, and a great many more ;" but he slept, notwithstanding, and dreamed, ay, of the last new ballet, and the charming danseuse who had warmed his fancy, when, alas! for mundane pleasures, he was aroused from the delightful slumber by some one shaking him by the shoulder.

At first, he thought the motion was caused by a carriage he had hired to go home in, and then he thought he must have fallen asleep in it, and the jarvey had taken the liberty of waking him up, to tell him he had brought him home, and to demand his fare.

But he was soon convinced of his mistake, for a female voice said, close to his ear—

" My lord !—my lord !—awake ! for Heaven's sake awake !"

" What's the matter?" said the earl, starting up into a sitting posture, thinking the house was on fire; " what's the matter ?—quick, tell me—tell me what is it ?" —" A girl," said the voice.

" Eh ?—what ?"—" A girl, my lord !"

His lordship opened his eyes, and rubbed them, and could not but think something was wrong in himself or the person who spoke to him ; and to mend the matter, his lordship having woke up in a hurry, and having had some wine, he was instantly seized with a splitting headache, which did not aid to make him any way happy in disposition.

" What the devil do you mean ?" said the earl.

He had hardly said the words, when he was soon made to understand the nature of the cause for which he had been disturbed, by the sound of a peevish cry.

" G——" exclaimed the earl, but he paused.

" My lord," said the nurse, " it's a beautiful creature—there, look at it, it's the very image of you and the countess, my lord ; she is very charming, but very delicate, poor thing."

As the nurse spoke, she placed in his arms the stranger, which began to squall, to the infinite distress and vexation of the earl, who was more than vexed; and could have said many uncivil things to her, but he paused, and looking at the nurse, said,—

" Well, it's all over, I suppose ?"

" Yes, my lord, Heaven be praised. We have done all that could be done for the poor countess, and she is likely to do well."

" Then I am not wanted," said the earl.

" No, my lord ; but we came to let you see your child—you would like to know when you became a father—an event so happy for your lordship and the countess."

His lordship much doubted the felicity of either party, and saw no reason why he should have been waked up out a sound sleep to be told what was not so new an occurrence to his lordship as some people were simple enough to imagine.

" Well," said his lordship, " that will do ; don't disturb me any more until I really am wanted ; the morning would have done quite as well as calling me up out of my sleep."

The nurse took the child away, and the earl endeavoured to fall again to sleep to escape the wretched headache his sudden disturbance had caused him, but for a long time it was in vain ; and, after more than an hour's tossing about, he succeeded.

* * * * * * *

The next morning there was much general disturbance; the whole street was carpeted with straw, and every one walked about as if in list slippers, with a cat-like motion and caution, and the earl was that morning indulged in more than ordinary quietude and loneliness at breakfast, for he sat with the papers lying about him.

It was very late in the day—twelve o'clock—he had not seen the countess, she had not sent for him, and he did not deem it decency to visit her without the invitation.

There was a carriage drove up to the door, and immediately a pair of creaking boots ascended the stairs towards the countess's room, where he remained for some time, until there was the same sound descending, and a servant announced the doctor. A tall gentlemanly man entered the room and said,—

"I presume I am speaking to the Earl of Crumbledown?"—"Yes, sir; be seated, if you please."

"I wished to see you for two reasons, my lord; one is, to tell you the countess is very delicate, but there's every prospect of a speedy recovery."—"Indeed!" said the earl, who might not have broken his heart if the reverse had been the case.

"Yes; but I am sorry to say I think your daughter's tenor of existence very precarious. I would not advise you to build your hopes too strongly upon her life."

"Indeed, sir! but what would you advise me to do?"—"I think, under the circumstances, the only chance there is—and that is only a probability—is in a change of air; if she were brought up by hand and sent to some place in the country, where the air is good, then that may produce a corresponding change in the child's nature. She is very weak and puny."

"I must adopt such a course as that you speak of," said the earl, thoughtfully. "It shall be done."

*   *   *   *   *   *   *

The medical man was gone, and the earl sat brooding over the news that had been communicated to him, and somewhat at a loss to understand what he should do; but feeling rather indifferent to all that was done, so far as it interfered with any plan or pleasure of his.

"Yes, yes," muttered the earl; "a good thought, a very good thought; she shall go to Mrs. What's-her-name—ay, Grove, that is it, and be brought up with little Emily Whitford—yes, yes, that will be excellent. I can kill two birds with one stone, as the saying is, and that will be a delightful piece of economy of time, and I can visit them both at once. I must set about it at once. I will see Colonel Bruce about it; he will aid me in this matter, and bring it about successfully."

Having now got an object in view, the earl left the breakfast-table, determined to go in search of Colonel Bruce, and communicate to him the result of his thoughts upon this affair.

This was easily done, for the colonel was found at the club, and to him he communicated the medical opinion that had been given him of the new-born infant, and then his own determination respecting it.

"Now, you see, Bruce," he added, "I can visit both children at once, and no remark will be made in consequence of my doing so."—"Very true, my lord," said Colonel Bruce, "but how will you contrive with Mrs. Grove? she will, in all probability, suspect something; the safest plan will be to make a confidant of her, and entrust her with the whole secret, which she will no doubt keep."

"She would do so," said the earl, "but yet it is some risk, and one that I would not willingly run, if it could be avoided in any way whatever. Could she not account for our preference any other way?"—"I think not; and, should anything be discovered at some future period, you may find much unpleasantness, and I am sure that she is trustworthy; and the conduct she displayed on the occasion of taking the child at first, rather than it should go to the parish, is a sufficient guarantee that she will act faithfully."

"I think there is much truth in what you say ; but it is, as I said before, some risk ; however, I think that must be run, and the sooner we see about it the better."—"I think so."

"Will you go down for me to Mrs. Grove, and state what you think at all necessary ?"—"I will," replied Colonel Bruce ; "and start off this very after-noon."

The earl then arranged with Colonel Bruce as to what should be done, and then parted ; the colonel went at once to the village by post, and determined on an interview with Mrs. Grove.

It was towards the evening when Colonel Bruce strolled out from his inn, and walked towards the cottage of the woman whom he desired to see ; and when arrived there, he paused a moment to consider how he should address himself to

Mrs. Grove, but he formed no resolution, save that of entering the cottage, at the door of which he now tapped.

Mrs. Grove herself came to the door, and then he inquired for her by name.

" My name is Grove, sir," she replied, with a low curtesy; " what is your pleasure with me ?"—" I wish to ask you a few questions," replied the colonel, " if you will permit me to seat myself for a few moments ?"

" Will you walk in, sir? there is a seat, such as we use. I fear it is not so soft as what you have been used to, but it is all we have."—" It will do very well, my good woman. I am a soldier, and have been glad before now, of a seat of any kind ; that is a nice little child there—is it your own ?"—" No, sir."

" Whose is it ?"—" The little girl belongs to some respectable people in London, who have left it with me for the sake of the air."

" And it seems to have thrived well, as yet. Would you have any objection to another child to nurse, on the same terms as you have that one ?" inquired the colonel.

" Another, sir !" echoed Mrs. Grove; " I hardly know whether I could do justice to them, or whether the parents of this one would altogether approve of my having another child to nurse."

" But if one were offered you by the parents of this same child," continued the colonel ; " would you not then accept it, and take charge of it as you have done this one ?"—" Certainly, I would, sir."

" Then I have come to make you such an offer," said the colonel, " for the father ——"

" Do you know the father of this little girl, sir ?" inquired Mrs. Grove, interrupting the colonel, in the surprise of the moment.—" I do."

" May I be entrusted with his name ?" inquired Mrs. Grove.—" You may, Mrs. Grove ; but, in doing so, I rely upon your fidelity and prudence in not making it known ; he is a nobleman of rank and wealth, and this child you have must be a secret to all the world besides yourself."

" It shall, sir. I have so little in common with my neighbours, sir, that I have not even the temptation, much less the inclination, to play the gossip."

" So much the better," observed the colonel ; " I am glad to hear it. You remember the circumstances under which this child came into your hands at the first ?"

" Yes, sir, very well. I little thought, then, that I should have had such a handsome and liberal allowance made me, I am sure."

" That will not be forgotten in that which is to come," said the colonel. " You remember all about the death and burial of the mother, poor thing, as well as the disappearance of the father when the child was supposed to be left destitute ?"—" I do, sir."

" Then you can imagine the situation of the lady with regard to the Earl ——"
—" Is he an earl, sir ?" said Mrs. Gore, looking at the child ; " and is this an earl's daughter ?"

" Yes ; but there is one trifling misfortune which will not permit the earl to allow this to become known ; independent of the accident of its birth, high family connections have made a marriage necessary between himself and a lady of equal rank in society ; but, were it not so, the illegitimacy of the little girl would be a constant source of unhappiness to her ; whereas, under your care, she never need know it, and yet be as well provided for."

" Then this little girl is, as I understand you, sir, a love-child ?" said Mrs. Grove.

" Exactly, that is precisely the case ; the earl formed an early attachment to the mother ; they were both imprudent, and she quitted her father's roof ; the journey was terminated you know how—fatally to the unfortunate mother."

" Alas ! poor thing, it was," said Mrs. Grove.

" And the earl himself, at the time, was very much grieved for the death of one he certainly loved. Well, after this, certain family arrangements have compelled him to marry a lady, as I have just told you, of great beauty and of high rank."

" And this is a child of hers that you speak of ?"—" Yes, it is. The infant is very weakly, and may not live. The only hopes the doctor gives is in country nursing; it is with that object the earl wishes it to be brought down here and intrusted to your care."

" It will be a half sister to this poor little thing," said Mrs. Grove, compassionately.

" It will ; but none must know of that, you understand. You solemnly promise me you will not divulge the secret to any human being, until you have the permission of the earl."—" I do."

" Then we shall be satisfied ; you must know nothing about this, if the countess should ask any questions?"—" Of course not, sir ; but how is the child to be placed into my hands, or how am I apply for it? or, indeed, am I to do anything, or wait patiently till it comes?"

" Of course," said the colonel, " the countess must not know that any application has been made ; you must come and apply in the ordinary way, and the earl will take care you are chosen ; that will be his care."

" When shall I have to come to town, sir?" inquired Mrs. Grove.—" I will write to you, and then you must come to town, and forward your address to me, Colonel Bruce, at the Traveller's Club. I will, however, in all probability, meet you on your arrival in town, and communicate with you at once."

" You have not told me the name of the gentleman to whom I am so much indebted for his liberality."—" It is the Earl of Crumbledown who is the father of both children ; while the mother of the one you have not yet seen, is the countess, whom you will probably see."

" How soon, sir, do you imagine all this will come to pass? inquired Mrs. Grove.—" As speedily as it can be accomplished ; as soon as I go back and see the earl, and acquaint him with this arrangement, you will be sent for, and everything put in train ; and I dare say all will be as agreeably arranged as you can desire."

" I am sure everything is quite agreeable to me," replied Mrs. Grove ; " nothing could be done more than has been done "

" The earl will have the advantage of visiting both his children at once, which will be a great convenience. The two sisters must not be given to understand that they bear any relation to each other, for it will do much mischief, and no possibility of avoiding it."

" I will be entirely guided by you and his lordship," replied Mrs. Grove. " Whatever you say will be law ; for, besides my promises, my interest, also, will induce me to do so ; they will not from me ever hear anything his lordship might desire they should not."

" And, with regard to your neighbours, your own good sense will tell you how little of the confidant any of them would become."—" Indeed I would not trust them, sir, with anything I did not wish to be public to the whole village."

Some more conversation ensued between them, and, after that, the colonel left, and returned to his inn. That very night he threw himself into a carriage and posted to London, where he arrived in due time.

CHAPTER XLIV.

MRS. GROVE COMES TO TOWN AND SEES THE COUNTESS OF CRUMBLEDOWN, AND THE EARL AND COUNTESS VISIT MRS. GROVE. — THE CONSEQUENCES OF PROSPERITY.

THE Earl of Crumbledown was waiting with some impatience to see the colonel, as early as he could, for his presence in London was now necessary to the plans that he had formed. Already anticipating the success of his application to Mrs. Grove, he had drawn out an advertisement for a nurse, and had arranged in his own mind the mode of action he would pursue. These advertisements were ready for insertion the very day that Colonel Bruce should come to town.

The Earl of Crumbledown sat in the club-room thinking over some events of his life, when the colonel entered the room, but he did not perceive him until he had walked up to him, and said,—

"This meeting, my lord, is fortunate."—"Oh, Bruce, is it you? I am glad to see you; you are doubly welcome at this moment. I did not expect you so soon."

"I am but just arrived, my lord, and I thought that nothing could be better than to put you in possession of the news—the facts of the case, and let you know how I succeeded."—"You have succeeded?" said his lordship.

"Yes, she will undertake the care of the child and be conformable to your wishes throughout the transaction; and, moreover, be discreet and faithful, both from inclination and interest."

"You think she may be trusted then, Bruce?"—"I do think so," returned the colonel; "she is, for her station, a very sensible and well conducted woman."

"I believe it, and I will trust her. Have you given her to understand that there is any secrecy to be observed?"—"I have possessed her of the entire circumstances and she knows all, and is quite willing, as I before said, to act entirely according to your wishes."

"Do you think it was safe to entrust her at once with the whole truth, and was it the best?"—"Not only safe, and the best course, but, it was in some measure necessary, and certainly prudent. Had you left it for a discovery, there would have been still the obligation for security that there is now—a promise has been required and given."

"Certainly."—"And, besides, she would not have known that it was necessary or desired, so there would have been risks run from more causes than need have been incurred at all."

"Certainly, certainly; you are quite right Bruce, quite right, I am glad it is done. I will advertise this night. Where is Mrs. Grove—in town?"—"No, waiting your pleasure as to the precise instructions," replied the colonel; "I knew not what arrangement you might deem it necessary to enter into before she came up."

"None, none; I have settled about advertising for a nurse, with the countess, and will advertise immediately; but you had better write by this post to Mrs. Grove, and I will put off advertising until to-morrow—that will give her the advantage of a post at least, because I have advertised for country persons elsewhere."

"That will limit the number of persons who will apply."—"Yes," said the earl; and, moreover, I have ordered the applications not to be at my own house, but at that of a tradesman in the neighbourhood, where the applications, should there be many, will be sifted, and I can mention the fact to the countess, that she comes from him."

"That will be a recommendation for her, which ought in the countess's case, to bias her in her favour."

"I shall make use of it as an argument, if there be one wanted," said the earl; "but, I have no doubt about determining the choice in her behalf."

The affair being thus far settled, the earl and Colonel Bruce passed some time in conversation about other matters, and the evening was spent agreeably enough by the earl, who, for the moment, had no care upon his mind. The colonel wrote by that post to Mrs. Grove to come to town, and sent her money by the same letter, to enable her to perform the journey by the first coach that came through the place, telling her when she could start, and he would meet her at the coach office—he would, moreover, be there each time the coach came in lest she should come before his letter came to hand.

This done, all was put in a fair way, and nothing could be hurried on faster. Events will have their own way, and must have their appointed time, and Mrs. Grove could not reach London before the letter reached her, and the next coach could bring her.

To that time the earl was compelled to look with some degree of fidgetiness, approaching anxiety, for he desired to see the matter well settled and out of hand.

The exact feelings of the earl would be difficult to define—more than ordinarily interested as he was in the care of his love child. Perhaps, the unhappy fate of the mother might have caused some compunctious visitings of his conscience, and caused some latent desire to render a reparation to the child which came too late to save the mother.

* * * * * * * * *

The day arrived when Mrs. Grove came to town, and true to his word, Colonel Bruce was there by the time the coach came in, and then met Mrs. Grove, who instantly recognised the person of the colonel as he stood in the booking office.

"Mrs. Grove," he said, as he walked up to her after she had alighted, " you have travelled many hours without rest and refreshment."

"Oh, I have something I brought with me," said Mrs. Grove; "I have taken care of myself."

"But not enough for such a journey; come into the hotel, and I will order you breakfast, and will talk to you the while."

"Oh! sir, have breakfast in this large place," said Mrs. Grove, as she entered the hotel; "and all these fine gentlemen to wait upon me?"

"Yes; they are paid for their services, and look remarkably well here, but that is the extent of their glories. There, sit down at this table, and they will bring you some refreshments in a minute or two."

The colonel then called to one of the waiters and spoke to him, and in about ten minutes Mrs. Grove had such a breakfast as quite puzzled her, for everything was served up in silver, and of the finest description.

"Now, Mrs. Grove," said the colonel, "you see a nurse has been advertised for, and you are to apply at this person's house for the direction of the earl, which he will give you."—"And this gentleman?"

"He is a milkman, that serves the earl's household. It is to prevent any trouble at his own house, that the advertisement is addressed there, and your going there is a mere matter of form, and you will be able to say you have come from him, when you see the countess."—"Very well, sir," said Mrs. Grove.

"Here is the advertisement," said the colonel, pointing it out in a newspaper, which he gave her to read.

Mrs. Grove read the advertisment, and having done so, returned the paper to the colonel, saying,—

"I understand clearly, that I am to apply as if I had done so in consequence of having seen this advertisement only?"—"Exactly."

"Then I suppose I shall have the care of the child," said Mrs. Grove, "immediately?"—"You will; and I expect you to carry it down, after passing a night in town," replied the colonel; and then, observing she had made an end of her meal, he continued,—

"If you have finished, I will at once conduct you to this man, and then you can go to the earl's?"—"I have done, I thank you, sir," said Mrs. Grove, with some timidity; "I have made such a breakfast as I dare say may astonish you, sir, but I have travelled, you know how far, and the air has given me a good appetite."

"I am glad you feel satisfied," said the colonel; "you have done nothing at all out of the way; but, come with me at once, and then we will go to this man's house."

As he spoke, he arose, and having discharged the bill, left the hotel, to accompany Mrs. Grove to the milkman's, where the persons who apply for the responsibility, are to make inquiries. Mrs. Grove made an application in the usual style.

"Well," said the milkman, "I believe they ain't got suited yet; they are plaguy hard to please. They've had about two hundred and fifty after the berth, so, I suppose, they are tired of it; I am, I know, and there's the address."

So saying, he gave her a card of the earl's.

"I don't know if you have any particular qualification, but, if you have not, I think your journey will be useless."—"I cannot tell what may happen, till I try," replied Mrs. Grove; "but, as I have come so far, I may as well try."

"Well," said the man, "you may, as they haven't made up their minds; but I couldn't have believed that everybody wanted a nurse-child. I am sure that there are more nurses than children, in London."—"There may be so, but I will try."

" I wish you luck—good morning," said the milkman, as he emptied a can of water into the milk-pail.

Mrs. Grove took the card, and after much inquiry, she found her way to the lordly mansion of the earl, where there were all the signs of a recent indisposition. She then rang at a bell, which she saw was placed on one side, and then awaited the opening of the door, which, to her surprise, was done immediately, by a tall man in knee-breeches and stockings, who seemed to be kept there on purpose.

" Who do you want ?" inquired the man.—" Is this the Countess of Crumble-down's ?"

" Yes," drawled the hall porter.

Mrs. Grove at once gave the card she had received into the porter's hands, and on looking at which, the man put a very genteel grin on, and said, as he picked his teeth,—

" Ah ! you've come after the juvenile Crumbledown. I wish you may get it, my good woman."—" Thank you," said Mrs. Grove, with much simplicity, though she didn't like the man's manners ; " I hope I may."

The hall porter laughed, and opened his eyes, as much as to say, well,—you are precious green ; but he turned to a female, who came very deliberately up the kitchen stairs, and said,—

" Mary, there is some one come to see after the stranger. I suppose we are never to have done with the tribe of dry nurses. I declare I am quite exhausted by the exertion of constantly opening the door to them, hour after hour."—" You want the steam arm," said the female.

" I want something,—the strength and constitution of a horse," said the hall porter ; " this is dreadful. Sit down."

These last two words were uttered in a tone of command, and Mrs. Grove at once obeyed them. After a time, she was desired to go up stairs, and then had an interview with the earl, who, after some conversation with her, walked with her to the apartment of the countess, to whom he introduced her saying.—

" Here is another applicant, my lady, respecting the infant. Will you see her ?"

" Have you asked her any questions, my lord, as to who and what she is, and where she lives ?"—" I have, and they appear to me to be highly satisfactory. The place and persons appear to me to be exactly what the medical man appeared to think were most applicable to the case."

" Of course," said the countess ; " that is the main point to be considered. Well, my good woman, do you understand the rearing of children ?"—" Yes, my lady," said Mrs. Grove, modestly.

" I don't mean boors," said the amiable countess ; " I mean delicately nurtured children—children who are not as easy to rear as the pigs in a farm-yard, or such places."—" No, my lady ; I have had gentlefolk's children, and they have thriven well with me, I am happy to say."

" Have any died ?"—" None," said Mrs. Grove ; " the air is so pure and good, that we have little or no diseases which can be laid to the score of a bad neighbour-hood, for the people about our place are very healthy."

The countess put a few more questions, and then agreed to commit the charge of the infant to Mrs. Grove's keeping ; and, having settled that matter, Mrs. Grove had another interview with the earl, who settled with her respecting the charges, and then said,—

" Now, Mrs. Grove, you had better rest yourself by sleeping one night in town, and then, to-morrow morning, you can return at an early hour with the child."—" How shall I go back, my lord ? I shall have the child with me, and it is very cold travelling."

" It is ; you shall have a post-chaise."—" A post-chaise, my lord !" exclaimed Mrs. Grove. " What will the people in the village say to it ? They will think all sorts of things."

" Let them think what they will," said the earl ; " the child cannot go by com-mon coach travelling ; for if it were you could not make the necessary stoppage that you thought requisite on the road ; besides, you would be much colder."—" It is very true, and, as the child is weakly, my lord, there might be some danger in it, now I come to think upon it. However, it may be the best, my lord."

" I think it will. You had better be here early in the morning—or, stay, you had better sleep here, and then you can leave here early. My steward will see you want for nothing, and then in the morning you will be put into a post-chaise, and go direct away."—" I thank you, my lord."

" You have no lodgings in town, I suppose ?"—" None, my lord ; for I had just got to the coach-office when Colonel Bruce met me, and brought me here, or, at least, to the milk-man's."

" Exactly. You remember all the colonel said to you, and the injunctions he gave you ?"—" I do, my lord, and will faithfully abide by them."

*   *   *   *   *

That was satisfactory to the earl, and Mrs. Grove was given over to the care of some of the principal domestics, who found her in all the requisites, of which there were so many in the earl's establishment; and next morning she left the earl's mansion, and proceeded in a post-chaise, with the infant daughter of the Earl and Countess of Crumbledown, to her own humble cottage.

CHAPTER XLV.

MRS. GROVE'S RETURN.—THE ENVY OF HER NEIGHBOURS.—VISIT OF THE EARL AND COUNTESS TO MRS. GROVE'S COTTAGE.

MRS. GROVE'S journey was rapidly performed, and with an ease which she herself could scarce have credited, had she not for once experienced the mode of travelling the wealthy indulge in. However, Mrs. Grove reached her own native village, and was once more installed into the cottage, in which she enjoyed more peace and comfort than ever she had before experienced ; for, not only had she more means, but the absence of the drunken sot, Jack Grove, gave her an opportunity to enjoy, for once, ease and quietness.

It is not possible for any one suddenly to become respectable in a village without exciting remark—that is, causing some envy. By " respectable" we mean to insinuate, better means, or more of the circulating medium than they have been in the habit of having in their possession heretofore. They either become objects of caresses or hatred.

Now Mrs. Grove was like to become suffocated with many of the caresses bestowed upon herself and the child ; but as these were always treated with only cold civility, then she became an object of dislike to those whose officious friendship was slighted.

Mrs. Grove had too much discernment to permit her cottage to become a beer-shop, by those who would have no hesitation in drinking at her expense ; and this caused some anger in those who could not enjoy the benefits derived, and intended so to be, by Mrs. Grove. However, she kept her own counsel, and an even course, and she was likely to derive all the benefit that such a course was likely to produce.

*   *   *   *   *   *

The time came round when the countess said she was quite able to travel, and therefore she determined she would see how the child got on in the country, and whether it throve or not.

For some time the earl did not precisely acquiesce, but at length it was agreed between them that they should take a post-chaise, and go at once down to see the infant. The post-chaise was afterwards changed into their own travelling carriage.

The earl and countess arrived, one fine morning, before the door of Mrs. Grove's cottage, much to her surprise and amazement. The countess alighted, and at once unceremoniously entered the cottage, and introduced herself by saying,—

" Mrs. Grove, I like to take people by surprise ; I have then an opportunity of judging of people's conduct and manners. Where is my little daughter ? I have come on purpose to see her."—" Here," said Mrs. Grove, producing the infant; which, fortunately for Mrs. Grove, was in such a state that they could make no complaint of, though it was at an early hour they called.

" Ah! I see; well, she certainly does thrive, though very little, as yet; but she will grow. I am glad, now, we came down here. Don't you think the child thrives, my lord?" said the countess to the earl.—" Yes, I do," replied the earl; " she has thriven very much, I think, and, considering the little, weak, puny thing she was, Mrs. Grove deserves some commendation; she has certainly been fortunate in her care and treatment, as yet."

" She has; but—ah! you have an older child there?"—" Yes, my lady."

" Whose is it?"—" Why that, you see," said the earl, stammering a little, in some confusion—" is—is—a child—altogether another child."

" Well, I dare say it is," replied the countess; " but whose is it? Do you know, my lord?"—" Who—I—I—why, how should I?"

" Whose child is it, Mrs. Grove?" inquired the countess.—" It is the daughter of some wealthy people in London," replied Mrs. Grove. " A Mr. Smith."

" Ah! Smith—ah, well! there's a whole directory of them in London. There is not a street but what has a Smith."

The countess paused, and gazed upon the child for some minutes, as if endeavouring to form some conjecture, or to trace some resemblance; but after a vain endeavour, she dismissed the subject from her mind. After passing a couple of hours at the cottage, they left to wend their way back to town.

CHAPTER XLVI.

FIVE YEARS ELAPSE.—THE DISCOVERY.—THE POSITION OF ALL PARTIES.

Now that we have drawn this veritable narrative to the point in which it presents itself to the reader, it becomes our duty to pass over a period of time occupying really the space of no less a number of years than five, in order that we may the sooner arrive at those circumstances which resulted from what we have already recorded, which will be found as interesting as they are novel.

The proceedings of the various parties who form the *dramatis personæ* of our tale during those five years, we can very briefly, or, at all events, within the limits of this present chapter, detail.

The consequence will be, therefore, that while the reader misses nothing that is essential to the full and particular development of the story of the love child, those events which are of minor importance are only related, instead of being detailed and described at length in all their more minute ramifications and relations the one with the other.

And by pursuing this course it will be in our power, within the reasonable limits which we have allotted to ourselves, to enter more fully and at greater length into events which, for stirring interest, have scarcely a parallel, even in the strange collection of circumstances which brought the love child into an existence of so anomalous a nature.

First and foremost, then, let us take a glance at the Earl and Countess of Crumbledown. That most ill-assorted pair had gone on wrangling as usual, occasionally; while, before the public eye, they were better than they had been at first able to subdue anything like an exhibition of the very small amount of consideration they had for each other.

Absent sometimes from each other for months together, they each took the course that seemed best calculated to ensure some degree of contentment. In fact, although certainly real agreement to such an effect there was none, there seemed a sort of tacit understanding between them, that if he, Lord Crumbledown, was in London, the countess would be more comfortable in Paris. And, on the other hand, if the earl were on the Continent, the countess took that opportunity of being for a time in London.

When the earl—and that was not very often—wanted, from any reason, to know

where the countess was, he generally consulted the newspapers, for the conductors of them knew much more of the movements of his lady than he did.

And thus living together, as far as the appearance to the world of so doing went, did this most incongruous, ill-mated couple exist. Now and then, certainly, something would occur to make a serious disagreement between them, and that was generally something connected with money affairs, and on those occasions they would manage to have about as pleasant a quarrel as any persons, be their condition in life what it may, could have.

But then the world knew nothing of these little affairs, and, probably, on the evening of the same day which had witnessed one of the most serious of the occasional matrimonial differences between them, they would meet at some ball or route with all the civility in the world towards each other.

The countess did not present the earl with any more " pledges of affection " than what the reader is aware of, namely, the one child who, by a combination of circumstances, had found a home along with its half sister.

The Marchioness of Fanfaronade still lived, but not all the skill she brought to bear upon the subject, and we freely admit that it was considerable, could hide now the insidious marks of old age. She looked the veriest wrinkled hag that ever lived. Every one of the bad selfish passions that had characterised her long career, seemed to have hung out upon her countenance some token of its power over her, and no one could look upon her for five minutes without feeling that in her was seen a specimen of all that was unloveable in woman.

And her temper suffered severely as age began, despite all the power of all the cosmetics in the world, to make itself so powerfully conspicuous. She got in a rage at the fact of getting old, and in her secret heart, no doubt, she railed at that providence which had given her length of years, because, forsooth, it had not, at the same time, inverted the order of nature, and bestowed upon her perpetual youth.

She knew, too, that she had passed through life without making one friend—without attaching one heart towards her. She could not, among all the list of persons whom she knew, name one who would give even a sigh of regret for her memory.

And her own children, too, she could not expect to love her. They knew well—it was impossible that they should not know—they knew well what she was, and what a mass of intrigue her whole existence had been. And although they could not but acknowledge that the greater part of the chicanery that had characterised her conduct had been exercised on their behalf, yet, such a knowledge sapped the very foundations of affections, only to rear instead a kind of admiration of the worldly cleverness of an intriguing woman.

Perhaps—we only say perhaps—there were moments when even the Marchioness of Fanfaronade felt that it would have been wiser to have pursued a different course. If such reflections really ever passed through her mind, they must have brought with them a vast amount of agony, and no one need wish for a greater retribution than that which she suffered.

But brought up as she had been among a vicious, a narrow-minded, and, in many cases, a brutalised aristocracy, it was not likely that at the decline of life the germ of any such feelings remained within her bosom. Such must have been destroyed long, long ago ; and the misery she felt arose, no doubt, from the fact that would press daily, ay, hourly upon her attention, that she was going from the world, and already was numbered, among her own set, among the stars that had been.

Thus, like a living corpse almost, did this proud, bad, ambitious, but wretched woman, struggle on towards the end of her career—a career not marked by any one incident which could be related to her benefit, or any one act untainted by the leaven of the grossest selfishness.

The only one of the Fanfaronade family who was happy, as the world goes, was Julia. She had really loved the man who had gained her whole esteem, and quite sufficient of her approbation, to lay a good and solid basis for domestic felicity. And he who could not have retained the kindly affection of such a being as Julia, must have had a cold heart, indeed. Such was not the case as regarded her husband, for he told her, that although he loved her before she became his, he was not aware of the real value of the treasure he had won, until she had been his wife a considerable time.

The town mansion of the Earl of Crumbledown was one of the largest in the metropolis. They had long since removed from the house that the cunning marchioness had furnished for them, and during the London season, some of the most brilliant of the assemblies of rank, beauty, and fashion, that took the metropolis by storm, and were recorded at great length in the " Morning Post," were held at the Earl of Crumbledown's.

On these occasions, and on these occasions only, did the Lady Julia Fanfaronade, by which name, by-the-bye, we ought not to call her, but the Honourable Mrs. Ratford, visit the earl's mansion. The fact was, that she had no feelings or sentiments in common with the Countess of Crumbledown, who, whenever she had an opportunity of doing so, launched out into bitter raillery against the connubial felicity of Julia.

But this the latter always bore with a dignified composure. It touched her not; but still the animus with which her sister spoke was the same, and therefore she did not wilfully throw herself in the way of hearing such words frequently spoken.

And now next in importance, if indeed they ought not to have been first, we shall proceed to notice the condition of the children, who were still with Mrs. Grove. It may appear extraordinary that these two children should have remained there so long; but the fact was, that so great an improvement took place in the health of the Lady Alicia, as the only daughter of the Earl and Countess of Crumbledown was called, that Mrs. Grove was removed from her cottage home, and placed in a small villa that happened to be to let in the immediate neighbourhood.

There in that villa, which was called Holly Lodge, a small sort of establishment was kept, of which Mrs. Grove had the command. The physician who had advised the change of air and country nursing for the young Lady Alicia, when he made a visit to Mrs. Grove and saw the child, was astonished at the improvement that had taken place in its health. He candidly told the countess that he had not at all expected the child to live; but that now he as little expected anything to occur to mar its progress, as if it had from the first been the healthiest child that was ever born.

It happened that the year after the child was born, the Earl of Crumbledown received some official appointment which required his presence at the Spanish court for a period of about six months, and although he had quite in imagination luxuriated with the idea of six months at Madrid by himself, what was his agony and mortification, after he had been located there about two weeks only, to have his countess one morning announced to him.

An angry meeting took place between them, during which she told him that she had a great desire to pass some time in the capital of Spain; that she had not the least intention of interfering with him; but that, as he was resident there, it gave her the opportunity, without seeming to have come alone, to gratify the wish she had to see something of Spanish life.

What could he do? His official duty—a duty which was of the most honourable character—forced him to stay; so he had just to do what, without making any disturbance about it, he had better done at once, that is, tolerate her ladyship's presence, and make the best of it.

But he was not condemned to endure her society during the whole period of his stay, for when about half of it had elapsed, there came a letter to him from Colonel Bruce, enclosing another from Mrs. Grove, stating that an epidemic disease, that had been much about, had seized on both of the children, and that they were, at the time of her writing, hovering between life and death.

Most awkwardly it happened, that the earl had just succeeded with the Spanish court in accomplishing one of the most important objects of his mission. That is to say, he had really accomplished it, although not officially, for some delays of old Spanish etiquette stood in the way, and he dare not leave a public duty thus half done on any consideration.

He communicated the subject of Mrs. Grove's note to the countess, and urged her immediate departure for England. There must have been some affection in her heart for her child, notwithstanding all her cold-heartedness towards all the world besides, for she set off instantly, and travelled post all the way.

The earl wrote to Colonel Bruce, expressing equal solicitude for both the children, although the colonel could see, from the tenor of his note, that it was the offspring of his first love, the poor, lost Emily, to whom he clung with the largest amount of fondness, and concerning whose fate he was the most anxious.

We do not mean to say that the Earl of Crumbledown was so unjust as not to love his child by the countess, because he loved not her; but we do mean to say, and nature will in all cases prove the assertion, that love for the mother is a great ingredient in love for the child.

He associated Emily Whitford always with his dreams, and his remembrance of all that was beautiful and good. Her very death had sanctified her to his heart, and the child she had left him he clung to with a different style of affection, but still as great an one, as he had felt for the unhappy mother.

He implored Colonel Bruce to see that nothing was spared; to personally go to the villa where Mrs. Grove had the children, and see that nothing which wealth could bestow upon the children was wanted. To congregate around them the best medical advice that could be got, and, above all, to write to him by each mail, telling him what was going on.

This letter reached England just about the same time that Lady Crumbledown did, so that she and the colonel, which she thought a little strange, met at Holly Lodge. By this time, however, a favourable change had taken place, and the children, although dreadfully weakened, were declared out of danger.

By having her anxieties relieved, as regarded the sad sickness of the little Lady Alicia, to whom the countess had flown at once upon her arrival, without paying the least attention to the other child, she was better able to turn her attention to the rather remarkable fact of finding Colonel Bruce making himself so busy at Holly Lodge.

Colonel Bruce was not one whom Lady Crumbledown liked much to mention, or much to talk to. She had a sort of disagreeable feeling on her mind that he thoroughly understood her; that he knew what a cold selfishness she really had; and that, joined to a full conviction that, as the confidential friend of the earl, he knew how Crumbledown had been inveigled into the marriage, made any one's face more welcome to her eyes than his.

When she met him, therefore, at Holly Lodge, she treated him with civility, and seemed completely to accept his explanation, that the earl had requested him to call there occasionally during his absence, to look to the child. But, before she left, the countess took care to question a servant closely, and she learned that Bruce often came, and that, somehow, his principal attention was directed, not to the Lady Alicia, but to the other child which Mrs. Grove had to nurse, and about which there appeared to be so much mystery.

And this circumstance completely threw the countess off the right scent; for she, after hearing all she could, and giving to the subject some patient consideration, said,—

"Oh! it's his own child, of course, and that accounts for everything. The earl might as well have told me; it could have made no difference; but I can see now as plainly as possible that that is the secret of Colonel Bruce's visits here."

The Countess of Crumbledown, like most ladies of her class, looked upon immorality in something of the light that some people do thieving—it's all very well if you are not found out; so Colonel Bruce lost nothing with her by the supposed discovery of his lapse of morals, while it cleared up a seeming mystery that had several times given her an uncomfortable twinge.

The recovery of the children was as rapid as had been their complete prostration by the disease that had laid so violent a hold of them, so that they soon became no special care, and by the time the earl came back to England they might be said to be completely restored to health.

Time had rolled on now, until, as we now think of again opening the events of our story, the Countess of Crumbledown had serious intentions of taking the Lady Alicia home.

The Whitford family, worn out by disappointment, and able to obtain no intelligence whatever of their lost child, had sunk lower and lower still in the world. Old Mr. Whitford had died heartbroken, and surrounded by poverty, and the mother and daughter had not been heard of for some time, even by Jonathan Willoughby, who had taken up his articles as a solicitor, and become quite a famous man among thieves, as their advocate at police offices.

From time to time he had procured supplies of money from the persecuted earl, but not of late, for he really was doing too well much to care about such small sums as he could extort, and he turned all his attention to endeavour to become the solicitor and agent for the earl's large property, a situation which, in itself, would have been a very good independence for any one. This, however, was a post of trust that the Earl of Crumbledown was not at all disposed to bestow upon Jonathan Willoughby, so that we consider his hope in that quarter as very faint indeed, although he does not.

And now with respect to Jack Grove; what can we say of him, but that he had become the mere creature of Willoughby. Half idiotic from drink, he had now got so accustomed to rely entirely upon the judgment of Willoughby, and to obey his orders, that it was only on some occasions that he, in a drunken fit of consequence, would beard him to his teeth, and kick up what he called a row.

But it was only noise; Jack Grove never did anything actually contrary to the injunctions of Willoughby. His very soul seemed to be too much enthralled, and he played the part of messenger, light-porter, and odd-man at Willoughby's offices, for which he got a stipend, that just enabled him always to keep himself in what he called a comfortable state—i. e., a drunken one.

And yet with all his folly, and with all his drunkenness, he somehow continued, as Jonathan Willoughby found, to keep secret what the clerks in the anti office made repeated attempts to get from him, namely, the nature of his connection with him, Willoughby, and how, and where, and when they became first of all acquainted.

The fact is that in his sober moments Willoughby had so pointed out to him the consequences, in the shape of nothing to drink, and no hope of anything, if he once divulged what he wished kept secret, that, if possible, Jack Grove was more on his guard when he was drunk than when he was sober.

And part of Willoughby's plan of operations, as regarded the Earl of Crumbledown, was to show him that he could not only secure him, the earl, from the consequences of the intrigue, but that he could likewise protect Mrs. Grove and the child even from the visits of the drunken fellow who had caused so much trouble and inconvenience at the first.

This, in addition to what he paid for on his own account, the earl had to pay for likewise, which he did with not such a bad grace as might have been expected, for he dreaded some scene of violence, perpetrated by Jack Grove, which might awaken the countess to the real circumstances regarding the love child.

Thus then we have tolerably clearly, we hope, sketched the position of the different parties with whom we have any principal concern in this narrative, and having so done, we shall be better able to proceed to our own and the reader's satisfaction.

CHAPTER XLVII.

MARRIAGE A LA MODE.—THE DISCOVERY.—A DOMESTIC RIOT, AND ITS CONSE-
QUENCES.

EVERYBODY has seen Hogarth's picture of "Love a la Mode," and if it was a la mode then, it is as much so now, when mere natural drapery has displaced the cumbrous hoop of the ladies, and gentlemen no longer dress like the lord mayor's footman.

Fancy a stately apartment in the house of the Earl of Crumbledown, which was situated in one of the most aristocratic of the west-end squares. The room is replete with every luxury that the refinement of modern taste can heap into it.

There is nothing omitted that could tend to make it perfect, and the quantity of gorgeous litter with which it was strewn, certainly, while it gave it a little the appearance of the warehouse of a dealer in bijouterie, said much for the wealth of its occupier and owner.

Upon a couch half sat, half lay Lady Crumbledown; a book was held in her listless grasp, and, from the expression of the lady's face, it was evident that some subject of contemplation, of a very interesting nature to her, occupied her mind completely.

At one of the windows sat the Earl of Crumbledown, reading some letters. He had turned his back to the countess, for he was not very ceremonious with her, and from the absorbed attention which he gave to some of the epistles which were before him, it was evident their contents were to him of a deeply interesting character.

But they were such as we need not trouble the readers with. The fact was that a change of ministry was on the tapis, and the Earl of Crumbledown, who had made lately several most vigorous and unexpected speeches from the opposition side of the House of Lords, expected fully to be named among the new appointments, should they actually take place.

And now the countess's eyes are turned upon him, and she is evidently upon the point of speaking, little caring whether she disturbs him or not.

"Crumbledown," she said, at length, " I have been again thinking of bring Alicia home."—" I have no objection," he said, without looking up from the which he was at the moment then perusing.

"I should be somewhat surprised if you had any objection. My objecti all along been against the child remaining where she was."—" Indeed! Has she not thriven well?"

"She has; and such has been the sole reason why I so long have endured an association which I look upon with dislike."

The colour rose slowly up the cheeks of the earl as he repeated the word, "association."

"Your look of surprise is well enough put on," she added ; " but it is useless, my lord ; I know better ; I tell you I know all."—" You know all, my lady?"

"Yes. The child which that woman, Mrs. Grove, has to nurse, is no fit associate now for the daughter of a countess."—" Indeed! And pray who may have made themselves so busy, madam, as to take the trouble of instilling this idea into your mind, may I ask?"

"You may ask; but my answering is quite another question. Alice is now getting of an age to make associations, and the one which she runs a risk of making where she is I cannot endure the thought of ; disgrace is in the very idea. I shall remove Alicia immediately."—" Disgrace, madam !"

"Yes. What else than disgrace can the legitimate daughter of an earl encounter from such an associate child, though she be as the base-born brat who shares the cares of that woman with her? What else but disgrace?"— "Madam," said the Earl of Crumbledown, and now he grew pale with passion, "madam, you may, of course, as you have been careful to do all your life, trample upon the best feelings of any man, because you know you are safe from the consequences of such temerity. But there is a limit to human endurance."

"Is there, really?"—" There is, madam ; beware you do not pass it. I say, beware you do not pass it. It is not often that you follow my advice, you know ; and it is not often that I offer it to you ; but, in this instance, I do think proper to offer it, and it would be well for you to follow it."

"And do you fancy that I am to be subdued, and my form of speech dictated to me? I said that child was a base-born brat, and I say it again—ay, again and again ; since the phrase does not seem to please you, you shall have enough of it. A base-born brat."

The earl advanced two steps towards the countess, and his aspect looked actually threatening, so much so indeed, that she rose and said with vehemence,—

"Why do you hesitate? You can strike a woman if you please. Why do you hesitate, my lord? Is this your courage? I do think that you are the stronger, and, consequently, have not much to fear. Strike, then, if you choose. Coward as you are for the thought."—" You wrong me, I had no such thought."

"Oh! I crave your pardon ; I did really think that the Earl of Crumbledown, in defence of his friend's bastard, could have struck his own countess."

"What—what mean you?"—"Oh! you know well. That woman—what is her name, Grove—is nursing a child of Colonel Bruce's."

The earl, with a feeling of great relief, sank into a chair as he said,—

"A child of Colonel Bruce's," and then catching at the suggestion, he hastily added,—"Oh! so you found that out, my lady, have you? Well, you know, I was bound to keep the secret as best I might, you know. I—I am glad you know it."

"I do know it, and, although you might have no objection to such an association for your child, I have every one. I shall remove Alicia at once, and she will then forget the early companion of her infancy, and not disgrace herself by making a friendship, perchance, of that romantic character, which at times arises between young persons thrown accidentally together, and which may become the bane of their future existences, and shall remove her."

It was an immense relief to the Earl of Crumbledown, to find that the countess was on so completely wrong a scent. In another moment or so, had she continued the dialogue, without uttering the name of Colonel Bruce, there can be no doubt but that he would have betrayed himself, for he inferred from the first, by what she said, she knew all.

"What an escape," he said to himself; "what a wonderful escape!"—"You seem discomposed," said the countess. "What is it, may I ask, that so much troubles you?"

"Nothing, oh! nothing. I assure you I am quite well, only it did not before occur to me, that there might be some of the danger of association you have mentioned, and on the whole, I am inclined to agree with you, that it would be just as well to have Alicia home now."—"I am glad, my lord, that for once we agree in anything," said the countess, sarcastically. "I shall myself take, steps to remove Alicia, at all events within a few days from the present time."

"As you please. I will leave the matter entirely in your hands, madam."

"A gentleman, my lord, wishes to see you," said a servant, coming into the room, and handing a note to the earl, who opened it hastily and read,—

"My lord, cogent reasons induce me to wish to see your lordship immediately.
"I have the honour to be, my lord, your obedient
"JONATHAN WILLOUGHBY."

"Is he waiting?" said the earl.—"He is, my lord."

"Say I will come to him shortly."

Lord Crumbledown crumpled up the note which Willoughby had sent, and, heedless of the presence of the countess, he paced the room with steps that showed much agitation, for he had not had now a visit from Willoughby for a considerable period of time, and he dreaded that something had occurred calculated to disturb his peace of mind.

"Perhaps those confounded Whitfords," he thoughts, "have turned up again. Nothing can be more likely. By Heavens! I do think I shall never live to see the end of this affair! 'Tis monstrously provoking. Other men can engage in intrigue without all those fearful and tormenting consequences arising therefrom."

The countess watched him with a feeling more approaching to curiosity than any other. She felt confident that something much disturbed him, and she would have given a considerable sum, for she estimated everything by money, to know what it really could be.

The visit of any one that could awaken so much apparent anxiety in the mind of the earl, was worth consideration, and that was what she fully made up her mind to give to it.

When the earl left the room, which he did without exchanging another word with his countess, he proceeded direct to the apartment into which visitors, who were to be seen, were always shown; and then, no sooner was his back turned, than the countess rang the bell, and desired her own maid, Jenkins, to be sent to her. When that official personage made her appearance, the countess said,—

"Jenkins, you will put on some street costume, which shall not attract any attention, and follow a man who is now with the earl. I want to know where he lives, and who he is, without the trouble of asking. You perfectly understand me?"—"Yes, my lady, certainly."

"Go, then; for I have no notion myself, as to whether this interview is likely to be a short or a long one, so go at once and get ready, or you may miss him."

Thus urged, Jenkins "at once set about a piece of duty which she was eminently well calculated to perform; and as for Mr. Willoughby eluding her vigilance, for she was an intriguante of the first water, it was quite out of the question, even had he been aware he was dogged.

But of that he had not the smallest suspicion. All his attention was concentrated upon the earl, and he did not consider for a moment, that the countess gave him a passing thought.

When Crumbledown entered the room in which Willoughby was waiting for him, he found that individual occupying his favourite position—namely, with his back to the windows, so that while his own features were thrown into comparative gloom, he had a good opportunity of remarking those of any one with whom he might be conversing.

"Well, sir," said the earl, "I thought you and I had parted to meet no more, when last I gave you a sum of money, which ought to have settled all amicably between us."—"And so did I, my lord. But, if you think that I now come for money, you do me a great injustice."

"Then to what am I indebted for the honour of this visit?"—"A zealous regard for your lordship's interests."

"Indeed!"—"Yes. Any other man than myself would not be well pleased with the sneer that your lordship chooses should accompany your mode of speech. But I am far above such common considerations. The Whitford family have come to London."

"You told me yourself that Whitford was dead."—"And I told you right. But the mother is not dead, nor is the second daughter, Mary, so that there are quite enough to worry you. I don't know how it is, but they have become possessed with the idea that Emily Whitford must have been murdered; and, so strongly is it implanted within them, that they purpose making such a public disturbance as shall call full attention to the facts of the case."

"Instigated by you, no doubt."—"My lord, I will not lose my temper to please your lordship. On the contrary, I have done all that mortal man can do to delay their purpose, and have succeeded, to a certain extent, in so doing."

"For all of which a certain sum of money, of course, is required," said the earl, bitterly. "That, I presume, is the climax of the whole affair, for the getting-up of which, I, of course, give your ingenuity full credit."—"That will do," said Willoughby. "Let it go, then. What care I?"

He took up his hat as he spoke, and at once left the room. The earl stepped a few paces after him, and then he paused.

"No, no," he said, "I know my man. He has left only that I should follow him. Then he would return, of course, with double power. No, no. That may not be—let him go. How absurd. Murder—suspect that Emily Whitford is murdered. Pshaw! at this distance of time, too. A good six years ago. Oh, no, no, Jonathan Willoughby, you are a clever fellow, and can act a thing well, but that will not do. You have paid yourself amazingly well already from my fears, and I cannot permit you to do so any further—ha! ha!"

But although the earl thus affected to think lightly of Jonathan Willoughby and his powers of mischief, he was in reality very much disturbed at this visit, and blamed himself for precipitancy, as regarded it, very much. Willoughby had not actually asked for money, therefore, he, the earl, certainly had no right to suppose he was about to do so.

"I might have heard him out," he thought, "instead of sending him away in such a manner; but the fact is, I was not master of myself. Although I should have been, for the only once, when I did fairly, as now, quarrel with Jonathan

See p. 244.

Willoughby, he soon showed me what, in his anger, he could do, for it was upon that occasion that he paid the memorable visit to my father, which induced the most infernal will, that forced me into the detestable marriage that I have been writhing under for these six years past."

These were not at all comfortable reflections for the Earl of Crumbledown; but while he is indulging in them, we will follow Mr. Willoughby, and see what course of action he thought proper to take upon the occasion.

Of course the reader does not for one moment give Jonathan credit for the liberality of feeling he affected to the earl. He did not, it is true, come for money, but he thought that the circumstances which he came to relate, were such as would suffice to convince the Earl of Crumbledown that it was not too much, in the way of a recompense, to give to him, Jonathan Willoughby, a good share, if not the whole management of the leases, &c., belonging to the extensive Crumbledown property, situated in different parts of the country.

Now Willoughby was an older and a wiser man than he was, when the earl, then Lord Warelock, knocked him down in May Fair, and he had got in the habit, when he felt himself in something of a passion, of going to his chambers, and shutting himself up to think, instead of doing the first thing that his discursive imagination suggested to him.

But the state of anger that had come over him, in consequence of being heated as he had been by the earl, was quite sufficient to get a strong enough hold upon him to make him regardless of little matters, which otherwise might have attracted his attention. One of those was, that he was closely followed by a female, attired in a cloak, and with a thick, black veil over her face.

This was Jenkins, the countess's waiting-maid; and, without the least trouble, she succeeded in dogging Jonathan Willoughby to his chambers. It was only where he lived that she needed to trouble herself to inquire; for his name was known to the servants of the earl's house, so that Jenkins went back to her mistress possessed of the two facts, that the Mr. Willoughby, who visited the earl, and whose visit so much disturbed him, was a lawyer, and that he resided in Lincoln's-inn.

Further information she had no opportunity of acquiring, nor had she any orders to do so. She must leave the future proceedings wholly to the consideration of the countess, and very well satisfied was she that she had discharged her mission.

CHAPTER XLVIII.

THE TWO NOTES TO JONATHAN WILLOUGHBY.—THE CHOICE.—A DOUBLE GAME.

THE earl, however, got so much disturbed concerning what Willoughby had hinted to him, and he so deeply regretted sending that worthy individual away in the manner he had done, that, after some hours had elapsed, he sent him the following note :—

"The Earl of Crumbledown will see Mr. Willoughby to-morrow morning at twelve, when the earl prefers coming to Mr. Willoughby's chambers."

This was a most welcome epistle to Mr. Willoughby, who congratulated himself more than ever upon the manner in which he had abstained, in the first flush of his anger, from committing any rash act of revenge. But what was his surprise when the next post brought him a note, which ran as follows :—

"The Countess of Crumbledown's compliments to Mr. Willoughby, and desires to see him at eleven, to-morrow, on professional business."

"What the devil does this mean?" said Willoughby. "What does she want with me? Can she suspect me? Has any one given her a hint that I am in possession of information that may be deeply interesting to her? Surely it must be so. I must be careful, now, how I play my cards. I have a good hand, but I must take care how I use it. Surely, out of all these family affairs, among people who have tolerable means, I ought to be able to do some good for myself."

This was what all the cogitations of Jonathan Willoughby always came to. What good can I do for myself? was the grand question in his mind; and, perhaps, he is not very singular in that idea. Before he would answer either of the letters, he gave the whole affair the most attentive consideration that it was possible to do. He felt that one false step now in it, would involve him in the most serious consequences, and, probably, defeat all that he had been attempting to do.

"I must be more than cautious," he said, "or all is lost. If I act rightly, I ought to make money—and plenty of it, too, from both parties; but, if I am foolish enough to do anything hastily, all is lost."

With such impressions as these upon his mind, it may be well imagined that when Jonothan Willoughby did do anything, it would be done amazingly well, and be productive to him, at all events, of felicitous results.

After some hours of reflection, he wrote notes to the earl and countess, merely saying to the former, that he should be most happy to await his promised visit at chambers ; and to the latter, that he would do himself the honour of calling at the hour she had specified.

He congratulated himself not a little upon the fortunate circumstance that the interview with the countess was to precede that which he was about to have with the earl, because much that he would say to the latter, might depend upon what passed between him and the former.

He certainly felt some degree of hesitation about going to the house of the Earl of Crumbledown, and asking for the countess ; but when he came to reflect upon what he knew, and upon what he had heard of the character of that lady, he soon made up his mind that she had duly considered all that, and had provided against every contingency that might arise.

And he was right there, for the earl was never at home at the hour she had mentioned, inasmuch as he always, even when he breakfasted at home, a meal that he did not take invariably in his own house, managed to get out to his club a little before eleven.

Therefore, Mr. Willoughby's visit was one which could take place with the most perfect security, and he need have been under no apprehensions of meeting with the earl. But still he cudgelled his brains not a little, to find out why it was she had sent for him, for he knew of no one who could have given her even a hint that he knew of anything that was calculated to interest her, and yet upon what other subject was it likely that she wanted to speak to him?

All was in vain. Mr. Willoughby could come to no satisfactory conclusion, except one, and that was, that with a full and entire confidence in his own presence of mind, and his own downright impudence, he was ready for anything that might by possibility grow out of the circumstances in which he was at present entangled.

As may well be supposed, Willoughby was punctual, and he found that orders had been left in the hall, to show him, when he came, into a small apartment on the drawing-room floor.

He had not many minutes' leisure to look about him, when Lady Crumbledown made her appearance, and the interview which Willoughby looked forward to with so much interest and curiosity, commenced.

The Countess of Crumbledown was a woman among a thousand, or she never would or could have ventured to make the bold experiment she now did upon human nature. Confronting Willoughby with a look that he almost shrank from, she said,—

" Sir, I have sent for you, because I am inclined to believe that you are in possession of some secret of the Earl of Crumbledown's, which it would be, perhaps, as much to his interest that I really know all about, as to any one. You are a lawyer, I understand, and therefore knowing that you cannot be a friend of the earl, I am tempted to believe that your allegiance to him is contingent upon what profit may arise from it. You shall gain by letting me know what it is that the earl keeps so industriously from me, and why it is that your visits always so much and so evidently disturb him."

" What a remarkably clever woman," thought Willoughby.

" Do you understand me, sir ?"—" Perfectly, madam, as far as you have gone."

" What do you mean by as far as I have gone ?"—" You have stated that I should not lose by betraying a secret of the earl's ; but you cannot as yet be aware of the amount of my gains by keeping it."

" That is information which you can give me. You admit that there is a secret?" —" Madam, we all have our secrets."

" Nonsense ; I did not send for you to make general observations. What are the terms for putting me in full possession of the affair upon which the earl seems in so ungracious and enforced a manner to consult you ?"—" The first condition, madam, must consist of an assurance upon your part, that you will not, whatever use you may make of the information, betray the source from which you got it."

" I promise you that."—" If you do so betray me, it will be to your own prejudice, as I shall be able to convince you at once, or, at all events, before we part.

And the second condition is, that you hand me a couple of hundred pounds, in case I should be put to any expense contingent upon what may arise from my telling you."

"And, after all, your information may not be worth the money."—"Of that you cannot judge until you know it, madam; but if you will believe me, you will find it in value, and in curiosity, so far exceeding your expectations, that I am certain you will not think it dear."

"You shall have the money. Say on."—"A-hem! of course I cannot doubt your ladyship's word as regards the cash, but if you were to forget it."

The countess cast on him a look of withering scorn, and then, without another word, she went to a desk, from which she took two notes of one hundred pounds each, and handed them to him in silence. Willoughby bowed, and placed them carefully in his pocket, after which, he said,—

"Madam, I will not keep so good a paymaster in suspense, I assure you. The subject upon which the earl and I have meetings occasionally, is concerning an illegitimate child of his."

"A child?"—"Yes, madam. She is now at nurse with your own."

"With the woman Grove, at Holly-lodge?"—"Preeisely."

"So, so. Indeed—indeed! I thought—I was led to believe that that child might look to Colonel Bruce for protection. So this accounts for all the earnest recommending of this woman. This accounts for all the mystery, and all the agitation. This is news! I once suspected it some years ago, but again I gave up the idea. I do feel the greatest resentment that he should have dared to bring up a child of mine along with one whose mother must have been most abandoned. Does that mother yet live?"—"That is doubtful," said Willoughby.

"Do you not know?"—"Not for certain; I rather think she does."

Willoughby had made up his mind to insinuate that Emily still lived, because he considered that by such a course he kept a firmer hold of some fears of the countess's, which we shall see he had well matured a plan for awakening.

"She lives!" muttered the countess. "His mistress and his child! Well, well—so much for my Lord Crumbledown. Oh, I will make abundant use of this information. My lord, beware—beware!"

"Before," said Willoughby, "you do make abundant use of this information, my lady, let me beg of you to pause yet awhile. I think I can show to you good cause to induce you not to do so. Not so much as to mention it to the earl, but to let him continue to flatter himself with the idea that he is keeping his secret well."

"What reasons can you give to me for such a course, when the knowledge of this circumstance will give me a power over him that ——"—"That you may push too far, madam. What real power can it give to you, except such as he chooses to cede to you? What, if to-day you reproach him with the fact, and he looks you in the face and asks, what then?"

"There is truth in that."—"Beware of so much as hinting at it—I say beware, as you value all that you hold dear—all that you see about you that is pleasant and luxurious—all that makes you what you are."

"What mean you?"—"I mean that I am inclined to believe—you are sure that we cannot be overheard—you are quite sure of that?"

"Quite—quite. Go on."—"Then, Lady Crumbledown, I am inclined to believe —although I would not, and, indeed, cannot assert the fact—that before the Earl of Crumbledown, then, as you know, Lord Warelock, triumphed over the virtue of the mother of the child we speak of, he—married her!"

The Countess of Crumbledown turned of a death-like paleness. This was a master stroke of policy on the part of Jonathan Willoughby, and he soon saw the effect it had produced upon his auditor.

For some few moments she could not speak, so absolutely stunned was she by this most unexpected piece of intelligence—a piece of intelligence that certainly she had not, for a moment, anticipated. It took her completely by surprise, and when she did speak, it was in so different a tone to that which she had formerly used, that no one could have supposed it came from the same person.

"Hush, hush!" she said; "speak low. You—you cannot mean what you have stated. You have no proof."—"No direct proof, certainly; but from what has dropped from the earl's lips, and from the dread he has of any exposure of the affair—a dread far exceeding anything that any man could feel concerning an intrigue—I am in a situation to come to a strong opinion upon the subject."

"Gracious Heaven! this is a fearful secret indeed—a most fearful one."—"It is; and the child, you perceive, who is at nurse with your own, would, in that case, be the Lady something Crumbledown, while yours would degenerate into what you may now call that—a love child."

"Love—love—love for him! I hate him! Do not use such a word of mockery to me, sir; I never loved him; I never loved any one, never—never; and I never shall."—"I beg your pardon, madam; I was only about to remark, in the most delicate way in which I could put it, that your marriage with the earl would turn out to be a mere nullity, if it be true that he was previously secretly united to the mother of this child in question."

She rose and paced the small apartment with agitated steps. She wrung her hands, and showed how keenly even her haughty spirit was at length touched by the dreadful fact that had been thus communicated to her.

"Can this be possible?" she said. "To be deceived thus by the man of all others whom I thought I had so successfully deceived. To be made the town's talk, the jeer, the gibe, the jest of every shallow fool who can laugh at the misery of others. Oh! I will have revenge—some deep and terrific revenge! When the story is told, and the question is asked—as asked it will be—'And what did the countess do?' the answer shall be one at which no human being can afford to smile."

"Hold!" cried Willoughby. "You have an intellect, Lady Crumbledown, which should, and which, I am sure, will enable you to think over this matter more calmly. I do not wonder now, that, in the first flush of your indignation at being thus most cruelly deceived, you should speak as you do; but you must see that a better course is open to you."

"What better course?"—"To keep the secret which, unless you breathe it, will probably die with those in whose possession it now is. Keep it fast in the inmost recesses of your heart."

"Say on—say on."—"The earl, of course, is interested in keeping it close. How he has silenced the mother of the child, if she be living, I know not; but she may be dead."

"Then what have I to fear?"—"That she was living, and can be proved to have been living at the time of your marriage. That will be amply sufficient to invalidate your union."

The countess groaned.

"Nay, madam, remember that, with the one exception," continued Willoughby, "that you now know your danger, whereas before you did not, all the circumstances of this affair are just as they were. Keep but your own counsel, and what have you to fear? The same means by which the earl has hitherto succeeded in keeping his secret, will keep it still."

"And yet you have betrayed it to me."—"Certainly I have, madam, for a consideration."

"And would betray it to another, likewise, for some consideration."—"What other," said Willoughby, answering her question by putting one—"what other would pay me so well for divulging this family secret as you and the earl will for keeping it? Do you take me for one who is so foolish as to take his wares to a bad market, when a good one lies on his path before him? No, madam; you are quite safe with me."

"I would rather," said the countess, "have to deal with a man like you, than one possessed of those troublesome feelings called honesty and honour."—"Madam, you are too complimentary; and but that I never retort upon a lady, I might say that I have dealt with you thus far upon a similar conviction. You have now but to keep your own counsel, and you cannot come to injury."

"What was the name of the child's mother?"—"Emily Whitford. The daughter of a solicitor; a girl of education and manners. Her child would grace, doubtless, the high destiny from which you can exclude it."

" Enough—enough. When I want to speak to you again about this affair, I will send for you. Be secret as the grave, and make what exertions you can to discover for me if the mother be living or dead."—" I will, you may depend; and as for the expenses ——"

" I will pay everything; spare nothing."—" Madam, that is just the liberal and comprehensive order that I admire. I have now the honour of bidding you good morning."

The Countess of Crumbledown coldly inclined her head, and rang for an attendant to show Willoughby out. In another moment she was alone. And when she fairly felt that, without a spectator, she could give vent to the storm of dreadful passions that had been awakened in her bosom, she did so most frightfully. She gnashed her teeth, she clenched her hands till the effort was absolutely painful, she would have shrieked—for she felt all the inclination to do so—but that she knew such a proceeding would alarm the whole house; and at length, exhausted by her own passions, she retired to her own apartment, and locked herself in for hours.

That the Countess of Crumbledown will be enabled to pursue the quiet and pacific policy pointed out by Willoughby, we very much doubt. The information she had now received she fully believed—although the reader knows it to be false—and it seemed to have altered her whole character and disposition.

Perhaps, instead of saying that it altered her character and disposition, we should say that it had altered the mode in which that character and disposition was manifested. She could no longer command her passions as she had done; but, instead of the cold, calculating, ironical woman she had been, she seemed now to be on the verge of becoming one of the most violent.

What will be the result of the deliberation she now held with herself upon the assumption of the news she had had from Jonathan Willoughby being all true, we shall soon see; but, in the meantime, it will be recollected that Willoughby has an appointment with the Earl of Crumbledown for twelve o'clock, and that that hour, after the interview he had had with the countess, must have been very near at hand.

CHAPTER XLIX.

THE EARL FRIGHTENED.—MR. WILLOUGHBY FEATHERS HIS NEST.

WILLOUGHBY found that it was within ten minutes of twelve when he left the countess, and he had to make good speed to the nearest coach-stand, where he procured a vehicle to take him to his chambers. He had the satisfaction of reaching them about two minutes before the earl arrived on foot. He did not give his name to Jack Grove, who was in the outer office, and who little suspected that there, at last, he was face to face with the father of the child his wife had to nurse; but he merely desired that Mr. Willoughby should be informed that a gentleman wanted to speak with him.

This was a measure of precaution that such a man as Willoughby would have been the last to disapprove of, and, guessing it was the earl, he ordered that he should be admitted instantly. In another minute they were together in Jonathan Willoughby's private room, which was protected from any listening by a second door, made of a frame-work with red cloth upon it.

When they were seated, Willoughby first spoke, saying,—

" I would fain spare your lordship the trouble of saying anything with reference to the rather unpleasant little meeting we had yesterday. Pray let that lapse."—" Very well," said the earl; " I was hasty, I dare say. And now, Mr. Willoughby, what is this story about the Whitfords which you have to tell me?"

" Simply this, my lord. The mother and the daughter Mary are inclined to be troublesome. They are impressed with a notion, in consequence of repeated murders that have lately been committed, and which have taken a m hold of their minds, that Emily must have fallen a victim to some such deed.

" But what is that to me ?"—" Only this much : if they go before a magistrate they will state when Emily disappeared, so that a description of her, and the date of her leaving them, will go the round of the press, and the consequence may be—I do not say it will—that some meddling fool from the village will put this and that together, and state what there occurred on that eventful night when she breathed her last."

" But the effect of that would be to do away with the ridiculous charge of murder." —" Yes, my lord ; and to append to the whole affair an accurate description of you likewise.   Fancy, then, all the worry and the dread of an exhumation of the body, for the purposes of identification ; provided it has, for so long a time, resisted the progress of decay."

" Yes, yes," said the earl, despairingly, " I can see all that ; but how, in the name of Heaven, are these people to be quieted ?"—" It is an uncommonly difficult task. One don't know really how to deal with women when their prejudices are concerned in any affair.   It is a most troublesome piece of business, I assure you.   The fact is, the more one says to them of a character to dissuade them from making such an attempt, the more they feel inclined to persevere in it."

" What is to be done ?   Doubtless, you have thought of something.   Indeed, I was inclined to think you have something to propose to me."—" Only this, my lord.   I have found out that they are egged on by a young fellow who is looking for a situation, but he won't take anything that is not tolerably good.   Now, I was thinking, that if I gave him a good salary to be here, in my office, I might so far acquire an influence over him as to stop the affair ; for, as he is a lover of Mary's, and the old woman thinks him a second Solomon, if he advised that the matter should drop, why drop it would."

" Try it, then, at all events."—" Very good ; I cannot give him less than one hundred and fifty pounds per annum, and you may as well pay me the first year in advance—or, I tell you what, my lord—a happy thought, by which you shall not be one penny out of pocket."

" That's an uncommonly happy thought," said the earl, " and as rare as it is happy.   Pray how is it to be realised ?"—" As thus : I really have not employment for him, but you can give into my hands the management of some of your property, which will make employment for him, so that I can give him his salary myself."

" Willoughby," said the earl, " I am well aware that what you have been panting for has been to get the management of my property into your hands.   But if I were ever so much inclined to gratify you so far, upon what pretext could I take it from the respectable firm who for years have had the trust ?   I cannot do it."

Willoughby looked much annoyed, as he said,—

" The more respectable the firm, the less consequence it is to them, and the less would they think or care about such a change."—" No, no, I cannot ; and, at a word, Jonathan Willoughby, I will not sacrifice my character with persons whom I respect, by acting in such a manner towards them.   I will not do it ; and, for the future, whether we meet seldom or often, you will find it but a waste of time to renew this theme, for I will not consent to it."

" Very good," said Willoughby, but he said it with a bad grace ; for the fact is, that the idea of becoming professional adviser and steward in general to the earl, had been one of his pet projects.   " Very well ; then we will say no more upon that head, my lord."—" I wish no more said upon it."

" Very good, indeed.   You must be aware, then, that I look for profit somewhere, at all events."—" I am quite aware not only that you look for profit, but that you look for it everywhere as a thing of course.   I know well that the services of Jonathan Willoughby are not to be procured for nothing."

" My lord, I am quite certain that your wisdom must have taught you that services that are got for nothing, are generally just about of that value.   In a commercial country like this, my lord, everything fetches its price ; and if you really do want anything, you must, in one way or another, pay for it.   The only thing in relation to that which strikes me forcibly is, that you had always better pay for it in money, and at once, because then you really do know what it costs you."—" Well,

well," said the earl, "I do not want particularly any of the fruits of your peculiar philosophy. I am not in a situation to say that the danger you have mentioned to me does not exist, and I have every reason to believe that you can avert it, if you think proper."

"I will try."—"Which I take it is tantamount to a knowledge that you know you will be successful; and, as this is a commercial country, you say, pray tell me at once what is your price."

"That is coming to the point, my lord, in a business-like way. Two hundred pounds is my price."—"Moderate, upon my word."

"Yes," said Willoughby, purposely affecting not to notice the sneer with which the words were uttered; "yes, I thought you would say so."

"And have you really the conscience, Mr. Willoughby, to place such a price upon your services?"—"Who, I, my lord? Oh, dear no, I do not set the price. You will excuse me, there. It is your lordship who fancies my humble services are worth that amount of money."

"I, Jonathan Willoughby?"—"Most certainly, my lord. And you will give the only practical proof in your power that you do think so, by paying the amount. Remember, that I do not say, for one moment, that keeping the Whitfords' secret is worth anything like the money. Indeed, my honest opinion is, that it certainly is not worth it; but, if your lordship thinks it is, your lordship will pay it. On the contrary, if your lordship thinks it is not, why, of course you won't pay it."

"Willoughby," said the earl, " you know that I have no resource but to pay it. You are as well aware of that; as I am. But your demands are none the less imprudently exorbitant, for all that. If I pay to you two hundred pounds, you undertake, I presume, that what you have hinted at as a probable proceeding of the Whitfords', will not occur."—"I think I may pledge myself."

"Very well; give me pen and ink, and I will write you an order for the amount; but remember, if you once play me false, I can never again trust you in the most trivial affair."—"I cannot afford to play you false, my lord."

The earl, with an air of vexation, pulled on his gloves, and then, with a slight nod to Willoughby, he left the chamber.

"So," said Willoughby, when he had gone, "that's over, and I have not the least chance of ever making a good thing of being attorney to the Crumbledown property. Well, it's of no use making oneself miserable about what might have been; I must just make the best use I can of what is."

Jonathan Willoughby was rather a man of his word. What he said he would do and named his price for doing, we will do him the common justice to say, he made a vigorous attempt to accomplish. So, when he had arranged what business was necessary for the day in his office, he prepared to go at once to the Whitfords.

As for the earl, it was with a feeling of great vexation that he walked back again to the club which he had left, for the purpose of attending to his own appointment with Jonathan Willoughby.

The money that from time to time that deep and designing individual had extracted from him, was about the most unsatisfactorily spent of any that he had in his whole life got rid of. He would rather, ten times over, have lost such an amount at the gaming-table.

"Confound the scoundrel," he said; "first and last, he has had of me somewhere to the tune of a thousand pounds; and for what? just to hold his tongue, and not go out of his way to do me an injury."

This was certainly extremely unsatisfactory. But how was it to be helped? How was he to avoid it? for whenever Jonathan Willoughby did demand any money of him, he brought forward onerous consequences contingent upon a refusal, that the only wonder was that he had really been so moderate as he had been.

That night had been set apart for an entertainment at the Earl of Crumbledown's; for holding, as he did, a tolerable position in the political world, it was absolutely necessary that occasionally he should open his house to a number of persons, for whom he did not care one rush, but who would have found themselves most grievously disappointed, indeed, and thought it marvellously odd if they had not been invited.

But these fetes were to him most abominably tiresome, inasmuch as they compelled him to a certain extent to do the amiable to his countess, whom he hated with a cordiality that only can exist between man and wife.

As ten o'clock approached, the square was filled with carriages, and the noise and confusion of a route began to show themselves in all their horrors to any one peaceably inclined.

See p. 251.

But peaceably inclined people do not go to live in fashionable places, but are content with the security and the solid comfort of some part of the town not sacred to the *beau monde* men, at the risk of the dreadful reproach of being out of the world.

The earl was compelled to show himself at some time during the evening, and he did so at about eleven o'clock.

"Thank God," he said, as he traversed the rooms, "there is such a crowd that I can get away again without being missed."

As he was gradually making his way to the door, some one took hold of him by the arm, and the voice of his friend, Colonel Bruce, met his ear, saying,—

"Don't go, Crumbledown, for another half hour."

"Oh, are you here?"—"To be sure. Her ladyship ticketed me duly, and so here I am. Have you seen Julia?"

"Julia Fanfaronade? She is not here. I understood they were on the continent, where they intended making a protracted stay."—"True enough, but you know the old woman went with them, and I expect that circumstance has had no inconsiderable effect in inducing a speedy return."

"Like enough."—"You know she would tire out the very devil himself."

"She would—she would."—"Then you may depend, Crumbledown, that such is the reason of the sudden return of Julia and her husband. I wonder you know nothing of it. Really, for a family man, you know about as little of what is passing around and about you as any one very well can."

"The fact is, Bruce, I never inquire of Lady Crumbledown."—"And she don't volunteer, I know, any information but that which she is well aware will be strikingly unpalatable. But come; she is in the back saloon, will you not speak to her?"

"Why, you know, Bruce, that I am no favourite in that quarter, and therefore had perhaps better not go. I would rather go away. You are the only man in the world who is at all aware that the Lady Julia did really occupy a place in my heart."

"Well, there's all the more reason, then, why, you should civilly go and ask her how she is. Come on—come on."

"I hesitate."—"I see you do, but that is no reason why you should go on hesitating. Come, my good fellow, you will surely not be so rude as to leave your own house without paying some sort of compliment to her, who has, despite some circumstances that might well have kept her away, become your visitor."

"Well, well. If I must, I must."

Colonel Bruce led the reluctant earl to the adjoining saloon, where he found Julia looking, if anything, far more radiantly beautiful than he had ever known her to look. Oh, what pangs of deep regret now came across the heart of the Earl of Crumbledown, as he thought that he might have been happy with her whom he could have esteemed had he so chosen.

He forgot for the moment all those powerful golden reasons which had induced him in the first instance to accept the almost proffered hand of the Lady Annabella, and his voice trembled as he said,—

"I am much gratified by the presence of—of——"

For the life of him he could not bring himself to pronounce her new name. No. Like the "amen" of Macbeth, it seemed to positively stick in his throat. He could not say it, so he finished his sentence by a bow.

The Lady Julia showed much more self-possession than the earl. Possibly the new situation in which she found herself as the wife of another, had enabled her to strip from her heart all feeling for one whom she really could not much esteem, or else women are better actors in these affairs than men; but she certainly carried off the awkwardness of the interview far better than Lord Crumbledown could.

"Come away, now," whispered Crumbledown to Colonel Bruce; "I have two or three things to consult you about, so come away."

They bowed and left the apartment just as four or five of the guests, who were acquainted with the Lady Julia, made their appearance. The earl would not pause for a moment, until he got fairly out of the place, and then, when he breathed the fresh cool air of the streets, he drew a long inspiration of exquisite relief, and said in an odd tone,—

"I do believe, Bruce, that I am, out of all question, the most miserable dog the world ever saw."—"Do you really?"

"Yes, I may say that I am sure of it; look at me now."—"Well—I do as distinctly as I can. Wait till I have given an extra polish to my eye-glass, and I shall look at you better still."

"Pho—pho! You know what I mean. I did not mean look at me with your corporeal eyes, but with your mind's eyes, am I not surrounded by every circumstance which can tend to make a fellow thoroughly miserable?"—"No!"

" No—no ; you say no because you cannot see as I see ; but I forget you do not even know all that perplexes me."—" Perhaps I don't, but I hope you have not been so imprudent as to get up any further cause of misery. Really, Crumbledown, you alarm me with the thought that you have some other little responsibility somewhere, besides the one that Mrs. Grove takes such care of."

" Oh, no—you are quite wrong there, I can assure you ; but those Whitfords, they seem as if, to the end of all time, they were determined to torment me."

The earl then duly informed his friend of what is already known to the reader regarding the reported intention of the Whitfords to make a public disturbance, even at this long distance of time from the commission of the acts that had led to the disappearance of Emily, upon the subject.

" Oh, surely," said Colonel Bruce, " you must be misinformed ; it is too long ago now for anything of the sort to be apprehended. You allow this fellow, Jonathan Willoughby, than whom I verily believe there is not a greater rogue unhung, to obtain too strong a hold of you."

" Perhaps I have, but I cannot help it unless I murder him. Jonathan Willoughby has been my evil destiny."—" You have made him so by your own fears."

" No—no ; only consider, now, the circumstances in the regular rotation in which they have occurred, and you will see that such has been the case. By his interference with my father, I was virtually disinherited and compelled to marry this desperate woman, whom I am condemned at least to be civil to."—" My dear Crumbledown, she purchased you, and gave a very handsome price for you, so you ought really to be flattered."

" Flattered too !"—" Hush ! come—come. Remember, at all events, who and what you are. You really, to my apprehension, need have no fears of this Jonathan Willoughby. When next he attacks you for money, turn him over to me, and as for your domestic affairs, now that you are assuming a position in the political world, which, without any flattery to you, I will say, you are eminently calculated to fill with honour, you will soon be able to withdraw your mind from minor subjects."

" I wish I could."—" Who is this ? some one is crossing over the road to us."

The Earl of Crumbledown looked in the direction which Colonel Bruce indicated, and he saw the hated form of Jonathan Willoughby approaching him with haste.

" It is Willoughby," he said ; " my tormentor ! the fiend, Willoughby. He of whom I may well say ' Of all men else I have avoided thee.' "

" What does he want, I wonder ?"—" Heaven only knows, but probably more money !"

Willoughby hesitated a little about speaking when he saw Colonel Bruce, but as the earl said, rather sternly, " Well, sir, speak—what do you want with me ?" he did speak out.

" My lord," he said, " when a man does his best, he does all that any other man ought to require of him. I have striven to turn those pig-headed Whitfords away from their purpose of making a confusion, but I cannot."

" You cannot ?"—" No, my lord, for once in a way I do confess that I have failed ; but, after all, you will see, that the evils we anticipated from such conduct on their parts were not necessary and contingent ones, sure to occur but only possibilities—perhaps you may call them probabilities, and that is all. I thought it but fair and proper to come and inform your lordship of as much, that you might not be taken by surprise when you found an account of the affair in the newspapers."

" The newspapers !"—" Oh, yes ; those busy vehicles of gossip will rejoice over such a theme as will be supplied to them by the Whitfords. But do not despair ; I will still do my best to throw them off any scent which they may fancy they may have upon the subject ; and, notwithstanding all the risk you may run, you may really escape unscathed completely."

" Confusion ! and you have taken £200 of me for nothing."—" No, my lord, not for nothing."

" Then, pray, what for ?"—" To fail at anything that I attempt," said Jonathan Willoughby, sententiously counting off his words at his fingers' ends; "to fail at anything that I attempt is much more difficult, troublesome, and disagreeable, than to succeed, so that I certainly have earned— I may, indeed, say more than earned—the money which your lordship gave me."

"And you mean, notwithstanding the ill success of your fancied exertions, to keep it, I presume, then."—"No money returned, my lord," said Willoughby, with a bow.

Colonel Bruce could not forbear laughing to himself at the mock gravity with which Jonathan Willoughby pronounced these words, and he whispered to the earl,—

"Come away, come away; do not prolong an interview with this fellow, which can do you no good really. Come away at once."

The earl, as he turned from Willoughby, said, "I have my suspicions that in this affair you are playing a double game. If you are, look to it, for there is a limit to even my patience, although you may think to the contrary from what you have observed."—"I have the honour of bidding your lordship a very good night," said Willoughby, and he turned away abruptly, and walked down the street.

As he did so, he fancied that he saw some one pass into a doorway, as if to avoid being seen by him; and Jonathan's suspicions were at once aroused, that he was being watched for no good purpose. That was a thing that he was not at all likely to put up with, so he crept forward very slowly, and hid himself in another doorway. A bolder, fiercer spirited man would have made an immediate attempt to discover who it was, but Willoughby was one of those who never did anything boldly that could be done by finesse.

He had not waited many minutes when the man who had hidden himself made a sudden appearance again, and after looking anxiously about him, he walked down the street rapidly, closely followed by Willoughby, who pursued him as quickly as he could.

The chase lasted for some time, as the pursued was very swift of foot. He took his way towards Park Lane, down which he went until he reached nearly as far as Grosvenor Gate, when he suddenly paused, and turned so completely round that Willoughby was face to face with him, and almost ran up against him before he was at all aware of the fact that the pursued had paused.

It so happened that the full glare of a lamp light fell full upon the face of the man, and the moment Willoughby saw it he uttered a cry of terror, and shrank back, with every appearance of the most abject fear.

"Good God!" he said, "Is it—can it be?"—"Beware!" said the man, in a strange, deep, hollow voice, and then he slowly turned and walked away, being quickly hidden from sight in the gloom and darkness that was around.

Willoughby was glad, indeed, to clutch the railings near which he stood for support, or he would have fallen, as he muttered,—

"I thought that he was dead long ago!—I thought I had certain information that he was dead!—Why—why, what has become of him now for years past? —are there such things as ghosts?—No, no! oh, no! impossible!—and yet, can it be a real personage of this world that I have seen?—No, no, no!—I have stood upon that man's grave, and spoken to those who saw him placed within gloomy bounds."

With a shudder he turned away. He did not make the least attempt to follow the man, if man, indeed, it was, but he shrank, as it were, within himself, and, full of the most abject fear, he returned to his own home.

Jonathan Willoughby could not sleep that night. He had seen quite enough to disturb his intellects completely for a time. The sight of that man had produced an effect upon him such as, perhaps, nothing else in the world could have done.

The particular episode in the life of Jonathan Willoughby to which the existence of that person belonged, was one with which we need not now trouble the reader. Let it suffice that it was one that he might well tremble at; one that made this dismal effigy of it become most terrific in his sight, and filled him full of fears.

When the morning came, he much blamed himself that he had not followed the seeming apparition, and he busied himself in looking through some papers, one of which was a letter, that contained the following words :—

"SIR,—The person G., whose continued existence, I am well aware, has been to you a source of great discomfort, is no more. He expired last evening, and, according to custom, we shall have an early funeral, and so make an end of the affair as quickly as possible. He was a little more sane a little before his death, and spoke rationally enough; and, among other things, he mentioned your name, accompanied with some expressions that might have led any one not acquainted with you to believe that you have done him some great injury. The expenses up to now, including the funeral, will be £30; which, if you will be so good as forward, you need give yourself no further concern about G.

"I am, sir, your obedient servant,
"F. NICHOLLS,
"To Jonathan Willoughby, esq.   Ford House Asylum."

Willoughby paused for a few moments after he had read this letter, and then he said,—

"Now, one would have really thought after this, that the person spoken of was quiet enough in his grave, and was not likely to confront me in Park-lane, London. Besides, I went down, not certainly in time to see him dead, but they showed me the mound of fresh earth that covered his grave."

Jonathan Willoughby was evidently much disturbed; but he strove with all his might to shake off the disagreeable impressions that had been made upon him, for it was just one of those, that if not shaken off, will grow into something gigantic in a short time, and prevent the individual obnoxious to it, from pursuing his ordinary avocations.

The bustling events in which Willoughby was so soon to be engaged, completely enabled him, if not to shake off the memory of the affair that had awakened almost for the first time in his life superstitious fears, at least the dread with which it was connected. But he had not yet seen the last of his dead friend.

The proceedings of the Whitfords now demand our utmost attention; and the troubles of the Earl of Crumbledown, instead of being upon the decrease with the progress of time, appeared to be quite the other way. He was doomed to pass through scenes and events which he could not have dreamt of as at all possible, or if he had, he would, at his first waking moments, have rejected them, as the wildest chimera of an excited imagination.

His troubles, in fact, as regarded Emily, may be said almost now to be actually beginning in their full intensity, and where they would end, he scarcely, after a time, dared even to form the faintest conjecture.

CHAPTER L.

THE REMOVAL OF THE LADY ALICIA TO THE METROPOLIS.—THE INTERVIEW BETWEEN MRS. GROVE AND THE EARL.—THE ATTEMPT OF THE COUNTESS, AND ITS FAILURE.

THE removal of the Lady Alicia from the care of Mrs. Grove being agreed upon, and being, moreover, a thing the countess had resolved upon, she determined that what was to be done should be done at once. There was no doubt some wisdom in acting promptly; but when she was at Holly-lodge, she had thriven so well, that there seemed little wisdom in removing her; but it was deemed necessary, and, therefore, it was done.

The countess, therefore, at once, proceeded to Holly-lodge, where she saw the two children, where Mrs. Grove was now living. It was quite a surprise to see the countess at all so suddenly, much less did she anticipate losing her little charge so soon.

"Mrs. Grove," said the countess, "I have come to take your little charge, Alicia, away."

"Indeed, my lady!" said Mrs. Grove; "I am sorry to part with her, for I now feel as much attached to her as if she were my own child. I hope you are quite satisfied that I have done what I ought to do by her."

"I am quite satisfied, Mrs. Grove, and shall speak to the earl about rewarding you suitably for your treatment and care of the child."

This was gratifying to Mrs. Grove, who desired that she should stand well with the countess, because she knew it would please the earl, and because she wished that those who entrusted her with a charge, should be quite satisfied that her conduct was what it ought to be.

"When do you take the Lady Alicia away?" inquired Mrs. Grove, with something like regret.

"At once, Mrs. Grove," replied the countess; "you, surely, do not regret my doing so—do you?"

"I ought not," replied Mrs. Grove; "and yet I have so long had her, that it seems painful to part; but that, of course, is not to be thought of, my lady."

"Why, you have another little one to console you, have you not, Mrs. Grove?" said the countess.

"Yes, my lady, I have; but one may get attached to more than one, especially to children."

"Whose child is that?"

"The father lives in London, my lady," replied Mrs. Grove.

"But who is he?" inquired the countess; "do you not know anything about him?"

"I do not, my lady; he pays me regularly, and that is all that I know about him. I had the child a twelvemonth, or, at least, it was getting on for a twelvemonth old when I had the Lady Alicia."

"Indeed! I suppose he has some motive in thus acting; for my part, I cannot understand it. Have you ever seen the mother?"

"I did once," replied Mrs. Grove.

"What sort of woman was she? Handsome, or otherwise?"

"I cannot now say, my lady; but, as far as I recollect, she was a very pleasant woman."

"Young?"

"Yes, my lady, she was, I think, rather young," said Mrs. Grove, in rather a cautious manner, lest the countess should be induced to ask too many questions. Indeed, she had already asked more than Mrs. Grove at all desired should be done; however, the countess said no more upon the subject, but proceeded to speak of the Lady Alicia.

"I intend she should go to London," said the countess; "that is, I intend to take her there myself. She is now growing to an age when children begin to take notice of what is going on around them, and, of course, a time when their education should begin under competent teachers, and this cannot be done anywhere so well as in London."

"I dare say, my lady; everything can be done in London, I believe; I never saw such a place. It seems like a piece of enchantment. Before I came to London, I never could form a notion of what it is."

"No; people who live in the provinces, cannot do so; but get the Lady Alicia ready, for I do not intend staying here any longer."

Mrs. Grove immediately arose, and it was not long before the Lady Alicia was ready for travelling, and when she was so, Mrs. Grove took her into the apartment, saying,—

"My lady, I give you up my little charge. I hope she will grow healthy and strong, and that London may agree as well with her as the country."

"I hope so, too," replied the countess.

"She is now ready, my lady," added Mrs. Grove ; "and I think you will find she has benefitted by my care."

The countess having made some acknowledgments to Mrs. Grove, led the Lady Alicia to the carriage, and with her own hands she placed her on the seat, and then entering it herself, desired the driver to drive on, which was immediately complied with.

Mrs. Grove stood on the steps, and could distinctly hear the words the countess uttered to the driver, and the rattle of the wheels struck upon her ear, but she continued watching them until they were quite out of sight, and then she turned with a sigh, and entered the lodge.

"They are gone," she muttered to herself. "Well, I have one left—but no matter, all things are in the hands of destiny."

This was true enough, for destiny being in general the objects and ends of life that are accomplished here, it is rather difficult to escape destiny, seeing it is not such until it has been accomplished.

* * * * * * *

Many days had not elapsed after the removal of the Lady Alicia from Holly-lodge, when Mrs. Grove was again surprised by the arrival of the Earl of Crumble-down

"My lord," said Mrs. Grove, "I did not expect to see you so soon as this, since the removal of the Lady Alicia, whom the countess came and fetched away."

"Yes, I am aware she did so, but I have come to see how the other child is. How is my first daughter, Mrs. Grove?—let me see her."

"Very well, my lord," said Mrs. Grove, after some hesitation. She left the room to fetch the little girl to him, as she had been permitted to be in the garden attached to the lodge.

In a few moments she returned, and then taking the child up to him, said, before she let go the little girl's hand,—

"There, my lord, you see she is very well, and I hope the care I have bestowed upon her will meet with your approbation. I hope your lordship is satisfied."

"I am quite satisfied," said the earl ; "you have done your duty, and more. You have done all that could be desired."

As the earl spoke, he lifted the child up, and placed it upon his knee, and caressed it. There seemed to be a strong sympathy between the earl and the child, for he exhibited more affection over it, than he ever had done upon any former occasion.

The remembrance of the unfortunate end of its mother, no doubt, caused some feelings of sorrow as well as recollection of the past, to spring up in the mind of the earl, and the fears that a similar fate might await the womanhood of the unfortunate child.

This thought was a bitter one, and which he would sometimes endeavour to chase away by plunging into dissipation ; but it was not of long continuance that these fits of remorse remained, far from it ; but it was hardly sorrow for the past, but chiefly the future.

Regret for his conduct to the mother occupied his mind ; it was the fear of the future for the child that seemed to disturb him most.

"I would," said the earl, after a few moments thus spent, "that you were in London, nearer to me."

"My lord?"

"I wish, Mrs. Grove, that you would come to live in London, so that I may see the child oftener. I could visit it and see it, but now my absence is noticed ; and, moreover, it would never be noticed then, when I have so many places to call at, and so many odd hours I could spend—I should be glad to see you in London."

"Well, my lord, your lordship's wishes are certainly only those that I need consult upon this matter. I will come to town, if your lordship pleases."

"Do so," replied the earl ; "you must take lodgings somewhere or other that are respectable. I will see you properly supplied with money. When will you go?"

"To-morrow, if it please your lordship," replied Mrs. Grove; "the countess took the Lady Alicia away."

"Exactly; and now she is gone to London I shall be more away, and have less time on my hands; and the consequence is, I shall not be able to see her so often as I have done. I will now give you some money, and I will myself obtain you a lodging in town, where you will afford me an opportunity of seeing my daughter, whom I love."

"Certainly, my lord. I will do it immediately, my lord," said Mrs. Grove, "if it is your wish."

"It is my wish; but it can't be done immediately. I will write, or come down to you."

This was agreed, and the earl then left Holly Lodge, and at once proceeded to seek out the lodgings he desired Mrs. Grove should have, and, with the aid of Colonel Bruce, they were procured, and Mrs. Grove comfortably established in them.

* * * * * * * *

The new lodgings of Mrs. Grove became no secret, for the countess was cognisant of the fact, and took no interest in her welfare. One morning, before the earl had gone out, at breakfast, the countess found her way into the same room, and there, while the earl was tossing over some of the papers, she declared she thought she should find him as she had something to say to him.

"Mrs. Grove is in town, my lord. She has left Holly Lodge and come to London."

"You took the Lady Alicia away, and then she had no further occasion to remain there; she had no occasion to remain there, you know. She was, in fact, dismissed, since her functions have altogether ceased."

"It is not every one of Mrs. Grove's situation, my lord, that would have such forethought, especially as she did not say anything to me about it when I took my daughter away."

"Oh, very possible; but I know nothing about it. She is now in town, you say?"—"Yes."

"Well, she has acted for herself, and upon her own responsibility, and the thing is done."

"There can be no doubt about it; but, my lord, has she not been a very faithful and careful servant to us?"—"She has."

"And ought to be well rewarded for her services, which were very great; for you know the little Alicia was not expected to live, she was so very weakly."

"I know it all," replied the earl, wondering what was about to happen, or what the countess could be about, or say.

"Well, I think the good woman has hardly been sufficiently rewarded. I think we ought to provide for her, so as she would be secure from want for the remainder of her days."

"I have no objection to such a course," replied the earl. "What did you propose to do—buy her an annuity? You have funds ample to do so if you will."

"I did not mean anything of the kind," replied the countess. "You have ample means of doing so without laying out money."

"Have I so?"

"Yes; have you not estates in Ireland? You keep up some kind of establishment at Ballybogbottom, could you not place her there? Ireland is a very hospitable country. Your lordship shrugs your shoulders, but all the world are against you."

"It may be; but I will be no party to sending out any female used to this country to that. It's out of the question. I should as soon think of sending her to Egypt."

"She would be well cared for. She will have got an independence, and I'll warrant me a husband, if she will have another."

"I imagine, my lady, one is enough; at least so according to law. She has had such a one, too, that would, I think, destroy all taste for another. Besides that objection, this would present itself to her, the father of the child would not like his daughter to be sent to such a place. Can't she throw up the child, and have nothing more to do but to retire?"

"No—no; I will have nothing to do with it at all," replied the earl peremptorily. "If you want to show your respect to the woman, do so; I have no objection to it as your own affair, but I will have nothing to do with transporting her to Ireland."

"I cannot see what objection you can have."

See p. 263.

"I have stated all I have any intention of saying," said the earl, rising. "I have business to attend to and must leave."

The earl left the room, and the countess remained in the same posture for some minutes, with her eyes fixed upon the ground, as if in some deep musings, from which she could not withdraw herself for some minutes; but there seemed to be no pleasure in them; for her features appeared set and harsh, as if something were dwelling upon her mind, and had displeased her—possibly the refusal of the earl to do what she desired had caused her disappointment.

No. 33.

CHAPTER LI.

THE APPEAL OF THE WHITFORDS TO THE MAGISTRACY.—THE RAGE OF WILLOUGHBY,
AND HIS QUARREL WITH GEORGE ALICANT.—THE EARL'S ANGER AND DISAPPOINT-
MENT.

WILLOUGHBY found the Whitfords at home, that is, mother and daughter—but
not alone, for George Alicant was with them.   He would have dispensed with the
latter, as it was evident he had seen too much of the world, and had, moreover, a
keen perception of what was real and what was mere pretence, or in common
language mere humbug.

They had very decent lodgings—more than decent, we might say genteel, and
with many conveniences that they had when last in London, never even dreamed of
but now, with the altered prospects of the daughter there came a hope that they
might yet once again appear in as good a station as that in which they moved
before the lamentable downfal of their family.

It was strongly believed by them that the unfortunate Emily Whitford had been
murdered; that she was dead they were sure, because she never could have been
so looked for, and yet have remained undiscovered; and this fact threw a shade
over their joy.

Mary Whitford was now Mrs. Whitford's only hope, she looked upon her as her
last stay in life; upon her were placed all prospects of life—a home save such as
she could offer her.

And then, as for George Alicant, he was a liberal young man—a young man of a
liberal education as well as sentiment, and his love for Mary was by no means
selfish, but disinterested and enduring.   He looked upon Mary as his future wife,
and he looked upon Mrs. Whitford as his mother, and as such treated her.

It was upon his means they were enabled now to take the place in so respectable
and comfortable a style; and Willoughby, when he entered the place, had a passing
thought that they were not in the same abject state they had been in when he last
saw them before their disappearance, and that it might so happen that there was not
the same motive to remain inactive in a matter which, though long since passed, yet
it concerned them nearly.

"Ah, Mrs. Whitford," said Willoughby, "I am glad to see you, I am sure, it does
one good to see you so comfortable; why you seem younger than you used to be."

"Lor, Willoughby," said Mrs. Whitford, "What are you talking about?   I am
more comfortable than I used to be, and misfortunes have some time passed away,
and not so sharp."

"Oh! that's right—that's right, there can be no doubt that when one once throws
the causes of sorrow behind one, we are in a fair way to get over them, and add so
many years of happiness to one's life; I am glad you are so sensible."

"That may be true, but then, you see, we are not obliged to forget them."

"No, no, we can remember them, certainly," said Willoughby, "though the
seldomer the better.   And there's Mary, she is the picture of what you were when
young, and at her age, she is a very beautiful girl; I'm getting old now, and may
say so."

"Ah, she is not less good than she is beautiful," said Mrs. Whitford, "she is my
only stay now, and Mr. Alicant, he is a son in every sense of the word, and to
complete my happiness I only want poor Emily."

"Ah! poor thing, she is gone beyond recovery, no human power can recal her.
that is, save by accident, and that can only be ascertained in the course of years."

"But by searching we increase the number of chances of discovering something
of her."

"Oh dear, no, that is a very popular delusion—quite a mistake, as any man of
the world must know; it only causes confusion and perplexity by dividing the
attention, thus weakening the main object."

"I cannot exactly see the force of your argument;" said George Alicant, "it
seems to me to amount to this, the more means you exert, the less you have a
chance of success."

"You may over-reach yourself," said Willoughby.

"There is nothing more true," said Alicant, drily, "but certainly not in this case, for here is nothing required but what may be attained, without taking from others more than we are entitled to."

"There can be no over-reaching in a matter like this, you know, Willoughby," said Mrs. Whitford.

"No," said Alicant, "now, had you any desire to suppress the truth, and laboured to do so, you would run some risk of over-reaching yourself, in exerting too much cunning."

"But here are five or six years elapsed, and nothing has been heard of her."

"There must be some one who knows something of the circumstances," said George Alicant, "and it seems to me the most proper and energetic means were not adopted in the first instance."

"What means?" enquired Willoughby.

"Why, application ought to have been made at the police offices immediately, and advertisements, giving a description of her. I am convinced, that had Mr. Whitford any friend to advise him honestly, and with common sense, that such a course would have been pursued at the out-set."

"All was done that could be done—rewards were offered, and bills posted, but yet nothing came of them, and as for the magistrates, I know, as a lawyer, that, however they might have been urged, they would have done little more than take a memorandum of the occurrence."

"I doubt if they would have done so little; they would neglect their business if they did not transmit notices to their subordnate agents, and thus, there was every opportunity given, and she might have been heard of."

"And she might not, which is very possible, and more likely, for the officers are very hasty in searching out matter, the bringing to light of which procures them a reward."

"That is very true, but I still think that all means were not adopted, and thus it is there is always the uncomfortable reflection, that something has been neglected."

"That I know was not the case," said Willoughby, "for Mr. Whitford did all he could, poor man, he was not in a state to do much; I know I did everything man could do, and therefore as to any neglect being allowed it was not."

"Granting all that you will be bold enough to affirm, has it produced any results?"

"None in the way of finding my niece."

"Then as it has not been successful, your attempts may be a strong motive why it should not be received."

"I think so."

"I do not! and because you say all methods, save one, have failed; so you argue that that one, the untried one, ought not to be tried?"

"Your reasoning is too nice, sir, and you stick more to terms than to meaning, and you will not see that all the others include that one, and therefore by implication, that has been tried, or at least, so much of it as could produce any result."

"It will not do, sir, you argue against making any application, as if you wished to prevent any inquiry from being made; it surely cannot matter to you, sir, what is done towards regaining any intelligence of a lost child."

"Matter to me? do you think me uninterested in the recovery of Emily Whitford."

"I cannot say, you do not appear indifferent, but be that as it may, I strongly advise that an application be made to the metropolitan magistrates upon the subject."

"I think it unwise."

"Why?"

"Because the matter has blown over now several years, and nothing has been heard of her; it is useless now to bring the family before the public, or to publish the misfortunes of the family."

"But I am sure she has been murdered, Willoughby, I am sure of it, she never would have removed away such a time without letting us know she was alive and well, though she refused to see us, or let us know where she was."

"Ah! that is all very well in thought, but depend upon it, all these years of silence would never have passed, had she ought but shame to communicate to you; it is useless so to blink the past, but it is my opinion."

"Well, to know even that," said Alicant, "is at least to set at rest the constant harassing conjectures that are continually being formed by those who regret and mourn her absence."

"But consider the feelings of the family, sir, in bringing such charges to light, nothing can be gained by it, and I am at a loss to conceive what can be the motive for raking up matters, that have so long lain dormant."

"Because they have lain dormant so long, would be a very good notion indeed," said George Alicant, "but as for the other insinuation, about the feelings of the family, all I can say is, I think they are much more likely to feel poignantly, the fact that she may have been murdered, and her murderer may have escaped condign punishment."

"The inflicting of that punishment is very doubtful, a clear case must be made out, and I think a man who has done so much must have a hell in his own heart, a far greater punishment than any that could be inflicted."

"That may be, I will not deny it; but his internal sufferings are no warning to others, which you know is one object in making laws for the protection of life and property."

"This is an individual case, sir, and not one of such general importance that private feelings should be violated, and the misfortunes of a family needlessly made known."

"I think otherwise."

"Permit me to think, and advise too," said Willoughby, "I have a right to do so." and then turning to Mrs Whitford he continued, "you will do unnecessary violence to family feelings if you pursue this matter, let me advise you not, for on my conscience I believe it useless, had it been otherwise I would have found her out before now."

"That may be all very true Willoughby," said Mrs. Whitford, "but I can see no family feeling that can be hurt."

"You cannot!"

"No, all those who have any connection with us know it well, and others are of no consequence."

"I have many connections now, whom I should not wish should know it, it would injure me."

"This then is a selfish motive on your part."

"Not at all, it is a proper family pride."

"And mine is love for my children Willoughby; I think, now, that if more exertion had been made, a different result might have been produced."

"This is all the thanks one gets for exerting oneself. If one's exertions had been successful it would have been a very different thing, everybody would have been thanking me and asking advice, and nothing would have been done without it—and now it is quite reversed."

"People do not act under one set of given circumstances: they do under other totally different circumstances," said Alicant, "and, the difference between success and non-success is so great, that I cannot wonder at people acting differently under such very dissimilar cases."

"My advice is," said Willoughby, "do not attempt to stir the magistracy, as you will have much trouble—it will be like the old proverb, 'Much cry and little wool,' as the devil said when he sheered the pig."

"Be that as it may, I have made an appointment with the magistrates at the principal office," said Alicant, "and shall see them upon the subject this very day."

"Well," replied Willoughby, "wilful people must have their own way, I can do no more."

"It would be useless to attempt it," replied Alicant, "for, as I have told you I have an appointment with the magistrates upon the subject, when the matter will be formally laid before them."

Willoughby made no reply, but took up his hat, saying, as he left the apartment " I wish you had been advised otherwise ; however, I bid you good morning, and wish you success."

" Thank you, Willoughby," replied Mrs. Whitford, " I do hope yet to hear of my poor dear Emily, if it be only to punish those who have murdered her, for I am sure of that."

Willoughby left the place, without saying more, evidently much chagrined at his want of success in the persuading of the family to refrain from stirring in the affair.

" I cannot help wondering," said Alicant, " why Mr. Willoughby should set his face against the making of this matter known."

" It is strange !"

" And yet he is a lawyer, too, and ought to be averse to such a state of things, but make all the efforts for justice."

" Willoughby was always an odd man, and had his own ways," said Mrs. Whitford, " but I think he may be mistaken as well as other people, especially in this matter."

" I think he is ; the way we are now about to adopt ought to have been taken at the first, and then, something would in all probability have come of it : at least, it would have been a better chance then, than now : but even now it is the best that can be adopted."

* * * * * * * * *

The hour at which they were to be at the police-office now arrived, and Mrs. Whitford and George Alicant left the house, accompanied by Mary, who had expressed a desire to see the inside of one of these much-talked-of places—a police-office.

When they arrived there the magistrates were engaged, and they heard the case through, it was one of those cases which are too frequent :—A man, through distress, had taken some things that were not his own, he had stolen them to sell, and procure subsistence ; but, inasmuch, as the articles were not of themselves food, the magistrate committed the unfortunate wretch to trial, when he would, in all probability, be transported for years.

Another case was called on, in which the affair turned upon an assault, which some person had committed in a midnight freak, and had nearly killed a poor woman—so much injuring her that she would be prevented from working for some weeks, when he was fined five pounds.

The difference in the penalty was great ; the rich man could buy impunity with ease for his brutality, while the poor man got a terribly severe and long punishment for obeying the overpowering impulses of poverty and distress.

George Alicant was now informed by the officer, that he could now address the magistrates upon the subject he had called upon them to ask their advice.

He at once stepped into the witness-box, and detailed the fact, that Emily Whitford had left her home and had never been heard of since.

" Have you no suspicion as to the cause of her quitting her home ?" inquired the magistrate.

Here Mrs. Whitford replied, she had made an acquaintance with some person with whom it was at first imagined she had left her home, and then detailed the exact circumstances that occurred at that time, and that were known to her only, and informing him what steps there had been adopted.

" Well, " said the magistrate, " it would appear she must have eloped with some one, but it is certainly very strange that she should not have once communicated with you."

" Certainly, we thought it very strange, and it made us yet more unhappy to find she would not let us know how she was, especially as we were a very united family, and never did an angry word pass through our lips."

" It is very strange—what do you imagine could be the cause of her silence ? Do you think she would commit suicide."

" No sir, I don't think she would."

"Mrs. Whitford fears, sir," said George Alicant, "that seduction was the probable cause of her leaving home, and that the cause of her silence is murder, possibly by the man who seduced her, to hide the evidences of his criminality."

"Well," said the magistrate, "I cannot do anything in the matter, but as the reporters will give publicity to these proceedings, which I have no doubt they will do, something by their instrumentality may turn up to clear up the mystery. The police, will of course, be on the alert, and should anything transpire, a message will be sent you."

After that, as the newspaper reports would say, the parties bowed and retired from the office.

This was hardly correct, for as they turned from the magistrate's bar, they encountered Willoughby, who had entered the office some little time previously, and had heard the concluding remarks of the magistrates.

"I am surprised," he said, "Mrs. Whitford, that a woman like you, should then, for no useful purpose expose the weak points of your own family, and to publish your own shame."

"No, Willoughby, I never did that yet that I need be ashamed of, and, therefore, you have no right to say that."

"Your daughter's honor would be yours too, I think," said Willoughby, sharply, "at least it used to be so considered."

"It may be my misfortune, Willoughby," said Mrs. Whitford, "for I can feel their evils deeply, but I cannot say I feel the same shame as if I had been the evil doer. When we commit an unfortunate——"

"Pshaw," said Willoughby, abruptly," "still, you have done some wrong—decidedly wrong, in this affair—decidedly wrong."

"You are wrong to say so," said George Alicant, decidedly wrong, sir. I take upon myself the responsibility of the deed, if there be any. I advised it, and maintain it was proper."

"I thought Mrs. Whitford could not of herself have adopted such an unadvised course as this. It was the act of one who had but little care for the good name of the family."

"I will not yield to you, sir, in that."

"You may not, sir; but I judge of men by their acts. I am a lawyer, and know you have put people on their guard, rather than aid in the discovery of what you desire."

"It is not every one who is so cunning as you, Mr. Willoughby; and, therefore, not so clever. This is, however, an honest, straightforward course, and one likely to be productive in a result, be your opinion what it may—you are not over anxious to discover who it is that has robbed a mother of a child."

"I am not to be chastised by you, sir."

"Nor I brow-beaten by you, and I will not be questioned; if any one has a right to feel and advise upon this matter, I have ; and, moreover, I will not shrink from acting."

"Here, Mrs. Whitford, I wish you joy of your new acquisition, but you cannot expect that I shall at all submit to interfere from such a quarter as this."

"Why Willoughby," said Mrs. Whitford, "you have done no good, either in advice or otherwise, and Mr. Alicant I look upon as my son. You cannot expect we should sit down quiet with an injury that may be redressed, or the evil-doer punished. You can have no interest, surely, in keeping things quiet. Eh, Willoughby!"

"No madame, since you have chosen your own course, you had better pursue it, for I shall cease to have any further communication with you on this, or any other subject."

"You must do as you please, Willoughby," said Mrs. Whitford.

Willoughby seeing there was no prospect of changing things from what they were, and undoing what had been done and being; moreover, in a towering passion, he quitted old Whitford's with many angry words, which did not make the matter any better.

CHAPTER LII.

THE NEWS FROM THE VILLAGE.—THE JOURNEY OF THE WHITFORDS.—THE EXHUMATION OF THE BODY OF EMILY.—THE STRANGE PRESERVATION.—THE INQUEST.—THE EARL'S FEARS, AND VISIT TO THE VILLAGE.

THERE was but little to disturb the even tenor of village life, especially that in which Mrs. Grove had once resided ; and even the vagaries of drunken Ned Grove were forgotten, and his disorderliness no longer disturbed the monotony of village life that was there the usual routine.

Sometimes, indeed, a stray poacher would be tracked through the village, or some petty thief ; that, and the scandal of the place, was all that offered itself in the way of active life.

The still life was the same as it had been years since, and was likely to be the same. True it was, on some occasion, the papers brought down the intelligence that something out of the ordinary way had happened, but the excitement produced by this was very evanescent and very trifling.

However, there was something in that for them, and when they did see it, the news spread like wildfire, and the village rose, en masse, as though they had anticipated a sudden revolution, or an invasion of the French, or some calamity for which the world has no name.

It was one evening, when the villagers had done work for the night, and were assembled around the tables in the inn parlour, discussing various matters that were on the tapis, when the postman brought the landlord the newspaper.

" What news—what news ?" inquired a dozen voices.

" That I can't possibly say," replied the landlord, " by looking at the direction, for I have not yet opened it further than that yet. Do you think I can look through the paper ?"

" To be sure you can, I know I could ; why can't you ?"

" Because I can't look through a millstone, as you can ; but I'll bring it in presently, when I have seen what is in it."

" Come, come, now, that is not the thing," said a man in a straw hat ; " you ought to sit here and read it out."

" And so I would," said the landlord, " if you could be quiet ; but as you can't, why I can't help you to the news."

" Order, order," said some others.

" Come now, landlord, just look over it, and be sharp, and allow us to come at the news any way you please."

After looking over the paper from side to side, he came suddenly to a paragraph headed—

" Mysterious Occurrence."

" Hallo ! that's the thing for our money," said one ; " plough away, landlord, you'll be in the furrow directly if you go on."

The fact was, the newspapers had, with great avidity, seized upon the statement of Mrs. Whitford, and dressed it up as follows :—

" Bow Street.—Mysterious Occurrence.—One of those strange and mysterious occurrences have just come to light, that astonish mankind ; but, unlike most of them, as yet there is no solution to the mystery ; all is dark, and at present unknown.

" About five or six years ago, the daughter of a respectable attorney left her home. The circumstances were singular, and show that it must have been the lure of a seducer that took the child from the parent, for a more united family hardly ever lived.

" Miss Emily Whitford, for that was the name of the young lady, had made an acquaintance with some person—but whom could not be told, for he effectually concealed himself from the knowledge of her father and friends. She left her home, and has not been since heard of.

" She was seen by one of the family, either getting into, or in a carriage, about that time; but since then, she has not been seen or heard of by any one of the family.

"What makes it peculiarly strange, is the fact, that the daughter was, up to this circumstance, affectionate and dutiful, and the feeling of Mrs. Whitford is, that her daughter must have been made away with—murdered—for she was not one at all likely to commit suicide, and she loved her parents too tenderly to have kept them all this time without, at least, of informing them of her being alive and well, if the latter were the truth.

"Since the daughter's departure from home, the father has dropped into the grave with a broken heart.

"Mr. Whitford's object in coming forward, and giving publicity to the circumstances, is to ascertain the fate of her daughter, and to bring to condign punishment the destroyer of her innocence and life; for the same hand that polluted the one, in all probability took the other.

"Emily Whitford was a beautiful young woman, and amiable,—she was retired in her habits, and the reverse of what would have been imagined by those who have to form the habits of those who could be easily induced to quit the parental roof.

"There can be no doubt that it was not the lure and glitter of fortune that drew her away: on the contrary, it must have been deep feeling and confidence in the man who abused it so cruelly."

There was a pause of a moment or two, every one present looked in each other's faces, and the landlord looked round, and his eye encountered the landlady, who at that moment was in the room, and had heard the whole of the paragraph.

After that there was a description of Emily, and the address of the Whitfords, who would be glad to receive any letter which would give them some information of the missing Emily.

"It is her," exclaimed the landlady.

"It is who?" inquired the landlord.

"You fool," said the landlady, "don't you know, isn't it the unfortunate young woman who came down here with a post-chaise, and who died in child-bed."

"Oh!" exclaimed the landlord, "I see now, but a man isn't a fool because he can't tell what you are about to say, you must speak before people can understand what you say."

"You've no gumption."

"That may be."

"Never mind," never mind," said one of the guests, "if you go on in that civil way, you'll come to punching heads next, what's the use of arguing with a woman, she only gets out of temper the more you say."

"Yes, yes, come, come, landlord, don't say any more."

"Well, but I have said nothing already that could at all make anybody angry, I am sure of that."

"Oh, but that don't always follow, you know; however innocent what you say, yet, because you speak at all you are not safe from giving offence."

"I believe it," said the landlord, "here's a precious storm a brewing, all because I didn't know what she was going to say."

"Well, this is a pretty way to be treated," exclaimed the landlady, "but I'll serve him out for this, there's no God in heaven if I don't."

"But what were you abrut to say to this account ma'am," inquired a visitor.

"That it must be the young woman that died here, and was buried in the churchyard, and over whom the coroner's inquest sat, and returned a verdict of —— I forget what now, but something that meant nothing, I expect."

"Very likely."

"I always thought," said another, "that we should hear something of that job, it was a bad job, a very bad job, and the fellow's getting away showed that no good was meant."

"That is what I say," said the landlady, "he ought to be punished for his wickedness."

" So he ought."

" What's to be done now," inquired the landlord, " it doesn't seem as if we were any nearer than before. No one knows him. He ain't been traced. If this be th e person, we have found out the injured parties for once."

" W ell, can't we let the mother know what has happened, she may be able to find out the person who came here with her. Who knows, indeed, but she may have been murdered."

" But, who will write to Mrs. Whitford, and inform her of the occurrence, for unless we do so, there will be no chance of her finding it out of herself."

See page 273.

" I will, said the clerk, I will write to her, and inform her of what has happened, and direct her here for any further information she may require upon the subject."

" That would do very well," said the landlady, " and inform her that the child when seen was alive, in the care of Mrs. Grove, who has gone away, I don't know where."

" Oh ! that is very true !" said another ; " I had forgot all about the child—the grandmother will be glad to find it."

No. 34.

" Very likely the grandmother would be glad enough to have nothing to do with it ; the child can be no great pleasure to her, but a great deal of plague and sorrow."

" So it is likely to be to any one."

" Ah ! but," said the landlady, " the father pays for the child, and could be found out that way, no doubt ; because he is living, and can be traced by that means, if no other."

" Right again !"

Here next arose an endless hubbub and bother between one and the other, until it all became one scene of confusion worse confounded, and which was increased by every one giving his opinion in the loudest tone he was capable of.

The excitement it produced in the village was very great ; there was not a house that could be entered that was not completely haunted by a vision of the unfortunate Emily Whitford : everybody spoke of her, and everybody declared how they should like to see the bottom of that affair, and know who was the author of all the mischief.

This, considering the extent of human curiosity, was only a laudable manifestation of it, and one in which they were perfectly secure in their expression of their desire to know more about it.

The person who had undertaken the task of writing to Mrs. Whitford, to qualify himself for the arduous duty, visited the grave of the stranger—the presumed Emily Whitford, and then made minute inquiries as to what had occurred ; and this done, he retired to his own abode, and tucking up his cuffs, began the task of literary composition.

There can be no doubt that he thought that the task could only be properly performed but by himself, and that done he would deserve great praise and be considered a literary character.

* * * * * *

The Whitfords were at home in the sickening hope that something would turn up, and wondering much upon the course pursued by Willoughby, whom they considered to have acted in a most extraordinary manner.

" It seems to me," said Mrs. Whitford, " that he is angry because we have taken the matter into our own hands."

" It would seem to me," said George Alicant, " that had there been any cause to suspect him, that he might have reason to wish to slight inquiring into the matter."

" I cannot think so," said Mrs. Whitford. " Willoughby, I dare say, means well enough, but at the same time he did not do what was requisite."

" He did not, indeed," replied Alicant ; " that is not all, he endeavoured to prevent the proper means from being taken by others, which you must admit was really too bad."

" It was—but—dear me, there is the postman !"

" It may not be for us, mamma," said Mary ; " there are other people in the house besides ourselves."

" That is true enough, Mary ! so I won't flutter myself with any notion that I am going to receive any letters."

At that moment the door opened, and the servant brought the letter in and placed it before her.

" For me !" exclaimed Mrs. Whitford, " from ——"

" Yes, ma'am ; at least the postman said so. I can't read myself, and so I am not sure."

" Yes ; it is for me sure enough."

The girl left the room, and Mrs. Whitford opened the letter, and began to read, when she became agitated, and giving the letter to George Alicant, she said, in a hurried tone—

" There, read it out, George ; my eyes are too wet with tears—I can't see, and I can't hold the letter still."

The fact was Mrs. Whitford was so agitated she could not hold the letter steady, and was unable to read it.

" It is about Emily—George read it."

And Mrs. Whitford held the letter towards him. George Alicant was much surprized at the emotion of his intended mother-in-law; but he took the letter and read as follows, which explained the mystery.

"To Mrs. Whitford.

"MADAM,—A paragraph has appeared in the newspapers of these last few days, by which we are given to understand that, at some time since, you lost a dughter.

"Now, we do not say we have found out the person you want; yet to us, the inhabitants of this place, we have a strong suspicion that it may be so.

"About the date of which you speak, somewhere over five years ago, a lady and gentleman drove down here in a post-chaise; they were travelling further, but the lady being taken very ill, they stopped at the inn, and there she was attended to as well as the exigency of the case would permit. After some hour's illness, she died, but the child was saved.

"The mother was buried in the village churchyard, and the infant given into the charge of a woman of the name of Grove, once an inhabitant of this place; she has now left it, but yet she might be found if necessary.

"The child is yet alive and is believed to be doing well, and the nursing is, we believe, paid for by the father, of whom we can say nothing, he being careful not to be seen. The whole affair was over in so few days, that there was no regular order adopted throughout. He also was scarce seen, there being much excitement, and though all the expenses were defrayed by him, yet he did it not in person, a third party was employed.

"We would not have troubled you with these details, but so soon as we heard the account in the newspapers, we felt assured that there was more than suspicion in its favour.

"Should you require any further particulars you can have them by applying at the inn where she died, and can visit the grave where she lies buried.

"I have the honor to be, Madam,

"JOHN NUDGE, Parish Clerk."

There was a dead pause of some minutes before either of them spoke. The contents of the letter were so astounding, and they gazed in each other's faces without being able to gather therefrom the import of their thoughts.

"Well," at length, exclaimed George Alicant, "this I imagine is at least a discovery—there are few things can equal this. Mr. Willoughby should have been here to listen to it."

"Do you think it can be Emily they mean?"

"Yes, I do;" replied Alicant. "It seems to me to be the most likely—it bears an appearance of being her—the fate—the reason for stopping at all—the absence of any male protector or husband—all seems to bear the character that gives a greater probability to the whole affair than it would otherwise wear."

"So I feared," said Mrs. Whitford, sobbing, and in vain endeavouring to stay her tears. "So I feared; alas, poor girl: her's has been a short, but sorrowful career."

"It has indeed, mother," said Mary, "but may we not hope that there may be some mistake about it, and that it may not after all be Emily, and we may yet see her."

"Never again, my love, never again;" replied Mrs. Whitford. "She has been taken from us; I have no doubt but that it is her; I cannot have the least hesitation in saying so."

"Nor I," said Alicant; "I think it most probable; but you will go down there, I presume, and see if anything remain to be done, and if possible, to find a trace of the scoundrel who could have brought her to such a pass."

"And the little child, too—we shall find that—poor little thing, how I long to see it."

"Ah, poor thing, poor thing, that must be seen to; there is but a poor aid to help it through such a world as this—where many are ready to injure and beat down the helpless."

* * * * * * * * *

It was agreed between them that they should all go down to the village, and make a personal inspection of the place, and to make inquiries there respecting the truth of the contents of the letter, and to endeavour to trace the father of the child.

It was deemed advisable to go to the magistrate's first, before they went; and George Alicant, when he saw a pause in the grief of Mrs. Whitford, said to her :—

" We have been to the magistrates for advice and assistance ; so far we have evidently done right, for, from that we have obtained this communication. We ought to go and see the magistrate, and show him the letter that we have received, and ask his further advice,"

" If you think it necessary, do so," said Mrs. Whitford, " I do not think I shall be wanted there, and I must say, I shrink from going to the place at all."

" I will go for you," said George Alicant, " there will be nothing more to do, or say, than give him the letter, and ask his advice."

" Then do so," said Mrs. Whitford, with a deep sigh. " Alas ! poor Emily—what a sad fate has yours been—to be cut off in the early spring of your existence."

*   *   *   *   *   *   *   *

Poor Mrs. Whitford was much affected by the letter which George Alicant bore to Bow-street police office, where he found the magistrates sitting ; and, as fortune willed it, disengaged.

George stepped forward, and informed the magistrate of the object of his visit, which was at once attended to.

" In consequence," said George, " of the publicity given to the affair by the public press, we have received this letter, which contains some information, in consequence of the papers having been read in the country upon the subject."

The magistrate took the letter which was handed to him, and then read it through very carefully.

" I wish to inquire, your worship, what your worship thinks the better course to pursue in such an emergency. I am myself of opinion that we had better go over there and make inquiries upon the spot, and see what traces there are of the father."

" It will be decidedly the best course to pursue," said the magistrate ; " the easiest, the readiest, and by far the most secure and safe that can be mentioned."

" Thank your worship. I think it will be the best myself ; but I was unwilling to pursue any course until I had acquainted your worship with what had been done, and the result of the first attempt made."

Bowing to the magistrate, George Alicant left the office, not before, however, the letter had been copied by the reporters. He then pursued his way back to Mrs. Whitford, whom he informed of the whole of what passed at the magistrates, and then urged an immediate journey to the village, there to ascertain what had been done, and what yet remained to be done.

To do this, she exhibited no reluctance, and the next morning saw the whole of them, mother and daughter, and lover, on their road to the spot where so long had been confined the body of the unfortunate Emily Whitford, and to whose little community was known the unhappy fate of the unfortunate girl.

Here they arrived at the self same inn in which she was taken while upon her journey, and incapable of aiding herself—far from friends, save from him whom she had most trusted, and by whom she was most abused.

After they had entered the inn and tasted of some refreshments, George Alicant desired the landlady to come forward.

" I am here, sir," said that-worthy.

" Do you remember, about five or six years ago, a lady was taken ill, and died ?"

" Oh yes, sir, very well, the same that was mentioned in the newspaper the other day."

" How do you know that it was the same ?"

" Oh, the description was as good as if it were a picture," said the landlady, " it was the same, there could be no manner of doubt—and I am sure of it."

" From the general resemblance."

" Yes, exactly ; and moreover, I heard the gentleman call her—I think Emily."

" Ah, that is her name, sure enough, where is she buried?" inquired Mrs Whitford.

" In the village churchyard," replied the landlady, " there were many people there at the time."

" Well, well, but I must see it, where is the child? The infant that was saved, I believe—and placed to nurse with some person here abouts."

" Yes, she was ma'am, but she is gone away, and nobody knows where she has gone to."

" What, the woman ?"

" Yes," Mrs. Grove, " nobody can tell where she is gone ; first, her husband went, that was drunken Jack Grove ; and after that, she had another child to nurse ; and after that, ma'am, she went away ; and after that, ma am, we never heard on her."

" And the child——"

" Went with her of course," replied the landlady.

" And you can't tell where she went to, then," said Mrs. Whitford with some regret ; " then I am again disappointed."

" Did you expect to find the child ma'am," inquired the landlady ; " did you expect to find it here ?"

" I did."

" Ah ! it isn't here, poor little thing," said the landlady ; " and I don't know where it is now, somewhere or other I dare say."

This was very true, there was no gainsaying it, every body could affirm such a proposition as that, and there was a pause of some moments, when George Alicant said to her—

" Can you tell me who it was that wrote this letter to Mrs. Whitford."

" Oh yes, sir, that was the parish clerk."

" Can he be found, I should be glad to see him and learn some of the particulars from him."

" Yes, sir, I can send for him to come to you, sir ; he's a very pleasant man, and will come I know, especially here, sir, because you see we sell good liquors."

" Very well, send for him if you please."

The landlady now left the room to put in force her promise to send to the parish clerk who was so pleasant a man, and who had no objection to come to a place where they sold good liquors, and that place was that in which he stood.

George Alicant understood that clerk's services were to be bought at a price, and that, unless he was paid, his information was very little indeed.

Pending the arrival of the parish clerk, George Alicant endeavoured to moderate the sorrow and excitement of Mrs. Whitford, which seemed called forth afresh, as she believed herself in the house where her unfortunate daughter, Emily, had breathed her last.

At length, however, the parish clerk came, and introduced himself to Alicant as the author of the letter referred to.

" Are you in possession of any more information," inquired Alicant, " than that which you have given us in your letter ?"

" That is a collection of the whole of the circumstances that are known respecting it," replied the parish clerk.

" You had no interview with the unfortunate lady before she died—you saw her not, I suppose ?"

" No," replied Mr. John Nudge ; " no, she was much too ill to be seen by any one, save by those about her ; and I believe she said nothing to them that was of any consequence."

" Can you point out the grave ?"

" I can," replied John Nudge," she was interred very respectably, and there was a stranger on the ground."

" Would you know him again ?" inquired Alicant.

" Can't say that I should," replied the clerk, " and yet won't undertake to say that I couldn't ; mind you, it's a long time ago, between five and six years ago, nearer six years than five as I take it, time flies fast, sir, though we sometimes complain of its going slow."

" It goes slow enough when anything is to be attained, but fast enough if we have to do anything,—but was there not a coroner's inquest held upon the body ?"

" There was."

" I should like to see the coroner," said Alicant ; " he may be able to give me some information, or tell me what was done, the weight of evidence, and the impression of the jurymen."

" The same gentleman that was coroner ain't coroner now, sir, and there's only the records of the office."

" They must be appealed to then."

" But you can see the present coroner, sir ; he's a nice active man, a gentleman of some experience, sir ; never lets anything pass without a careful examination, from a cow"s tail to an elephant's tooth, it's all alike to him, he's sure to hold an inquest upon it.   Ah ! he's a rare man, he is."

" I will see him," replied Alicant ; " was there no medical man who was present when she was so ill ; surely there must have been some one to whom, in her extremity, she would confide."

" There was a medical gentleman, sir, who waited upon her ; but then he's dead, and there's no helping that ; but there is a very clever man, sir, as practices here now."

" Yes, but he can do no good."

" I don't know that, sir ; he's an extraordinary clever man, sir, and has done a few things here, I can assure you, sir."

" He may be ; but he can't inform me what took place on the occasion that I allude to ; however, I must see the coroner, perhaps he can tell me something more about the affair than any one else, seeing he has the coroner's papers and books."

" Undoubtedly."

*   *   *   *   *   *   *   *

The same afternoon, George Alicant, and Mrs. Whitford, and Mary, took a walk out and examined the tomb of the unfortunate Emily.   How many emotions of sorrow and pity for the hard fate of one so good and so young, and who suffered for what might truly be called her only offence, her only fault—dearly had she expiated the crime of loving one she believed, and of trusting him.

The grief they felt was somewhat mellowed, perhaps checked, by the fact, that there was some uncertainty as to the simple question, as to whether it was Emily's grave or not ; but, at all events, it was one, whose fate seemed to be so similar to what might have been Emily's, and what, in all human probability, was her end, that it was enough to excite a lively sympathy in their mind.

" There can be no benefit derived in remaining here," said George Alicant to Mrs. Whitford, " we had better go to the coroner, and ascertain what he has to tell us."

" If you please," said Mrs. Whitford, who implicitly acceded to any proposition that emanated from George.

When they had taken a lingering look at the tomb, they left the grave-yard and its peaceable inhabitants to their quiet repose, and walked to the residence of the county coroner, who, in this case, happened to live close at hand.

It was not long before they arrived and were admitted to the coroner, who offered them chairs, as he had some business to transact before he could speak with them, but when he was at leisure he turned to Alicant, saying :—

" I am sorry that I have detained you, but I like to be precise, and to do one thing at a time, and finish it before I begin any other, so I seldom make mistakes.   In what can I be of service to you ?"

" I have called to inquire a few particulars respecting an inquisition, held upon the body of a young lady, who arrived in a carriage with a gentleman, and died in child-bed at the inn."

" How long ago was that, sir ?"

" About five or six years ago, nearer six than five."

"That was before my time; but I remember such an occurrence, and there was little or no evidence of any consequence, the case was but very lightly got up."

"Indeed, I suppose there was no one willing to say anything about her ; and those who did know, and were willing, were not at hand."

"There was something in that, I believe," said the coroner, "but permit me to inquire if you are interested in the decease ? "

"We are, if we can identify the body, and should it turn out as we expect it will, we shall have the most direct interest in her ; and this lady, Mrs Whitford, has lost a daughter, who seems to resemble what this young person was represented to be—so strongly, that there seems to be but little doubt of her being the same."

"The question, as far as it relates to you, is one of identity ; you desire means to enable the young lady's mother to recognize the body."

"It is."

"How to do that, is the difficulty," said the coroner, thoughtfully. "Have you any reason to fear she was unfairly dealt by ? "

"I cannot think she was fairly dealt by ; some foul means were made use of to get rid of her, I am convinced. I have had it upon my mind long since, that something bad has happened to her, and my own heart tells me she has been badly treated—unfairly used—some advantage must have been taken of her state, to cause her death—it must have been to the interest of her seducer to have got rid of her."

"Certainly, there seems some probability of that," said the coroner. "Do you think you could bear to look upon the corpse, if it were exhumed ; would it not be too much for you ? "

Mrs Whitford was silent and trembled.

"Will it be far advanced in a state of decomposition ?" inquired George Alicant.

"That I can't say," replied the coroner ; "but it may not be so far gone as you may imagine, I have known bodies see twice these years and to be perfectly recognizable."

"Then," said Mrs. Whitford, "I should be glad to see the lady—much as I fear it will cause me unhappiness—yes, I am sure I would sooner feel all that, than endure the misery I at present feel not knowing what has become of her."

"There is a great deal of truth in that, my good lady," said the coroner ; "there is nothing so bad as being in doubt, especially upon such matters as this."

"Can anything be done to ascertain what was the cause of death ?" inquired Mrs. Whitford.

"She died in childbirth," said the coroner.

Mrs. Whitford shook her head, and then, after a deep sigh, she said, "You see, sir, any kind of death can be carried off under such a name, at such a time, and no one thinks of inquiring further into the matter, but there may be much more in it than meets the eye."

"Certainly," said the coroner ; "little more is thought of them, and I have often considered in my own mind how easy it would be to cause a death at such a moment, undiscovered."

"A little poison ?" suggested Mrs. Whitford.

"Yes, a little poison," said the coroner ; "how easy it would be ; but I will write an order for exhumation ; you desire to see the body, and I will have a fresh inquest."

"I think," said George Alicant, "it will be the most advisable means of disposing of the question and of finding out the cause of death, for many things may come to light, that would never be heard of under any other circumstances."

"That is very true, sir ; shall I make out the order."

"If you please."

"Well, then, if you inform me where I shall communicate with you, I will inform you when the body is disinterred."

"I will attend the ceremony myself with your permission ?" said George Alicant; "I should prefer being present."

"Oh, certainly ! I am glad of it. It will be all the better if you are there, and every thing can be deposed to."

" Certainly ! then I may consider the matter in progress while in your hands."

" You may rely upon me," said the coroner. " I flatter myself, sir, but little now escapes me. I never omit having an inquest where there is any doubt about the death."

" Very proper."

" Extremely so. You see I am considered one of the most active men in my line that has ever held the coronership of this county, and dareth undertake to say, that this occurrence would never have been passed over in the manner it has: of that I am sure. There are circumstances of great suspicion about it."

" At what hour to-morrow will the disinterment take place?" demanded George Alicant.

" I will send and let you know this evening. We must see the authorities, and then fix a time."

* * * * * * * *

It was late that evening before George Alicant received a note from the coroner, stating, that ten o'clock next day would be a convenient time for the authorities to disinter the body, and requesting his attendance, and that of Mrs. Whitford, if she chose to attend, which he thought would be necessary.

" Will you go ?" inquired George of Mrs. Whitford.

" Yes, George, I think I had better go ; however painful it may be, yet it must be done, and it may as well be done first as last; so I will go, and may God give me strength to go through the trying scene I am about to witness."

" You must recollect that I have agreed to go through this affair, Mrs. Whitford," said George Alicant; " and you must exert your strength of mind, for I cannot disguise from myself that the examination of the body may shock you much."

" It will, but I am resolved to go there. It may give me a shock and great pain ; yet I owe it as a duty to poor Emily, to bring, if possible, those who have brought her to this pass to justice. Poor girl, she is more sinned against than sinning."

" I hope," said George Alicant, " that whoever was the cause of her sad fate will yet repent the misery they have inflicted, and receive something like punishment for their misdeeds."

* * * * * * * *

The morrow came, and before the hour that was appointed for the disinterment of the body had arrived, Mrs. Whitford and her daughter Mary were prepared to quit the inn to seek the village grave-yard, there to be present at a sad and mournful scene.

There were all the appliances for the work that was to be done; and they arrived in company with George Alicant, a little before the appointed hour, and entered the church-yard. The grave had been dug out, and there was the face of the coffin to be seen through a very thin layer of soil.

It was a painful sight to both Mrs. Whitford and Mary, and George Alicant could hardly withdraw her from the scene ; and they wandered about, visiting one grave after the other, speculating upon the deceased persons, until the hour of ten chimed, and struck upon the village clock.

" We are in good time," said George.

" Yes ;" replied Mary, who was with him, " but who are these coming yonder— we are to see the coroner, are we not ?"

" We are ; this is the coroner and some persons with him ; come this way, you will probably go into the vestry until the body is raised, and then, I imagine, it will be placed in the bone-house, or some such place, where they are accustomed to deposit the dead, when any such accident happens."

To this there was no dissent ; and Mrs. Whitford, with Mary, were accommodated with a seat until their presence should be required. They, however, begged that George Alicant would be present, and witness the whole process of raising the body, from first to last.

Returning, therefore, to the grave, he determined to stand by until the coffin was on the surface.

"You see, sir," said the coroner, "I have brought a medical gentleman with me, who will make an analyzation of the contents of the stomach, and tell us whether there has been any poison administered to the deceased."

"A very proper arrangement," replied Alicant; "how long will they take in viewing the body? it must be a troublesome affair."

"It is a very troublesome affair; especially when the grave's deep and the soil heavy as this is; but half an hour at the most, will put an end to this, and we shall have the body then carried into the church, and there unscrewed."

"Have you ever had occasion to disinter bodies in this ground before?" inquired George.

"I think we have."

See page 274.

"Do you usually find them decay very fast, or do they preserve their form and features any length of time?"

"Well," said the coroner, "that is a thing I can hardly answer. I have seen some cases of very rapid decay, and some quite the reverse; but we can form no general rule; but I should imagine you would be able to recognize the deceased. Certainly, there is no telling, she may have decayed; something may be said as to the manner of death, too, that may make a difference. I should imagine, now, that there would be a more rapid decay in one dying under the circumstances which she died, than when the subject died from natural causes."

By this time the coffin was partially raised, and then with much difficulty it was raised to the surface, when there was a pause.

"Now," said the coroner, "let the body be taken into the church, and then it can be opened."

"I think," said the parson, "that it had better be taken to the bone-house, and there opened."

"And why, sir?" inquired the coroner; "surely, it is no desecration of the sacred edifice to carry the body in."

"It may not be so," replied the curate, "but it will spread such an effluvium over the whole place, that it will take weeks to get rid of it."

"That will hardly be the case," said the coroner; "but if you won't have it in, why, I can't help it; let it be taken to the bone-house, where it can be unscrewed."

This was accordingly done, and when there, the operation of unscrewing the coffin took place, and then the lid was removed; when George Alicant stepped up to view the body, and was much struck with its state of preservation. Her features were undisturbed; but there was an expression of pain and sorrow on them, that gave a melancholy sweetness to all who looked upon her.

"Do you recognize the body, sir?" inquired the coroner.

"I can even now see a likeness; but I will fetch both mother and daughter, and they will be able to do so, I think, from the preservation in which the body appears."

"Yes, I never saw one so little disturbed; it seems as if death made no difference in her appearance. Surely, the hand of decay must have been withheld for the purpose of enabling her to be recognized, and the wicked man punished for his misdeeds."

"I will fetch her," said Alicant; and as he spoke he returned to the church, where he found Mrs. Whitford and Mary, growing very impatient at the delay, and waiting his return.

"You are now wanted," he said; "the body lies in the bone-house, and is wonderfully preserved from decay."

"Thank heaven!" said Mrs. Whitford, "if it be my poor Emily; thank heaven, that her mother has not to look upon the disfigured and terrifying sight of a decayed mass of human flesh."

"Be under no apprehension about that," said George Alicant, "do not alarm yourself, you will see her as if she had been through a long illness. But come, I will aid you; if you have the power, go through this scene with what courage and fortitude you can."

"I will, I will! Mary—"

"I am here," replied Mary; and she took hold of the arm of George, with something like fear."

"Do you think you should know your sister, Mary, if you were to see her again?"

"I think I should; in fact, I am sure I should, mother; she would still be the same under any circumstances."

"She would, child, she would! But hasten, we shall keep them waiting for us. I never thought this day would have come. Do you think it is our Emily, George?"

"I am not able to tell with anything like certainty, but my opinion certainly does incline to that side. I cannot help fancying there are certain lines of likeness to you."

They were come to the bone-house, and Mrs. Whitford entered the place; those who stood round the coffin immediately made way for the unfortunate lady. She walked calmly up to the coffin; the lid was removed, and she gazed upon the countenance of the sleeper, and then fixing her lips upon those of the corpse, she kissed them.

"Emily! Emily! it is my poor unfortunate girl," she murmered in a low tone, but loud enough for every one to hear, and then she sank upon the floor insensible.

She was immediately raised up and carried back to the vestry-room, and those who were about her offered her the best aid they could give; but it was some time before she recovered from her swoon, and then only by the aid of the doctor who had attended.

As for Mary, she had stolen to the side of the coffin, and was satisfied that the features she saw were the same as those of her long lost sister, but they were different from what she had seen her, while alive. She had never wore the same sad look, and the same expression of pain and sorrow had never been a characteristic of hers; far from it, but there was yet a sufficient remembrance in her mind as to what she had been, to tell Mary what she saw there was once the living form of her sister.

Some allowance must also be made for the change that must be effected in the grave for six years, yet the preservation of the body was wonderful considering the time it had lain; however, she had not time to contemplate it before her mother's fall recalled her to herself, and she left the charnel-house with her.

After seeing her recovered, George Alicant returned to the body, and found the coroner and some persons standing there yet.

"I hope Mrs. Whitford," said the coroner, "is getting better. I saw she had plenty of attention, and therefore did not come to offer any aid, as I believe in those cases too much aid is as bad as none."

"That is very true," said George Alicant, "she is quite recovered from her insensibility, but she is very much shattered."

"Oh, that is to be expected; but there can be no doubt now as to the identity of the body. That, sir, is one point gained. It is, sir, what a great statesman might call, a great fact; and the next thing we can do will be to hold the inquest."

"Aye, but ought you not to have a post mortem examination made, and a chemical analysis made of the stomach, or of its contents, and then you know you will have all things in readiness, and every precaution will have been taken to render the whole affair capable of attaining its object—which is a great thing, you know."

"It will be as well," replied the coroner, "therefore do you do it, doctor, and let it be done to-morrow; for we should have the inquest held by twelve o'clock, and we shall want all the evidence you can bring."

"Then, sir," said the doctor, turning to George Alicant, "you are willing this analysis should be made?"

"If it be necessary for the purpose of detecting the cause of her death, I think, I may say, Mrs. Whitford will not object to its being done. But do not allow the body to be injured more than is absolutely necessary, as it may excite the feelings more than they are."

"I will take care, sir, that nothing but what is necessary shall be done."

"Thank you," said George, "and now, as I have done all that need be done until the inquest, I will bid you good day."

There were immediately many salutations exchanged, and George Alicant returned to Mrs. Whitford and Mary, who were anxious to leave the church and return to the inn, the truth about the unfortunate Emily now being so palpable, and there was now not a shadow of a hope that she might live. No, she was dead, and there was nothing to expect, and nothing to look for.

Yes, there was one thing that could be sought, and, by perseverance, it might be attained, and that was justice. It was in a fair way of being meted out to her. The mother and sister were now at the grave of that unfortunate girl, and they would now make the whole affair complete, and place it before the world. But as yet they could not, however, fix upon the guilty party; he was not known, nor could he be traced, by them at least.

He, however, was not without his apprehensions; his fears were excited—but more of that anon.

The inquest was to be held at twelve o'clock the next day, and at that hour the respectable and enlightened jurymen were drawing together in a crowd round the inn door; and some of them stepped into the inn itself, with the intention of moistening that clay which was so soon to be employed on public affairs.

It is astonishing what great men people are when they are thus employed; they feel, no doubt, as consequential as a parish beadle, who feels proud and honoured by the delegated trust of her majesty.

Jurymen, too, are in the habit of hearing themselves styled respectable and intelligent; the consequence is, they are by far too cunning for ordinary men, and haven't brains enough to be above them.

There was much bustle and excitement when two strangers drove down to the door, and stopped; one of them got out and looked very carefully at the horse's feet, and then he said to the other,—

"Yes, yes, she must have rest; that shoe must be taken off before we go further." Then turning to the ostler, he said,—

"Have you good quarters here for a horse?"

"Yes, your honour, none better. I'll put her in a stable, and then I'll look to her feet, your honour; perhaps she's hurt herself with a stone only, and wants a day's rest."

"I dare say that is all; but she went lame, and that must have been caused by something."

"Sure enough, there's truth in that," said the ostler; "shall I take her into the stables?"

"Yes, yes, take her up; I can't ride behind a lame horse. What a mob of people; let's go in, and see if we can obtain accommodation of some kind or other."

* * * * * * * * *

The letter that Mrs. Whitford received from John Nudge, the parish clerk, in due time reached the Earl of Crumbledown's hands, not by the post, but by means of the newspapers.

It was the morning after the communication of the letter of John Nudge to the magistrates, that the earl sat down to breakfast. The 'Post' was placed in his hands, when he came to the paragraph headed,—

"Mysterious Affair.—The occurrence detailed in our paper a day or two since, respecting the sudden disappearance of an attorney's daughter, has been productive of the following reply, and thus exhibits another point, which is so far satisfactory, that the parties intend proceeding down to the spot at once."

Here came a copy of the letter of John Nudge, which was the letter that the Earl of Crumbledown read through, with great signs of discomposure; and when he had done so, immediately arose and dressed himself for the streets, which done, he made the best of his way to the Traveller's Club, where he met Colonel Bruce.

"Colonel," said the earl, "I came on purpose to see you; I have just seen the Morning Post."

"And so have I," said Bruce.

"Then you know, exactly, what I have come about," said the earl, setting down in a chair, beside him. "I have seen this infernal letter from some fellow, called Fudge, and I wish it was all fudge; but I can't help thinking there will be mischief come of it now."

"Fudge, is that the man, my lord?"

"Ah! well, Nudge or Fudge, it is all the same to me. I am afraid now, that something or other will turn up, to make this matter notorious; and, probably, I shall be marked out as the object of all the vituperation it can incur from the press."

"Very possible, my lord, but there seems to me, to be one slight bar to that, and not easily to be over-stepped."

"And what is that, Bruce?"

"This—whatever they may do about the girl, they cannot find anything amiss with the means taken to preserve her under the circumstances ; and, moreover, you are entirely unknown to these people, you cannot be traced; personally unknown, and your very name, a secret."

"Yes, yes."

"And, moreover, you had no go between ; you are free of all persons, whatsoever—so you see, my dear earl, your fears are groundless. I am sure, you may make yourself at ease, on that point."

"Well, well, I hope so, but there may be something or other which I may know nothing of, some of the thousand, and one accidents that so happen upon these occasions to mar the best managed schemes in creation. It is always so."

"You are needlessly, apprehensive, my lord, but what course do you intend to pursue."

"That is what I have come here to consult you about, what to do, I don't know. You see, I know nothing now, I can't learn anything, until I have seen it in the papers, and it would be too late to attempt to avert the storm, when the papers gave me the first intelligence of its having broke over my head."

"Whence do you expect it?"

"I suppose, if it come at all, it will come from the village, of course. There will be the most infernal hubbub. The mother and daughter are gone with some friends down with them."

"Then go, too, my lord," said Colonel Bruce.

"Well, it would be no bad plan, and yet, what could I do—that would be a very good plan—but, we may betray ourselves, and then it would be making bad worse ; and, moreover, we may be remembered by some one of those old fools about the place, who have nothing else to do."

"There are not many who will do that, my lord, but still I should advise you to go, for two reasons ; the first is, you will be tranquilized; and the second is, you will know what is going on, and you will not imagine the danger to be greater than it is."

"Well, well, I begin to agree with you ; I had better set off, and that to-night, and then we can know the worst."

The earl and the colonel did set off the same night, and arrived by post at a small market town, in the vicinity of the village, and then taking a gig, they drove over to the village, where they arrived a little before the inquest begun.

The two strangers came up to the inn, and examined the horses feet, and declared they could go no further.

The landlady being in the way, the colonel inquired of her if she could afford them any accommodation, beyond the setting-room or parlour?

"You shall have the best my place affords, sir. But my house has several visitors above stairs, two ladies and a gentleman. Then, there's the large room upstairs ; they are going to hold the inquest in that very room, but you can set there if you don't mind it."

"Oh, yes," said Colonel Bruce, "that will do very well; "it will be something to think about, and pass the time away, until the room is empty, or something else turns up to attract our attention."

"Oh, sir, it's a very sad affair before you.; but there, we all don't feel alike," said the landlady.

"Certainly not; but, at the same time, we as yet know nothing of the whole affair, and cannot be expected to feel much sorrow for what we don't know."

"Oh, no, in course not."

"Is the room above ? because we will go at once, and take possession of our seats, as we may get none, if the room is to be filled to an overflowing."

"Oh, no, sir, only the jury, and a few more."

"Which few more," said Bruce aside to the earl, "will, I dare say, comprise half the village—a mass of nothings—who will sit down in chairs, and complacently hear themselves called 'intelligent and intellectual beings !' Faugh !"

"You may well say so, Bruce; for a greater mass of human stupidity were never collected together, than what I have just now set my eyes upon."

He entered the room, and sat down on some wooden chairs, which seemed all the fashion here, since there appeared no others about; and these were scooped out to fit the person. The room was a long, low room, with several windows facing the street, or main road, as it really was. Branches were arranged, or rather fixed in, or built in the wall, while on the outside of the tables were placed the chairs before-mentioned.

"Well, Bruce," said the earl, "what do you think of this place? It is not quite in the style of the Traveller's Club, is it?"

"Not quite; but it is very good, of its sort—quite for the purpose to which it is appropriated."

"No doubt; but here comes the coaches. Well, we have got our wine here and are safe—they can't very well dispossess us, as we must be entitled to a share of the room."

"We must endeavour to keep it; but I dare say they will not be over particular about it."

At that moment the "gentlemen of the jury" came tumbling up the stairs, which groaned and creaked beneath the tread of their feet, as one after another they reached the top of the landing; and, after hesitating a moment at the appearance of the two strangers, they summoned resolution and entered the room.

It required but a few minutes to fill the room from one end to the other, and when the coroner took his seat, he glanced at the earl and his companion. Upon which he said to the coroner,—

"We are strangers passing here, when an accident happened to our horses, and we were obliged to stop. Am I intruding here?"

"No, sir, no," said the coroner; "this is an open court—I like to see publicity given to the proceedings that have once taken place here, though, now and then, it may be necessary to exclude strangers; but then, it's only for the purpose of furthering the ends of justice, and not under any other pretext whatever; gentlemen, you are quite welcome to stay."

The colonel and the earl bowed their acknowledgments; and then, notwithstanding all the eloquence of the coroner respecting the publicity of the court, he ordered out about a score of useless people.

"I am obliged to keep the court to a certain degree clear, for we could not perform our duty unless we heard, and had the room to breathe in, which we should. Now, then, officer, keep the door locked. Perhaps, Mrs. and Miss Whitford and their friend, would like to be present. Let some one or other inform them of the fact that we are sitting."

This was a very great fact, and an uninteresting scene; and while the messenger was gone, the coroner began to tell the jurymen the causes of their meeting there.

In doing this, he gave them to understand that an inquest was holden, some five or six years before, upon the same body; but that, according to his notion of things, there had been no proper diligence used in the conducting of that inquest.

Be that as it might, the body was then unknown; but now evidence would be adduced to show who the deceased was, as well as some other facts, which made the case a peculiarly suspicious circumstance—this would not be lost upon an intelligent jury, like that he saw around him on that occasion.

The earl, and Colonel Bruce, exchanged glances, the former seemed very uneasy and the latter looked serious, but whispered in his ear, and they both listened to what was going on.

"I have ordered a chemical examination of the contents of the stomach, as there seemed reason to believe, that there might have been unfair play used towards the deceased."

The jury were called over and sworn, and the coroner took his seat and proceeded to make some memorandums in a book which he kept for that purpose. The door then opened, and George Alicant, leading in Mrs. and Miss Whitford, entered the room and were handed to a seat, not very far from that on which Colonel Bruce, and the earl, were seated; the latter looked at them very hard, and his heart beat quick as he looked upon Mary Whitford, and could trace a strong resemblance between her and the unfortunate and deceived Emily. He could not but feel that she had been cut off in the pride of her youth and beauty—in the spring-tide of life—at a moment too, when there could have been no doubt, she would have entered life, and had all the prospects of a long and virtuous one—a time of joy and happiness—a time, that to her was lost, and of which she had been robbed under the false colours of love and affection. No man could be so utterly senseless as not to feel this; and the earl, when he gazed upon the mother, of whom he had robbed a child—on a sister, whom he had deprived of a sister—could not but feel repugnance and sorrow at the part he had acted.

Mrs. Whitford knew not her vicinity to the man, who had caused all the evils she was now suffering, and who was, in fact, the murderer of her own child—the cause of the death of her husband—the cause of all her misfortune—for, the first grand cause of all the subsequent incidents was, the elopement of Emily. Had she known this, it is hardly possible that she would have set there coolly—she would have become insensible—or she would have flown at him like an infuriated mother for the protection of her child; but, fortunately for all parties, nothing of this kind was known; we say, fortunately, for the bereaved mother could have gained nothing by the knowledge though she suffered more.

There was now some motion among the jurymen and Mrs. Whitford was desired by the coroner, to inform the jurymen who and what she was; and also, all she knew concerning her daughter.

Mrs. Whitford then stated, how, about six years ago, her daughter left her home, suddenly, without the knowledge and consent of her parents, and that she had been sought after ever since but never heard of, since she had been seen once by a neighbour—and that was on the day she had left home—enter a carriage with another person. Mr. Whitford had since died, and the first thing she had heard of about the unfortunate child, was a letter she received from this village, describing what had taken place; upon that she came down, the body was exhumed, and was that of her unfortunate child, who had, according to the verdict of a former inquest, died in child-bed.

" Do you think, there was any motive for putting your daughter out of the way, by her seducer?"

" I have no doubt, sir, but that the person who effected her ruin, at last wished her dead, and the wish may be father to the deed; and, at such a moment, death is easily effected."

" You think, had she not been dead, she would have written to let you know where she was, or how she was?"

" I am sure of it; or, if she had been at such an extremity of danger—had she any knowledge of it—she would have written to me some account of it."

" Then you infer, her death was so sudden, or unfair, as not to permit of either."

" I do, sir; she would have insisted upon some one writing to me to let me know. This was not done, and there must have been a motive for keeping of her death a secret from me."

" And this is all you know about her?"

" All. I have seen her in her coffin, and knew her in an instant; the features wore an expression of pain."

" You have seen the body, gentlemen, and have noticed that the body is in a wonderful state of preservation."

" Yes—yes—we have," said the jury, with one accord, and the Earl of Crubmle-down looked thoughtful.

Then several witnesses were examined; who deposed, that a lady and gentleman came to the inn, about six years back; the deceased was the lady, and she was very ill and remained so for some hours and died; the gentleman, as soon as he saw what was the end of it, left the neighbourhood; but left a friend, or solicitor, to act for him, it was difficult to tell which.

"Who was the gentleman," inquired the coroner.

"Nobody knew; but it was said, that he was a Mr. John Smith, of London; who paid all expences."

"There was a child, I believe," inquired the coroner.

"Yes; and it was put to nurse, and has been paid for ever since. Mrs. Grove had the care of the child."

"Where does she live?"

"Nobody knows; she used to live here, but now she has left these parts, and nobody knows where she has gone to; most likely to London, as all other people do who are doing a little better than ourselves."

"Then, of the child; at present, nobody knows anything at all?"

"No, sir."

There was a stand-still for evidence, nobody coming up, they all seemed as if there was a great hiatus in the evidence; something more was wanting, but which could not be had; at length there was a movement at the door, and a person entered with several odd looking bundles and laid them upon the table.

"Oh, Mr. Bell," said the coroner, "are you ready, we are waiting for you now."

"I am sorry if I have kept you waiting, but the time was very short to complete my tests; they require some hours to go through them properly, however, I have got through them very carefully."

"Well, Mr. Bell, state the result of your experiments to the jury."

"I will, sir."

"But first, you may as well state who and what you are, as the jury may be better satisfied as to your capabilities as a chemist, and lecturer on chemistry."

"Certainly, sir. I am Doctor Bell, I have studied chemistry sixteen years, and have lectured in most of the principal towns of England, and have often experimentalized."

"Now, sir," said the coroner, "have the goodness to tell the jury the result of your experiments upon the stomach of Miss Whitford, the unfortunate deceased. What have you found?"

"I will briefly relate it, sir. I found there was the probable presence of several poisons, sir."

"Were they each enough to cause death? or their united effects only."

"Each would have done so, no doubt, if they had been in sufficient quantities;" replied the chemist.

"And what quantity of poison was there in the stomach?" inquired the coroner; leaning his ear towards the witness, for the purpose of catching the answer, clearly.

"I didn't analyze the whole contents, only a part of it," replied the chemist. "I had no reason to do so, in case any further tests were necessary, they could not be done."

"Well then, sir, what was the relative result, be particular;" added the coroner, putting his hand to the back of his ear, fearful, lest he should lose a part of the answer.

"Why," said the chemist, "the relative quantities, stated in accurate terms, were seven-eighths of a per cent of nine-tenths of an unit of poison in the stomach, submitted to my operations."

"Seven-eighths," said the coroner, noting it upon the paper, "of a per cent of—dear me—what was the other part of your extraordinary calculation, Doctor Bell, eh?"

"Seven-eighths of a per cent of nine-tenths of an unit."

"Oh, very well; but its an uncomfortable calculation for country jurymen," muttered the coroner to himself as he put the answer down on paper, and then proceeded—

"Now, sir, having arrived at the conclusion that there was poison, how did you arrive at that truth, and what are the poisons you detected amongst the contents of the stomach?"

"The process—"

"Yes, describe the whole process, and the jurymen will be better able to judge of the mode of doing these things, and place more reliance npon the results that you give them."

"I will do so now, sir. In taking the stomach, I took out a certain portion of its contents, and that portion is divided into so many portions, that each may be subjected to its own proper test, for the discovery of the different poisons that are suspected as being likely to be administered to the subject."

See page 290.

"Good; now go on, sir."

"Now, sir," said the chemist, straightening himself on end, and holding his thumb and forefinger up in the air, and half shutting his eyes, lest the moonlight should come into them; "now, sir, I take a small quantity of indigo and place it in some water, with the smallest portion of the contents of the stomach, and then I add a little gamboge; the result is, a change of colour—it becomes green."

"What do you infer from that?" inquired a juryman.

"The presence of white arsenic," replied the chemist, solemnly; and the jurymen looked in each other's faces, and the coroner gave a fatherly look over the whole brood of intelligent beings.

"Well, sir, proceed," said the coroner, who seemed to think the jury had had time enough to digest that fact, and appeared to like to jog on a bit.

"Sir," said the chemist, "I then added a little vermilion to the mass, and another change is produced—a cloudy brown is the immediate result, with a little stirring."

"And what may you infer from that?" inquired the coroner, with some anxiety; for the lecturer betrayed frequent desire to pause and collect the admiration of the jurors, which he appeared to consider pleasant to look upon.

"That produced the presence of laudanum; yes, gentlemen, there was the result as plain as the clock of St. Paul's; but let me go on again, gentlemen, I have more to tell you yet."

The jurymen gazed at each other in speechless amazement and indignation at the bare thoughts of such a being existing as could attempt to kill a young female by such a medley of poisons; but the fact was so clearly demonstrated that they couldn't doubt it for once. It wouldn't bear thinking about.

"Now, gentlemen, I took another portion of the stomach, and allowed it to dry by means of a great heat in a crucible; and the consequence was, it dried up to dust. This was placed in some water, and some acetous acid put in; and then, after a time, a little carbonate of potass added to it, and the result was, an immediate effervescence."

"And what does that prove?" inquired a juryman, with a very blank face, for he had drunk such compounds.

"The presence of prussic acid."

There was a great sensation in the room, while the earl and Colonel Bruce gazed at each other in intense amazement. They never had heard anything like this; the provincials had astonished them—they could hardly hear of anything like this anywhere.

"Now, sir," said the coroner, "do you think there were sufficient quantities of any one of these poisons to cause death?"

"Of the last poison," said the chemist, "any quantity will cause death; for if you drop the smallest portion upon a sore place on the flesh, when the skin has been knocked off, you will cause death."

The jury was a country jury, and they were too much amazed and astonished to make any inquiries, and their minds were so far confused, that they were scarcely able to take into cognizance any more facts; these had occupied all the energies they possessed.

"Have you any questions to ask this gentleman?" inquired the coroner of the jurymen, who, however, shook their heads; and it was plain that they did not understand enough of chemistry to ask anything.

"Then," said the coroner, "you are of opinion that she died of poison?"

"It seems that was the cause of death. There is the poison, and the subject died; what more can we have in the way of proof?"

"The jury must be satisfied of that, sir," said the coroner; upon which the jury brightened up, and rose one per cent. in their own opinion.

"You may retire, sir; I have no further questions to ask you. Will you be good enough to remain in the way, lest we should want you again""

The medical man agreed, and left the room.

The next witness called was the landlady, who gave it as her opinion that the lady had died in childbed, but she couldn't say but what something else might have been the cause as well; and declared she had taken several warm liquids.

This produced a great sensation.

"Now, upon your oath, don't you think that poison might have been given to her in those drinks?"

"Yes, there might,' said the landlady; "but I didn't think there was any at the time; for I tasted them myself, and found no evil effects from drinking them."

" The poison might have been put in afterwards ?"

" Well, it might; though I can't think there was any ; I fancy I should have been ill too, if there had been any ; in fact, I am sure I should."

" But you can die under the care of the doctor or nurse," inquired a juror, with great composure, and a shew of dignity ; for he evidently thought he had put a severe question.

" If I had," said the landlady, looking hard at the juror, " I should have been in my coffin, and not here."

" That is very true," said the coroner; " where is the medical man who attended her upon that occasion ?"

" Hear, hear, hear !" exclaimed several of the jurors, who thought the suggestion a good one."

" That is what I want to know, gentlemen ; and I dare say you do, too.— (Hear, hear.) Well, gentlemen, I think there's nothing like having a thorough examination, when you have one at all ;—(Hear, hear,)—and that now we are here, we may as well understand what we have come about ; and, moreover, we will, to that end, thoroughly sift the matter through a very fine sieve."

This was highly applauded ; everybody thought the coroner a clever man, and a good speaker ; while the coroner told the jury they were respectable and very intelligent. Thus they went on for an hour or two, when they were in a high state of good humour with each other.

" Now, gentlemen, I want to know, where the medical gentleman who attended upon Emily Whitford is ?"

" Oh, to be sure, so do we."

" But where is he, does anybody here know? Nobody know where he has gone to? He has left these parts some time ; and nobody, it appears, knows anything of him."

" He has not been heard of since he left the village, about four years ago ;" said a voice.

" It is my opinion, gentlemen, we can't go on until he is found. We must endeavour to trace him."

" We must adjourn," said one of the jury ; " and endeavour to trace him out, and thus obtain his evidence."

" I think the suggestion a good one," said the coroner; " I cannot but think the gentleman may be found. Surely his departure was not so sudden but some one knew of it before hand. He most probably communicated his intention to proceed to some part of the country ; and, if we can only discover to which, then you know we can write to that part of the country and make inquiries."

" Certainly ;" said several of the jurymen.

" What is your opinion, gentlemen, of an adjournment for a week or so? we may give publicity to what has past, and the knowledge that we want may be obtained ; it may reach some one's ears who may be able to give it—and willing, likewise."

" Aye, let's adjourn, master coroner," said one fat, fine old fellow, up in a corner ; " I am nation dry, and am sweated to death here ; and if I stop much longer I shall melt, and you have to hold an inquest upon me—you'll find ' I am over done.' "

This was a sensible speech ; but the coroner frowned, and said, " the gentlemen must do their duty, at whatever personal risk or inconvenience it might cost them."

There was a pause of some moments, when the coroner said :—

" I shall be sorry to displease any of you, gentlemen, but I must beg you to withdraw, for I have a few words to speak to the jury, which I think are necessary."

Colonel Bruce, and the earl, and many others now left the room, for about three minutes ; and then, when they returned, the coroner said :—

" Gentlemen, the inquest is adjourned to a future day; in the meantime, you may gather what information you can."

There was now much conversation being carried on among different persons who were collected in the room; however, Colonel Bruce left the apartment, and informed the landlady that they should be glad to be alone; and, as the inquiry was at an end for the present, therefore, she might inform the guests the room was engaged. This was at once done, and acceded to; then the room was evacuated, as a matter of course; and, not a little glad was the earl, and Colonel Bruce, when they once more found themselves alone."

" This begins to look a very disagreeable affair," said the earl; " I don't at all admire the perseverance of these people."

" But I do admire the learning of the chemist—people about this part must be uncommon clever people; what this fellow was I cannot imagine."

" Nor I, and were it not for the fact, that something might arise of a very unpleasant nature, I could sit down and laugh till I got ill; but, really Bruce, turn the affair in what way you will, it presents but too many unpleasant phases."

" Well, but I see no danger yet."

" No, I see not much immediate danger; but yet, I suspect it must be known to some few, and I am liable to be betrayed. The fact is, these people are determined to exert themselves to the last, to endeavour to have. me; and so, as it is known to some, it will be an easy matter to come at me."

" Whom are you known to here, my lord?"

" No one I know here, but they know Mrs. Grove, and if they were to trace her, they might put her upon her oath, and then she would be compelled to tell the truth."

" I would not harass myself with needless apprehensions, my lord; I am sure your lordship has, as yet, no cause for fearing a discovery at this present moment, for I see no danger."

" I hope there may not be, but there is no certainty whatever; I would, I could feel sure that it was so."

" As for Mrs. Grove, I don't think she is likely to be traced, for there is no trace whatever of her left here. Nobody knows any thing about her, where she is gone to, or what she is, or what she is doing; so there seems but little probability on that score."

" No, I hope there may be none; but, she may be discovered yet. Some one may accidentally pass her, and follow her, and then out comes the whole secret," said the earl.

" That, however, is but a distant probability, and no means can well be taken to prevent the occurrence; however, it is useless to contemplate such a chance as that. I am annoyed at the inquest—it is a very singular affair, and if one were not otherwise engaged would be quite a study."

" So it would, but then the corpse—they have exhumed that, and it would seem in a state of great preservation. I should very much like to see it—poor Emily! it was an early end, but I was not the controller of her fate. I could not tell what was to happen before it really did occur."

" No man can look into futurity; that is, he may look, but he can see nothing of it—but I do not know how you can see the body at all."

" Why not? I have managed worse affairs than that before now, Bruce. I must say, I have a very strong desire to see her, especially, as she is so strangely preserved from decay."

" I would advise your lordship to do nothing of the kind. It can answer no useful purpose—and the only result will be, your lordship will feel more uncomfortable after the view is over, than you do now. The sight of a human body, that has lain in the grave for six years, under more favourable circumstances than any ever known, is not one that will at all restore the tone of your lordship's mind."

" And yet, Bruce, I should much like to see her. She was a sweet girl; and if she should cause me to feel a pang, it shall not be an unwelcome one, for I have certainly deserved——"

"Will not your lordship be persuaded? It can do no useful purpose, and it may entail some evils that you would be glad to escape. Look, before you leap, my lord."

"Advice is very good, Bruce, but honestly, I cannot follow it in this case, and I must chance all and procure the means of seeing her body; some how or other."

"Very well; if your lordship is resolved upon going, I will accompany you. I have nothing to fear, but your lordship has, and that was the motive which induced me to advise your lordship to avoid this attempt to see her body."

"I must, I will, Bruce."

"Be it so, my lord, I will go with you; and, having determined upon the line of conduct, the next is, how it shall be carried out. Where does the body lay?"

"In the bone-house, or charnel-house, I believe they call it," replied the earl. "I asked one of the intelligent jurymen, and his answer informed me of that much."

"When will you make the attempt to visit the coffin?" inquired the colonel. "At what hour?"

"At midnight."

"Well, I suppose the worthy and intelligent inhabitants of this place will by that time, be in their deepest slumbers; it is a hour, too, that is sacred to church ghosts and charnel-houses, we shall not, I think, be disturbed in our work."

"No, no, there will be no risk. I am convinced," replied the earl, "I am sure we shall have no interruption whatever. I long to see my once-charming Emily, now cold, and many years in the grave. It seems strange to me that she should be so wonderfully preserved from decay."

"I should not think much of that, my lord; some accidental circumstance has been the cause of that, something, quite independent of the body itself; though it is gratifying to the living to know that what they once loved, has not so rapidly as others, decayed."

"It does seem strange though, Bruce, very strange; it appears as though there were some special care from the hand of Providence in this case. Yes, yes, I will see her."

"How shall we get into the charnel-house?"

"That is a question we can only settle when we get there, Bruce; we must be guided by necessity, and not make our plans so minute and undeviating, lest we spoil all; but, I suppose, there are doors, windows, or roofs, at every one of these places we can get in."

"So we can," said Bruce; "but we shall want some instruments, such as a crow-bar and a lantern."

"A lantern, but nothing more; we could not obtain one without a suspicion that something wrong was intended, and then there would be a watch set upon us, which would spoil all and make something like a disturbance, and our stopping here might have its disadvantages as well as other matters."

"So it would; however, we must have a lantern, one can be procured in the house from the ostler or some one about."

The matter was arranged, and they both sat down to wile away the time until midnight should arrive.

* * * * * *

The hour of twelve chimed from the old fashioned steeple, and the Earl of Crumbledown, accompanied by Colonel Bruce, quitted the inn; and they both made the best of their way towards the village church-yard, which lay at no very great distance, perhaps less than half a mile from the inn-door. The night was calm and starry, but there was no moon, and though there was a light above, it was of that character below, that you could not tell a rise in the ground, from a hole; every thing seemed about the same size and form; it was therefore dark, and they could not see far beyond them.

"This is a beautiful night for such a purpose," remarked the earl as he walked along.

"It may be," said Colonel Bruce," but I don't know the ground, and am in a state of continual tremble; a very agreeable night to walk on a tower, or a meadow when you know all the holes and impediments blindfold, but not otherwise."

"Then we have not far to go," said the earl; "scarcely a hundred yards more.'

"That is news worth hearing," said the colonel; "I am glad of it, for the sooner we are out of this main road the better, suppose any one was to pop upon us now, but stop, you are going past, is not that a gate?"

As the colonel spoke, they came up to a gate at which they stopped for a short time to listen, but nothing could be heard—not a sound reached them of any description.

"Yes, Bruce, this is the place," said the earl, "this is the church-yard; we may as well get in as quiet as we can, our chance of discovery, if there is any, will be less there than if we remain here."

Accordingly, they both got over the gate, and walked amongst the tombs and upon the grass, until they came to the back part of the church, and there was a small old-fashioned building attached to it. This was the charnel-house, where all the odd matters that belonged to the church-yard were usually placed, and where people were laid out in, when death ensued to a stranger by any kind of accident.

"Is this the place we have to get into?" inquired Colonel Bruce.

"Yes, this is the place," replied the earl; "and I fancy it can be no difficult matter to get in."

"No, I should imagine it's easy enough," said Bruce, "especially when we find that the key has been left in the door on purpose for our accommodation, I presume, for I can see no other that it can be left for."

"Some one did it by accident, I suppose," said the earl; "but we can profit by the accident and enter the place; but let us first listen, and ascertain that no one is in before us, for thus we should be walking into a lion's den, where they would be just ready to receive us."

"Exactly," replied the colonel; "it would be above a joke to walk into a pit of that description, and as it is as well to keep out of the hands of the Philistines, I will just peep in very carefully."

Then, with great caution, Colonel Bruce walked to the door, and listened attentively for some time; but he heard nothing, and then opened the door and peeped in. There was no sound, no moving object that met his view; and after waiting thus a few minutes to ascertain with certainty the truth of any one's presence, became assured of the fact.

"Come in now," he said; "the coast is clear—no soul is here—we have it all to ourselves."

The earl followed, and they both entered the charnel-house, and came to something that suddenly brought them to a stand.

"What can be in the way now," said the colonel; "we had better have a light, I have the lantern;" and as he spoke, he produced it from beneath his cloak, and by means of some matches, he soon obtained a light; and then the cause of the impediment was soon discovered, which was nothing more than a heap of coffin wood. This had been taken out of the grave-yard when they dug new graves, and the old ones interfered with the making of the new ones. It is an ordinary custom to burn the coffin wood in the charnel-house, or somewhere near at hand, because they have a peculiar odour which betray their origin. The consequence was an accumulation of wood, against which the colonel and earl had run, and found a kind of impediment they could not understand in such a place.

"This is very odd," said the earl; "how these broken pieces of wood smell of dead bodies."

"That is because they are parts of coffins that have been dug up to make way for others—it is common enough, and an affair that ought not to excite surprise; because, when the grave-yard is full, the parson won't say so, for he will be curtailed in his profits arising from the burial of the dead."

"But where is the body, Bruce, my unfortunate Emily, where is she? Alas. this is a sad, sad place to look for her. The charnel-house, one would think, was no place for such as she had been; but, alas, what is she now, and who made her so?"

"You take the matter in too serious a light, my lord, for the freak of a moment, and that too when the passions are wildest, and both are willing."

"Yes, Bruce, I know all about that ; but when the results are so palpable to the senses as this, when the consequences are so dreadful ; then, indeed, we are induced to examine the justifiableness of one's own conduct."

"Undoubtedly, the result has a great influence upon the mind when you come to look back, and I am far from saying your lordship has done right ; but the wrong is of that description that is, in some measure, entailed by our very nature, and it being so, renders all retribution impossible, unless voluntary, as in your lordship's present case, for such I consider your sorrow."

"So it is, Bruce."

"Besides, were she living, I need hardly suppose you would act towards her with that liberality that would place her beyond the reach of all ordinary necessity—in fact, so that she would be independent of all personal exertion."

"Certainly I would."

"And in that case, she would be better off than if she had been married ; and, perhaps, had to drag on a life of misery and wretchedness, besides all kinds of injuries."

"We cannot foresee that."

"No, no ; but the end she came to could not be well imputed to your lord- ship—far from it. It might have happened under far different circumstances."

"True, true ; but I am impatient to behold what I most dread to see, and that is the altered form and face of Emily. Where is the coffin, Bruce— where is the coffin ?"

"Here," said Bruce, "here ;" and as he spoke, he pointed to some tressels that supported a coffin, the covering of which was torn and soiled with clay and mud."

"Aye, there it is," said the earl ; approaching it softly, as though he feared to awake the slumber of the dead.

He approached the coffin, and lifted off the pall, which had been thrown over it with a hasty hand, as if they had deemed it necessary to do something, but had as yet done nothing with that solemn care that is used when the body is first placed in. Was it because the body had so long lain in the ground, that it was not worth the care that was ordinarily bestowed upon it ? It might be so.

Now, Colonel Bruce assisted the earl in lifting off the lid, which had been secured by one or two screws, partly turned in ; but the tool was at hand, and the coffin lid removed. The earl trembled, and could not avoid shrinking back, as he looked upon the features of the corpse.

"It is Emily's, is it not, my lord ?" inquired Bruce.

"Yes, yes. Oh, God ! oh, God !" he exclaimed, placing his hands before his face, "I was not prepared for this. How strangely every form—every feature, should be so preserved. I could not mistake her ; but, oh, what an expression of sorrow and bodily anguish do they not express. It seems as though her last moments were painful, bodily and mentally, and they stamped the emotions upon her face."

"Poor thing," said Bruce, "she does seem to feel her sorrows ; but that, you are aware, arises from the contraction of some of the muscles at the time of death."

"It may be so ; but its preservation is so strangely perfect."

"That will not be of long continuance, my lord, since the air will now get to it, and aid in the work of decay—it has been in some tenacious soil that has not admitted the atmospheric influence to penetrate it."

"So I perceive," said the earl. "Alas, alas ! that so much beauty should come to such an end. She was as amiable and lovely as she was confiding, and her only fault was that of believing in one who has thus cruelly deceived her, and caused this unfortunate end to her, who would have died to have saved me from any evil. It is a bad return, and a sad acquittance for such love as she bore me."

"My lord."

"Nay, Bruce, it is the simple truth, and I cannot gaze upon these sad remains, and not feel—feel, deeply too, how far I have been guilty in causing all this misery ; and at the same time I am free from all deserved punishment, save that which lurks in my own breast—unseen but not unfelt."

"But this, my lord, can avail nothing, that is the coffin ; now, come away, you have been here long enough."

"I should not expiate my crime were I to pass the remainder of my life beside this coffin, and should only be doing a deserved penance—the more I think of this —the more I feel the baseness and enormity of my own conduct."

"Say no more, my lord."

Colonel Bruce would have said more, but he was suddenly stopped, by the sound of voices and feet, and on turning round, beheld three or four men rushing at them with staves in their hands, exclaiming:—

"Here they are, the body-snatchers—the sacrilegious robbers—they are all of 'em thieves—hoorah—sieze 'em boys—capture 'em—that's the way to do it."

"My good friends ;" said Colonel Bruce.

"Bother good friends; you are no friend of mine, I knows ; said a tall fellow— I never had a friend in such a state, and wouldn't for a crown piece."

"Well, but," said the earl, "we are no robbers."

"Of course not—who expects you cry stinking fish—but we have catched you, and that is all—and we'll try if we can't keep you, so come along—come along —it ain't no use resisting the strong arm of the law—we means what we says."

"Well, we have no intention of resisting," said the earl.

"Of course you ain't, who said you had ; but it would be all one as regards that, we should be down upon you, and tie you both together, neck and heels, here's a pretty go, howsomever."

"Well," said Colonel Bruce, "what are you going to do with us, we have done no harm, and no wrong."

"Aint you tho'—well his worship will tell'ee more about that in the morning, so come along.

"Where to ?" argued the earl.

"Where to ? why to the cage to be sure, where else did'ee expect to go to, eh?"

"If we are to be taken into custody, let us be taken before a magistrate instantly."

"Ah! ah! a very likely thing indeed, how his worship would swear at us for our pains. No, no, that will not do, it is no go, no go at all my good sir, I tell'ee what, it would be more than our places are worth to do that."

"I'll warrant you against all evil consequences from the act, if you will at once carry us to the magistrate."

"And what would he do ?"

"Discharge us immediately."

"Ah! ah! that is good ; but come, come, I haven't got time to waste in this fashion, either come along or say you won't, it's all the same, we are paid by time, and will carry you gently, neck and heels, until you come to the cage."

"We will walk," said the earl, since it must be so ; but allow me to tell you, you don't know whom you have seized, and will be sorry for it when you come to know, you would be glad if you had taken my advice, but we have done no wrong, we have done nothing that you can charge us with,"

"Yes, you came here for felonious purposes, that's very plain, and broke into the church, which is sacrilege."

"We have not broken in, for the door was open, the key being in it ; and moreover, there was no intention of committing any wrong, whatever ; you can say what you please, my friends, but you are wrong in what you are about,"

"We'll see about that, come along, and we will place you all right, if we can do nothing else, we shall be all right in that at all events, come on."

"There is no help for it, Bruce," said the earl ; "come along, we shall be free in the morning, they dare not detain us, but—I do not wish to be recognized."

The earl, and Colonel Bruce, suffered themselves to be taken into custody and walked towards the cage, where they were deposited without any more being said, either by themselves or the posse that had them in custody. Some little while afterwards, when they heard the footsteps of the men retreating, the earl seemed to awake out of a dream.

"Bruce," he said, "this is a very awkward affair. Here we are locked up, and what to do I cannot tell."

See page 298.

"Why, my lord, I think we shall have to endure this now until the morning; we are safe here, so safe that we cannot escape were we inclined to do so."

"There is no need of doing that," said the earl; "we have committed no wrong, and I am sure they cannot do anything to us without accusing us of something and proving it too."

"Your lordship is not aware of the perversity of country magistrates. 1 have seen some extraordinary things done in my time by the unpaid; it is uite extraordinary to see the extent of ignorance and prejudice that exists among such men."

" Well, we must go through it somehow or other ; and, if we can do so, we must not allow our rank and names to be known—it would be desirable to remain incognito."

" There can be no doubt of it, my lord ; but the question is, can you do so, and get clear of this scrape ? it strikes me we must give some explanation or suffer some imprisonment, for you may depend upon it these wiseacres will never let us go without being fully satisfied, especially if they imagine there is any secret in the affair ; they are hot-headed and prejudiced."

Thus the Earl of Crumbledown and Colonel Bruce passed the hours, from midnight till morning, in very uncomfortable speculations as to the probability of their fate, and the amount of explanation that would be required, and also the exact position in which it would place them when it was known who it was. There, of course, could not be evidence that he was interested in the inquest then going on ; but then would come the question, what took him to the bone-house, and why did he desire to see the body? All these things came across his mind, and the earl wished he had not been so indiscreet as to have gone at all. However, there was no mending the matter ; now they must remain, and get through it in the best way they could, and spend the hours that remained between this time and morning in the best manner they could, and the best was but very indifferent. Morning came, and with it some aggravation to their case ; for several countrymen climbed up to see, the " two chaps what wanted to rob the church." This, by no means mended their prospects, or made them any better pleased with their situation.

" This is very uncomfortable, Bruce ?" said the earl, " pacing about in this confined space ; I wish they would come and fetch us, and not leave us here in this manner to be the sport of every gaping fool who chooses to look in at us."

" It certainly does seem that we are objects of curiosity, and our presumed crime makes it a matter of some importance to the villagers to have a glimpse of such daring adventurers ; however, I would willingly dispense with this. I wonder what hour they will return and fetch us away. I really begin to feel tired and hungry ; this kind of imprisonment seems to increase all my wants."

" It arouses my impatience," said the earl, " and that is all ; I can feel I am exhausted as well, I must admit, but what will be the end of this affair I cannot tell."

*   *   *   *   *   *   *

The time passed heavily on their hands until they heard the sound of approaching footsteps, and then a key was thrust into the lock, and then the door opened, and the constable thrust his head in, and looked at them both with a knowing wink, saying,—

" Safe bind, safe find, eh ! old fellow ? I say, the cage is a pretty place for pretty birds like you, eh?—gallows birds, eh ! he, he, he !—nice place in wet weather."

Neither the earl nor the colonel made any reply to this facetious appeal ; but looked at each other with chagrin expressed in their countenances.

" Come, come, old fellow, don't be down upon your luck ; you may only have two months at the wheel, and you know that is soon got over—keep up your spirits."

" When do you intend to take us before the magistrate ?" inquired the colonel, suddenly.

" Oh, are you in a hurry to be committed ? because the magistrate will commit you like smoke."

" My good fellow, you had better carry us before him at once, and not detain us here with your absurdities ; you will be sorry for this insolence."

" Ah, you are a wise man to rob a church, aint you ? I tell you what, you won't see him these three hours."

" I'll give you ten shillings if you'll carry us before him in less than half an hour."

" Eh ?"

" I'll give you ten shillings if you'll get us to speak with the magistrate directly," said the colonel.

" You will?" tip it up then.

"If you get me the interview, not else ; because I should have no value for my money."

" You want me to trust you do you, and yet you will not trust me ; very well, the bargain's off ; I could not ask it of you if you refused, so far—all well, I won't be done, that's the plain truth, I won't be done, I will have nothing to do with it, you must take your turn among other prisoners."

" Will you promise to obtain it, if I give it you now?"

" I will promise you to do my best; and, at all events, you shall be the first to be served—no one else shall see him before you, so I'll make that bargain."

" Very well," said Colonel Bruce, " how long do you think it will be before you can get us to speak to the magistrate?"

" About an hour—perhaps only half an hour," replied the constable, as he held his hand out for the money which Colonel Bruce counted out; and when he had got it he said,—

" Well, you aint bad chaps neither—but, however, I must do my duty; you must come at once, and I will place you in safe keeping in the magistrate's house, where you will remain till I can persuade him he must see you, and hear what you have to say before he takes the trouble of understanding the charge."

With the prospect of such an interview, and the results which might be expected from the character of the magistrate, they were cautious to remain quiet, and follow the constables, who did not use them so roughly as they had at first seemed inclined to do. It was a fine morning, but it was early, and there were not many people about, and those few who looked at them where a great annoyance to the earl, who could have dispensed with such impertinence as he called it; he did not like to be looked at in such company. As for Colonel Bruce, there was a soldier-like dignity in his manner and demeanour, that caused him less inconvenience than it did the earl; at all events, he did not shew himself either angered or daunted. But they arrived in good time at the magistrate's mansion, for such it really was, the unpaid leaving mostly large incomes, or estates. Here they were placed in a strong room with constables outside to take care of them, in case they were to become unruly. While here, the earl, and Colonel Bruce, waited patiently until they should be brought before the magistrate, and were in ignorance of the efforts that the constable made to get them a hearing from the magistrates at once —and he succeeded.

" Now then," he said, " come along, I have done your business with his worship, though I think you are wrong, but I promised I would do it, and I have done ; its made him angry though."

However, as the earl, and Colonel Bruce, did not seem to fall down in a fit at the thought of his worship's anger, they followed the amazed constable into the presence chamber.

" Well," exclaimed his worship, with Falstaff-like demeanour ; " well constable, what have you here?"

"Two disorderlies, your worship, who got into the bone-house last night, with intent—"

" Well, and what then constable?"

" We took them into custody, your worship."

" Oh! abominable sacrilegious wretches, who would rob the church, or dead body of its teeth ; what did you do there, answer me that, if you can ; what did you do there?"

" Nothing, replied the earl, coolly."

" And you, he added, turning to Bruce, where you doing nothing, too.'

" No ;" said Bruce, " I was not. I was only helping."

" Insolent, as well as guilty, I perceive. I'll commit them at once and save trouble—had they anything about them?"

" Nothing, your worship, but a dark-lantern," replied the constable, " nor had they done anything, save look at the dead body."

" Ah, I see, you were too soon for them ; well, I can only punish them as rogues and vagabonds, and give them two months to the mill ; it will do them good. Who are you ?"

" If you will grant me a private interview I will tell you."

" A private interview !" exclaimed his worship, " what do you mean ? you are body snatchers !"

" I shall be able to convince your worship that we are something else, if you will favor me with the interview I ask, I have a particular motive for what I say, and if you are not satisfied that it ought to be communicated to you in private, you can punish me by publishing that which I am unwilling should be made known."

" Well," said his worship, who was somewhat overawed by the ungentlemanly tone of Colonel Bruce, at the same time there was so much command in him that he began to have some idea he must be mistaken in his estimate of the occupation of the two gentlemanly strangers—they might not be London thieves upon a country excursion and prowling about—" well, then you shall have it," he said, as he arose, " I am not sure that I can do wrong—step this way."

The earl, and Colonel Bruce immediately followed, and the amazed constable opened his eyes ; and by the time he was convinced he was awake, the door was closed before him.

" Here," said Colonel Bruce, " is my card," and he handed his card to the magistrate, and the earl did the same.

" We are here out of curiosity alone, that is, I should say, we went to the charnel-house out of curiosity alone, and the key was in the door and we opened it, certainly."

" But what induced you to do so, my lord ? a bone-house is not the place for a young peer," said the magistrate, half doubtingly.

" No ; but we had been present at the inquest held yesterday, and had heard part of the strange preservation of the body, we determined to gratify our curiosity, without asking leave, as we were travelling for pleasure, incog." said Bruce.

" But how am I to know you are what you represent ?"

" Send to the next market-town and inquire where my carriage and servants are left—then you may be satisfied."

" That is enough, my lord," said the magistrate, who made many apologies for the detention, and was sorry they had not sent to him in the night and he would have ordered them to have been released. After some conversation they returned to the outer-room, where his worship said, aloud, " these two gentlemen, having their curiosity excited at the inquest, by the tale of the preservation of the body, determined to see—the door was open, and they did see it ; there is no charge against them—they ought not to have been detained—you must be more cautious, constable."

Great was the constable's amazement, he was stupified, and could not speak, but a woman's voice instantly said, " your worship, I remember that gentleman very well, he's the same man that brought the unfortunate young woman down in a post-chaise, who died at the inn, and on whom they held the inquest yesterday he's the man, I can swear to him."

" But there is no charge against the gentleman."

" No charge against him !" said the woman, growing angry and red, " no charge against him—isn't seducing a young female to death, nothing, then—well, I am sure, what are men, now a-days ?"

The magistrate, however, not being called upon to answer such an extra-judicial question, he merely hinted, that he required order in the court, and that he would require the absence of any one who talked without his permission—he declared the gentlemen free. In the argument of the constable, the earl, and Colonel Bruce, left the court, loaded with civilities, and not at all looked upon in the light of wronged doers.

The Earl of Crumbledown, and Colonel Bruce, being once more at liberty, determined to make the best use of their time, and made no remarks on the inconveniences suffered by the misadventure; for they had not, as yet, had either sleep or refreshment, both of which they stood in need.

CHAPTER LIII.

JACK GROVE PLAYS MRS. WILLOUGHBY A TRICK, AND QUITS HIS SERVICE.—HE IS APPREHENDED, AND MR. WILLOUGHBY COMES OUT IN AN ENTIRELY NEW CHARACTER.

JACK GROVE was not quite so satisfied, as he looked; he was one of those, who, under a stupid exterior, could look and remember a great deal; especially, if that were to turn out useful to him in any way. He was cunning, in fact, one might say, he had a great deal of York about him—he could do much, provided nothing in the shape of drink was to be had; drink, was Jack Grove's enemy, that certainly stole away his wits, for when drunk he was, to all intents, mad. While Willoughby could frighten Jack, or while Jack, was in need or had nothing better—but he had learned a little of Willoughby himself, so good a master in rascality as he was, was not easily found within the precincts of London or its liberties, and it was not in human nature to remain under such tutelage and not become instructed. Do what you will, however, nature never stagnates, it either progresses or retrogades, after a certain time; and, in the words of the comedy, "what's bred in the bone must come out in the flesh." Now, Mr. Willoughby, however he might affect to become a man of character, the cloven foot would peep out, and he cared not how often, provided he was assured that it was at all beneficial to him in its results. Now, Grove had an inclination to follow in the steps of his master, indeed, like master like man, was very true in their case, they both shone in their respective stations; Grove had long thought there was some means of paying Willoughby off, and leaving the house.

Jack argued that he was tired of that kind of life, and that if he had some money, and the means of procuring more, he should be able to enjoy himself for some time, and then it might be time to obtain another supply; however, that he thought needn't be, they seeing he hadn't got the first supply made up—had he spent it? Therefore, it was, he discarded the latter part of the transaction, and only troubled himself about the first, namely, the raising of the first subsidy.

I know pretty well how to manage that, he thought—and by the doctor's wig I'll have the means some how or other; if I were to take it without asking his leave, he mightn't like it, but if I ask him he is sure to say no, so I may as well not ask him.

Willoughby had taken Jack Grove into his employment, at a very small remuneration, for the purpose of preventing him from getting drunk; and, certainly to an extent he had succeeded in doing so, but it was not because sobriety had any charms for drunken Jack Groves. No, the reverse might be said to be the case, and he never would have been sober had he the means to do so.

It was a part of Jack's duty to go every morning to Willoughby's room, and receive his orders before he stirred out, and to carry them to his office, for he lived some distance away from the office. Imperiously, enough, did Willoughby treat his humble servitor; and regret often entered the breast of Grove, that he had ever entered his service, but then he always asked himself "how could I have helped it?" This was a question he could not satisfactorily answer himself, and he, therefore, concluded that it must have been inevitable; this was a reasonable conclusion and one very natural. Each day Jack became more and more discontented with his position, he wanted more money, but he was not like to get any here; he wanted less to do, but he had a much better chance of getting a great deal more. This was unsatisfactory, and Willoughby made it still more so, by giving him all the trouble he could, and by being as personally displeasing to him as he could; in fact, being, as Jack Grove himself said, as infernally disagreeable as if he had been allowed to turn sour. There was much that was annoying to Jack Grove. Willoughby, had for a time frightened him to a certain extent, he led him—to use a familiar saying, he had him under his thumb; but Jack now began to rebel, he thought he had been long enough with Willoughby, and it was time he tried some other scheme.

One evening, despite all prudential considerations, Jack Grove determined to spend his evening in the nearest public-house. Thither he repaired, and seated himself in one corner.

"Now," muttered Jack, "I shall have a comfortable hour's private conversation with myself, and I think I may be lively enough over it, for they sell good ale here, and that's one great comfort; I wonder how much I could drink at one sitting."

This was an abstruse calculation, and if begun now, would have to be performed with insufficient data; but, at the same time, there was every chance of his putting the truth to the proof, making actual experiments as to what he could bear.

This was one way to test the powers of his sobriety; but he was not fated, as the romancist would say, to become the victim of his own skill.

His draughts turned quite a different way; and, as he drank, he began considering in his own mind what would be the best course, with the object in view mentioned before, that he could pursue. He would do anything that would give him money.

"Well, I'm in a pretty fix," said Jack Grove; "here am I—I can't even get drunk now—what am I to do, I should like to know? When I was yonder I could get drunk, but now I can't; there's no freedom here, that's certain."

This was plain to the mind of Jack Grove, who put the thing down as settled in his estimation. That was one point gained, and he now travelled on to another.

"Its quite clear," he said, "that if I stay as I am, I shall not make the genteel independence I expected. No, no, hard work and little pay, that's the dodge at Willoughby's mansion—for such it really was—and I must try some scheme to make it better."

"But what? Let me see; he generally has a tidy lot of cash in his purse. Then there's plenty of rings, watch, chain, and a good many more things. Why, I do believe, I could raise a hundred pounds myself upon 'em."

This was a thing that he could not very well forget; no, no, a hundred pounds was a heavy sum, if he could only get that. Why, then, he should never want money again. Only think what a quantity of ale a hundred pounds would buy. There was a matter for consideration. Who could tell what could be done with such a sum in that way? Certainly, Jack Grove could not do so, and what's more, he had not the remotest intention of trying. He was resolved that he would not trouble the mysteries of arithmetic upon the subject.

"I know what I could do if I could break into the iron chest at the office. I might have as much as that in money at once, and I could take the jewels afterwards—but might as well break into Newgate as into that—I should be as well off. No, no, the iron chest is safe, and so is a block of stone."

Just at that moment some persons entered the room in which Jack was seated. One of them was a Jew, and another was a female, and a servant in livery. They all three sat down together, and looked cautiously round; and Jack Grove pretended to sleep. They called for some ale, and they all began to drink.

"I tell you vat it ish, ma tear," said the Jew, "you have a fery hart place of it; they don't pay enough—not at all vat you deserve, dat's certain, take my word for it; take Apraham Moses' word for dat, if for noting else."

"Well," said the man in plush smalls, "that is very true. I do indeed work very hard, very hard, indeed; but I don't get enough money to make things agreeable."

"Then take money, my tear."

"But I can't; they have none save what they have in their purses, and I can't get at them, you know, so what I am to do," said the man, sulkily, "I don't know."

"Take anything, no matter vat; tings will bring money, my tear—they be money's wort, you know. I will give you a goot price. I can't give you as mosch as if they was new; but, you know, I will give you all dey are wort."

"There is something in that," said the man; "there's only the chance of being found out, and that is——"

"Very small; yes, as my name is Apraham Moses; so I am sure, that if you take care, my tear, you can't get found out—always keep your eye open, and never be cotched."

"Ah! Jack," said the woman, "when are you going to give me that new gown you promised me; you know you promised me that four months ago, and now I am as far off as ever?"

"I don't know that," said the man; "at all events, I am sure of this—you have had a good bit one way or another. Why, last holiday I was out, I spent near thirty shillings; you had fifteen besides, so how can I do it. You can't have your cake and eat it."

"Ah! well, if I'm only to have a show on a holiday, Jack, and be sown up in a sack all the other time, we must cut our sticks back; it wont do for me. I thought you a better man than that comes to, at all events. I must look out for another. There's slippery fingered Bill; he's the man to make money."

"Well, well, I will do the best I can; but there is an end of it for the present. What will you give me for this watch?" inquired the man, pulling out a silver hunter and chain.

"Ah!" said the Jew, "them's the things: I could get rid of a pushel of such tings. Let me see: capped and jewelled—all humbug, know all about that; going fuzee—ah! very good; case light—the works old—put into modern case; ah! very well; dare say—good and useful watch, but not de ting to sell. How much you want?"

"Why, three pounds are only half its value, and barely that: you ought to let me have that at the least."

"He, he, he! My tear, when did you learn dat funny way? 'Three pounds!' —oh, my conscience!—you'll get more for dat! I tells you what I will do: I will give you von pound."

"That be d——d," said the man: "I'm not going to run all sorts of risks, and then be chiselled in that way. No, no!—that won't do for me"

"Well, my tear, you may take it back again: but, as you are a friend, I don't mind straining a little hard, and saying five-and-twenty shillings. Come, come, will five-and-twenty shillings do?"

"No it will not."

"Then I can't help it," said the Jew, and he resigned the watch.

"Come, come," said the woman, "you are not a-going to do that, Jack. Have money anyhow, and not higgle for a few pence."

"But it is a few pounds."

"That is all very well, but in the way of bargain, you know you can't always get what you ask."

"Nor anything like it," retorted the man. "I don't mind taking two pounds, but I can't do less."

"Ah, my tear! you are very hard in a bargain: but you forget that I am obliged to sell to another, who has to sell again; he wants his profit, and I can't do without mine."

"Ah! between one and the other I get nothing."

"Yes, yes, my tear, you gets yours without any risk. Come—there's thirty shillings, and that's a handsome price. Anybody knows Apraham Moses for an honest man," said the Jew, complacently.

"You thundering old rogue!" said the man, as he took up the money. The Jew smiled, and the woman laughed outright. They all three arose and walked out, leaving Jack Grove solus.

"Well," thought Jack, as he got up from the recumbent posture in which he had been lying, "well, I think I could do better: but as for getting anything upon the sly, and then staying in the house afterwards—that won't do for me. If I have money I like to spend it: and if this Willoughby was to lose a sixpence, and I stopped away, he would swear I had it. I know he would; but I might as well be hung for a sheep as a lamb—so I'll have enough to keep the pot a-boiling for a month or two. I"ll see a trifle of life. I'll have a good turn-out, when I do leave; and, by the parson's nose, it shall be to-morrow morning. He's got a purse."

Jack Grove seemed lost in thought for some moments: and then he struck the table with the empty pot before him, which seemed to rouse the genius of the place—and, when he came, Jack said—

"Another pot—let it be of the best: I'm going to treat myself—so let's have no humbug."

"Very good, sir. Anybody going to drink with you?"

"Yes: I'm in partnership with myself", said Jack Grove; "so, I and myself will drink together. Do you hear?"

"Yes," said the man; and he left the room, muttering something about a good sort, and shutting the door after him; when, in a minute or two, he returned with the supply of moisture required.

"Well," said Jack, "this will do. Now, here's success to to-morrow morning. I don't care. I wish I may die if I don't have a go in at old Willoughby. It aint no use grumbling—he'll never give me anything by that motion. I'll take the law in my own hands: if I don't, why cuss me—that's all about it."

Jack Grove drank his ale, and staid very late—too late to get into the house: and so he got into the stable, where he lay very comfortably, as sleeping in a hay-loft was no hardship to Jack Grove; indeed, it was a common thing to him—he had often slept in a much worse situation than that. In the morning, Jack arose early, and set about preparing for a hasty departure; and as soon as any of the inmates were up he walked in, to their amazement.

"Well, Grove," said one, "you have got into a pretty mess, now. The governor has been asking for you, and he swears all sorts of vengeance."

"Does he now," said Jack.

"Aye, he swears he'll give you the sack."

"Well, I hope it won't be an empty one. Where is he now?"

"Up stairs—he went up stairs: he wants you as soon as you come in, he;; so you had better go up, and have it out once."

"Well, you may as well tell him I am here, and I am coming up as soon as I have had my breakfast."

"Not I; you had better take those messages yourself, he'll wait for you; I dare say, he won't come down on purpose to see you, so you may as well take your own way."

"It's all the same a hundred years hence, I should say."

This was a consolatory reflection, and Jack Grove immediately began to help himself to some cold meat, and all that was in the house under the care of the cook; but, as the cook was not up, Jack did not wait to ask a permission, he knew would be denied him, so he set to work, and ate and drank heartily. When Jack had done all he desired in this way, he walked up into the sitting-room, and took several articles of value from the mantelpiece—such as the time-piece, and any portable article that was of some value.

"This will do for a beginning," said Jack, "I'll now go to the governor's room, and hear what he has to say."

Acting upon this resolution, Jack made his way to Willoughby's room, and shutting the door behind him, walked up to his bed. Willoughby turned, and saw who it was, and in great anger asked him where he had been?

"Enjoying myself," said Jack.

Willoughby opened his eyes, but instantly afterwards contracted them, saying,—

"Enjoying yourself, eh! That means getting drunk. Well, I'll have something like satisfaction, for this, you dle infernal scoundrel; but I'll talk to you presently. Where's my boots?"

"I don't know," said Jack, coolly.

"Don't know?" roared Willoughby, "but you shall know."

"Can't," said Jack.

"Damn your insolence," said Willoughby, hardly able to contain his anger, and starting up in bed, "I'll teach you something better than this, or I'll know a good reason why."

"Come, come," said Jack, "I'm sick of you, and intend to have an alteration; now, be quiet, or I shall be obliged to do you some mischief: will you be quiet, or won't you, now?"

See page 301.

"Get out of the room!"

"I shan't," said Jack very coolly, at the same time he gave Willoughby a back handed blow across the mouth.

"You villain!" exclaimed Willoughby, jumping up, "you villain! I will punish you for this."

"I'll have my turn now," said Grove, "and will command at once, so here goes for a good one."

As he spoke, he levelled a couple of straight blows at Willoughby's eyes, both of which took effect, and laid him instantly on his back in the bed, stunned and bleeding.

"Murder!" he called in a very faint voice, "murder! murder! thieves! help! help!"

"Stop all that," said Jack, "now give me your purse, I have entirely done with you; I'm going, but I shall help myself before I do go, and unless you are a fool you will lay quiet while I do so, for I'll make no bones of cutting your throat."

"Good God!" said Willoughby, alarmed, "the man's a murderer."

"No I ain't yet, I may be soon, and you'll have the honour of being my first victim; what do you say to that? Will you now lay still and be quiet until I have done?"

"Yes, yes, I'm quiet," said Willoughby, "I'll be quite quiet, but you are not going to rob me, are you?"

"Well you may call it so, but I call it helping myself, and I intend to take away as much as I can, and should you make any noise, I'll do for you, you may depend upon it."

As Jack Grove kept talking, he walked about the room, opened this thing and then that, took Willoughby's clothes, and rummaged them over and over, to the owner's great chagrin and annoyance.

"Give us your keys," said Jack, "which on 'em opens the secretaire, eh? come don't fumble in that way, and don't give me the wrong one, for if you do, I'll hit you on the head with the whole bunch, I will indeed, and no mistake."

Willoughby did not like the job of pointing out the means of opening the secretaire, and did not do it so willingly as Jack Grove seemed to think he ought to have done, so he seized him by the ear and shook him violently for several minutes.

"Now will you give me the key, or must I do it again for you? I'll be the death of you."

"There, that is it, that is it," said Willoughby, holding up the key, "that will open it."

Jack Groves took the key, and applying it, found it did open the secretaire, and immediately set to work, to rummage over and over the contents of the piece of furniture.

Willoughby kept a watchful eye upon him, and Grove upon him in return, so much so, that Willoughby was convinced he had no choice but must let the affair run its own course, and wait until Jack was gone before he would make any attempt to have him secured; for he felt, that Jack was as good as his master, or rather in this case, he was somewhat better.

"Where's your watch, come just hand it over, will you? There it is over your head, don't persuade me you don't know, or that you can't get it. I will help you, at all events, and then I know you'll be able to get it."

Willoughby again assisted Jack to despoil him of his own property, and Jack placed the watch in his fob, and stowed away a great many other articles about his person besides money.

"Now," said Jack, "I believe I shall do—what do you say—eh! don't you think it will?"

Willoughby thought it would do for once, and accordingly he said so, and he really thought so—he was sincere.

"And now," said Jack, buttoning his coat up—now I'm going, but I want to give you a word of advice—are you in a fit state to listen and remember it?"

"Yes, yes, what is it?"

"This, that you keep your tongue between your teeth, seeing, if you do not I'll cut it out; now, remember this, that if you make but one sound of alarm

I'll come back and fracture your skull, that will save all future trouble. I don't see why I should not do that now, and save all bother."

"No, no," said Willoughby, "you may depend upon me, I'll make no noise or disturbance whatever."

"Very well," said Jack, "I'll take your word for once, but mind you if you do break forth I'll be the death of you."

"Ah, Jack, you need not fear me!"

"No, I don't; but you'll have occasion to fear me, if you give me any provocation, said Jack."

Turning the key in the door, he walked back to the bed, and once more threatened Willoughby with all the evil consequences he could think of if he made any disturbance. He then left the room and locked the door, taking the key out, and then gradually walked down stairs and bade some of the servants good bye, saying "he was going," and left the house.

"So you've got the sack, Jack," said the cook.

"I have," said Jack, "but it won't hold all I can put into it; however, good day to you."

Willoughby no sooner heard the door locked, and the sound of his feet descending the stairs, than he jumped out and began dressing himself in great haste, and threw up the window to watch for Jack's coming out of the house, which happened in less than two minutes.

"Thief, thief, stop thief," roared Willoughby, as he saw the form of Jack Grove issuing from the house. "Stop him, stop him! stop thief! hilloa! stop him!" Grove was not prepared for that, and scarcely knew what to do; it was no use going back—the mischief was done, and people could secure him if he went back to punish Willoughby—his only course was straight ahead, and away he ran; but was suddenly caught in the arms of a tall constable, who informed him he was his prisoner; and then, as Grove seemed inclined to contest the matter, the tall constable took out a pair of handcuffs out of his pocket, and with the help of another officer placed them upon Mr. Grove's wrists.

"There, now, my young feller, you may as well come back quietly and hear what the gentleman who's bawling out of the window has to say against you—eh?"

"Why there's no choice, I suppose," said Jack, "so I must when the devil drives me—Hobson's choice—eh?"

"Come, come, young feller, if you ain't civil, you will be handled a little; that's all I have to say to it."

Jack went back to the house, and Willoughby, after some delay, broke threw the door and came down. He gave him into custody for robbery; many of the things were found upon him, and he was forthwith hauled along to the office at once.

"You had better follow on quietly, sir, said the officer, who, I."

"Yes, 'cause you see the magistrates are sitting, and they will most likely commit him at once, or discharge him"

"I'll follow on immediately," said Willoughby; "the scoundrel deserves to be transported for his conduct."

"Aye, and so he will too," said the officer, who led Jack away, in company with the other officer.

It was some time before they reached the police office, and then he was placed in a cell until Mr. Willoughby should arrive, so that the case should be complete.

"Well," thought Jack Grove, "I'm here, fast enough; but yet, I think there is a chance for me now; I'll try—I don't think Willoughby will prosecute me in this case; I'll try and persuade him privately, not to do so on this occasion."

However, there appeared but little prospect of anything in the shape of mercy flowing from Willoughby. He would rather rejoice in the event of his being transported than otherwise. He would consider it in the light of a fortunate accident, that had removed a troublesome person out of his way.

"Now, young feller, your turn at the bar is come."

"Very good," said Jack Grove, "I'm called, eh?"

"Yes, and I expect you'll be grinding soon; so come along—comealong, I'll help you to a good place, where you can see what is going on all around you and where you can be seen by others."

"Very likely," said Jack; "do you stand beside me?"

"Yes."

"Very well, then they'll see a handsome man alongside a fool, eh? come, I am ready," said Jack.

In another three minutes Jack Grove was placed in the dock, and Mr. Willoughby then stepped up into the bar, to give his evidence.

"What's the charge?" inquired his worship.

"Robbery, your worship."

"Proceed with the evidence," said the magistrate; who, thereupon, placed the paper before him, and began to read.

Willoughby then began to to recount how he gave employment to Jack Grove, and how he had that morning returned the obligation, first by insolence, and then by putting him in fear of his life; and lastly, by robbing him of his watch, his money, and his jewels.

"What have you to say in answer to the charge," inquired the magistrate; "I am willing to hear you."

"I wish just to say one word to Mr. Willoughby," said Grove.

"You can't do so," said the magistrate, "you must say, what you have to say, before the bench."

"I will do so," replied Jack; "I only want to say it in Mr. Willoughby's ear; he wouldn't wish me do otherwise."

"You—you villain! I wish you—you would say I would connive at your villainy, I dare say."

"One word, sir, about the property. You'll never know the rights of it, if you don't, there's the fact on it."

Willoughby inclined his ear to Jack Grove, and the latter jerked his head towards the former, and he whispered something in his ear, and the effect was perceptible to all present, for Willoughby seemed uneasy.

"Well, sir" said the magistrate, "what have you to say?

"Why, your worship" said Grove, pointing to Willoughby, "he knows very well, he gave me what I took; he told me to do so."

"Eh?" said the magistrate.

"Yes," said Willoughby, looking unutterable perplexity; I—I—that is—there's a mistake about the matter—I don't wish to prosecute."

"But you have sworn to the charge."

"Oh have I?

"Yes, and we cannot permit you to compound a felony; you must proceed in this business, you know, the public are interested in this master; really, I don't know what to think of it."

"Oh he was drunk, sir," said Grove. "You were drunk, eh?" added Grove turning to Willoughby, "and then you told me to do what I did."

"Yes, yes; I had a little too much wine."

"And knocked your head against the bed-steps, eh? that was it, eh?"

"Yes, that was it, your worship; I must apologise; but I didn't recollect all that passed, until I was reminded it was the wine I was oblivious, and I had better make an early confession than commit an injustice."

"Yes, that's honest and fair," said Jack.

The magistrate looked first at one and then at the other, until he gathered breath enough to speak, and then he said, in a severe tone :—

"This charge never ought to have been brought here; I do not think I could receive another from the same party; I am astonished and disgusted at this proceeding. I beg you will both quit the court together."

"I ain't done nothing wrong," said Jack; "ain't I honorably acquitted what do you mean, then, by talking to me in that way?"

"Begone, sir! If you speak again, I'll construe it into a want of respect to the court, and have you committed."

"You may construe what you please," muttered Jack Grove, as he and Willoughby were both hustled out of court together; "you may construe what you like, but you can't construe my riddle."

CHAPTER LIV.

JACK GROVE'S INSOLENCE TO WILLOUGHBY.—MENTAL DISQUIETUDE OF THE COUNTESS OF CRUMBLEDOWN.—HER INTERVIEW WITH WILLOUGHBY.

THE morning sun shone through the splendid and elegant boudoir of the Countess of Crumbledown. All that was costly and glittering, proper to the place was there. No expense spared to procure those luxuries and refinements, which only the age and excellence of art could supply, to administer to the wants and acquired necessities of the wealthy. The softest carpets to the tread, well stuffed seats and ottomans, cases curiously inlaid with costly material, and constructed by yet more costly workmanship—all which shone here in their proper sphere. The blinds were down, and the sun's rays entered the apartment with diminished force, and shed a subdued and pleasant light through the whole room—a warm and glowing tint, one that would add to the feeling of enjoyment, which the owner of such a mansion might by ordinary mortals be supposed to enjoy to the full. But such was not the fate of the noble and opulent owner of the mansion, for the Countess of Crumbledown was in no mood to enjoy any one of those things, she was agitated by no ordinary feelings. The pride and all the feeling that animate a woman, were at war with a state of things she could not bear to reflect upon, but which yet met her thoughts, turn which way she would, and endeavour to avoid them how she could. She struck her hands passionately together, and stamped her foot on the carpeting, while her face and neck seemed crimson, and her features were strained to a look of agony, and a tear started from her eye, from the violence of her own emotion.

"Heaven!" she exclaimed, "I cannot endure it—wrong and deception surround me, and yet, like a victim at the stake, I am bound hand and foot. What on earth can be done?—What am I?—What can be the end of all this? One single false step, and I am lost, irretrievably ruined."

She paused a moment, while her features assumed an ashen hue, she sunk back in her chair, exclaiming softly—

"And what am I, if this woman lives? God of Heaven, what am I! I should be compelled to retire from life. I could not enter society again, for my dear friends would sympathize so much with me, that they would exhibit their joy in tormenting me. But, no, no, I will not do that; and yet, to remain inactive is dreadful, what to do I know not."

The countess arose, and paced in an agitated manner the boudoir; her hair hung dishevelled from behind her and over her shoulders, her eyes seemed red as if with weeping, and yet no tears seemed to be shed. She at length appeared to be exhausted and sank on an ottoman. Restless and fidgetty, she knew not what to do; she could not sit still, and she became wearied with emotion and her thoughts distracted, for she was scarce able to maintain her senses. She had a disposition to faint, and to hysterics; but she fought against her feelings, and succeeded in maintaining her consciousness, but at the same time it was at the expense of an agony of mind.

"I cannot bear it!" she exclaimed, after an interval of thought; "I cannot bear it. I must see that man and set him to ascertain if this woman be alive. I will visit him and ascertain what he knows; anything is better than this terrible state of indecision and torment. I will not remain in doubt—if she be alive, why, I am not the Countess of Crumbledown. Oh! heaven, what can I do! Nothing, literally nothing."

Overwhelmed by this thought she buried her face in her hands; but in a little while she arose, and taking a damp cloth she applied it to her eyes, and then sitting down, with her back to the light, rang the small silver bell that lay on the table. In a minute afterwards an attendant entered.

"Order the carriage to be ready in half an hour," said the countess.

"Yes, my lady," replied the menial.

"And do you come and assist in dressing me; I want to go out," added the countess, in a low tone.

"Yes, my lady," said the menial, who departed at once to give the necessary orders to the proper domestics; and then, in a short time, she returned to give the required assistance to her lady. This, when accomplished, occupied the time until the carriage was brought to the door, and the countess entered it, desiring the coachman to drive to Willoughby's office, where she determined that she would have an interview with the trickster. The drive was not a long one; and, when the inquiry was made if Mr. Willoughby was at home, and the answer was that he was, the countess descended from her carriage and entered the attorney's private office.

Now, Mr. Grove had been exceedingly independent in his behaviour to Willoughby; he was remarkably easy in his manners, and never thought of disturbing himself any more than he chose upon any occasion whatever, however urgent it might be.

"I say, Willoughby, what a stupid fellow you must be to think you could come it so strong over me at the police office the other morning. I tell you you you are all very well with some people, but not with me you know. You remembered the affair, eh?"

Willoughby did remember, but could not get the better of Jack Grove, so he said nothing but he spoke volumes, and Jack Grove went on,—

"I say, your eye looks better than it did; but you should have a raw beef steak applied to it."

"Will you mind your own business?" said Willoughby, growing angry.

"Yes; and so I am minding you, and can I do anything better than look after you, day after day, and see you don't do anything very foolish—but, I say, I'm blowed if there ain't a carriage drove up to the door, who can it be, I wonder?"

"Never mind who it is; go and answer the door."

"They ain't knocked yet, and I shan't be in a hurry; you ain't in a hurry, are you? I say, Willoughby, what would you say if I were dressed out in jewels, and rolling about in a carriage?"

Willoughby was too indignant to reply, though the answer was on the end of his tongue; he had a mind to have said he would have looked as much like a hog in armour as anything he could well understand. There was no time now to speak; for a thundering peal at the door announced the arrival.

"Is Mr. Willoughby at home?" inquired the powdered lacquey.

The answer being yes, the countess immediateey stepped out, and entered Willoughby's office. Of course, he knew her in a moment, and Jack Grove lingered in the office; the countess looked at him, and Willoughby turned with anger to Jack, saying,—

"Leave the room, Grove, leave the room."

Jack Grove did leave the room, and, as he did so, walked most audaciously in the face of Willoughby; and, when he shut the door, Jack applied his ear to it, and listened with great perseverance.

"Mr. Willoughby," said the countess, "you may be surprised to see me; but the fact is, the affair which you have informed me of has made me very uneasy, and I wish you to obtain some further information for me respecting this person."

"My lady," said Willoughby, "I am at your service; anything I can do I shall do with the greatest pleasure."

"I expect as much from you Mr. Willoughby," said the countess, "and I do not desire you should work without a proportionate reward."

Willoughby bowed, and the countess continued.

"I am naturally anxious to learn something about this affair, in which I am so much concerned, the point which I wish to ascertain, is this, does the mother of the child yet live? there is no certainty about the information I possess."

"Nor I my lady, though I have some suspicion that she does; I dare say, I can make some enquiries that may make it a matter beyond a doubt."

"I wish it to be done, but you really think that the mother lives, then?" inquired the countess eagerly."

"I do my lady."

"What is your reasons for so thinking, Mr. Willoughby?"

"They are difficult to explain, my lady, because I cannot allege one fact that may not be disputed as being any evidences but I may say, my impression decidedly is, that she is yet living, and is only kept quiet—I cannot precisely say how."

The countess shook, her whole frame seemed convulsed by a spasm; but it passed away, and she said—

"Do you think you could obtain any authentic information respecting her existence, because I should know how to guide myself in this affair what to do, or at least, what to abstain from doing."

"Exactly, that is very discreet of your ladyship, I do think I could obtain some information if I were to set regularly about it, heart and soul, and invest it with all my resources."

"What do you mean?"

"Why, my lady, I must spend a good bit of money, I must employ men to make inquiries, and must approach matters in an indirect mode, to prevent suspicions; and, lastly, I must be satisfied in more ways than one, of the truth of my information."

"That is very just," said the countess, "here is a fifty pound note, I will double it the moment you bring me the information I require of you; in the meantime money is no object, do your best, and whatever you require, I will furnish you with."

"Your ladyship deserves success, and a better fate,—I will do all that your ladyship desires, I will do what I can, though this will go but a short way towards defraying the expenses, as only descreet people can be employed, others are of no use, and it may be days of expense, before we can get even a hint, where she is to be found."

"Then you had better add this to it," said the countess, who handed him another fifty-pound note; "and now use what dispatch you may, for the state my mind is in is such, that I shall go mad if it continue many days longer thus."

"I will be as expeditious as the nature of the service will permit," said Willoughby, as the countess arose, and left the office.

Jack Grove opened the door with marvellous rapidity; indeed, had there been time for thought, there would have been a suspicion that he had stationed himself on the outside for the express purpose of ascertaining when the countess was about to quit the place.

"Mr. Tompkins," said Jack Grove, "walk in, Mr. Tompkins; Mr. Willoughby is now disengaged;" and Mr. Tompkins forthwith obeyed, and met Willoughby full in the face.

Willoughby saw Grove following the countess to her carriage, but was so completely absorbed and taken away by Mr. Tompkins's conversation, that he hought no more of the matter.

"I say, ma'am—my lady—countess—I know all about it."

The countess turned around with an air of anger, but was soon more terrified than angry; when Grove caught her by the arm, and winking very hard with his right eye, looked very wide-awake with his left; and said, in a low tone—

"I say, my lady countess, I have heered it all—I have listened at the blessed key-hole."

"Good God," said the countess, alarmed.

"Oh! my lady, it's all that infernal fellow Willoughby; but don't mind Willoughby, I know more than him."

"Who? what?" exclaimed the countess.

"I can't tell you here—he'll see me, and you won't know all; and he'll make you believe black's white. I'll get into the carriage, and tell you all as we go along."

"You had better get up behind," said the countess, drily; "but I hardly think I am doing right in believing what you say."

"You are the Countess of Crumbledown; and you come to know all about the young woman as the earl had a little girl by, I believe. Oh, that's the dodge, my lady countess."

"Yes, yes; get up behind, and I will talk to you when I come to a fitting place."

"Oh, very good," said Jack Grove, "I'm willing, if you are agreed. You ride inside, and I'll take an outside place—all's one to me; but, I say, young fellow," continued Jack, as he ascended the foot-board behind, "lacquey, don't you have a seat here."

The gentleman in plush breeches looked hard at Jack Grove, as if wondering what sort of animal he was, but he got but little out of Jack, save a stare in return.

They rolled rapidly on—the countess's carriage dashed forward, and the blinds were drawn up, and the countess leaned back in deep thought. She was bewildered and amazed at Jack Grove's conduct; and yet, situated as she was, she knew not what to do. She did not dare reject any probable or possible source of information; she was in a similar predicament as the drowning wretch, who would sooner grasp at a straw than sink without an effort. They soon arrived at Hyde Park, and there the countess commanded a halt, and then got out, ordering Jack Grove to descend; and then seeing that no one was at hand, she desired Jack to follow her towards the interior of the park—

"I can meet with no one I know here," she said, "and though passengers cross, they are strangers and pedestrians."

There was a pause of some moments, and when they had got about a hundred yards from the carriage, Jack Grove got alongside of the countess, who turned to him and said—

"Well, my good man, what have you to tell me—speak out honestly and boldly, and I will reward you."

"Thank you, ma'am—my lady. Mr. Willoughby does very little in that way, though he don't object to receive very largely. I knows what you came about to him, very well—I have heard of a few things since I came to him—I listen, you know."

"But that is very wrong."

"Can't say I see it is; at all events, I shall do it as long as I get a chance. Well, I was telling you I know what you came about. You wanted to know if Emily Whitford is dead."

"Emily Whitford?" said the countess.

"Yes, the lawyer's daughter—the young woman that the earl took up with, and the mother of the little girl."

"Ah, yes, I did. Do you know anything of her, eh? did you see her?"

"No; I never saw her, but my wife did, she and the earl came down to the inn, where I came from—they came down in a post-chaise and she was confined with this little girl there—it was done all in a hurry, a few hours after she stopped, and all was over."

"And the mother——?"

"What! will your ladyship, stand—"

"Stand!" exclaimed the countess in amazement, "I don't understand your country words, speak so that I can comprehend you."

"I mean, what will you give me for the secret that I can now, at this moment, give you, and which you have paid willingly for, and will have to pay more before he tells you, if he ever do so."

"I understand you now," said the countess, putting her hand into her reticule; "whatever this purse contains," she said, "is yours." As she spoke she opened the purse and turned out the contents of it into the hands of John Grove, who saw, with sparkling eyes, a very fair sprinkling of sovereigns amongst the silver.

"Well," said Jack, "I'll tell you, the young woman died in child-birth, the same time the young 'un saw the light."

"What do I hear," said the countess, delighted to an excess, "do you mean, truly, to say she's dead?"

"I do, and she is buried—I know the tomb."

"And Willoughby?"

"He knows it quite as well as I do, but he prefers drawing the money to making inquiries, and therefore he has not, nor would he, tell you the truth—I know it—he's a humbug—don't be led by him, or you'll find he's too much York for you."

The countess paused a moment—there was much that was incomprehensible about Jack Grove's speech—but then the general meaning was understood, and the countess said, after a while, "but did you see her a corpse?"

"I saw her tomb—I know those who saw her alive, and who saw her dead, an who followed her to the grave—there was an inquest held upon her, too."

"Indeed; then I need not fear her—dead—dead—aye, dead."

"Yes; dead enough, I reckon," said Jack Grove, who looked rather amazed at the countess, as she kept repeating the word, "dead," with a fervour and pleasure that never witnessed the like before.

"And Willoughby, too, he has practised upon my credulity."

"Lord bless you, my lady," said Jack, with great composure, "he'll practise upon anybody as would be fool enough to let him."

"I will go back and see him—I will tell him of his baseness, and expose him at once, the pettifogger; but may I rely upon what you say? Are you sure of all you have told me?"

"As sure," said Jack, composedly, "as you have got a head upon your shoulders. The earl and the young woman, as I said before, stopped at the village inn; the young woman was put to bed, the child was born, and the mother died."

"All passed very rapidly."

"I believe so; the next day, or the day after, an inquest was held, and she was buried, and my wife had the child to nurse. All this I know happened, and Willoughby knows it too, for I told him."

"Where was the earl at this time?"

"I don't know, but he wasn't there. I believe there were strangers down there at the time," said Jack; "and some of 'em might have been his friends, as I partly believe they were. He kept out of the way—it wouldn't have done for him to have remained. They would have asked him too many questions, and it wouldn't have been pleasant."

*　　　*　　　*　　　*　　　*　　　*　　　*

The countess said no more upon the subject; she, however, gave Jack some more money, for she was too well pleased with the information she had received to feel niggardly upon the occasion, and then, turning away abruptly, she returned towards her carriage, into which she entered, desiring to be driven back to Willoughby's office.

"The double-dealing villain," she muttered, "to extort money and play with my fears in this manner! Here have I suffered such torments that no tongue can describe, and all to no purpose. I would I could—that I dare punish him—but that cannot be done. I will, however, tell him I know him. I am well aware of his deception; he shall know that."

Angered as she was by the duplicity of Willoughby, yet her satisfaction at the intelligence that Emily was no more—this was salve to a severe wound that she had received; but it was not applied by the same hands, and she determined he should become acquainted with the fact. The ride in no way tended to soften down the angry passions that had been excited in her breast by the knowledge that she had been imposed upon by one whom she trusted. However, all things have an end, and so had the ride back to Willoughby's. Willoughby himself was at home, and awaiting the return of Jack Grove, whom he suspected to be playing him some trick.

"Oh, my lady," he exclaimed, as the countess entered the apartment, red and flushed with anger, "have I the pleasure of again seeing you?"

"I have come, sir, to tell you I have discovered your base and mercenary conduct; you have acted basely, sir."

"My lady—"

"Well, sir, you took money of me to discover if Emily Whitford was yet living, or dead."

"Yes, my lady, I did."

"And you knew that she had been dead ever since the birth of the child at the village inn—"

"I—I know she was dead?"

"Yes, I am credibly informed; I am assured she died at the birth of the child and has been buried there since that event."

"Your ladyship is misinformed entirely, I can assure you—I can convince you in one moment of the fact; I—I act dishonourably towards your ladyship; impossible, quite morally impossible!"

"Mr. Willoughby, this is absurd. I have neither time nor patience to bestow upon such matters; you have deceived me, I will never trust you more; it is the more culpable, as you must have been aware of the interest I have in the matter, and the mental disquiet I should feel."

"Do not name your rank, my lady—do not mention your name, and express no surprise at what I can show you; you shall be convinced—step this way, madam, step this way."

Willoughby beckoned her forward, and she in much amazement followed him across the apartment and opened a passage-door, there was another on the other side, and a glass in it.

"Here, my lady, look through there, and you will see if my opinion be correct: the true Countess of Crumbledown—she has called upon me quite unexpectedly, and now you have proof I do not deceive you."

The countess looked through the window and saw a young female dressed handsomely, weeping; but sitting, as if waiting for some one. The countess felt sick at heart; she at once sunk into a seat. Willoughby advised her to depart, saying, the young female—the countess, might come out, and an introduction mightn't be desirable; the countess had better retire to her carriage, which she did, trembling with apprehension—in fact, she was hardly able to command an appearance of equanimity.

CHAPTER LV.

THE CONSULTATION OF LADY CRUMBLEDOWN WITH HER MAID.—THE DREADFUL SUGGESTION.—THE WATCH SET UPON THE EARL, AND ITS RESULTS.

LADY CRUMBLEDOWN had an "own maid," named Margaret Manners—one who, under the guise of affection, contrived to become possessed of the confidence of the mistress she served—and, with a peculiar cunning, adapting herself and her counsel to what she believed the ultimate tendency of the wishes of her mistress led her to desire and to hope. But more than this was Margaret Manners a dangerous woman—she had much art about her. Cunning and unscrupulous at the same time, she possessed a hardihood and devilish disposition that well became one of her class, so situated, with regard to such a mistress as the Countess of Crumbledown. This woman became acquainted with the nature of the countess's conference with Willoughby. She had wormed the secret out of her mistress, who had but little motive for keeping it from one, whom she entrusted with many of the private opinions of her friends. Besides, something had been overheard—and the matter must come out some day or other; so it happened that her "own maid" Margaret was well acquainted with the fact. Lady Crumbledown was much harassed by the reflections that were consequent upon the recent communication she had received upon the subject of the child of Emily Whitford.

"My lady," said the maid, "you seem thoughtful; more—you seem as if you were grieved about something or other: you will spoil your eyes."

"Ah, Margaret! my mind is so much occupied—I have so great a cause to harass and destroy my peace of mind, about this affair of my lord's ——"

"Oh! the young female and her child?"

"Yes: that child may destroy our peace, and all hopes of enjoyment. I would I knew what to do!"

"Do you know where it is, my lady?"

" I do not : and if l did, I know not what I should do. The child, so long as it lives ——. What to do I do not know. It is quite a question as to what could be done, under any circumstances; for that child may mar all the hopes of my own."

Margaret was thoughtful for some time : some dark thoughts passed through her mind, but she spoke them not ; but she did say, in an insinuating tone—

" And while this child lives, my lady, your own daughter's prospects in life, as well as your own, may be marred."

" Undoubtedly."

" Then it follows, if she were dead you would be relieved of all these dreadful considerations. You would once more look as you used to look—free, and unembarrassed by any thoughts, save that which should be your only care—your daughter's education."

" 'Tis just so, Margaret," said the countess, laying her head on her hand, and relapsing into deep thought.

Margaret thought over several things at that moment ; and she did not disturb the cogitations of her lady, but kept herself busied about her ; while the countess herself appeared embarrassed, and scarcely to know which way to turn for help.

" Yes," she repeated aloud, as if she awoke up from her reverie, and during which she had been contemplating the same state of things she had been speaking about before. " Yes, Margaret, that is precisely what I would most desire ; but, awaiting the course of nature is uncertain, and terribly tedious ; and who knows the result?"

" Certainly, my lady, who does know the result ?" said Margaret Manners. " You yourself may die first ; and then you leave behind you an unprotected daughter—perhaps I might also say an orphan, if it should turn out so that the earl fancies the other child."

" True—very true."

" And then all you can fear while living is almost sure to take place when you are dead," said Margaret.

" It would : but what I can do to change such an awful state of things, I do not know," said the countess. " It is beyond my skill to indicate my way out of such a dillemma."

" It is hard : but I remember a fellow-servant of mine telling of a precisely similar case."

" Indeed ! I thought that such another case it would be impossible to find in the country," said the countess.

" No one knows, my lady, what is going on in families. It is all carefully hidden from ordinary eyes."

" That is most true."

" It is needless to fill the ears of every common body," replied Margaret ; " but the case that I am alluding to occurred not many years since in this country, and I believe in London."

" Who were the parties ?"

" There your ladyship asks more than I can tell, for she would not name the parties, it might result in mischief," she said, " and she would never name them."

" Well, she was right."

" Yes, my lady, she was, for it is not proper to divulge confidence. Well, there was a former child by a former wife—a secret affair, I believe ; but it was always in the power of the head of the family to place it in that position which her own child ought to occupy—he could make her heiress."

" Indeed, Margaret, that is my position."

" Aye, my lady, but here it was in the power of another person to do the same, by divulging the secret ; therefore, she was not safe, do what she would. If her husband died first, she had no security ; he was aware of the secret, it is true, but she could not be satisfied ; but, however, those might be well aware of that, she desired none should be implicitly informed."

" That is the case with me, Margaret. How singular, two such unfortunate persons should exist in the same age, or in the same century—it is amazing."

' Truth is stranger than fiction, my lady."

"I believe it; but what did this lady do in her case, which is so similar to mine? "

"Why, after much consideration and thought, she came to the full belief, that so long as the child lived, so long she would be unable to have one hour's repose, and at her death she should be unhappy and wretched, because of the uncertain fortunes of her daughter. Therefore, she thought if the child died first, all this would be satisfactory enough, and a great change take place ; and, moreover, that the sooner it took place the better ; but, to wait for the course of nature would be quite useless, therefore, she adopted the expedient of destroying the child."

"What!—murder it," exclaimed the countess, with a shudder.

"She did, my lady," said Margaret, coolly ; "she poisoned it, or something of that sort; nobody knew anything about it."

There was a long pause, during which the countess seemed to be considering the matter over in her mind; but she shrunk from the thought that there must be a violent death to relieve her from the object of her fears, but that object was a paramount one to her, and one that, as matters stood, she could not well accomplish by any other means that she could at that time imagine, and notwithstanding its repulsiveness, yet it was an only alternative, dreadful as it seemed to her mind ; but she shuddered at doing, or having any connection with an act that would have death for its result.

"No, no ;—I could not do that," said the countess, "though, Margaret, it would free me from my embarrassment."

"It would; there would be no fear of the future, only it's a desperate and uncomfortable thing."

"It is desperate."

"But sure," said Margaret Manners, abstractedly.

"Yes, sure, but how dreadful ! had I the will to do it I could not, for I do not know where she is—I am ignorant where the earl has placed her."

"That shows that he sets some store upon her—that he is taking great care of her, for some purpose or other."

"It does," said the countess, bitterly, "it does."

"Did not a Mrs. Grove have charge of her?" inquired Margaret; "I thought she had her as well as your own infant daughter, my lady."

"She did, but she has mine no longer ; she has, however this child. I believe she left her late abode suddenly and secretly, at the same time the child went with her, no doubt."

"Then she is somewhere that is discoverable, I must believe."

"But how can it be discovered? it would not do to ask the earl, that would betray oneself."

"Oh no, it is not to be expected he would do so, my lady, and it would, moreover, be imprudent to attempt it."

"It would ; but what can be done? "

"Oh, that is easily answered," said Margaret, "easily—the earl, no doubt, visits his child occasionally."

"Yes, that is certain."

"Then set a watch upon him, and follow him about from place to place, until he has been traced to the one you want to find out, then you will know, at the same time he will know nothing about it at all," said Margaret.

"That is certainly a very good plan—a very excellent plan, but I do not know how to adopt it.

"Why not, my lady?"

"I know no one to whom I could entrust such a commission with," said the countess, thoughtfully.

"But I do, my lady ; and one too who is at least well calculated to perform such a job well ; he is a distant relation of my own, he is out of situation now, and has therefore time enough to spare to follow the earl about, for days, if need be."

"Well then, Margaret, you shall tell this person what is wanted of him, and he shall be paid handsomely if he succeeds, but at the same time tell him no more than is at all absolutely necessary, nor even who requires it of him."

"Exactly, my lady; I will take care that he is properly instructed and set upon his watch."

"Then do so—do so, as soon as you can," said the countess.

*   *   *   *   *   *   *

The same evening Margaret Manners had an interview with her relation, who was a footman out of place—just the man capable of performing such a service, or any other piece of knavery, that would bring him in any money and give him an idle life. He had left his last situation for some peice of misconduct, and now was hanging about, living as best he could. It was with something like pleasure that he received the instructions that were given him, to ascertain if the earl went to visit a Mrs. Grove and a child, or any place where there was a child, that was the object of his visit; this done, he was to inform her of what had taken place, and where the earl had been to, and the name of the place, with every other piece of information he could obtain, that bore at all upon the points they desired to be informed of.

"Now," said the man, "I don't know the earl; what shall I do to see him? I must have him shown to me."

"That is easily done, he is at home now; you can watch him go out, and meet him full face to face; you will be sure to know him again; he will not remain in long."

"If I fairly see him once, it will do; but I have seen him, I think, at all events I don't know him now, I may when I come to see him a little, for there aint many people I don't know something of," said the man, with a grin.

"Well, do this piece of business well, and you'll get well paid for it."

"That is just what I like; I'll stick to him like a leech; if he attempt to double I'll double too, and so we will dodge till we are tired, and he goes to the house of the young lady."

"Mind you don't be seen or betray yourself, for you will spoil all, and get yourself into trouble to boot."

"Never fear me; I will be caution itself."

With such a promise the man left the place, and went and stationed himself at the door of the Earl of Crumbledon's mansion, and there awaited his coming out. For this he had not long to wait, for the earl was dressed for walking, and left the house. As he came out he was met by an acquaintance, who, touching his hat, said, "Good morning, my lord!" and passed on.

"Oh," thought the man, "now I am sure of my bird, I will stick by him until he goes back again."

The earl walked down the street, and after him as a shadow, but at some distance, and followed him thus through some streets until the earl stopped; at this place the earl looked round and saw the man look after him. This was the Travellers' Club House, and after a moment the earl went in, and when he had vanished, the spy walked up the steps, and seeing the porter alone, said to him—

"Has the Earl of Crumbledown gone in?"

"He just went through," said the porter, "not a minute since."

"Thank you, I will be in immediately."

And so saying he left the club-house, and stationed himself in the immediate neighbourhood, so as to command a view of the entrance of the club-house, so that no one could go in or out without his seeing them do so. Here he waited for upwards of an hour, and yet the earl came not out, and the spy began to wax impatient—but yet there was no help—stop there he must, lest the earl come out, and he should, by missing him once, lose the whole of the day's labour, and perhaps many more. After about another half-hour the earl came out, and proceeded in another direction until he had gone some distance, when he turned round again suddenly and looked at the man who was following him, but he seemed to be thinking of something, for he looked one of those peculiar looks in which people look without seeing, fixing their eyes upon an object while the mind is so occupied that it receives no idea or notion of any object by means of the external senses.

"He doesn't see me," muttered the fellow to himself, "he doesn't see me, I know, he's in a brown study."

The earl turned round, and walked in the direction he came, and he once more entered the Travellers' Club House, where he remained for some time longer.

"Confound it," muttered the man, "here's a pretty go; will he remain here for another hour and a-half? he will, I dare say, but there's no help for it, but—but I am mortal dry."

This reflection caused him to look around him, and on the opposite side of the way he perceived a small turning, at the corner of which was a public-house; he could make a sudden dash, it wasn't far, and the earl could not very well escape him; it was close at hand, and—and he would make the attempt. He was very hot and very dry—what could he do?—he was tired to extremity.

A moment more, and giving a look at the club-house as though he would have pierced the walls, had eye-sight been able to do it, and then made a sudden dart across the road, one more look, and then bolted into the public-house.

"Hilloa!" said a man, "where the devil are you coming to?"

"I'm in a hurry."

"Well, then, I aint; but what does that signify to me? I am not to have my beer knocked out of my hand because you are in a hurry! You'll get to the gallows too soon, I'm afraid."

"Well, well, I didn't go to do it—I'm sorry for it," said the man, as he walked up to the bar, not wishing to get into a quarrel at that moment, which was the most inconvenient he could possibly find, to have any cause for detention; "a pint of ale," said the man.

"Yes," replied the barmaid; "where's the pot a-going to?"

"Not far."

"Where to?"

"To my mouth, miss, but I won't swallow it."

The young lady behind the bar took the money, and watched the progress of the ale down his throat; he took two-thirds before he stopped, and then only for breath; and while he did so, he worked the pot round with the contents, and then, after breathing once or twice, he drank down the remainder and set the pot down.

"Well, I'm blowed," said a coalheaver, "if you warn't dry. If I had done that I should have been on the floor: you've a strong head, and you are foracious."

"Well," thought the man, "I was dry, and I never tasted anything I liked so well."

Without waiting to reply to any remark he rushed out of the house to his former position. At the same time he cast an eye to the right and to the left, to see if the bird in the bush had flown, but seeing nothing of him, he again ensconced himself in his place of espial, and then waited more patiently for the earl's appearance.

"Well, he does make a long stay," he muttered; "if he's going to stay much longer I shall go to sleep. Ah! it's all through the ale, I have no doubt about it; I shan't be able to help myself — to sleep I shall go — and no mistake about it either."

He nodded fearfully, and tried to keep his eyes open, but he was scarce equal to the task; however—suddenly the next moment, just as he had shaken himself and forced his eyes open, the earl again came out and walked away.

"There he is, by Jove!" said the fellow, "just in time—I should have been asleep in another minute. I'm off now. I'll keep on his track as close as a tiger cat; I'll be on to him in double quick time, but I'll be very cautious."

He was so cautious, that the extremity of caution which he used caused people to look at him; and, eventually, the earl looked around and watched him a few moments. He walked on again for some distance, and then again he turned round, and on he went as before.

"Where the deuce he can be going to I don't know, but I'll follow him. I'll warrant he is going to the place they want to find out; it's quiet and retired enough here, just such a place as one would select for hidden purposes, if he wanted to be quiet and snug."

He pushed on, however, very close after the earl, the ale having emboldened him, and believing himself to be perfectly unnoticed, he came up close to the earl in the middle of a very quiet street, expecting to see which house he was about to enter, when the earl suddenly turned upon him, and said,—

"Fellow, who set you to watch and dodge me?"

"Who? I—oh! yes—that is—no—I—nobody told me to do so, my lord."

His lordship, however, was well convinced by the confusion of speech that came over him in consequence of the sudden and unexpected interrogatory of the earl, that he was quite unprepared for anything of the sort.

The earl did not wait a moment hardly for an answer, but in the next minute took the cane which he carried and laid it about, suddenly, his head and shoulders, that he was confused, stunned, and unable even to cry out, much less to make any resistance to the assault, which was continued with great vigour and perseverance.

"Mercy! mercy!" he at length called out, but not in a very loud tone; "I am done, I am done! I'll never do the like again—I'll go another way, I will, indeed!"

The earl finished the chastisement with a hearty kick that sent the unlucky spy flying into the road; he then turned round and walked slowly away from the spot.

"Oh, Lord! oh, Lord!" exclaimed the unlucky spy, getting upon his legs; "well, well, well, I am done, regularly done, I hadn't a chance! What can a man do when another man wollops him over the head with blows, and gives him no chance even to take care of myself?"

He brushed the dirt off his clothes as well as he could, and propped himself up against a door to wait awhile till some of the effects of the ale, and the severe drubbing he had received, should have worn itself away and left him a little more of the use of his faculties than he had at that moment.

CHAPTER LVI.

THE INTERVIEW BETWEEN THE EARL AND HIS CHILD.—THE RESIGNATION.—
THE SPY'S ACCOUNT OF HIMSELF.—THE COUNTESS'S ANGER.

WHEN the earl had thus got rid of the impertinent spy who dodged his footsteps so closely, he walked on for some time in deep and painful thought—painful, because now he felt quite convinced that the countess had all her suspicions by some means aroused, and had taken that means of discovering his haunts.

And yet being, as he was, in complete ignorance of all the affairs connected with Willoughby and her, he could not imagine in what way she had managed to possess herself of information.

If, however, there ever was a time—when, with great safety and a total absence of all fear of being dodged to his place of destination, he could visit his child towards whom his best feelings always tended—it was now—now, that he had discovered and got rid of the spy that was following him.

Accordingly he bent his steps at once in the direction where Mrs. Grove had taken up her abode with the little innocent, which such a strange combination of circumstances had placed in her motherly care.

"I must endeavour to ascertain fully," he told himself, "what is the meaning of the system of *espionage* to which I am, it appears, subjected. I really need scarcely care whether or no the countess is aware of that episode in my life, which will ever be so great and so bitter a resource of regret to me; she has no feelings to outrage, and she can do nothing."

Still, although he was able to argue thus, and although what he said was perfectly true, the earl had no desire that his countess should know anything of the affair of Emily Whitford, because it was one which, day by day, he had though more seriously of ever since its occurrence, and the more he saw of the world the more he bitterly repented of the part he had taken in the transaction.

"I do not want," he thought, "to hear her name uttered by unfriendly lips; I do not want to answer the bitter sneers of contempt with which she would make some remarks upon the matter, and, perchance, characterise e innocent child by epithets I would not hear from any lips, and yet have no effectual means of stopping her from uttering."

For these considerations, then, and not from any feeling that the virtue of the countess would be so much outraged, or her affections wounded that she would suffer any pangs, the earl was still most intent upon keeping secret that intrigue, which, in one respect, had terminated so fatally, and which had yet, although he did not think so, to produce results of the most awful and the most agonising character that can be imagined.

The distance from the place he had had the fracas with the spy to where Mrs. Grove and the child was staying was rather considerable, but as the earl felt inclined for walking, and the full occupation of his mind prevented him from feeling any symptoms of fatigue, he proceeded, on foot, until he came to the hous which he had provided for her, and where certainly every comfort was prepa ed fo the Love Child.

His voice at the door soon procured him admission, and Mrs. Grove received him with all her usual courtesy.

In answer to his first inquiries, he was at once informed that the child was in perfect health and spirits, and that not the least alarm of any sort had arisen which could by any possibility be construed into a belief that mischief was meditated; so that the earl felt perfectly certain that in being followed as he had been himself, nd in discovering and defeating that intention, he had most probably discovered in the outset the projected danger, and put an end to it.

Nevertheless, he told Mrs. Grove that he had reasons to suppose efforts were being made for the purpose of discovering her place of residence, and that, consequently, he wished her to be more than usually careful and circumspect in her intercourse with strangers.

As our readers may well suppose, the child was now of an age to distinguish individuals well, and to observe and make a number of comments upon circumstances and upon people, with all the freshness and originality of intellect which belongs to the young.

And children seem to have an intuitive kind of perception concerning the real character of caresses.

They quickly discover those mere lip-words of kindness—which civility puts into the mouths of those who address them—from the real accents of genuine affection; and thus it was, that although the child knew not of the closeness of connexion between it and the earl, it clung to him ever with a fondness of manner that touched him to the heart.

"I cannot," he whispered, as he bent over it caressingly, "I cannot now alter the circumstances attendant upon your birth, my child; but I can and will bestow upon you the means of making life glide gently onward, and of lifting you very far indeed above those sad disasters and changes of time and circumstances which affect those who have to cast themselves into the vast arena of society to battle for an existence: I can and will do that much for you."

"And why should she not be happy?" said Mrs. Grove, who could not help overhearing some of the earl's words. "Why should she not be happy, under such circumstances?"

"I hope she will be happy. The age is getting more liberal than to visit directly upon the heads of the children the sins of the parent."

"Most certainly, my lord; and now that you are here, there is one subject concerning which I wish to speak to you, and upon which I hope I shall receive from you a favourable answer."

"Say on, I shall attend most willingly to all you have to utter."

"I wish to know what you intend doing as regards the education of the child."

"It is a subject I have not reflected upon; but by your manner, I presume you have already formed some opinion."

"I have, my lord; I should certainly advise that some unexceptionable boarding-school in a distant part of the country be chosen for the child."

"You are willing, then, to resign your charge?"

A slight flush of colour came across the cheek of Mrs. Grove, as she replied,—

"I am, for my charge's advantage most certainly, because I think that I cannot myself hope to impart to her anything beyond the mere rudiments of education, such as I am sure it is your wish she should receive."

The earl was a little surprised at the readiness with which Mrs. Grove was willing to part with the child, but he nevertheless promised her that he would take the subject into consideration, since she had mooted it, and give her an early and decisive answer; but after this, she surprised him still more by a request she made him.

"I have been thinking," she said, "that when the child leaves me, I shall be dull and spiritless, and therefore should wish much to adopt some line of life that would rescue me from such a state of things. The misconduct of my husband makes it to me a matter of great congratulation that he knows not where to find me ; and I was thinking, if it would be consistent with your arrangements, that I should like much a situation in your household."

" Indeed ! you surprise me."

" I have been accustomed to occupation all my life ; and as my own child has now gone down to one of the midland counties to reside with some relatives, I am sure I shall feel lonely."

" Well," said the earl, " I see no objection, except the great difficulty of me interfering in the employment of any female domestic, but that I will likewise consider, and if it can be managed you may rely upon it it shall, for I owe you too heavy a debt of gratitude not to endeavour to do all I can to meet your wishes."

She seemed well satisfied with this promise, and the earl shortly took his leave, but he could not conceal from himself that there was something in the conduct of Mrs. Grove that surprised him, and the impression began to steal over him that she must have been planning something, the reasons for which she chose to keep to herself. Knowing the great antipathy that she had to his countess, he was wonderfully surprised that she should ask for a situation in his household, which would bring her into contact occasionally with her in a manner that she would find it difficult to defend herself. Besides, there was all the chance of the countess knowing her, and that consideration almost decided the question in the earl's mind, making him think that the proposed scheme would be highly imprudent.

*　　　*　　　*　　　*　　　*　　　*　　　*

While the earl was thus engaged, the spy which the countess and her maid had employed for the purpose of dodging the footsteps of the earl, sufficiently recovered to be thinking that it would be necessary to give some account of his mission. The disappointment which was likely to ensue from his failure was nothing to him in comparison with the stop that might be put to his supplies of ways and means in consequence ; and not being the most scrupulous person in the world, he resolved upon concocting some tale which should carry with it an appearance of probability, although it really had none.

He accordingly proceeded to the earl's house, and when he saw Margaret he shook his head with great gravity—an assumption of wisdom, however, which did not deceive her in the least, for she saw, in a moment, that he had been indulging in what she had before suspected, although he had always stoutly denied it—his besetting sin, drink.

She heard him patiently to an end, and his story was this :—

" I have found out the earl," he said, " and followed him closely, but yet so closely as not to excite the least suspicion ; and he proceeded for some distance towards Brompton, when suddenly, at the corner of a street where there was a livery stable, he stopped and blew a mysterious whistle, when out came a chariot, drawn by two cream-coloured horses. He got in and drove off, at fourteen miles an hour ; and, although I ran after him six miles down the Uxbridge-road without stopping, of course I could not come up with him going at the rate he was, and now, as you may very well suppose, I am thirsty."

" I dare say you are," said Margaret.

" Yes, I am, I assure you."

" Very good ; of course we highly appreciate your great services ; but it so happens that we shall not require them any further."

" Not require them ?"

" No, we shall give it up, since the earl takes such extraordinary precautions to prevent himself from being followed ; and, as it is quite out of the question to go after a man who drives at fourteen miles in an hour, we shall not attempt it any further."

" But don't you think it's a pity to give it up ?"

" Most certainly I do ; but you have supplied us with such a good reason for doing so that I cannot perceive how we can do otherwise."

" Well, but perhaps he didn't go quite at fourteen miles."

" Oh! if you have any doubts about the accuracy of your statement, I am quite certain that it will not do to have anything more to say to it; so the best thing you can do is to drop the whole affair and think no more of it."

" Confound it! that's rather hard."

" I cannot perceive that it is so; and, what is more, my time is too valuable to be taken up in frivolous conversation with you."

So saying, she walked out of the room, leaving him to digest his disappointment as best he might, and to find, like most exaggerators of the truth, that he had only thereby succeeded in deceiving one person, and that was himself; for, probably, had he stated the simple facts and promised amendment, he might have had another trial given him; but the mysterious whistle and the two cream-coloured horses, going at fourteen miles an hour, completely did the business altogether. The waiting-maid was much vexed at the issue of this affair, because she had selected the spy; and she resolved to keep it from her mistress until she could think of some better means of accomplishing the object of the Countess of Crumbledown.

CHAPTER LVII.

THE MYSTERIOUS COMMUNICATION TO THE EARL.—THE CONSULTATION.

WHILE these things were in agitation, and while the feelings of Lady Crumbledown were in that state of alarm and agitation which we have depicted, and while, we fear, she is revolving in her mind the commission of some very serious offence, for the sake of freeing herself from what she considers unjust embarrassments, a circumstance occurred which had a material effect upon the mind of the earl.

One day that he was sitting alone in his library, and ruminating over affairs that were not of the pleasantest character, it was announced to him that a man earnestly desired to see him upon particular and private business, which he could and would communicate to no one but himself. Of course persons in the situation in life of the Earl of Crumbledown are subjected to a great number of annoyances which people in an inferior station escape, and they are forced to make themselves difficult of access to strangers.

" You can tell him," said the earl, " that I cannot and will not see him unless he declares his business, and it must then turn out to be of a nature that I choose to attend too, but not otherwise."

This message was, no doubt, duly delivered; and a reply was brought back that the earl would be the last person in the world to wish him to declare his business to any one but himself, and that, if his lordship was not then at leisure to see him, he must call again and again until he was.

The pertinacity with which the stranger thus adhered to his purpose awakened a curiosity in the breast of the Earl of Crumbledown which made him half resolved to see him; and, after a few moments' consideration, he said to the servant who had brought the message, " What sort of a man is he?"

" He is what we generally call shabby-genteel, my lord; he looks as if he had seen better days."

" But is there anything of the blackguard or ruffian about him?"

" No, my lord; I cannot say there is."

" Then show him in here at once; I will see him."

The Earl of Crumbledown waited with some sort of curiosity the coming of his visitor, and he almost trembled, as a sort of dim feeling came over him, that possibly some sort of communication was going to be made which would be uncomfortable in its character and very unpleasant for him to hear. But then, strange to say, these are not the sort of communications from which human nature shrinks, but the very things which, on the contrary, people take the greatest possible pains to get at; and, when once the notion came across the Earl of Crumbledown that this stranger might have something uncomfortable to say regarding his affairs, the resolution to see him became fixed and unalterable.

He waited, with his eyes fixed upon the door, the appearance of this man, who yet, for all he knew, might only be some extremely artful beggar, who adopted that mode of awakening curiosity, and getting admission by such means to the mansions of persons of wealth and rank. Indeed this was too likely to be the case ; and so confident did the servant who came to announce the shabby-genteel man feel upon that subject, that before he delivered to him the message to the effect that the earl would see him, he said,—

"If it's any charity affair, I should advise you not to see his lordship, for you will only put him in a passion, and get nothing from him, in consequence of coming under false pretences."

"I am very much obliged to you for your caution," was the reply, "and do not in the least take it in bad part, but it is not so, and, therefore, I do not expect a rebuff of that description."

The servant, thereupon led him at once into the library, and, not a little curious himself to ascertain what it was he came about, although he dare not take any steps to satisfy that curiosity, he left the stranger with the earl.

There was something of the appearance of a decayed gentleman about the man, and, as he looked in the face of the Earl of Crumbledown, it seemed as if he hesitated, even now that he had gone so far, whether he should make a communication or not, which was probably calculated to give pain to him who heard it. The earl was rather struck with his manner, although he did fancy that he saw something about the man, which bespoke the fact of dissipation, being one of the most prominent causes, if not the principal and only one, of the present decayed state of his fortunes.

"Pray, be seated, sir," said the earl, ' you have expressed a desire to see me upon important business ; I need not say that my time is very much occupied, and therefore, before you commence, I sincerely hope that it not only is important business that brings you to me, but that it is that which likewise concerns me, otherwise, I must request of you to leave me at once."

"I have no doubt, my lord," said the stranger, "that you are subject to quite sufficient annoying visits to make it necessary that you should give utterance to some such speech, and, if my business were not of an important nature, and did not concern you, I do not think that I should be proof against what you have said, but should go at once."

"Then, sir," "said the earl, "I am sure you will excuse me for making the remark I did, because it cannot apply to you in any respect. I shall listen with great attention to anything you have to say."

"Very good, my lord, very good, and yet I scarcely know how to begin."

The stranger hesitated for several moments, during which time the Earl of Crumbledown employed his imagination in speculating as to his age, &c. He appeared to be verging upon sixty, at the very least, and yet to have had one of those constitutions which, with ordinary care, would long have withstood the assaults of time, only that it unfortunately happens, people who are blessed with such great physical energies like men with large fortunes, take but little care of that which seems inexhaustible, and at length find themselves complete bankrupts in health, while the man of only ordinary powers, who has all along felt the necessity of being careful, completely beats them out of the field.

When he did speak it was in a voice rather tremulous, that he said—

"I have not been long in this country, although an Englishman born and bred, but, during the short time I have been here, I have made some careful inquiries concerning you."

"Concerning me !"

"Yes, my lord, concerning you, although I never heard your name till three weeks ago."

"Indeed :and pray what interest can my affairs have for you?"

"That I shall proceed to tell you: and, in the first place, I wish your lordship would contradict me, if what I have heard is not true, and likewise excuse the freedom with which I feel myself compelled to speak."

"Say on," said the earl, whose curiosity was strongly aroused, "say on—what is it?"

"It is this: I have heard that you do not live the happiest of lives with your wife."

"You are right enough, sir," said the earl, "in characterizing that as a very singular question to come from a stranger, for a more remarkable one I certainly never heard."

"It would be a most insolent one," said the man, "if I could not supply you with some excellent reason why I ask it, but, as I can supply you with such a reason, it loses that character. I do not ask you, my lord, to answer me in the affirmative, I am quite satisfied that you do not instantly deny the fact, and, therefore, I feel that I can proceed, at once, to explain to you what I mean."

"Well, sir, proceed."

"I do not think it is in my power, completely, to undo your marriage with the countess, because the means I possesss involve some points of law, which, certainly, have been disputed, but I learn that she is proud and haughty, like her mother, so I think I can give you a power over her of such a character as she will not feel inclined to dispute."

"This is a madman," thought the earl, "and my best plan, I suppose, will be to get rid of him as quietly as I can."

"Well, sir, may I ask what means they are to which you allude?"

"I will tell you. You are aware that the Marquis of Fanfarronade was not the cleverest man in the world, in fact, a more blundering idiot could scarcely have been conceived, and when he married he little guessed the state of subjection in which he would be kept by one of the most imperious women that ever stepped. They went to reside for some time abroad, and there are, possibly, even now, some old servants of the family who perfectly recollect that the lady Arrabella, now your wife, did not go with them, but yet that suddenly she appeared in Rome as part of the family, being then only three years of age."

"Suddenly appeared!" said the earl, "at three years of age—is not that rather a remarkable phenomenon?"

"Very, if it were not accounted for; but she was brought from England, and at once domesticated in the family."

"But do you mean to tell me that she was not the daughter of the Marchioness of Fanfarronade?" cried the earl, growing deeply interested in what the stranger said.

"I do not mean to tell you any such thing," he replied; "on the contrary, I hope to be in a position to prove to you, in spite of any doubts that may be attempted, and they will be attempted to be thrown upon that fact, that she unquestionably and incontestably is the daughter of the Marchioness of Fanfarronade."

"I know she is—you speak in riddles to me."

"Riddles," said the stranger, "which a very few words will, I think, suffice to explain. May she not be the daughter of the marchioness without, as a matter of actual necessity, being likewise the daughter of the marquis?"

The earl started and drew his chair back several paces, as he cried—

"Not the daughter of the marquis! then who, in the name of all that's damnable, is her father?"

"Your very humble servant."

"Oh! absurd, absurd!"

"I quite expected you would say that."

"This is the height of improbability."

"And that, too, I quite expected you would say; but a plain tale shall set the question at rest. There was a time when I called myself a gentleman, and held a captain's commission in the Guards—that was four years before the marriage of the Marquis of Fanfarronade with his wife. After that they went abroad, and she, by dint of violence and that sort of control which a strong mind possesses over a singularly weak one, enforced upon him a consent to receive what she first represented as an orphan child confided to her care, but which she afterwards, with unblushing effrontery, declared to be her own, and you may guess the great and singular power this woman had acquired over what might be called her poor victim, the marquis, when he actually put up with this insult, and kept the secret until the day of his death, I am convinced, from positive fear. When he was dying there can be no doubt but he would have made a disclosure had the marchioness not kept close to him, and even in his last moments his habitual dread of her was sufficient to close his lips upon a matter which it would have been just as well if you had known a year or two ago."

The earl rose and paced the room with agitated steps, and then he said—

"The mere word of a stranger cannot suffice for such a tale as this."

"I know it cannot, and whenever it is required I can produce such condemnative proof as shall convince you."

"But if this be true, she whom I have married, not being the person represented, surely cannot in law be my wife."

"The point has been disputed, but I think you are wrong, and an error in the name of a party will not invalidate a marriage. I think, therefore, that the only power this circumstance will give you will be a power to make yourself more comfortable by exercising a kind of control over the woman who is now so high and so haughty that she attempts to exercise such control over all who come within her reach."

"But do you think that she is ignorant of the circumstances?"

"Let's think so; but whether she be or not, it is your knowledge of it, which will give you power, and you will be much to blame if you do not use it."

"You take me so by surprise, sir, by the communication you have made, that I know not what to say to it. I am perfectly astonished, for, until now, I never entertained the remotest doubt of the legitimacy of the countess."

"Nor should you now, but that I ascertained how unamiable her conduct was; had she been like Julia Fanfarronade, who, I have heard, is the soul of honour, and as amiable as she is beautiful, I should never have interfered to mar her happiness, by a recital of these circumstances."

"Peace, peace! do not name Julia Fanfarronade to me"

The earl pronounced these words in such an agonized tone, and sunk into a chair with such a deep sigh, that the stranger looked at him with surprise, and then broke a short silence, by saying—

"Is it possible that you loved Julia Fanfarronade, and yet wedded her not?"

"It is possible—it is true; I did love her, and had taken pains to awaken in her breast corresponding sentiments, but a set of circumstances, over which there is no control, forced me to become her sister's husband."

"I have heard of the singular will your father made, and of its result, and I felt that although the news I brought you was such as you ought to know, and that if it was properly used it would give you a power you have not yet possessed of controlling the actions of your countess, it would yet bring with it a pang of another kind."

"A world of pangs—a world of pangs!"

"Believe me, I was not aware, in the slightest degree, of the attachment between you and Julia."

"She despises me now, she utterly and entirely despises me, and the last time our eyes met, her face wore the look of deep contempt she felt for the man who sold his heart for gold."

"And you, likewise, now must have the reflection, that although aware your wife is not the person she was represented to be, cannot free you from your matrimonial fetters; it would, both in law and in equity, have completely set aside your father's will."

"And I should have inherited everything."

"Everything, if you had wedded, as your heart dictated, with Julia Fanfarronade, and just struggled through these few years without your princely fortune; yon would have recovered every penny of it, because you perceive you would have proved that.'

"Peace, peace! Do you want to drive me mad? I know it all—I see it all. I require no suggestions upon the subject, for, dependent upon the one condition that you are able to prove what you assert, I might have been the happiest of men, instead of being, as I am, the most wretched."

"Wretched!" exclaimed the stranger; "do I hear aright? and have I been so long repining at my own indifferent fortunes? Do I hear a man, with an earl's coronet upon his brow, and an income that is enormous, call himself wretched?"

"Yes," cried the earl, vehemently; "and from me and my career let all men learn that there may be as aching a heart beneath the glitting star of an emperor's breast as within the bosom of the poorest wretch, who goes from door to door solicing the means whereby he may support the current wants of nature, learn from me that it is but a wild delusion to suppose that wealth and contentment walk hand-in-hand together."

"It is true," said the stranger, as he rose; "but believe me, my lord, I have not come to you to awaken awful reflections. I have myself passed through a long life of error, and have nearly reached its close without having the felicity of being able to tell myself that I have done six things throughout my whole existence that I can look back to with pleasure."

"I wish you had not come and told me this intelligence."

"If you say so, I wish I had not; but it was with a view of bettering your condition that I came—to give you the power of curtailing an imperious woman, for, although she is my daughter, I have had enough to make me mourn for what she is, and wish that the arrogant pride which possesses her should be mingled with some sort of humility."

"Listen to me! since you have come and made to me this communication, there must be no doubt left upon my mind upon the subject; I must have proof—ample and substantial—such proof as it is impossible to doubt—a proof that shall not leave the shadow of a loop-hole for hesitation."

"That you shall have; I will not and ought not to deny it to you."

"You have not told me who you are?"

"But I will do so: my name is Moffat, and I am nothing now but an adventurer; I was, as I mentioned to you, something very different, but that is long ago, very long ago."

"Do you require assistance of me?"

"I do not; I manage to make a subsistence by a cultivation of a branch of the arts in which I was once a proficient; and, if I were now to ask of you any assistance of a pecuniary character, it would be at once to throw discredit upon any exertion that I might make to be beneficial to you, and upon the motives which I have alleged I had in making to you a communication such painful interest as that which I now make. I will call upon you, my lord, at any time you please to appoint."

"Leave me an address where I may write to you, and you shall hear from me as soon as I have got my mind in such a train that I can really enter into the subject calmly and dispassionately."

The stranger left a card, containing his name and address, with the earl, and then at once departed from his house.

"Alas, alas!" murmured the Earl of Crumbledown, when he found himself alone; "am I not now justly punished for the evils I have done? Oh! Emily, Emily! if you could but look up from your grave and see how truly wretched I have become, even you would see that a retribution had overtaken me, and I should have your full forgiveness for the errors of the past."

CHAPTER LVII.

THE CRIME STILL CONTEMPLATED.

It is one of the phenomena of the human mind that it may become familiarised with anything by use, and so at last rob it of all the colours that it had first wore.

So it was with Lady Crumbledown, as she revolved in her mind the means of getting rid of that most obnoxious of all existences to her—the Love Child.

Tortured as she was by a thousand doubts with regard to its actual position, and having, as she had, more evidence, a great deal presented to her to make her think it a dangerous rival for her own child; the thought never left her, by night or by day, that she should know no peace while it was in existence.

With all her pride, with all her arrogance, and withal, what we may call her insolent ferocity of temper, the lady had certainly not yet ever contemplated, until these circumstances arose, going so deeply into iniquity as actually to take the life of any one who stood between her and her desires.

She was capable of achieving a great deal, but scarcely that it was a reach even beyond her to dream of; but now that by degrees she gradually got familiar with the frightful notion, she began to entertain it with a degree of force and power such as she never expected it could have possibly assumed to her mind.

It became the one prevailing notion of her intellect, overpowering all other considerations, and rendering them completely nugatory as regarded the production of any actual mental result.

She would sit for hours together brooding over such thoughts, until she almost felt a kind of insanity steal over her that was frightful to contemplate

"What am I to do?" she said; "am I to submit to all the degradation which may be in store for me, or shall I, by a vigorous opposition to it, place myself in a far different position? What is a life when it stands between me and such objects? Are not hundreds and thousands of human existences sacrificed for the most trivial purposes, and shall I not achieve as great an object as I have in view by the sacrifice of one? shall I hesitate at a matter of such paramount importance that it comes next me and my very heart, because a life stands in my way, no—I will not —I cannot—it shall not be said that I was bold enough to project what I was not bold enough to execute. I will achieve something, or in a vain endeavour to do so, perish!"

Such were the sentiments which actuated this desperate woman, and from what we know of her we can well suppose that no feelings of mercy or consideration would withhold her arm, if she chose to strike a blow. Unhappily we know amply sufficient of Lady Crumbledown to feel assured that no feelings of mercy —of compassion—ever found a home within her breast, and slowly but surely she came to a resolution frightful to think of, but one which certainly, if carried out with the full and entire boldness that characterised most of her proceedings, would be eminently calculated to accomplish her object: it was a resolution that murder should not be wanting for the purpose of getting rid of those obnoxious individuals who threatened the stability of her position to a continuance of the proud eminence. in which she found herself, and which, we are well aware, she had made such immense exertions to obtain.

A remarkable change took place in her very manner; her lips became compressed, as if she dreaded that the frightful secret of her terrible resolves should escape at some moment when least expected by herself, and when she was off her guard.

It would have been impossible for any one to have looked at that woman for a moment without being acutely sensible of the fact that something was upon her mind of a serious character which she was extremely anxious to keep from all the world.

And such then was the condition which crime—and the contemplation of crime—threw this desperate woman into.

"I will collect," she said, "every minute and necessary fact to enable me to act with positive certainty; there shall be nothing left to mere chance or fate, but whatever is done shall be done clearly and decidedly."

It is an awful interesting period for one who contemplates a great moral offence to be debating upon the best means of accomplishing it with safety, and it was now an unquestionable fact that Lady Crumbledown was turning over in her mind the best means of being the death of whoever stood in the way between her and the continuance of her own position and the sure prospects of her own child.

She felt that there was time for action; she did not anticipate any sudden danger from the peculiar circumstances which surrounded her, so she could, of course, consider of the safest and the best mode of accomplishing her purposes.

She had read of those Italian poisoners who had the means of giving their victims some dangerous but immediately fatal drug, which slowly, by degrees, like the insidious progress of some distemper, supplied the springs of their existence and made them live a short life of anguish and then drop into the tomb unsuspected of having been murdered.

" If," she muttered to herself, " if I could but procure one of those rare decoctions all would be safe, and I might pursue a career which would make me the mistress of the destinies of all around me."

The difficulty, however, of procuring poison of any kind without an accomplice was so great, that although the use of it presented itself to her in rather pleasant colours, she shrank from it, and began to think that what must be done must be done by her own hands.

" Why should I shrink?" she said. " I have a bold spirit, or I should not dream even of commencing such an enterprise ; and therefore that same boldness which enables me to contemplate it, should and will give me courage for its execution. It shall be done—it most assuredly shall be done !"

There can be no question but that the Lady Crumbledown was entirely ignorant of the remarkable fact that had been alluded to by Moffat, or she might have altered her line of conduct ; and when she and the earl met, which they did for a wonder at dinner that day, it was a strange thing to see the aspect which each of their countenances wore, in consequence of each being in possession of secrets of great importance to the other and yet unknown to each.

The earl looked with feelings of detestation at that woman, who certainly had been, beyond all question, the bane of his existence. He felt how he had snatched at the shadow of happiness instead of its substance, and he saw before him, in the person of his lady, decidedly what might be considered his evil genius. The few words that passed between them were of a constrained and artificial character, and when he left the house, to proceed to his club, it was quite as great a relief to him to depart as it was to her to see him do so.

The Earl of Crumbledown, however, had a greater facility for throwing off disagreeable thoughts and fancies from his mind than his lady had ; and, perhaps, this arose not so much from philosophy on his part, as from a certain carelessness of intellect, which we have more than once had occasion to notice as forming a portion of his character. Yielding, therefore, without much opposition, to an impulse which came over him, he took his way to the Opera ; and knowing that there would be no one in his box but himself, he thought that he might as well sit there and think, if he were disposed for thought, while there was the advantage, if he could cast off disagreeable impressions, of sufficient amusement, if he chose to seek it. The building was crammed to excess ; and after he had sat for some time, his attention became riveted upon a countenance in an opposite box which in a short time absorbed the whole of his attention. It was the countenance of a young female, and it was not so much that she was beautiful that he gazed upon her, as it was that her beauty recalled to him the memory of the past, by putting him vividly in remembrance of one who was now no more.

Yes, if ever there was a living likeness in the world of Emily, who is now no more, that likeness sat before him and claimed the whole of his regard. For more than an hour he looked upon that countenance ; and at times—but that the progress of years rendered it impossible, and that he knew too well that the grave had closed over her whom he had once loved—he could have supposed that Emily sat before him looking as she had used to look before the blight of his affections fell upon her. In the dim obscurity of the box in which she sat he could not tell by whom she was accompanied ; but when, after the Opera, she rose to go, he, being familiar with the house, got round to the box door before she could possibly leave it, and then he saw her emerge along with two elderly women, who seemed to be bestowing the most vigilant attention upon her.

The earl was determined to follow them, not so much that he cared particularly or wished to engage in any adventure consequent upon those circumstances, as because he thought it would be pleasing to him to know what house in London contained one whom he could look at with a feeling that she so closely resembled her whom he had lost for ever. To his surprise they walked away on foot ; and from this circumstance he gathered they were not regular frequenters at the Opera, but most likely were in a much more humble condition of life, and had only been admitted that evening by some special favour. They walked rapidly, and finally halted in one of the second-rate streets in Soho, where they knocked at a door and were admitted.

As the earl paused for a moment, he felt some one slightly touch his arm; and then turning suddenly, to his surprise he beheld Jonathan Willoughby.

"You here!" cried the earl; "what means this insolent intrusion?"

"Intrusion! surely, my lord, you forget that you are in the public streets? I have been to the Opera; and from the pit I was so astonished at the remarkable likeness of a young lady who entered this house to Emily you know who, that I could not refrain from following her."

"Do you know her?"

"I do not; but if your lordship expresses a wish that I should get you information upon the subject, you have but to say so."

"No," said the earl, "no; I have nothing to do with you, Willoughby; nothing to say to you. Do not presume to address me, or I may punish the insolence I cannot always, perhaps, repress."

"As you please, my lord, as you please."

The earl walked on, and Willoughby looked after him for some moments in silence, which at length he broke by saying,—

"It has cost me no little trouble to manage this affair nicely; but if it succeed, as I hope and trust it will, I shall not grudge that trouble, had it been twice as great. My appearance has scared him a little; but, for all that, this is an adventure which he will pursue, or else I am a wonderfully worse judge of human nature than ever I thought myself. He will pursue it, and he shall pursue it, and it shall answer my purpose yet; I know you, my lord of Crumbledown, better than you know yourself, and at all events, if I cannot get amply and well paid from you, you shall immediately, and without knowing that you are doing so, assist me in my designs against your lady's purse, which is a tolerably full one, I know."

The earl, although he had treated Willoughby so haughtily in this transaction, certainly felt an irresistible desire to look again upon that face which reminded him so particularly of the past. It seemed to him as if a vision of her who had been so completely sacrificed by her affection for him had passed before his eyes at a moment when his thoughts were in the greatest state of confusion from a variety of causes, and his mind was embittered by the saddest reflections.

Probably, had he not met Willoughby at that moment, he might have made some further effort to ascertain who and what she was, but the presence of that man, whom he certainly so cordially detested, and whom, it must be confessed, he had no cause to regard with friendly eyes, deterred him most completely.

"At some other time," he said, "I must manage to make further inquiry with regard to this fair and beautiful being. I did not think that there was one in the whole world who could have reminded me so strongly of her who is lost to me for ever. I could not have believed it possible that I could have looked upon the face of any human being with such an interest again. What was that?"

The earl paused as he spoke, and looked upwards, for a sudden peal of thunder had come upon his ears, and then, before he could tell himself that some remarkable change in the weather was going to occur, there came down a sudden deluge of rain, which forced him, thinly dressed as he was, to take refuge where he could, and accordingly he darted into a gateway leading to some low buildings, occupied by some of the vilest specimens of humanity that London could produce.

But, at all events, he was in shelter, and the cool, damp air that blew in upon him from the now drenched streets was rather a matter of congratulation and pleasant feeling than otherwise, and he inhaled it with pleasure, even accompanied as it was by dashing gusts of rain, which blew furiously in his face, and sprinkled him with watery particles.

He might easily have left his place of shelter and procured a conveyance, but as he there stood he fell into one of those deep reveries which neither time nor circumstances will control—reveries which steal over the mind when they are least expected, and which, when one should be glad to have them come, will not obey the bidding.

He seemed to travel mentally back to those days when, in consequence of the very limited income allowed him by his father, the eccentric old earl, he had been thrown much more into ordinary society than he was now, and he could not help asking himself how much the happier he was for the change; and the answer, accompanied by all the bitterness of regret, was, that in those times, when he was forced to look at shillings instead of pounds, he was in every respect happier than he had been since, although now he had around him all that could be of a tempting character, and was surrounded by those insignias of wealth and rank which were coveted by so many, and which, before he possessed, to him had had a thousand unknown charms, but which now, alas! had found their due level in his mind.

Whilst these reflections were passing through his brain he suddenly heard the sound of rapid footsteps behind him, and almost before he could turn to see from whom they proceeded, some one clutched him by the arm, and the voice of a young girl exclaimed—

"He will die, he will die. Oh, sir, come and listen to the last words of one who should have merited a better fate."

There was a musical cadence in the voice which struck sympathy upon his ear, and he found himself following his unknown guide before he had expressed to h mself a single word in reference to the danger of so doing.

"This way, sir," she cried, "this way. I know that he has something to tell with his last words, which more than one person ought to listen to. Follow me, sir, now and at once, and Heaven will bless you."

This was just the sort of appeal that was likely any person would respond to, unless it should happen to be one of the most suspicious nature, and that the earl certainly was not; for his movements were, generally, to tell the truth, rather too impulsive, and it would have been better if he had exercised a larger amount of caution in transactions, the real nature of which he knew nothing of. When the young female—for she was young he guessed, by the slight glance he got of the retreating figure—passed suddenly through a doorway into a dark passage, he did not scruple to follow her, although he so little knew, or rather did not know at all, where that place might conduct him.

A man does not advance far in total darkness and uncertainty, and the earl was no exception to such a general rule; for he paused almost immediately, and at the moment that he did so pause he heard a door slam violently behind him, and an indefinite feeling of alarm began to take possession of him.

CHAPTER LVIII.

THE EARL'S DANGER, AND SOME NEWS OF MR. WILLOUGHBY.

To turn abruptly, and attempt to make his way back again, was the impulse of the moment with the earl, after hearing the door closed, and no doubt it would have been the impulse of any one under similar circumstances. But he found that, in consequence of the profound darkness, or of the similarity of the inside of the door to the remainder of the passage-wall, that he could find no trace of it; and he began to feel extremely uneasy, inasmuch as a death-like stillness reigned in the place, into which he began strongly to suspect he must have been entrapped.

He was completely unarmed, and had not the remotest means of effecting anything in his own favour, should he be attacked, except such feeble resistance as he could offer with his hands to any one who might proceed to violence. When he again turned from his fruitless search for the street-door, he saw a faint gleam of light some distance off, and apparently at the further end of a narrow passage, which presented itself to him. The light seemed to come from a half-open door, and he walked towards it with extreme caution, listening attentively as he went, if he could hear any sound of voices, and perhaps with yet a faint hope that the adventure might not be dangerous.

The sudden disappearance, however, of the young girl after she had succeeded in inveigling him into the house was not a matter which could be passed over unnoticed; and so, with a feeling of alarm, rapidly obtaining strength in his bosom, he made his way towards the place from whence the light proceeded.

He found, as he had surmised, that it came from a room the door of which was partially open, and, after listening a moment, and hearing no sound from within he entered the apartment, and found that it was of small dimensions, and that the gleams of light proceeded from a miserable candle placed upon a table, which was the only article of furniture that the room possessed. He took not a moment to survey this apartment, with the exception of a cupboard, which the earl made a vain attempt to open.

"It's very odd," he said, "that I can see nor hear no one here; but, at all events, this light will afford me the means of finding the street-door, and so escaping —for I must confess I am not at all partial to the aspect of the place."

Just as he raised the candle from the table, he had a convincing proof that his movement was not unobserved, for the door of the apartment was closed, and he heard a key turned in the lock, after which he began to hear the murmur of voices in the next apartment; and presently these voices rose so high in contention that he could hear distinctly what they said.

"Dead men tell no tales," said one, "and we don't know what dangers we run, by letting anybody go. I opposed it before, and I always will oppose it."

"Nonsense, nonsense," cried another; " ours is a trade which must be carried on; but, as sure as fate, it must and will be found out. We ought always to be providing for that evil day; and, as Master Willoughby has told us long before now, our best defence, if we are taken up, is that we use no violence if no resistance is offered."

"Rank cowardice," cried the other. "Cut his throat, I say, and have done with him. Besides, it's as bad to be transported as hung."

" You know better than that."

" Why, don't all the newspapers say so?"

" Yes, they may; but if you were to ask the ingenious gentleman that wrote the sentiment which he would sooner be, there would be no mistake about it. It's all twaddle, and we all of us know well enough that it is so. It aint pleasant to be transported; but it's a great reprieve from being hung; so I say no violence, and then you are sure to have the judge with you, if things should go queer, and you get to the bar of the Old Bailey."

"Well, that's your way, and the other way is mine; I don't mind saying what I think and believe, and that's just that it's rank cowardice, and nothing else. Cut his throat, say I, and make the most you can of every rag he has upon him, but I suppose I am going to be cried down now with some rubbish about sanguinary humanity."

"Well, then, put him out of the world at once," said another, who had not yet spoken, "and as for Willoughby, what the deuce has he to do with it? and if we pay him our subscriptions regularly, as we do, to defend any of this association as may happen to get into trouble, I don't see that he has any right to make a fuss about it, so cut his throat say I, and put him in the cupboard along with the other one."

This was a most uncomfortable conversation to overhear, and the Earl of Crumbledown at once perceived that he had got into one of those dens of infamy with which London abounds, and where, no doubt, many a stranger has lost his life, concerning whom no inquiry has been made, and who has thus, with perfect impunity, been made the victim of the most abandoned ruffians. But what was to be done?—was there any means of escaping of himself, or could he hope to offer those ruffians a sufficient inducement to allow him, after he had heard what he had heard, to leave unscathed. He felt the perspiration standing upon his brow,—it was the perspiration of mortal dread, for what could his resistance amount to against three, or even two armed ruffians, intent upon his destruction?

"And is this," he said, "to be the end of my brief career? is this to be the end of all the hopes and fears that have agitated me? am I to come to so despicable a death as this?"

He was recalled from these reflections by the continued conversation of the ruffians in the adjoining apartment, and one of them said—

"Well, I suppose that's agreed upon, it has to be done, and I hope it may be done at once. Let's have no squabbling, but fell him instantly. We have the means, and then let's leave him till day-time, when we can more conveniently get rid of him than now, when we know we are watched."

"Will you do it?" said another.

"Yes," he said, "I'll get in very softly, and mallet him."

There was now a buzz of conversation among them, in so low a tone, that the earl could not hear it, but as well as his seared and scattered faculties would let him, he began to think if it were possible to adopt any means for his own security. He made another attempt at the cupboard, which had before resisted his efforts, and he found that on the former occasion he must merely have turned the handle the wrong way, for now it opened with considerable ease, and the moment it did so a most terrific and ghastly object presented itself.

Seated in a strange, doubled-up posture, on a chair that was within the cupboard, was the body of a murdered man, in whose forehead was the mark of a deep indentation, where some frightful blow had been struck, that had caused his decease.

The earl recoiled with horror, as well he might, with the candle in his hand, and for some moments all his faculties were frozen up in a contemplation of the fearful spectacle before him.

"Gracious Heaven!" he said, but, even in that mood of terror, he was mindful not to let his voice reach those in the next apartment; "gracious Heaven! and this is the fate destined for me! Oh, grant that some happy thought may occur to me, by which I may have a chance of avoiding this frightful death."

It seemed as if his prayer, almost at the instant of its utterance, had been heard; for the thought did strike him, that there was a chance of success by resorting to a plan that only the desperate circumstances in which he was placed could have invested with the least appearance of probability.

It was no sooner thought of than carried out; for, in such a direful emergency moments become precious and were not to be trifled with.

By an exertion of strength which he scarcely believed himself capable of, he succeeded in lifting the chair, with its ghastly contents, from the cupboard, and placing it at the table. He found that the corpse had stiffened in the posture in which it sat, and, as he turned its back towards the door, it must have had all the appearance of a living person sitting by the table.

He then placed the light in such a position that most of the frightful figure was thrown into darkness, and he himself took up the position in the cupboard from which he had taken the corpse.

Scarcely were these preparations completed, before he heard a whispering outside the room-door, and he became aware that the murderers were near at hand.

His situation now was certainly one of the most hazardous description, and the agony he suffered while he was thus awaiting what might be a very awful doom— for he could not be at all certain that the plan he had adopted would in any case succeed—can be better imagined than described, for it certainly was of the most awful and intense character.

He dared not keep the cupboard-door open, to see what was going on, lest that state of things should be noticed; so the only sense he could bring to bear upon the occasion was that of hearing, and the dangerous situation in which he was rendered that most painfully acute, enabling him to catch the slightest sound, and to become vividly conscious of everything that took place.

He could be now well aware of how it is that those deprived of sight seem, in many cases, to make up as much for that great deprivation, by what might be called a double or treble exercise of the other senses.

He heard the door carefully and slowly unlocked, and not the slightest whisper escaped him. He heard one of the murderers and robbers say,

"He must have been drinking before he came here, for, I'll be hanged, if he hasn't sat down and gone to sleep, for there is his hat beside him and he don't hear us in the least."

"Sat down!" said another, "I thought there was no chair, except what was in the cupboard, and I am sure he is not likely to have got that out."

"I told Kate to place another," said the first speaker, "and she told me to do it myself, so that I am rather surprised to find she has."

"He is fast asleep—who will hit him?"

"I!" said one of them, "and then let him get cold, which he can do, while we are taking our supper."

There was a momentary pause, during which not the slightest sound disturbed the stillness of the place, and then the earl's heart sunk within him, and he could not forbear uttering a deep groan as the frightful sound of a heavy-crashing blow fell upon his ears, and then there was a fall—a confusion of feet—the loud bang of a door—and all was still.

* * * * * *

The plan had succeeded, and the doubly-murdered man lay upon the floor of that small apartment with as frightful and as deep an indentation at the back of his head as he had before received at the front. The stillness that reigned in the room was that of death, but yet it was many minutes before the Earl of Crumbledown, with trembling limbs and feelings so utterly enervated that he could scarcely drag his feet after him, slowly emerged from the cupboard and looked around him at the horrible scene that room presented.

The candle was nearly expiring and there lay the body—he thanked Heaven that it was upon its face—that had saved him from destruction, and as he there stood grasping the wall for support, for he felt sick and weak, he could hear again the murmur of voices from the adjoining room and felt that he had not yet achieved his deliverance.

Then, after a while, nerving himself up with the conviction that if he still had a chance of safety it must wholly depend upon his own presence of mind and fortitude, he stole on tip-toe till he got to the door to see if it was fastened.

It was only on the latch: the villains who had so recently left it, thought they had but the dead to contend against, and, therefore, that it was unnecessary to put a lock upon the door.

He crept out into the passage so noiselessly that he felt conscious the most attentive ear could not possibly catch the remotest sounds of his footsteps, and then he saw that the door of the front room, that is to say a room nearest to the street-door but opening from the same passage, was partially unclosed, and a bright stream of light came from it enabling him to see the street-door well, with all its fastenings, while he could hear quite plainly the conversation of the villains, who were discussing in a loud and ribald strain the various chances and changes of their fortunes, and boasting of that prowess it should have been their greatest boast to have wholly abstained from.

There was nothing in their conversation which he was inclined to listen to, and his whole thoughts were bent upon escape.

While, however, he felt that his best chance of leaving the house was now at once, while it was believed he had mingled with the dead, and while he was so near the street door, that the continued effort of a few brief moments must suffice to open it, he yet shrank back, as anyone might well do, perfectly appalled at the amount of danger to be encountered in the progress of such an action.

They did not carry their conversation on in that quiet strain which was likely to make them good listeners; but, on the contrary, they all talked together, and now and then it would seem as if they were almost trying to outbawl each other; although, occasionally, there was a lull in the conversation, during which, if the earl had made any sound above almost the lightest, he must have been heard.

But he advanced still towards the outer door, slowly, and with a world of deliberation, moving one foot after the other with such extreme caution that he felt confident he made no noise; but yet how hazardous it looked, for now he was standing

within four paces, at the very outsides, or men who would think it necessary, for their own preservation, at once to take his life.

The passing of the door was the most nervous and agitating thing in the world; and he had just accomplished it within a few inches, when one of the men cried—

"I'll run down stairs and get another bottle of the ale."

"I am lost," thought the earl; and he shrank back as he spoke as much into the gloom as he possibly could; "I am lost!"

The door was flung open, and one of the men came staggering out; for, since

committing the deed of blood, they had drunk deeply—a proof that, even harden
in iniquity as they were, they yet found it necessary to drown reflection in son
shape or another.

The earl felt that part of the light, that came now from the wide open doo
actually fell upon his face; and that, if either of the men who were still sitting ar
talking in the room, were to turn their heads in that direction, they must see him
and he told himself, at that awful moment, that if he escaped the observation of the ma
who was about so soon to return, it would indeed be next to a miracle.   Urged t
this sense of danger, and feeling that now or never was the time to attempt som
thing for his release, he retreated backwards until he got to the door; and the
suddenly turning. he, with agitated and trembling hands, began to unloose th
fastenings.   He took down a bar which was across it, and then he stooped, an
drew back one bolt, which, as it went into its socket, made a shrill, shriekin
noise.

One of the men immediately sprang from the room, and stood face to face wit
the earl.

"What's this?" he cried.   "Is it you, Joe?"

The earl lost not a moment, for he knew that his life hung upon a thread, bu
with the strength of almost madness and despair, he seized the ruffian by th
throat and hurled him along the passage with such excessive force, that, comin
against the other one as he did, who was just returning with the ale, the
both rolled down the kitchen steps together with a tremendous clatter, of cours
thoroughly arousing the third villain to a sense of his danger.

But the earl did not wait for him.   The other bolt was withdrawn in an instant
the door yielded, and he dashed into the court, which led by the covered way wher
he had taken shelter from the storm, into the street.

The hour now was so late, that but few chance passengers were about; never
theless, the earl felt so anxious that the villains should not escape, which the
would no doubt attempt to do, now that they knew their own danger, that he woul
not leave the mouth of the court, but stood there crying—

"Help, help, police!" until several people congregated around him, and on
produced a constable's staff, saying—

"What is it, sir, what is it?"

"There are three men," cried the earl, "that I wish to give in charge for
murder."

"I'll go," cried a young man, "and if we three honest men can't take three
rogues, it's a hard case indeed."

Instead of three, however, the party increased to eight in a few seconds, and
the earl led the way toward the murder-house, from which he had just escaped.
Altogether, he could not have been absent from it above ten minutes, and then
the door was perfectly fast, and the young man who had joined the party in the
first instance, consumed some time by going to borrow a crowbar, for the purpose
of forcing it open.   When this was done, the passage within appeared to be in
complete darkness, and the people in the court, who were applied to for lights,
appeared much more unwilling than willing to produce them; but at length they
were procured, and under very different auspices indeed did the Earl of Crumbledown re-enter the house, in which he had incurred such great danger, and been
so near losing his life in so frightful a manner.

They found that the room where the murderers had been seated was completely deserted now, but that there was abundant evidence that they had been
there, in the glasses and bottles that were still upon the table.   They did not
search further than that apartment, for it was evident at a glance that it contained
no secret places, but directed their attention to the next room, on the floor of
which they found the murdered man.

This sight inflamed the feelings of the people so much, that, forgetting all
caution, they rushed over the house in search of the murderers, but no trace of
them was found until they came to the cellars beneath, and there lay one man
with a broken ale-bottle scattered over him, and a fractured skull.   It appeared as

if, when the two villains had rolled down the kitchen staircase together, they had fought, each thinking the other in fault, and that the one who was armed with the ale-bottle had succeeded in thus injuring his companion, and then making his own escape.

This man was not dead, but he was labouring under concussion of the brain and was perfectly insensible, so that he had to be carried out, and was taken at once to the infirmary of a prison, for it was thought to be by far too serious a matter to encumber a hospital with.

As may be well imagined, when the earl told who he was he received all that world of difference which in this country is ever extended to the privileged classes and to rank, and the affair altogether threatened to make about as serious a noise as anything of the sort had ever done.

It was a proof of how little domestic felicity the Earl of Crumbledown enjoyed, that he never for a moment thought of going to his own home to appease any anxious fears that might there be entertained concerning him, but on the contrary he repaired at once to his club, where he took a bed for the night, feeling much more at his ease by so doing than if he had been at his own mansion, full as it was of everything that was costly and beautiful.

" No," he said, " I have no home, although I have a house that calls me master, and the countess may hear how likely she was to become a widow by public report, but she shall not hear it from my lips, for she does not deserve such an amount of courtesy."

CHAPTER LIX.

THE COUNTESS'S NEW SPY.

THE countess was too anxious to wait long for her report from the spy who had been employed to dodge the footsteps of the earl, and to endeavour to discover where the Love Child was to be found, for Margaret to keep long secret from her the failure that had been made, and when closely questioned upon the subject she admitted, that although she had employed a person on whom she thought she could rely, he had most certainly failed her.

" My lady," she said, " it is almost always the case that persons who accept such employments as these are not the sort of persons one can rely upon to carry them out properly."

" It seems so," said the countess, " but what am I to do? Am I to continue ever thus at the mercy of a set of circumstances of which I know not the fearful import but am continually guessing the worst?"

" No, my lady, that shall not be. What I have promised I will perform. I said that I would discover the residence of the earl's child and of its mother, if a mother it have living, and I will keep my word."

" But how?"

" Rest satisfied that in a short time I shall be able to bring you the intelligence you require."

" I can make certain of it, for one most special reason."

" And what may that be? It seems to me that it's quite as likely you may be deceived by any other subordinate whom you may employ, as the one who has already failed you."

" Most unquestionably, my lady; but I mean now to do myself what I before trusted to others. I can be certain of myself, but of no one else; I can manage to dress myself, so that if the earl sees me, he will not recognise me; for, as your ladyship is well aware, he is not sufficiently often at home to be intimately acqnted with his own household."

" That is true enough."

" I will follow him then, and you may make sure of speedily obtaining the information which is essential to your peace. Be assured that now there will be no disappointment."

" I have a better hope ; but, whatever you do, mind that you do quickly, for my anxiety is day by day destroying me."

" I cannot sleep, and the ordinary affairs of life pass by me, and I heed them not, for my whole thoughts are fixed upon that one subject; and I earnestly ask myself am I to be subjected to a degradation, such as before never had presented itself to me, even in a dream, for the frightful fear that the mother of this child is really the earl's wife, comes across me, now and then, with such a strange and astounding belief in its reality, that at times I am not mistress of myself."

" You shall get rid, my lady, of all these thoughts and fancies. It is but a short road to the grave, and there is no occasion on earth why those persons should not take it who stand between you and what is due to you."

" Set about your mission quickly, and bring me tidings, I pray you, of where the earl has secreted these persons, or this child alone, if it be true that the mother is no more."

" I will, this very day; and I do hope that, by perseverance, I shall be able very shortly, perhaps within twenty-four hours, to bring you some satisfactory intelligence ; and be assured I shall not fail for want of perseverance, for personal danger shall not even deter me."

" Do but succeed, and then name your own reward, and you shall have it. I have set my whole existence upon this matter, and I must and will succeed in it. Is it to be borne, that I, who have accomplished so much—I, who have carried things with such a haughty hand, and forced myself into the position I at present occupy—should live to be crushed by such a set of circumstances as those which now oppress me ? I say it shall not—must not be !"

" It shall not be, my lady. Be of good heart in this transaction ; and as for putting the child out of the way, I don't see that you need scruple about that, for people who have no right to be in the world, have no right to complain at being put out of it."

" Listen to me—I have thought over all ; but I have thought over it until my brain has been in a perfect whirl of frenzy, and I have come to a conclusion I will do the deed, and influential considerations now only pause about the manner in which it is to be done, and not the deed itself."

" You are right, you are right, you are quite right, my lady ; and I cannot help telling you that I rejoice to see you in such a mood, quite rejoice. The life of a child, what is it ? a creature unconscious of what it gains by existence, or what it loses by death,—'tis too absurd to think of it for a moment."

" Peace, peace, I want no further argument, I want to know nothing more on such a point, to hear nothing more ; my mind is completely wrought up to a stern determination—it is one which cannot be strengthened by anything that you can urge, nor can it be weakened by aught that can be uttered against."

This was tolerably true, for the fact is, that Lady Crumbledown knew perfectly well that what she purposed doing was unjustifiable by every law human and divine, and she knew that no course of argument could reconcile her to an act that was only one of stern necessity, which nothing but a strong appreciation of her own interest could have any effect upon. She knew that it was wrong—she knew that what she contemplated was one of the most diabolical crimes of which she could be guilty—a crime alike denounced by heaven and by earth—such a crime as humanity might well shudder at, for it was a murder of the deepest and the blackest dye—the murder of a child an—innocent being, who of itself could have done no wrong, and who in its very helplessness was entitled to universal protection. And could it be supposed for one moment that such a woman as the Countess of Crumbledown, could be the happier for such an act ?

How strangely singular it is, that such persons forget how short is the tenure of human existence, but that they go on committing crimes for the accomplishment of fancied objects, as if they actually had an immortality of human life before them. What could she hope for if she completed all the deep iniquity she contemplated, well aware as she was that perhaps a few hours more might see her a corpse, and that some slight vicissitude in the season, or the merest accident in the world to the complicated machinery of the human system, might lay her on a bed of death.

But granting that she lived, admitting that she reached to an age even beyond the ordinary lot of humanity, what kind of enjoyment was it likely to produce to her, when her thoughts must be continually reverting to the frightful scenes of the past, and her dreams must be haunted by such hideous spectres, as would be calculated to appal the boldest imagination that ever existed in this world?

But these are not considerations which induce the wicked to pause in their career, and it is one of the strangest phenomena of the human mind, that while they bring abundance of talent to bear upon their schemes they never discover the impolicy of their conduct.

CHAPTER LX.

THE EARL AND COLONEL BRUCE ESCAPE TO LONDON WITH SOME DIFFICULTY.

UNQUESTIONABLY the greatest danger which the Earl of Crumbledown and Colonel Bruce had run of absolute detection at the village where the unfortunate Emily Whitford breathed her last was when, at the magistrate's, a woman denounced the earl as the man who had before shown himself there with the supposed murdered person while in life. Had this untoward event occurred at the village instead of where it did, it is very likely indeed that some serious consequences would have resulted from it. As it was, however, it had the immediate effect of convincing the earl and the colonel of the desirableness of getting away as quickly as possible.

This woman, who had been so tardy with her accusation, happened to be one of those who were so bitterly disappointed upon the occasion of the Love Child being put out to nurse; and she had ever held that circumstance in the liveliest remembrance: consequently, she had, in her own mind, thought over every possible particular connected with it, and had a strong and a vivid mental picture of the Earl of Crumbledown.

Hence was it that she made the exclamation she had done, and denounced him at once as the supposed murderer.

"You may depend," remarked Colonel Bruce to the earl, "that she will give us some some trouble, if she can."

"But how can she?"

"By inciting a pursuit for us, of course. Did you not hear with what excessive bitterness she spoke when she said she knew you?"

"The recognition was certainly not made in the gentlest manner; but let us get road-horses, and be off at once."

They procured with some difficulty their steeds, and proceeded on the London-road at a smart trot. Many a time they looked behind them as they came to raised portions of the road, which commanded a good view, to see if there were any symptoms of pursuit; but, as all was quiet, they began to think that the idea of following them either had never been at all entertained, or had been given up as dangerous or impracticable.

After thus proceeding about ten miles they halted at a road-side inn, for rest and refreshment, both to themselves and to the horses. It was a pretty rural spot, and they remained, perhaps, rather longer than prudence dictated. In about two hours, however, and just as they were thinking of starting again, a horseman reached the door of the inn, and called out, in a loud voice, to a man who was loitering near to it, and who belonged to the establishment—

"Have you seen two gentlemen ride past here on horseback?"

"No, I haven't; but I see two stop here."

"Indeed! Both tall are they, and one with moustachios?"

"Ah, to be sure, you have hit it. That's about the truth, and no mistake. They have put up here: and here you will find them at this present moment of time, if you take the trouble to go into the parlour."

The horseman looked very well pleased at this intelligence, and at once dismounted and walked into the house, making his way to the parlour, into which he entered without any further ceremony than a slight tap at the door.

"Gentlemen," he said, "I have to beg your pardon for this intrusion, and I trust that the errand I come upon will plead my excuse."

The earl and the colonel looked rather amazed at this exordium, and the stranger continued—

"My name is Potts, and I reside in the village where certain circumstances have taken place that I need not more particularly allude to; and the object of my present errand, gentleman, is to tell you, that a woman, who says that in one of you she recognises the gentleman who came in the travelling carriage with the young lady who died at the inn——"

The earl started, and the colour rushed to his face, so that if Mr. Potts had been in any doubt as to which of the two his message was the most interesting, such doubts would have been at once dissolved, and he would have been able to place the saddle upon the right horse.

"This woman then, gentlemen," he continued, "is raising a popular commotion, and some of the young farmers of the neighbourhood, when I came away, were talking of mounting and pursuing you on this road; and, as some of them keep good cattle, you would, in all likelihood, be overtaken before you had got many miles further."

"Sir," said the earl, "I am grateful to you for the information."

"You are welcome."

"Although I am completely innocent of any wrong-doing as regards this young creature, whose death no one can more bitterly deplore than I do, I do not wish that any greater trouble or publicity should be given than at present to the affair."

"I think," said Mr. Potts, "that I understand the whole circumstance pretty well, or I should not have gone to so much trouble to warn you about it. Your generous conduct towards the child, that was left in the care of Mrs. Grove, was quite sufficient to convince me that all was right, at all events, as far as concerned the death of the young lady being natural."

"You have taken a correct view of the subject," said the earl, "and, amid general distraction, I have to be very thankful that I have found one person who is disposed to behave towards me with some degree of liberality."

"Oh, don't mention that, I am really very glad to do so; but I should like to hear how the child is, if it be not asking an impertinent question."

"Not at all—not at all. The child is perfectly well, and still in the care of Mrs. Grove, who likewise is quite well, and has never ceased to attend upon it."

"I am glad to hear such good accounts, and now, I advise you to mount and take some cross road as soon as possible."

"We will; and if you will be so good, Mr. Potts, as to oblige me with a note addressed to me in London, letting me know how affairs have gone on in the village, there is my card, and, by my handing it to you, Mr. Potts, I give you the best proof I can of my entire reliance on your friendly feeling towards me."

The earl, as he spoke, handed his card to Mr. Potts, who, although he was by no means one of those persons who looked with a slavish sort of homage upon nobility, was yet not ill-pleased to find that he had obliged a nobleman of such high rank as the Earl of Crumbledown."

"My lord," he said, "I shall do myself the honour of writing to you, ad I beg again now to urge your immediate departure from home, for some of those who were talking of pursuing you have horses, that by a little feeding will take them a good fourteen miles in an hour of time."

This was really good advice, and the earl and the colonel were soon on the road again; and. accompanied by Mr. Potts, they rode on for some distance till they came to a lane, down which he directed them to go, saying—

"If you pursue that lane, you will find it will bring you out on quite another road to London, where, as it ranges to a great extent, you will be able to proceed with safety, for I will myself return and mislead any of your pursuers whom I may chance to meet on my road homewards."

After duly thanking Mr. Potts for his kindness, they separated; and had the earl and the colonel been a witness to his meeting with half-a-dozen well-mounted young men some short time after, they would perhaps better still have appreciated the kindness he had done them.

"Hilloa, Mr. Potts," cried one, "is that you?"

"Yes, it is," he said; "and I suppose you have come on the same errand that I have."

"We are riding after the two fellows that were taken up in the Bone-house."

"Then you may spare yourself the trouble on this road, for I have ascertained that they crossed a hedge about a mile higher up to the left, and then rode away southward through the open fields to Heaven knows where."

"Thank you for your news," said one, "for we should have blown our horses for nothing."

"But are you quite sure?" added another.

"Yes; I met two men separately, who saw them, and described most accurately, so that there can be no doubt upon the subject whatever, and I have tired out my horse for nothing, which is a thing I don't at all like doing, I can tell you."

"I don't suppose you do, Mr. Potts," said one, "for I know well you are as careful of him as you are of yourself, and perhaps a little more so. But we may as well now come back at once, for I don't see what good is to be done now; and as for riding across the country on a wild-goose chase after men who, by this time, if they are well mounted, will have a dozen miles the start of us—I for one decline it."

"One of the men who told me he saw them," said Mr. Potts, "told me he never wished to look upon finer cattle than they were mounted on, and that it was that which attracted him to give his particular attention."

This assertion settled the business, and the horsemen, one and all, turned round, but it was with great difficulty that Mr. Potts prevented them from all stopping at the same inn where he had himself overtaken the earl and the colonel, in which case there certainly would have been a strong likelihood of some incidental remarks being made that would have made the party aware of how they had been imposed upon.

He did, however, by breaking out into great praises of another establishment, get them past the door, and after that there was no danger to be apprehended as regarded the part he had taken in the earl's escape.

This proceeding of Mr Potts was altogether founded upon reasoning of his own, with regard to the singular affair that had come under his investigation. He was, as the reader is well aware from his conduct in the early part of this narrative, a very eccentric character, and not one of those persons who are at all in the habit of pinning his faith to the sleeves of ordinary persons, but, on the contrary, always exercising or endeavouring to exercise an independent judgment. The circumstances connected with the coming to the village of the Earl of Crumbledown, whom he thus, of course, knew not along with the young and beautiful creature who gave birth to a child at the inn and then died, were all facts in his recollection; and he knew from the surgeon himself, who had attended her, that her death had arisen from purely natural causes. Being thus a man always opposed as much as possible to vulgar prejudices, he had resolved upon throwing the woman, who, from purely motives of long-cherished personal anger at missing the considerable sum of money which had been left for who ever undertook to nurse the Love Child, had now endeavoured to do all the mischief in her power.

The Earl of Crumbledown and Colonel Bruce now proceeded towards London without any interruption worth recording; and then the former sent to the market town for his carriage, which had been there waiting, but which afforded no clue to him, inasmuch as no one but the magistrate—and he kept all to himself—knew that it belonged to the same parties who had been arrested for their intrusion into the bone house. To be sure something like a disturbance was attempted to be made with him for letting the two men go who had been apprehended and brought before him, but he only replied that he was quite willing an application should be made to the Secretary of State upon the subject, when he would defend his conduct; and so the matter dropped.

The remains of the unhappy Emily Whitford were a second time placed in the grave; and although, as a matter of course, the affair was still talked of as a most mysterious one, the real secret, with the exception of Mr Potts, remained in the same hands that it had been in before.

When this state of things arrived, Mr Potts wrote a note to the Earl, in which he stated that all was tranquil, and stating that, if any more disturbances took place, he, the Earl, might depend upon hearing from him about it.

Thus then was it that the Earl and the Colonel got out of a hazardous adventure; and, by recording how they did so, we have filled up what looked like a hiatus in our narrative, but which in reality was left, in order that the progress of more important events might not be delayed; and we feel now that the bad and malignant passions of the Countess of Crumbledown are fast bringing us to a description of events which we shudder to think humanity, especially in the shape of a woman, could be guilty of. But as an impartial historian, and relating from carefully collected and authentic words what really did take place, we feel that we must not shrink.

CHAPTER LXI

SHOWS HOW THE COUNTESS'S MAID DISCOVERED THE LOVE CHILD.

AFTER the failure of the spy who had been employed by the Countess of Crumbledown's maid for the purpose of discovering where the earl had hidden the Love Child, it will be remembered that that worthy personage had promised her lady that she would herself undertake the task of dogging his footsteps and ascertaining whither he went.

So intent was she upon securing the reward which she perfectly well knew would be hers if she succeeded in inciting the countess to a commission of a crime she contemplated, and yet, at times, shrunk from with horror, that she was extremely likely to succeed in her object of tracking the earl to where Mrs. Grove resided. It was not a present and immediate reward that this designing or unscrupulous domestic of the countess looked to as what would pay her for what she was about. No, far from it; but it was the prospect of having the countess completely in her power, as she undoubtedly would be after the commission of the deed, and the being enabled, consequently, to make a continual profit of her, which induced this wicked and designing person to aid in the perpetration of so much cruelty.

Having procured then the full and free consent of the countess to play the part of spy upon the earl, she fearlessly set about it, and resolved that not a day should pass over her head without her having followed him somewhere, and at least attempted to make some discovery of importance. She had no fear of detection on the part of the earl, for as she had herself remarked, he came so seldom to his own house, and when he did so, he paid so little attention to any domestic affairs, that nothing could be more improbable than the fact of his recognising her, even should he see her apparently close upon his track. She did not suppose that he visited very frequently or continually the child, concerning whom the countess was anxious to obtain information, so she rather suspected than otherwise that the task of following him might be a long one, but as it could only be accomplished with a certainty by the greatest perseverance, she made up her mind to bestow upon it so much time and attention as should make the result almost a certainty.

Accordingly, dressing herself in an ordinary unobservable costume, which was not likely to attract the smallest share of particular attention, she followed the earl upon an occasion, when, as the fates would have it, he was upon the point of proceeding at once to visit Mrs. Grove, for the purpose of giving her some answer regarding what she had said to him upon his last visit. In point of fact,

what she had stated upon that occasion had given him some uneasiness, because it had looked to his mind as if she had suddenly become anxious to get relieved of that trust which, at one time, she had certainly regarded with so much complacency, and appeared to take so great a pleasure in performing the duties of.

This was a state of things, which he could not reconcile to his knowledge of Mrs. Grove's character, and hence it gave him considerable uneasiness. He had promised to let her know shortly what he thought upon the subject, but he certainly had not anticipated going to her again quite so soon, and his object for so doing was rather to get from her something fu ther concerning her own thoughts and feelings, than to inform her of any conclusion he might have arrived at in the matter that he viewed with so much anxiety.

It was unfortunate, we say, that upon this occasion of all others he should have been followed by the waiting-maid of the countess, for we must confess we should have liked to have given that individual a world of trouble before she succeeded in discovering any of the matters which it lay so near her heart to become acquainted with. But there is no fighting against facts, and certainly in all these affairs the earl seemed to be labouring under some unlucky fatality, and that nothing went exactly right with him. When the mind is intensely occupied likewise, it forgets those ordinary cautions, which in general would exercise a marked influence on its conduct, and never upon any occasion of his visiting his child did the earl proceed with less caution than upon the present occasion, when really the most was required. But this was a state of things purely natural, and although, when he did come within sight of where Mrs. Grove resided, he looked around him, and saw a woman suddenly start in consequence of being so close to him, he took the circumstance to be accidental, and had no suspicion that that woman was his countess's own maid, not as usual attired in the cast-off finery of her mistress, but remarkably quietly dressed. That she looked ten times better than she usually did in her borrowed plumes, there can be no doubt whatever ; but as the earl did not know her either in one state or the other, he had no means of making the comparison. He entered the house, and after caressing the child for a short time, he said to Mrs. Grove—

" I have been thinking over what you said to me on my last visit, and I have come to ask you, plainly and distinctly, if you wish to rid yourself of your charge."

A momentary flush of confusion came across Mrs. Grove's face, as she repeated the words, " Resign my charge ?"

" Yes," said the " earl, I wish you to be candid with me, and I hope you will, for if you are still willing to continue to act a mother's part towards this desolate little creature, I shall not feel myself so anxious or so hurried in procuring for it better instruction, than you are yourself qualified to impart to it ; but if, on the contrary, you called my attention to the matter from any wish to resign your charge, tell me so at once, and it shall no longer be a burden to you."

This was plain speaking, which from her manner Mrs. Grove neither expected nor seemed exactly to like, but still, after a few moments' pause, she said very firmly and distinctly—

" No, I have no wish to rid myself of my charge, or I would say so at once, and, therefore, I leave the matter entirely in your lordship's hands, to do with it as you shall think proper, bearing it in mind merely as a suggestion from me, which I think and hope is for the child's welfare."

Notwithstanding this, the earl could not convince himself but that Mrs. Grove's affection for the child had suffered some diminution, although what was the cause of such an effect he was entirely at a loss to imagine, for all the circumstances appeared to be much the same, with the one exception, that the child was certainly old enough to be exceedingly engaging and companionable, a fact which one would have thought likely to have a completely opposite tendency.

However, he was so far satisfied with the declaration she had made, that she did intend to imply a wish to part with the child, by what she had said, that he felt he could dismiss the subject, at all events for the present, from his thoughts, so as to leave him time to duly weigh and consider other matters of greater moment and intense anxiety.

One of these matters was the singular story that had been told him by the stranger, who claimed to have such an intimate knowledge of his wife's mother.

He could not quite decide in his mind whether or not that circumstance was one which he would like to use by way of increasing his power and authority over her or not, but he had reserved it for careful and mature consideration.

Before he left her, Mrs. Grove said to him—

"My lord, on your road hither did you observe any one follow you?"

"Certainly not," said the earl; "I am always careful, I think, indeed, careful to an excess, and I have seen no one."

"I asked the question, because since we have been talking the face of a female has twice appeared at yon window, which looks into the street."

"Indeed! are you certain?"

"I am—I cannot be mistaken; I should not have thought much of it, because people frequently look in as they pass, but the head-dress is the same."

"Indeed, it shall be looked to. I will now leave you, and probably shall not repeat my visit for a week, although, should anything occur to require my presence, of course I will come to you, at an hour or two's notice, on receiving a note from you to that effect."

The earl now left. And as he took care to get to the door very suddenly, he observed a woman move hastily away from the window, and walk with quick steps in another direction than that which led towards his residence.

"This, probably," he said, "is nothing but idle curiosity, and there are so many persons who are fond of interfering in the affairs of others, that one can scarcely wonder at a thing of this sort happening occasionally."

Banishing it then completely from his mind, he walked homeward at once, and sat down in his library, as chance would have it, very close to a window, which commanded a view of the door-step of his house.

It gave him rather a start of surprise, upon accidentally happening to cast his eyes towards the step, upon hearing a violent ring at the bell, to see that the person demanding admission was the same female whom he had noticed walk away so hastily from Mrs. Grove's window.

This was a discovery which immediately altered the whole aspect of the affair, removing every possible doubt connected with it at once, and convincing him that he had been followed, and not only followed, but discovered.

He rung his bell, and desired that a man, of the name of Edwards, who was a groom, who usually went out with him, and upon whose fidelity he thought he could depend, should instantly appear before him.

When this man came, the earl ordered him to close the door, and then said—

"Who was it, Edward, that came in just now?"

"My lady's own maid, my lord, and she is giving herself such airs in the kitchen now, that I fully expect the cat will be sick."

"That will do, Edward; be ready in five minutes' time to take a note for me. Go on horseback, and ride fast."

"Yes, my lord."

Within the specified five minutes Edward was at the door, and mounted, and then the earl sent out to him a letter, addressed to Mrs. Grove, and which merely contained the following words—

"MRS. GROVE—Remove from where you are within a few hours after the receipt of this, and let me know by post your new address.

"CRUMBLEDOWN."

Having despatched this letter, he felt a little more satisfied in his own mind at the prospect, that at all events, unless the countess was exceedingly prompt in her measures—much more prompt than he expected her to be, or that she could possibly imagine there would be any necessity for being—she would be foiled, for he doubted not but that with all imaginable promptitude Mrs. Grove would take care to remove in obedience, to the order he had sent her to do so.

"Now, my lady," he said to himself, as he sat alone, "now, whatever may be your designs as regards the child to which you entertain so deadly a hatred, you shall find that others can plan and plot as well as you, and that it is not because you have an artful waiting-maid that you are to succeed in everything you undertake."

As he sat he kept his eye fixed upon the door-step, and his object in doing so, was to feel certain that the countess did not slip out upon any expedition to the annoyance of Mrs. Grove; he was far, very far, from suspecting her of entertaining the notion upon the subject that she really did.

The outside act to which he thought her malevolence would carry her, was a visit to Mrs. Grove, and sundry threats and remonstrances to her if she did not forthwith inform her, Lady Crumbledown, of the full particulars concerning the child of which she had the care.

Being ignorant of the strange machinations and intrigues by which his lady was surrounded, the earl could have no idea of the very serious aspect which the matter had assumed to her mind, and therefore he looked upon her conduct as being that of a mere unworthy malevolent spirit, for that she should be impressed with any belief of the unfortunate Emily Whitford being his wife, it never entered into his imagination to suppose it possible for one moment, or else he might have been a little more lenient in his strictures upon her conduct than he was, and he might possibly, likewise, have taken the trouble to disabuse her upon that head, because it affected his own honour as much as hers.

He waited until he saw his groom come back, and when this man told him that he had delivered his letter correctly, he felt more at his ease, and there was a little of the gratification of victory, for victory's sake in his mind, as he thought of how he had got the better of the countess.

"She will find," he said, as he rose, "that circumstances can play against her as well as against me, and there is one good, certainly, which will arise from this affair, and that is, that it places me doubly and trebly upon my guard. I shall never again proceed so incautiously to visit that child of misfortune, to whom I owe so much duty and affection, and towards whom it shall ever be my study so to comport myself, that if it cannot praise its father, it shall at least respect him. It shall say in after years, that I did what I could to repair a grievous error—not persevering in wrong, or seeking to derive satisfaction from it, but, on the contrary, repenting of its commission, and doing what I could to repair the consequences."

These were the thoughts of the Earl of Crumbledown. What were those of his lady under the circumstances, we shall quickly be in a position to perceive; and we can imagine what a feeling of disappointment is likely to possess her, if she should really make an excursion to Mrs. Grove's residence, and find the bird flown she expected to find so snugly in its nest, and only awaiting her to crush it.

CHAPTER XLII.

THE REMOVAL OF MRS. GROVE TO HAMPSTEAD HEATH, AND AN UNWELCOME VISITOR.

THERE was quite sufficient in the earl's note to Mrs. Grove to make her feel that it required the most prompt and vigorous measures, and considering one circumstance in connexion with another, she had not the smallest doubt on earth but that the earl had discovered he had been followed by some one, and had taken that means of foiling some projected mischief.

From what the reader already knows of Mrs. Grove, it may be clearly enough deduced, that she is a woman of quite sufficient promptness and decision of character to meet any circumstances that might occur, and consequently, when she received the earl's letter, she at once procured a vehicle, and placing herself and the child in it, she proceeded towards Hampstead, as it was the springtime of the year, for the purpose of seeking out some abode that would be pleasant and grateful during the summer season.

When she reached that delightful suburban locality, and saw it in all the green freshness of early spring, she was inclined to feel quite grateful for the necessity that existed for changing her present residence for one in that new locality.

But not to waste her time, when, for all she knew, minutes might be precious, she made immediate inquiry for some furnished cottage, and was soon informed by a house-agent of several.

In half an hour she had fixed upon one, on the very Heath itself, surrounded by all the natural beauties of hill and dale, and wood and meadow, with which that locality abounds; and, as it was a furnished cottage, and let weekly, the payment of a small sum in advance sufficed, together with a reference to where she had lived last, to give her possession.

It was astonishing with what celerity the whole movement was executed, for in two hours and a half after receiving the earl's letter, Mrs. Grove and the Love Child had changed their residence completely, and she was engaged in quietly putting to rights the few articles she had brought with her from her former abode, that she could call her own.

Her next act was to post a letter to the earl, giving him her new address, and detailing the promptitude with which she had removed to it; at the same time expressing an earnest wish to see him soon, in order that she might know the nature of the danger which had threatened, in order that if it presented itself in any other shape, she might be prepared to cope with it.

* * * * * * *

While these energetic proceedings were going on under the direction of the earl, Margaret, the waiting-woman, was making her report of what she considered her great success to the Countess of Crumbledown, who received it with every demonstration of satisfaction.

"You perceive, my lady," said Margaret, "that when I myself set about any business for your ladyship, it is sure to be well and promptly done, although you can trust no one else."

"I am fully alive," said the countess, "to the fact that you must have contrived this very effectively."

"There was immense difficulty in doing it, for the earl must needs look round at almost every half-step he took, and seemed so suspicious all the way, that I don't wonder at any ordinary person not succeeding in discovering him."

"I told you you should have any reward you chose; and, therefore, if you will name what you consider an equivalent for the great service you have rendered me, it shall be yours."

"Oh! we won't say anything about that yet, my lady, for there is more to be done, you know."

"There is, indeed, more to be done."

"Well, then, my lady, when that's all over, and everything is completed, we shall be able to talk about rewards; but I think at present we may as well leave that part of the subject for a further consideration."

"As you please," said the countess; and then, after a slight pause, she added, "truly, there is indeed much more to be done; for all that requires courage, perseverance, and desperation, has yet to be accomplished."

"And yet, my lady, why should it not be done? Is it to be borne for a moment that one like you should put up with such a state of things as that into which you are thrown? No, my lady, it cannot be—it must not be—you ought to do something, and I am sure you will do something to rescue yourself from such a state of affairs. Are you to put up with the child of one belonging to the lower classes of society coming in, perhaps, all of a sudden some day, and telling your daughter that she is illegitimate, and consequently, of course, good for nothing, and that she, who comes in thus suddenly, is the rightful heiress of the Crumbledowns?"

"It not only is not to be borne, but it shall not be borne! Did you fancy I was going to bear it?"

"No, my lady—no; but—but—"

"Peace—peace! Say no more, my mind is made up; and that child, which for my comfort and happiness should never have lived, shall surely die. But stil we have come to no decision. It is the deed we have decided upon, but not the mode of operation, that remains yet to be considered."

" Yes, it does indeed, my lady ; but I am inclined to think it might be done with poison."

" With poison ? but how to administer it, that is the question."

" From all I can see it seems a commonish sort of person that has charge of the child, and it is very likely she knows nothing of you by sight, and would feel very much flattered if you were to call."

" Have I not told you, over and over again, that she knows me well ? Have I not informed you that she is quite familiar with my face ? for she had my own child to nurse, and she has reason to dread me, from what I said to her when I took it from her."

" I had forgotten ; and certainly that makes it an awkward affair, because I was thinking that it would be a remarkably easy and comfortable thing to call and pretend to admire the child, and give it a cake or an orange, or something of that sort, which contained poison, so that something might be done in that quiet way without exciting any suspicion."

" You are unknown to her, and consequently can do it."

" Who—I, my lady ? I am sure, I—I—that is, I should not exactly."

" I understand you; you can recommend the deed but shrink from its execution. Be it so ; perhaps you are right. I have no business to expect any one, at all events, to do more than assist me in the execution of such a purpose ; so say no more about it, but let us together consult upon what is to be done.'

The consultation certainly was held, but we cannot say that it was productive of anything very satisfactory to the countess, who could not herself hit upon any plan of operation by which she could securely take the life of the Love Child, nor could she hear anything suggested from the lips of her confidante that was likely to succeed.

Murder looks easy, but when the deed has to be considered in all its bearings it is quite another affair, and the difficulties come, like Macbeth's troubles, in perfect battalions.

Besides, the countess knew that Mrs. Grove, from the little she had seen of her, was not a woman exactly the most easy in the world to deceive, and as to corrupting her in any way, so as to make her an agent in the infamous transaction, that was quite, she considered, out of the question.

The result of this first deliberation, then, which the countess and her bad adviser had upon the subject, after they supposed themselves to be in possession of the secret of the place of abode of the object of their enmity, was to wait a little to see what circumstances might turn up to assist them ; and in the mean time she, the countess, determined to go, accompanied by the maid, to see herself the precise situation of Mrs. Grove's residence.

Little, indeed, did they suspect the sudden and most extraordinary change which had taken place in the abode of Mrs. Grove, or that the earl had acted with so much promptness and energy, as had actuated him upon that occasion.

The self-sufficiency of Margaret fully sufficed to convince her that she had managed the matter too well to have exposed herself to the least chance of detection, and when the earl emerged from Mrs. Grove's house, walking away in another direction, she thought she had completely smothered suspicion.

Had she been content to have merely followed the earl, which she had succeeded actually in doing with the most perfect success, all would have been well enough for her purposes ; but, like most persons of her stamp, she must needs do something more, and that was, look in at the window until she attracted the attention of Mrs. Grove, in the manner we have already related. And then she was detected by trying to do too much. What will be the results of her folly, we shall soon see ; but now we must turn our attention to a most unwelcome circumstance that happened to Mrs. Grove in her new place of abode.

One might have fairly thought that so long an impunity as she had enjoyed from every persecution that she had suffered from time to time at the hands of her husband, that ingenious gentleman had given up all idea of making even any energy concerning his decidedly better half, for better she was in every signification of the term.

In fact, Mrs. Grove, if she had not been much better than her husband, would certainly, in our estimation, have been no very brilliant specimen of humanity.

But as it was, the difference in the character of these two persons was strong and marked.

So long indeed had it been since she had heard anything of him, that she had quite taught herself to give him up, and almost to consider him as among the has beens, instead of an actual living member of society.

Now and then she did think of him, but we cannot take upon ourselves to say that it was with the smallest possible amount of regard.

How such a woman came to marry such a man was one of those mysteries of society which occurs sufficiently frequent to induce people to consider that marriages are not matters of choice, but, on the contrary, affairs of pre-arranged necessity on the part of those who are compelled to undertake them, and that they are the victims of a set of circumstances, over which they have themselves no control.

It would seem most particularly that the marriage of Mrs. Grove with such a man as drunken Jack Grove was one of those matches, for otherwise who could believe it possible that she would have united herself to one who could not in any way make himself entitled to her commonest consideration, but who was a man so despicable in his conduct in every respect, that if it be possible for one person to disgrace another, then most certainly did he achieve that object as far as she was concerned.

She felt it was rather a strange circumstance that after she had moved, and had succeeded in putting a few things to rights in her new home, her thoughts should suddenly revert to him, and with a painful sort of impression, too, of some undefined evil in connexion with him.

Such a feeling as that is always annoying, for it rapidly affects the imagination, and conjures up a host of greater evils than are at all likely to ensue.

The day wore away, and she was beginning to get rid of the uncomfortable impression regarding her husband, when, as she stood by her cottage-door, she heard some men laughing and talking as they walked along the Heath, and from their frequent mention of the name of a tavern in the immediate neighbourhood, she guessed that they formed a portion of some riotous party which was going there to regale.

She took no notice of the proceeding, and walked into her house, but she was quickly summoned to the door again by some one wrapping at it with a stick, and a loud voice cried—

"Hilloa! missus, how far is it to Golden-green, and which is the way?"

Mrs. Grove clasped her hands in dismay, and well she might, for in that voice she recognised at once the tones of her recreant and drunken husband.

Terror deprived her for a few moments of the power to speak, and then reflection kept her silent, and she thought that if she made no answer he might go away, suspecting nobody was in the place, or that, if they were, no one was disposed to give him an answer to his question.

But Jack Grove had seen a female form standing at the door of that cottage, and consequently he was not to be abashed, but, on the contrary, at once made his appearance within the door-step, saying—

"You might as well give a fellow a civil answer, whoever you are."

Mrs. Grove felt that there was no help for it now, and that although she would have given worlds to prevent it, the much-dreaded recognition must take place.

She was not a woman, when circumstances of difficulty actually occurred, to make them worse by shrinking from them, and accordingly she now advanced, and, with an air of great dignity, she confronted the man who had been the bane of her existence.

" My wife !" he cried; " the devil ! This is a chance. Why, Mrs. Grove, where have you been hiding yourself all this while ?"

" Where I hoped," she said, " to continue hidden from you, and the only favour that I can ask at your hands is, that you will leave me and forget me."

" There is a pretty go," said Jack Grove, looking around him ; " and I must say that, as far as I can see, you seem tolerably comfortable here, and everything looks as pleasant as possible. Upon my word, Mrs. Grove, you seem to me to have brought your pigs to some uncommonly good market, and perhaps you won't have any objection to explain."

" How dare you," said Mrs. Grove, with indignation, " how dare you speak to me of explanations, when you yourself deserted me, leaving me to seek a living by any means within my power ? Your effrontery in appearing before me at all, after the conduct of which you have been guilty, almost exceeds belief. Begone at once, and let shame keep you miles from this spot, and any other upon which I may reside !"

" Very good," said Jack Grove, as he sat down; " there is nothing like carrying things with a high hand. I admire the principle; and as I have been in the law since I last saw you, I am a better judge of those sort of matters than I was."

" You in the law," said Mrs. Grove; " but I understand you. The law has, no doubt, exacted from you some penalties for your vicious conduct. Begone, sir, at once, begone !"

" No, I thank you, that won't do now. I aint half such a fool as I was when we used to live at the village ; I know better now my own interest, and how to manage matters. I am forced to live upon my wits now."

" I should say then, indeed," said Mrs. Grove, " that you get a poor subsistence."

" I thank you for the compliment," said Jack, " but I suppose a man may inquire after his own flesh and blood, so I ask you what's become of my son, who will be heir to all my property."

" I sincerely hope that he will be heir to none of his father's vices. You will find him at his grandmother's in the country, who has had charge of him for the last twelve months."

" The deuce she has ! Well, well, as the old lady and I never did agree, I think it is better for me not to go."

" It is better for you not to go, for you are perfectly aware in what contempt you are held by those poor but honest people."

" What is it to me what they think or what they say ? and now let me ask, as I am here, what became of that child, that you got such a precious load of money for taking care of ?"

" Once of all understand me, I will answer no questions whatever of yours. You have long ago forfeited all right to ask them, and I will not answer one."

" Give us hold of some money."

" Not a farthing ; not a fraction of a farthing."

" You don't mean to tell me you haven't got any ?"

" I have told you no such thing, for I have plenty, and yet you shall not have a farthing of it; and if you dare to make yourself to the least extent troublesome, I can and will get the assistance of one who will soon rid me of your annoyance."

Jack Grove was a little staggered at the bold course that was pursued by his wife, and by adopting it she showed that she knew well the individual she had to deal with, who was a mixture of cowardice and audacity, and just one of those slaves who will always act the tyrant when they can.

It suddenly struck him that his wife could not possibly know all that had occurred with respect to the exertions that the Countess of Crumbledown was making to discover her place of retreat with the earl's child, and he thought that to be sure now, by carrying such information to her ladyship, he should earn from her some very handsome reward, but that if he alarmed his wife to a great extent she might hastily remove, and so defeat his intentions.

Accordingly, Jack determined now to temporize with her and to affect a moderation of sentiment and intention he was very far indeed from feeling.

" I tell you what it is, Mrs. Grove," he said, " of course it aint very pleasant to visit one's wife after all these years, and get nothing but bad words from her. You know that as well as I. I don't want to interfere with you, for I am an altered

man now to what I was, and I'll go away at once to convince you that it is so, and then you will see whether I want to annoy you or not. I shan't come near you again for a month, so that you wi.l have time to consider what sort of a reception I ought to have."

So saying, Jack Grove turned upon his heel and walked from the cottage, leaving his wife certainly immensely astonished at what could be the causes of his conduct, although far from being deceived by it into any feeling of false security, for she well knew he must have some design in saying what he did.

CHAPTER LXIII.

MR. WILLOUGHBY GIVES LADY CRUMBLEDOWN STARTLING EVIDENCE.

"MR. WILLOUGHBY, my lady," said a servant on that evening, laying a card before the Countess of Crumbledown.

The countess started, for she did not expect that Willoughby would have the effrontery to call upon her at her own house, but she began to find that she must, in common with every one else who made them, reap the consequences of having low accomplices, and with some degree of confusion she ordered that Willoughby should be shown into a private apartment, where in a few moments she went to him.

He was quite sufficiently versed in the countess's character to perceive at once that she was ruffled at his visit, and considered it as rather an outrageous thing, but this did not deter him, and putting on his look of utmost audacity, he said to her,

"Madam, knowing the great anxiety which you must be labouring under regarding the circumstances connected with the earl's supposed previous marriage, I have come to you to inform you that I have absolutely discovered the fact of their union, that is to say, the union of the earl with the mother of that child who is kept so mysteriously concealed."

"But concealed no longer," said the countess, "from me."

Willoughby started, as he said in a voice of some confusion,

"Have you then, indeed, discovered the abode of the Love Child? Where has he succeeded in so long and so ingeniously concealing it?"

"Mr. Willoughby, I pay you for bringing me information, but it has never formed any portion of my plans to give you any."

Willoughby bit his lip as he replied,

"But madam, it may, for all I know, much facilitate my getting information for you, that you should give me what news you can upon the subjects that are of such great interest to you."

"I will take my chance of that," she said, "and as I can well suppose you have not come here, Mr. Willoughby, without some motive, allow me to ask you at once what it is?"

"Most certainly you shall hear from me, madam, all that I know, without the smallest reservation. If the earl and this young person were really married, it struck me that the ceremony had most likely taken place somewhere in the immediate vicinity of London, and I accordingly made it my business to visit all the little suburban churches for the purpose of examining their records, to see if anything in the shape of an entry could be found relating to the earl's marriage with the party your ladyship has so much cause to dread, and I have found that at an obscure village church called Kingslake, about fourteen miles from town in a northerly direction, the earl was duly married in the name of Warelock to Emily Whitford."

"Warelock is his family name."

"It is, and it adds to the legality of the marriage, although his being married in any name would have made the matter equally dangerous."

"Can you assure me of this fact; and how is it that it was not communicated to you by the mother herself, since it really seems that she came to you as a client?"

"I lost her confidence, and lost her custom."

"How?"

"She saw your ladyship's equipage at the door of my chambers, and that finished the business, but I can produce evidence of a satisfactory nature regarding what I now tell you. The entry of the marriage is in the parish register, which can be produced as evidence at any time, but your ladyship knows enough of me to feel assured that I'm not one who is likely to come to you and propose a difficulty, without at the same time having in my mind some means of overcoming it."

" What means are those ?"

" Why, my lady, in law, when a fact stares us in the face, and we cannot get rid of it as a fact, the only thing we can then do is to discover some means, if possible, of quashing the evidence of it."

" But how can that be done ?"

" I have not only ascertained how it can be done, before I came here, but the price at which it may be done."

" Go on, sir ; go on, sir."

" A leaf torn out of the registry of that church might contain the very entry, which it is so important to you should never appear. I was too well watched to tear it out myself, but the party who watched me will tear it out, and bring it you for a consideration."

" And what is his price ?"

" He considers he is doing it cheaply, when he asks a £1,000 ; as for my own remuneration, I shall leave that to be named by your ladyship's generosity."

" And who is this man who sets so high a price upon his services ?"

" He is the beadle of the parish in which the church is situated. I run great personal risk in proposing any such thing to him, but without entering into any particulars with him, or even pointing out the precise leaf which I wished to be torn out from the register, my zeal for your service induced me to ask him at what price he would do such a thing, and my confidence in human nature made me think that he would not scruple if the reward was high."

" This is nothing but a statement from you to me," said the countess, " and you cannot be surprised that I entertain doubts upon the subject which it is for you to satisfy."

" I know not, my lady, how I can satisfy them, except by saying, that not a sixpence of the money named is required of you, until you actually have the document I have named in your possession. Make what inquiry you like in the meantime, and satisfy yourself in every possible way you can, consistent with security, but do not go so far as to endanger the real secret, because upon the leaf of the register, which I shall require the man to tear out of the book, there are no less than four marriages recorded, and although I will indicate the leaf which is to be torn out, see no occasion whatever for indicating the special entry in which we are interested."

" Certainly not, certainly not ; I will consider of this matter ; but may there not be other evidence, I mean the evidence of living persons, of the fact of that marriage taking place?"

" I cannot tell, but it is most unlikely, because, as may be well supposed, the marriage would be conducted as privately as possible, and it strikes me that by destroying the legal evidence which would be afforded by the registry, you will most probably succeed in destroying all evidence whatever of the fact."

" And you will require for your services in the matter—"

" I certainly, madam, should not like to take less than a parish beadle."

" I will consider of it," said the countess, rising, " and let you know the result of my determination. It seems strange to me that you have not succeeded, with all your resources, in discovering where the earl hid the child, while I, with no resources at all, comparatively speaking, may certainly congratulate myself upon making such a discovery."

" I give your ladyship all the credit possible for having made it, and I can only very much regret that you do not think me sufficiently entitled to your confidence to share in the information."

The countess returned no answer to this whatever, but just left Willoughby to draw what inferences he liked, to his great aggravation, for he could not help suspecting, from the whole of her manner, that she was in possession of more information than he exactly liked to think she had, upon those subjects which he was endeavouring, with such an abundance of art, to turn to profit.

She, likewise, always suspected that Willoughby never told her more than was just sufficient to answer his own purposes, and thus was it that these two persons, each of them as unprincipled as they could possibly be, perplexed and annoyed each other, creating much confusion, and, even when they spoke the truth, each one believed that it was quite the reverse, because, associated together, as they might now be considered to be, for the most vicious purposes, it was quite impossible that anything like confidence could subsist between them.

CHAPTER LXIV.

THE EARL CONSULTS WITH THE COLONEL CONCERNING THE STRANGE COMMUNICATION, AND THEY DETERMINE UPON ALARMING THE COUNTESS.

Now that the earl had, as he supposed, got rid of any danger as regarded the child of whom he was really so fond, he turned his attention to the strange communication which had been made to him by the stranger, who had represented himself actually to be the father of the countess.

He knew that he could not by any possibility get better advice upon that subject than his friend Colonel Bruce would give him, and he accordingly detailed to that gentleman all that had been told him, and concluded by saying,—

"You see, Bruce, that after all there appears to be a kind of retribution in this affair, and that I have a power of completely confounding Lady Crumbledown just upon the very high ground which she assumes, in this unfortunate affair of mine with Emily Whitford, to confound me."

"I see that; but yet you must remember what a woman of strong passions she is, and that by anything of the kind you only set her scheming brain to work to counteract what she considers an evil. I think it well that you should know such a circumstance if it can be proved, because, in the event of any open rupture with her, at all events such a secret places you in a good position, and effectually prevents her taking any advantage of Emily Whitford's case."

"Yes, it would have that effect, and my only doubt was whether it would be better to keep the thing for the present perfectly quiet, and wait until some circumstances arose to make it of importance, or to let her know in some way that I am in possession of a dangerous secret to her, which I will only keep so long as she holds out an inducement to me to do so by her own behaviour."

"Well, there is something in that, and perhaps the latter course would not be amiss. She will, of course, set all her ingenuity to work to endeavour to discover what it is, that is to say, provided she be really ignorant of it, which to my mind is an extremely doubtful case."

"The experiment shall be tried, and this very day too; and I will, at all events, speak daggers to her, as Hamlet says, although I am now convinced that she knows much if not all of the affair connected with Emily Whitford."

"Likely enough; and you may be further convinced that she has got some scheme of persecution in her mind, which, if it can be nipped in the bud by persuading her that you have a power to detail something that will make her uncomfortable, would be a most desirable thing, but it would be a thousand pities to throw away, in the shape of a mere threat, this affair which has been communicated to you and offered to be proved, at all events, if it was not really so. Break the matter very gently to her, extremely gently, indeed, so as to give her not the slightest power of guessing what it is, while, at the same time, she shall have no possible excuse for not believing that it is the truth, and not only the truth, but a very important truth."

"I will do it—I will do it! and I will watch her very countenance and her very expressions that flit across it as I speak to her, so that I may be able to judge most distinctly and clearly if what I have to say to her be entirely fresh news or something that she has some previous idea about."

"Do so; and if she know it, the fact of your knowing it likewise will touch her to the quick; but, before you take that step, it is due to yourself that you should call upon the individual who has given you the information for more-proof of his assertion than his simple word suffices to surround it with."

" I will do that; he offered me such proof, and therefore I have no reason to believe he will shrink from giving it to me."

" The countess little suspected, while she was plotting and planning to see in what way she could maintain that exalted station which she thought was to act in quite a different quarter to what it really was—little suspected the mine, so to speak, upon which she was standing, and which might at any moment blow all her dignity to the winds by branding her with that very appellation of " bastard," which she was so ready to bestow wherever she had a notion it was due.

Ever since Willoughby had made to her the last communication, her mind had been in a state of the greatest possible excitement short of that amount which would have disabled her from thinking at all upon the subjects nearest her heart. It certainly presented itself to her in pleasant colours—the idea that she might be enabled now to crush both mother and child of that unhappy pair, which she believed created for her annoyance.

" If," she thought, " I could succeed without suspicion of encompassing the child's death, while at the same time I deprive the mother, if she be living, of the power of proving her position, I shall certainly have achieved wonders."

Maddened and angry, however, as she was at the earl, it was a source of great bitterness and great regret to her that she could not make him fully suffer all the legal consequences of his double marriage. This would, indeed, have been delightful to her spirit, but she was forced to save him in order to save herself.

And now we cannot help remarking what a tangled web of difficulty, falsehood, and dissimulation both these persons, the Earl and the Countess of Crumbledown, have got into for the want of a little candour. Had either of them been wise enough, for candour is wisdom—we say, had either of them been wise enough to smother for one half hour all feeling of resentment, and to state fairly and exactly what they knew and thought about this Love Child, all must have been well.

The countess's resentment would have vanished into indifference, could she but have been aware that Emily Whitford was not only dead but that she had no claim to call herself the earl's wife; and he, on the other hand, would have been free from the annoyance of fancying that she was continually meditating something againt his child, because it was his child.

But in people circumstanced as they were, and with such thoughts and feelings, what tools for his ambitious ends and designs did such a man as Willoughby find! Had the earl and countess been for half-an-hour candid with each other, Willoughby's functions would have been gone. But the villain knew well that such was not the case; he knew that there was too lasting and excellent misunderstanding between them to be readily patched up.

We have seen with what adroitness he managed, when he found that the earl would no longer pay him, to turn the countess's evil passions to account, and how cleverly he succeeded in making her believe things that were only the suggestion of his own brain, and conceived for his own profit.

When we add to all this the cleverness with which he had kept the Whitford family quiet, and the tact he had displayed, at all events for some time, in keeping Jack Grove out of mischief, we are inclined to regret that so much ability was thrown away upon so bad a subject, and to wish that there had been even such a fragment of honesty, which, alas! there was not in the disposition of Jonathan Willoughby, attorney-at-law, and about as great a scoundrel as that profession, which enjoys an unenviable popularity as regards the production of such characters, could furnish.

*   *   *   *   *   *   *

The earl, as he had made up his mind that he would—let what his lady's feelings were on the matter connected with the assented fact of her own illegitimacy, be—thought that there would be no harm, notwithstanding the advice of Colonel Bruce, and the sort of half promise that he had made, not to stir in the business until he had obtained something like positive proof of what the alleged father of the countess had asserted, in just hinting at the matter. He was the more inclined to do this at once, because of a little circumstance that took place in the course of the day.

That circumstance was this. While he, the earl, was at home for the short space of time that was required to dress to go out again, which generally comprised the amount of time he spent in his own house, received a message from the countess to say she would be glad to speak to him. This was common enough between them, although virtually residing in the same house, and being in the near relationship to each other of man and wife. If the earl had anything to say to the countess, and that, Heaven knows, was not very often, he used to send a servant with his compliments, and she in the same manner sent to him.

Upon this occasion he sent word back that he would see her in the receiving room in three minutes.

When he got there, and he took care to go with his hat in one hand and his riding-whip in the other, to show that he was going out, and therefore wished the conference cut as short as possible, he found his lady waiting for him.

"I shall not detain you a moment," she said, as she glanced at his preparations for leaving the house; "I merely wished to tell you that I give a party to-night, and that, of course, if you are disengaged, I should be happy to see you."

"I shall have great pleasure," said the earl, in a tone of much civility, "in accepting an invitation so graciously given to me in my own house."

So saying, he turned upon his heel and left her at once, while she bit her lips with vexation, as she muttered—

"So he means to come, does he, and trouble me while I have got my intimates here? I expected anger; but if he begins in the sarcastic style, I must alter my tactics towards him. And yet, I do not regret his determination to come, for it will give me an opportunity of annoying him, surely, in some way or shape. What if I were to hint to him something about the child he takes now such care to conceal from me—or—or perhaps I might arrive at some correct conclusion about the fact of his marriage to the mother of that creature who stands so much in my way; if I were cautiously to say something that would touch him to the quick, and then watch his countenance. Let him come, I will do it."

It will be thus seen that the earl and the countess felt disposed to hurt each other's feelings a little, for he, when he left her, said to himself—

"Yes, I will go to this party of hers. It will surely afford me some opportunity of saying to her what I wish, and if she really knows anything of her real condition, I shall have the satisfaction of spoiling her pleasure for the evening."

* * * * * * *

The entertainments of the Countess of Crumbledown were always well attended, and of the most gorgeous and costly description, but strange to say, in her invitations she mostly looked out for those people who she thought would be angry instead of pleased at the glittering display she, with her ample means, was able to lay before them.

If she could excite a powerful feeling of envy she was quite delighted.

And we make bold to say, that in the class of society in which the Countess of Crumbledown moved, she did not find much difficulty in exciting such feelings, for if envy be a passion that deforms all classes, it certainly is not found to its least extent among the idle and unworthy, who, as some critics have said, have nothing to do but to make a comfortable hot bed for the cultivation of all the vices of human nature.

With the ample means she possessed, it is no wonder that the entertainments of the countess were of that description that the Morning Post delights to allude to and describe in the glowing diction peculiar to that journal, and as she was by no means a woman wanting in taste or talent, we certainly must admit that when she did give what she called an entertainment, it was a something in every way worthy of the name, and conducted upon a right royal scale indeed.

We do not mean to take up the reader's time at the present juncture with any laboured description of the entertainment given on the occasion by the Countess of

Crumbledown. It will be sufficient for us if we briefly state what she and the earl said to each other on the occasion; and although the latter said he would be at the party, he did not make his appearance until very late, and then it was only for the express purpose of making the experiment he intended upon his wife's nerves.

When he entered the room he was himself surprised at the glittering throng she had succeeded in collecting, and it was some time before he found her in such a large assemblage of persons.

When they did see each other, however, their desire to meet was mutual, and, consequently, the meeting soon took place.

" You have a gay assemblage here," he said, "and it is not one of the least advantages of birth, that such persons can be collected together under one roof."

" It is a great advantage of birth," she replied, " and it shows how careful persons of rank should be that they do not in early life contract disgraceful alliances which they are afterwards ashamed to own."

She looked in the earl's face as she spoke, but he never winced in the least, and for a very good reason too, because the reader well knows that he could not be at all affected by the hint, inasmuch as he was not at all open to the accusation, and the only thing that surprised him was the pointed manner in which the countess chose to make what appeared to him so common place a remark ; and, after a moment's pause, he said—

"I quite agree with your ladyship, that nothing can be worse than a misalliance of the character you mention, except it be when some person, with wonderful audacity, assumes a rank and station which the accident of their birth, if it happened to be well known instead of being kept a profound secret, by no means entitles them to."

The earl now watched the lady's countenance as he spoke, but he saw nothing there but an expression of surprise, and he began to think it was just possible he might, after all, be misinformed.

And so these two very cunning persons continued looking at each other, rather puzzled to know what to do or say; for they each felt themselves disappointed at the manner in which the other had received their questions.

They made up their minds mutually that there was much more in what they said than met the ear, and that it would be worth while inquiring into each other's meaning, if they had been on sufficiently good terms to do so ; but that they clearly were not ; and so, after a few more common place remarks, they separated, mutually dissatisfied and disappointed with the result of what had taken place, which had left them just where they were, as regarded the subjects concerning which they were so anxious.

The countess had never given the earl great credit for the ability to conceal his real thoughts and feelings ; but now she began to think that it must have been an effort of great art that had enabled him to answer the question, or rather the remark, that came from her lips with so apparently frank and unembarrassed an air and manner.

He, on the other hand, was inclined to believe that she was really quite ignorant of the matter to which he had alluded, and he did not know, very well, whether to feel pleased or angry at that supposition, although he felt convinced that it enabled him, when he used the fact, to use it with much more stunning effect upon her that as if she were already acquainted with it, and looked forward to it coming out, some day, in evidence.

" She knows it not," he said, " she knows it not, and so will its effect be all the greater, and when it does come upon her, in all its full force, she will feel herself overwhelmed by its consequences."

CHAPTER LXV.

JACK GROVE INFORMS THE COUNTESS OF THE RESIDENCE OF THE LOVE CHILD.

THE day following such an entertainment as that which the Countess of Crumbledown had given must surely be one of listlessness and *ennui*.

She did not rise till very late, and after she had made her appearance in the drawing-room and had been reclining upon a sofa for some time, Margaret, her confidential maid, came to her and said, in a mysterious whisper—

"My lady, there is a man below, who, they say, has been waiting for about two hours and a half to see your ladyship, and he will not disclose his errand to any one, but says that it is important he should see you, for that he has something to tell you which you will be pleased to hear."

"I do not know," said the countess, "that I ought to see him, and yet, situated as I am, I scarcely like to refuse. Show him into the small room adjoining the dining-parlour, and say I will come to him."

This order was promptly obeyed, and the countess, after revolving in her own mind all the possibilities and the probabilities as to who it was likely to be, at length, with no small amount of curiosity, repaired to the room into which she had directed he should be shown, and when she saw him she at once recognised in him the individual who had cast such doubts upon the testimony of Jonathan Willoughby, concerning the continued existence of Emily Whitford.

She concluded that he had come to offer her some new evidence on that head, but such was not the case, as she soon discovered.

"Well, ma'am," said Jack Grove, "I don't know whether you have been trying, or others have been trying for you, to find out where my wife has hidden herself with the child, but I have discovered it."

"Indeed! I think your information comes to me too late to be of service, for that is a discovery I have already made."

Jack Grove looked rather blank at this, for he certainly had expected some very handsome reward for bringing that news of his wife's residence, which we know he had acquired by such mere accident, but which he was quite willing to turn to as good an account as possible.

"If," said the countess, "you have any further proof that the mother of the child is dead, I will listen to it; but I am assured she is living and that you have been deceived. You admit yourself that you were out of the way during the period?"

"Why, yes," said Jack Grove, "I certainly did have a little misunderstanding with some of the county magistrates, and as might, you know, is right, my lady, they very unjustly sent me to the county-gaol, but when I came out I heard all about it."

"You may have been misinformed; and I have to assure you that Jonathan Willoughby has given me such strong evidence upon the subject, that there is scarcely room left to doubt."

"Jonathan Willoughby! why, you are never going to believe anything that he says? I should doubt if I had my head upon my shoulders, if Jonathan Willoughby was to set about proving it. You don't know what a rogue he is!"

"I cannot help it, but must be guided by circumstances, and all I can say to you is bring me any facts that you can and I will amply reward you, but surmises are no use to me, and, as you came upon this occasion to give me a piece of information, which it appears I by mere accident became acquainted with before you, I will not disappoint you of some reward. Here is money for you!"

"Well, my lady, that's liberal enough of you," said Jack Grove, "because I certainly have no right to expect to be paid for what you know already. It's a pretty situation that my wife has got upon Hampstead Heath."

"Hampstead Heath!"

"Yes, my lady; the cottage where she lives, Bellender Cottage it's called, and its windows look quite over the heath."

"This is very strange," said the countess; "are you certain you are correct?"

"I have been there, seen her, and spoken to her, and she as good as told me to go to the devil, so I came here as soon as I could."

Lady Crumbledown rung the bell, and when a servant appeared, she said,—

"Tell Margaret I wish to speak with her."

In a few moments the waiting-maid entered the room, and then the countess turning to Grove, said,—

"Tell her where your wife resides."

"Why, on Hampstead-heath, to be sure," said Jack Grove, "in a pleasant-enough little place called Bellender Cottage."

"Indeed!" said Margaret; "I can tell you, sir, that you are much mistaken, for I saw her in quite another place."

"Damn it," said Jack Grove, "I spoke to her, and ought to know my own wife, I think."

"It is no matter," said the countess, "it is no matter; this is merely some little mistake which, no doubt, can be readily rectified. Mr. Grove, whenever you have anything to say to me in the shape of information, I shall of course be glad to see you."

So saying she rose and walked from the room, whispering to Margaret as she went,—

"Get rid of him as quickly as possible, and then come to me."

This was done; and when the mistress and the maid were again together, the countess said,—

"I can understand all this perfectly. It is quite plain to me that you have been observed in watching the earl, and that in consequence the woman Grove has changed her residence. Of course, this is merely my supposition at present, but it can be easily ascertained."

Margaret looked a little mortified that this should be the case, for she thought that she had acted in the matter so very cleverly that the earl had had no suspicion whatever of her dodging him, but still she felt that it was far better her ladyship should imagine such to be the case, than that she (Margaret) had deceived her, for that would have been a very uncomfortable idea, although she could have proved probably in a short time that such certainly was not the case.

"It is possible, my lady," she said, "that I may have been watched, because for all we know he may have somebody in his employment to look out and see if any one follows him; and if that be the case, it is as your ladyship supposes, no doubt the fact that she has removed suddenly, in order to baffle us."

The countess remained in thought for some minutes, and then as she was about to speak, a card was brought to her, on which were written the words,

"A lady wishes to speak with the Countess of Crumbledown."

"Who can this be?" she muttered to herself; "go, Margaret, and s e. Ascertain, if you can, who the intruder is. What if it should be —"

"Who, my lady, who?"

"I am almost afraid to say the word; but what, if it should be the earl's first wife!"

"Gracious Heavens! couldn't we manage, my lady, to smother her, or something of that sort?"

"No. Hush! nothing must be done—nothing attempted. Do you hide behind yonder screen when she comes here, and over-hear what passes; I will send for her to this room."

All this was done as the countess projected, and in the course of a few minutes, a fashionably-dressed female of considerable personal attractions was ushered into the apartment.

She and the countess regarded each other for a few moments in silence, and then the visitor said,

"Madam, in thus intruding upon you, I cannot help feeling a large amount of diffidence under the circumstances, but as I have a communication to make to you which I think has been too long delayed, I trust you will excuse the abruptness of this intrusion."

"I hope," said the countess, "that I shall have the pleasure of knowing with whom I am conversing?"

"It is for no other earthly purpose, madam," said the visitor, "but just to tell you who I am, that I came here."

"Indeed!"

"Yes, it is to make known to you a secret which the solicitations of another, and a wish to spare your feelings, have induced me to keep, I fear, much too long locked within the recesses of my own breast. It is a secret which ought to have been told to you long ago, and I cannot but greatly pity the unhappy circumstances that have made it a matter of such deep interest to you."

"I pray you go on, madam," said the countess, dissembling her agitation as well as she could ; "go on, madam, I am not aware of any particular circumstance which can largely interest me that any stranger can possibly have to communicate."

"It is that feeling of conscious security which your entire ignorance of what I have to relate to you gives you, that I have been loth to disturb, but it must be done, and I can only ask you, madam, to prepare yourself for a shock."

"I have tolerable nerves," said the countess, "pray proceed."

"I am glad you have good nerves, for the knowledge of that fact gives me greater confidence to tell you that I am the Countess of Crumbledown."

"You!"

"Yes; compose yourself. Some time before your marriage with the earl, I was wedded to him at a little obscure country church, called Kingslake; and my daughter consequently is the heiress presumptive of the Crumbledown property."

The countess made a successful effort to conceal the feelings of strong emotion that came over her as she said—

"I cannot assert that such a thing is impossible, but you will hardly have come to me with such a tale, unless you were provided with proof of its accuracy."

"The clergyman who married us is dead, as well as the only other person who was present at the marriage besides the earl and myself, but the church registry will of course prove the fact."

"And that," said the countess, rather eagerly, "and that is the only evidence."

"It is surely sufficient; and I should certainly, before this, have presented myself to your ladyship, had I not been kept back by a lawyer, whom I employed, and who I began to think had private notions of his own in suppressing my just claims, for he has more than once urged me to abandon them altogether."

"And that lawyer's name?"

"Is Willoughby."

"Yes, is Willoughby. Madam, without attempting to throw any discredit upon your story, or in the smallest degree casting any doubt upon your veracity, you must feel that I can take no step in this matter without abundant proof, but as I shall be out of town for ten days or more, there will be no occasion to trouble you to produce that proof or even to set about procuring it till my return."

"I understand your ladyship. I shall not do anything hastily or take any measures which shall wear the appearance of harshness, towards you who are the most innocent person in the whole transaction, and deserving of the greatest amount of consideration. On the back of the card which I sent by your servant, you will find an address at which any communication will reach me."

"In about ten days," said the countess, with something of an abstracted air and manner, "in about ten days you shall hear from me, and if you can then prove that you are entitled to call yourself the Countess of Crumbledown, I shall be the last person in the world to oppose your assumption of the title."

"This is great liberality under the circumstances ; in fact much greater liberality than I ought to have expected, and of course it shall be my earnest endeavour so to shape my conduct in assuming the title which I must dispossess you of, so as to give you as little pain as possible."

"You are considerate," said the countess, "you are very considerate, and I will think upon what can be done so as to give me as little pain as possible."

The strange visitor now rose to depart, and Lady Crumbledown rung the bell for a servant to show her out, and had her ladyship been close behind her as she walked down the street, she would have heard her say—

"I think old Willoughby ought to stand something very handsome for this, for I never acted anything better in all my life, and whatever may be his design in the matter, he can't say but what I have played my part well."

"Margaret, Margaret," cried the countess, when her visitor was gone, "you have heard all. Tell me, do you think this woman will really give us ten days for action ?"

"She promised it, my lady, and I think she will, she seemed so astonished at the calm manner in which you took her information."

"She did, and at all events she has given me one piece of important information, and that is, that the church register is the only evidence it is in her power to produce. You heard her say that the witnesses were dead."

"Yes, I did."

"Give me writing materials at once. Quick, quick, Margaret, give me writing materials, I must address a note to Willoughby. I have now proof that in this transaction at least he is honest. Yes, I must write to Willoughby—I must write to Willoughby at once."

CHAPTER LXVI.

THE BEADLE OF KINGSLAKE PROMISES TO AID THE COUNTESS, AND SHE PAYS A LARGE PRICE FOR A PAGE OF WRITING PAPER.

Mr Jonathan Willoughby was not very likely to neglect any message that might be sent to him by the Countess of Crumbledown, and the fact of his receiving a note from her to come to her as soon as possible, as quickly after he had employed the actress to call upon her ladyship and personate the mother of the Love Child, convinced him of the complete success of that plan which had entered into his prolific brain.

He was quite in glee at the thought that he was about now, with such real ease, to get possession of so large a sum of money—a sum such as in no other way could he have hoped to persuade the countess to disburse, although, really speaking, it was not to her a very formidable amount, when we come to consider the immense fortune which the death of the old Earl of Crumbledown placed within her grasp. In the course of an hour Willoughby was with her, and they were closetted in a private apartment.

"Mr Willoughby," she said, "I have sent for you because a circumstance has happened which so far confirms the statements I have received from you, that I am willing to embrace the course you propose."

"What course may I ask, madam?" said Willoughby, affecting an ignorance of the precise meaning of the countess. "What course, may I ask, madam, do you allude to?"

"The course as regards the registry of the earl's former marriage at the church of Kingslake. That registry must be destroyed—destroyed at once."

"It can be so in the manner I have suggested, madam. The price which I shall have to pay to the beadle of Kingslake for undertaking such a thing, is one that I have named to your ladyship; and, although it sounds large, yet when you come to consider what a serious risk he and I run of bad consequences in case of detection, I am quite certain that your ladyship will—"

"Enough, enough, you shall have the money; but I must see the man who is to do the work. I wish to have an interview with this beadle of Kingslake, who, you tell me, has promised his concurrence in the affair."

"That you shall have, madam; and it will be much more satisfactory to me that you should, because I think you ought to know by sight always any one whom you may employ in an office of such importance as this is, and who may eventually to a greater extent be—"

"When can you bring him? I wish to do everything with the greatest caution, but, at the same time, I wish that what has to be done, should be done as quietly as possible, and without the least shadow of an unnecessary delay."

"Your ladyship has but to name your own hour, for he is in town, living now at my expense, awaiting your decision upon the matter; and I think you had better come privately to my chambers, so that you will see him without him at all knowing who you are."

"But can his knowledge of who I am be avoided?"

" Yes ; as I before mentioned, there are several entries of marriages upon one page of the church registry, and I indicate to him the page I want torn out, and not the particular entry which has become of importance to quash."

" I understand, I understand ; I will be at your chambers in two hours' time from now."

" That will do excellently well, for it will give me time to get the beadle of Kingslake to meet you there, and you can ask him what questions you please. I can only say for myself, that I am most happy to be able to do your ladyship this service; and my advice to you is, to pay no money whatever until you actually see the leaf of the register which contains the notice of the earl's former marriage, and have it placed in your possession."

" That is advice which is judicious, and which goes far, coming from you, to prove your fairness in this proceeding. I will take such advice, and until I do have the leaf of the register placed in my hands, I pay nothing."

"You may adopt such a course as that madam, with great propriety, because there can be but the most trifling expenses incurred in carrying out the matter, and, therefore, there is no excuse for demanding money beforehand."

This apparent fairness and candour on the part of Willoughby went far towards convincing the countess of the general character of the affair, and it is a remarkable trait in the character of this most imperious and strange woman, that she was so much more ready to believe what gave her trouble and uneasiness than the reverse.

It will be observed, that although the story told her by Jack Grove was one which, in its very simplicity, deserved to be believed, she must have dismissed it from her mind in favour of the more laboured suppositions and statements of Willoughby, who she might well have suspected of possessing both the will and the power to deceive her.

There can be no doubt but that she pondered over the chance of Willoughby's statements being true, until she convinced herself that they really were so.

In her progress to the chambers of Willoughby now, she dispensed altogether with the services of any of her carriages, and got Margaret to procure for her a hackney coach which waited round the corner of the street for her, and then conveyed her with all imaginable secresy to the place of destination.

Willoughby, in the mean time, had not been idle, and from the interview that followed, we may see that he had, with considerable tact, selected his confederates.

The uncomfortable ricketty old coach drew up at the door of Willoughby's chambers in due time, and telling her waiting maid who went with her, to wait for her in the vehicle, Lady Crumbledown entered alone the legal emporium of that most tremendous scoundrel.

Of course, Willoughby was within, and, of course, he had given private orders so that the countess could at once be shewn into his room which was so well provided with double doors in order to stop the possibility of any strange sound or observation issuing therefrom, and enlightening the clerks who did duty in the outer office, as to what was going on in the inner one.

All this was very proper and very satisfactory, no doubt, to the countess, and with some little flutter of spirits only, and a very slight notion that it might have been better if she had left the matter entirely in the hands of Willoughby, and not have mixed himself up in it at all, she waited his appearance, which took place almost immediately.

" Madam," he said, " you are punctual, but I have the party here whom it was your pleasure to say you would see here in my humble chambers."

The countess inclined her head, and Willoughby continued :—

" You will find him quite a specimen, madam, of his class—an ignorant man, rather inflated with the idea of the importance of the situation he holds, and fond of using language which he considers fine, but which, unhappily, he does not understand the meaning of, and so constantly misapplies as a matter of course."

" It matters little," said the countess, " what he is, so that he performs faithfully

the service I require of him, and afterwards keeps profoundly secret the whole proceeding."

"Oh, that he is quite certain for his own sake to do, inasmuch as he could only,
beyond all dispute, accuse himself, and, in consequence, draw upon upon his head
the vengeance of the law, while he would find it, I rather flatter myself, a difficult
matter to prove anything against your ladyship, between whom and anything at
all disagreeable, I consider it to be my duty to stand."

"Very well, very well," said the countess, in a slight tone of impatience, "I do
not, at all events, as yet, see that I have any occasion to be dissatisfied with you
as regards this transaction, so let me see the man at once."

Willoughby walked into the small room in which the countess had been made to
believe, on her former visit to those chambers, she had caught a glimpse of her most
dangerous rival, as regarded her coronet, and said, in a voice that fell quite distinctly upon the countess's ear—

"Mr. Brown, the Mrs. Smith whom I mentioned to you is here now, and
wishes to see you if you will follow me."

"In course," said another voice, "I shall follow you, sir, with all the pacifica-
tion and obstropolousness in the geological universe."

"And remember, Mr. Brown," said Willoughby, "that the lady you are about
to see is one who will much prefer a plain and intelligible answer to what she says,
than any display of your learning."

"I shall be quite miraculously adjectative," said the beadle; "the lady may
depend upon my promiscuous behaviour, Mr. Willoughby, but as for quite hiding
that I knows what I knows, I don't think as how I can astronomically do it."

"Well, well, only be as brief as you can."

"I'll be as brief, Mr. Willoughby, as the collusion of affairs will let me, I assure
you; so without any more quadrupedal conversation let us go on like a stratum."

"And," thought the countess, as she heard the profound remarks of the beadle,
"and is anything in which I take a strong interest to be submitted to the guidance
of such an idiot as this. Heaven help me! Heaven help me, if I have no better
tools than these with which to work. But what resource have I? It must be done
as he, Willoughby, has suggested, for while that church register exists, I can know
no peace in this world. I have now thrown myself into a stream, from the current
of which there can be no escape, and from which I dare not even attempt to emerge,
and I must go as the wild waters choose to hurry me."

In another moment the learned beadle was introduced to the presence of the
countess, to whom he made a profound bow as he observed—

"I hope, ma'am, as you is quite resuscitated."

The countess had already heard enough of the beadle's peculiarity of diction to
be fully prepared for anything extraordinary he might say, and, therefore, without
repeating the word resuscitated, she replied that she was, which further encouraged
the beadle to say—

"I hopes, ma'am, as all your family is in a state of *plumbosity*."

"Yes, yes," replied the countess, rather impatiently. "I presume, Mr.
Willoughby has duly informed you of the service I require from you?"

"Yes, ma'am, he has; and all I can say, ma'am, is, that so far as my electrical
ideas is concerned, it shall all be done as you wants it, ma'am. It's leaf No. 153,
Mr. Willoughby says as you wants out of the old register book of Kingslake, ma'am,
and, of course, *gustatively* speaking, I can take it for a consideration, you see,
ma'am; not as it's exactly a part of my duty as beadle, to have nothing to do with
the registry; but if ever there was a beadle as was considered a confidential
character, it's me, rather, above a bit, ma'am."

"And you think you can do this, then, easily?"

"Oh, yes; 'tis easy enough done, ma'am; that's the problem, you see. But if
it's found out, it will all lay between me and Mr. Bumwraugh, the churchwarden,
and in course he will lay it upon me, and then I may get transported, and then
what's to become of all the little Browns? I've got nine of 'em, ma'am, and looking
up to me continually for good advice and bread and butter."

"Do not entertain any doubt," said the countess, "as to your reward. You shall have it, be assured, upon producing to me the document which it is of importance to me I should become possessed of."

"Then, ma'am, we will, if you pleases, consider this matter as settled, and I'll go back to Kingslake at once, ma'am, and do the little job for you. But how am I to get it to town, because you see, ma'am, living there, as I does, I don't want to incite suspicion by coming to London again."

"You are right there, and it will be much easier for me to come down to Kingslake than for you to come to London again. My movements can excite no suspicion, and no one has any right to inquire into them, so if you will arrange a place and hour I will be there."

"Let it be at night," said Willoughby, "and then there will be much less danger of being observed. Suppose we meet in the church at night. No doubt you, Mr. Brown, have the means of admission to that edifice."

"Rather," said the beadle; "I believe that whenever I pleases I can go in promiscous."

"Well," added Willoughby, "it is dark at eight now, and I propose we agree, all three of us, to meet at the church-door of Kingslake at nine o'clock precisely and be sure you be punctual, Mr. Brown, and not keep Mrs. Smith there waiting, because otherwise she might be exposed to much disagreeable remark."

"You may depend upon me always," said the beadle, "and I'm glad we have settled everything, so that I can get back now at once; for, to-morrow; fat old Perkins, the malster, is to be buried, and I would not be away on any account. I'm safe to get a silk hat-band given me, and that's not a sort of thing a man likes to miss exactly; and besides, the next day Mrs. Groggs is to be married to Marks, the butcher; and if I don't get something by that, it will be an odd thing indeed. Oh! there's rare doings sometimes at Kingslake, I can *insure* you, ma'am; and you wouldn't believe what a *pathological* place it is."

"I can easily imagine," said the countess, "that such is the case where you have any authority, and now we have but to name the day as we have named the hour."

"To-night," said Willoughby, "by all means. Things of this sort don't get any the better by keeping. I think, for the safety of all parties, it is better done at once."

"Yes, fractionally," said the beadle. "Always do every thing fractionally; that's my principle."

What idea he attached to doing things fractionally, the countess could not imagine, nor did she stop to inquire; but being satisfied that all the necessary arrangements had been made, she rose to go, and again sought the hackney coach in which Margaret was waiting with no small amount of impatience to ascertain the result of the rather prolonged interview with the beadle of Kingslake.

Foolishly, we must say, the Countess of Crumbledown had now taken this woman sufficiently into her confidence to tell her every thing, consequently she was duly informed of the conversation that had occurred and the agreement that had been made to meet at the church of Kingslake on that evening.

"It's rather quick," said Margaret, "but perhaps, as your ladyship says, it is better over and done with at once. and then there is no more trouble about it, and it is off your mind. But won't it be troublesome to get there?"

"I must leave you to arrange all that for me. You must procure at some livery stables a conveyance which may be depended upon, to take me to Kingslake, which is no great distance, and a pair of horses ought to do it well enough with no great burthen behind them."

"Oh, no doubt of that, my lady. But I shall be dreadfully uneasy unless I go with you."

"You shall if you wish it. I shall be glad of your company; for i have, as Heaven knows, no very pleasant thoughts to fall back upon when I am alone."

This was all arranged then precisely as we have stated it. The waiting-maid was to procure a coach, and the countess was to be ready in sufficient time to get them to Kingslake by the appointed hour, in order to meet the beadle, and secure that important document, which was to be such a security to her against the dreadful consequences of a first wife of the earl's making her appearance,

"I shall be more at ease," she thought, "by such a proceeding; I shall feel that I am not, as now, tottering upon the brink of such a fearful abyss as that which now even appears to be yawning before me. I shall perhaps then be able to sleep at night, which now I cannot, except when I drop into that strange, feverish slumber which brings with it no refreshment, and which is peopled with frightful images, as if dimly shadowing forth a career yet to come."

CHAPTER LXVII.

THE CONFEDERATES.—THE FORGERY OF THE REGISTRY-LEAF.—THE JOURNEY TO KINGSLAKE.

"WELL, Willoughby," said the sham beadle of Kingslake, when the countess was gone, and he and that disreputable vagabond were alone together, "well, Willoughby, candidly speaking, now don't you think I played my part really to perfection, and that it was quite a sublime piece of acting ?"

"I give you great credit."

"Ah, that's liberal of you; well, there's nobody else in the world that will give me ever so little credit, therefore I am proportionably grateful."

"But don't you think, after all, the affair might have been managed without dragging us all down to Kingslake ?"

"No, I think not; you cannot tell what wavering ideas of doubt may have been in the mind of the countess, and I contend that my proposition of going down to Kingslake, and my enumeration of the duties I had to perform there, gave a kind of truthfulness to the whole affair, that, to her mind, you may depend, was decidedly important."

"Well, well, it may be so, I am not prepared to dispute such a fact for a moment, —it may be so; and after all, it is only a little personal trouble, and you know I am not the sort of man to grudge that; so let's think about manufacturing the document we want."

"Oh, that's easy done, I should think, by you."

"I grant that there is no difficulty about it, but it will take a little time. I have some old skins of parchment, out of one of which I shall cut a piece, about what one may suppose to be the size of a church registry-book, and then, by a chemical preparation, the secret of which I have, I can remove from it any writing that may be in the way without destroying the marks of age which the parchment will have."

"That will do."

"Then we can make several sham entries of marriages, and among them the one upon which the countess will quickly enough fix her eyes."

"No doubt she will; I never saw a female face in which was exhibited such passions, struggling with such pride. I am quite sure she was on the point, several times, of launching out, and giving us both a taste of her quality. But come, as you say the little document will take some time in preparation, the sooner you set about it the better."

"I will now at once, and you shall get for nothing, an amazingly useful lesson in the preparation of such little matters as sham deeds, wills, &c., which are much oftener done than any one supposes."

"Is it so ?"

"To be sure it is; why for one case of such a nature that comes to light there are about a hundred that don't, and that one never hears of.'

"That sounds reasonable enough, Willoughby; and you, of all men that I know, are just the one to be well acquainted with such matters. But as regards the fact, that criminality of that sort is not found out above once in a hundred times, I have no doubt about it; for many people don't mind what they do in that sort of way."

Willoughby now set to work in earnest, and produced a very old parchment deed, from which he contrived to remove the writing that was upon it; and then he cut it into the shape of a quarto leaf of a book, making holes in it to show where

the binding-threads were supposed to have nipped it; and after that, he wrote four entries of marriages upon it, and among the rest, one to the following effect,—

"John Herbert Warelock, to Emily Whitford, Aug. 10th, 18—."

"I think this will do," he said.

"Do!" cried his confederate. "It's capital. It could not be better; and now, suppose we think of going down to Kingslake at once. It will be but a pleasant ride, after all ; and we can dine there, you know, or tea, or sup—call it what meal you may."

"Agreed.   I will order my chaise, and we can go at once."

This Willoughby did ; and the precious pair at once started to be ready to keep the appointment which had been made to the deluded Countess of Crumbledown.

We call her deluded, but she need not have been, had her own passions not combined with Willoughby's schemes against her; but yet we do not so thoroughly and so heartily condemn her in this affair of the church registry, as we do regarding those dark and terrific thoughts which were finding a home in her heart as regarded the child, who, at all events, was the most innocent person in the whole trans-action.

Nevertheless, the same spirit of unscrupulous criminality which induced her to make such arrangements as she had done for annulling the supposed marriage between the earl and Emily; or, at all events, destroying the supposed evidence of its having taken place, would be amply sufficient to induce much more desperate acts, and probably may be taken as a fair indication of that desperate character which she had, and which was willing enough to strike down all the barriers of morality which usually act as restraints upon human passions.

The countess's maid was an old hand at any sort of intrigue, and well able to manage anything that was entrusted to her care, so that she had a private carriage ready in good time, to convey her mistress to Kingslake, and two good horses, which, their proprietor assured her would perform the journey rapidly and easily, although he could not say, that they could come back again, under at least, one hour's rest, so it was an understood thing, that such an amount of rest at Kingslake was to be accorded them.

The countess was in a feverish and excited state when she started, and yet, there was about her face an expression of triumph, for she considered that she was accomplishing something which would enable her thoroughly to discard her fears, and to defy fate to place her in the position she dreaded to think the caprice of the earl might at any time have forced her to occupy, although he would have done so at the expense of the consequences to himself likewise.

The dreadfully dangerous visit of the presumed mother of the Love Child, had made the risk so great, that it was impossible longer to stand against it, so that if this means had not presented itself to the countess, of getting out of the supposed difficulty, there is no knowing what she might have attempted.

During the rapid drive to Kingslake, she was more than commonly silent, and answered very shortly indeed, all the remarks, which, from time to time, were made to her by Margaret, who, not being at all oppressed with anything, but a desire of making as much money as possible, was only intent upon doing so in the best way she could as regarded her own safety, and so went on talking for the sake of getting what hints she might regarding the personal feeling of the countess.

"I don't see, my lady," she said, " why you should not make use of your know-ledge of the earl's marriage, when once you have destroyed all testimony and evidence of it, in order to threaten him."

"What do you mean ?"

"Why, my lady, I suppose he is open to the law of the land, as well as anybody else, and therefore, if it is found out that he has committed bigamy, he may be punished."

"Such a threat would have but little effect upon him, you may depend, for well he knows how much more to me the consequence of such a state of things must be than to him.   But I have been thinking that I will keep the leaf of the registry when I get it, and not destroy it as was my original intention, for heaven only knows what circumstances may occur even to make such evidence as that useful."

"Certainly, I would keep it, my lady.   It's bad policy to destroy anything whatever, for at some time or another, it is almost sure to become useful, so of all things in the world I would keep that leaf of the registry, that contains such an important announcement.   I would never destroy any paper on which anything is written, that may by any possibility be useful."

"It is good as a principle not to do so, you may depend; and therefore will I keep that leaf of the church registry, of Kingslake, which is worth to me a larger sum of money, than probably so small a document ever cost a human being."

"No doubt of that, my lady, unless it was some will by which people were to get something."

"That of course is a different case, but it does seem hard to have to pay two thousand pounds for such a simple thing as the leaf of a book."

It was indeed a heavy price—a price which none but one accustomed as she had been to considering money in large masses, ever since her marriage, could have thought of paying; but still, if she did purchase for that amount, such peace of mind and such immunity from danger as she expected she was purchasing, and intended to purchase, how very cheap, really, was that small piece of parchment to her!

The many natural beauties of the road through which the carriage travelled, were entirely lost upon the Countess of Crumbledown and her maid, for they were both by far too worldly minded to have any appreciation of such beauties, and by far too much absorbed in their own thoughts, of the present and the future, to be able to enjoy any of those charms of nature, in which the environs of London abound, and which, to those who can seek them, afford the purest and holiest of gratifications.

Pitiable, indeed, in our estimation, is the condition of those, who, from want of sympathy, or from the tumult created in their breasts, by their own bad passions, have no appreciation of the many charms of nature that to those who can enjoy them are so delightful and so full of pleasant reflections.

And there were two other persons likewise, traversing that road, who were as little alive to the beauties of it as the countess and her maid. Those persons were Willoughby and the actor, who had played so well, according to his own opinion, at all events, the character of the beadle of Kingslake. But, whether those worthies were likely to agree for long, is a matter which we cannot attempt at present to determine, although, we think that we can clearly see the evidences of future discord between them.

It is not likely that they should for long agree, when we come to consider that they are leagued together for no other object than what may be called downright robbery, for the swindling transaction in which they were engaged, as regarded the Countess of Crumbledown, cannot be called by any other name.

In due time they arrived at Kingslake, and we will now suppose that the dark of evening is slowly creeping on, as, according to the arrangements they had made, the countess and her attendant got out of the carriage, about half a mile from the village, to walk the remainder of the distance to the church, in order to avoid observation and remark.

CHAPTER LXVIII.

THE STORM AT KINGSLAKE AND DESTRUCTION OF THE CHURCH AND THE SHAM BEADLE.—THE FRIGHT OF THE COUNTESS.—THE CONFESSION.

THERE was an odd appearance about the sky, as the countess and her maid left the carriage to walk the remainder of the distance to Kingslake church. The clouds appeared to come across the heavens with more than the usual speed, and in a short time, lowering black clouds which seemed to droop towards the earth, came up with a very ominous speed and appearance that more than threatened a storm, and the countess had not gone above a third of the way when she paused, and looking up at the sky, said

"I fear we shall have a storm before we reach the church yonder, now; it looks very heavy."

"But there we can get shelter, my lady," suggested the maid, "for if not, I am sure we shall be sacrificed—washed away in the torrent of water that will pour down upon us."

" Pshaw !" said the countess, " a storm will pass away, and a few hours after restore things to their wonted appearance."

"Ah ! well if your ladyship doesn't mind, I am sure I don't see why I should ; only it spoils my things, and they cost money, and one is not used to such rough things."

This latter part was uttered in too low a tone to be heard by the countess: though, had it not, it would not have been heard by her, as she was too deeply engaged upon other matters that furnished her with abundant food for reflection, and which now occupied her mind to the exclusion of all other subjects ; and so great was her anxiety to obtain the leaf of the register, that she was determined to brave the storm, if storm it be, but she would have that which she sought. It was of the highest moment to her—so much of the future depended upon it that she would sacrifice anything for it.

She walked rapidly forward, while her maid, not used to such pedestrian feats, or who would have it appear that she was by far too delicate to contend by the side of her more robust mistress (such is human nature—female nature at least). "Dear me," she muttered, "dear me, what could induce her to walk at this rate ? I am sure she would not have done so had she been in town : I never saw her do the like before—but there's no accounting for her humours."

Thus did the maid pursue the thread of her plaints, groaning as she every now and then struck her thin shoes against a hard stone or clod of earth, and winced from the effects of the blow.

The path they pursued led them direct towards the church, and they could see it through every break in the hedge and among the trees, and the church spire was seen topping all the surrounding trees and other objects.

There was now but a short distance intervening between the Countess of Crumbledown and the church of Kingslake ; but the countess's eyes were strained to catch a glimpse of the objects she most desired to see, and that was no other than Willoughby and the sham beadle, whom she expected to see and to hear too— but at that moment the form of Willoughby and the beadle were seen waiting near the gate of the church-yard.

" It is they," she muttered " I—"

Then she walked along more rapidly than before, indeed she now thought that there would be an end to all the fears that she had so long been a prey to. The sight of Willoughby and his confederate at once brought recollections to her that were both pleasing and painful.

She thought then that at that church was the ceremony of marriage performed, which made her marriage a mere mockery, and her present state might be called by names that conveyed but little of what was pleasing to think of ; but now she would be able to render herself secure, for no marriage could be proved to have taken place, and in the absence of all proof to the contrary her marriage must be held to be legal.

There was sound reason in that and upon that she relied, and thought now she would place herself in a position to act with some effect, for she could not be toppled down from the eminence upon which she stood and from which her friends would, no doubt, have foretold her fall, at the same time they would have felt much satisfaction in the event.

Then she would have been subject to worse misfortunes than even the earl had subjected her ; bearing the taunts of her own friends was more insupportable than even the misfortune itself.

" There they are," she muttered as she came near enough to recognise their features, " yes, there they are. Now, now, I am safe, and the earl cannot turn round to tell me I am no wife, for he cannot prove me otherwise."

She felt herself exulting in this matter which did not concern her personal feelings towards the earl, they were in the same state as before.

They now met, Willoughby raised his hat as the countess neared him, but she took no notice of the salutation, while the beadle gave a fine flourish that would have done honour to a master of ceremonies.

" Good evening, my lady," said the unabashable Willoughby, " it is fine at present though a storm does threaten, but it will not be here yet."

" I came, as you know, Mr. Willoughby, about this matter—this leaf of the registry—that contains this certificate that I wish to see destroyed."

" Certainly, my lady.'"

" Have you all ready as you said you would when I last saw you, and are you prepared to exhibit to me the leaf of which I have been speaking to you?"

" Yes, here we have it, my lady; but is your ladyship prepared to advance us the money we demand?"

" I am," said the countess.

At that moment the clouds which had, until now, held up, suddenly discharged their load of moisture, preceded indeed by such a sudden burst of thunder as seemed to rock the very earth and caused the countess to start, the maid to utter a suppressed shriek, and even Willoughby and his confederate felt as if they had rather that it had not happened.

" Dear me," said the countess, " it is very unfortunate?"

" Unfortunate! it is perfectly horrible," said the maid. " I hope we may get away alive again?"

" Yes, yes, I hope we may," said the beadle. " I hope you may I am sure, but as for me why I am at home, quite at home, I am used to the thunder in these places."

" Your ladyship had better come into the church," said Willoughby, " you will run some risk of getting wet here, the wind you see drifts along and carries so much rain with it too."

The countess entered the church which Mr. Brown opened, having provided himself with a pick lock-key easily used.

" I may say, your ladyship is welcome," said Brown, with an air of much complaisance, " I may say you are welcome here, for there is only another person in the village who could have offered you such an asylum."

The thunder now rattled and roared in terrific volumes of sound from one end of the place to the other, and with such fearful noises and sounds that it was impossible, for some time, for them to hear each other speak.

This, however, they contrived to do, though at the risk of being misunderstood, or not heard.

" My lady, would you like to have this leaf of the register now? this I presume to be the proper time and place for it, seeing my worthy friend, Mr. Brown, might be called upon to perform some one of his many functions elsewhere, and then another appointment would be necessary."

" Yes, my lady, I am much in request in this locality. I am—though I say it—of some importance in this suburban retreat—I am often required to become more than omnipresent, and sometimes I am compelled to admit that I am a little less——"

" I should say you were, Mr. Brown" said Willoughby. " Will you favour my lady with a sight of the document we have taken possession of."

" I will, " said Brown, drawing out a piece of parchment very much like a leaf of a book, and bearing the appearance of having been used as such for some time.

" Is that the leaf?" inquired the countess.

" Yes, my lady, I'll warrant it—yes, I—Brown the beadle, do warrant it."

" Let me examine it. Yes, there is the entry—ah! what is this above?"

" Oh! those, my lady, are merely other entries which have been made before and since that occurrence."

" I see, and this is genuine, Mr. Willoughby. Have you seen the registration yourself?"

" Indeed, I have my lady, and I vouch for the genuineness of the document, There can be no doubt about it—it is genuine from it's very appearance ; but I saw the others. We took care to take it out with all imaginable precaution, because had we not done so some suspicion might have produced discovery before we were well prepared for it."

" And how long has this been done ?"

" Not long, my lady. Mr. Brown and myself performed the operation very skillfully, for the reasons I have told you, and, I have every reason to believe, it will remain unnoticed for years; but, at all events, you must not use that yet awhile else some mischief will happen."

" I shall not use it all—but destroy it; but, give me the document and the certificate."

" And then, my lady," said Willoughby, with laudable anxiety, " for the circulating medium."

" There," replied the countess, as she pulled out a handsome purse, and displayed some gold; " there, and now let me have no more trouble; but let me have the leaf."

" There it is, my lady," said Brown, giving the required document; as Willoughby took the cheque, which he placed in his pocket and buttoned up his coat; and, allow me to observe, that you are most fortunate in finding a beadle who is so accessible to reason. I am sure you would not have found one so much so else where."

" I dare say some might not have been so hard as to price," said the countess, " and I imagine you have had a very profitable job, which you would like to remain undiscovered."

" Certainly, certainly," said the supposed beadle; " but, I understood it should remain so from Mr. Willoughby, else I wouldn't have had anything to do with it upon any account whatever, for it would cause me the loss of my place, besides being dangerous to the liberty of all those concerned."

" So it will remain," said the countess, " do you remain silent, and all will be well."

" I wish the thunder would remain quiet," said the beadle; " I declare it makes a most awful noise. I never heard so much crushing and crashing in all my life."

The thunder certainly did appear to keep up an incessant play from all quarters of the heavens without any cessation whatever. The rain, too, fell down in such torrents as to darken the air, so much so, that you could not see but a short distance from where they stood. The hail, too, now began to make dreadful havoc upon the glass, and many panes were broken, and most of the side glasses were knocked in, and lay scattered about in profusion.

There was, too, such an incessant play of lightning that it would have been light enough to have read small print, had it been but thus in the dead of the night.

However, as it was, the flashes appeared to play right through the church, from one side to the other, as though it had been but a very common matter.

The whole party, now they had attained their ends, seemed and felt somewhat annoyed at the storm. Not a hope of it clearing up appeared to exist. The countess sat down and looked through the window

" Dear me," she muttered, " when will this end. It has been very violent; but I have got the document, she muttered, which I will destroy when I have reached home. It is a heavy sum, but as nothing when compared to that which I should have lost had I not obtained it. Nevertheless I will obtain it when I get home, and then I can destroy it when I am more at leisure."

She hid her eyes involuntarily, for such a flood of lightning came across her that she thought she must have been struck by it; but, at the same time, she arose and staggered forward, and sunk near the church-porch with a scream.

Her maid had lingered near the church-door while Willoughby was walking towards the porch to ascertain what probability there was of the storm giving over, and its clearing, for he wanted to leave the neighbourhood now as quickly as he could.

But the flash that had so alarmed the countess stopped him for a second, for he felt blinded by its brilliance, for he could not see.

Then came the report of the thunder. The heavens seemed to open and shut, and the very earth seemed to have been stricken, for it shook, so awfully loud was the report: the church-bells were set ringing, and then a sudden vibration was felt, mingled with a babel of sounds, and the number of other sensations that no human being could describe: so great was the shock that they were all thrown down, and covered with dust and dirt: the church filled; the whole of the steeple had fallen into the body of the church which was now filled with one body of bricks and mortar, wood-work and stone, to such an extent that the walls seemed to bulge outward.

The whole affair had happened so suddenly, that they knew not what had happened, but something very dreadful they were aware.

For some moments they were immersed in the blackest darkness of midnight, and almost choked with dust—there was scarcely any possibility of breathing.

The first person that recovered his senses was Willoughby. He sprang to his feet, and, in a moment, comprehended that some great calamity had befallen the place, and he saw the countess struggling to her feet, and seizing her by the arm, he led her out of the place, as well as he was able, and then he felt the refreshing effects of the rain and the cool air.

He gasped again for the cooling draught—he had never yet felt the refreshing virtue of the pure element before, but he did now.

" Did you hear that, my lady ? " he gasped—" are you hurt? you are not hurt, I hope."

" No, no ! at least 1 think not—I think not—but—but what has happened ?—where is my maid ? "

" Why." said Willoughby, " why, the lightning has stricken the church and knocked the steeple off, and filled the church with bricks and mortar; well, well, I never expected so narrow an escape as that."

" Where is my maid ? "

" I don't know," said Willoughby ; " but if you'll sit down here, I'll try and get in and see if she's hurt or not. She was near the door, and had a better chance than I ; but there is no knowing how the bricks fell. I was knocked down by the rush of winds."

As he spoke he saw the countess seated upon a grave-stone a few yards from the church, far away enough to escape any falling matter from the church, and Willoughby now went cautiously to the church-porch, with the intention of ascertaining the state of the other actors in this scene.

When he entered the church-porch, he saw the countess's maid employed in recovering herself by means of a smelling bottle, and her dress by dusting it. She had been deterred from going out, for she had seen a brick or two thrown down.

" Come out," said Willoughby, " you are not hurt—you are not hurt—your lady wants you. Do you hear."

" Can she expect me to go out, and bricks falling down in that way. Gracious me ! I must give notice."

" You will have a discharge without notice, if you remain here much longer : besides, the porch is falling down, and you'll be smashed to a certainty."

" Goodness ! " she exclaimed, as she got up—" is this the end of the world? Has the day of judgment come? What has happened? Oh! my lady, are you hurt? I am dying with fright. Oh! how dreadful this has been !"

As she spoke she rose and went to the countess, who appeared to be in a state of great nervous excitement and terror; she shook and trembled violently ; and though it rained hard, yet, she never attempted to escape its fury.

" Help me, " she said, " help me to reach the carriage, if that is yet remaining ; I cannot stay here any longer."

The attendant attempted to assist her, but she was incapable of rising to walk.

" I must wait a moment," she said; " where are my salts. I am quite dizzy; how dreadful ! how dreadful !"

She was attended to by her attendant, but at the same time, Willoughby again went into the church, to look after his confederate, whom he had not seen since the accident had occurred, and whom he shrewdly suspected must be either killed or detained against his will by some one of those extraordinary circumstances, which, at such times, and under such circumstances occur.

However, no extraordinary circumstances occurred on this occasion, but one very likely, and that was the unfortunate impersonation of a beadle lying down with a load of rubbish lying upon him, but which was by far too heavy to be easily removed.

Indeed, he was crushed, bruised and bloody, and he turned up his blood-shot eyes to Willoughby, with an expression of the most acute speakable anguish, and said, in a husky, broken voice,—

"Willoughby, Willoughby, I am a dead man. I am dying. Give me water—water—water—"

"I will get help," said Willoughby, as he rushed out of the church, and seeing the countess there he said—

"The beadle is dying, my lady; I must get assistance somewhere or other. Will you remain till I come back, or you had better endeavour, my lady, to reach your carriage; for I see yonder is assistance coming. They have doubtless seen the fall of the steeple, for they must have heard the bells."

The Countess of Crumbledown cast her eyes towards the village, in which direction Willoughby pointed, and at once felt for the paper she had received, and being satisfied that she still had it, she at once rose leaning on the arm of her attendant, and left the spot with what speed she was able.

Willoughby at once comprehended the situation in which he was placed, and ran towards those who were coming, shouting for help as loud as he could.

"Why, what's the matter with you; you ain't killed, be ye?" inquired a countryman.

"No; but the church—the church steeple—"

"Aye, we know that as well as thee, man: we know all about that as well as can be. We saw the steeple struck, and heard the bells ring."

"Very well," said Willoughby, "perhaps you have seen the man that's lying beneath the heaps of rubbish and stones."

"No, we haven't."

"Then make haste and help him out; he's suffering horrid agony, crushed and mangled in the way he is lying."

"Come on—come on," said some of the peasants, as soon as they heard that there was a man lying crushed in the church beneath the mass of rubbish. One or two were despatched for spades and pickaxes, while the others hurried forward to see what could be done before the others would arrive.

They soon came to the church, and after a little hesitation, for at first they declined to enter, seeing the porch was in a very tottering condition, the groans of the unfortunate man inside determined them, and they rushed in, and beheld a sight that paralysed them for a moment.

"Save me! save me!" cried the unfortunate man, groaning, gasping between whiles.

The men paused for several seconds, when one said,—

"Take the rubbish off—it can be lifted by degrees—lift it all off—it will kill him."

The men set to work to lift and clear him out from the rubbish, which held him down as if he had been secured in a vice.

"Water! water! water!" gasped the soi-disant beadle.

"For God's sake get him some water," exclaimed some of them. "It is horrid to hear him call for it in that state."

Some water was got and given him, and after about a quarter of an hour's work, they had lifted off all the mass that had fallen upon him. It was merely mortar, bricks, and stones; but no large beams of wood. However, they had bruised him very much, and for a few minutes he looked worse, and fainted away.

The cool air, and the plentiful application of cold water, having re-called his fleeting life, he looked around for some moments from one to another, and said in a low voice,—

"Is there a clergyman near?"

"There is one at hand. Do you wish to see him?"

"Yes, yes—I am dying—I am dying!"

"Fetch the rector—fetch the rector," said one or two; and in [another moment

two or three started forward to fetch the man sought for. He was, however, close at hand; it could not have been more opportune, for, as he advanced to see what had happened, several men called out,—

"This way, sir—this way. You are wanted here. This way, if you please."

Thus urged, the rector walked rapidly towards them, until he came to the group that were kneeling round the unfortunate man, who seemed to be growing weaker each moment, and less able to speak. His breath grew shorter, and large gouts of blood came up as he spoke, and they were compelled to sponge his mouth with water to enable him to speak.

His breath grew shorter each moment, and he grew fainter and fainter; but he was urgent for a clergyman.

"Do you seek aid of Heaven, my good man? It will grant its mercies even to you, if you seek it in a spirit of meekness and true repentance.

"I do—I do."

"Look to Heaven."

"I—I—have something on my mind," he said, raising his head, and gasping from exertion.

"If so, I beg you will confide in me. Do not die with any weighty matter weighing down your conscience, like a load that must in time bear you down. Confess, I beseech you, if you have aught to ask forgiveness of this world."

"I—I will—I will," said the man, with sudden exertion; and then such mouthfuls of blood came up, that he was compelled to wait until it was cleansed.

"Speak, I beseech you."

"I—I came down here to—to—"

"Yes, my man, I listen—to what, eh?"

"I—I—and he—to me—"

"Who?"

"We came down together—they came, and we all—— Oh, God! oh, Heaven! I'm dying!"

"Confess first."

"I will—I do—I have committed a deed without a name—a gross fraud. I have been a party to it with—with— Oh, Heavenly Father! mercy, mercy! Oh, what agony——"

The unfortunate man's sufferings were of so acute and dreadful a character, that he trembled with agony. The curate stood by, watching the return of a moment of ease, to obtain from him the confession. He presumed he had some crime in view—some deed that had been consummated, and which he wished to confess to, but life was ebbing fast, and it soon became apparent to all who were there, that there was no chance of his ever being able to speak another word. His glazed eye became fixed, and the blood frothed in his mouth, he gave a convulsive shudder, and all was over—he was dead.

CHAPTER LXIX.

THE EARL'S ADVENTURE IN THE PARK.—THE ENCOUNTER WITH THE COUNTESS.—THE QUESTION AND ANSWER.

WHILE the Countess of Crumbledown was thus pursuing her schemes, the earl met with a new adventure which arrested his attention. It will be recollected that an attempt had been made by Willoughby, to once more ingratiate himself with the earl, by drawing his attention to a young girl who so closely resembled the unfortunate Emily Whitteford, as really to awaken in his bosom, again, some of those emotions of affection he had felt for her before.

Since that occasion, however, upon which such an attempt had been made, many things had occurred to put it out of the earl's remembrance that he had ever looked upon such a creature, until on the morning of that same day on which the countess determined to go to Kinglake, for the purpose of getting possession of what to her appeared to be so important a document, he was doomed again to encounter the being who put him so much in mind of her who was now no more.

He was riding, at a slow pace, along that bit of road in Hyde Park, which leads from Oxford-street to Kensington Gardens, when his attention was arrested by observing a young female in an attitude indicative of great grief, sitting upon one of the seats, with her face covered by her hands.

Now, the Earl of Crumbledown could not be called one of those men who are ever ready with, perhaps, more of real personal vanity, than any other feeling, to rush into adventures ; and he might, after a pitying remark to himself, have ridden on, had she not suddenly removed her hands from her face, and looked up.

Then, in an instant, that countenance flashed across his eyes, and he knew that it was the same, or else one most wonderfully like that with which he had been struck at the theatre, on the occasion when Willoughby had so politely offered his services to him.

He did not then pause, **for** there were several persons passing at the time, but he continued on to the gate, close to Kensington Gardens, and then he dismounted and told the groom who followed him, to lead his horse by the open road-way to Oxford Street, and there wait for him.

When he had completed this arrangement, he walked back among the trees to where he had seen the young creature in whom, for her likeness to Emily Whitford, he felt so deeply interested ; and it was a gratification to him to see that she had not removed from the spot she had occupied when he had ridden past before. But now came the difficulty as regarded how he should address her, so as to make her believe that he was not one of those ordinary frivolous flatterers about the parks, who think it manly and great to annoy any unprotected female they may happen to think possesses some personal charms.

He cudgelled his brains in vain for some plan of operations, but after a time he found that there was really no other plan open to him, than just to trust to what he should say, and the manner in which he should say it, to disarm her of any fears she might entertain as regarded the address of one who was a perfect stranger to her.

While he was thus considering, however, of a difficulty which appeared to be insurmountable, accident befriended him, and he advanced his object in a manner which at once placed him on a good footing as regarded the unknown.

It happened that a young fellow who had, no doubt, come to the park to make an exhibition of his attractions, became, in his turn, attracted by the fair stranger who occupied the seat in the walk in the shrubbery, and without feeling any of the doubts or hesitations of the Earl of Crumbledown upon the subject, he at once walked forward, and flinging himself, with a careless air, into the vacant portion of the seat, it was evident, from the sudden start of the young lady, and the self-satisfied looks of the intruder, that he had made some remark which he thought uncommonly clever, but which she, perhaps, thought uncommonly rude.

This was followed by an attempt to take her hand, which was indignantly rejected ; and, although the earl was not near enough to hear what was said, he could well perceive that the annoyance of the impertinent stranger, was getting to a height that would soon warrant him in interfering.

This, if he had planned it himself, could not have been better, inasmuch as it at once, and in the most natural way in the world, got him over all his difficulty about how to introduce himself to the fair object who had, from her resemblance to another as fair, so much attracted him.

She now rose, as the stranger showed no disposition to cease his troublesome importunities ; and as good fortune would have it, she walked in the direction the earl was waiting.

As they approached him—we say they—for her persecutor followed her closely, he could hear the style of remonstrance in which the gentleman indulged.

" Really now, this is *monstrous* unkind—'pon my soul it is—aw—aw—my dear, aw, I love you, 'pon honour, *to distraction.*"

" But," said the earl, stepping up just as the would-be fashionable was abut to place his hand upon the lady's arm—" but it seems, sir, that the passion is by no means reciprocal, and, consequently, you will allow me to suggest that your best course will be to cease your unmanly persecutions of one who was an unprotected female, but who is so no longer. Do you understand me, sir ?"

"Eh! what—do you know the—the—individual—I—aw—aw—don't want to poach on anybody else's manor, pon soul."

"I do not know the lady, but still a lady persecuted by a coxcomb is entitled to the protection of every gentleman."

"'Pon soul, do you *threaten* me?"

"Precisely I do."

"Oh, aw, aw—I look upon you as quite beneath me—aw, and as for the young woman, she aint half so killing as I thought she was, so you may have her if you—aw, aw—if you particularly wish. I don't want to have anything to say to you."

So saying, the puppy turned and made off in another direction as quickly as he could, for there was something in the earl's looks which a little awakened his prudence, and made him think the adventure, if pursued any further, might probably become much more dangerous than pleasant. So to use his own expressive language, "'Pon soul," he got out of it as quickly as he could.

"I hope," said the earl to the lady, in as gentle a tone of voice as he could assume, "I hope that you have not been much annoyed by that man, who is no gentleman, although in the affected garb of one."

"I have to thank you for preserving me from the annoyance, and to blame my own imprudence for lingering here, and consequently subjecting myself to it."

She made a slight bow as she spoke, and was passing on, but the earl again spoke, saying—

"I do trust that you will, at least, let me feel the gratification of having protected you through the park, but so little wish have I to make you think that you have exchanged one troublesome person for another, that if it be not endurable that I should walk with you, I will follow you in silence if you wish."

There was scarcely any resisting such an appeal as this, couched in such language, and coming from one who had certainly done her a service; so the young lady hesitated, and as young ladies, on the authority of some cynic, are said to be lost when they hesitate, the earl placed her arm within his, and they walked along as comfortably as if they had known each other for years.

The great object of the earl was to ascertain the name of his young companion, for young she was, as well as most beautiful, and he said, after a few moments' pause,—

"Let me assure that, in asking you to tell me who you are, it is not mere idle curiosity that actuates me, but a desire to know the name of one who reminds me so forcibly of another, that I could almost fancy it was herself risen from the grave to walk the earth again, and show to the wondering and admiring gaze of all beholders what beauty really is. I implore you to tell me your name."

She was silent for a few moments, and then, when she did speak, it was in a well-remembered tone that stole upon the ears of the earl like the memory of some dream, so closely did it resemble the voice of her who was in the tomb.

"My name," she said, "is Whitford."

"Whitford? God of Heaven! did you say Whitford? You—you had a sister, then?—Whitford! Oh, how that name thrills through my brain! It must be so—the likeness, the voice——"

"Oh, sir, speak again; you have mentioned my sister. Yes, yes, I had a sister—the long-lost poor Emily. If you know aught of her, speak to me, I charge you."

The earl shook for a moment or two, and seemed unable to speak, then he, when he did recover sufficiently from the shock which the sudden surprise had given him, to speak articulately, said—

"Farewell, farewell for ever; I hope to Heaven we may never meet again. Farewell, I have nothing to tell—I know nothing. All is past now, and knowledge of evil can avail you not. Ask me no more."

"Oh, sir, be you who you may, let me implore you not to leave me thus a prey to reflections which you have awakened again; let me beg of you, if you do know anything of my sister Emily's fate, to tell me, and at once, too, and so end the deep anxiety of suspense. Do not leave me."

"I must, I must. Rather let me implore you to ask me nothing. Would to Heaven we had never met."

The groom with the earl's horse was now close at hand, for they had walked so far down that the gate of Kensington Gardens was within sight of them, and now, as the earl made a gesture with his arms, the groom came up, and he flung himself on to his horse, exclaiming—

"Farewell, farewell. For your own peace, as well as for mine, speak to me no more, should we ever meet again, here or elsewhere. I know nothing for you to hear."

He turned and cantered on towards Oxford Street, but he had not gone far before he met the countess in a barouche, and to pass her entirely without notice, thronged as the park was by people who knew them both by sight, was out of the question, but still he hoped to pass her with a mere recognition, but in this he was disappointed, for she pulled the check string, and the barouche stopped, so that he could not but perceive she wanted to speak to him, and he paused at the side of the carriage. There was a strange expression, as if of subdued passion upon her face, as she said in stern, but low accents, so that they reached no ear but his—

"You parted just now with a female. Understand me, I do not care one iota for that as a fact, but I do care to know her name."

"Her name," said the earl, confusedly.

"Yes; I want to know if her name was Whitford. Ah! you need not speak; I am answered. Your face has already given me too expressive an affirmative. Now I know the worst, and—no matter, no matter. Coachman, go on, go on."

She flung herself back in the costly vehicle, as she muttered to herself—

"Willoughby is correct, and may be trusted, but as regards the non-existence of the mother of that child, who is the bane of my existence, the man Grove has either been grossly deceived himself, or he has attempted most grossly to deceive me. How do I know but he may have been authorized by the earl."

*　　*　　*　　*　　*　　*　　*

The reader will now readily perceive into what a series of mistakes the Countess of Crumbledown has fallen, and how easily circumstances were deceiving her. Of course she at once now imagined that she had the most absolute proof that possibly could be of the fact of the continued existence of the mother of the child that was under the care of Mrs. Grove.

And not only had she proof she considered of that fact, but the additional conviction was forced upon her that the earl was in communication with her—perhaps, indeed, actually keeping her quietly somewhere in London. The only thing which it seemed difficult to reconcile with such a circumstance was the visit of the presumed first wife of the earl, which that individual had made to her, but even for that, after a time, she managed to find a reason, and she thought that an ebullition of anger after some temporary disagreement might have produced all that effect, for which now probably the mother of the child might be very sorry.

And we must state that the countess's barouche was quite far enough off from Mary Whitford and the earl to prevent her seeing how much younger she was than the person who had called upon her. All she could see was, that the earl had been in conversation with a female, with whom she saw him part, and the idea that it was she, who was so much to be dreaded, crossed her mind at once, and induced the question which the earl had felt so much confused about.

Now, then, the countess had no doubt whatever, and from that moment we may safely reckon the complete determination which she made to be the death of the child, which was the fruit of a connexion he could not but regard with the bitterest feelings.

But while this little episode in the park had the effect of convincing the countess of the great faith, as she considered it mistakingly, of Willoughby, it had quite the contrary effect upon the Earl of Crumbledown, for he, of course, could only conclude that Willoughby had betrayed him, as there seemed to be no other means that he could conceive for the countess to acquire the knowledge she had. If Willoughby had not, despite all the money he had received not to betray him, how, he asked himself, could the countess become aware of the name of Whitford, and evidently, as she did, attach to it such serious meaning?

Thus, then, were they both confused and tormented by a thousand doubts, fears, and surmises which, we cannot help saying, so far as regarded their own discomfiture they amply deserved to feel, but the result of which we do indeed tremble to think of.

CHAPTER LXX.

THE MURDER OF THE LOVE CHILD DECIDED UPON.—THE COUNTESS'S DISGUISE.— THE VISIT TO HAMPSTEAD-HEATH.

WHEN the countess reached her house, she at once closeted herself with her confidant, and announced that all hesitation had vanished, and that she had from that time made up her mind that the child, which, while it lived, would be inimical to her peace, should most assuredly die.

To this, always provided she could manage to keep herself clear of the deed, Margaret had no objection whatever, and when we say that she was anxious to keep herself clear of the deed, we rather ought to say that she was anxious to keep herself clear of any of the personal consequences of it, because, as regarded the deed itself, she had no sort of compunction whatever, for into her disposition there entered no human feelings of compassion.

"What's the life of a child of seven years of age," said the waiting-maid; "of course it will be all the happier when it is gone, and especially when one comes to consider that—"

"Peace, peace! I want no arguments," cried the countess. "Let it suffice, that from what circumstances do actually exist, I have made up my mind that the child shall surely die. The present is not a time to consider of that part of the question, but to consider how the deed can be done."

This was a matter that did indeed require the very strictest attention, because anything in the shape of failure would be most fearful in its consequences, and if an act of that kind was to be committed, the countess felt the necessity that it should be committed completely and surely,

After a considerable time thus spent in thinking and talking over the affair, it was determined that she (the countess) and Margaret should attire themselves in common ordinary apparel, and go to Hampstead, for the purpose of reconnoitering the cottage and its vicinity, and endeavouring to discover the personal habits of Mrs. Grove, as to whether she ever left the cottage, and when she did so as to what she did with the child.

We shall now follow the Countess of Crumbledown on this dreadful and desperate mission of hers. She succeeded without observation in leaving her home along with Margaret, and she took with her a packet of poison, which she had procured with some trouble in small portions at a time. It was the deadly arsenic, that fell foe to human existence; and she hoped for some opportunity of mingling it with the child's food, so that the death she wished to inflict should occur after she had left, and not in her presence.

A hackney-coach sufficed to convey them to that village, the environs of which are perhaps the most truly picturesque and beautiful of any that can be found in the neighbourhood of the metropolis—that village of laundresses and of their drunken, idle, dissolute husbands; and on the borders of the heath they got out out of the vehicle, and dismissed it.

"Do you think," said the countess. "candidly speaking, that I am sufficiently disguised to be able to appear before Mrs. Grove, always bearing in mind that she has seen me a number of times?"

" Then, my lady, candidly speaking, I do think she would know you, for there is a something in your countenance which is not easy to forget, and it certainly would be hazardous for you to make your appearance in the cottage; but I have thought of a plan which may succeed."

" What is it? Name it at once."

" It is this. I was thinking that if you were to wait among the shrubs and trees, which are about here in such great abundance, while I go to the cottage, and, complaining of indisposition, endeavour to induce Mrs. Grove to leave it for the purpose of getting me something to take from a chemist's, or one of the public houses, you might, upon seeing that she had so left, make your way into the cottage, and the deed might be done, and you gone again before she could possibly return."

" That can be tried, and, at all events, it is one of those plans, which, if it do not succeed, will not bring any great risks in its failure. If she refuses to leave the cottage to aid you, you can but affect gradually to recover, and come away, when we can consider of some other plan of operation."

" Most certainly, most certainly, my lady. As you say, there will be no harm done even should it fail of success, which I don't, however, think it will exactly; for it seems so natural, and unless she is a woman much beyond her station in life, it is almost certain to succeed."

" She is a woman beyond her station of life as regards intelligence: I have seen enough of her to know that; and if she had any suspicion of such an act as that which we project, your plan would fail; but having no such suspicion, she may fall into the snare at once, even were she ten times more observant than she really is. Go at once and make the experiment."

The Countess hid herself among some fir-trees that grew in great luxuriance near to the cottage, which was in the occupation of Mrs. Grove, and there waited with considerable impatience, the result of the base scheme which was being attempted to be carried into effect by Margaret.

" Oh! if but for one moment the Countess of Crumbledown could have been endowed with philosophy enough to feel how much greater evil she was preparing for herself than any she was by such means endeavouring to avert, with what horror would she have flown from that spot, and relinquished the frightful plan by which she expected to ensure—what! happiness—peace of mind—serenity? Surely, surely not. Could she really be so mad as to imagine that, for the most fleeting possible period of time, she could call such feelings hers after the commission of the act, which she was now bending all the energies of her iniquitous mind to consummate. Oh! fatal—fatal—horrible delusion!"

But let us see how fared the bold and bad *confidante* of the Countess.

Summoning to her aid all the artifice she was mistress of, and that was no mean stock; for, from early life she had been nurtured in deceit, she walked to the open door of Mrs. Grove's cottage, and assuming an appearance of great exhaustion, and, clinging to the door-post as if she were compelled to do so for support, she in a few moments attracted the attention of Mrs. Grove, who came to the door to see what was the matter with the person who really seemed so ill on her threshold.

" I—I beg your pardon," said Margaret, in faltering tones, " for this intrusion, but I am very weak and unwell, and if—if you would let me, for a moment or two, sit down to recover myself, I should be truly thankful."

" Certainly, oh! certainly," said Mrs. Grove, with ready humanity. " Why did you hesitate for a moment? Walk in. Could you doubt that you would be welcome? I hope you are only fatigued, and not seriously indisposed."

" I owe you many—many thanks," said Margaret, as she affected to totter into the apartment, and sat down upon the first chair she came near. " I have walked a long way to see my husband, who is a soldier, and has been abroad these five years; but, I have been given to understand that his regiment will be landed this day at the Tower of London. I—I—"

" You seem absolutely sinking."

"I—I—am not well, and if you would not mind going to the nearest doctor's or me, while—while—I take—take care of your little girl here and your cottage, you—you—might, perhaps, save my life."

Mrs. Grove could scarcely be said to have any suspicions aroused; and yet there was a something about the manner of the woman that she did not like, admirably acted as was her illness.

"I cannot," she said, " go myself, because I have made a fixed resolution, which to me, amounts to all the solemnity of a vow, that I will not leave this child for a moment in the care of any one whom I do not know; but I have no doubt, that if I stand at the cottage-door, I shall soon see some boy who, for a few pence, will be glad to go."

These few words were sufficient.   The scheme, artfully concocted though it had been, had completely failed ; and the chagrin the waiting-maid felt for a few moments, excluded almost her power of hiding it from the observation of Mrs. Grove.   After, however, such a failure as this, the next best thing undoubtedly was, not to create suspicion, so she said, in a faint voice,—

"I thank you kindly : you are quite right, you are very right; and I think that the little rest which I have already had has done me good, and perhaps, with a glass of water, will enable me to get on again."

"I am glad to hear you say so—there is some spring water, and I hope you will not think me unkind in not going as you wished to the nearest surgeon's, but the child you see here is not my own, therefore most specially am I bound to be particular as regards it."

"You are right—you are very right; and I much blame myself for being so thoughtless as to ask you to do otherwise than remain yourself by it.   Pray excuse me, for I can fully enter into your feelings, and ought not to have requested you to leave your home.   I am better now, and as my anxiety to get on is very great, I will now, thanking you for your courtesy, make another effort."

As she spoke she rose, for now she was quite as anxious to get out of Mrs. Grove's cottage as she had been before to get into it, and she found it very up-hill work indeed to play the part of the fatigued invalid, when she was not in the least advancing her object by so doing, but only aiming to ward off suspicion, in order that some other attempt might be made which should be more successful.

Mrs. Grove too, to her great aggravation, watched her from the door, so that she had no opportunity of joining the countess, who saw her come out with feelings of great chagrin, because it showed her at once that the plan had failed, and that up to this point all that she had done was of no avail, and that it would require something of a bolder and more dangerous character, before Mrs. Grove's care of the child could be got over."

Margaret, in order to keep up appearances, was compelled to proceed towards town, which placed her at a still further distance from the countess, who, when she saw Mrs. Grove had retired from her door, ventured, but not till then, to walk rapidly after her waiting-maid.

This, one would have thought, would have been sufficiently humiliating to her, but it only tended to influence her anger ; and when she did join company with Margaret, she almost alarmed even that unscrupulous individual by saying, with a vehemence that was almost demoniac,—

"I am resolved to stake my life upon this matter, and will, now that I am here, stay and endeavour, when night comes, to effect something."   You surely could not be in the cottage, even the short time you were, without making some observation ?"

"I saw," replied Margaret, "that it was an inner room on the ground floor in which the child slept, for I observed a motley got-up couch there close to a window, which seemed to look out into a garden belonging to the cottage.   If anything of a violent nature was to be attempted, it might at night be done through that window, if it could be opened without creating an alarm."

"It shall be so—it shall be so.   Did you ascertain if the woman slept in the same apartment ?"

"I fear she does. The room looked like the principal bed-room of the cottage, and as the door was opened, I could not see the whole of the apartment; but I should think that from what I did see, that there was a bedstead against the wall behind the door."

"Never mind. What can we do with ourselves for the few hours that must intervene between this and nightfall? Surely there will be some sort of accommodation, however humble, to be found in this place."

"Oh, of course, my lady, there are inns, and I daresay a private room can be got, and some refreshments that your ladyship will be able to eat, at some of those places, although we cannot expect the sort of accommodation that *we* have been accustomed to."

At one of the inns in the immediate vicinity of the heath, they, upon showing an ability as well as a disposition to pay, had abundance of accommodation; and then the Countess and Margaret waited until they could, under cover of the night, perpetrate an act at which humanity might well shudder, and which we dread the task of describing to our readers.

CHAPTER LXXI.

THE MURDER OF THE CHILD.

SLOWLY but surely came the night, and all the beautiful landscape, in the midst of which was the countess, became veiled in obscurity. The songs of the birds had ceased, and gradually the heath and its beautiful vicinity had become cheerless and deserted. Immense clouds came up from the south, stretching over the whole face of nature like a black pall, and involving in one common darkness trees, houses, roads, and water-courses, so that nothing could be observed, after a time, but an universal blackness.

There was no moon visible, and altogether a night more favourable to the execution of the design which the countess had in view, could not well have been devised, for it was, of all nights, just the one upon which such a guilty action might be committed, and the perpetrator of it escape punishment most completely, by plunging into the obscurity around.

Here it was that with silent and stealthy steps the Countess of Crumbledown and her associate, the wicked Margaret, left the hotel where they had been staying for several hours, and betook themselves towards that part of the beautiful heath where the cottage of Mrs. Grove was situated, and proceeded with such caution and circumspection as they could bring to bear upon the question, to possess themselves of a knowledge of the precise locality of the garden, its extent, and the mode by which it was fenced in from the rest of the common.

They found that at one part of it there was a small lake of water, which was an effectual defence against any intrusion; but on another side, a low park paling was the only thing which separated the highly cultivated little spot of ground from the remainder of the heath, which, without doubt, it was a reclaimed portion.

There could be no possible difficulty, then, in getting into the garden, and Margaret and the Countess stood by the low paling conversing, their only doubt was whether it was not much too early to commence operations, and whether it would not be desirable most decidedly to wait awhile until there was something like a certainty that the parties occupying the humble dwelling had gone to repose.

As yet, however, all was uncertainty in the mind of the countess as to the precise mode of accomplishing the dreadful deed she had in view. That she would rather perform it without the necessity of anything in the shape of personal violence, there could be no doubt, as that would be the most easy course for her to adopt, as well as the one least of all productive of danger to herself, but if unforeseen difficulties were to present themselves, and actual violence should become necessary, we do believe that woman, as she is, will not scruple to have recourse to it.

"Shall we wait," she whispered to Margaret—"shall we wait until there is something like a certainty that she has retired to repose, or shall we at once proceed to make the attempt which we have lingered here so long in the hope of succeeding in?"

"I see nothing to delay," was the reply, "our getting into the garden; for you must bear in mind that, let what will happen, we are two to one, and if this Mrs. Grove should discover us and attempt to make a resistance, I do not see that, of necessity, such a fact ought to deprive us of the power of action: for we can and will resist too, and if needs be, why should she live to tell a tale, the smallest particulars of which had better never be uttered by mortal lips? And besides, it is more than probable that, as the child"s bed-room lies actually in this direction and looks into the garden, it will retire to rest at a much earlier hour than its nurse."

"That circumstance, then," said the countess, "would make an early attempt safer by far than a late one."

"Much safer. I have seen, from my visit, that the child's bed is near the window. And after all, would it not be an admirable thing if we could perpetrate the deed, burning the nurse in the very house, so that she could have no tale to tell of how the deed was done, and could not prove her absence at the time of the commission of the deed."

" I perceive your meaning: you would ask upon whom would suspicion fall but upon her."

" I would—and is there anything that could be better than another calculated to make the deed a safe one than the conviction and perhaps the very execution of another person for it ?"

The countess was silent for a few moments—but even that frightful suggestion did not make her shrink altogether as she ought to have shrunk from the contemplated crime. When she spoke it seemed as if instead of addressing her, who from a domestic had grown into a companion, she was communing with herself, for the tone in which she spoke was subdued, and her eyes were cast strangely downwards, like one forgetting the presence of any auditor to those words which came so slowly, but at the same time with such fearful meaning, from her lips.

Margaret listened to her with profound attention.

" It is surely safe—very safe; what harm can come to me? There can be no other but this one to whom I have given my confidence, who can ever be cognizant of the deed; I should need to have betrayed myself before any real risk could accrue. No, no; there will be no danger, and the deed be safely and surely done,"

" It may," interrupted Margaret. " You may be assured it may; and I am only surprised that your ladyship can hesitate for a moment."

The countess started and uttered a half cry of alarm; thus betraying the fact to demonstration, that she had fallen into one of those strange waking reveries which it is said that persons upon whose minds there is a load of guilt, actual or intended, are peculiarly subject to.

" I—I had forgotten," she said, " I had for the moment forgotten even where I was. But we will now proceed to the work we have in hand. I hope that if occasion should actually arise for active proceedings I may count upon you an assistant, Margaret."

" Your ladyship may count upon me, of course, for is not my own safety concerned in the matter? I tell you candidly that I will not do the deed so long as it can be done by you—but if such danger should accrue as requires activity, I will not be found backwards in any course that may become necessary to free us both from such a dilemma."

" I am satisfied, Margaret; and now even if when we get within the precincts of the garden, we should see reason to conclude that we had better wait awhile, we can surely wait there as securely as elsewhere."

" More securely. There is no dog, or we should have been discovered before now; and the darkness in the garden is such that our discovery is not at all likely, while out here we do run a momentary risk from some one seeing us lurking about; and if questioned we should find it a very difficult matter to justify ourselves, or to say what we are about or who we are."

" True, true—it would be a complete stop to the enterprise at once, if we should be seen and questioned."

Acting upon this view of the question, which was certainly a very true and just one, so far as their interests were concerned, they commenced getting over the low fencing that we have stated defended the garden of that cottage from the common land.

This was easily accomplished, for the fence was very low, and indeed it was in such a state of decay that any person possessed of ordinary strength could have broken it down with their hands with the greatest possible ease.

When they were once in the garden the enterprise seemed to be truly begun, and the countess at once lost all the hesitation, which during the preceding half hour had from time to time come over her, and imparted to her sentiments that air of irresolution which we have noticed.

She seemed so fully to have wrought herself up to the dreadful resolve of her mind, and to have in one moment banished from her mind all those thoughts akin to humanity—she became transformed from all that should characterise a woman, to a demon thirsting for the blood of the innocent being, who never by word or look had given her the least offence, but whose misfortune it was to stand between her, as she thought, and those objects of ambition which always occupied so prominent a place in her regards. For the sake of wealth, of name and station, she was willing to do that deed, which, if discovered, would consign her to infamy, and which, undiscovered, must surely implant in her heart that thorn which never can be eradicated—the dire and dreadful remembrance of an evil deed, which was calculated to awaken the severest pangs of a terror-stricken conscience.

The garden they were now in was unquestionably darker than the heath, because it was crowded with all sorts of luxuriant vegetation, as well as several tall trees, all of which added to the general gloom of the little spot of ground, and made the security of those who were there ten times more secure, for not the most attentive observer looking from the cottage could have seen them, and even had Mrs. Grove, which was a most unlikely thing, come into the garden, there were a hundred hiding places, where, with the most perfect security, any one could have taken up a position to the complete defiance of discovery.

No light came from the back window of the cottage, which looked into the garden, and just as Margaret had made a whispered remark to that effect to the countess, and intimated that it was a proof that the occupants of the place had retired to rest, there came a flash of light from a window, as if some one had suddenly passed it on the inner side with a lighted candle. Then, before a remark could be made upon that point, it came again, and a curtain was drawn across the very window which belonged to the child's bed-room, and which Margaret was able to declare to be such, in consequence of the observations she had been able to make in the front apartment of the cottage.

Through this curtain there came now the steady faint glimmer of a light which was but just sufficiently strong to show itself through the material of which the curtain was made, and yet scarcely sufficiently well to define the whole of the window.

"Is that the room?" said the countess. "Are you certain that is the room?"

"I am quite certain, and it is evident to me that Mrs. Grove is now putting the child to bed. Let us approach. We can do so with perfect safety, and we may overhear something that will be interesting."

Treading as softly as foot could fall, they both proceeded towards the window, and when they got close to it, they found that there were several portions of the window which the curtain did not fit closely, and which enabled them to see clearly into the apartment.

A glance was sufficient to show that the supposition of Margaret was correct, and that the child was going to bed, for it was already in its night-gown, and Mrs. Grove was talking to it. They heard her quite distinctly say, "Ask me no more questions, for I dare not tell you more than I have told you, my dear, and when at night you pray for your father and mother, you must be contented to do so without the necessity of my telling you any more about them.

"But I want to know, dear nurse," said the child, "who my papa is."

"The knowledge will come some day, and in good time too. He is a gentleman, and your future fortunes, I dare say, will be a splendid contrast to your present ones."

They then heard Mrs. Grove say to herself, as the child closed its eyes and gave unequivocal symptoms of repose having stolen over it—

"Yes, the secret must come out some day, that is evident. I will not myself die without declaring it. It would be most wrong and wicked of me to do so, and I hope I shall get the pardon of Heaven for the part I have played in a transaction, which must, sooner or later, come to light, and which I can only be the most decisive evidence of. The earl has evidently a strong affection for the child."

"Do you hear," whispered the prompter of evil; "Margaret, do you hear? Can you have any doubt now?"

"Hush! oh, hush! she speaks again."

" You shall know some day of the injustice that is done you, and then it will most probably be a time when you will be able to enjoy by contrast all that will become yours by right ; for you have rights, although you know them not."

" You hear ; you hear, again," whispered Margaret.

" Yes, I do ; yes, yes, and this is all such confirmation of the dreadful truth, that it but works my purpose up so strongly that nothing shall stay me in what I have commenced ; she shall die ! she shall die !—the child shall surely die !"

" Look, my lady, look through this small crevice here, and you will see that, in a few moments, the child will be alone, for the woman is about to leave the room. Now—now she has gone, gone most probably for some hours."

" And how is the deed to be done ?"

" Most easily. You have but to open the window, and one blow with a knife —"

" A knife ?"

" Yes ; do you not see that there actually lies one upon the window, just within there ? Do you not observe it, and with what ease, too, may this convenient window be opened ! You perceive that the frame-work merely consists of pieces of lead which the fingers will turn aside, so thin, and old, and rotten are they. Hush, hush ! she returns—surely she is not about herself to retire to rest at so early an hour ?"

The small door which communicated between the front and back apartments of the cottage was now opened again by Mrs. Grove, and she came into the room in which the child was sleeping, carrying in her hand a jug of milk and some slices of bread and butter cut up, all of which she placed upon the same ledge, just within the window, where Margaret had already observed that a small knife was lying.

" How sound she sleeps to-night," said Mrs. Grove. " I suppose though, as usual, poor little thing, she will wake with the dawn of day and feel disappointed if her milk and bread be not within reach of her ; so there it is, although it is a habit that must be broken soon, indeed, almost immediately, for she is getting of an age to know better, and to wait the regular hours for meals now."

Mrs. Grove then again left the apartment, taking particular care to close the door of communication between the two apartments, no doubt with the kind intention of preventing any sound or any ray of light from destroying the repose of the child, who slept—alas ! the last sleep it was ever to know in this world.

" Would not," whispered Margaret to the countess, " would not this affair altogether, as it has proceeded, be called under any other aspect providential ?"

" Hush ! do not use that word. If our dealings be in evil do not profane such a word as that by using it. No, no ! Oh, no !"

" But do you not perceive how suddenly all the difficulties have vanished in the way of your plan ? Do you not see that the means so obvious, so clear, and so easy for carrying out the object of your visit here, are now precisely before you ?"

" How—how do you mean ?" Are not the same difficulties now existing that there were before, as well as the same facilities ?"

" Yes, as regards the facilities, but not as regards the difficulties. What now is to hinder you from placing in the child's milk the poison which you have ready ?"

" I see—I understand you. Nobody, nobody. There is *nothing* to hinder us. The deed shall be done ! I—I do not hesitate now. Oh ! no—no ; it must be done. Tell me again that it must be done ; let me hear some other voice than my own proclaim that fact."

" It need not be done," whispered Margaret, " if you will be content to take the consequences of leaving it undone—if you do not mind the loss of name, rank, wealth, and if you do not mind seeing another take your place as the Countess of Crumbledown, and this child come and displace your child, while you are covered with contempt : it need not be done, but ——"

" No more, no more. You mistake me ; I did not waver."

" I'm glad to hear it, my lady, for your sake. See there, and there, and there ! How easily these panes of glass are taken out, and how easily these little leaden frames are turned aside. Now is not the passage to the action which will make you secure free and open to you? When his child is dead the earl can have no motive for disturbing existing arrangements, and ——"

The child spoke in its sleep. It was an infant prayer, taught to it by Mrs. Grove, that it lisped in soft and gentle accents, such as should have been sufficient to move any heart, and which for the moment did appear to have some effect even upon the countess, for she clasped her head with her hands and uttered a deep groan.

The prayer was one for a blessing upon her father and mother that the child uttered. It was one of those genuine and guileless effusions that, in our opinion, will find better acceptance and favour in heaven than the most elaborate compositions of an archbishop or the most exalted specimens of applications to the Deity in G flat or A something else that are ever perpetrated within the saintly atmosphere of Exeter Hall.

"Did—did you hear that?" whispered the countess.

"Yes, oh! yes."

"Well—well. Do you—hold to the purpose. God help us! God help us!"

"You now do shrink, I see, my lady; and if that is the case I advise you to go round to the front entrance of the cottage at once, and tell the woman who you are and who you know the child to be—that you look upon your own marriage with the earl as a mockery, and your own child as no better than a bastard."

"No, no; oh, God! no."

"Then what other course have you to pursue but ——"

She pointed significantly through the window to the child, as it there peacefully and now silently slept the calm sleep of innocence; thereby intimating that its destruction was the only other course at all open to the countess.

These few words did indeed recall to the mind of that imperious and haughty woman all those worldly things which made up the sum of what she considered to be desirable, and the temporary touch of feeling which had for a brief moment exhibited itself, passed away. She was again resolved.

"Say no more, say no more," she muttered; "I am myself again, and it shall be done."

"You have but, my lady, to stretch your hand now through the window, and to place in the jug of milk that is standing on the window ledge the poison you have brought with you, and the deed will be complete. Can anything be conceived easier to be done?"

"Or more difficult to undo," said the countess, as she produced a small packet of white powder, and with trembling hands unfolded it. Indeed, she shook so that she spilt some portion of it upon the ground at her feet, which Margaret observing, she stamped into the earth in order that there should be no such evidence that the deadly drug had come from any one outside the house.

It did take but a moment to perpetrate that dreadful deed. The Countess of Crumbledown had only to place her hand within the window, and then, in another moment, the poisonous drug was shaken into the milk that had been placed there by Mrs. Grove for the child's refreshment.

"'Tis done!" she said, "'tis done!"

"Come away, then, at once," urged Margaret. "There can now be no object gained by staying. Come away at once, I charge you."

The countess stood like one transformed to stone, with the paper that had contained the arsenic in her hand, until her confidante, who now felt that her power over her wretched mistress was fully consolidated, snatched it from her and concealed it; at the same time that, in hurried and anxious accents, she kept on urging her now to leave the spot, a proceeding which the other really deemed almost too much prolonged, by the deed she had done, to adopt."

"Are you mad, my lady?" added Margaret; "are you mad, that you do not move? Do you wish to stay here until detection is certain?"

"No, no—what do you say?"

"What do I say? Why I say come away, of course. Is this the resolution which has induced you to do so much as you have already done? Surely you have forgotten that by this act you have saved your own child from such disgrace, which would have clung to it through life. If it had been a boy, I don't know that it would so much have mattered, although then he would have lost the title."

" Hush, hush! It is done now. Say no more—it is done—it is done!"

She now suffered Margaret to lead her away from the spot, and they removed the short palings which separated the little garden from the heath, and stood in comparative safety after the perpetration of one of the most horrible deeds that could disgrace humanity.

At this moment the clock of the old church at Hampstead struck ten.

" We must get to town," said the countess, whose confidence, as she increased her distance from the scene of the murder, seemed to increase likewise, and she hurried on towards the London road with a speed that made it difficult even for Margaret to keep up with her, notwithstanding she was as anxious as the countess could possibly be now to place as much space between her and Hampstead as possible.

"We had better walk," said the countess, " and then we shall have less chance of recognition when—when——"

" When what, my lady ?"

" When the diligent inquiry commences which the proceedings of this dreadful night will be sure to provoke. You need not have asked me the question, for you must have known to what I alluded."

They walked on until they came to Camden Town, and then they procured a hackney-coach, for by placing such a distance as the whole of the road between Camden Town and the heath between them and Hampstead, they considered they had broken the thread of any evidence that might otherwise have been produced against them.

Of course, the mere fact of two women coming from Heaven knows where, taking a hackney coach in Camden Town, could hardly be construed by the most active imaginations into having anything to do with a murder at Hampstead, so they considered now that they were tolerably safe ; but, to make assurance doubly sure, they did not order the coachman to drive to the earl's house, but to the street adjoining, at the corner of which they got out, and having paid the coachman his demand, which was very moderate, for it was only three times what he was entitled to, they saw him drive away before they moved from the spot on which they had been set down.

The countess's great anxiety now was to get into the house without observation, and she directed Margaret to enter first, and then introduce her afterwards by opening the street door for her herself, and telling the hall porter not to trouble himself, as it was a friend of hers.

There was one thing that the countess felt perfectly easy about, and that was that no inquiries of a very close or anxious nature had been made concerning her, for she was not so stultified by the adulation which was paid to her mere rank, as not to know that it was paid to that, and nothing else.

One thing too was quite certain, and that was that the earl was not likely to have gone into any great grief on account of her being away all day, if, indeed, he knew it at all.

The scheme, then, of sending Margaret in first, succeeded very well, only that the hall porter made a remark that he rather considered she Margaret was " coming it," to have her friends calling at eleven o'clock, and past at night, after she herself had been God knows where. To this he had a reply in the shape of a volley of abuse which quickly made him feel how little of a match he was for his opponent in that species of oratory which consists in the stringing together of a number of expletives, and launching them with great volubility at the head of some one unlucky individual.

He accordingly, after a weak and vain effort in the way of a reply, sunk back into his huge leathern chair, crying " Well, well, damn it, hold your infernal tongue, and let in who you like or what you like for aught I care."

Having obtained this victory, Margaret opened the street door, and admitted the countess who succeeded in quickly passing through the hall undetected, and in a few moments she gained her own dressing-room, the door of which she instantly closed even against Margaret, for after the terror and excitement of the day, one of the most dreadful she ever passed, she wished to be alone.

Soon, however, she discovered that solitude had no charm for her, and that, perhaps, one of the most perfect things that for her future existence she would have to dread, would be to be left to the undisturbed company of her own dreadful thoughts and fancies.

CHAPTER LXXII.

THE DREADFUL NIGHT PASSED BY THE COUNTESS.—THE DEMANDS OF MARGARET.— THE VISIT.

Yes, the deed was done---that deed which could never be recalled---that fearful act which, when once accomplished, could not again be undone by all the wisdom, all the science, and all the power of the whole world,---a deed which the united exertions of an universe could not undo, or prevent the consequences of.

The Countess of Crumbledown had accompanied the converse of that proposition which has puzzled the learned for ages past, and will puzzle them for ages to come, namely, the production of vitality! In vain may human science attempt to grasp and to grapple with that gigantic mystery: it cannot be achieved; and that existence, that power of thought and of action which may be destroyed in a moment, and by the merest child, cannot be restored by the greatest sage.

What an awful situation was that into which she had recklessly plunged herself; and why had she done so? What were her inducements to outrage the strongest of God's ordinances, as well as violate one of the most stringent of human laws! No one commits a crime but with the hope of gaining something by its commission— something which shall produce peace of mind securely, and pleasurable sensations which shall be preferable to the thoughts and feelings which existed before the act of criminality; and yet, good Heaven! what awful mistakes do criminals commit in setting about their purposes!

Can any one suppose for an instant that any natural ill to which a human being may be exposed, could possibly come near to that frightful agony of soul which such a woman as the Countess of Crumbledown must feel whenever her thoughts should revert to the fearful act she had committed?

Can any one suppose that it was an escape from pain to her to have done that deed? Alas, no. The thing will not bear a moment's reflection; but it appears so monstrous that we can only wonder how a person possessing the intellect which that woman of strong passion did, could have been so misled by those passions as to engage in an enterprise, all the worst consequences of which must ultimately fall upon her own head, and upon none other.

But thus it is ever with people who dye their hands with human blood. They do not reason until it is too late. The frightful pangs of terror and remorse can find no home in the heart until the deed is done that calls them forth, and then they come too late to be of practicable benefit to the trembling wretch, who finds too late the frightful error he has committed.

But not quite yet had this state of things arrived as regarded the Countess of Crumbledown. The excitement of the whole affair had not yet subsided, and the danger she had run, and the means she had been compelled to adopt for the purpose of endeavouring to overcome it, had all kept her mind in a state of ferment and turmoil, such as prevented, in a great measure, thoughts from rising up, and presenting to her her real position in all its horrors.

The period of reaction, however, was not far distant—it could not be far distant.

Strange to say, when she reached her own chamber, the first feeling that came over her was one of fatigue, and she took off a portion of her apparel and flinging herself upon her sumptuous couch—a sumptuous couch which the veriest wretch that ever slept upon dried herbage in the open air need not have envied, she dropped into a deep sleep.

We have heard of men condemned to death sleeping calmly and soundly, and why should not the Countess of Crumbledown do so notwithstanding the foul crime with which her soul was oppressed?

But the condemned wretch awakens to the consciousness of who and what he is, and when exhausted Nature has claimed her due, and the deep sleep has done its work, imagination begins to paint in all its brilliant colouring—brilliant alike for joy or for woe—the period of horror and dismay that is to come.

So was it with the Countess of Crumbledown. She slept for about thre hours, and then, just as the clocks from the neighbouring church steeples were sending forth the hour of three, she awoke.

At first there was but an undefined, dreamy sensation upon her mind, that she had something unpleasant to think of, for the memory had not quite shaken off the lethargy of sleep and resumed its functions ; but that comparatively blissful state was little more than momentary, and then she awakened to a full and an awful sense of what it was she had to recollect, and of what it was that while the warm blood should continue to circulate through her veins, she could have no chance—no hope of forgetting it, except it might be for such a fleeting moment as that which had just passed away.

Besides, she might be said never to forget, for even if sleep sometimes would come over her—such deep dreamless sleep as that from which she had just now awakened, and when she did arouse herself from it, memory came back again. Memory may be said to be continuous, for sleep, it it lasted for a century, takes no count of time, and the last sensation upon closing the eyes in repose, and the feel upon awakening, are linked together without an interval.

But now she was awake, and she heard the clocks strike three. Memory, with a full flash, like an overwhelming tide, brought to her all the proceedings of the previous day, and the early period of the night. She knew what she had done, and with a scream of horror she sprang from her couch, and stood like one suddenly driven to madness, on the floor of her apartment.

Margaret slept in the next room, and the cry of despair that came from the lips of the Countess, could not fail to reach her ears. Indeed, it did not fail to reach the ears of others, as well as hers, for many of the servants in the house were startled from their sleep by it, and shook with terror, fearing that some dream had either made them utter the sound themselves, or that it was altogether a delusion.

None but Margaret really understood it, and were able to say as she did.

"That is the Countess !"

As she said these words she rose and at once opening the door of communication passed into the chamber of her mistress, in which a faint night-light always burnt, and by the dim rays of which she saw the Countess standing in the middle of the floor with her hands clasped, and her lips parted, while her eyes seemed unnaturally distended. Indeed, her whole appearance was that of one in some perfect trance of terror.

"My lady ! my lady !" said Margaret, reproachfully, "what is the meaning of this ?"

"Hush ! hush !"

"I hear nothing ; what are you listening to ? This is some dream you have had."

"Oh ! God, if it were only a dream ! But no—oh ! this is a hideous reality— one of the most awful of realities—God help me. No, no, what right have I to call on God ?"

"What is the matter ?"

"Can you ask ? You—oh ! let me look upon you ; come nearer to the light that I may see if you be human, for it was you who prompted me to that dreadful deed which there is no recalling. And yet you seem calm, your features are not distorted by the horror of your conscience, as it pictures to you that which you have done."

"And why should they ? for in the first place I have really done nothing, and in the second, I do not see that the life of a brat of a child is of such consequence as to make anybody, with a grain of sense, uncomfortable."

"God made it."

"Pshaw ! you should have thought of all this, madam, before. I could not have believed you would have begun preaching afterwards. It's too late now, and of all people in the world I must say, I should not have expected this of you."

The wretched Countess sunk into a chair, and covering her face with her hands she rocked herself to and fro, uttering deep groans expressive of an immense amount of mental anguish.

Margaret looked at her for some moments in silence, and then she spoke sternly and in a low determined tone of voice.

"Listen to me, my lady," she said, "listen to me. This is the beginning of something, which if you do not check it, will make you uncomfortable while you live. It is what people call remorse—a foolish feeling for a necessary deed. You have had certain reasons for a certain act. You knew what the act was before you did it, and you knew what your reasons were for doing it, and therefore you ought now to be above such folly as this."

".The Countess moved her hands from before her face, and said with an unnatural calmness—

"Will you kill me?"

"Kill you! I kill you! why should I kill you, my lady? You don't know what you are saying, that is quite clear. You have had some ugly dream that has affected you in this way."

"Oh! if it were but a dream. Tell me though by what bribe can I tempt you to take my life?"

"By none; why should I take your life?"

"Because I am so weary of it that I could bless the hand that took it from me."

"Oh! pooh! nonsense, you will think differently in broad daylight, I'll be bound. These are just the sort of fancies that come over people in the night-time, and you will be a different creature when the sun is shining."

"It ought not to shine upon us."

"Why do you say us, my lady—you cannot say that I did the murder?"

"And can you," said the countess, solemnly, as she fixed her eyes upon the face of Margaret—"can you flatter yourself that because your hand was not the one that placed the poison in the cup, you are free from the stain of guilt—oh! fatal delusion. Your own reason, if you have no feeling, will tell you differently, and at the judgment-seat of Heaven your name, as well as mine, will be mingled with the shriek of accusation that will rise against us."

Margaret shrunk back, for there was something awfully prophetic in the manner of the Countess. There was a deep and solemn truth in what she uttered, that the guilty creature could not for one moment avoid perceiving, and after a pause of several minutes' duration, she said, without attempting to contradict what the Countess had said,

"This is idle talking, and indeed, it is a sort of conversation which I will not indulge in. The deed is done!"

"But Margaret, Margaret—is it now too late?"

"Too late for what?"

"To go back again. To seek that garden—that latticed window, and the poison cup which is placed by the child's bed. Oh! think for me, and say if even yet there may not be a chance of snatching from death that little one. Tell me there is yet time, and I will fly to drag away the draught of death."

"This is positive madness—such madness as I certainly never did see equalled."

"No, no. All that has passed; but this, for the last twenty-four hours, you may call madness if you will, but this is a gleam of reason breaking through the mist. Yes—oh! yes, Heaven, in its mercy, may have yet given me the last chance of redemption. It may have awak'ened me from the sleep into which my many fears fell, on purpose that I might conceive this thought. Yes, yes, there is a hope."

"What would you do?"

"Go at once to Hampstead. Quick, quick, Margaret, procure a horse—anything, anything. Oh! be quick, and we may yet save ourselves from years of horror and an eternity of woe."

"No," said Margaret as she rushed between the Countess and the door. "No, this is folly—sheer midsummer madness. It must not be, and well for you is it that you have got me to think and to act for you, or else I can easily perceive you would do something that would be your total destruction."

"Do not stay me, Margaret, I command you."

"No, my lady countess, the time when you used to command me has passed away—we are equals now. You have got me to aid you in the commission of a crime that involves my safety as well as yours, and you shall not do anything, therefore, that shall hazard either. I command you to remain where you are, or if you will not, I here declare that I will raise the house and at once myself confess all that has been done."

"Confess?"

"Yes, confess, and seek safety and impunity myself by impeaching you. What is to hinder me doing so? I shall not altogether, perhaps, avoid punishment by such a course, but the consequences to me will be as a feather in the balance, compared with the consequences to you. Be warned, therefore, in time, and do nothing rash."

The Countess had made a movement towards the door of the chamber, but these words made her pause, and she stood trembling and irresolute before that menial, who, but a few short hours before, would not have dared to speak in such a tone, or to use such words of defiance to one, who then had the power of dismissing her, but who as certainly had it not now.

And this was one of the consequences of her guilt, which the Countess had to endure, and, so far as regarded those words of Margaret's, which expressed that she considered herself now upon an equality with her former mistress, and would not be commanded by her, for guilt, like death, levels all artificial distinctions, and makes the beggar and the king equals.

"I say again," added Margaret, who was determined to console her indignancy if she could; "I say again, that it is madness to think of such a thing, and that, by preventing you, I show myself to be the best friend you have."

She turned the key in the lock of the door as she spoke, and then, taking it out, she placed it in her own pocket.

"Now, my lady," she said, "when daylight comes, and you get rid of these vapours, you will thank me for this."

The Countess staggered to one of the windows, and opened a shutter. A faint streak of light came into the apartment, and she saw the new day was rapidly coming.

"It is too late," she moaned. "It is too late."

"Of course it is," said Margaret. "By the time you get to Hampstead it will be broad daylight, and the deed you would find done, so that all you could do would be to quickly give yourself into custody for that act, the consequences of which you are really, if you do nothing imprudent to draw suspicion upon you, as safe from as if you had never stirred from your own house."

"Yes—yes—I think I am safe."

"I am sure you are. Who knows it but I? You are quite safe, and have most effectually succeeded in removing every impediment now to your continuing in your present position. You have the leaf of the registry, which alone could prove the Earl's marriage with the mother of the child, so that you prevent her from dislodging you from your position."

"Yes—yes."

"And the child itself, which, some day or another, the Earl might have taken it into his head to acknowledge; for, I'll be bound, he thought much more of it than he did of the Lady Alicia, is, no doubt, now no more."

"Hush! Margaret, hush! Do not speak of her."

"I hope you are convinced, then, that this, what shall I call it, sudden passive weakness that came over you was most dangerous to your peace, and to your safety. See how the morning light increases."

"Yes; all is over—all is over."

"At Hampstead, you mean, all is over, there, I have no doubt, and you should, instead of putting on that face of woe, congratulate yourself upon the full and complete success of what you have done."

"I cannot do that. Congratulate is not the word. But I will endeavour to seem calm and satisfied, even though my heart be racked with agony. No one shall gather from my countenance that it is but a mask to hide the consciousness of such guilt, as is sufficient to draw reason from its throne."

"Time will dissipate all such feelings, and you will learn to look back with wonder upon such a night as this. I would advise you, my lady, to give some splendid parties—to see more company than ever; and since, now, you are quite certain—thanks to me—that what you possess cannot be wrested from you, I would advise you to use it royally."

" I will—I will. It is only in a crowd, and in the excitement of life, that I can hope to have a moment's calmness. Solitude will be, henceforward, horrible to me."

" There is no occasion to court it; and, as for myself, if you will call me your companion instead of your maid, and allow me to dress like a lady, I can mingle with your company, which, of course, hitherto I have not, from the situation I have held, but which I hold now no longer, been able to do."

" Companion did you say, and dressed like a lady?"

" I did say so, and I mean what I say. I am your companion and not your servant. You have made me, I again say, your equal, but do not for a moment mistake me, my lady."

" What do you mean? You speak plain enough."

" I mean do not mistake me by imagining that I shall presume, upon my new position, so as to become an annoyance to you. No. To you I shall always be the same, but I shall have the satisfaction of no longer being considered the equal of the domestics of the house, and you will not find me intrude upon your friends either."

" Were you a stranger," said the Countess, " I should make no objection, but the awkwardness consists in your being known to have been my maid and then coming out suddenly in your new character."

" That is an awkwardness which cannot be avoided, my lady. There are very few affairs of life which have not some drawbacks connected with them, so we must put up with this one as best we may."

This was an argument which the Countess found it difficult to reply to, so she did not attempt it, but finding that she was completely in the power of her former servant, she bowed to circumstances and gave up the point. She certainly had one consolation in the affair, and that arose from a conviction which had been from the first gradually growing stronger each hour since she had become so familiar with Margaret, and that was, that she was a person of actual enterprising intellect, and one who was likely to be a valuable confidant, for her powers of scheming were certainly great.

Moreover, the Countess of Crumbledown now began to entertain that strange feeling which is found soon to take actual possession of all persons who have given way to the impulses of guilt, namely, a desire for some one who, knowing the whole circumstances, they can converse with without fear of by a stray word committing themselves.

But for Margaret the Countess would have found herself completely isolated from all confidential conversation with any one, and she would have lived in constant dread that some stray word she might utter would betray her.

Thus was it, then, that the more she thought over her peculiar position the more she was induced to look with complacency upon the demands of her confederate, and even when, in the course of the next hour or so, Margaret intimated that a sum of money would be acceptable, the Countess gave it to her without making any grudging remark.

But with all this, and although, as Margaret had prophecied with the increasing light of day, some of the mental terrors of the Countess had vanished, there was a frightful dread on her mind of something which was certain to come.

That something was the riot and confusion consequent upon the news of the death of the child at Hampstead.

CHAPTER LXXIII.

THE COUNTESS, IN CONJUNCTION WITH THE MARCHIONESS OF FANFARONADE, GETS
UP A MASKED BALL.

THE Countess of Crumbledown now, with and by the advice of Margaret, her privy counsellor, so to speak, resolved, in order to ward off the possibility of suspicion, to be so engaged in matters merely connected with pleasure, that the idea of her having anything to do with a murder should appear quite preposterous.

As soon, therefore, as the arbitrary rules of custom would permit her to do so she ordered her carriage, and at once went to pay a visit to her old hag of a mother the Marchioness of Fanfaronade.

As far as regarded keeping secret from her what had been done it may be considered to be much more a matter of choice, on the part of the Countess, than a matter of necessity; for as to the Marchioness of Fanfaronade being shocked at anything, it was quite out of the question.

She had passed through such a long life of heartless selfishness that the taking the existence of a child for any object that was at all connected with the maintenance of those things upon which she had, throughout her whole existence, set her heart would, no doubt, have really appeared to her but a very small matter indeed, and, probably, she would have listened with equal composure to the account of the murder at Hampstead, as to the comparatively menial offence of getting possession of the leaf of the registry of Kingslake Church.

But, although the Countess of Crumbledown no doubt was well enough aware she might with safety have made a confidante of her mother, she did not do so, because there was nothing in the world to be gained by so doing, and she was not the sort of person to make quite a gratuitous confidence with any one.

What she went to the Marchioness for was, to arrange with her the particulars of a brilliant *fête*, which she intended giving, and she knew well that her mother was willing for any arrangement of an expensive character, provided the cost came out of anybody's pocket but her own.

We have already hinted, that time had not done anything for the personal appearance of the old Marchioness of Fanfaronade, of a favourable character, and it is scarcely going too far, although it may sound a little ungallant to say, that she as closely resembled an old female baboon of unusual size, as anything could.

Late hours, cosmetics, the glare of lights, and positive age, had made dreadful ravages in her looks. Her skin was shrivelled and wrinkled, like a piece of old parchment, and her sunken eyes gleamed with a strange sort of preternatural fire, while her sharp, imperious voice, sounded like a prelude to snapping somebody's head of, with the the two rows of brilliant teeth she possessed, the only drawback to which was, that they were all artificial.

She was always well enough pleased by a visit from her daughter, the Countess, because, in her she recognised a congenial spirit to her own, and that she could give free utterance to the grossly selfish feelings of her heart to her, without the slightest risk of being thought worse of on that account.

Of course, what the pure and gentle spirits of the world understand by affection —that sort of holy and beautiful affection, which should subsist between mother and daughter—was unknown to this precious pair, who, if their personal interests had at all clashed, would not have hesitated a moment in sacrificing each other in any way.

But as it happened, their means, feelings, and interests, rather coalesced than otherwise, so they agreed tolerably well.

" I am thinking, we have been rather dull of late, at Crumbledown House," said the Countess. "What would you advise as novel now, in the way of an entertainment?"

" A masked ball," said the Marchioness.

" Indeed !"

" Yes, it succeeded *à marveille* at the Duke of Dunderhead's, last week. You see that there are a number of people with tolerable figures, but frightful faces, and a masked ball suits all of them so well, that it is sure to be popular."

" Well, it's a good idea enough. But, the worst of it is, the amount of preparation it requires."

" I don't see that at all. Those milliner and dress-making people, who are such necessary nuisances, may as well sit up all night as not; as far as I can see, I think the four-and-twenty hours' notice is quite enough to get up a thing of the sort. You had better leave it to me, and I will manage it for you. Your rooms will hold a hundred people, I think, well enough?"

" Oh! yes, certainly they will, and a few more, if any eligibles should be thought of after the cards are issued."

" Very good. Then we will fix it for to-morrow night, and you need not take any trouble about it, except what you are going to wear yourself. By-the-by, Crumbledown is in town, is he not ?"

" He is."

" But how odd you look, now I come close to you. What's amiss? I'm sure there is something. You seem as if you were full of suspicion, and I have noticed, since you have been here, that you start at the slightest sound. What's the meaning of it? You may as well tell me at once. Come, I know there is a something to account for all this, because it is contrary to your usual habit, for I am proud to say, that I brought you up to care for nothing and nobody."

" You are mistaken."

" What! you don't mean to tell me that you have a passion ?"

" No, no, you mistake me—you mistake me, I say—you are mistaken as regards me having anything to say, or anything to keep secret. You are, you know, naturally suspicious, and that makes you think so."

" Oh, very good," said the Marchioness, " very good; I am not at all offended, my dear. I asked you candidly what was the matter, and if you had as candidly said you would not tell me, I should not have been hurt in the least. Everybody has a right to keep their own secrets, and you are of an age now to have secrets, as well as to have discretion enough to keep them."

" I have no secret."

" I don't care if you have, so we will drop the subject; and depend upon my arranging your *fête* as it ought to be; and there is always an advantage in another person sending out invitations—and that is that some objectionable people can be overlooked, and afterwards the matter explained away as a mistake, you know."

" Yes, that is handy."

" Oh very handy, indeed. Of course, in all classes of society there will be objectionables, and I do know some that I would rather walk a .mile, and that's what I very seldom do, than meet."

" And I likewise ; so cut them out of the list without mercy. I don't want anybody who don't come up to the mark completely, you know. But you are acquainted with my favourite aversion, as well as I am myself, and so can, I know, manage the whole affair with perfection."

" I can, and will. I suppose you don't see any more of the Earl than usual, and the affair of the Love Child sleeps ?"

" Yes, sleeps," said the Countess with a shudder, " it sleeps."

" A good thing—for these matters, however handy, you see they become as weapons of attack on domestic life, soon lose all their edge, and most decidedly they do mischief if they become public, because they destroy that prestige, that feeling of reverence which the common people ought to be taught to have for the nobility."

" Yes," said the Countess, " it sleeps."

" Eh? what makes your keep on repeating that word 'sleeps' for ?"

The Countess gave such a start, that she surprised her lady mother, and looked hurriedly and anxiously around her as if she fully expected her eyes to be blasted by some horrible vision, she said :—

"No, no, I did not say it—I did not say it. What have I to do whether it sleeps or not? No, no, you are mistaken."

"Oh," said the Marchioness, with a toss of her head, "it's no business of mine—none in the least—so I don't want to make an inquiry; but you may as well try to persuade me that it is not now daylight as that there is not something on your mind; and all I can say is, that if you are going to make any more morning visits, and do not wish to create the same impressions at every house you go to, you will alter your style, my dear."

"Alter my style?"

"Yes, to be sure, and try to behave and to look a little rational, and not as if you expected each moment to see an apparition spring up before your face. Why, if you had committed a murder last night, you could not have been more strange."

This was a random shot, but it hit the Countess of Crumbledown home to the very heart, and the only way in which she could overcome for the moment her agitation was to rise and make a great bustle about going, as she said—

"I am nervous, and not very well to-day; I suppose I must ask Alford's advice. A bad night always does disturb me in in this way in the morning."

"Then, my dear, you must generally have amazingly good nights, for I never saw you so disturbed before, and my only anxiety is, that you should not show it to any one but me. It is so very low and common: o seem moved at anything, really.

"Thank you, thank you, good morning! mind, and forget nothing connected with the masque."

"You may depend upon me."

"And is it so?" said the Countess, when she was seated in her carriage, " is it so? Do I indeed carry about with me in my manner and in my countenance the appearance of having done the deed that stains my soul? She said, 'murder!' Yes, she used the word 'murder!' What made her think of that?"

These reflections, as may be well imagined, were far from being the most agreeable in the world to the Countess of Crumbledown, but they forced themselves upon her, and even if she had not been intent upon returning home after she paid her visit to her mother, she would have been fearful, after the remarks which the Marchioness had made, of making any further calls, lest by so doing she should, to some persons who would remember them to her prejudice, exhibit some of the symptoms of uneasiness that had so strongly attracted the Marchioness's attention.

There was something uncommonly annoying to the self-love and pride of the Countess in the thought that on the only occasion when she most required that self-possession she thought she possessed in abundance, she should completely break down and lose all command of her features. It made her feel humiliated beyond anything she had ever thought could humiliate her, and probably, now, amid the crowd and the bustle of the streets and the broad glare of daylight, she felt more provoked at her own want of confidence than shocked at the remembrance of the fearful crime she had committed.

When she reached home she crossed her threshold with a feeling of positive dread, for she expected that she should hear something at once of the occurrence which, by that time, she fully believed must have taken place at Hampstead; and when the hall-porter advanced with a silver waiter, on which were the cards of those persons who had called during her absence, she shook so, that the man was amazed, and showed upon his countenance that he was so.

By a great effort she managed to say,—

"Let the cards be brought up to me at once—I—I—yes, let the cards be brought up to me."

Before, however, she could proceed any further, she was intercepted by the housekeeper, a prim old lady, who had had possession of the keys and the uncontrolled power over the domestic affairs of the establishment for some time.

She dropped a profound curtsey to the Countess, as she said,—

" May I have the honour of a few moments' conversation with your ladyship?"

" What about, what about?" said the Countess ; " has any one—come this way, into this room ; well, well, what is it? what do you wish to say?"

" If you please, my lady, the conduct of your ladyship's maid is so extraordinary that I think she must be out of her wits. She has taken upon herself to order a couple of rooms to be got ready for her own separate use, and she has

had her milliner and her mantua-maker here, and says that for the future when she rings she expects one of the footmen to answer her bell. Thinking, my lady, that she must be out of her wits, I have said nothing to her, but considered it best to wait till your ladyship came home."

The Countess's cheeks burnt like a living coal as the housekeeper made this speech, and it was only by a great effort she managed to say,—

" I will speak to Margaret myself, and see that everything is arranged properly."

" Thank you, madam ; I have to apologize for troubling your ladyship.'

" Oh ! not at all ; not at all."

" And this," muttered the Countess, " is another of the penalties of my transgressions. Can I now wonder how crime begets crime, and why it is that people are ever so anxious to destroy the tools by which they have worked out their purposes ? If by a word or a look I could bring death upon this woman, who is evidently inclined to presume so much upon what she knows, would I hesitate ? No, no, not for a moment."

When the Countess reached her own room she was met by Margaret, who had a wonted complaint to make of the manner in which the servants had hesitated to obey her.

" Can you wonder ?" said the Countess. " How are they to know the altered circumstances in which you stand to me ? How could Mrs. Andrews, the housekeeper, be aware that I had special reasons for acceding to your demands ? If you have brought trouble and censure upon yourself, it has been by your own foolish precipitancy."

" My precipitancy !"

" Yes; what else can be the reason ? It is your conduct which looks strained and unnatural, while that of the domestics, who have looked with contempt upon your orders, is but just what might have been expected."

" My lady," said Margaret, bitterly, " if you, after having made a certain arrangement with me, had done as you ought to have done—that is, told your housekeeper of it—all would have been well, but you left that for me to do, and now you are surprised that it was not believed. Of course it was not ; and it is I who have to complain of your neglect."

An answer of passion was upon the lips of the Countess, but she repressed it. She felt that she dare not quarrel with her servant, and without a word more she passed into her own chamber.

Margaret looked after her with a strange expression of countenance, as she muttered—

" I perceive it will yet take some time to consolidate that power I have been grasping at, but I will have it. Yes, I am determined I will rule here, and there is not a servant in the place but shall feel my rule; and if there be any one who strenuously objects, that one shall go as certain as that the sun will set to-night."

The Countess had no resource. She was compelled to yield, and at the risk of much more unpleasant consequences, she was compelled to go through the humiliation of telling the housekeeper that henceforward Margaret was to be considered as her companion, and was to be accommodated with two rooms, and her bell was to be answered by one of the footmen whenever she chose to ring it.

The answer to all this on the part of Mrs. Andrews, the housekeeper, was merely a respectful notice to quit her ladyship's service in one month from that date.

And so that affair ended apparently, although not really, as we shall in due time perceive.

CHAPTER LXXIV.

THE SUSPICIONS AMONG THE SERVANTS.—A BRILLIANT CONVERSATION.—THE HALL PORTER MAKES A DISCOVERY.

It must not be supposed, however, that all these affairs passed off without exciting something like surmise and suspicion among the domestics of Crumbledown House.

On the contrary, the mysterious absence of Margaret had from time to time afforded abundant food for curious speculation, and on the occasion when the Countess herself was away from home the whole of the day on that expedition to Hampstead, which had had so horribly successful a result, although they had not noticed her leave the house, still it soon became a matter of profound mystery where she could be gone.

No carriage was ordered, no message left ; but the Countess had, in fact, just disappeared, and that was all any one knew about the mysterious affair.

In vain did the servants ask each other where she could have gone. In vain did the little Lady Alicia's own maid endeavour to get from that really beautiful and intelligent young creature, for such she was, some information. Alicia had none to give her, and was to the full as ignorant as any one else could be of the movements of her aristocratic and eccentric mother.

And thus the whole day passed away, the only controlling powers in the house being the housekeeper over one section of the household, and the butler over another, for (as it indeed frequently happened for days together) the Earl did not put in an appearance at his sumptuous mansion.

It was undeniably the general opinion, that wherever the Countess was there likewise was Margaret, her maid; and many were the curious surmises hazarded regarding the whereabouts of each of them. The butler at last, although under ordinary circumstances he considered it a long way beneath his dignity to speak to that functionary, condescended actually to walk into the hall, and talk to the porter about it.

"Ah! ah! Samuel," he commenced, "I wonder you don't feel dull where you are. You look just for all the world like a snail in a shell, Samuel."

"Thank you, Mr. Griffith, all the same, but I don't feel dull a bit; and don't see how I should when the house-door is so continually opening, and all sorts of people coming in and out."

"Oh! ah! there is something in that, Samuel. But don't you think it strange, eh?" and here the butler inclined his mouth closer to Samuel's ear; "don't you think it strange, eh, that we see nothing to-day of the Countess, eh, Samuel? What do you say to that?"

"Nothing."

"Well, but don't you think it strange, and odd, and all that sort of thing?"

"No."

"You don't. Well, then, Samuel, all I can say is, that I have been deceived in you, and you are a greater fool than you look."

"Am I, Mr. Griffith? All I can say, then, is, that I have been deceived in you, for you are not quite such a fool as you look, though pretty near it."

"What do you mean, you rascal?"

"Nothing, you stealer of wine, and carrier away of it in a cart drawn by a horse with a rat tail, and driven by a man named Johnston, living in a mews not a hundred miles away from Blackfriars. Don't you think all that's odd, eh, Mr. Griffith?"

The butler turned rather pale and staggered a little, then he said, with a forced laugh,—

"Oh! very good—very good joke. You—you know I was only joking, Samuel, of course. You know that, my boy. I was not in earnest at all. I—I hope you did not think so, Samuel?"

"Oh dear no. No more was I. 'Live and let live,' say I, Mr. Griffith ; only you do sometimes call me a fool, and I just wanted you to know that a fool might have his eyes open, you see."

"Oh! ah! thank you, thank you—and you have not, I suppose, seen anything of the Countess to-day?"

"No ; and as you ask the question in a civil sort of way, Mr. Griffith, I have no objection to say that I haven't the least idea of where she is, or of where she aint ; no, nor of Margaret either. But you may depend something is going on that might be rather odd and curious to know, Mr. Griffith."

"Yes, Samuel, you are right ; and I am much afraid that in this house, Samuel, there are wheels within wheels."

"I'm sure there is, Mr. G. ; I'm sure there is. Don't the commonest people in all the world come here and ask for my lord and my lady, and don't they see 'em ; and it was but t'other day that Mr. Tomkins, the coachman, told me, on his word, that her ladyship got out of the carriage, and held quite a long talk with a man who belonged quite to the lower classes."

" The lower classes, Samuel ! Well, I never. If there is anything I hate, it's the lower classes."

" So does I. They is regular brutes, and don't know what polite society is. Now we, Mr. G., as does live in the higher circles, of course knows a thing or two."

" I believe you, Samuel—I believe you; and you may believe me or not, as you like, but I assure you that I have seen some of the lower classes actually eat green peas with a knife."

" The horrid low wretches ! "

" You may say that, Samuel. But, however, just you keep a look-out, and if you should happen to discover anything, you know, about what's going on, I should be very glad if you would let me know, for it's a serious and a dreadful thing to think of sacrificing oneself by living in a family, you know, Samuel, that aint quite *commy foe !*"

" Aint quite what, Mr. G. ? " said Samuel.

" *Commy foe*—it's French, Samuel, for being just the thing, you know—the ticket, and all that sort of thing—you understand."

" Oh, I see, but I don't know any French ; though I ought to know something of it, for my wife's uncle was a Frenchman."

" Ah, Samuel, that shows it was in the family, you know."

" I believe you. But, however, as you say you would like to know what's going on, Mr. G., and as it's no more than you ought to know, you may depend upon me doing the best I can to find everything out about it."

" Thank you, thank you. You know it's a serious thing for a butler to be compromised in any way, a very serious thing, you know ; and if one don't know what the family is about that one's living with, only think how we may be almost done for without being aware of it. And besides you know, Samuel, it's a dreadful thing to think of that you should be obliged to open the door to low people—a very dreadful thing."

" So it is, damn it, I didn't think of that."

" But you ought to think of it, Samuel, for the respectability of hall-porters. You ought to think of it, Samuel, that you ought ; and I only hope, now I have mentioned it to you, that you will think of it."

" I will, I will, you may depend ; crush me if I don't ; I'll think of it, and what's more, I'll make others think of it likewise, I will. The idea of me opening the door to anybody : that is not the thing, when there's the *hairy* bell for 'em to ring."

" Go it, go it—you are quite right, Samuel, you are very right indeed—I can tell you."

" I'm a desperate hall-porter, and for half a pin's head the next time her ladyship comes through the hall, I'll tell her to open the door for herself—I would, ah, that I would."

" And quite right too," said Mr. Griffith walking away, and then adding in an under tone, " the stupid animal will get himself discharged I hope, and a good job too. The idea of his hitting upon that little affair of the twelve dozen of wine I took away, when I thought I had done it so uncommonly snug ! Curse him, he shall go by fair means or by foul, or else my name aint Griffith."

The butler now betook himself to his own pantry, which had a small door of communication into the kitchen, so that from there he could, if he pleased, see what was going on in the lower regions, as well, as when he was peculiarly amiably disposed, address a few words to the inferior creatures as he considered them, who were there employed.

Still intent upon worrying everybody for information, Mr. Griffith now condescended to talk to the footman, and soon the whole of the kitchen servants were assembled, and seemed as if they had resolved themselves into a commission of inquiry as to the causes of the absence so mysteriously for the whole day of the Countess.

"Well," said the cook, "I can't make it out. There's no dinner been ordered."

"And no carriage announced," said the coachman.

"And no list of calls sent down to me as usual," said her ladyship's own footman.

"And no nothing," remarked a lad, who was there to make himself generally useful, but this remark by general consent seemed to be not a thing that came within the sphere of his duties, so he was kicked by one, and cuffed by another, until he was expelled the kitchen, and forced to take refuge in the scullery.

"I'll tell you what it is," said Griffith, "we shall all have to leave here, that's flat. It's quite impossible we should compromise ourselves by staying, unless her ladyship explains her conduct."

"Certainly, certainly," said everybody.

"I tell you what I'd do," said the boy, popping his head in from the scullery, "I'd discharge her ladyship, I would, and when she did come I really wouldn't let her in."

"You rascal, how dare you speak?"

"*Rally*," said the cook, "that boy is more troublesome every day of his mortal life, he is,—there's no such thing as bearing the remarks as he makes. It's *wice*, that's what it is.—it's *wice*."

Everybody agreed to this proposition, and the butler gravely informed the boy that he might consider himself discharged, and might go as soon as he liked, but, before he did go, he desired he might come to him, (the butler,) and have his ears pulled.

"Thank you," said the boy: "I'm very much obliged—of course I'll go, because I know what a dog's life I should lead if I was to stay; but before I do go, I shall just speak to the Countess, and tell her what we all think of her behaviour, I will!"

"What do you mean, you rascal?"

"Why, just what I say—I'm not going to see everybody imposed on in this sort of way, I'm sure, I won't have it, not I! It's *monstracious*, it is, so I'll just tell her of it, and what you think of her, Mr. Griffith—and what you think of her, cook—and you, coachman—and you, John; I'll tell her, too, how all of you say you won't put up with such goings on."

"Oh, gracious, providential, providence!" cried the cook, "he will be the ruin of us all."

"Good God!" said Mr. Griffith, "what an uncomfortable idea."

"We should all get the sack," gasped the fat coachman, "as dead as bricks."

"*Unkimmon!*" said the footman: "here's a pretty go."

Mr. Griffith now smiled at his compeers, as he made some telegraphic signals with his hands, in order to convey a general idea that he meant to do something that would get the whole fraternity out of the scrape in which they had entangled themselves, and then turning to the boy, he said :—

"Ha!—ha!—ha!—ha!"

"Eh? what do you mean by ha! ha?"

"Oh, I was laughing only at the joke, you know, the devilish good joke."

"Oh, was you? I don't see it myself, Mr. G. it's no joke to be turned away, and have one's ears pulled, for nothing at all."

"That is the joke. Come now, how dull you are sometimes! You don't suppose, now, for a moment, that I meant it. Why, I was only having a little laugh, I wonder how you could have been taken in by it."

"I don't, it was so uncommon natural."

"Pooh! pooh! You know how we all notice you, and wouldn't part with you on any account. Come, come, I find I must tell you another time, when I am only jesting, for fear you should look upon it as earnest. Forget it. It was nothing."

"Oh, well then," said the boy, "in that case, I shan't interfere, and it aint worth my while to say anything to the Countess about what you all think, only I thought as I was going away, it would have been just as well to have done you all a good turn if I could, you know, Mr. Griffith."

"Yes, yes, yes, of course. Come, now, I know you like sherry, and you shall have a glass—a glass all round, to heal up any little differences of opinion. That's the proper way to do things."

This was a proposition that was not likely to be otherwise than assented to most cordially, and by the time the glass of sherry had circulated all round, a wonderful feeling of unanimity seemed to be prevailing amongst them.

The boy had gained his point, though, and now he felt that he knew even how to manage the great Mr. Griffith himself, who was so much in the habit of threatening to pull his ears, and had on several occasions ventured upon saluting him with a kick.

It was at about a quarter to twelve that night, while the servants were taking their supper in the kitchen, and rather enjoying themselves than otherwise, that Samuel, the hall-porter, made his appearance among them with such a mysterious expression of face, that everybody at once knew he had something odd to tell.

"What is it, Samuel?" exclaimed the butler.

"Give us a drop o' something first."

"Yes, yes, take it—take it, but tell us what it is as soon as you can, there's a good fellow. Don't keep us in suspense all night."

"No, I won't. Here's towards all of your remarkable good healths! Bless you all!—a very nice drop of ale, to be sure. Ah! it's quite refreshing."

"Well but, Samuel, what have you got to tell?"

"Something that will make you all open your eyes like so many dying cod fishes, I can tell you—something that I found out all out of my own head."

"It must be something uncommonly hard then," remarked the boy, with an appearance of great simplicity that, however, did not impose upon Mr. Griffith, who shook his head and made a mental determination to get rid of him as quick as he could.

"Yes," continued Samuel, "I have been putting this and that together in my own head, and I quite agree with you, Mr. G. when you say that in this house there is wheels within wheels, for I know now as there is."

"Of course there is," said the butler; "I saw there was when first I came here. But what's the news, Samuel, what's the news?"

"Look at this," said Samuel, as he produced a white cambric pocket handkerchief from his pocket. "Look at this, all of you, with a lace border and a coronet in the corner—I say, look at this!" and Mr. Samuel shook it about like a flag.

"Well, what of that?" said one of the housemaids. "It's a handkerchief belonging to the Countess, of course I'd know 'em by sight anywhere."

"Very good," said Samuel, "that's where it all lays."

"All what lays?" cried Mr. Griffith, fairly out of all patience.

"Why just this here. About half an hour ago who should come in but Mrs. Margaret? Well, she wasn't quite so out-and-out smart as she usually is; but, however, that is no business of mine, so I took no notice of that, and as I and she aint the best of friends, I didn't say nothing to her at all."

"Well, well?"

"I'm a coming to the *pint*, so don't hurry me. Well, as I was a saying, her coming in wasn't of no consequence at all, but it was of consequence what happened *arter*, and what do you think now that was—just try and guess now?"

"How can we possibly? Do tell us at once, Samuel, what it was, will you?"

"Well, then, it was just this. No sooner had she, I mean Margaret, been in about five minutes than she walks into the hall, and goes up to the street door and opens it. 'A friend of mine,' says she, in quite an off-hand sort of way, and she lets in a woman shabbily dressed, such as you might see in the streets in a low *neighbourhood*."

"Indeed!"

"It's a *melancholic* fact, I assure you, and of course I had no call to say nothing about it, and should not, only as that ere female woman passed through the blessed hall she dropped this here handkerchief."

" The devil!"

" No, the Countess."

" Well, it's much the same thing."

" Oh ! I shall positively leave," said Griffith ; " I can't stand such things. Oh, dear no ! the idea of living in a family where the lady comes home shabby and on foot at near midnight don't suit me. Oh ! no, I shall give them a month to-morrow and have done with them altogether. My character is not to be taken away in that manner. Oh, no !"

" Yes," added the hall-porter, "you can just fancy how I looked, but you can't fancy what I thought."

" What did you think ?" eagerly inquired the housemaid.

" Nothing, for hang me if I knew what to think."

This incident, which, if the Countess had known of it, would certainly have given her some disquietude, occupied the attention of the servants for another hour at least before they retired for the night, and perhaps it may yet become of importance as other events arise to make it so.

CHAPTER LXXV.

THE DEATH, THE EXCITEMENT, AND THE DETERMINATION OF MRS. GROVE.

THE morning following the night which had made the Countess of Crumbledown a murderess at length came, and the sun's cheerful rays broke over the Heath of Hampstead, lifting the dews off the grass and leaflets, causing a moist to arise from the earth that indicated a heavy dew and an approaching fine day.

Mrs. Grove awoke that morning by the child complaining of thirst, and, as was usual, she arose to give her the milk that had been placed ready for her over-night ; she gave the milk to the child, who drank it off as usual, and then expressed a desire to sleep.

Mrs. Grove herself went to sleep again, as it was yet early, and she could not well rise without disturbing her charge ; however, she lay meditating for some time on the past, and then she fell into a deep slumber.

When she awoke she thought the child was somewhat restless or convulsed, and she watched it with the tenderest care, but she could not but think something was the matter with her, yet she had no suspicion of what was really the case.

She herself was up and dressed before the child could move about—it was not yet awake—she drew up the blind which closed the room, and let in more light.

The morning was delightful—the birds sang merrily, and the trees glistened in the sun—nothing could be seen or heard save the notes that rang from the birds on the trees.

The grass was yet wet with dew, for the sun was not strong enough, and had not risen long enough to effect the clearance of the moisture, and in the distance the mist rendered every object more and more indistinct.

A sudden groan from the child recalled Mrs. Grove from the contemplation of the scene before her, and she turned to the child and saw it was in pain, and gradually awakening.

" Well," said Mrs. Grove, " well, darling, what ails you this morning ? You are very restless."

" I'm so bad," said the little sufferer, at the same time she turned in her bed, with more like a writhe than an attempt at a change in position for ease.

"Goodness me!" said Mrs. Grove, as she watched the motions of the child; "what can be the matter with her? Nothing serious I hope, and yet I never saw her do the like before."

Her uneasiness was increased when the child complained of sickness and thirst. She grew worse and worse each moment, and at length unable to speak or express her feelings. Her sufferings were very great—she groaned and heaved, and appeared in great pain.

Mrs. Grove immediately set about calling for assistance, and getting the inmates of the cottage to get up, and obtain such aid as she most required.

"I will run to Hampstead and fetch medical assistance. Something very bad has happened to the infant, and she is violently unwell."

She began at that moment to show signs of sickness, retching succeeded to other symptoms, and was so violent for a few moments, that Mrs. Grove did not like to leave her.

The paroxysm was very violent, and when it ceased the child fell off to sleep, more from exhaustion than from any other cause; then she determined to run to the village for assistance.

She immediately quitted the cottage and made for Hampstead, to the shop of one of the principal practitioners in the village, who, however, was not up; but Mrs. Grove's application at the night-bell soon caused him to appear.

"What is the matter?" inquired the worthy surgeon.

"Oh, come, Mr. Mason, as quickly as you can, to the Heath—there is a little girl dying."

"What is she dying of?" inquired the surgeon.

"I don't know," said Mrs. Grove. "I come to you to see what it is that ails her."

"How long has she been ill?"

"Not half an hour, or perhaps, a little more."

"God bless me, it is very sudden! How is she affected?"

Mrs. Grove then detailed to him all that she had noticed, and then Mr. Mason said,—

"I don't know, but it appears to me she must have been poisoned. I'll come at once with you; but wait a moment, and I'll provide myself with some matters that may be useful."

In a very few moments, the surgeon having provided himself with such instruments and other matters that he believed he should want, if the case turned out to be as these symptoms appeared to indicate, and then he followed Mrs. Grove, and they both walked quickly to the cottage.

"What has the child been eating or drinking lately?" inquired the surgeon, as they walked along.

"Nothing but she usually takes," replied Mrs. Grove; "and nothing since last night, which was a little milk and some bread and butter, at the same time she has had some milk this morning, about a couple of hours before I came away."

The surgeon said nothing, but he could not attribute such sudden and violent indisposition to such viands.

They soon arrived at the cottage, and then Mr. Mason was ushered into the room in which the little girl lay. She had just such another fit of sickness on her as she had before Mrs. Grove went out of the cottage to fetch the surgeon.

There was not a moment to lose, and the surgeon immediately requested some warm water, and proceeded to employ the stomach pump for the purpose of discharging the contents of the stomach, and then forcing some warm liquids.

However, the symptoms became more and more violent; her eyes swelled with exertion, and her complexion became ghastly pale, and she could not utter a word.

"She must have taken something internally," said the surgeon to Mrs. Grove, "to cause all this disturbance. It could not have arisen from simply any natural illness."

"She had nothing but what I told you, sir."

"Have you any suspicion that she could have been unfairly dealt by—or any thing given her in her food?"

"Nothing of the sort: I am sure she could have had nothing given her; she had been so strictly under my own care, that I am sure no one could do anything of the sort."

"Well," said Mr. Mason, "it is very singular—very strange—the symptoms

are those of poison, decidedly; and I cannot conceive that they could have been produced by any other cause."

"Do you think she is in danger?"

"Yes, she is in very great danger indeed; so much so, that there is not one moment in which you can say she is not in danger."

"Do you believe she will recover?" inquired Mrs. Grove in great alarm, of the surgeon.

"Indeed I do not think she can; but she might rally—and yet I cannot tell—

she might rally and recover; but I fear she is too far gone; the poison has got too deep a hold upon her system to be easily ejected by any effort of art or nature."

"Good God!" exclaimed Mrs. Grove; "what can have been the cause of this? she in such good health, too?"

"Ah," said the surgeon, "it is very sad; but at the same time, I fear, the more I look at her the less chance there is for her—she is, in my opinion, sinking fast."

Mrs. Grove sat absorbed in grief: she could not but believe that the child had been seized with some sudden and malignant illness, of what character she could not say, but it was so from the effect; and the surgeon acted, she thought, upon an erroneous impression. Poison was a thing she believed it was impossible could have come near her; and she taxed her brains to ascertain in what manner she could have seized hold of any food, or how any could have been given her without her knowledge and consent; but yet she could not find, or satisfactorily point out to herself, any such possibility.

Again the child was seized by another fit of the convulsive heavings of the stomach, while its features were distorted with pain—and even these efforts of nature, painful as they were, were feeble in comparison to what they had been.

"Her strength," said the surgeon, "is not equal to the purpose of throwing off the poison; she will sink from exhaustion alone, even if she were not existing under some virulent poison, and yet had the same symptoms."

Mrs. Grove's grief was great, but she did all that she could imagine would alleviate the sufferings of the unfortunate girl. She attended to her with a mother's care—and yet it was evident she was sinking fast—she could not hold out any longer.

"Well," said the surgeon, "I fear a few minutes more will put an end to all her sufferings."

"She is not dying, I hope," said Mrs. Grove, whose own fears tended to produce the same impression upon her mind.

"She is."

The unfortunate creature was seized with a sudden spasm, and in the next moment she had ceased to exist. She was dead ere Mrs. Grove was aware of it.

"Is—is—she dead?" she asked, as she looked into her features and saw the fixed gaze of the unfortunate little child. Her eyes seemed to protrude from their orbits, from straining and pain.

"Yes," said the surgeon, "she is now dead and beyond all human aid. I feared so from the first."

"Good God! how sudden and how unexpected!"

"It is sudden," said the surgeon.

"What can have caused such a catastrophe?—when she came to me early in the morning, she asked me for drink; she appeared well enough then, save a little thirsty."

"She complained of no pain?"

"None; but fell asleep again—and in about an hour or so afterwards she awoke with pain and sickness."

"Ah!" said the surgeon, "the milk disagreed with her."

"It would seem so—and yet it never did so before; I cannot understand it, I am sure. It is a dreadful calamity."

"Yes," said the surgeon, rising, "it is;—but it seems to me to have been hastened by some means that are not apparent. I cannot but express my opinion that the child has died of poison."

"How could it be given her?"

"I cannot inform you that," said the surgeon; "but I should advise you, on no account, to attempt anything towards the burial until the proper authorities have inquired into the affair."

When the surgeon said this he arose, and again looking at the corpse, he left the room full of thought.

In a few minutes more he had left the cottage, and proceeded towards Hampstead. It was now late in the morning—the shops opened and people hurrying about—

coaches passing through and from, carrying people to business in town—people who resided about the spot.

On his way to his own shop, Mr. Mason met with a gentleman who was known in the town very well, and after some few compliments he proceeded to say to him :

" Do you know the cottage on the Heath, south of the Highgate-road ?"

" Yes, very well ; it is against the pound—that is the one you mean, is it not ?" he replied.

" Yes. Well, there is a most singular and strange occurrence there—I hardly know how to act."

" Oh ! it's a strange affair—but that woman appears to have been placed there to take care of that child."

" I believe so myself ; her name is Grove, I believe ?"

" Do you know that of the child ? "

" No : but no matter, the child is dead, and has died under very peculiar, and, I may add, suspicious circumstances."

" You do not mean to say," said the gentleman, " that she has been unfairly done by—do you ?"

" Yes, I do ; and my opinion is that the poor little thing has been poisoned— and I cannot help thinking, from all I have heard, that this woman, who had the charge of her, has done the deed ; indeed, I cannot conceive how it could be otherwise. She admits that there was no sign of the child's illness overnight, nor in the morning when she awoke, and that no one could have given her anything without her knowledge."

" And you think she murdered her ?"

" I am of opinion the matter ought to be inquired into, and that a coroner's inquest ought to be holden upon the body, and a thorough investigation gone into, to sift the circumstances."

" You will communicate the circumstances to the parish, I suppose ?" said the other, with a look of importance.

" Yes, certainly."

This was the end of the conversation, which Mason well knew was enough to set the whole village of Hampstead in a state of ferment and excitement, from one end to the other.

The gentleman, of course, went and related the matter to at least fifty persons, in the course of the next half-hour, and the whole town was in a state of excitement in a very short time ; and, before long, it reached the summoning officer, who being a parish dignitary as well, thought it incumbent on him to proceed to ascertain the truth of the report that had reached his official ears.

When, however, he did become acquainted with the report, he determined to proceed at once to Mr. Mason, and inquire of him what was the meaning of what he had heard ; and to this purpose he posted along the high street, on either side of which he could observe the gossips coming out and talking to each other ; and moreover, he could see that their looks were, ever and anon, directed towards himself, which was a gratifying acknowledgment that he was a man of importance.

In a short time, without deigning to speak to any one, he entered the shop and presented himself to Mr. Mason.

" Good morning, Mr. Mason."

" Good morning," replied the surgeon ; " you are the person I most wished to see ; how fortunate—you have saved me a walk, and time is money to me at all events."

" I am glad of it, Mr. Mason," said the officer ; " but I have heard of it, and I am proud to say there aint much that happens in Hampstead that I don't hear of, and that very speedily too."

" I do believe that," said the surgeon ; " you are correct—very correct in your' supposition. You are a very active personage indeed, and I think there is more than one person in the parish that knows that to be true."

" I dare say, sir ; I try to do my my duty. But what is it I hear about a family of seven persons being poisoned this morning—is that true, Mr. Mason, or false ?"

" False."

" And what may be the truth, sir ? '

" You shall know. A little child, whom I was called to attend to, has died under very suspicious circumstances."

" Indeed, sir ! "

" Yes : my own opinion is, that she was poisoned, and that, probably, by the woman in whose charge she appears to be placed ; for I cannot see by whom it was administered : according to her own account, no one else was with her."

" Indeed !—how dreadful ! Well, there must be an inquest, that's certain—an inquest."

" Yes, of course."

" I'll set about that immediately. I'll give notice to the jurors and the coroner—"

" When you please, sir : I have some other calls just now—excuse me—good morning."

"Good morning, Mr. Mason," said the important functionary, as he left the shop, upon this hint, and proceeded to consider the matter over in his own mind, as he walked along."

*   *   *   *   *   *

Mrs. Grove, when left alone, appeared stunned at the event that had taken place : it was, to her mind, totally incapable of explanation ; she could prove that the opinion of the medical man was decidedly inimical to the supposition that it was no natural cause of death that had carried her off, but some unfair means—poison had been resorted to to cut her off.

How that could be effected, she could not see nor believe ; she had never yet left her : what could have been the occasion of all this she could not tell—but there was the dead body before her, and that told her a sad but true tale. What could be done ? She was bewildered—lost in a maze of conjecture—what ?

What would the earl feel at such a bereavement—what would he say ? how could he know it, unless by accident ? She was resolved that she would go the earl, and watch for him at his door until she saw him and communicated with him—informing him of the loss he had sustained in the death of the child.

———

CHAPTER LXXVI.

MRS. GROVE NARROWLY ESCAPES BEING MURDERED, BUT ULTIMATELY ARRIVES AT THE EARL OF CRUMBLEDOWN'S MANSION.

Mrs. Grove having made up her mind as to how she should act, at once deter¯ mined to leave the house regardless of all other considerations, and proceeded to dress herself for her walk, which she did with a heavy heart, and it was not without a sigh she left the room in which the little child lay a corpse ; but she had other duties to perform, which, to her mind, would admit of no delay, or the interference of any other feelings.

She quickly, however, arrayed herself and walked up to the bedside of the unfotunate child, and, taking a last look at it, left the room and then the cottage, proceeding at once towards town for the express purpose of seeing the earl.

Mrs. Grove had few selfish feelings, and it was from no fear of the consequences of the mysterious death of the child that she left the cottage, for she well knew the rectitude of her own conduct, and had nothing to fear from any deed of her own.

Indeed, it was not every one who had the same singleness of purpose, nor every one who could bear the same scrutiny of conduct—indeed, she could have divulged her own thoughts, and been tried by their purity, and she would have been triumphant.

What had caused the death of the child she at that moment could not tell—nay, it would be utterly impossible to tell, but something much too extraordinary to be easily unfolded. She determined to tell all to the earl without reserve, so that he might, if he could, solve what appeared to her such an enigma.

Mrs. Grove pursued her way to town : in sorrow and in silence she plodded her way onwards until she came to London, until she reached the Camden Town side of the canal, and then, coming down to Camden Town, she turned down some streets to the right, which took her across some fields, which she crossed with the intention of getting to the West End by a nearer cut than the direct road.

It was a pleasant enough walk, but Mrs. Grove saw not that she was by far too much absorbed to notice anything about her ; she was deeply meditating upon the recent event that we have detailed.

There was at that time not the masses of houses and streets there are now—it was all open fields, and nothing could be seen save hedges and ditches, and fields filled with cattle or shut up for grass ; but there is a very different appearance there in these days—indeed, on many spots it would be very difficult to see anything in the shape or the colour of a blade of grass.

However, Mrs. Grove pursued her way, but she was not at all aware that she had been followed by a couple of men, for some distance, across the fields. They were two ill-looking men, with sticks under their arms, and their hands in their pockets, as though they had no particular object in view but to enjoy themselves.

When she approached near the houses they came up closer and closer, but yet she noticed them not—and, if she had done so, she would have paid no attention to them, seeing she was getting nearer the houses, or, wretched as they were, she would have considered them as a protection to her.

She now crossed out of the fields into a lane, in which was a high hedge on one side and a deep dyke or ditch on the other—and at that moment the two men quickened their pace and came after her very quickly, but they did not decidedly overtake her, keeping only a few yards behind her.

About two-thirds her way there was some miscellaneously built out-place, which might of itself have been considered a cottage or a lumber place—about a hundred yards further up the lane stood an old public-house.

When she arrived at the first place (the cottage) they set up a shout to Mrs. Grove to induce her to stop, and she turned round, but at the same moment she found a handkerchief thrust into her mouth, and she herself seized as well and forced into a shed, or some place at the side, for she had not noticed what the building was, as she came up to it, but in she was forced by the men.

"Speak but one word," said a gruff voice, "and you are a dead woman, if you had a hundred lives."

"Mercy !" she faintly articulated, "mercy."

"Be quiet," was the only reply.

She was then forced into another and inner place, where she was carefully secured in a more systematic manner, and fresh threats made use of when the handkerchief was removed to admit of other fastenings being used to secure her.

"Take all I have," she said.

"We mean," said the men, interrupting her roughly.

"Take all I have," she said, "all—all ; but spare my life—spare my life ! I promise never to give you the least trouble about this matter, I do not know you—let me go.

"No, no, not yet ; you must remain where you are ; there is no time to spare in bothering with you ; stand quiet ! You will suffer for it, depend upon it."

"I mean no harm," said Mrs. Groves ; "but you know not what you do. I have left a house where there is a child lying dead, and want to see its only parent."

"Gammon !"

"As Heaven is my witness, I mean what I say ; let me go. It will be a worse things than you think for, if you detain me. I am, like yourselves, poor."

"Knock her hard, Jem," said one of the men to the other, which was readily

^acceded to by the other, who immediately did as he was requested, and struck Mrs. Grove a rather heavy blow on the head with a knobby stick, that nearly stunned her, and brought her to her feet.

" Now, my good woman," he said, " you will hold your tongue. You women never do as you are told at once asking, that's the truth : married or single, you never do as you are told; it's the worst of women they are so cursed obstinate, they will have their own way, and all you can do is to hit them a topper upon the head."

" Ah! that's the way to do it."

Mrs. Grove saw there was little to be expected but ill usage from these people, and she was compelled to remain silent, and in a few moments she was seized again, and a cloth bound over her head and a handkerchief stuffed into her mouth, and her hands and feet tied together.

Fearful that this was a prelude to some fearful tragedy, she resisted so far as to get one of her hands free, and to take the handkerchief out of her mouth, to scream out for help and assistance.

" Another knock, Jem, damn it, do it at once!"

" Wait a minute, don't be in such a hurry, there's nobody at hand, I know, for the signal would have been given."

" Quick !"

" There, will that do ?"

As the man spoke he struck Mrs. Grove a heavy blow on the head, and she instantly became insensible, and what took place afterwards she could not tell.

It was some time afterwards when she came to herself that she found herself in a reclining posture in the dark ; but there was a great noise close at hand by her ; though she could see nothing, it seemed as though several men had met and were conversing over their exploits.

She lay some time motionless trying to recollect her situation, and it was some moments before she could really recollect the past, so much was it in the character of a dream.

" Well," said one, " I don't care what it is, but I have done my share, and if I aint lucky to-day I may be to-morrow."

" You may," said another voice.

" Then why shouldn't I have my share to-day ?"

" Because you aint half a man, and shrink from doing your share of the hard work."

" I say it's a lie ; I do as much as any man, I don't care who he is," replied the other.

" That's a lie, Jack, and you know it."

" Say when, then, I didn't. I tell you what it is, you have a good haul, and you want to keep me out of it ; you are doing what's not right, and it won't prosper with you."

" You might have taken part ; but, Jack, you are a sneak, there can be no two minds about it ; when there's hard work to be done you are without bearing, that's the truth; we have had some hard knocks for this. Recollect the affair of the lane the other day, you were out of that ; and yet you shared along with us, that's true, you know."

" What affair of the lane ?"

" You know as well as we do. Why, when the man came over from town the other day, we stopped him, and a devilish heavy job we had of it too."

" Aye."

" Yes, he had nearly got away from three of us, and no mistake ; and had we not, at last, have knocked off his hat, we should never have stunned him, and he would have got away."

" Couldn't you three secure one man ?"

" No ; he was a great man, and had a good stick, and I'm hanged if he couldn't make use of it, too, for we all had a taste of it, and went down one after another as if we had been shot ; however, we got up pretty well, and then we came behind him and knocked his hat off his head, and so, when we got a rap at his head we made him feel it, and had it not been for that we should have been done for once, at all events."

" Well, then, you needn't have grumbled so much the other day, when I found one man too many for me. You know I told you, if I hadn't taken to my heels, he would have nabbed me. I had to make devilish quick work of it, I assure you."

" Well, it might have been the same."

" Most likely ; but he was a stout, active man, a good height, and of fair complexion, and light hair."

" Aye, the same."

" He had a light blue coat on."

" Yes, he had, and a well-filled purse too. He didn't fight for nothing, for he had about sixty guineas in gold."

" Was he much hurt ?"

" Much hurt ! There you go ; you are such a cursed sneak, that nobody can depend upon a word you say. You want to make out you didn't know he was done for. You know we knocked his skull in, and you want to make out you didn't know it."

" Well, you know very well it isn't my place to know what doesn't concern me. If I don't know much, I can't tell much ; and so, you see, I'm not a man for a split."

" You be d——d !" said the other ; " there aint another man like you for a split in the whole country. Why, you hanged Jack Trowbridge."

" Did I ?"

" Yes ; but you got got out of it by saying you were his friend, and you had been concerned in another affair, and had been hurt, so you couldn't help him."

" It was the truth ; but I have the mark on my right arm now. I had been in an affair, in which I stopped a man and woman : this woman, cuss her, had hold of me somehow by the arm here, and she stuck her teeth into me like fury."

" Aye ! aye !"

" Well, it was the truth ; the marks are here, and they'll tell their own tale. Now, just look here : I went into the lane, to wait for some likely people. There was a fair a few rods off, and sometimes people came down this lane. Well, I stopped one or two on that night, and had a good haul, I can tell you."

" Go on."

" Well, this man and woman came down. I challenged 'em—they wouldn't give up the tin, anyhow. They had a booth at the fair, and had sold out, and were coming home to take care of their cash, and to buy more goods. I had heard all about it, for I was in the fair for a short time."

" Well, as I was saying, he wouldn't tip up the browns, and I hit him a crack and he came at me like a bull at a gate, swearing he would do for me and a dozen more if they were at hand, but Lord it was all talk, you know."

" Just hear him ! Did you ever hear such a fellow in your life ?"

" Not I."

" Did you ever see him, or know him to strike a blow ?"

" Never."

" You mind your business, I know mine. Well, I hit him another crack on the head, and he turned over, and I was about to give him another taste of the same, but the old woman seized me by the arm, and fixed her teeth into it like a she tiger. By Jove ! she made me stagger a bit, I can tell you."

" I can believe that."

" Well then, I tried to shake her off, but it was of no use. I couldn't use my arm—I was regularly done up, and she was like a vampire sucking my blood. At length, with a desperate effort, I struck her off, by kicking her shin till I broke her leg."

" That'll do."

" Well, when she fell, she set too screaming like a wild cat, so I hit her a crack o' the skull—quite a fancy one, I tell you, and it quieted her. Well then, I set too and rifled them and got clear off. I heard a row after me, but I wasn't going to rush back."

" Perhaps the old man got up."

" Not he—he was done for. I saw that before the old woman laid hold of me."

" Aye ?"

" Yes, and if he hadn't, he'd abeen up, and I should have been nicked sure enough—I could have made no resistance at all. I was of no use at all."

" You never are at a pinch."

" Now, I tell you what : you want to pick a quarrel upon me, to do me out of my share, that's it. You think you can do it easily, that's what it is."

" I tell you what you are, a sneak, and you want to sell us all. I know it well enough. You've tried it before, and you have tried it for a week past. I have watched you about, and now will have it out. It's no use your denying it, because it's all out. We've done for your friend the officer, but we made him confess all first. You were to have a hundred pounds, and a pardon for the job."

The man no sooner heard this, than he sprang to his feet, and made a rush to the door, with the hope of getting out before any of his comrades could seize him.

But his effort was a vain one, for they had secured the door, and before, or by the time he had got it unfastened, he received a blow on the head that brought him to his knees.

" Mercy, mercy!" he cried.

" No, no ; no mercy for the sneak."

Again the wretched man got up, and endeavoured to get out, but he was beaten back. The blows fell fast and thick about him, and, with a loud shriek, at length he sprang towards the door, and rushed out; but it was only to go a few yards, and then fall dead, for he had received a stab in his back.

There was then some horrid conversation carried on, and they all rushed towards the door, and in a few moments more the place was quiet and still.

Mrs. Grove began to think she was forgotten in the heat of the fray ; and that, if she delayed leaving, she should be remembered, and she would not escape.

She struggled to her feet, and found that most of her bonds had been undone—that being the case, she presumed they believed her dead. She got out of the place, and, passing through the passage, emerged into the open road by the passage which appeared to have been designed for the occasion.

She saw no signs of the body. Doubtless the gang of robbers and murderers were busily engaged in concealing the body, and she made the best of her way to town.

CHAPTER LXXVII.

THE MASKED BALL.—MRS. GROVE'S INTERRUPTION OF THE FESTIVITIES.—THE ACCUSATION OF MARGARET.

THE same day the countess, as soon as she had returned to town, which she did unperceived or noticed by any one, issued a number of invitations to a grand masked ball or entertainment. That she could give such an entertainment at such a moment might excite some surprise ; for though she was bred up a heartless being, yet it could not be expected she could be so callous to crime.

This, however, is a matter not well understood by many people, who affect to believe that people in high life have too many sympathies to be able to commit such an act ; but their life is one of deceit, and an attempt to destroy feeling and sympathy—they have no exercise for them.

After a while the place was immediately put in order. The rooms were large splendid. It did not require much time to get together the necessary essentials for a splendid *fete* of the most extensive and *recherche* character, especially by those who had such ample means as the Earl and Countess of Crumbledown.

Nor were they likely to want visitors, since the very *elite* of the aristocracy willingly came, and, long before the appointed time, there was every prospect of there being an ample attendance.

The rooms were filled with beautiful ornament work of all kinds, lights and glasses shone from side to side, from end to end, and all that was beautiful in flowers was shere.

Side-tables were spread, and there indeed was the richest wines and viands that

could be produced in London by the magic influence of gold. The hall was lit up. The splendid saloons shone in a blaze of light from end to end.

The house gave a feature to the whole neighbourhood, and there was an orchestra ready erected for the musicians, who would fill the house with those dulcet sounds which would enliven so many hearts, but which would also for a time still at least one guilty conscience, but at the same time sweet sounds will not last for ever; there will be a day when the still small voice will be heard, though a trumpet were to sound.

The hour came round; the street began to fill with carriages, and the whole street was in an uproar from one end to another, arising from the sounds of wheels, horses, and the eternal knocking at the door, which kept up such a clatter, that these combined sounds might well be a nuisance to every one else.

The company now arrived, the saloons began to fill, and many were the beautiful faces hidden behind grotesque and fancy masks; many a youthful and faultless form was hidden beneath many a fanciful costume.

However, the place, though apparently filled with visitors, yet it was evident the arrivals had by no means ended. The knocker still continually rattled, and the carriage-steps were continually sounding up and down with a clatter that would be astonishing if one did not know that it was done on purpose.

In the midst of all this shone the countess with all the gorgeousness that wealth could procure, with all the additions that could, under the circumstances, b obtained—and what was there that she could not?—all the gems that could be purchased from the East.

The sounds of music came from the house, and the hearers stood on the outside and listened to the luxury, which the wealthy alone could purchase, and which they could only occasionally listen to.

Among the crowd, who stood on the outside, was a female, whose grave and anxious countenance showed that these sounds found no responsive chord in her heart.

" What is the meaning of all this?" she inquired of the bystanders.

" It is a masked ball," said one.

" Whose house is it?" she again inquired, after a pause.

" The Earl of Crumbledown's."

The woman made no answer. She stood some time by the door and watched it narrowly, but she saw no one whom she recognised, and all was strange to her.

That woman was Mrs. Grove.

Presently, seeing one of the footmen come down the steps to enjoy a little of the cool evening air, she determined to walk up to him and speak to him, to make an inquiry.

" Is the Earl of Crumbledown within?" she said, when she got near enough without being heard.

" Yes," said the man.

" Would you do him a service by telling him that some one is waiting who would be glad to speak with him?"

" Oh, I fancy I see myself," said the footman, jerking himself on his heels, and looking admiringly at the calves of his legs—" yes, I think I see myself on such a fool's errand."

" You would be doing an act for which he would commend you. I must see him—it is most important, both to you and to me, to let me see him immediately."

" Oh, it may be; but it can't be done."

" Why not?"

" Because his lordship will be engaged until, I dare say, daylight; and then he'll go to bed, damme!"

" Good Heavens! I cannot see the earl now?"

" No, you must wait."

" I cannot wait until such an hour—it would be impossible to wait so long; and if you will not call him out, I will go to him—ay, even among those by whom he is surrounded."

" Ah, ah! a devilish good idea. You'd be taken for a mask. My eyes, what a sensation you would create! but there would be the unpleasant consequences of a watchhouse in perspective."

" I must go."

" No, you can't; and if you atempt to pass me again, I will give you into custody, and have you locked up, and no mistake about it."

Finding this useless, she left the man in the livery, and walked away to watch her opportunity. Apparently well pleased with having shown his importance and being perhaps conscious that his duties would require him elsewhere, he walked in, and began an interesting gossip with the other servants at the farther end of the hall.

While this was going on, Mrs. Grove watched her opportunity, and walked quickly up the steps and up the first-floor tairs, when she was first noticed by the enraged flunkey, who called out in desperation, as he hastened after her,—

"See there! damme if that mad woman won't go into the ball-room, and I shall get the bag for not keeping her out. Oh! you obstinate cat, you know you are wrong."

However, before he got more than half up stairs, Mrs. Grove entered the ball-room. The music had ceased, and there was a crowd of the most distinguished guests near the door. Mrs. Grove quietly curtsied, but nobody noticed her; but the earl in a moment saw her, and came towards her—her pale face could not escape his observation.

He pulled off his mask and said,—

"Grove, good Good! what do you want here?"

"She is dead, my lord."

"Who?" cried the earl; "speak!"

"The child, my lord, died this morning; and I fear, too, by poison. Yes, it must be so."

There was little in all this that was intelligible to anybody, even if it had been heard, but two figures turned round and unmasked themselves, as did almost every one else, when they saw the deep emotion of the earl.

These two figures were the Countess of Crumbledown and her maid, Margaret Manvers.

How this woman came to take part in the masked ball was easy to divine. She had her mistress's life in her keeping, and now threw off all the restraints which are usual to all in her station of life. She made herself her equal; and the countess dared do no more than frown, of which Margaret Manvers took no heed, save now and then to make a sarcastic remark.

No doubt one or two of the guests saw this; but their attention was riveted to two objects, the earl and Mrs. Grove, the latter of whom, raising her finger and pointing impressively to Margaret Manvers, said to the earl, in an audible voice,—

"And may Heaven judge me, but that woman is the murdress! I have seen her linger about the spot. I knew her not, else I might have suspected. But now I see her, and full well can judge the motive of this most foul act."

There was a pause: no one of the numerous guests moved or spoke; their silence was impressive. And what afterwards took place, we must reserve for another chapter.

CHAPTER LXXVIII.

THE CONSTERNATION AT THE BALL.—THE JUSTIFICATION OF THE GUILTY.

It would be almost impossible to find any language that would be sufficiently strong to convey an adequate idea of the strange scene of confusion which ensued in the magnificent saloon of the Earl of Cumbledown when Mrs. Grove made the most unlooked-for and extraordinary charge which she did against Margaret, the countess's maid once, but companion now.

The state of bewilderment in which all the guests were with regard to the subject-matter in dispute was such, too, that not one could comprehend what it was all about, and what it was that could produce so remarkable an effect upon the earl, whose ashy countenance and trembling limbs showed that he was for a time completely overpowered by some terrific mental shock.

What to think he knew not ; who to accuse, or who to justify, he knew not, for the news that such a catastrophe had taken place came across him with such a stunning vehemence, that for a time his mind was in a state of the most terrific confusion.

But perhaps the most remarkable-looking person now in the whole group was the countess. She had been rather liberal in the bestowal of paint upon her cheeks, in order that, at the assembly, she should present no symptoms of languor and weariness ; and now that this most sudden and alarming scene ensued, the perspiration from her forehead, when it suddenly broke out, rolled down her cheeks, carrying with it long streaks of the carmine which she had used so freely.

Her lips, too, were of a most complete and ashy paleness, so that in a few moments she really looked like some North American Indian in his war paint.

No one could, with unprejudiced eyes, look upon her for a moment without a feeling of certainty that she knew more of what was going on than she chose to reveal.

As for Margaret, it would almost seem that she had beforehand calculated upon every possible contingency, and that the coming of Mrs. Grove to the ball was one for which she had duly prepared herself, for, although pale, she was far more composed than the countess.

And thus for a short time they all stood in attitudes confronting each other, and with such strange expressions of countenance, that had they been all delineated in some picture, the spectator would have gazed in wonder to know what strange circumstance had so suddenly affected them.

Mrs. Grove spoke, and she pointed to Margaret as she did so, saying,—

" I accuse that woman ! I accuse that woman ! "

There was now a general movement forward among all the guests, as if the sound again of the voice of Mrs. Grove had broken the spell which had for a time held their faculties in bondage, and then Margaret replied, saying,—

" Of what do you accuse me ? "

" Murder ! "

" The murder of whom ? "

" Of—of——" Mrs. Grove glanced at the earl before she proceeded further, and he stepped forward, interrupting her in so strange a voice, that those who knew him best started and looked fixedly at him, to be sure that it really was from his lips the sounds came.

" No, no ! " he said ; " oh, no ! oh, no ! "

" I—I am dumb," said Mrs. Grove, and she shrank back.

" What is the meaning of all this ? " said the Marchioness of Fanfaronade ; and then, before any one else could say a word, some wonderful revulsion of feeling seemed to have come over the earl, for he spoke in a voice that rung again through the place, exclaiming,—

" Speak, and speak freely ! The temporary hesitation has passed away. Speak freely, I say ; and, in the sacred name of justice, I implore you to speak truly. Henceforward let there be no concealment. All shall be known, and all shall be understood. Speak, Mrs. Grove ; you have my full permission to tell all."

" My lord, are you mad ? " whispered a voice in his ear.

" No, I am not mad, Jonathan Willoughby," said the earl, suddenly turning upon the man who spoke to him, and tearing the mask from his face before he could escape, which he made an attempt to do.

" Jonathan who ? " said the Marchioness of Fanfaronade. " There is no Jonathan anybody on my list, I am sure. Who is this man that has intruded himself here uninvited ? "

" It matters, not madam," said Willoughby, with great effrontery, " since you see his lordship knows me, and, consequently, you may, by a little stretch of your ladyship's active imagination, suppose that I am his guest."

" Peace, peace ! " said the earl. " All this is idle talking. Mrs. Grove, I charge you to speak out."

" So commanded," said Mrs. Grove, " I of course obey. There has been a murder done. The child which was committed to my care by the Earl of Crumble.down has been poisoned."

"What," said Margaret, "could induce you to do the deed?"

"Those words," said Mrs. Grove, "are not worth refutation, and you know they are not when you utter them. I accuse you, for you came to my humble home under false and suspicious circumstances. I therefore, seeing you now here, and recognising you, have the strongest suspicions that you are concerned in the deed. Who was your instigator is best known to yourself."

"This is fine talking," said Margaret; "what is there in all the world so easy as to bring a charge of this sort against any one? and, if the accusation against me rests upon the fact of my having been at Hampstead—"

A shriek came from the countess's lips, and at the same instant Mrs. Grove clasped the wrists of Margaret, and, looking her sternly in the face, said, in tones of the most startling description,—

"Who mentioned Hampstead but yourself? Who named Hampstead? Guilty wretch, out of your own mouth came the materials of your accusation."

Margaret quailed at this, as well she might. It was a frightful slip of the tongue she had made, and from that moment a strange aspect of despair seemed to sit upon the face of the countess, but yet Margaret recovered her self-possession much sooner than most persons under the circumstances would have done, and she replied, with apparent calmness,—

"I cannot see that what I have said affords you any triumph over me. I know you by sight, and I know that you live at Hampstead. I know that what you call your humble home is there situated, and that you are in the employment of the Earl of Crumbledown, in capacity of nurse to a child; that, knowing all that, when you said you had seen me, I instantly denied having been at Hampstead."

The earl, at this juncture, stepped up to the countess, and laid his hand upon her arm.

"Come with me," he said, in a strange, preternatural sort of voice, "come with me, come with me!"

She shuddered, but she allowed him to lead her into one of the small rooms which had been laid out for refreshments, and then he tried to close the door, but something prevented him, and, upon looking to see what was the obstruction, he found that the Marchioness of Fanfaronade had followed them, and was endeavouring to effect an entrance.

"Madam," said the earl, sternly, "I have some few words to say in private to the Countess of Crumbledown."

"Well, but——"

"Madam, I will have no audience."

This was decisive, and the mortified marchioness was compelled to leave, and in another moment the small door was shut in her face. She lingered a minute or so, and muttered to herself, "I will be revenged upon him for this as well as many other slights; but revenge is a commodity that will keep very well indeed."

When the Earl of Crumbledown was alone with the countess he turned his gaze upon her, and there was such a strange lustre in his eyes that she shrunk back with an undefined fear that he might intend some personal violence. She knew her own guilt, and although, as yet, nothing in the shape of the most distant insinuations had been breathed against her, she knew how much she had to dread the truth.

And people may say what they will of dreading falsehood and detection, and of dreading what the wicked and the designing may say of them; but can any of these dreads come near the dread of the truth?

Most horrible is the position of that person whose reputation can only be bolstered up by falsehood, but who lives in continual and in horrible fear lest the sacred, immutable tongue of Truth should utter an accusation against him. Such was the position of the Countess of Crumbledown—wretched woman that she was. She knew herself to be guilty, and she needed no accuser to make her tremble as she looked upon the face of the earl.

"I have brought you here, madam," he said, with a horrible calmness, "I have brought you here, madam, because I have something to say to you which ought to be said to you only by me, and the answer to which ought to be heard only by me. Do you understand me?"

"I hear you," she said faintly.

"'Tis well—I do not expect you to say more than that. 'Tis well. I have, first of all, a revelation to make to you which, although I have reason to think you are already acquainted with it, ought now, and must now, come from my lips. The woman Grove, whom you know well, had two children to nurse ;—one our child, now in this house ; and the other a child which you supposed, or affected to suppose, was the child of Colonel Bruce, but which I now tell you is—no—no—I must say was mine."

"Go on—go on."

"You know that?"

"I suspected that ; but you ought to be the last person to blame the prudence that induced me to keep such a suspicion to myself. I did know it, if you prefer that term."

"I—I thought you did. Well, that is no matter now. You have heard, from what has passed to-night, that that child is now no more, and the question I have to put to you relates to the deed which has placed it in the arms of death. The woman who has been accused of the deed is your grand confidant—your spy---your sycophant—the creature who waits upon you to do your bidding ; and, therefore, I ask you, in the face of Heaven, and as you hope for peace here, or mercy hereafter, to tell me if you are, or are not, privy to the deed?"

Nothing but the state of extreme excitement into which the earl was thrown could at all have so stultified his judgment as to make him forget the character of the person he had to deal with, and fancy such an appeal as that would have the slightest effect in inducing anything like a clear and truthful answer from his countess.

He of all men, who had had such experience of her conduct, ought to have known her better.

In fact, it was an immense relief to her to find that that was all he had to say.

"My Lord Crumbledown," she replied, with the most frigid coldness, "the gross insult of being asked such a question would be quite sufficient of itself to justify me in refusing an answer to it ; but as that might lay me under a misconstruction, and as I am inclined to think you are really in too great a state of excitement to know that this question is of so insulting a nature, I answer it most clearly and distinctly in the negative."

"If you have spoken truth," said the earl, "Heaven will sooner or later justify you in that truth : if falsely, so surely as we are now here, the day of retribution will come."

"Indeed," said the countess with a sneer, "how long is it, my Lord Crumbledown, since you have turned so pious? I have not so often heard the name of Heaven from your lips, since I have had the honour of your acquaintance."

This was spoken with such an expression of hearty contempt, that the earl made no reply to it, but at once left the room, feeling that, at all events, at that time, he was really no match for his cool, calculating, impious lady.

While he was gone, but little had transpired in the ball-room worthy of note. The guests had separated themselves into small groups, and were conversing in suppressed tones about what had happened, whilst Mrs. Grove had sat down upon one of the gorgeous couches that were in the apartment, and leaning her head upon her hands, she was almost unconscious, in the agony of her reflections, of where she was.

She remained in that state some time until some one touched her, and, starting round, she saw that the old Marchioness of Fanfaronade had sat down by her side.

"Mrs.—a—a—what's your name?" said the marchioness.

"Grove."

"Oh yes, Grove. Pray oblige me by a call to-morrow morning. Do you know where I live?"

"No—no," said Mrs. Grove, "nor would the information be of any importance. I do not wish to know, nor can I think of calling upon any one at such a time as this. If you have anything to say, say it now."

"Do you know who I am?"

"Yes, you are the Countess of Crumbledown's mother, I believe, but that fact does not alter my determination in the least."

"Are you aware that this, from you to me, is great insolence?"

"Call it what you please, madam, I have not inclination nor spirits at present to contend it with you. I only pray of you to leave me alone, for I will satisfy the private curiosity of no one."

"Very well," said the marchioness. "It strikes me that you are in a very ticklish position, and that a friend might have been of some service to you; but if you think otherwise, so be it. You may have counted one who could and who would have secured you from an enemy."

The old marchioness waited for a moment or two to see what effect these words would have upon Mrs. Grove; but as she returned no answer, it may be fairly presumed that they had no effect at all; so the marchioness rose with a look of vexation upon her face, and left the couch upon which this brief and very unsatisfactory dialogue had taken place.

"Close is she," she muttered to herself: "I should like her to be hanged for this murder, that they say has been done, although I don't think her guilty of it, but have my own private thoughts upon that matter."

What these private thoughts were the reader may very well divine. Probably she thought that a little inquiry would alter the aspect of affairs completely, and enable her to judge of who was the real culprit; but since Mrs. Grove chose to put a stop to such inquiry, and to say it should not be conducted through her, the old marchioness was rather troubled to know what source to apply to.

But when she came to think of the appearance of her daughter, the countess, on the morning when she had come to her about the masked ball, she could not but feel some very powerful suspicions, the propriety of keeping which to herself she did not for a moment question.

Not that the Marchioness of Fanfaronade felt any degree of virtuous indignation at the possibility of such a horrible fact as that her daughter had instigated another to commit a murder, or had committed one herself; but she could not but condemn what she in her own mind called, "the horrible imprudence of murdering anybody."

And this was the only remark that her ladyship had to make concerning one of the most cold-blooded and deliberate murders that had ever been committed.

Upon the earl's return into the ball-room he walked direct up to Mrs. Grove; it was quite singular and amusing to see how every person there present affected to be quite at their ease and to be talking about something else. Indeed, some went so far as, when he passed them, to make aloud an indifferent remark about something, as if they had really quite forgotten or never noticed that anything amiss had taken place. This was what, no doubt, they considered good breeding, and we must say that it was highly preferable to the betrayal of an idle and vulgar curiosity, and a wish to pry into another person's affairs.

"Mrs. Grove," said the earl.

"Yes, yes, I am here," she said, starting at the sound of his voice, "I am here!"

"You can remain here until all the guests are gone, and then we will talk of what is to be done."

"Anything you please; I am wretched—most wretched. Dispose of me as you please; I am really mad. But I pray you to believe what I have said."

"As regards what?"

"As regards Margaret, as I hear she is called, your lady's attendant. She was at Hampstead, and came to the cottage, representing herself to be fatigued with long travel. She wanted me to go to the nearest public-house, so that she might be left alone with the child; but I would not do so, and have no doubt she lingered about the place intent upon the murder."

"Hush, hush! not so loud—it shall be seen to. You will find a small room yonder to which you can retire now, and so avoid the observations of my guests. Hold no converse with any one."

Mrs. Grove did as the earl desired her, with a heavy heart, for she feared that he was not acting with that energy and promptitude which the dreadful circumstances demanded.

In this, however, she was much mistaken, for the earl had made up his mind to a particular course, and he was resolved to pursue it; so, when he had thus bestowed Mrs. Grove in safety, he whispered to one of the servants, who was in the ball-room, and the man, with a bow and a "certainly, my lord," at once left the place.

"Crumbledown," whispered Colonel Bruce, "what on earth do you intend to do?"

"Hush—step this way. Do you think you could, without making it seem as if it came from me, whisper it about among the guests that under the circumstances they had better go?"

"Oh, certainly."

"Then pray oblige me by doing so?"

"Of course, you shall soon have a clear house; indeed many have, with an intuitive feeling that strangers were in the way, already ordered their carriages. Do you not hear?"

As Colonel Bruce spoke the earl could hear the rattle and dash of the carriages as they rolled up to his door and took up different parties of his guests, so that he could not doubt but that the whole of them, by the assistance of the colonel, would soon be upon the move, and that then he would have leisure to do as he pleased.

The colonel went among the guests and spread it about that no doubt it would be better to break up the party,— a feeling which was almost universally responded to; and the few who would have stayed found themselves in such a small minority that they were, in a manner of speaking, compelled to go.

Another half hour elapsed and the last carriage dashed off from Crumbledown House, and quiet and repose reigned in those brilliant saloons which but a short time before had been crowded with such a gay and glittering assemblage.

CHAPTER LXXIX.

THE INTERVIEW BETWEEN MRS. GROVE AND THE LITTLE LADY ALICE.

It was one of the greatest possible releases to Mrs. Grove to be able to leave the magnificent ball-rooms of the Earl of Crumbledown and to find herself in the comparative quiet and retirement of the small apartment which he indicated to her.

She sat down, and, after a deep sigh, she clasped her hands and commenced a mental review of the past and the present of the most painful description.

She could see nothing now at all cheering in the prospect before her, and it seemed as if all at once life had changed all its hues and prospects as regarded her fortune and that nothing now awaited her but trouble and discomfort.

And, as is the case always with people when an evil is done, she blamed herself and suggested to herself a hundred ways by which it might have been avoided, forgetting, at the time she did so, that it never had been in the smallest degree contemplated, and, therefore, that none of the simple means of averting the evil

which now presented themselves to her imagination were at all likely before t°
occur to her.

The dreadful crimes that had made that cottage home of hers a scene now of
such sadness and melancholy she told herself would be ever before her mind ; and,
as she sat alone in that little room, she more than once, with deep anxiety, wished
that she were dead, and so spared the multitude of evils which destiny seemed to
have in store for her.

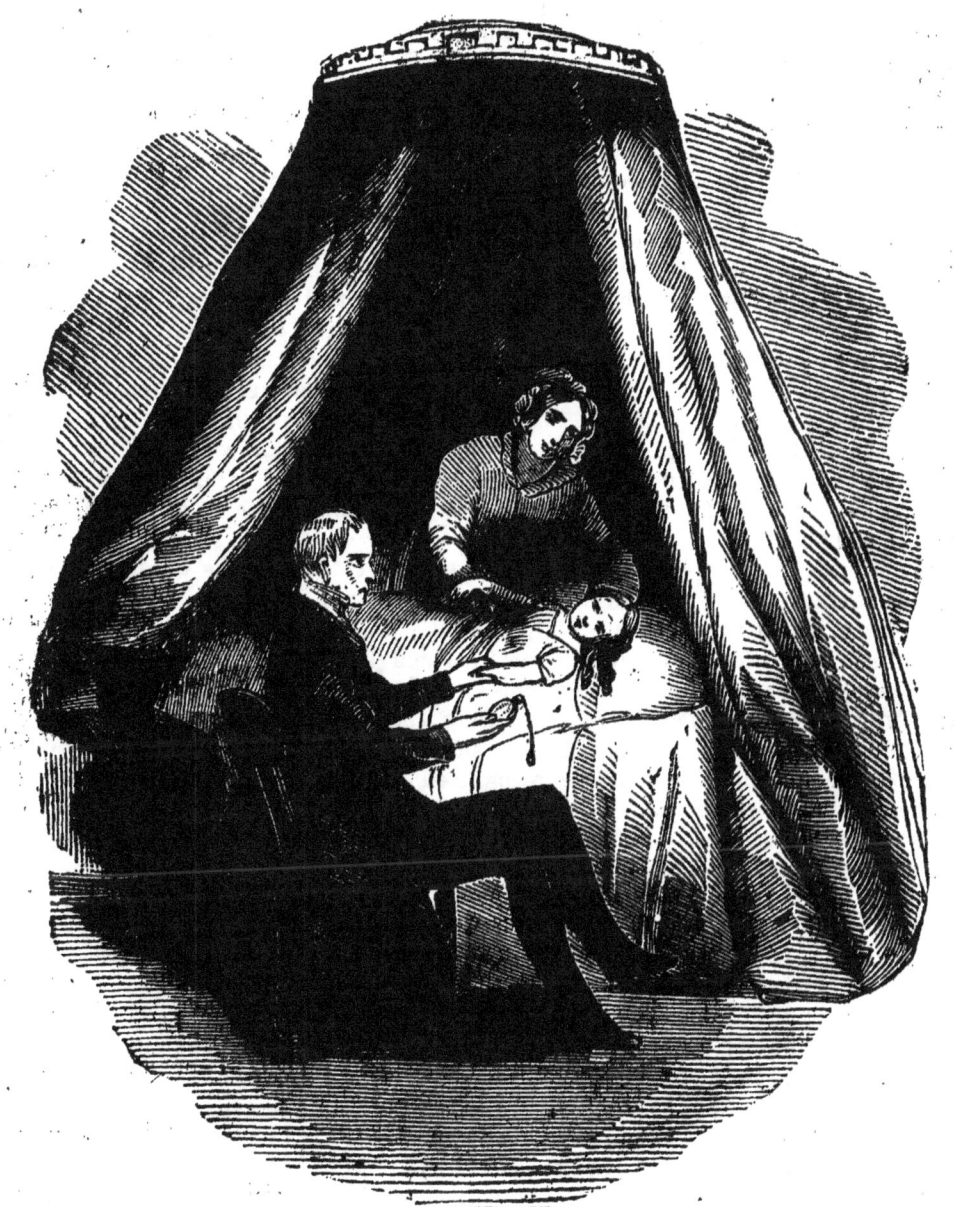

The few words, too, that Margaret had said in the ball-room awakened a new train
of thought and new ideas. "What if," she asked herself—"what if, after all, the
earl should be induced to suspect me ? Oh, what horror that would be ! I have
no evidence that the deed was done by another, save my own mere asseverations."

This was one of those thoughts which, when once it takes possession of the
mind, is likely to stay there for a time ; and each moment, in the imagination of poor
Mrs. Grove, it seemed to assume a more horrible aspect, and she became painfully

alive to the slightest sound which might have a tendency to encourage such an idea.

If she heard a more hasty footstep than common in the ball-room she began to fancy it heralded the approach of the officers of justice, coming on the unjust and mistaken errand of apprehending her. If she heard a door shut suddenly the sound jarred upon her nerves and caused her heart to palpitate painfully. And such sounds, as the guests were rapidly leaving the earl's splendid mansion, became each moment more frequent, until, at last, all her senses became absorbed in the sound of whispered voices, which suddenly struck upon her ears in close proximity to where she was.

Glancing in the direction from which these whispered tones proceeded, she heard plainly voices, and saw that there was another door to the apartment which she had entered, and which seemed to lead into the more domestic portions of the house, and it was from some apartment beyond that door that the low sounds came. And how strangely and how acutely one of those voices strikes upon her ears! It was the voice of a child, but it was one that she knew well; for it was the child which the countess had taken from her care. It was the little Lady Alice.

From the moment that she made this discovery the whole soul of Mrs. Grove seemed to be completely absorbed in listening, and the simple but sweet accents of that little one appeared to have in them a charm sufficient to chase away all the agonized thoughts that had found a home in the breast of her old nurse.

" 'Tis she—oh, yes, 'tis she! 'Tis the dear one whom I have not now seen for so long!" exclaimed Mrs. Grove. "She will surely know—she has not yet forgotten—one who never uttered to her an angry word. The voice comes like music on my ears—I cannot be mistaken: it is the child which was torn from me by that woman."

Mrs. Grove, as she spoke, rose, and, forgetting that what she was about might be considered as a very serious intrusion, she laid her hand upon the handle of the door and opened it.

She was right; for in an apartment to which that door led her was the Lady Alice along with her nursery governess, and both started at the sudden and most unexpected entrance of any one from that direction. It was only for one moment though that anything like the shrinking of alarm showed itself in the mind of Alice, for in the next she recognised Mrs. Grove, and with a cry of joy flung herself into her arms.

The nursery governess was both surprised and shocked at this sudden ebullition, for she had never found that it occurred, as regarded herself, in the least; but, alas! she had not the tact of finding her way to the hearts of the young, although there was nothing at all objectionable in her conduct.

"Oh, my dear nurse mamma!" cried the child, as she kissed Mrs. Grove repeatedly; "where have you been all this time, that you have never come to see me?"

Mrs. Grove's emotion would not allow her to speak for some moments—she could only caress the beautiful young creature who clung to her.

"Have you come to stay with me?" said Alice. "Oh, tell me that you have come to stay with me?"

"That, my dear child, I cannot; but I bless the fortunate chance that has brought me into this part of the house, and so enabled me to see you, whom I have been so much longing to see."

"May I take upon myself, mem," said the governess, "to ask who you are?"

"And so," said Mrs. Grove, scarcely hearing, and, if she did, not heeding the question which was put to her, "and so, dear, you are glad to see your poor old nurse again?"

"Glad!" said the little creature, "glad! I am very glad indeed, dear nurse; and you must stay with me,—you must, indeed. My papa says kind things to me sometimes, and I will ask him—I wonder if I could find him now?"

"Really, Miss Alice, you must not think of such a thing," said the governess; "it really must not be. You know you teazed me until I brought you into this room, where you could just hear the music from the ball-room, and I should be blamed if it was found out that I had kept you up so late I know: and as for this person, I really don't know who she is."

" " My name is Grove," said Mrs. Grove, whom this long speech had awakened to something like a perception of the necessity of at all events making some explanation. " I was the nurse of this dear child for a long time; indeed, until it was lately, and only lately, removed from my care by the countess."

" Oh, indeed !" said the nursery governess, in one of those unsatisfactory sorts of tones in which people speak who are not over well pleased, but who don't exactly wish to say as much, although they have no sort of hesitation in implying it.

" Yes," added Mrs. Grove ; " and no wonder that I loved her, for a gentler little lamb there could not be than she was ; I ought to know, when I have watched her from her earliest years."

" Very good ; oh dear, yes — ahem ! I suppose her ladyship the countess knows of your being here ?"

" I know not, and care not."

" Care not ! Care not for the countess ! Upon my word that is a most extraordinary speech for you to make. Not care for the countess ! I must say then that I think you are - ——"

What the nursery governess thought Mrs. Grove was, was cut short altogether by the sudden entrance of the earl himself, who had come into the spare room into which he had shown Mrs. Grove, and not finding her there, but seeing the door of the next apartment open, he naturally supposed she was to be found in it.

He started back with rather a look of surprise when he saw her caressing the child ; but what he came about was too urgent to be delayed, and he said to her at once, in a voice which pretty plainly evinced the great struggle it cost him to control his feelings—

" Mrs. Grove, follow me ; there is a work of justice to do."

She gave the child several hurried kisses, and then followed the earl from the apartment into the now nearly deserted ball-room—in fact, it was by then deserted by all the guests, although there were several persons in it. The countess, for instance, was there, and her wicked designing confidante too, the waiting-maid, Margaret, who had taken so dangerous and slippery a path to her ambition ; and likewise, standing a little apart, as if undecided what to do, there was a man roughly dressed, and of rather coarse aspect and appearance generally, and who, from the occasional glances he cast around him, seemed quite a stranger to the gorgeous place in which, for some reason, he now was, in all likelihood, for the first and last time.

Several of the servants, too, of the family, in the rich liveries of the Crumbledowns, stood near the door, and the whole of these persons were silent, as if they were awaiting some event which should break the spell that seemed to be cast over them.

The entrance of the earl with Mrs. Grove seemed nearly to have that effect, for there was not one present who did not shift his or her position ; but nothing was said by any one until the earl had spoken, and he said with a clear voice—

" There has been a murder committed in the house of this person, Mrs. Grove by name—the murder of a child ; and she has accused a person here present of the deed."

" It will be my duty, my lord," said the strange, rough-looking man, now suddenly stepping forward, " it will be my duty, my lord, of course, to take any one into custody against whom anything like suspicion is entertained."

" Then take that woman named Grove," said Margaret, " for she I suspect most strongly."

" Upon what grounds ?" said Mrs. Grove.

" You, and you only, lived with the child."

" I have done so for years; and, besides, had every possible motive for wishing its protracted existence. I appeal to the Earl of Crumbledown for my character and for my exculpation."

"I exculpate you," said the earl, "wholly and completely. I never, for one moment, entertained the remotest thought that you could be guilty, and I never shall. Speak, Mrs. Grove, and say freely what you have to say."

"Then," added Mrs. Grove, "I charge that woman with some knowledge of the deed, if not with its actual perpetration; and I do so, because I saw her in disguise at my house, which she entered under false pretences. God and her own conscience can tell if she be guilty, and Heaven forbid that, without abundant evidence, I should say she did the deed; but there are circumstances of grave and most serious suspicion against her, which I now urge freely—for why should I shrink from the truth?"

"'Tis false," said Magaret, "'tis false."

"Can you positively swear to what you have just said?" said the officer, "because if you cannot it will be of no use my interfering in the matter at all. Can you positively swear you saw the woman you now point out in the neighbourhood of your house? for if you can it will justify a remand on the part of a magistrate, but if you cannot I had better abstain from taking her?"

"As Heaven is my judge," said Mrs. Grove, "I can positively swear to the circumstance."

"Very good! then who charges her?"

"I do," said the earl, "and pledge myself to support the charge."

Margaret put on a look of contempt and glanced at the countess, who by this time had rubbed the paint off her face, and looked as pale as death itself. She tried to speak twice before she succeeded in doing so, and then she said,—

"This woman Grove is mistaken. God knows who has done the deed; but it is not this person in my employment, for she has been in close attendance upon me for the last three days, and except upon trifling messages has not been from my private apartments. The accusation against her therefore is a mistake, if nobody else, and I presume falls to the ground."

At this moment there emerged from one of the windows the old marchioness, who said,—

"I happen to be aware of that, and can confirm what the Countess of Crumbledown has just stated."

The officer looked rather staggered, as well he might, at these direct contradictions of what Mrs. Grove had said, and he evidently hesitated what to do next; but the earl cleared him of his difficulty by taking the responsibility wholly upon himself, and pointing to Margaret he said to him,—

"It is sufficient for you that I charge this person under suspicious circumstances with being guilty of, or at all events accessary to, a murder."

"Certainly, my lord, that is amply sufficient for me," said the officer. "You will please, ma'am, to consider yourself my prisoner."

He touched Margaret lightly upon her shoulder as he spoke, and the touch seemed to thrill through her whole frame with an electric effect, for she shrank back and trembled from top to toe; but this was but momentary, and she soon recovered her self-command as she said,—

"My Lord Crumbledown, you will have to repent of this. I know that I am hateful to you because I enjoy the confidence of your lady; and for that, and that reason alone, you will willingly inflict if you can some annoyance upon me."

The earl made no answer to these words, and considered it beneath him, as indeed to an enormous extent it was, to hold any conversation of such a nature with one in the position of Margaret; but he could not help being struck with the awful appearance of the countess, who suddenly stepped up to him and said,—

"My lord, if this conduct towards a servant of mine be not dictated by ill will to me, why is not my word taken for her innocence, since I have declared it?"

"There is the oath of another against your word," said the earl.

"But I too will swear."

"It is not for me then to judge who is perjured."

"Enough," said the countess. "If you are resolved upon this monstrous act of having my waiting-maid in London arrested because some crime has been committed in Hampstead, you can do so, but sooner or later the consequences shall fall upon your own head; I feel myself bound to afford her, as a servant of mine, my protection in every possible way, and I will do so."

These words were uttered aloud, for they were intended to reach the ears of Margaret, so that she might be assured that she would be protected, and that by keeping the dangerous secret which she had locked in her bosom she would lose nothing.

"Be it so, madam," said the earl: "I need not be particular in pushing a charge against that person, since I now know she enjoys so much of your protection, for you can easily take measures to prevent any injustice being done to her. Officer, I think you had better at once remove your prisoner from this house."

Upon this hint the officer motioned Margaret towards the door of the room, and then once again she glanced towards the countess, who could not but understand the appeal, and she said—

"You shall hear from me at the earliest possible hour in the morning."

With this Margaret seemed tolerably satisfied; and she even tried to cast a look of contempt upon the earl, but he did not see it; as well done as it was, it was thrown away altogether upon him.

CHAPTER LXXX.

THE CONFERENCE—THE ONLY FAVOUR—THE EARL'S VISIT TO HAMPSTEAD.

WHEN the waiting-maid had been thus taken off, the Countess of Crumbledown though t evidently that nothing could be lost, if nothing was gained, by making, for once in her life, a direct attack upon the sensibilities of her liege lord.

She accordingly walked up to the earl and said in a low tone of voice,—

"I wish for five minutes' conversation with your lordship."

"Certainly," he said; and he walked into the small room which he had so recently left; "certainly: I shall have great pleasure."

It was quite evident, from the peculiar and very strange manner in which the earl uttered these words, that he did not by any means attach to them their ordinary meaning, but that his thoughts were far away from the present scene. Heaven help him! perhaps he was thinking of what a dreadful sight remained for him to see at the cottage at Hampstead.

The countess, however, followed him into the little room, and she carefully closed the door after her. Then, as she stood facing the earl, but scarcely looking at him, she spoke in a tone such as he had never yet heard come from her lips—yes—yes, he had heard it once; and it was unlucky for the countess that at that moment he was put in mind of such a circumstance—he heard her speak in such a tone when she made the mock generous proposal to restore to him the whole of the fortune of the old Earl of Crumbledown in her mother's house—that proposal which had looked so noble, so generous, that it had taken the earl's imagination by storm.

But at the same time he recollected that she had told him afterwards how that was merely a piece of acting, and she had actually to him congratulated herself upon its success.

It was most unfortunate then, that, upon this occasion, the countess should have by her voice brought to the earl's mind such a most damning reminiscence for her, but she did do so.

"My lord," she said, "I think you will do me the justice to say that I never asked a favour of you in all my life."

"Well ?"

"I am about to do so now."

"Go on, madam."

"I ask you, knowing, as I do, the entire innocence of my waiting-maid of the crime which is laid to her charge, to consent to her immediate release."

"Indeed!"

"Yes—I ask you that, my lord, as the first and last favour that I shall ever require of you; and in asking it, pray understand me, I do not wish to impute to the woman Grove, who has played the part of her accuser, anything but a mistake, a common everyday mistake of identity, to which we are all liable, but which it is very dreadful to adhere to."

"I cannot understand," said the earl, "why the release of this woman should be asked of me as a favour, if you are in a position to prove that she is innocent by showing that, being here with you at the time mentioned, she could not have been on Hampstead Heath."

"Still, my lord, I ask the favour. It is a piece of bad taste for you and I to come into collision at a police-office."

"It may be so—but we must all bow to circumstances."

"Do you refuse me this small simple matter?"

"I am compelled to do so. I cannot blow hot and cold with the same breath. A charge has been made, and that charge ought, even in common justice to the accused person, to be thoroughly investigated. I cannot call that matter a simple one which involves the death of—my child—yes, my child: I do not see why I should hesitate to say the words."

"Then I am to understand that you will persevere in this most absurd charge against my waiting-maid?"

"God forbid that even in an affair like this, in which my feelings are so largely interested, I should commit an injustice to any one! Nothing can possibly be further from my thoughts; but at the same time I will say God forbid that justice should not be done! and I declare that, so far from consenting to smother this investigation, I will stir heaven and earth until I arrive at the truth of it!"

"You will?"

"As Heaven is my judge, I will."

"I am answered. It was but a small matter after all—a very small matter, and one which surely might have been granted to me: but it is no matter; I am, as you say, in a position to prove that Margaret was with me."

"And where were you?"

The earl had no idea beyond the mere words themselves in propounding this question, but it gave the guilty conscience of the countess such a shock, that she uttered a half-scream, and then had to cover her confusion by instantly adding,—

"In my chamber."

"When?"

"I shall not give you, who stand in the light of a prosecutor of one whom I know to be innocent, an opportunity beforehand of examining the witnesses for the defence; at the proper time, and in the proper place, sir, I will prove that innocence—to your confusion—as it must be; but I will answer no questions that you can put to me."

"Beware!" said the earl; "beware of what you do. There have been instances of the ready tool performing the work it knew its master or its mistress wished done, before the order came to do it."

"What mean you?"

"I mean that your waiting-maid may be guilty in act, while you were only guilty in thought. Did you wish my child dead, and did she fly to execute the deed?"

"This is madness; and a conversation which it is alike beneath you to urge and me to maintain. It is enough that I have asked of you what you will not grant, and henceforward let us be strangers again."

"Yes, strangers as we have ever been—strangers ever in thought and in feeling as we have ever been, and as we ever shall be. My lady, I never yet cursed an hour of my existence but that one which introduced me to you, and that I have cursed and do curse, with all my heart and soul. You have been the bane and the blight of my existence. You and your evil passions have kept me on the constant stretch of impatience; but now I cast away all disguise, and I tell you, unhesitatingly and firmly, that from this day, even the seeming bond—which in the eyes of the world has held us together—shall be cut asunder. We part actually as well as virtually."

" I am profoundly willing."

" 'Tis well. There need be then nothing pass between us but what can be settled by our respective solicitors."

The earl walked at once from the room in which this brief but certainly rather animated conversation had gone on, and going into the ball-room again, he said to the first servant he saw,—

" Order my carriage."

" Yes, my lord."

Then, turning to Mrs. Grove, he added in a tone of deep pathos—

" Wait for me—wait for me; I will go with you to the cottage, for I must look once again upon that face I loved in life, even although now the stillness of death is upon it."

" No, no," said Mrs. Grove ; " perhaps it would be better not, and, yet it is almost a duty that you should do so.

" It is quite a duty, it is quite a duty, and it shall be done. But, while you are in this house, be careful, and engage yourself in conversation with no one. Answer no question, let it sound as trivial as it may."

" I will be careful. I know the necessity there is for care. I shall not utter one word to any one here save yourself."

" That is right. In a short time the carriage will be ready to convey us to Hampstead ; until then be still."

The countess came to the door of the small room in which the rather agitating conversation between her and the earl had taken place, and beckoned to her mother, who obeyed the summons, and that mother and daugher, who were so particularly worthy of each other, retired together.

In a few minutes the carriage was announced, and the earl with Mrs. Grove were soon rapidly whirling along towards Hampstead Heath, on the melancholy errand of looking upon the face of the dead.

* * * * * * *

These occurrences, rapidly as they had transpired, had consumed an amount of time which threw the night on one side, and brought once again the bright and beautiful morning to gladden the earth.

As the carriage passed through Camden Town, and rolled along that suburban thoroughfare, which is one of the most popular, as well as, certainly, one of the most beautiful out of London, the slant first rays of the morning sun began to catch the tops of the tallest trees, and to shine upon some of the house windows that happened to look towards the east with a faint but yet a beautiful lustre.

Thousands of birds shook off the drowsy influence of night, and, springing upwards in the faint misty air, until they could catch a glimpse of the glorious coming luminary, they burst into song, making the air vocal with the melody of their small voices.

And the soft tinge that crept across the surface of the earth was full of refreshing coolness and sweet odours, for it bore upon its wings the soft breath of millions of sweet flowers.

Had the Earl of Crumbledown not had his mind so full of the unhappy scene he was about to visit, he must have seen and welcomed the world of beauty in which he was. But, alas ! his heart and soul were blighted, and, as he had truly enough said to the countess before his departure, she had been the bane of his existence, for little peace indeed had he known since that time when he had, in a moment of enthusiasm, said that she should be his.

Oh! if he had had then but half the appreciation of her character he had now, how gladly would he have abandoned all the wealth which the mean spirit of the old earl had so strangely left, and endeavoured to seek happiness—the happiness of contentment, at least surely in some diplomatic employment, which would not have been refused by any minister to one holding his high rank in the peerage of his country.

At least, this was what he told himself, now that he was satiated with all the enjoyments that such wealth could afford him; but the reader will remember that his feelings were widely different when he was simply Lord Warlock, and sighing for some portion of that wealth which the old earl took such especial care to keep from him.

To the well-conditioned and fresh horses of the earl, the trot to Hampstead was nothing, and in a very short space of time indeed they reached the Heath.

The earl was not desirous that his servants should know the exact house to which he was going, so he got out of the vehicle at some distance short of Mrs. Grove's cottage, and with her walked towards it.

His state of nervousness and agitation was painfully apparent to Mrs. Grove, and yet, what could she say to comfort him? She could not tell him, that where he was going there was not the sight he had come to see; and if she could not tell him that, how could she in any way soften the anguish he was likely to endure?

Alas! in no possible manner could she hope to be able to make him feel less that dreadful truth, which was so amply sufficient to awaken every source of harrowing reflection.

They therefore walked onward in silence, for the earl could not speak. Mrs. Grove had left the cottage in charge of a woman and neighbour, and she now from the window, seeing the child's nurse approaching, accompanied by a gentleman, hastened to open the door for their reception, and in another moment or two the earl stood beneath the same roof as his dead child lay under, in the calm deep sleep of that death, which, after all, although it is the most deplored calamity of which human nature is capable, is yet that which ought to awaken the least possible amount of regret.

Are not the dead to be envied as having paid that debt of nature which all must pay, and as having, by so doing, escaped at once and for ever from "the thousand natural shocks that flesh is heir to?"

Why should we mourn for the dead, whose life is so full of evil? Is there really a little envy at the bottom of the feeling which makes human being assume such expressions of profound grief, when one of their number has passed away?

The cottage wore a strange and melancholy aspect. It was singular, indeed, what an immense change had been effected by the death of that little inmate of that humble abode. Everything wore an aspect of neglect and untrimness; all the different articles, which were strewn about the place, looked as if they were tossed promiscuously into the positions they occupied, and owed nothing to the attention of their owner.

And beside this, there was such a stillness there present—that strange, preternatural stillness which, by some means or another, always infests a place in which the dead are lying. Perhaps this is as much owing to the whispering manner in which people accustom themselves to speak, and the quiet footsteps with which they move about, as anything else.

The woman who was in the cottage verified this idea most remarkably, for her manner was all that of one who feared, by an incautious word, or by a footstep louder than common, to awaken some one who slept profoundly, and upon whose continued repose hung some very important events.

Insensibly, too, the earl himself was impressed with this seeming necessity for silence, for he trod as softly as he could over the floor, and followed Mrs. Grove into the chamber of death.

She did not speak to him, but she knew that he would follow her, and that he fully understood where she was leading him. The room was a small one, and even the little window which looked into the garden was darkened. It is strange that people should, so sedulously as they do, shut out the daylight from a corpse, as if there was anything in it inimical to the repose of the dead. But it is a fashion, and so it had been done in this instance.

And now we cannot give to Mrs. Grove too much praise for an act of instinctive delicacy, and that was the leaving the earl alone in the room with his dead child. She felt that the father's grief was of too sacred a nature to be trifled with, or even witnessed by any one else, and she at once, after drawing on one side the blind from the window, left him alone.

With tottering footsteps this proud noble made his way to the side of that little bed, where lay one of the principal ties which bound him to the world. A sheet was covered over the whole body, but it had shrunk to the still proportions of the face, and there it lay, exhibiting, but too plainly, the presence of the destroyer.

With faltering hands the earl turned that covering that was over the face of the dead; he turned down the sheet, and then he saw the pale face of his beautiful child in that sad stillness of repose which is eternal.

He clasped his hands, and a gasping sob came from his lips—such a sob as none who did not feel the very height of heart anguish could have given utterance to. Then, for about five minutes, he gazed upon the face of the dead ; after which he stooped and kissed the cold lips ; then he turned aside, and, walking with the strange, uneven pace of a drunken man, left the room.

Mrs. Grove was standing in the outer apartment waiting his coming. She had dismissed the woman who had, during her absence, had the care of the cottage ; and then, when she saw that the earl had emerged, she placed for him a chair in silence.

" I—I have taken," he said, " my last look in this world upon that being who was dearer to me than, until now, I thought ; my last, last look! Oh, Emily, Emily, you are avenged now."

Mrs. Grove said nothing. What could she say to such an appeal ? She had no consolation to offer, and she felt that the common ordinary words in which people express consolation would be, under the present circumstances, a mockery. At length, after a silence of some minutes' duration, the earl spoke again, saying,—

" Tell me, now that I am here, fully and particularly, all that passed. Begin with what, now that you know the sad result, seems to you to have any connection with it, however remote, and tell me every minute circumstance that happened from then until the time when I saw you in my house last night."

Thus questioned, Mrs. Grove did commit to him everything that had happened, commencing with the visit of the pretended soldier's wife, and the request which the woman, whom she recognised to be Margaret, made,—that she, Mrs. Grove, should leave the cottage, in order to procure her something from a public-house ; she then detailed the death of the child, as already known to the reader.

The earl listened with the most profound attention, and when she had concluded he said—

" Now tell me, have you any doubt whatever of the identity of Margaret, with the person who came here ? "

" I have not the smallest doubt in the world upon that point; and when she spoke, I knew the voice again in a moment : she could not conceal that so completely but that there were some tones of it that struck quite clearly upon my ear."

" Then that is beyond all doubt ? "

" It is in my mind ; and besides, if it were another person who called here, that other person can easily be induced to come forward and declare such to be the case, in which event I should see my mistake at once, if I had made one, which I do not for one moment believe or think that there is any chance of."

" True, true; she professed, I think you told me, to be going to the Tower in search of her husband, and an inquiry there would soon test the truth of that statement, and so add a strong confirmation to your opinion."

" It would, my lord. But can you believe it possible that that wicked woman has not been most powerfully instigated to the crime? Can you think that she herself would be sufficiently interested in the circumstances so interesting to others, to do a deed which is of so terrible a description, and which really in its consequences involves so much personal danger? "

" I scarcely dare," said the earl, with a shudder, " turn my thoughts in that direction."

" I understand your lordship; the thought is a terrific one, but still it is one which cannot but occur to you, and it is one, too, that will occur to all who in any way interfere in the affair. Such a deed is not done without strong, overwhelming, personal motives, and when it is so, that motive is either one of passion or of interest."

" Yes—yes."

" What motive, then, of passion could the countess's waiting-maid have to take the life of your child ? "

" None—none."

" Then she must have derived her impulse from interest ; she must have been well paid to do the deed, and the frightful question then arises of, by whom was she so well paid?"

"A horrible question! A most horrible question!"

"It is, my lord; and yet it is one which in the course of the full and immediate inquiry which must be made into the affair, will have to be met. It is a question, that however it may be for a short time repelled, will force itself to be heard, and will most certainly force itself to be answered. It is well to consider such questions beforehand."

"It is so. You awaken in my mind the most dreadful thoughts, and yet——"

"Hush, my lord; do you see yon persons coming?"

The earl glanced from the window of the cottage and he saw several people advancing.

"Who are they?" he said.

"The jury. There will be an inquest held upon the body, at which I shall have to repeat all the evidence I have recounted to you, and at which I may be compelled to declare the child's parentage."

"Yes—yes," said the earl; "oh, into what a tangled web of perplexities these proceedings have plunged me! I dare not think of the issue."

CHAPTER LXXXI.

THE PROCEEDINGS, ON THE PART OF THE COUNTESS AND HER MOTHER, FOR THE DEFENCE OF MARGARET.

FROM the first moment that the Countess of Crumbledown found that the earl was firm in his notion of having a searching legal investigation into the alleged guilt of Margaret, she felt her danger.

She came instantly to the conclusion that in Margaret's safety lay her safety; and, indeed, that look which Margaret had given her when she was taken by the officer, was quite sufficient to convince the countess that if Margaret stood upon the brink of a precipice, down which she should find she was likely to be thrown, she would most assuredly drag her, the Countess of Crumbledown, after her.

Of course none of the parties had at all expected that the nurse of the Love Child would intrude herself into that gay and glittering assembly, of which Margaret's insolent pride had induced her to make one; and, least of all, did the countess think that, under such difficult circumstances, Margaret would be identified by Mrs. Grove, who was a much keener observer than she, the countess, or Margaret, gave her credit for being.

Had Margaret, however, been content to remain in the position which she had before occupied, she would most certainly, by not coming in Mrs. Grove's way, have avoided the recognition which had so unexpectedly and so uncomfortably consigned her to a prison.

But in all these affairs now, the countess at once felt that she required a confidante; and towards whom could she look with greater certainty to act such a part than towards her mother, the marchioness?

She was the more induced, too, to take the old marchioness into her confidence in the affair, because she strongly suspected that she already had a strong suspicion of the fact, and therefore was it that when she beckoned to her, she fully meant to disclose to her the rather awkward position into which her violent passions had thrown her.

Perhaps the marchioness guessed as much, for when they were in a private room together, the old lady said,—

"Well, I suppose this is really some very unpleasant piece of business?"

"It is," said the countess. "I do not mind whispering the truth to you; but my personal safety is concerned."

"How could you be so imprudent?"

"You do not know the provocation."

"Well, but no amount of provocation should have induced you to make a confidante of your waiting-maid. If it seems really necessary that anything unpleasant should be, never trust anybody that is about you. It's really the very worst thing in the world to do, I can assure you, quite practically. Now, you see, you are quite in the hands of that woman."

"I am: but listen to me, and you shall know all. Since I have told you something of what has taken place, and since you know something of an effect, you ought to know the causes which   to it."

"Well, of course I'll listen; but you must tell me something very particular indeed to justify a step of so much danger as—as——"

"Call it by its proper name—I do not shrink from it: it is a murder!"

"It's very unpleasant to say; but I suppose it is a murder. Come, let me know all about it. Really I can feel for you when low, common people become troublesome to any one in the higher circles of society. I suppose you were quite troubled?"

"You shall hear."

The countess then related to her mother how, step by step, she had discovered what she still considered the fact of the earl's marriage to Emily Whitford, and how she had actually got up such a chain of evidence upon that subject, with the assistance of Willoughby, that there was not a link wanting in it at all; and that then she had set to work to counteract the possible evil consequences of such a state of things.

"You will readily perceive," she said, "then, how it became necessary and desirable, first of all, to destroy all evidence of the marriage, so that the wife could not come forward, as she showed an inclination to do, and substantiate her claims; and secondly, to deprive the earl of all motive for doing so himself, by depriving him of the offspring of that first marriage."

"Go on—go on."

"With this intent, then, I procured the leaf from the registry of the marriage of the earl with Emily Whitford,"

"And that, then, I presume, you have?"

"No. Do you think I was likely to keep such a document as that?"

"Well, it certainly was not a desirable thing to lay about, I will fully grant; but are you sure of its being original?"

"Quite—quite."

"Well, well, there is something in that. Pray go on. Do not hide anything from me now you have once began to be confidential, for a half confidence is one of the most dangerous things in all the world."

"I will conceal now nothing from you, for I devoutly believe in the sentiments you have just uttered. In plain language, then, Margaret and I were both at Hampstead, and did compass the death of the child, the earl's bastard."

The old Marchioness of Fanfaronade could not be said to be taken by surprise by what the countess had said, for she really fully expected to hear such a revelation, for, as some people say, putting this and that together, she had made up her mind already that the deed had been done by somebody, and she could very well conceive that somebody to have been instigated by the countess.

Probably the only piece of information that her daughter's words now absolutely conveyed to her was, that she had herself been to Hampstead and had a personal hand in the affair.

"Really," she said, after a short pause, "you have been very ill-advised in this matter."

"I cannot be said to have been advised at all," said the countess: "I did what I did, because I considered that it was quite, in a manner of speaking, inevitable to do so. I could not get Margaret to do the deed."

"And yet she is the party recognised."

"There are thousands of persons," said the countess, with bitterness, "who would hold a light while a murder was doing, but whose rank cowardice would prevent them doing it themselves."

"Remarkably true; you have some very just ideas of society at large, and wi h such I am only amazed that you should have placed yourself in your present awkward circumstances. You ought to have known that Mrs. Grove was one of those very troublesome people it is really not safe to interfere with. It's horrid at any time to have anything to do with the lower classes, but there are some who are particularly noxious and dangerous, and I look upon that woman as one of them."

"But what could I do?"

"Well, of course it's very easy, I know, for people to give advice, who have not been placed in the peculiar circumstances of others, and who consequently cannot exactly see all the difficulties in the way of following it; but, as far as my impression of the business goes, as I hear that poison was used, my only subject of great regret is, that you did not manage to give some to the woman Grove, as well as the child."

The countess shuddered.

"There has been enough murder," she said; "there has been, God knows, quite enough murder."

"Don't mistake me. I do not wish you now to engage in any enterprise of the sort, for I assure you I should look upon such, as extremely hazardous indeed. But I only express my regret, that, while you were about it, something of the sort was not achieved at once."

"Yes, yes, I own all that. It would have been as well, perhaps better, perhaps much better, to have been so; but it is now too late—it is now much too late, I tell you; and the only thing you can effectually advise me is what to do with Margaret, and how to manage matters for her defence. She must be defended from the charge brought against her."

"She must."

Yes, you feel with me the importance of that, I hope; you feel with me that upon a successful defence of her must all my own hopes of preservation depend. She is to be depended upon as long as she is safe, but she is not for one moment to be depended upon, if her interest pulls her in another direction."

"Ah, to be sure not; that, you see, is the inevitable consequence of trusting low people with any dangerous secret. The fact is, that you are completely in the power of this person now, and she will let you see that you are. You will find that whenever such a person gets a knowledge that she has any power over her superiors, it will be so delightful to exercise it, that she must do so."

"I can cloak that."

"No, no; you may fancy you can, but you will too soon find out your mistake. You will too soon discover that to such a person as this waiting-maid of yours the consequences of a full disclosure of all that has occurred are immeasurably less than the consequences to you of such a disclosure."

"Well, well, what would you have me do?"

"Nothing, in particular, but what you yourself have stated that you see the necessity of; but there is no harm in reasoning upon such a matter, and pointing out its noxious bearings. Therefore I say, that to the extent that a disclosure of this affair is of more importance to you than it is to her, will she always triumph over you."

"But is it not, even in its most limited point of view, too important to be spoken of by her at all? Does it not, in its result, involve her very life?"

"No; because the press—the people—she herself—the council—the judges—all would be led to believe that you were the tempter of her, and that she was induced by you to commit a deed, which I dare say she advised."

"She did—she did."

"But who will believe that—who, but myself? I believe it, because I know the woman, and think it highly probable; but at all events, that is not the immediate question. We are quite agreed that she must be protected and defended from the accusations now brought against her—she must be rescued; and now, let me ask you if you really think this man Willoughby, who has made himself already useful, is a man of sufficient ability to be employed?"

"I think he is, and I think he may be trusted likewise."

"We won't trouble him so, for I can see no necessity on earth for trusting him; let him guess what he likes, but tell him nothing."

"Then how can we proceed?"

"Thus: tell him that your waiting-maid is apprehended on suspicion of a murder on Hampstead Heath—tell him that the only evidence against her is that of Mrs. Grove, who says she saw her there on that occasion, but that you can swear she was here with you hours before and hours after the time Mrs. Grove will mention, and that I will corroborate the statement."

"But the servants—will they not know that I was from home—will they not know that you did not call, and that Margaret was from home?"

"Oh that is all of no consequence—the servants will not be there, and Margaret must be discharged; besides, servants have the worst memories in the world, and after a day or two has elapsed they will get into such a confusion as to dates that they will not be able to depose to anything distinctly if they were all put upon their oaths to do so."

"There is something in that. You would advise me, then, to employ Willoughby?"

"Yes; he is an attorney, you tell me."

"He is."

"Then he is of course just the sort of person to employ—an unscrupulous attorney; and besides, you have the advantage of not mixing up any other person in your affairs. No doubt he already knows enough to be dangerous if he likes, and if he is overlooked now upon this professional occasion he would have some right to think himself slighted."

"Be it so then; I will send for him at once. There is nothing at all unnatural or out of the way in my wishing to defend my servant from a charge of this nature."

"On the contrary, you will do yourself much credit by it, and universal suspicion will point to Mrs. Grove herself as the author of the deed of blood."

"Hush! hush! do not speak of it in such terms; for a murder, it was done as quietly as could be."

"Pray excuse me; at the moment, I really did forget that you had anything personally to do with it, or I should not have so characterised it, I assure you. But send for Willoughby at once."

The countess wrote a short note, requesting Willoughby's immediate attendance at Crumbledown House on business of importance, and at once despatched it by an attendant to his chambers.

"I will wait here until he comes," said the marchioness, "and then I shall be able to judge better of him, for although I certainly have seen the man I have not had much opportunity of coming to an accurate opinion concerning him or his abilities."

To say that the countess was grateful for the support which the old marchioness gave her in this matter, would have been a profanation of the word gratitude most completely; but she certainly was glad of her mother's company, for she began to have that dread of iniquity—the horror of being alone.

She found, too, that the marchioness was capable of taking a cooler and a more collected view of the matter than she was, in consequence of not being so deeply interested, and, therefore, she was glad on that account to have her there in the ensuing interview with Willoughby.

The period between sending for Willoughby and his appearance, although the latter event took place much quicker than could or ought to have been expected, was a most anxious one; for there was nothing to talk about but the probable and the possible consequence of what had taken place, and that was a theme which, while it had a great interest, was certainly full of terror. The marchioness got the countess to relate to her the exact particulars of the murder of the child; and when she had concluded that dreadful narration, the former remarked, with all the nonchalance in the world—

"Well, I must say, that if it had to be done at all—the wisdom of which I am not quite clear about—it was done as well and as cleverly as it could be."

"I presume, too, with as few chances of detection."

"Yes, yes, as it turned out. It's still a great pity that you had not an opportunity of placing some of the poison in something that Mrs. Grove was going to take. Do you know, I have really a great antipathy to that woman? she is one of your sharp, low creatures, that think themselves clever, mistaking insolence for ability. Oh, if she could but have been but put out of the way, it would certainly have been a matter for great congratulation."

"Mr. Willoughby is in the drawing-room, my lady," announced a servant.

"Tell him I will be with him immediately."

"Yes, my lady."

The countess and her unprincipled mother both rose, and proceeded to meet Jonathan Willoughby, who was rather alarmed at the peremptory message he had received from the countess, and had really hesitated about complying with it for a moment or two; but he was a man of quick resolves, and when he did make up his mind to obey the summons, he made no further delay in doing so.

He bowed, with what he, no doubt, considered quite a courtly air, when the ladies made their appearance; but it was a bow which had much vulgarity about it for all that. Bowing is not very easy.

"I hope, my lady," he said, "I have the honour of seeing your ladyship quite well—I believe I have the honour of recognising the Marchioness of Fanfaronade?"

"Yes," said the countess, "this is my mother, who will explain to you the professional business which has induced me to send for you on this occasion."

Willoughby muttered something about how happy he was to be of service in any way, and then the marchioness clearly and distinctly told him what it was he was wanted to do, namely, to undertake the defence of Margaret, by employing counsel or otherwise, as he thought proper, against the charge of Mrs. Grove, and to call upon them as witnesses to prove the *alibi*, which must have the effect of clearing her from the charge.

Willoughby promised to attend to the matter; and although he had his own thoughts about it, and would have been glad to ask a question or two of the countess, the presence of the Marchioness of Fanfaronade restrained him, and he merely contented himself with making the visit a strictly professional one, because he could not tell how far the marchioness had been taken into the countess's confidence—if, indeed, she had been taken into it all; so it might, for all he knew, have been dangerous to speak at all on other matters.

CHAPTER LXXXII.

THE INQUEST ON THE CHILD, AND THE VERDICT.—MRS. GROVE'S LONELY NIGHT IN THE COTTAGE.

THE Earl of Crumbledown of course, both from feeling and from policy, had no inclination to come at all in contact with the persons who had been summoned to attend the inquest, which was about to be held on the remains of his child, and he got out of the way as quickly as he could. To be sure, some questions were put by one or two of the more curious of the jury to ascertain what he was, because there was certainly a sort of air and manner about the earl which convinced them that he was no common or ordinary personage, and that, in looking upon him, they were regarding somebody who, as one of the jury remarked to another, was a somebody. But they soon found that Mrs. Grove was not the sort of person to gratify their curiosity, so they were compelled to give up their questions.

The coroner evidently viewed the case as one involved in great suspicion, but, before the inquest commenced, Mrs. Grove placed in his hands a sealed letter, with a request he would read it at once.

This letter was from the Earl of Crumbledown, and had been written by him for the protection of Mrs. Grove, in case any one who did not know her so well as he did, should fancy that there were sufficient grounds of suspicion against her in the transaction, to return a verdict at all reflecting upon her. The letter was precisely as follows :—

"Sir,—Feeling, of course, deeply interested in the inquiry which you will feel it your duty to institute into the death of the young child at the cottage inhabited by Mrs. Grove, I think it my duty to inform you that it is my child, and was at nurse with Mrs. Grove from the period of its birth, in consequence of the death of its mother within a very short space of time after that event.

"My principal object, however, in writing to you this note, is to assure you that I am entirely free from the remotest suspicion regarding Mrs. Grove herself, who, I know, was not only tenderly attached to the child, but whose best interests are all compromised by its death, and would have been not so by its continued existence.

"Upon the testimony of Mrs. Grove, of which I have not the smallest possible doubt, I have already given a person named Margaret Manners into custody for the offence : God knows whether she be guilty or not, but circumstances, to my mind, are strongly against her.

"The child's name, of course, must be that of its unhappy mother, and as further concealment is now as useless as impossible, the child may be called Emily Whitford. Trusting that you will consider this letter as a strictly confidential one, and by no means to be allowed to be seen by any one but yourself,

"I am, sir, yours very obediently,

"Crumbledown House.   "CRUMBLEDOWN."

The coroner read this letter very attentively, and the jury and two reporters who were present sat upon the tenter-hooks of impatience to know what its contents could possibly be ; they fully hoped and expected that when he had finished the perusal of it he would show it about ; but when they saw him fold it up very carefully and put it into his pocket, their feelings amounted to perfect agony, and they could not conceal their vexation.

"Aint that ere letter nohow," said one of the intelligent jury, "got nothing to do with this here murder?"

"No," said the coroner.

"Oh ; perhaps you wouldn't object to let us see it?"

"I do not see, sir, what you can have to do with a private letter to me. Suppose, now, it was to invite me to dinner somewhere, what could that be to you, sir ?"

"Oh, I only asked ; I thought it might have something to do with the murder, and, if so, of course we should all of us like very much to hear all about it, you know, sir."

"Sir, I have said that it is a private letter, and I have nothing whatever to add to that statement, sir,"

"Oh! very good."

"And now, gentlemen, we will proceed to the inquiry, if you please ; and I do most sincerely hope that the result of it will be to bring to justice the really guilty perpetrator of this most diabolical offence."

We need not trouble the reader by going through the whole of the evidence which was produced at the inquest : suffice it to say, that Mrs. Grove gave her evidence after the body had been looked at by the jury.

She deposed to the indisposition of the child, and to her calling in medical aid, and to its ultimate death. And she did so with so much feeling, that long before the end of her evidence, the coroner was fully of the earl's opinion, that she was completely innocent of having any hand in the affair.

When she had concluded this direct portion of her evidence, the coroner said,—

"You are the nurse of this child; have you any objection to say whose child it is?"

"None, sir; for I have been empowered to say so by him who, if he had desired me not, I should have felt it my duty to obey."

"Oh, stuff!" said one of the jury, "you must tell us you know. You are on your oath."

"I have yet to learn," said Mrs. Grove, calmly, "that to refuse to answer a question is perjury."

"Answer me, if you please," said the coroner, with a rebuking look at the juryman, who seemed to think that he possessed the inquisitorial power of making any one say what he pleased.

"The father of the child," said Mrs. Grove, "is the Earl of Crumbledown."

This announcement caused what the newspapers call a sensation among the jury, and they began to view the matter with much greater interest now that they found how distinguished—on one side at all events—was the parentage of the child, whose melancholy death they had met to inquire into.

"And its mother?" said the coroner.

"Its mother's name was Whitford. The child was called Emily from its birth."

"Then, gentlemen," said the coroner, "the object of our present inquiry may be named Emily Whitford; and now, Mrs. Grove, have you anything to add to your testimony, which is calculated to remove any of the mystery in which this affair is enveloped?"

"I have," she said.

The coroner and jury now listened with the profoundest attention while Mrs. Grove related how she had been called upon by a person representing herself as the wife of a soldier, and who was so wearied that she begged to be allowed to rest herself; how this person had made an endeavour to induce her to leave the cottage for a few moments; and how, upon her refusal so to do, she had got suddenly better and walked away.

Then she concluded by stating how she had recognised and meant to swear to this person as the same whom she had seen at the Earl of Crumbledown's house, when she went to tell him of the murder.

"You are certain, are you?" said the coroner.

"As certain as human judgment can possibly be on any point of identity. I am willing to swear to the fact as a fact, for I have no doubt whatever upon my own mind."

"But what possible motive could she have for the murder?" said one of the jury.

Mrs. Grove was silent, and the coroner said,—

"I think the witness exercises a sound discretion in not entering into the subject of motives at all on this occasion, except so far as she is herself concerned. It is not for her to find out, or even to hazard any guesses, as to the motives of other people in so serious a matter as the present.

The evidence of the medical witness, who was now examined, was quite conclusive as regarded the fact, that the child had died from the effects of arsenic.

"I never saw a clearer or more decided case," he said, "of poisoning by arsenic. The child took enough to have killed half a dozen grown persons. There can be no doubt about it whatever; and I think that there is no necessity whatever for opening the body, but of course I will do so, if the jury wish."

The jury declared themselves satisfied with this direct testimony, and negatived, to the great relief of Mrs. Grove, the proposition to open the body; for although she was almost as free, as any non-medical person could be, from any absurd prejudices about dissection, she did shrink from the notion of the knife of the surgeon touching that delicate and beautiful form she had so often fondled in her arms.

"Gentlemen," said the coroner, "it appears to me in this case, the evidence is all against one individual, and as against that individual, Margaret Manvers by name, it is but slight; inasmuch as it wholly depends upon what testimony can be brought forward in corroboration of the conclusion that she is the murderess.

"In the first place, it does not follow that she is the criminal, because she was upon Hampstead-heath on the day on which the deed was committed, notwithstanding there may be the most ample evidence of such a fact, as well as that she came to this cottage and gave a wrong account of herself.

"And after all, whether she was here or not altogether is a subject of identity, and you are all aware how the best of us are liable to be mistaken in such a matter as that, so that although the conduct of this woman, Margaret Manvers, the waiting-maid to the Countess of Crumbledown, is not without suspicion, it does not absolutely follow that she is guilty of what is laid to her charge in any degree, and my own opinion is, that we should scarcely be justified in returning a verdict of wilful murder against her."

" What are we to do then ?" said one.

" Why, gentlemen, of course you will do what your judgment dictates ; but the great thing in all these matters is not to do too much. Now, we know that a murder has been committed—of that fact we can have no doubt at all. And therefore, I put it to you, if it would not be safer to return a verdict of ' Wilful murder against some person or persons unknown,' than to append any one's name upon slight and inefficient evidence."

" But will she escape ?" asked one.

" Not at all. Our verdict has nothing whatever to do with any proceedings that may be taken by the police ; and I can inform you, that the woman, Margaret Manvers, has been already given into custody by the Earl of Crumbledown, so that you may feel assured that the most searching inquiry will be made ; only, I think that we have not sufficient evidence before us to justify us in such a course as the verdict of wilful murder against her would commit us to."

This was all so reasonable, that it could not but be acquiesced in ; so the jury, after some little conversation among themselves, returned a verdict accordingly of " Wilful murder against some person or persons unknown."

There, then, the proceedings terminated ; and, even although Mrs. Grove was strongly impressed with an opinion of the guilt of Margaret, she could not but acquiesce, in her own mind, in the propriety of the verdict, because it was quite impossible that the jury should have the means she had of coming to a correct conclusion upon the subject, for they could only guided by the bare evidence which was brought before them.

" This verdict, of course," said the coroner, " permits the burial of the child, Mrs. Grove, whenever its father thinks proper ; so that your and his feelings need not be harassed upon that head."

" I am thankful for that," said Mrs. Grove,—" I am very thankful."

" It is certainly better; and now, gentlemen, we may consider our labours to be at an end, and I can only sincerely hope that the time will come when all that is mysterious in this affair will be brought to light, and thoroughly known; and that whoever has really been guilty of this most wicked act will meet with the punishment due to their crime, but if they should miss that punishment in this world, they may rely upon it in the next ; where no evasion or subterfuge will avail them, but where the guilty will be duly judged."

With these very proper remarks the coroner left the cottage, after giving Mrs. Grove a written authority to get the child buried, and the jury distributed themselves about the tolerably numerous public-houses of Hampstead, to relate each in his own particular idea what had taken place at the inquest, and to fill the ear of wonder with the statement that Mrs. Grove's nurse-child after all belonged to a real earl.

Here was food for gossip and for speculation—here was food for all sorts of absurd conjecture upon the parts of the gossips of the place ; and, in the course of an hour, there was not a person in the place who did not know all about it.

The jurymen became quite, for the time being, the heroes of the different public-house parlours, and related such wonderful remarks that they had made, and such things that the coroner had said to them individually, of a complimentory character, that, by constant reiteration, they began almost to believe them themselves.

In fact, there had not been such another knot of gossips Heaven knows when in the place, and it seemed, from the mystery in which the affair was still enveloped, to be calculated to last for a considerable time longer.

Poor Mrs. Grove was the only sufferer, and she, when her cottage was left, and she once again found herself alone with the dead, suffered from all that desolation of spirit which such a state of things was likely to produce.

And now she began to blame herself for not, by some act of foresight or care, preventing the possibility of such a catastrophe occurring to the child ; and she began to render herself wretched by accusing herself of neglect, and by fancying that she ought to have been much more careful, and that the earl would think so himself upon calmer reflection. The reader may easily comprehend what a dreadful thought this was to such a person as Mrs. Grove, and how much she must have suffered from the mere existence of such a supposition.

And in such cases as these the imagination becomes preternaturally active in making food for its own annoyance, preying upon itself, as it were, until it conjures up thoughts and images that really have no connexion with truthful reflection. The state of solitude in which she was, too, combined to make such a state of mind more probable, and that solitude was not an ordinary one, for the presence of the dead makes up a feeling of loneliness of a very different character from that which ensues from a mere absence of the living.

" Oh, why did I not be more zealous!" exclaimed Mrs. Grove. "Why did it not strike me as a truth, that the child had bitter, irreconcilable enemies to contend with, and why did I not cast about in my own mind for any possible means by which they might effect a murderous object ? If I had done so, I must have seen with what facility that little window, opening from the garden, could have been made available for murder."

Thus, with what might almost be called a species of ingenuity in self-torment, did Mrs. Grove perplex herself upon the painful subject of the death of the Love Child—a subject which she felt she should never forget while life and the commonest power of reflection belonged to her—a subject which would always, spectre-like, step between her and every joy that she could be susceptible of feeling.

CHAPTER LXXXIII.

THE NIGHT-WATCH.—THE WRONG HOUSE, AND THE RESOURCE.—MORNING AGAIN.

THIS was a painful and agonising state of mind for poor Mrs. Grove to fall into. Over and over again, she wished that the poison, which had sapped the young existence of the earl's child, had taken her life instead, and so freed her from a world in which, for a long period now, she had known nothing but care and anxiety.

It was certainly true that, since she had been in the service of the Earl of Crumbledown, she had not been compelled to have any thought with regard to the means of subsistence ; but others, and, perhaps, really more harassing anxieties, had taken the place of that ordinary one. She had always had upon her mind a dread of her husband, and of late too, there seemed to be some secret cause of uneasiness, which she dreaded even to whisper to herself.

As the dawn of morning approached, she did hope that she should be able to get some repose, but that hope turned out to be a fallacious one, for, if anything, her misery increased ; and she, at length, without scarcely knowing the meaning of what she read, until, after a time, when the mere act of reading withdrew her mind a little from her own woes, sat down to the perusal of a volume which had been lent to her by a neighbour.

It consisted of a series of short sketches of human life ; and opening the book at random, for she could have no choice, she cast her eyes upon the first page that presented itself to her observation, and commenced an anecdotal sort of narrative, which in a short time engaged her attention more than she could have thought possible.

*　　　*　　　*　　　*　　　*

It ran thus :—

" The time was," said a tall, but withered, lean old man, who was seated in the midst of some villagers—"the time was when young men bore more respect to their elders, and bowed to old age, as being revered, and entitling the aged to some consideration, were it only for the wisdom that springs from experience."

"That was in your young days, Gaffer Morris," said a young man, who came up to the throng, as the old man was speaking, and he threw himself upon the turf.

"Ay, boy, it was in my young days, when I was as young as you are, but not quite so heedless."

The old man was seated beneath an oak-tree that grew beside a village inn ; there were seats ranged round the oak, or the greater part of it, and then along the white wall that formed the back of a stable, while in front of the seats was an enclosed space of turf, upon which many of the rustics lay after their day's toil.

The sun was sinking in the west, and the side of the ale-house, for it was not much better, was illuminated by the declining rays of the sun, which sank, or was sinking, immediately opposite to the house,—threw the dark leaves of the oak into strong contrast with the white-washed walls, and the windows which reflected the glowing light of the sun in his own brightness and colours.

"Come, Gaffer Morris, you can, if you will, tell us of some of the exploits of your own times—why you must have seen something in your time."

"I have lived long enough, lad."

"And how old are you, Gaffer ?" asked an aged man. "I can recollect you as an old man these fifty years."

"And I," said another, "can recollect my grandfather, poor man, when he was alive, say that he and Gaffer Morris has had many a good day's spree together."

"And so we have."

"But what age are you, Gaffer?" said several of the young men about him. "I have heard people say you must be a hundred years old if you be a day."

"I am," said the old man, slowly taking his hat off, and passing his hand over his bald forehead and grizzled side-locks—"I am just one hundred and seventeen to-day."

"A hundred and seventeen," echoed several standing by ; "come, that is a good old age."

"It is a good old age," said the old man ; "and the better, because I have enjoyed good health, and the use of all my faculties, and can even now do a decent day's work, and no man can say I ever kept my bed."

"Well, that's true, as far as I know," added the other ; "for I can remember you a long while yet. I never remember hearing you complain, or lay idle a day."

"And how did you continue to be so well ?"

"By always eating and drinking moderately—not over-loading myself with one kind of food more than another, and being an old man in habits, when I was young I took care of myself."

"Well, you have done credit to yourself, at all events ; but, come, Gaffer, we'll all subscribe for some of the best ale round, in honour of your birthday, therefore give me your best ale upon the occasion."

"I will, lads," said the old man; "my time is nearly run—and it is many a long day since some deeds happened, of which I may now speak with safety."

"I was, like many more young men of my time, fond of adventure, more so than of sitting at home at work, and there was one little affair which I was engaged in, that happened here before this very door; but it was ninety years agone."

"It is a long day."

"Ay, lad, it is ; but even the longest day, though it last a century, will have its end, and when you have come to the end of it and look back you will find that it will look but a very short time too, much more so than you can believe."

"No doubt, but go on."

"Well, then, when I was young, the civil war raged about from one end of the kingdom to the other ; and sometimes here. Well, I wasn't much of a puritan—I liked the world and the king, and when I found he had got such enemies, I, as many others, forgot all his faults, and stuck to him through thick and thin."

"Bravo, Gaffer."

"Well, then I was about twenty ; but before that time I had fought in four or five battles—but it often happened that we were beaten, and had to make our escape from the field in the best way we could, and the consequence, after every such affair was, I left the field and made my way home again.

"I always came back here—I never got caught, but have run one or two very close chances.

"I had been away to the battle of Worcester, and had by that time enough of fighting, because we seemed to do no good. I never flagged while at it, and I never hesitated about being present; I always left the village when I heard there was a gathering of the king's friends, and I joined them always in time to do my duty, and it never cost him a shilling, unless I was compelled to march with others, and then I could not always provide for myself.

"However, before I went, I had fallen in love, as I may say all the young men do hereabouts—even since I can remember—even to this day."

"So they do, Gaffer."

"Well, as I was saying, I fell in love, and that too with one who was acknowledged to be one of the prettiest girls in the village. I thought her by far the prettiest of any, and I was not the only one either.

"There was but a short leave-taking between us, but she said she would be true to me if I were to her; but she told me to take care of her master.

"Her master was a puritan—a married man, with a family, and a virulent man against the king—and I had it in my heart to kill him out, for I thought I should have got rid of one of the king's enemies.

"I might easily have done so, he was often near where I was, and I could have killed him over and over again; but I didn't like to do it in cold blood. It looked too much like assassination for me.

"I therefore let him go; determined that if there ever was a quarrel between us, or a chance of a fair fight, I would not be the one to shrink from it.

"I had a strong suspicion that this man was but a wolf in sheep's clothing after all—his religion, and all that, being a mere blind; but other people said no, and I held my tongue, though I was right, as I found out.

"He had been endeavouring to get the better of my sweetheart, but had failed to do so, though she had not told me a word about it."

"Had I known it, I would have done for him, sure enough; and it would, in my mind, have justified me."

"So it would."

"And dead he would have been. Well, you all remember the fate of the king's cause at Worcester; we were totally routed and dispersed, and the king himself was compelled to fly.

"I got out of the *melee* as well as I could, and had a job to do so. At one time I lay down under a waggon as if dead, when a whole troop of cavalry came by; at another time I got under a heap of dead and saved myself.

"However, I got out of the neighbourhood of the battle after many hard struggles; sometimes I had to fight for it, at others, run—but I got clear off.

"Then I had to contend against the flying parties, who were sent out against us to take prisoners, but more often to kill those who had borne arms.

"I got back here after many dangers, to tell all which would be to occupy a week or two; but I got here at last safe and sound. However, I could not show myself; I had been known, and I believe my sweetheart's master had been busy in inquiring for me.

"I learned this from a friend.

"This compelled me to hide a bit, as there was a party quartered in the village, most of whom kept their head-quarters there where the house is now; but I kept quiet.

"Well, I had got to the end of my money; I wanted a supply; besides, I could not depend upon others; so I determined to see, if possible, my sweetheart.

"I knew her master's grounds very well; and I thought, if I could only get there, I could watch for my opportunity, and then I should obtain some aid from her.

"Well, now, his house did not stand ten hundred yards from this place, and was well wooded with ornamental shrubs and trees ; and a man could hide easily among the evergreens, unless he was carefully looked after.

" I thought there would be less chance of my being discovered in the grounds of a Puritan than anywhere else ; and that was likely enough, because they would never look for me—of this I was sure, and acted accordingly.

" I did hide myself there, and after a day, I saw my sweetheart, whom I terrified out of her life ; but she did not scream out, fortunately.

" Ah, Morris," she said, " what did you come here for ?"

" To see you," said I.

" Ah, they are looking after you everywhere !"

"Who ?"

" My master and some of his people. He is sure you are about and have been to Worcester."

" Ay, so I have."

" Well, but he will murder you as a rebel, for he says you are one. I don't know, but he swears you shall die if any man ever did."

" But why should he trouble you so much about me ? Does he know much about me ?"

"Not much."

" Then, what can I have done to have caused him to have so much ill-will against me ?"

" I don't know, but he is much changed of late. I don't know what to think but there is a strange alteration in master—I don't think I shall be able to stop."

" Not to stop," said I ; " why what on earth can be the matter ? they haven't said anything to you about me, have they ?" said I, getting angry at the thought, that one whom I loved should be subjected to such treatment on my account.

" Why, not exactly ; but you are in greater danger than you would be, but for me."

" I—?"

" Yes ; you see master has been saying more to me than I like of late ; he wants me to give up to him, and I won't—and swears he'll ruin you and me too.

" Never fear," said I, " I won't take him unfairly ; but you may depend he shall be unable to do so. He is the king's enemy, and yours, and mine, so he shall rue this."

" She then told me that she had suffered a great deal of torment and persecution on my account, her brute of a master having taken all the pains he could to ruin her wholly and solely.

" That was enough for me. I was determined I would be revenged. I was. I will tell you how I was.

" I got some food and some money from Mary, and, after promising her to take care of myself, I left her, determined only to wait until we came to hand-to-hand combat. I would fight him even then—fairly fight him—and fight him I would

" I laid up in the loft there, while the soldiers were below, and when they were all asleep for the night, I came out of my hole to take some exercise.

" Well, I stood under that tree for some time, when I observed a figure coming forward towards me in the moon-light. I waited a moment for him, for there was but one man, and I thought there would be a chance of fighting my man, for something struck me that he was the man I wanted.

" He was but a few yards from me, when I saw who he was, but he did not see me. He was muttering to himself, and I overheard him say to himself, angrily,—

" She may talk as she please, but I will have her. I can depend upon those men, they will carry her off to some place which I will name, and there leave her for me."

" You and I have a few blows to exchange before you can do that," said I, stepping out.

" Ah ! traitor—surrender !"

" Draw, and defend your worthless carcase," said I.

" Help, help!" he shouted.

" Coward!" said I, " take your doom."

" I rushed forward, there was no time to lose, and ran him through the heart. He fell dead, and I left the spot, where he was found next day. I and Mary were married a few days after. Nobody knew who killed him, though some of them suspected me."

Mrs. Grove closed the book, which certainly for a time had chased away some of the gloomy thoughts that her most sad and melancholy situation had oppressed her with.

She walked to the door of the cottage, and opening it, she looked out upon one of the most grand, solemn, and beautiful of all naturnal phenomena—the rising sun —the birth of a new day.

And nowhere within many a mile of London can such an effect be seen with so many accessories of the magnificent as upon the beautiful heath on which the cottage was situated. Here the deversified nature of the country imparts a thousand charms to the new day, which, in other regions, it could not possess. She saw the faint, long hue of greyish-looking light in the eastern horizon, growing each moment in strength and beauty. She saw nature, as it were, awaking from the slumber of the night, and shaking off the stillness and repose that had crept over it.

The warbling of the birds upon the tall trees began to be plainly heard, and now and then a lark, with rapid, circling flight, would go up—up—up into the clear, cold, morning air, until it was almost lost to human ken, and looked but like a small speck, hovering between earth and heaven ; and then, as it caught from its altitude a glimpse of the coming orb of light and beauty, it would burst into song.

All this Mrs. Grove saw, and at any other time she could have deeply entered into the full enjoyment of the beauty of such a scene, but she could not now, for she remembered how at times in the light vernal season she had brought that child who now lay in the calm of death to look upon such sights, and how, young as it was, she had spoken to it of Heaven and of Heaven's matchless works, teaching it to love God and not to fear him—teaching it a purer and more natural religion and adoration of the Creator, through his works, than any book ever yet inculcated.

Mrs. Grove was fully of opinion, that,—

" He prayeth best who loveth best.
Both man, and bird, and beast :"

and she simplified her theology into an adoration and an admiration of the Deity, whom she invested with far higher and far nobler attributes than the grovelling and brutalised intellects of what are called religious people can ever imagine. For is it not grovelling, to suppose that the Deity can be " angry ?" Is it not brutalising, to dream even of a hell?

But, alas! that young creature, to whom Mrs. Grove was enacting so kind a part was no more. The thought came upon her mind like a blight upon a flower. She walked slowly into her cottage again, and sat down by the side of the dead, and wept long and bitterly.

Those tears were, perhaps, the bitterest that Mrs. Grove had ever shed. A spirit of resistance had always supported her against the ill-usage of her husband ; but she was now completely subdued by the grief that took possession of her soul, when she thought of the calm, still form beneath the sheet, that now covered up the little cot from observation, over which she had often stooped to kiss the smiling face of the child.

Suddenly then she shuddered, as if a thought had come across her of a different complexion to those which were merely of grief, and she sank upon her knees by the side of the child's bed, and clasped her hands as she cried in a half-distracted tone of voice,—

" Heaven forgive me! Heaven forgive me, for that which I have done. There is yet a fearful secret which lies at the bottom of my breast. The time may come when it must be told. Oh! Heaven forgive, for an act which was the impulse of a moment, and which has implanted in my mind an undying regret."

What could it be, that hung so heavily upon the soul of this woman, whose whole course of conduct appears to be irreproachable. She does not appear to be a person likely o act upon mere impulse in any affair of moment; and yet, she accuses herself of having done so in some matter of the very first importance. We shall see, we shall see. Our narrative is drawing to a close, and we shall soon see what it is that causes ⸴ rove so much acute uneasiness and mental agony to think of.

CHAPTER LXXXIV.

THE EXAMINATION AND ACQUITTAL OF MARGARET AT BOW-STREET.

THE turn affairs had taken was a very untoward one, and was quite unexpected neither the countess nor Margaret had any supposition that there could have been any chance of the latter being given into custody, or even recognised as having beeⁿ in the vicinity of Hampstead. Had Mrs. Grove not come there at all, had Margaret not shown her face, all would have been well, but the impatience of Mrs. Grove drove her into the presence of the earl at such a moment, and it was surprise that induced Margaret to take off her mask, as it had done many other persons present on that occasion; moreover, it was merely the recognition of the moment that gave a direction to Mrs. Grove's suspicions, which had been vague and pointless.

However, there was but little fear in Margaret; she knew others too deep in the crime to think for a moment there was any danger; she knew, also, there was ample means to exert in her favour, even if such corroborative evidence as was required were to be forthcoming; yet, what between the countess and her mother, she knew she must be freed.

The morning came, and with it the usual bustle and excitement of a police-office, and at the earliest opportunity the prisoner was placed at the bar, and the office was crowded to excess by many persons anxious to hear the result of a matter that promised some food for the lovers of the mysterious.

Margaret Manvers was placed at the bar, and the whole party was ushered into court.—the countess being there as well as the earl and Mrs. Grove.

"What is the charge?" inquired the magistrate, taking his eyes off the newspaper for a moment.

"Murder, your worship," said the officer.

Thereupon Mrs. Grove was placed in the witness-box and sworn; she was then desired to tell her own tale in her own way and to be quick about it.

Mrs. Grove proceeded to detail circumstances that have been partially related, and some others which will be more fully spoken of hereafter; so that we will not go into her evidence now, but proceed to other matters.

"Has there been an inquest held?" inquired the magistrate.

"There will be one to-day or to-morrow, your worship," replied the officer.

"Then I think it will hardly be advisable to enter into the case more fully, but await until we know the result of the inquest."

"I think so, your worship, especially as there is no more evidence now to offer, but by that time I may be able to do more in the matter."

"There is quite sufficient for a remand. I shall not call upon the prisoner to make any defence, as this is a mere preliminary examination, but shall remand you until day after to-morrow, when you will be brought up here for re-examination."

"This is very hard, your worship," said a solicitor, who had been sent to, "there is no case against the prisoner, and if fairly accused is ready to meet anything."

"The evidence is incomplete," said the magistrate; "and therefore a remand is necessary."

"I submit, your worship, there is none," said the solicitor.

"We decide, there is sufficient to justify the demand for a remand, which we grant until the day after to-morrow."

"Will your worship take bail?" inquired the solicitor, knowing very well that his worship could not.

"Certainly not, sir. It is a felony."

"But the circumstances are the merest suspicion."

"Which may become certainties by the next meeting," replied the magistrate; "no—no, I cannot take any bail whatever. It is never done."

"I must submit to your worship's decision," said the solicitor; "but I am prepared with evidence to rebut every scorn that has been advanced, and my client's sex taken altogether makes the case one of great and peculiar hardship, and I trust your worship will take it into consideration."

"If you really believe I can alter the decision I have given, you must be in some ignorance of the law of the case, for you must well know I cannot do otherwise."

There was now a movement in the court, when the solicitor said,—

"I trust your worship will be more complaisant towards my next application?"

"State it, sir.

"It is that the prisoner shall have means of communication with her friends and her solicitor, as this is a serious affair, and she will have now some days to collect evidence."

"Certainly; you will have access to her at all reasonable times; I cannot interfere, if I wished, with the ordinary regulations of the jail."

"Thank your worship."

Then Margaret Manvers was removed from the dock and conducted through the court by the officers to a cell into which she was conducted and there left; but it was not long before her solicitor entered and had some communication with her, and then left her, after which he had an interview with the countess.

Mrs. Grove left the office also, the countess leaving in her own carriage without having any communication with the earl, or any one. Mrs. Grove, however, understood that she was to be present at the appointed day, but before she left the earl motioned her to follow him.

"Mrs. Grove," he said, "are you sure of what you have now related?"

"As sure as I live," she replied.

"You must be here on the day named. I will be here also and carry this matter out; I will send some one to attend to the inquest, in the meantime you will want money, take that and provide for yourself out of it. I am distracted at this moment."

He gave Mrs. Grove his purse, and then with Colonel Bruce entered the tilbury that was waiting for him on the outside of the office and drove away.

Mrs. Grove received the purse with feelings that can scarcely be described, and left the office and wended her way to some place where she could remain in security, for she well remembered the events of the previous day, the narrow escape she had the day before: all these things passed like a frightful dream before her; she saw she had passed the danger; she saw she was surrounded by enemies of one kind or another, and that day had succeeded in destroying the life of the child.

It was a terrible pause in the proceedings to all parties, for while they are pending none knew what to think of them, none could say how they would end.

The earl was distracted and bewildered; he had no doubt of Mrs. Grove's honesty and integrity; he was sure she could have no object in betraying him or his child; there was every reason why others should, and yet there was the greatest improbability of one so situated as the countess employing her own maid on such an expedition; he could not believe it possible.

"Yet with all that who else could desire the child's death? Suppose she had learned all and found out where it had been placed? Suppose—but there, suppose almost anything—what would it matter? it came all to the same in the end—one great uncertainty."

And who is there that can thoroughly understand or explain that which is yet uncertain and has yet to be dreaded by the future; it is a harassing reflection that we are compelled to postpone the solving of the most desired events; the explanations of which either make or mar us.

How the countess felt can scarcely be a matter of doubt; she was much staggered at the unexpected occurrence; she had never dreamed of such a thing, and she had nearly betrayed herself at first, but fortunately it was Margaret who had been recognised and accused.

This gave her great power of exertion; she could act effectually; she could and would save Margaret; nay, she felt that she must do so; despite even herself, she must save her, or she felt that Margaret would confess more than she knew would be safe either for her or for her objects; she would lose every point of the game for which she had played so desperate a part.

The countess knew well how matters stood; her measures were resolved upon and undertaken with the aid and counsel of that very respectable individual, Willoughby, who, however, would not appear in it; but at the same time, he was the man who urged the countess to take every precaution she could, such as counsel and solicitor, and to be witness herself, and to procure corroborative evidence as well.

Being thoroughly aware of the importance of the success of the plan, the Countess of Crumbledown determined she would leave no stone unturned for Margaret's safety.

* * * *

And Margaret, too, she was sent to Coldbath-fields, there to await the decision of the coroner's inquest that was to be holden at Hampstead. She had little or no care for the future,—she had perfect confidence in the countess, for she knew very well that she dared not neglect her.

"I am safe," muttered Margaret, when she considered over in her own mind; "I am safe, quite safe, the countess must swear through thick and thin to save me."

This was very true; but whatever was done would bind the countess, if possible, more and more to her, and she could not for one moment run any danger of which the countess did not have an equal or greater share; indeed, the more she plunged, the deeper she sank.

Being different from many of the females who are sent to that place, Margaret Manvers was well dressed, and had plenty of money, which was soon made known to the turnkeys, who contrived, by the aid of gold, to obtain for her somewhat more accommodation than is usual.

"I can't give you a place to yourself, ma'am," he said, "but I can do what's next to it."

"And what is that?"

"Only this, ma'am. You see, we are wery full, so I can put you in, as you are a 'spectable lady, a place where there is only one."

"And what is that one?"

"Oh! she's a decent innocent young woman; she's harmless."

"Well then, let me go there," said Margaret, "I dare say it's the best you can afford to give me, else you would do it."

"And so I would," said the turnkey, as he pocketed the money. "I wish I had such as you every day of the week, I'd treat 'em well, at all events."

He led the way to the place where she was to be confined, and then she was shown in by the turnkey, who said, in his way,—

"Come, now, young one, stir about, I have brought you a lady, who is a trump, she has proved herself one. Come, no snivelling."

As the turnkey spoke, he looked towards a wretched object of sorrow and dejection in one corner of the cell, and again said,—

"Come, come, it's no use being down-hearted about a trifle; you'll be better yet; here is a companion for you, good-bye to you both."

So saying the old turnkey hobbled out of the cell; and having locked the door, was heard retreating along the passage with a slow steady step, and humming a song.

Margaret found herself in a cell along with another young woman, who looked the very picture of misery and wretchedness. She sat down upon the bench that was placed at the side of the wall; and then leaning her back against the wall, hung her head down in sorrow and despair.

For some moments Margaret gazed at the unfortunate being in silence. At first she determined that she would not exchange any words with any soul within the prison; but the more she looked at the young creature, the more she became interested her—that is, she became curious to know what it could be that had brought such an one as she with so much grief to such a place.

"You seem grieved," she said to her, at length.

"And are you not grieved?"

"No," said Margaret.

"Then you are innocent, and have friends to make you happy."

"Yes," said Margaret, "I cannot be under any apprehension about my fate; I am only annoyed at the inconvenience I am now compelled to suffer by being incarcerated in a common jail, where I am so placed upon the charge of committing an evil deed."

" You are happy."

" I cannot think myself very happy," said Margaret.

" Not happy, and yet know you are innocent," said the young girl. " I cannot understand that ; but here I have been told there is no one perfectly happy."

" They may not be," said Margaret, " but I cannot say I am unhappy, though I can't call myself happy, when I am put to so much inconvenience and annoyance."

" And yet," said the girl, " conscious innocence ought to make you happy, because it presents the certainty of one's being able to prove oneself so before all the world."

" I am that, but that doesn't seem to me to be happiness ; but are you unfortunate enough to be unable to do so," inquired Margaret.

" I am innocent," said the young girl, " but I fear I shall have to suffer as though I were guilty."

" Indeed that is hard."

" Doubly hard, indeed, is it, when the nature of my crime is such that it makes me shudder, my very nature revolt at it," said the young girl with visible emotion.

" And are you innocent ?"

" I am."

" Then under what circumstances, and for what crime, have they brought you here ?" inquired Margaret."

" I will tell you ; but first tell me for what are you brought here ; I fear to name my crime, and yet why should I not? I cannot see why I should not do so; for I am conscious of innocence! but yet I have no friends ; and to be without friends is here to be almost equal to being guilty."

" I am here," said Margaret, seeing the young girl's reluctance, " upon a charge of murder."

" Murder !"

" Yes, I am accused of poisoning a child ; but thanks to my friends I am well provided with the means of proving I am entirely innocent of the charge. I was elsewhere."

" You are fortunate in having friends."

" Of course," said Margaret; " without them I must have sunk beneath the weight of the charge, but I can clear myself upon testimony they cannot doubt."

" And I am here for child murder. In a few days I shall be taken up and committed for trial, and yet, Heaven alone knows I am innocent."

" You are very young," said Margaret.

" Scarce eighteen," said the girl.

" You have indeed much to suffer, since you are thus early accused. This is your first ?"

" Oh, yes," said the girl, with a sigh that appeared to come from her heart, but so full of sorrow and sadness that even Margaret Manvers could not help feeling the influence of the feeling which appeared to be so fully developed in the young girl.

" What were the circumstances under which your present state came about ?"

" I will tell you," she said, after a moment or so ; " I will tell you, and you shall judge if I have not been cruelly used by those who ought to have treated me better."

" I listen," said Margaret.

The young girl paused a few moments before she spoke, and wiped away the falling tear from a cheek that was now thin and pale, but which, despite all that suffering could inflict, still betrayed signs of no ordinary beauty, which, alas, was the ruin of its possessor.

It is now about two years ago since the first of these unhappy circumstances took place; I was then not sixteen, ; I was near it, but not quite. I was always considered above my age, for my growth and beauty, alas, attracted those who lured me to my ruin—to my present state.   It is now a great horror to me, but I was proud of my looks then.   I knew I was beautiful, not because I was told so, because I heeded that but very little indeed, but because when I looked at myself and compared myself with others I felt it was so.

My self-confidence laid me open to many charges, and gave me many enemies, but then I had some friends, and none could accuse me of selfishness, or even of any undue attempt to make myself superior to my companions.   I was always ready to listen to the distress of others; thus it was I never had any money about me.

I was in service.   I was the attendant upon a young lady about my own age; she was very beautiful, and exceedingly amiable, but she had the advantage of accomplishments and of education, position and friends, whereas I had only my beauty as my dowry.

Girl-like, my thoughts often reverted to a lover; I often thought how happy my mistress must be, for she had a lover, and one who was received by the family as the future husband of my young mistress.   I must say there were times when I looked upon my mistress with an eye of envy, but it was quickly dissipated, yet at intervals it would return, and I felt that fortune favoured her who wanted her favours less than I did; and began to believe that they who had much always could get more, and they who wanted might always want, but there was little impartiality in Providence.

About that time there came a visitor to the house of my mistress; it was the brother of her lover.   He was a younger son, but I considered him the preferable young man of the two, and I saw, also, that he paid me some little attention.   I was well pleased at this; it was far too gratifying to the vanity of a young girl not to feel pleased at such an occurrence.

Well, I might be pardoned for my presumption; but I was wrong; and yet, when there are so many temptations to the young and inexperienced, what could be said?   Better than I have fallen, and older than I have been deceived.

I was well pleased with the attentions which were offered me by this young gentleman, who took some trouble to see me, and who vowed he loved me.

I believed him.   Who would not?   I who was young, ardent, and unsuspicious; I who had no experience in the way of the world.   I was not one who could find reasons for distrust in the admiration of a young and handsome man.   It was by far too flattering and too pleasing.

I had too much happiness to feel any desire to awake from such a pleasing dream.   I was well aware that if my intercourse was discovered I should obtain severe reprehension, and most likely an ignominious discharge, which would have ruined me entirely.

I, however, braved all this.   I thought him sincere.   I knew he would incur severe censure in his own family by any premature discovery that might be made; and yet he braved all.   Why should not I?   He professed he loved me, and where is the girl, who, loving a man, could believe that he was false?   I believed him true, because I loved him, and because I wished him to be so.

After a time, we used to spend our time together.   Whenever I could obtain an hour's release he was sure to be with me.   He was constantly at my side whenever I obtained leave of absence, and I knew he frequently put himself to great inconvenience to do so.

He often rode ten and twenty miles only to be an hour with me.

What could I attribute all this to?   I could not suppose that it was less than the most disinterested love that was ever possessed for woman.

I was, indeed, then happy—very happy, indeed.   I used to walk down the green lanes with his arm round my waist, breathing words of love and tenderness in my ears.

Who could then dream of falsehood?   Not I.

Well, weeks and months passed by.   He was the same attentive lover.   He promised me marriage; gave me a written promise of marriage, which he would undertake to perform as soon as his brother's marriage was performed, and as soon as he had secured some provision for himself.

This was but reasonable, and I believed him.

It will scarce be necessary to follow step by step my fall ; but fall I did. I fell a dupe to the deepest laid scheme of treachery and deceit.

Still I had no thought of anything ill. I did not believe that he would be so bad as he turned out. I even then did not doubt his honour and his word.

" He will never desert me; he will be true," I said to myself; " I know well that he will. What has happened has been done through excess of love ; and am not I as much to blame as he ?"

This was the view I took of the case, and it was a fatal one for me ; and had I then been suddenly awakened to a sense of my own situation all that has since happened would have been saved me. I might have been ruined. I was ruined, but at the same time I should never have been deemed guilty. I should have done what all women do under such circumstances.

" What is that ?" inquired Margaret.

" Have made some provision for the coming event."

" And you did not, of that you are most positive ?"

" No, I did not."

The young girl paused a moment or two, and heaved a deep sigh. She resumed her narrative, and then proceeded in a low tone as follows :—

When I found there was a probability of my becoming a mother, I told my lover of it, and he seemed much concerned, and yet declared his joy.

He was sorry, he said, because he was so situated that he could not perform his promise for some months ; for if he did so he would lose all the prospects which he had of making me and my offspring happy and independent for the future.

However, he was glad to be a father, he said ; he felt joy at the thought, and it made me dearer to him, if possible, than even I was before.

Could I be otherwise than happy ?

No, I could not ; I felt that I could not be displeased even with him, and looked upon my present circumstances as, at the most, but a temporary reverse, and which would soon be put an end to, and a long life of happiness afterwards would be the reward I should inevitably receive.

Oh ! how few can calculate upon the future ? I was not of that class ; I felt that I was safe in the arms of the man that I loved.

But how long does security last ? I was seated on a mine which might explode at any one moment, and I might be involved in the common ruin.

My lover had strictly forbidden me to make any communication of the state I was in to any human being, and if I did so, he said, I should ruin all ; I should destroy his own hopes, and his own prospects, and my future happiness, as he intended to arrange matters that very morning, and should appear much earlier than usual. He had the means of doing this, he said.

How it was to be done he did not say ; but that he would do it I had not the slightest doubt, and I felt rejoiced at it.

Indeed, it appeared to me as if he were as anxious for my honour as for his own, and this gave me additional cause for confidence in him, and I obeyed him implicitly.

I held no communication with anybody upon the subject ; I saw nobody, and I held myself aloof from all such of my companions as I had been used to communicate with. Indeed, I began to feel that there was a greater distance between them and I than I should be warranted in shortening, and by my conduct I gained their ill-will, because they saw it not.

However, there was something in my own mind that told me I was acting for the best, and that my husband would desire that such should be done, and that I should never hold any communication with them, save such as the situation I was then in compelled me.

Besides, had I done so, I could not have kept my state such a profound secret, which I had succeeded upon doing to the very last. I must have made some revelations, and then all would have been discovered, and in gaining their ill-will I saved myself from some observation and remark.

This was, of course, an advantage.

Time flew by, and I again urged my lover to adopt some course that would take me away from my present situation ; for I then told him I could not remain there.

" Well," said he, " have you given warning to leave ?"

" I have not."

" Then do so now, and keep it all a profound secret. I will have a place ready for you. You shall want for nothing ; but a marriage now would make me forfeit property that would be mine if I remain single to a certain age. If, therefore, you can do that, I care for nothing else ; be assured that what I am doing is for our united benefit and for our children also."

What could I say to this ? The case was too plain and evident for all argument, but I did venture to say to him,—

" I have not made the slightest preparation."

" And none you need. I have, as I told you, means, and, by the time you want them, you shall find all you can desire ; but stop to the last day, and then you can appear afterwards at some future time, and should the child not live it will never be suspected."

" True," I said ; " but I can hardly tell if I don't remain so long."

" Do the best you can, but let me know in time."

" I will," I said, " and I will do my utmost to keep the secret to the last ; but I fear it very much, for I shall not have a day to spare."

This was understood between us. Fortune favoured me so far that I kept my secret so well that I was not even suspected to the day in which I left. I was, however, very ill on that day, and could scarce keep about ; but, by dint of great exertion and resolution, I did so. I had held up so long I determined that, if any effort of which I was capable could carry me through it, I would make it cost what it would. Be the anguish ever so great it was not worth while to lose the advantage of all my previous efforts for the sake of a few hours. I was resolved, and the will did it.

I succeeded.

I was, however, too much exhausted to take away my own things, but said I would send for them ; and then I left the house to meet my lover. He had agreed upon a spot where to meet me, and then he would take me to a place he had secured for me.

I went along somewhat relieved of my fears and doubts, for I had some at times ; but now I was going to be released from all these ; I was about to go into the life I expected to begin, to have about me a home, and in a few months I was to be a wife.

I was well pleased with these thoughts ; I walked along, but at times felt ill. On one or two occasions I was compelled to stand still, and at length I was compelled to sit down by the way side, and at length I could go no further—all was over.

I was left there—I was insensible. I had fainted ; and, when I was found, my child was discovered dead by my side and I in a fit.

I was carried to an infirmary ; for I was placed in a cart and brought to London, and delivered up, and when all had become known I was placed in jail for concealing the birth with an intent to murder my own child ; and, God above knows, how innocent I am of any charge of the kind. I would sooner have died myself than have done or thought of so foul a deed.

" But what had become of the father ?"

" I believe he left the country on the same day I left my situation. Could anything be so base, so wicked as this deed ? It would seem he had contemplated the end I have now come to, that I should be so irretrievably ruined, that there is no hope of my ever rising again."

" But this will not affect your life ?" said Margaret.

" But it will."

" It is not murder."

" It may not be, but I shall suffer ignominious imprisonment. My shame will become known, all the world will point at me, and say I have escaped my doom ;

and besides, how shall I ever again look any one in the face? How shall I live? how shall I obtain the means of existence honestly? No one will have me! no one will take me! I am an outcast, and can never hope for serenity again!"

CHAPTER LXXXV.

THE SECOND EXAMINATION OF MARGARET.—THE TRIUMPH.—THE INTERVIEW WITH THE EARL.

THE office was crowded on the morning upon which it had been announced that Margaret Manvers would be brought up on a charge of poisoning a child. The situation of the parties, the curious mode of accusation, the disturbance of a masked ball, and, all things taken into consideration, there was enough to cause this to be deemed an interesting case for the papers.

The inquest had been holden.

There was a thronging company, the whole of the benches being occupied by persons of distinction, and, at the moment, it was reported that the countess herself had poisoned the illegitimate child of the earl.

There was, as usual on such occasions, plenty of scandal, a variety of reports, and none of them true, but that did not matter. Only one report could be true, but as there was a great many, some must be false, which is a matter, as we said, of little consequence.

There were several magistrates present, and an old lord, who often presides upon the occasions that appear more than usually exciting, and who offered his valuable assistance, which, of course, was accepted, though they were of no value at all, his lordship just occupying his seat, and that was all.

As soon as the night-charges were gone through, Margaret Manvers was placed at the bar, and seated at the table was a very grave counsellor, with his gown and wig, and by her side was her solicitor, all of which had been provided by the order of the countess through Willoughby.

The Countess of Cumbledown and the Dowager Countess of Fanraonade, the mother of the former, were present, besides some others.

The earl, Colonel Bruce, and Mrs. Grove were present.

"Now," said the magistrate, after a few moments' pause, so as to enable the respective parties to seat themselves and proceed in a methodical manner; "now," said the magistrate, "are you prepared to proceed with this charge of poisoning?"

"Yes," replied the usher.

"Then proceed," said the magistrate.

This was done by Mrs. Grove being called into the witness-box, and, being sworn, deposed as follows,—

That she was in charge of a child at Hampstead, near the ponds, in the Vale of Health, as it was called, from its healthiness, as known to the inhabitants of that place. The morning before the child died she was visited by a woman, who appeared to be very faint, and to be taken suddenly ill.

She entered her cottage and there sat down; she appeared to be very ill, and wanted me to go fetch her something from a public-house near at hand, but I refused to do so because I would not leave the child and a stranger by themselves.

She said she was the wife of a soldier, and had just come to England; she had travelled a good many miles, and was very faint and ill.

I said I would wait at the door, and as soon as I saw a boy go by he should go and fetch her whatever she pleased, and, at the same time, I should not be obliged to leave my cottage and the child; but, when a boy was coming near, she got better, and said she would have a glass of water, which, she said, was enough then, and, after awhile, she got better and left me.

"Is the prisoner at the bar that woman?"

"Yes."

"Are you sure? be careful what you say."

"Yes, I am sure. I cannot be mistaken. She was many minutes at my place, and I am as sure she is the woman as that I am now living."

"When did you see the prisoner, and on what occasion?"

"I saw her when I came to the Earl of Crumbledown's house, when I came to tell him of the nature of the unfortunate occurrence—the death of the child."

"And how did that happen?" inquired the magistrate.

"I cannot tell. She was taken very ill soon after she awoke in the morning, and when I found her symptoms becoming worse, I went for medical advice, which, however, was of no use. The poor little thing had died, evidently in great pain, and from some violent cause."

"That is as you judged?"

"Yes, sir."

"Pray, Mrs. Grove, after the person who called upon you at the cottage, and requested you to send to a public-house for some spirits, which you did not get, did any one have access to your cottage without your knowledge or consent, or with your permission."

"No one came in to me who remained there by themselves. I was there the whole of the time."

"Then they could do nothing that you could not see?"

"They could not, I am quite confident."

"You saw no one about your cottage during either day or night?"

"Nobody, but the prisoner."

"Now answer me, if you please, clearly and distinctly, and be particular in what you say," said the barrister, shaking his well-powdered wig; "for this is a matter of grave importance, especially as your testimony will be disputed—are you sure the prisoner at the bar is the same person whom you saw at your cottage and made the request you have related?"

"I am quite confident of it; there was no room for mistake; I could make none. If I had the smallest doubt of it I would say so, because I know it is a serious affair."

"And being a serious affair, Mrs. Grove," said the barrister, "it behoves you to be cautious in what you say upon this matter, especially as the charge affects life."

"The evidence of identity," said the magistrate, "appears to be conclusive and most positive; the witness has not hesitated or prevaricated from the first statement a bit."

"The witness's evidence, your worship," said the barrister, "can be refuted by the most unquestioned testimony. She was elsewhere the whole of the day."

"What induced you to believe the prisoner to have any hand in the death of the child?" inquired the magistrate; "and why did you charge her with the murder?"

"Because, sir, I saw her at the masked ball of the countess."

"That was nothing extraordinary," said the barrister; "her duty to her mistress rendered her presence necessary."

"The answer does not seem to me to be a very clear one," said the solicitor.

The barrister frowned, and the magistrate immediately said,—

"Tell me distinctly what induced you, seeing the prisoner at the ball, and believing you had seen her before, what induced you to accuse her? You had no suspicion before, that the woman who called upon you had any hand in the child's death I believe?"

"I had not," replied Mrs. Grove.

"Think well my question, and give me a straightforward answer, for to me the answer to it must be important, one way or the other," said the magistrate.

"I think so, too," said the barrister.

"I did not have any suspicion of her before I accidentally recognised her at the Countess's ball, I cannot perhaps explain why my suspicion was awakened suddenly otherwise than by the singularity of the cases, and the fact that disguise and falsehood had been used."

"In what respect," inquired the magistrate.

"In this :—It was strange that the Countess's maid should have appeared in the guise of a soldier's wife."

"So it was," said the barrister.

"And moreover wanted her to leave the place, she asserted falsehood in describing herself to me in the character she did, and her illness I now believe to be feigned; I had, I repeat, no suspicion at that time that she was otherwise than what she represented herself to be."

"Supposing all to be as you say it was," said the barrister, "can you tell us whether the prisoner at the bar could have administered the poison to the child."

"When people do those things," said Mrs. Groves, "they take care they shall not be seen."

"I do not ask you what people usually do then," said the barrister, with sudden and startling energy, "I ask you, what the prisoner did?"

"I cannot say, I saw her also, I should have prevented it."

"Very good, then according to your own shewing, the prisoner at the bar could have had no hand in the murder of the child under your care."

"I did not say that. If I saw anything wrong, I would have prevented it, but I did not; however, the fact of falsehood and deception being used, I do now believe that it was she who poisoned the child. The suspicion in my mind amounts to a certainty."

"But what on earth could she have done had she been there?"

"I cannot be expected to tell you that," said Mrs. Grove.

"No," said the magistrate, "that is not to be expected; cases may cause the witness to suspect a person, without her being able to give a detailed account of what took place on an occasion when no one is known to be present and see."

"But had the prisoner been there your worship, she could have done no harm, and why should it excite suspicion, if she were there? the countess's maid had nothing to do with the child, much less had she any ill will against it."

"Still," said Mrs. Groves, "she came in disguise; why assume a character she did not know? There must have been a motive for that."

"We can prove she did not."

"I cannot be mistaken, the countess herself may not look with favour upon the child."

"Witness," said the barrister, gravely, "you are travelling out of your way to bring other names in this matter that are above suspicion. Unless you have some charge to make, you had better not deal out any insinuations of a character so injurious and gratuitous."

"I am not doing so; I have only stated my full belief founded upon the fact, that the countess's waiting maid came to my place in an assumed character, entered into conversation, tried to induce me to go out, and failing in that, she got better and left, the next day the child is poisoned. She is the only person upon whom I can place any suspicion."

"And that is the only motive you have for making the charge."

"Yes, sir, the only one, but I do not doubt anything about what I have said. If I could do so, I would say so at once, sir."

"And this," said the magistrate, angrily, "is the whole of the evidence against the prisoner?"

"Yes, sir," replied the usher."

"Has there not been an inquest held upon the body?"

"There has, your worship," said an officer with a very red face and a fierce squint.

"What has been the result of the inquest?" inquired the magistrate.

"The verdict, your worship," said the same officer, "was wilful murder against some person or persons unknown."

There was now a pause of some moments' duration; during which the barrister consulted with the solicitors and his notes at the same time. Mrs. Groves was desired to stand down, but to be in readiness against the time she was called upon, in case she should be wanted.

"I presume your worship intends to call upon the prisoner for her defence?"

"Yes," replied the magistrate; "you have heard the charge against her, and the evidence—she can now offer any observation or explanation she pleases."

"Precisely, your worship; but do your worship think there is any case at all? I cannot see any."

"Yes, there is grave suspicion, which would warrant me in committing her for further time to prosecute en uiries, unless some satisfactory explanation can be tendered."

"I submit to your worship there is none; but I must bow to the decision of the magistrates. We do not offer any explanation of the circumstances detailed by the witness, but we insist she is mistaken, and deny altogether that the prisoner was ever in or near Hampstead, the whole of that day; if we can do this, I may, I believe, demand the discharge of the prisoner."

"Certainly," replied the magistrate,

"Then I shall be able to prove that not only at the time the witness has deposed to the presence of the woman who came to her cottage, that she was engaged with her mistress, the Countess of Crumbledown in her ladyship's private apartment, at her residence; not only, I say, at that hour, but for the whole day, from morning until the evening; that in short it is, to say the least, as clear a mistake in the identity, as any case that ever came before a bench of justice."

"Nay, sir, visitors at the house saw her. It is most fortunate that she was so employed on that day, for had it happened that her mistress had been otherwise engaged, such clear testimony could not have been given in her favour, but Providence has clearly in this case interposed in her favour, and placed her above suspicion, and has placed the means in her power of proving herself so."

"Call the Countess of Crumbledown," said the barrister as he sat down.

The Countess of Crumbledown at once stepped forward, and upon being questioned if she had any objection to being sworn, replied she had none.

"Do you know the prisoner at the bar," inquired the counsel.

"Yes, I do. It is Margaret Manvers, my own personal attendant."

"State, if you please, any circumstance you may recollect, respecting the prisoner in regard to her employment on the day in question; and also where she was."

"I can easily do that. She was with me the whole of the day, on which she is stated to have been at Hampstead," replied the countess, confidently.

"Can you state any particular reason why you recollect her being with you on that day?"

"Yes, I had it in contemplation to give a masked ball, which I afterwards gave, but before I did so, I was desirous of examining my wardrobe personally; to do which, required the aid of my maid. It took us nearly the whole day, and I did not go out on that day in consequence of my desire to finish the job on that day, and not to have it protracted to another, and for that reason also I was denied to several visitors, whom I could not see upon such an occasion as the one to which I allude."

"Then you had no visitors on that day, when you and your maid were so employed?"

"Yes I had, but none whom I remember; save, indeed, the Marchioness of Fanfaronade, my mother, who came, and was in the room with me some time."

"At what hour?"

"The same she was stated to be in this woman's cottage."

"And your mother, the Lady Fanfaronade, was present at that hour too?"

"Yes, she was," replied the countess, "and made some remarks upon our employment. I am confident as to the time, because I watched the hours as they went by, not believing the inspection would have taken so long by a great deal as what it did, and the day appeared to pass rapidly."

"Then you are sure that your maid was not absent on that day?"

"I am as confident of it as I am that she is here at this moment, charged with a crime she could not by any possibility be guilty of."

"What character does the prisoner bear in your establishment?"

"It is almost a needless question," replied the countess, haughtily; "had she any but the best, a day would have been too long a notice to quit. I never heard a complaint against her, and I never had one. Could I not repose the most implicit confidence in her, she should not be my personal attendant upon me; and one act that would disturb my confidence, must separate us."

"Have you any opportunity of judging of her principles and humanity?"

"I have, and believe them to be good; and I believe her to be much attached to children."

"I have no more questions to ask you, my lady; I do not know whether his worship may see occasion to ask you anything."

There was a short pause, during which the magistrate looked at some papers, and seemed to be thinking over some matters, but he said,—

"No, I do not see that anything is required."

"Then call the Marchioness of Fanfaronade," said the barrister, as the countess retired from the witness-box, and at the same time her place was supplied by her mother, who scarce deigned to look upon either magistrate or barrister, but stood mute.

"You are the mother of the last witness, are you not?"

"I am," replied the lady, with the most supreme indifference of all in court.

"Did you visit your daughter upon the day in question?"

"Yes," said the lady, with the utmost coolness.

"Pray will you relate what you saw on the occasion of your visit? I mean as to what they may have been about, or who may have been present."

"My daughter and her maid were at home, but I take very little notice of what people do. I never do anything myself—I leave it to those who have to earn their bread."

"And you cannot tell what they were about?"

"I should not have known anything about it, save that my daughter's maid made an exclamation upon some subject, to which I paid no attention; but my daughter, the countess, informed me that she was examining her wardrobe."

"A necessary employment sometimes."

"I really cannot tell—my maid inspects mine."

"Still are you sure that your daughter's maid was present—that is the prisoner at the bar? Have the goodness to look at the prisoner."

The countess turned slowly, and looked at Margaret Manvers with steady composure for some moments through her glasses, and then the counsel said again,—

"Did you see the prisoner on that day?"

"Yes, I did see her; I have seen her too often not to know her perfectly well. She is my daughter's maid, and she was at home on that day. I can state this quite positively—I am sure of it; I cannot be mistaken about the matter at all."

"You may retire, my lady, I have done."

"Yes," added the magistrate, and then after a pause, he added, "let Mrs. Grove be called—I have a question or two to ask her."

Mrs. Grove was recalled; she had not, in fact, been out of the court, and had listened to the whole of the evidence of the countess, and her mother, and she saw at once, that her testimony was overpowered by theirs, but it did not shake her opinion. She entered the witness-box again, as she was directed to do by the usher of the court, and the magistrate spoke to her.

"Have you heard the evidence of these two ladies?"

"I have, your worship," said Mrs. Grove.

"Think for a moment or two, we may all make a mistake, but it is better to rectify a mistake, especially a grave one, than to permit it to remain uncorrected, for you may avoid injustice by so doing, and commit a higher crime by refusing from doing so."

"Yes sir."

"Well then, now tell us truly—look well at the prisoner, and tell us whether you may not have been mistaken, in supposing the prisoner at the bar, the same woman, who came to you at the cottage at Hampstead, and feigned illness?"

Mrs. Grove did look steadily at Margaret, and then she, in a firm voice, said,—

"I have not the smallest doubt of it, sir." I have heard all that has been said, but it does not shake my belief. I recollect the prisoner too well, and I saw her and spoke to her for too long a period, to permit me the smallest chance of making a mistake."

There was another pause of some moments' duration. The magistrate appeared to be puzzled, and scarce knew what to do. The evidence appeared to be so positive on both sides, but the weight of it was by far too great on the side of the prisoner to permit him long to hesitate.

"This, your worship, I take it, to give it a mild word, to be as clear a case of mistaken identity as ever happened."

"Yes," said the magistrate, "there can be no doubt about it—Mrs. Grove must be mistaken. It is an occurrence that is by no means uncommon, but at the same time, I do not think Mrs. Grove is actuated by any, but proper feeling in the affair and I believe her to be perfectly conscientious in her testimony, but still she has made a mistake."

" Yes, your worship, she has, and a very grave one too, and had my client been less favoured by circumstances to prove her innocence, she might have been placed in extreme jeopardy ; at least, she would have had a slur cast upon her ch racter she would have found it difficult to have cleared herself of, and which might have had a very detrimental effect upon her future prospects."

" That might have been," said the magistrate, " and I am willing to add, she has been clearly and sufficiently exculpated from the charge brought against her."

" And my unfortunate client who had suffered here these four days' imprisonment in a common jail, can obtain no redress whatever; she must submit."

" There are circumstances of suspicion," said the magistrate, " and these were enough to justify a detention. It is not like a lesser crime, when the accuser is liable for any malicious or unjust accusation. In this case, you see, the crown is the accuser; besides, in matters of this kind, you cannot but be aware that, until an investigation has taken place, we cannot tell who is innocent, and who is guilty."

" Certainly not, your worship, but it is equally certain, that it falls hard, very hard upon the innocent, who happen to be wrongly accused."

" A certain amout of injury is inflicted upon all these occasions, and it cannot be avoided. Every investigation is hampered with it, and you cannot escape it. It is a hardship, but it is also one that must be borne for the good of the community, if circumstances of suspicion were to pass without investigation, no man would be safe, and he would never be clear from this suspicion which is cast upon him."

" Does your worship think any suspicion rests upon my client now ?" inquired the barrister. " If so, any course than cau be suggested, will be adopted, to purge her of it."

" No, there is no imputation. She is clearly proved not to have been there."

" Thank your worship."

" At the same time," added the magistrate, " there is no imputation upon Mrs. Grove, she has acted rightly; but to my mind, the whole affair clearly resolves itself into a case of mistaken identity. This I think is clear enough. The prisoner is not the same person who was at Hampstead."

" That is clearly my own view of the subject," said the barrister, " and though it is a case of great hardship for my client, more so on account of her sex, yet it is unavoidable, I presume she is now no longer in custody, and that your worship will discharge her ?"

" Yes, certainly ; she is free."

The usher opened the dock, and Margaret Manvers, without uttering a word, or deigning to look at Mrs. Grove, walked by the place where the Countess of Crumbledown sat the latter offered her maid her hand, and made a few remarks of congratulation to her which were received with becoming courtesy, and at the same time a smile of triumph played upon her lips, while, indeed, the whole party looked exceedingly gratified."

There was a long conference between counsel and solicitor, and the countess, and her mother and Margaret, all of whom were engaged in the conversation, until the usher politely intimated that it had better be carried on outside the court, upon which polite hint, they left the office.

" I hope," said the barrister' " that your ladyship is quite satisfied with the triumphant termination of this affair ? It appears most gratifying."

" Yes," said the countess, " but I am surprised nothing can be done with the woman Grove.'"

" That is to be lamented, your ladyship, but I tried a little in that direction, but the feeling of the magistrate was decidedly against me. They like to encourage a full explanation of all circumstances connected with such a crime, and, therefore, they will not hold the witnesses answerable, for any statement which they think they have conscientiously made, so it was useless to urge the matter."

"I see," said the countess; "I am much obliged to you, for your attention."
"Good morning, good morning, my lady."

"Margaret," said the countess, "come with me to the carriage.'

Margaret followed in silence, but with the air of an empress, and she entered the carriage of the countess, and sat on the seat opposite to her, and after being fully assured every one saw the triumph, they drove away.

*   *   *   *   *   *

The feelings of Mrs. Grove were of a strange and mixed character, and she stood musing upon what had happened, and quite unable to improve her own memory in the affair, or to come to any other opinion relative to this distressing affair. It was a mystery.

The earl too, he was completely staggered; he knew not what to think. He saw the plain and positive contradiction of the countess and her mother, and yet he saw Mrs. Grove was still positive, and did not, though she heard the testimony given against her, swerve from her original statements.

He determined to go to Mrs. Grove, and again question her. When this case was over, the earl walked up to Mrs. Grove in the outer office, and taking her aside, he said to her—

"Mrs. Grove, you have heard all that has been said and sworn to-day."

"I have, my lord."

"Well then, think calmly in your own mind, and tell me truly, if you have not one cause, or if there be no possibility of your being mistaken in the identity of Margaret Manvers."

"I have no doubt, my lord."

"It is very strange—very strange, indeed," said the earl, musingly, "and I cannot understand it at all. It surpasses all I ever heard in this way. And you cannot even now doubt, that this Margaret Manvers is the same person who came to you at Hampstead, the day before the child died.

"I am as sure of it, my lord, as I am that there is a Heaven above me. I could not be mistaken, I could not clearly, and at once have recognised her. I could not, in fact, feel so very positive, so clearly, so entirely convinced of the truth of my recognition, if I had the smallest doubt. I am unable to explain anything, but the fact of her being there I am most positive of."

"Well," said the earl, "I must say it is very extraordinary. The countess and her mother both swear, that she was at home on that day."

"They do, my lord," said Mrs. Grove, quickly.

The earl paused again to think. He was much distressed in mind and body; the death of the child and the circumstances attending it, had made him grave and thoughtful; what could have brought about this unusual state of things, he could not tell. The whole of the evidence was positively at variance.

He knew the countess could have no affection for the child; nay, she could not, but he supposed to have some feeling of dislike towards it; but he could not help feeling that murder was hardly a crime she would attempt, either by her own hands, or by proxy; neither would she and her mother purchase indemnity for their instrument of evil, by direct and wilful perjury.

"God of Heaven, into what a maze of thought and conjecture does this affair lead one!" he muttered to himself, "and yet, Mrs. Grove can have no motive for saying what she does, if she did not think and believe what she said, and feel as positive as she says. I am convinced of the honesty and integrity, but I am at a loss to reconcile all that I have heard upon this subject."

"Mrs. Grove," said the earl, "this is a serious affair. I have no doubt in you at all; I am satisfied with what you have done, but have you no doubt in your own mind? This becomes a matter of some importance, as it involves others in a grave and terrible charge, that of murder, and the countess, with either being principle in it, or at least concerned in it."

"I cannot look at the consequence of my testimony, my lord, if I did, I might have abstained from giving it, but I am sure of what I have said. It is the truth and only the truth. I have not even exaggerated it in the smallest respect."

"Well," said the earl, turning to Colonel Bruce, "it is a strange and uncomfortable circumstance, but I can say no more now; I must see you again some other time."

As the earl spoke, he and Colonel Bruce left the office in company, and Mrs. Grove herself quitted it a moment or two after.

CHAPTER LXXXVI.

THE HOUR OF TRIUMPH.—WILLOUGHBY'S EXACTIONS.—THE QUARREL BETWEEN THE EARL AND COUNTESS.

THE scene is changed; and instead of the noise and poverty-stricken meanness of the appointments of a police-office—its bustle, dirt, and its motley crowds—we see no kind of appearance, but now enter the boudoir of the Countess of Crumbledown where is to be found the Countess of Crumbledown herself and her mother, the

Marchioness of Fanfaronade, and attendant upon them was the countess's maid, Margaret Meavers. The whole three had the expression of exultation, and, if we m ght say so much of the aristocracy, the exhibition of what might be termed impudent defiance,—the joy arising from successful villany, when all attempts at discovery and detection have been defeated by mere might of observation.

"I had no idea of even so much happening as has happened," said the countess suddenly, after a long pause had taken place ; "it only occurred in consequence of that woman Groves recognising you, Margaret ; had it not been for that, even a suspicion could not have been raised anywhere, but it does not matter as it has turned out."

"No, my lady," said Margaret, "but who would have expected to see her here ? It was a mere accident that one couldn't guard against."

"It is true, but they are defeated, and may enjoy it among themselves."

"I am surprised you have disturbed yourself about it at all," said the marchioness, "I am astonished at it—quite ; at least I should be if it were possible for any thing to annoy me, but it isn't."

"But you see," said the countess, "it was of the utmost importance to get the child out of the way ; that was one object with me."

"And you have done so," said the marchioness, coolly.

"Yes, we have done so, and succeeded despite all opposition, and despite all attempts at discovery ; we have done it well and safely. Now I dare say the earl won't be quite so well convinced of the truth of what in law is proved, and yet he cannot be otherwise than convinced that there is something more in it than he found out, but at the same time I care nothing about that, it will only show him that I defy him, and care not for him."

"Very proper, my dear," said the marchioness.

"And now I have nothing to fear, I can look upon the future with complacency, and I can now enjoy the present to the extent of my means, which are not a few. I have no doubt but what this matter is entirely crushed."

"It ought to be. The testimony of persons of rank and distinction ought always to carry some weight with it, and crush all kinds of testimony of the lower orders, who ought not to be permitted to offer any opposition to what their superiors say."

"It were of no avail in this instance," said Margaret ; "I had no idea that she would have recognised me, and for all I can see I don't know of what use it can be to them to prove that I had been there."

"If they could have proved that much," said the countess, "it would have been considered a suspicious circumstance, and I cannot tell to what they might have turned it, but new you are safe and free from suspicion."

"We are safe now," said Margaret.

"And now," said the countess, with an air of exultation, "I will have a masked ball. I intend to give it on the very day that this brat of his lordship's will be buried. I will show my indifference."

"That can be done easily," said the marchioness.

"All shall be done, and moreover, I will invite the earl to be present. It will still be a note of triumph, and one that will sound melodiously in my ears, whatever it may do in his lordship's."

"And you need say nothing now about it," said the marchioness, "I mean about the death."

"But I have a word or two to say to his lordship, when he says anything about it to me ; I have at least a very good excuse to say something, and I don't see any propriety in my losing such an opportunity."

"Well," said the marchioness, "these family matters are not of much importance, and therefore there need be nothing premeditated—the occasion will suggest to all what must be said and done—it should be nothing more than extempore."

"Here is the earl," said Margaret, "his lordship is coming this way, and it will no doubt afford a very good occasion for a *fracas.*"

It was true ; the earl was coming to the countess's boudoir, and that without any formal announcement of his intention of doing so. He had determined to have some private conversation with his lady, though of its precise object he was unsettled and uneasy,—he felt in his own mind that there was something more than suspicion in all that had been done or said, and that the countess must be at the bottom of it.

He could not, at times, however, but think that there was some mistake as to the identity of Margaret, and that Mrs. Groves must have been mistaken. There could be no hope, however, of settling this matter. The child was dead, and all that he could think of was that there was an end to the whole affair. It had entailed some moments of poignant regret to the earl, which this sudden shock had by no means decreased; for indeed it was the remorse he felt to see to what a wretched end he had brought both mother and child—the unfortunate Emily and her child.

However, he entered the apartment with little or no marks of sorrow, though the countess could not but believe she saw signs that convinced her that grief was felt, and this rankled in her bosom; not that she cared what the feelings of the earl were, only the cause of them was what displeased her.

"Well, my lord," said the countess. "you have come to your confessional, I presume, and to repent of your evil ways."

"If my ways are a matter of importance to your ladyship, I dare say I should have heard of it before this."

"Oh, ay, love, you are satirical. You surely would not have me trouble you; but you see it is seldom the hypocrite is unmasked so completely as this. I had no notion your lordship had another family."

"It could matter very little to your ladyship as to what took place before the ceremony of marriage took place between us."

"Indeed! We usually consider people's characters in these matters."

"I am surprised at that, because I thought there were other matters that had mainly been inducements."

"Perhaps your lordship was induced by others—recollect yourself—and have you attributed the same to me?"

"I should be sorry to deny any such result that may be established by observance," said the earl with some composure.

"And I," said the countess, "have become acquainted with circumstances that I should never have known, had it not been through the intervention of a police officer."

"Perhaps not; and I dare say your ladyship's feelings will make it a matter of congratulation, now you do know it."

"A subject of congratulation that the individual whom the law allows to call one's husband should have been so base as to conceal from me a fact which I ought to have been made acquainted with at the first."

"I have no intention of entering into any discussion upon the affair, it is one in which I only am concerned."

"I am surprised," said the marchioness, "you should think anything about such people; it is a very low connection."

"Very," said Lady Crumbledown, "very; but, my lord, I am going to give a grand masked ball on Thursday next. This little affair of your lordship's being so peculiarly your own, cannot in any way affect me, and I shall hold my ball in the same manner as if nothing really had happened, for the individual was only a peculiar connection of your lordship's. Will your lordship be present?"

"I shall—I shall make no difference myself."

*   *   *   *   *

The earl had left the room but a few moments, when the conversation was resumed, and again did the notes of triumph sound from the countess, her mother, and each in its peculiar tone and manner, when they are suddenly amazed by the unannounced entrance of Willoughby.

"Oh!" he said, as he passed in at the door, "oh, I guessed you were here. You needn't disturb yourself on my account; look upon me in the light of an old and valued friend. I am always happy when with my friends."

"Mr. Willoughby," said the countess in explanation to the marchioness's look.

"Yes, my lady, Mr. Willoughby, a claimant upon your ladyship's treasury. There can never be a better time to make a just claim than in the moment of triumph—it is paid and received with so much greater pleasure than at any other time."

"And what am I in your debt, Mr. Willoughby? But understand I do not receive any visitors unannounced."

"Oh, as for that, my lady, you need take no notice of me. I want just the moderate sum of one thousand pounds from you to-night."

"One thousand pounds!"

"Just so much, my lady."

The countess looked for a moment in Willoughby's countenance, but what she saw there apparently induced her to comply; for, checking her anger, she gave him the sum, saying, as she did so,—

"This serves, then, to clear all matters up between us, and our communication ceases."

"For the present, my lady; but I shall occasionally call upon you when I want cash, for I'm sure your ladyship will see the utility of being just and generous to me since I am the depository of important secrets, and they are worth paying for. But adieu to you for the present."

CHAPTER LXXXVII.

THE MASQUERADE AT CRUMBLEDOWN HOUSE.—THE DECLARATION OF MRS. GROVES.

THE scene must again change. The various positions of our characters render it necessary that we should, as the lawyers say, shift the venue. From the boudoir of a countess, we must turn to the contemplation of more humble life.

Mrs. Groves, whom we left as she quitted the earl and the police-officer, was much saddened by the event that had occurred. It was an untoward and violent end for a child to come to, and she could not be supposed but to feel most poignantly at the event.

True, the child was not hers. It was not one connected to her by the ties of blood; but she was connected with her by the ties of gratitude. The earl had been a good patron to her, and the child had won upon her; she could not have nursed the child so long without feeling an affection for it.

Mrs. Groves sat in a chair before the fire at her own house. She appeared absorbed in deep reflection. She was actuated by some strange impulse, which every now and then found a vent in some exclamation, or in rocking herself slowly backwards and forwards from time to time, and then she would again fall into a deep fit of musing, but from which she would apparently awake, and commence rocking again.

"It must be done,—it must," she would mutter to herself. "Ay, there is every reason why I should do so. Who knows what may be the result; I know not, and, as far as I am concerned, I care not."

She appeared to be making some internal resolution which took her some time and some thought to determine upon. Her mind was busy, and no pleasing thoughts appeared to be there which she now had. There was some care and much sorrow on her countenance; but they were probably occasioned by the grief she felt for the hard and untimely fate of the nurse-child, the love-child, which had so long been under her care, and of which she could almost feel herself the mother, so great was the effect produced by constant association and care.

There was much of reflection in Mrs. Groves' manner, and the resolution which she came to was one that took some mental effort to get over, but she appeared to have made that determination, and whatever it was, it was unalterable.

" Yes, yes, it must, it shall be so," she muttered. "I must, I will do it. Even in the midst of triumph and folly there came a nerve that would change all joy into sorrow, all triumph into defeat. I am resolved it shall be done, and to make certain more so, I will not even give myself more time for reflection. I will go at this very moment."

She arose. It was night, and the streets had been lighted up some time, and she looked out of her window, but she saw nothing there that in any way altered her determination. She took her bonnet and cloak, and after a brief observation, left the house for the streets.

* * * * * *

That evening there was a disturbance in the street, in which the earl resided. There was a masked ball held at his mansion. The long string of carriages reached a great length, and the police were compelled to keep order among the high-bred, better-fed flunkies and coachmen who could understand nothing as being so aristocratic as disturbing peaceable people and giving all imaginable trouble to the public functionaries, who were compelled to be peremptory.

The knocker as usual appeared to be endowed with the perpetual motion, or for the time had contracted the disorder called St. Vitus's dance, for it was in incessant motion for a great length of time.

Carriages of all classes, and cattle to match, now occupied in double rows the whole street, and Heaven only knows how far they extended round the corner, that could not be defined.

Then the lights that shone in the mansion appeared as if more than usually brilliant—they were numerous and shone brightly. Could it have been studied on the part of the countess how much she should and would show her joy by making a most brilliant display upon the occasion.

Certain it was that if such had been her intention, it had so far succeeded, for never had the Crumbledown town mansion exhibited such a display of wealth and such an exhibition of splendour.

All that was costly and beautiful—all that could be produced by art and nature that was in season, and among that were exotics too—found their way into the mansion upon that occasion.

The visitors, too, were for some reason or other more numerous than usual, and the *elite* of the sphere in which they moved. Perhaps the countess had added something more than usually entertaining in the cards of invitation, or she had written additional notes—certain it was that many came.

The handsome furniture was lost amid the sea of human heads—the orchestra was hidden ; and the sounds of music came from without the room—the ladies' dresses were for the most part handsome in the extreme. There was an amount of youth and wealth and beauty that can scarcely be met with in any country in Europe on a similar occasion.

The countess was there, and entertained her guests more than usually graciously ; she appeared to feel more than the ordinary pleasure derivable from such a source, and many of her friends muttered to each other,—

" Oh ! the countess has obtained a victory over her lord, and thus it is she is so very pleased. Well, to be sure, I am amazed how some men will put up with anything from their wives. I dare say, poor man, the earl has lost what he placed his heart upon, and he does not see the airs of his countess."

Thus were made many remarks with the good friends they invited, who were envious of this display of wealth indulged in ; they made not a few—and they were not confined to either countess or earl, but some of them extended to other matters that had lately been made public.

There were many gentlemen present, and among them was Willoughby, who had entered, no one knew how.

" Oh ! my lady," said Willoughby, bowing to the countess, "you see, I am a dutiful attendant upon you ; I must really be constituted your shadow."

" This, sir, is no place for you," said the countess, haughtily, but in so low a tone that it reached nobody's ears but Willoughby's.

" Oh dear! my lady, it is quite good enough— quite good enough, I assure you, I am obliged to you for your consideration, and beg to reciprocate it—by the way, you must introduce me to some agreeable young lady for a partner for the dance."

" You!"

" Yes, my lady," said Willoughby, interrupting her, " yes, I shall positively dance, and I know it is in your power to recommend me to a lady who will greatly benefit me both by her beauty and by her wealth."

A sudden thought struck her, and she said,—

" Wait a moment, and I will shortly return with one—put your mask on."

" I am your slave, my lady."

Willoughby put on the mask, and the countess left that part of the room, and made for another part, where a number of persons were standing in masks.

" Margaret," she said, to one who stood dressed in a fancy dress of an expensive and lively character, " I have a partner for you, but you must make him keep by you all the evening, he is a gentleman."

Margaret followed the countess, who introduced her to Willoughby under assumed names. The latter immediately began to converse with his new partner with all imaginable politeness, when his eye was attracted towards the door.

" My lady," he said, gently touching the countess's arm.

" I have no more time to spare; I have done more than you have any title to."

" Pardon me for disputing the fact ; but who is that entering the room?"

The countess turned her eyes in the direction, and to her annoyance and amazement, she beheld the person of Mrs. Groves. There was such a look of astonishment on her countenance that every one was as much amazed as she. The earl, too, who happened to be near the object, looked upon her surprised.

Mrs. Groves, however, paid attention to nothing that passed around her, but advanced through the throng of astonished guests to the earl and countess, and said. —" I have been unable to refrain any longer from confessing a secret that you ought to have known before. When the countess took her child away from me, instead of her own child I gave the one entrusted to me by the earl, whose mother is dead, and that which has been poisoned is the countess's own daughter."

CHAPTER LXXXVIII.

THE DEATH OF THE COUNTESS.—THE FATE OF WILLOUGHBY.

HAD a thunderbolt suddenly burst among the guests, it could not have had a more astounding effect. The countess strained her eyes and ears—her brow was contracted, and she appeared spell-bound.

Willoughby and Margaret stood together, and both involuntarily unmasked when they heard this astounding declaration.

The earl was too much astounded to speak, and Mrs. Groves continued :—

" I repeat, the murdered child is the daughter of Lady Crumbledown, whilst that which she has cherished is the child of the unfortunate lady who died in the village. Knowing she was illegitimate, I thought she most required a protector, and I loved the child, and projected its future fortune in the manner I have told you—because I did love it. I can swear to the truth of this statement—so help me Heaven, it is true !"

The countess stood all the while Mrs. Groves had been speaking, in the attitude of one listening to fearful intelligence, and fearful of injury being done to her by the object to which she was listening.

Suddenly the spell broke, and she staggered back for three or four yards, all who were standing around her making a lane for her, instead of offering her any assistance; and as she thus staggered back, she uttered one of the most appalling and painful shrieks that such assembly ever heard.

Then, before any one could offer to stay her progress, she recovered herself, and darted out of the apartment.

There was a long and deathlike pause in the assembly—scarce a visitor drew a breath—the flutter of a feather might have been heard. The guests stared at each other, and none appeared able to answer the questions which the look of astonished inquiry seemed to make.

The earl stood motionless, and heaved a deep sigh; he looked round the room for a moment, until his eyes encountered Colonel Bruce, who at once stepped forward and stood by the earl.

"What can be done, Bruce! what can be done?"

"Really, I don't think anything can be done, my lord."

"But the guests—"

"Must act as they please. If they stop, as I dare say many will, out of mere curiosity, you have everything that can be expected; but they cannot expect you to remain—they will go or stay, as it pleases themselves. I would advise you not to trouble yourself about them; your lordship's wealth will not permit them to be very fastidious."

"True, Bruce, true; but this woman?"

"I will retire with her, if you please; or we can both do so. It may be as well, and will ease you of all further trouble."

The earl, without saying more, quitted the apartment, and was followed by Colonel Bruce, who took Mrs. Groves with him, and then, in a smaller and quieter apartment, the three sat to converse on this new occurrence, and to hear the confession or explanation of Mrs. Groves at length.

"I am amazed," said one of the guests to another.

"Did you ever hear such an awful scream?"

"Never; but the young Countess of Pinkerton also has fainted away, as soon as she heard there was nothing more to be known."

"I am not surprised at it. Who wouldn't faint on such an occasion? I declare I never could have believed that the human lungs could have emitted such a sound. It was quite unique, I declare."

"So it was, but it has spoiled the evening."

"What are you going to do? Do you think there are reasonably good places to be had at the Opera?"

"There are some empty boxes, I dare say."

"Well, then, I think I shall go there. I'm dying with *ennui*, and I must dispose of my time somehow or other. It is really horrible when one is thrown upon one's own resources in a way like this. I am sure, suicide is more bearable, abate the vulgar gaze of twelve men being fixed upon one's corpse."

"If it were not for that, I am sure suicide would soon become fashionable."

Of all those present there were none more amazed, or appeared to be more really interested in this strange announcement, than Margaret Manvers, the countess's maid, and Willoughy, both of whom remained for a long while speechless and staggered.

"Well," said Willoughby, turning to Margaret, "this is a strange occurrence—a very singular affair, eh? my lady. Oh, what, are you my partner?"

"Yes," said Margaret, putting on her mask; "and I see you are mine."

"I was not aware of it."

"I dare say not: but what is to be done now—I suppose you will see the necessity of withdrawing?"

"I really cannot see the necessity of leaving so many good things—which now remain. Suppose I suggest to you the propriety of your attending your mistress, and just seeing if she has done no mischief to herself. I will remain here at all events, until you return and inform me of how matters stand."

Margaret thought this was only reasonable, and accordingly left the ball-room and made her way to the countess's boudoir, but on reaching that she found the door fast and that she could not get in. She called but no answer was returned.

She immediately sought assistance, and for that purpose went straight to the earl's, whom she found closeted with Colonel Bruce and Mrs. Groves.

"The countess's door is locked and I can hear no sound within," said Margaret. "I have knocked but have had no answer."

"That is no affair of mine," said the earl.

"But she may have committed suicide—no one can tell," said Margaret; "but it is as your lordship desires."

"It is much better to remain here, Mrs. Groves," said the earl; "will you come with me? Sure we had better see about this—something may be wrong in that quarter too—I will have the door broken open—get the aid of a couple of men with a crow-bar," added the earl to Margaret.

In about five minutes more the assistance had arrived, and the earl advanced and struck the door with his foot, and called to the countess, but he received no answer, and after waiting a moment or two, he exclaimed,—

"Break it open!"

The men instantly set to work. The door was strong, and fitting well and closely, it was not easy to get a purchase for the lever—but after some blows given to the door, the hinges gave, and it was then soon forced out, and let the whole party in, the door having fallen with a crash that made the guests start again.

"Where is she?" exclaimed the earl.

"Here!" said Colonel Bruce.

As he spoke he pointed to a couch, upon which the countess lay with her eyes almost distorted, her lips slightly parted—she reclined on her back, and her arms hung down beside her.

"She is dead!" said the earl.

She was dead. On the floor lay a small phial, and from the smell emitted, it was plain that she had ended her days suddenly, by means of prussic acid. The room was filled with its odour; and Margaret, as soon as she saw the end of her mistress, went to some of the drawers, from which she took both money and jewels, and then left the apartment; she, however, entered the ball-room once more.

"What have you learned?" inquired Willoughby.

"That the Countess of Crumbledown is dead," said Margaret in a loud voice, so that every one in the room heard it, and when she spoke she quitted the apartment.

"Dead!" muttered Willoughby; "well, that is unfortunate for me; I had hoped she would have been as good as a bank to me—a life long annuity; but this is now no place for me, the time is over." As he spoke he quitted the room, and walked leisurely down the stairs, but by some means, his feet tripped or slipped, and he fell backwards.

The noise occasioned by his fall attracted the attention of several servants; and when they raised him up, they found that he had fractured his skull to a fearful extent.

A surgeon was instantly sent for, and when he arrived, after a slight examination, he at once declared that the unfortunate man could not live an hour.

Willoughby at length slowly opened his eyes and gazed with a wild, agonized look around him; then, he placed his hand frantically to his head, and again relapsed into insensibility. When his senses returned, the look of agony had passed away, but his eyes had grown dim and lustreless, and there was a fixedness about them quite painful to see. In a faint voice he spoke, saying,—

"I'm dying, I'm dying—let me see the earl."

"Is it my master you mean?" asked one of the servants.

"Yes, yes; I have something to tell him; but, quick, quick! or it will be too late!"

The man hastened to the room where he knew the earl to be, but when he returned to the hall, Willoughby was a corpse!

CHAPTER LXXXIX.

THE CONCLUSION.

AND now, gentle reader, do we come to the conclusion of our labours, and it remains but to say a few words respecting the final disposal of the individuals who have figured in this narration. The last chapter has shown how three of them were disposed of.

In the case of Willoughby, his death, though purely accidental, was an awful instance of retributive justice; and, perhaps, exhibited a more terrible example than if punished according to human laws.

The countess's death completely saved all this with her family; that was understood, no doubt. In a day or two an inquest was held, but it was a very quiet and well-conducted affair; the jurors being chosen from the immediate vicinity, and who were at all times willing to oblige the rich.

They viewed the body, and after a short inquiry, during which it was impossible to dispel the fact she had poisoned herself, especially as the earl made no scruple of saying so,—that was a matter ascertained at once, and admitted; the verdict was accordingly given—"That the countess died by taking prussic acid, but during a fit of temporary derangement, brought on by extreme nervous excitement."

This, of course, hid from the view of many the fact that she took poison in a fit of disappointment, through having committed an unavailing crime, and being foiled in the object she most desired to succeed in.

Mrs. Groves was immediately taken into the earl's establishment as an honoured domestic, and to be a companion to the child whose life she had been the means of preserving.

How that estimable woman blessed the day which had introduced her to the notice of the Earl of Crumbledown, and how thankful she felt that, in her anxiety for the welfare of her little favourite, she had exchanged it for the child of the countess, by which circumstance, most decidedly, its life had been preserved

The change, too, in her mode of living was particularly gratifying to her, and when she came to reflect upon the early years of her life, and upon the privations she had undergone, combined with the cruel treatment she had experienced from her drunken husband, Jack Groves, she could not help expressing her gratitude to that almighty power which had imbued her mind with those principles of kindly humanity, that had so strongly recommended her to the notice of the self-styled Mr. Smith, in the parlour of the little inn, at the time of the death of poor Emily Whitford.

The child she had been as a mother to in its infancy, loved her with a daughter's love when she grew up to womanhood and her declining years were smoothed by the kindness she experienced, alike from Emily and her grandfather. If she had one single thing more than another that cast a cloud over her tranquil days, it was the occasional remembrance of her husband, not as he was in his later years, as a drunken and degraded wretch, but as he was to her in his youth, before he had given himself up to the deadly fascination of the soul-destroying liquor. But these thoughts were only occasional, and her days glided away in tranquil happiness.

Jack Groves once more appeared, and was like to have been troublesome, but he was easily induced to go abroad, when there was a sum of money offered him to do so, and a pension given him by the earl, out of consideration to Mrs. Groves, who was alarmed at the bad thoughts of being in his power again.

This was, however, easily settled under such circumstances, and then Jack Groves left the shores of his native country, declaring that he was at last a gentleman, provided for during life—he had succeeded better than the cunning Mr. Willoughby, who had been cut off suddenly—he cared for nobody, not he, and but for his pension failing him if he remained, he would have gone back to the village, if it were only for the purpose of restoring the first shilling, and the kick he had received along with it, when he first raised a subscription to enable him to journey to London, and to taste once again the ale at the turnpike gate; but his bargain would not admit of it, and he left England.

After a time, however, he was missed, and no more money was called for, and it was immediately discovered that he met with an unfortunate end by drinking too much wine that had been drugged by some gamblers, who were tempted by the display of a whole quarter's money which he had received.

His end, which was never presumed, though upon good evidence was really ascertained, was rendered fully sure by the fact, that no claim was ever made afterwards for the pension—and it was moreover too characteristic of the man to excite much surprise in the mind of Mrs. Groves, nor even much regret.

The fate of the guilty Margret Manvers forms one of the most fearful episodes in the records of every-day life. As we have said, she secured about her person all the valuables upon which at the moment she could lay her hands, and then quitting the mansion in which such a strong contrast of life and death was to be found, she sought the residence of a young man with whom she had been long connected. With the proceeds of this robbery, Margaret and her paramour led a most dissipated life for a considerable time; the voice of conscience being stifled in the breast of the former, by the excesses into which she plunged. This mode of living was at length brought to a close by the desertion of her lover, carrying with him the remains of the property, and leaving her penniless and destitute. Step by step, she sank deeply into degradation and poverty, until at last, a homeless, starving, miserable creature, she wandered the streets of London to beg for bread.

One cold night in November, she found herself famished for want of food, and soaked with wet—in the neighbourhood of Hampstead. Despair had seized upon her, and she felt that if the means were at hand, she would willingly have resigned her life. By some strange fatality, her footsteps were directed towards the cottage once inhabited by Mrs. Groves, and in which the child was poisoned. It was now fast falling to decay, and the little garden around it was choked up with weeds. The unhappy woman seated herself upon the threshold, and gave herself up to the most maddening thoughts; the scene of her crime was before her eyes, and remorse played so busily round her heart, that she scarce cared whether she lived or died.

The darkness increased, and the rain still came down in steady torrents; there was no prospect before Margaret but death, in one of its most awful forms—that of sheer starvation, and exposure to the inclemency of the weather. Suddenly she started upon her feet, and with hurried steps made her way in the direction of the large ponds that are on one side of the heath. When she reached the brink of one of them, she paused, and in a beseeching manner, exclaimed "Mercy! mercy!"

There was a plunge, a shriek, a struggle in the dark circling waters, and then the quiet of that lonely spot was undisturbed; that form, whose short life had known so much crime, reposed in death beneath the surface of the pond.

The next character of whom we have to speak, is no less a person than the Marchioness of Fanfaronade,—she whose counsels had so much to do with the formation of the character of the Countess, and who, indeed, might be said to be the prime cause of all the untoward events that have occurred in our narrative. The death of the Countess, upon whose resources the Marchioness entirely depended, her own having long since been exhausted, threw her down from her lofty estate, and she was glad to accept a small annuity from the Earl of Crumbledown, which she contrived to eke by patronising, as she termed it, one of those families whose sole ambition it is to rank a "title" among their acquaintance. She died, as she had lived, without the respect of a single person.

Of Colonel Bruce, the attached friend of the Earl of Crumbledown, little more need be said than that the friendship they entertained for each other was continued through a long and valued life; and the greatest consolation for the past that the earl could find, was in talking over with him, the many happy days he had known with Emily, and in devising plans to promote the happiness of the love child.

The Whitfords were rescued from their poverty and misfortunes. The earl strove, as much as means could effect that object, to compensate them for the distresses and misfortunes they had endured, as well as for the loss of Emily.

Their thoughts very often turned upon their past misfortunes, yet they saw nothing with which they could blame themselves in the past—they were thankful and happy in the present, though they had a love for her whose spirit fled in a moment of distress and agony, and prayed for their welfare. It was, however, some consolation for them to know that her dear Emily's child was living—the image of herself—and that satisfaction was increased by the knowledge that the little Love Child was the acknowledged heiress of all the Crumbledown property.

The earl never again ventured within the bonds of matrimony, and their grand child was her father's delight, and the source of gratification to him in his old age and she never more had a rival in his affections or in his riches.

THE END.